THE PREFACE OF A WORTHY FABLE

The Preface
of a
Worthy Fable

a novel

by Astrid Axton

{BY.AA.PREFACE}

Fox Fairy Font

Cover Design by David Leahey
Illustrations by Savannah Drews
Fonts: EB Garamond, Courier, WW Designs

ISBN 979-8-9925394-0-0 (paperback)
ISBN 979-8-9925394-1-7 (ebook)

First published 2025

For You.

The author has decided to rate this book and disclose the following warnings:

Fantasy	**Content Warnings:** suicide ideation, self-harm, minor torture, mild language, childhood runaways, referenced train accidents
A-E	**Themes:** tortured artist analysis, conceptualizing silence, community, identity, chasing dreams, love, the Chosen One

for more information on F3RS (Fox Fairy Font Rating System) please visit:

foxfairyfont.com

PROLOGUE

The Dance

of the

Golden Dragonflies

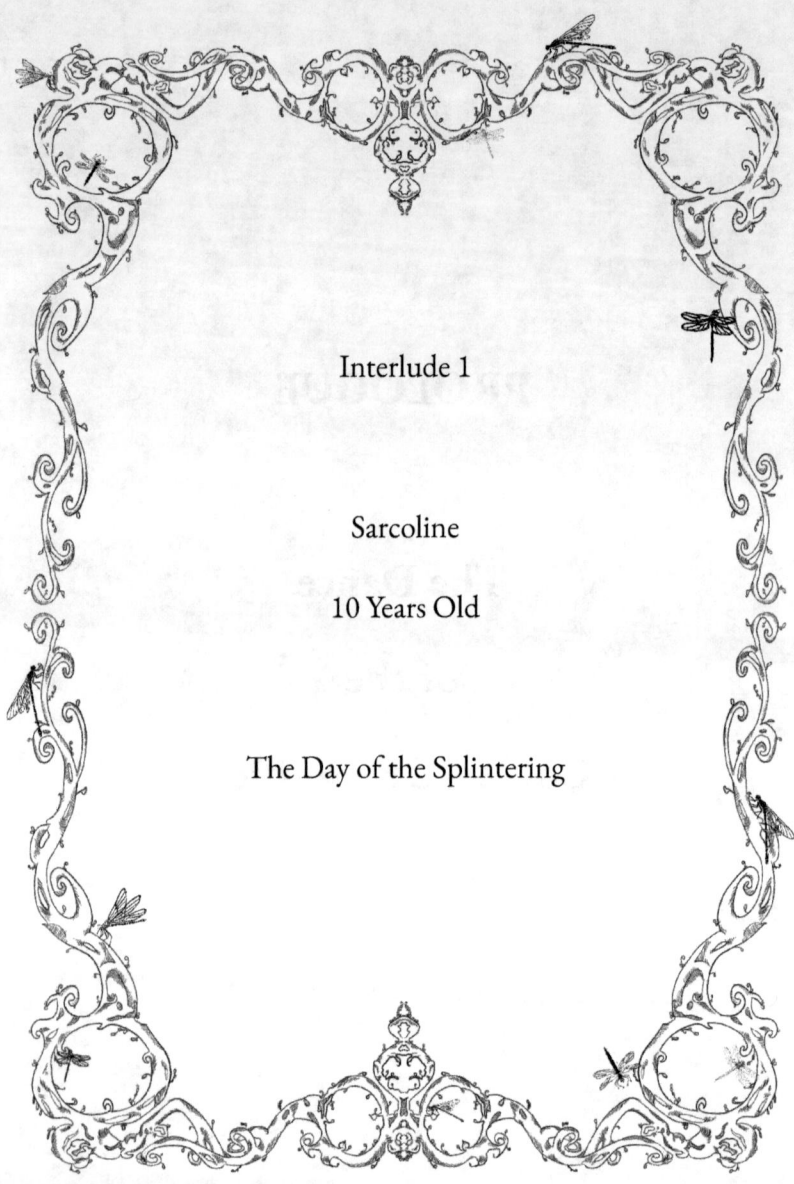

Interlude 1

Sarcoline

10 Years Old

The Day of the Splintering

If it meant he could dance forever, then he was going to do whatever it took to weave himself into a legend. Most stories could captivate an audience immediately but being interesting was never enough. The ones worth remembering, worth relishing over, could live in memory forever. Good stories told you, right from the beginning, how they would end.

Or so his brother said.

His brother also said the same could be applied to dance. Only for dance, the stories were told through the body. A good story when told through a good dancer took another form, took another life, became another dream. They were the ones that became legends.

He didn't much care; he just loved dancing.

The night of the Splintering started off as any other Ceremony of Chaos: the end of the year had arrived, the last event of New Dawn Day began, everyone was watching. Arco was dressed in his favorite mint green suit. It was rigid, like a beetle's hard exoskeleton, and always gave him luck. He had a mask on his head inspired by Vervain the Blythe, and a holly necklace around his neck. He hadn't slept all day and while his parents continued to tell him to nap, he couldn't. Not this year. This year was supposed to be special. This was the beginning of *his* story.

Arco stood in the crowd with his mother.

"Go. Go," he urged her to return backstage.

She shook her head. "I won't leave you here."

"But he *needs* you."

And he didn't need their mother. He was safe here.

"Your father and sister will support him from backstage and we'll watch from here." His mother smiled down at him, taking his small hand and squeezing it tight. She was nervous too. After all, his brother was dancing Powers for the first time at just fifteen, which made him the best dancer in the world.

For now, at least.

The Ceremony of Chaos began when the emcee walked out on stage. He began his usual yearly lesson about the Dances. Cameras flew around, through crowds, and above their heads. Projectors presented full three-dimensional renderings up in the sky, past the Weeping Stage's arch. Hovering speakers moved through the crowd, making the sound so close, Arco swore it was over his shoulder. Everything felt closer out in the audience, more so than being backstage.

This year the emcee added a joke about Vervain the Blythe. The audience laughed and he glanced up at his mother, giddy: the joke was added for his brother. He was unable to keep still and wanted to yell his brother's name into the crowd.

When Cardinal White stepped on the stage to begin the prayer there was supposed to be a hush over the audience. Yet, people continued to speak.

Arco took his hand from his mother and closed his eyes. He held both hands out, palms up and connected as if holding a large candle.

"The Saint recited the Chosen's words for all to hear. 'Upon you we grant bodies so that you may move, and live, and grow. Upon you we grant voices so that you may speak and change, and bond. Upon you we grant intellect so you may know our divine nature and worship our benevolence.'"

Arco recited the Prayer of Benevolence with Cardinal White. People continued to talk and scream the names of the dancers, completely ignoring the prayer. Refusing to backdown, because his brother would never back down, Arco continued louder. His mother's voice joined him.

"And they said, 'upon you we grant Blessings so that you may thrive, and so that our brilliance may shine through you. Upon you we ask of peace between yourselves and to the world around you. Balance and life are what we require. Upon you we ask for reverence in the form of twenty-seven dances given each year on the solstice, so that the bond between us may remain.' And so, it was. And so, it shall be."

When Arco opened his eyes, he was furious. The voices around him, the side conversations ignoring the prayer, were numerous and all encompassing. The complete disregard for the ceremony made it clear that these people only saw it as entertainment, with little value. They saw it as something meant to be consumed and never analyzed.

There was no decorum, no respect. How was it that so many people did not believe the Gods were real? His brother *heard* them.

Biting his lip in anger, Arco refrained from lashing out. He could not ruin this night for his brother. He could not.

His mother placed her hand on his shoulder. "Ignore them."

It was easy to do so as the first dancer began. The crowd was enthralled enough that their side conversations died. Arco clapped along with the music and smiled, knowing that one day he would dance on the Stage, himself. He'd narrowly missed the spot this year, but next year he would get it. He'd finally dance on the same stage as his brother. And like his brother, he'd be seen, be great, and become the best dancer in the world.

Dance to dance, Arco was enraptured by the spinning bodies and the flourishing fans. He knew every move by heart. He had memorized the histories that the emcee gave between each section. He recited all the names of the dancers and their history with the DHS. By the time that the emcee walked off stage, and the assistants rushed on to place the fans down for the Blue Rose Fears variation of Powers, Arco was screaming his brother's name louder than everyone else around him.

"Calm down," his mother laughed. "He'll be out soon."

But Arco was nervous. While it was close to midnight, and usually his mother made him go to bed by midnight, even on the Day of New Dawn, he was not worried about leaving. He was nervous for his brother: the best dancer in the world. What if he got nervous? What if he was scared? What if he didn't see Arco and didn't know that Arco was in the audience watching him to support him and be his focus. Arco told him he'd be his brother's focus point, but what if Arna didn't *see* him?

The fear was shorted lived, for the screams grew louder. His brother's name was an echo sent to the heavens.

"Incarnadine! Incarnadine!"

Arna stepped out on stage in the Blue Rose Fears ceremonial costume, and within seconds Arna's eyes were on him. Arco waved his hands wildly and smiled brightly. He screamed his brother's name and his brother smiled back, taking his spot on stage.

This was the greatest dancer of the Golden Generation. Everyone knew it.

The world froze as his brother started to dance. Each movement was practiced and polished. The snaps of the fans: crisp. The way he pulled the fabric with his Blessings to make it flow: perfect.

Arco breathed in time with his brother, having watched him enough times to know each muscle movement of his brother's take on the variation. For a moment Arco heard chimes and a storm began to surge around him. The shadows of the audience loomed over the stage forming six hazy figures.

Arco danced with the shadows in the crowd, losing his mother for a second. Instead, he was with older woman who was calming an older man who stomped his feet in protest of some decision yet unknown. Arco was with young girl who bounced around and a young child who was spinning and spinning and spinning. Behind Arco was a person who stood still, nervous and counting, but their nerves did not stop them from twirling the young girl and Arco. The last was a gentleman who stood with his arms crossed, head tilted, and smile growing wide. They celebrated his brother's success as brightly as Arco did.

Arco wanted to cry; his brother was so brilliant. His brother was everything that he wanted to be.

There was a flicker, as his brother spun, and his eyes landed on Arco.

Seconds were left in the last song of the Powers section.

Six seconds to midnight.

When their eyes locked, terror bloomed across his brother's face. The air was sucked from Arco's lungs, as a chill ran down his spine.

His brother's face fell: distraught.

His brother let go of the fans in his hands. The clock tower chimed; the new year arrived.

The fans clattered to the ground.

the KNOWLEDGE of

When you step, step with purpose. No hesitation.
When you open, open with meaning. Snap the world awake with sound.
When you dance, dance with heart: for the world and the Gods can see you.

— all first lessons begin like this.

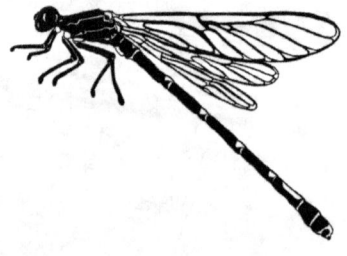

Dance 1

Destiny

Incarnadine

2 Poan

113 Days Left

"You were born for this."

Again.

Arna picked himself up from the floor, breathing deeply. He blinked back the sweat dripping into his eyes in frustration. The electric bulbs buzzed overhead, sensing his movement and wanting to turn on. His powers kept them off. Six candles flickered before him, reflecting and refracting in the mirrors that were dim in the night. Six candles sat four feet apart, on the floor, burning but not melting. Six candles were dyed unique sets of three colors—the first for their touch, the second for their voice, the third for their blessings, so said Saint Citrine—with the God's individual symbol etched into the wax. They were the only source of light in the dance studio that Arna had snuck into.

The hardwood floors were slick with his sweat, despite the windows being open to let in the breeze. Even so, there was no light from the outside, due to the blackout curtains he had placed. There was no sound either, his Blessings keeping everything muffled and the room free of noise, save that which he purposely created himself. Only the breeze remained. The door into the dance room was locked tight. A three-sixty circle of mirrors surrounded him, containing yet expanding, allowing him to examine himself into infinity.

Again.

Arna stood up straight, sliding himself back into his proper stance for the beginning of the dance. The candles stopped flickering and began to silently pop: one, two, three, four, five, six, seven, eight.

He lifted his arms.

He began.

The tempo was dictated by the candles. His movements created the music, aided by the use of his Blessings. The whoosh of his long sleeves, emulating the fans as they hit the air, were the strings. His sharp breaths: the percussion. His steps were the woodwinds, and his dripping sweat the bass. He was symphony and solo, all in one, crafting and creating as he moved.

Grimacing, Arna nearly missed a step. He hurried to focus on the candles and not on how heavy his body was. His eyes were blurry; his head swirling underwater.

The world began when. . .

Clarity would not come from reciting scriptures, but it would keep him focused. He could not mess up. Not now, not when he was so close to succeeding. Complete this test. Finish his variation. Get home. Save the world. He could do it.

Every form, posture, step, his expression, and the way he danced: it had to be exact, calculated, measured. Each snap of his fingers was the moment he'd open a fan if he had been allowed to touch one. He had weights on his wrists, to help with the proper weight distribution, along with the custom-made long sleeves all to replicate the feeling of the fans without holding them. He had collected much over the years to accomplish the impossible task of practicing perfection without the proper tools.

Step, slide, snap.

Arna breathed in time with the candles that pushed him forward, aflame, but not burning out. The flames were still despite the sound they made.

Twelve years and he had never been closer to perfection than he was at that exact moment. He could taste it on his lips. He could see it: locs tied back, dark eyes scrutinizing every move of his body in the mirrors. He was perfect. In this moment not even the Gods could interfere, just as they would not on the night he danced and saved the world. For he had to do this alone. He was the only one who could.

And to the mortals the Gods gave their child, neither mortal nor God. The Chosen Child for the mortals who could lead them to the future.

[Six figures sat in the reflection of the mirrors behind their respective candles, bored.]

Or what he had learned to identify as bored.

When they appeared to him in the day it was accompanied by the glare of the manufactured daylight. He only ever saw them in mirrors, video screens, and shadows as strange mortal-like shapes little more than an apparition. At night they were more tangible. Although, he had to be alone before they'd attempt to show him their form; not that anyone else could see them. Dim light and shadows helped. When he lit their candles? They almost looked *real*.

The six sat scrutinizing him. Their forms mortal-like crossed with animals, swirling and evaporating like fog off of trees. With antlers and eyes that changed from one to five to two, Ixxzal was Arna's focus center point as he spun and moved. Their candles popped in counts as the Gods bent their heads in the unheard conversations.

Then it was over, and Arna was breathing, breathing hard, breathing full deep breaths that echoed about the room in jagged disjointed gasps. His body ached, muscles sore from the overuse of his Blessings, and the long hours. He'd made a mistake with the second step during the twelfth song, although he'd caught himself. He probably would be called out for the near miss of a spin as well. Chances were, he'd have to do it again. Hands against the floor, Arna steadied himself onto his knees and bowed low until his head touched the ground.

"These Dances are my vow. May your benevolence smile upon the world for this Variance and all Variances to come." Only after completing the vow words, practicing them as he was taught, did Arna look up at the six again.

They all had to be impressed, Xeyaro, God of Dance, especially. If Xeyaro was not moved, he'd have to do it again. The popping ceased; only the false flickering remained. With quick hands, he wiped his face and body with the towel that hung on the dance bar before kneeling before the Gods again. It was beginning to smell in the hall despite the open window, which was not a good sign.

[*That was acceptable,* Xeyaro, God of Arts and Nature, spoke out loud.]

They spoke in the language only Arna could hear and understand.

Each muscle in Arna's body tried to turn to mush the instant it was said. Struggling, he maintained his kneeling posture and bowed a second time with great difficulty. He would need to ice his body tonight. They pushed him harder than they usually did.

"I thank you for your guidance." Once he heard the sound of acceptance from the six—the chorus of birds accompanied by something similar to chimes or the swell of a breeze—his focus began to drift.

He was tired. Annoyed at himself, considering that he had to do the dance three times more than usual. He continued to kneel and contain himself, waiting for their dismissal and approval. One more mistake and he'd be dancing again. However, he *wanted* to get back to his apartment.

Annoying them with complaints was not enough to get him there faster. Complaining would make them laugh and he wasn't in the mood for their banter. There was only one sure fire way to get them to cave first and that was to use scriptures they hated. He began reciting the Azzalite's Chaos Scripture resulting in a chorus of groans.

[*Please don't,* Pokk, God of Knowledge, hissed.]

Arna began to recite the Ixalites' Holy Dissolvement parable.

[*Stop! Stop!* Ixxzal, God of the Unknown, shouted.]

[*You have passed this test,* Pokk, God of Knowledge and Change, sighed.]

[*There is nothing more we can do here. You may go home,* Xeyaro, God of Dance and celebration, said.]

Blinking, Arna stopped and let the relief wash over him. He'd spent the last year on the test: perfect all five variations of The Twenty-Seven and be able to dance them all in a single day at a standard the Gods approved. The Twenty-Seven Dances of Worship for the Knowledge, Adoration, and Understanding of the Six Gods were separated into five sections: Appreciation, Knowledge, Powers, Understanding, and Worship. The first four sections were composed of six dances. The last section was comprised of three.

There were five variations of the dances, and when danced with only six seconds between a song and twelve seconds between a section the dances took between an hour and a half to two hours to complete, depending on the which variation was being danced. To dance one variation in one section, depending on the section, was enough to leave a dancer out of breath and their muscles close to over exertion. To dance from the beginning through twenty-four, could send most dancers to the hospital due to extreme exhaustion, or in worse cases, they could die.

[*You just had to start reciting that nonsense,* Ixxzal, God of the Unknown, groaned.]

[*It's a smart move. I would have,* Lumak, God of Balance, laughed.]

[*Recite something else! Maybe something from the Book of the Apostle? I like that one the best,* Azza, God Chaos, said.]

"And here I thought I was terrible." Arna chuckled, checking his body for how weak he was. His hand shook a bit as he held it out. His muscles screamed as he moved them through cool-down stretches.

Yes, he'd need an ice bath.

Most people did not have the Blessings to maintain the stress and strain the dances caused the body. Arna could, but that was because Arna had more Blessings than the average person. He had access to most of the seventy-two Blessings that existed. Even then, dancing all five variations in one day, perfectly, made his muscles shake and his head ache from the overuse of his powers. Yet, it was easier than some of the other tests the Gods had put him through in preparation for him to complete his variation of the Twenty-Seven: the sixth variation.

[*Please don't, Arna. Azza is only saying it to annoy me,* Zaynir, God of Emotions, complained.]

[*I'd never do that,* Azza said, lying.]

[*Are you trying to pick a fight with Lumak? If so, keep me out of it,*
Pokk asked at Azza's blatant lie.]

[*You should be on my side,* Azza said.]

[*No,* Pokk said.]

The brief relief that washed over Arna was quickly replaced by something more sinister. He had passed, which meant there was one step left: completing his variation. He had put his progress on pause for the year, as all his time had been dedicated to developing his body to withstand the exhaustion of the repetitive dancing. This meant he had to be the Chosen Child again and soon he'd no longer be able to hide. He still had much to do before he danced at the end of the year on the Day of New Dawn: his music, his fans, the dance steps and moves, the clothes.

imgoingtodieimgoingtodieimgoingtodieimgoingtodieimgoingtodie

Panic bubbled in Arna's throat. His muscles shook in the fear of what dancing meant, and he choked it back. Yes, he would die attempting his variation, but it did not matter. He clenched his hands tight and killed the fear.

He alone had to save the world.

breathebreathebreathebreathe

BREATHEBREATHEBREATHEBREATHE

breathe... breathe...

One. Two.

Three. Four.

Five. Six.

Seven. *I'm fine.*

Arna buried the emotion deep with the use of his Ch.Insight Blessing and got up from the floor. Discarding the weight of the twenty-seventh dance, changing his practice clothes to his hooded cloak, had never felt better. His whole body was light and airy. Packing his supplies away into his bag, he grimaced at having to wash it the next day between morning practice and work.

[*Arna? Are you okay?* Zaynir asked.]

"For you, Zaynir. I won't recited the parable." Arna smiled at the candles, burying every level of exhaustion and fear.

[*Playing favorites?* Ixxzal asked.]

"Unlike you, I doubt Zaynir voted to push me to dance extra tonight." Arna sighed irritated.

[*You'd be surprised*, Ixxzal laughed.]

"Did you?" Arna paused his clean up and stared at Zaynir, planting the biggest look of betrayal on his face for dramatic effect.

[*Don't lie! Lumak make them stop!* Zaynir snapped.]

[There was a chorus of laughter, including Lumak.]

Arna prepared to erase his existence from the room. Nothing could be left behind. Not a trace could remain, for he could not be seen. Every and any memory would be wiped.

Arna's heart began to race, and he clenched his fists hard. He flourished the Blessing to gain more power. *I'm fine.*

Arna collected his things in the same order as he always did. First, he gathered his bag for his dance clothes and placed it next to his outdoor shoes. He then gave a prayer to the candles so that they'd go out one by one. The Gods' vestige shimmered away as the room was left in pitch black.

[*Distant chatter, like that of birds and bells bounced across the glass.*]

Without having to see, Arna placed each of the six candles in their individual carrying case wrapped in velvet cloth dyed the same colors as their candle. His fingers traced the embroidered designs that symbolized each individual God. Each candle was cool to the touch, but there was a heat radiating from within.

He moved from mirror to bag by memory, placing each one of the six cases away. Then, and only then, did he remove the curtain over the window of the room blinding himself with the neon city lights. He was bombarded by the sounds of the world outside. Had it always been that loud?

[*Twenty minutes left until the next bus,* Pokk, God of Change, warned him.]

[*Hurry Arna, hurry!* Envious *is on tonight and we might make it back in time for the rerun,* Azza, God of Creation, urged him.]

[*I don't know why you watch it. You don't even like it Arna,* Ixxzal said.]

[*Liar. Lumak!* Azza complained.]

[*It's the truth,* Lumak disagreed.]

[*Arna! Since when?* Azza asked, betrayed.]

"I watch it because you like it." Arna shrugged.

[*Liar,* Azza cried.]

[*It's the truth,* Lumak mocked, *It's not a very good show. But he won't have time for anything if he misses his last bus.*]

[*I can do something about that,* Ixxzal said.]

[*You will not,* Pokk disagreed.]

Arna forced a laugh at the joke, trying to contain his grimace. Ixxzal did not have the ability to manipulate reality.

Not anymore.

"I can make it. Don't worry."

After the Splintering, the Gods only had so much energy they could use each day. Years ago, the prayers of the mortals kept the Gods strong, but these days their energy originated and ended with Arna. There was only so much they could do and as they approached the end, talking to him was the most they could muster some days.

Society treated the Gods as infallible, perfect, and all knowing, but the Gods Arna knew were messy, loud, deeply ignorant to most things, afraid, and dying.

Arna shivered. He clenched his fists tight and killed the idea of death. His Ch.Insight Blessing thrummed working hard, but with skilled precision.

[*We aren't disappearing any time soon,* Xeyaro said.]

[*But Ix might do something stupid if you miss that bus,* Azza giggled with Ixxzal.]

Arna chuckled at the empty threat, grabbed the mop, and began to hum to himself. The Gods joined him. Exhaustion started to rear its head, and he yawned.

Luckily, by the time he got home he'd have four hours of sleep—unlike the last week where he'd only had two—before morning practice, where he'd learn his new God-given task. With little more than three months left before the Celebrations, he assumed it was to complete his variation.

He had to be at work at ten, which left him an hour and a half for laundry. The issue would be afternoon practice. He'd agreed to a meeting with his boss in the afternoon, which meant he'd have to rush across town after. Arna hated rushing to practice, it always exhausted him more than necessary, but his boss requested the meeting—not that the man remembered his name.

They never did.

After practice, he'd be back across town to his second job, before he had third practice late that night. Third practice was always the hardest. He never had the energy for it; however, he'd been living on this schedule for a year. He didn't complain.

He could never complain.

Arna then pulled the window shut and moved back to his bags. He stuffed the curtain in his backpack. Dance shoes off, outdoor shoes on, Arna swung the bags over his shoulders: heavy as always. Arna gave the room one last glance before he unlocked the door and flourished his Blessings one last time for the night.

Arna's Fa.Mirrors Blessing, allowed him to disappear, or rather to make it appear as if he were *meant* to be in the room. Anyone playing back the footage from the cameras would assume he was *meant* to be there. Then they would forget him. Although Arna paid for the studio membership just in case, the hours of operation stopped far before his evening practice began. It had taken him years to master the ability as well as he had, but it had been one of the first ones he had to get to near mastery when the Gods demanded he dance without being seen.

He left the room door open so that it would air out. Past the night guards, Arna said nothing. Perhaps by this point he'd done it enough that they truly believed he was allowed to be there, despite the hours. Maybe they didn't think he was breaking and entering. Maybe they *remembered* he existed.

Arna clenched his fist tight, fingernails digging into his skin, and he calmed his heart with Ch.Insight.

Arna walked out into the brisk winter air, not another soul in sight. Up above, past the false sky, the residential districts were glowing a soft green like a borealis of ancient myth and curving about like the petals of a lily. He lived in the second ring, third petal, and from here there was no way to see his small apartment. The sky buzzed in light from the flickering far off city lights, displays and advertisements, drones making deliveries, and the glowing tracks of trains that looked like spider webs from where he stood. Billions of people lived in the city, living their interconnected lives.

As the city of the sea and water, Azis was filled with spiraling rivers tumbling through the sky, weaving through the skyrails, into spinning torrents of floating water kept up through a series of invisible riverways created through Blessings and advanced technology. There were shimmering lakes and forests littered throughout the petals. Islands floated in the sky as tiny dots, covered in trees: private homes for individuals who had enough money to have one installed. Even through the false sky, that turned the otherwise bright city: into the illusion of night, the water swirled with a beautiful faint glow of lime and red.

Ancient sea creatures and those of myth: whales, sea dragons, water snakes, eels, sharks, squid, and more floated through the air, crafted with nanotechnology to create projections. Some were flying robots delivering goods, people, and messages across the city. Hanging, glowing robotic jellyfish lights floated and hovered above. Robotic octopi flew off to assist people with maintenance.

More tech was created to fill the sky with not tools but decoration, swimming through the open air like they were under water. Actual animals followed suit and flying with them through the streams in the sky.

Arna boarded his river bus shaped like a river dragon that floated atop the waterway: large, metal, twisted in a spiral, and not actually floating on the water but hovering above it ever so slightly causing tiny ripples in in its wake. The reeds swayed out of the way from the air pressure. He nodded to the bus driver who ignored him. No one else rode the bus this late at night, and the bus driver did not so much as give Arna a hello despite the year they had traveled together. Arna never said a word either: secrets had to be maintained, and the man would forget him as soon as he stepped off the bus.

Sitting in his usual seat, Arna looked out the window as the bus started into the sky, flying away from the river to another, past the towering skyscrapers that were shaped like cones, waves, and crescent moons. Through seaweed and muscle farms, they flew towards the skyrail where he'd catch his next bus towards his apartment in the coral cove. Most of the homes on the third petal, second ring, were coral adjacent but his complex was a curling landscape of homes within concrete and metal structures shaped and colored like a reef.

They passed tall glass buildings that glowed in the colors of Azza, their city's God of choice: red, lime green, and forest green. Despite being the God of the sea, Azza was the God of Chaos and Creation firstly, and their colors reflected the sentiment.

There were large screens plastered to the false sky filled with televised announcements and reports. There was Rosmarinus' charming brown face: a soft smile accompanied by a number to call to assist in donations. Ebru laid next to perfume bottles on some fake beach, half exposed and sultry. Ginger talked excitedly, reminding the city of Azis to turn off their lights at night so the bioluminescent tech could glow brighter and that the public servers would shut down at midnight. The energy consumption of the internet and most things like, washing machines, were being heavily regulated.

Arna supposed that was due to some sections of the city having major power outages for days. Reports said that people would turn their lights off in the midst of one and be unable to turn them back on. Rumors said those that kept their lights on, retained the light. As if keeping the lights on would assure they couldn't go off. Arna never much cared for the dark, so he rarely turned on his lights to begin with.

Based on what Arna could read from the headlines and subtitles of the news reports: officials were speaking to the priests of Axis. As the new year approached and the Ceremony of Chaos, Arna had seen more priests giving their predictions and calls for prayers. Up to a duodecennial ago no one cared for the months leading up to the Celebrations. Now it was all anyone could talk about, with the twelve-year anniversary of the Splintering.

No Sign of Incarnadine.

Arna's heart sank as he read the lines on the marque:

Eburnean asked whether or not he shall take the mantle once again. Gingerline continues to struggle: the end of another Golden Generation dancer? Pervenche still not returning to dance. Is Phlox's new movie more important than her duty to the world?

"And we're back," the News Anchor's voice rang out over the bus radio after the commercials for the new augmentation lawsuit ended. Images floated in the air before him, of the talking heads and the grimaced faces.

"With me, I have Cardinal Song of the Church of Axis. Cardinal Song, as an Azzalite yourself, this year's Ceremony of Chaos, what can we expect?"

"This will mark the twelve-year anniversary since Incarnadine disappeared," The Cardinal said with a hollowed voice. "If Incarnadine returns, the prophecy of the Chosen shall be complete and we must anticipate the beginning of the Sixth Variance, marking the Fifth Variance to a close."

The Third Variance marked by Vervain the Blythe had been the longest Variance before the fifth marked by Ilex, although records were uncertain when Raven existed and the time between them and Watsonia.

"Many skeptics believe that he is dead," the news anchor responded.

Arna clenched his hands tight at the word, trying to ignore that it had been said.

[*Ignore them,* Azza danced with the talking heads like a shadow.]

Arna could not. The images vanished, no doubt due to the interference from the Gods, and the words became muffled.

"We believe Azza in her infinite wisdom shall lead him to what is needed."

"The Church of the One Truth—"

"We do not need to listen to those heretics who—" The voice was cut off as music replaced the noise, creating a softer ambiance. Arna looked up. The bus driver's eyes in the reflected glass were staring at him. For a moment Arna was seen, before the bus driver focused on navigating the floating ocean, once more.

With his Ch.Insight flourished to erase the thoughts, Arna clenched his fist tight. It was hot and warm and. . .

[*You made yourself bleed!* Pokk yelled.]

Arna released his hand, and his palm held the marks of his nails, bleeding and tickling ever so lightly. He didn't even feel it anymore. . .

[*Heal,* Pokk demanded.]

Arna lowered his head, and did so, by flourishing his K.Body Blessing. His body ached at the overuse of his abilities. *Remember,* he told himself.

He had been the one to break the world. He had invoked the world's greatest taboo and with it the Gods had been separated from mortals. He was the only one who could fix it.

Nothing else mattered.

Nothing.

Arna paused for a moment when he got off the bus, leaping from the doors to the platform, despite the holopathway that formed. He didn't trust the nanotech to keep the platform steady. He met the eye of the bus driver, who did not so much as glance to him before shutting the doors, cutting off any hope Arna had at a conversation.

He tightened his fists and hurried through skyrail station, trying not to cause himself to bleed again. Arna flashed his card at the gate to pass the security barrier to the platforms, the silver nano-gates dissolving so he could rush through and immediately reforming as he did. There were few others in the station: individuals who were alone and those who, Arna assumed, had nowhere else to be as they loitered near train doors but did not enter or exit.

Once on the platform, Arna was forced to wrap his jacket tighter around himself as the chilled air berated him. The cloak had holes again, which meant he either had to fix it or buy a new one. He was not sure which he had more time for—both required an allowance of flexibility that his current schedule could not give. He was already struggling to pay rent between the equipment costs, renting studio space, food costs, and virtual data plans. He had little time to do most things.

Time reminded him of sleep, then of music. That night he'd need to send Alis the new samples, most of which he'd not yet recorded. Alis would not be pleased.

Mobile Holophone out of his pocket, Arna opened his messaging app and clicked on Alis' name. Before him the screen appeared. His retinal augmentation, although old, was able to pick up the information in the air above him floating like a large screen only for his eyes.

Despite their array of possibility, augmentations had never taken hold over the main populace. No one had been able to develop an augmentation technology that perfectly balanced the capability of Blessings with the technology. It was unlike most of the nano and holotech that was powered and built by the combination of Blessings and science. Augmentations had to withstand Activation and Flourishing of Blessings from an internal place, working with the mortal's full capability. Like most things when reaching for the divine, the majority of Augmentations broke under pressure—resulting in death or injury to the user.

Retinal augmentations, and some replicated organs, were the only augmentations capable of withstanding the change for most people. Those who had Blessings that affected their eyes, however, found it difficult to use retinal augmentations. Arna supposed that would be nice, not being bombarded with constant advertisements, and *fun* facts, but without it most holotech was difficult to use. Jasi and Ebru wore glasses. Arna shook their names from his head.

Yet as he opened his mobile to message Alis, an ad popped up in the air. Ebru stood, wearing white framed glasses saying something that Arna did not care for.

Arna's eyes lingered on Ebru for a moment: bright white teeth, body hand sculpted, and—Arna closed the ad. He could not think of his family. He could not think of home. *Focus.*

He couldn't send messages with his eyes, as his augmentations were old and not sensitive enough, but at least no one else could see what he was writing. Arna had only one contact in his mobile. He logged into his messaging account for CrimsonFlesh, his online username, and clicked on the only chat that mattered. He sent:

Rosy: I forgot.

As Arna awaited a response, the first train arrived. A ripple of terror ran through Arna as he stepped back to let it leave. Agonizing minutes passed as he waited until the skybus arrived. Skybuses were more expensive, and slower as they did not ride along the skyrail like trains, but Arna did not trust the trains.

The all red whale was empty inside, save him. He checked his times again, the signs on the bus, and waited a few moments. They did not change, as sometimes the trains and buses did, randomly and without warning becoming different routes as soon as the doors closed. Always a consideration when traveling in Azis, one had to be prepared to end up somewhere they did not want to be.

As the bus began to move, the lights flickered, and the Gods formed before him seated in different rows. The six Gods were impossible to describe. They were constantly changing, constantly shifting: shimmering in and out of existence, with no face or corporeal form, like a reflection or mirage. Physical form was of little importance to them. They never appeared to him in the exact same form twice. This time they appeared similar to flower mantis, large eyes and with massive petals representing their individual plants.

The only consistency were their voices. It was not a pitch or frequency, but the tone and feeling they gave.

[*When we get back, we will need to be vigilant,* Xeyaro, God of Arts and Nature, said.]

Xeyaro was there and watching, observing, guiding, and loving. Usually kind, Xeyaro spoke when necessary and often gave out guidance, but could be sharp with their words and rarely was kind for the sake of being kind.

[*As if we aren't already. I don't like this plan,* Ixxzal, God of the Unknown, complained.]

Ixxzal was like one's worst fears matched with risk, adrenaline, and hope. They often spoke with a bit of sarcasm, rooted in deep meanings, a bit of humor, and cutting to the bone when necessary.

[*You were out voted,* Zaynir, God of Emotion and Souls, sighed. *Besides, it's time.*]

Zaynir's voice was the tears one cried when they were happy and smiles someone gave when they were pissed, a harmony of complexity. They were always extremely emotional and spoke quickly. It was almost childlike.

[*We shouldn't be talking about this where he can hear,* Pokk, God of Knowledge and Change, said.]

Pokk was the sound of wisdom—not that Arna could describe that to others. They rarely spoke unless they had to, and it was often filled with a hit of ferocity and anger. There was a deep fire in their voice and it swirled with the depths of the knowledge that they had.

[*He's not listening to us,* Azza, God of Creation and Chaos, disagreed.]

Azza was dissonance, a voice that hurt and healed. It was beautiful and horrendous all at once. They were often cheering, yelling, laughing, and the most talkative out of everyone.

"Should I be?"

[*You said that aloud, and* we *should be more discreet,* Lumak, God of Balance and Justice, said.]

Lumak was perfection, or what Arna figured perfection sounded like: skin tingling and disorienting. Lumak was kind, direct, and always responded when spoken to. They were often the voice of reason against the others and helped to stop the bickering between the others.

[The voices of the six became muffled as if they were speaking behind glass, far away.]

Arna did his best to ignore them. His phone buzzed.

    Rosy: I forgot.
    Alis: You have got to be kidding me.

Alis was Arna's one real connection in a world where he was forced to disappear.

    Alis: Again?
    Alis: It's been a year. I can't keep this project on
        hiatus.
    Rosy: Who is going to care? Me? Who else listens to you?
    Alis: I'll have you know that my followers have been
        berating me for the delay on this project.

Alis, short for Ivumalis, was the world renown composer who had always hidden himself. Only known by the image of an ancient, mythical aurora borealis done in all white tones, no one knew him. No one was able to talk to him, no one but Arna.

    Rosy: Wow. That's rude.
    Rosy: You should tell that guy to suck a dick.

Rosy: It might make him happy.

Alis: Go suck a dick, Rosy. Maybe it will make you happy.

With a laugh Arna sighed out, a tension at the back of his spine dissipated. Finally, he could relax. Thanks to anonymity, they had no true connection save the messages online. When Arna was dead, Alis would forget him easily, without Arna having to do anything. Alis was safe; the one person Arna could be himself with, at least for a fleeting moment.

Rosy: If it's yours it would. Immensely.

Rosy: You know what else would?

Alis: Driving me up a wall and ruining the little quiet
    I have?

Rosy: Yes.

Rosy: You against a wall screaming my name would be music
    to my ears.

Alis: Keep talking like that and I might have to hunt
    you down just to see if you're as skilled with your
    mouth as I think you are.

Rosy: Only for you

There was a moment that Arna was certain that the dirty talk would continue when Alis sent three song links, as well as a sample from a new song he was planning. Arna's stomach lurched.

Rosy: What happened?

Alis: Dad.

Alis: For some reason he expects me to complete this
    other project for his boss and I'm already at my
    limit.

The notification of a voice call came through and Arna denied it.

Rosy: Sorry, on the bus.

The small amount of guilt that he had, he shoved away. He could not get closer than he was, even if Alis was trying to call him more often these days.

Messages only, Arna reminded himself, *for Alis' sake.*

Rosy: What project?

Alis: My dad let it slip that I compose music and now his
    boss wants me to write a song for the celebrations.

Alis: For someone else to dance to.

Alis: I want to say no.

Arna placed his headphones on from his side pocket on his bag and started by listening to the music links. Alis usually sent the music that explained his mood, using the sound to explain himself better than words did. Closing his eyes, Arna listened to what Alis used as an escape. The music was like a dream, lofty and mystical, much in Alis' usual taste when he was a mess.

Who was Alis?

Arna drifted through hypotheses, for a moment: perhaps no one or someone from a city like Ixis, surely, or maybe... Ven...

Dreams, however, were a dangerous place for Arna to be after dance practice. Dreams led him to hoping for things that would not happen, missing those he cared for, and contemplating the possibility that had not been given to him. Dreams made him contemplate what happened after he danced in three months.

Not that he'd live to see it.

[Are you visualizing? Zaynir asked.]

Arna's eyes snapped open, and he glared at the ceiling, settling his heart. *Kill it.* Bury the fear. Ch.Insight came in to guide him down the path to clarity.

He slowly faced Zaynir who jumped atop the seats before him. Arna opened and closed his mouth three times trying to articulate that no, he had not, and even if he had, they would know. Yet he *was* thinking of Alis and Ven and. . .

"Alis is my muse," Arna spat. *I'm trying.*

[*No need to be so hostile, Incarnadine,* Ixxzal chastised.]

[*We are only here to support you,* Pokk said.]

Arna sighed out in grievance. It was true, but it did not make him any less nervous. Five variations of the Twenty-Seven dances existed. His task for the last twelve years had been to create the sixth. However, creating a dance that could compete with the other greats was easier said than done.

[*Being good, is good enough,* Azza tried to cheer him up.]

"Nothing is perfect." Arna turned off the music, discarding thoughts of his best friend and a life he could not have. The bus climbed through the sky, passing over the rails of other routes. The glow of the rail web brightened when trains moved: blues for receding and red for approaching.

The Rail Operators had a perfected schedule to ensure no crashes or delays despite the overlaps and crossovers. The trains twisted and spiraled up as they moved through the sky. His bus floated through them all to the next stop.

In his mind he heard screams. Once more he resumed the music, to drown out the memory. Silence cascaded around him as the volume was turned up and he forgot everything.

As Arna transferred from bus to bus his thoughts drifted to changes for his variation. Alis' songs were forgotten, and the ideas swept through him. The world rippled about him, calling him to dance. In the silence of the platform, a woman wept. Instinctively directing his attention to her, Arna froze and then forced himself to look back at the tracks. He knew better than to ask; it was a bottle better left sealed.

[*Her child was not blessed,* Pokk confirmed.]

[*Maybe you should comfort her,* Azza chastised. *It's your fault.*]

Arna flinched.

[*Not you, baby. Pokk,* Azza, God of Creation, corrected. *You know I didn't vote for the midnight test.*]

[*At this rate I think you are trying to fight me,* Lumak sighed at Azza's lie.]

But Arna dropped a fan and sentenced the world to rot. Pulling his cloak's hood up over his hair to hide it, Arna wished for the bus to arrive sooner.

[*Do not blame yourself.* Xeyaro's voice stopped the chatter.]

All at once the Gods disappeared from around him and Arna was left alone as they discussed further away. Arna opened and closed his hands trying to calm down, trying to find peace. His eyes traced the crescent shaped scars that were centered in his palms, as an anchor to reality. His thoughts raced with the what-ifs and the knowledge that no matter what he would never make up for what he'd done.

The mobile began to play another Ivumalis song and in it Arna found renewed silence.

As fate would have it, Arna made his last bus.

There were a few other passengers on the bus, surprisingly. Most people did not avoid the skyrail and trains the way that Arna did, and there was a more direct train that was scheduled to arrive ten minutes later.

The passengers ignored Arna as he sat. They spoke in hushed whispers about the Celebrations.

"—Heritage Foundation *again*?"

"—unable to heal because—"

"—without Blessings—"

"—I don't care who dances so long as Sarcoline dances Powers—"

"Do you think Incarnadine will appear?" One person asked too loud. Arna refrained from looking over out of feared of being recognized. Not another voice was heard.

Arna exited the bus at his stop then the station and walked along bridges that lined the frozen water ways with haste. In Azis, weather changed regularly, and while it was still winter throughout the whole of the lily, tonight his district was below freezing and his breath was a harsh white as he trudged through the snow. He did not have the clothes for the weather. But by tomorrow it would be a more temperate winter; he hoped.

Above him, past the false sky and in the heart of the flower city, laid the central district that was alive in light except the dark void in the very center. The core of the flower was cast in total darkness from the lack of Everlit candles, just as it was in every city. There, Harmonious Six priests—and perhaps others from religions, although Arna doubted it—would be maintain endless worshipping. Their Gods would not respond.

They had not responded to mortals' pleas in the last twelve years.

Arna's apartment was the largest he'd lived in for the twelve years on his own, but it was small all the same. The studio was the cheapest space that he could rent as a person without a name, a real job, or a degree. The walls were lined with photographs and news articles of those he loved and cared for: Ven, Ebru, Ginger, Arco, Phlox, Aureolin, Jasi, his parents—what little of them he could find—and even Rosmarinus, who he did not know very well. Not an inch of blank space was left.

The only bookshelf had a series of scrapbooks dedicated to them: each a different color for a different person. He wanted to leave the books to them, in some sort of repentance, to prove that he'd been watching and supporting them the whole time.

He planned for them to only get the books after he danced when he was dead.

Sometimes he wished he'd be able to see their reaction, but it would never happen.

Kill it. His Blessings did the work and the worry dulled.

He swallowed and immediately picked up a bucket, to go outside.

After gathering enough snow for his bath, Arna finally locked the door. Arna unpacked his bag carefully, placing the candles on their altar: a set of six metal flowers designed to look like the six mortal cities. He'd stolen the altar, candles, and holders on his first month on the run. The priests hadn't needed them.

He hung up his dance clothes to air them out before he threw them in the wash. They needed to be cleaned, despite how washing wore them out too quickly and they were expensive. He owned just enough clothes to get by in two weeks without someone realizing he was wearing the same thing in a cycle. Most of his wardrobe money was dedicated to the dance clothes.

He had one hundred and thirty-five robes each a different weight and each a different color. The robes, different from any of the official ceremonial clothes, had massive, long trailing sleeves that were difficult to fold and travel in. They were necessary for practicing the dances for they emulated real dance fans the best. He had adjustable wrist weights of different types in a drawer. There were ribbons that he could use in arcs to practice his movement when the robes were too hot.

Arna sat in the bath for enough time for his skin to scream at him in pain and fire. Only then did he get up and begin working on his nightly routine.

Arna first made himself a nutrient shake and worked his muscles. He used a tool he'd created that could replicate the fan's snap of opening and closing. His wrists could not be weak.

He reviewed his schedule for the next day, drank his shake, opened his computer, and started the upload of the sounds to his and Alis' shared drive. He grimaced both at the time of the upload and his list. He'd have to go shopping for food soon, much to his dismay. Food shopping was always more of a hassle than laundry. Arna could not order it to be delivered without having to sign for it and he was never home.

The upload would take an hour at least because of his horrible connection. He checked his messages.

```
Alis: ???
Alis: Hello?
Rosy: Just got home. Files up in the morning.
Alis: I thought you didn't get anything.
Rosy: I'm missing the final few chimes. I can get them
      in the morning.
Alis: I suppose you're reliable after all.
Rosy: You won't hate me?
Alis: Don't press your luck.
Alis: Get better internet.
Alis: Sleep well.
Rosy: Love you too.
Rosy: Message me if you need me.
Alis: I know.
```

Checking everything once more, Arna drew his curtains on his window and prayed to the candles. They lit up immediately. The candles were useless for anything mundane—cooking, warmth, good lighting—but he had to keep them lit as it was the only way to keep the Gods powerful. They filtered his prayers through the flames to feed themselves. Without them, they sustained themselves off of him directly. There was only so much divine energy a soul could take before it fractured, which was part of the reason he needed to dance in three months.

Only when he was certain the candles were not burning, did he lay down. He watched Azza's show, laughing with her. He checked Zaynir's favorite comics and listened to Ixxzal's favorite podcast. He read the updates on technology for Pokk and legal cases for Lumak, all before thinking of his dances one more time for Xeyaro, even when they didn't ask.

Alarm set, he closed his eyes. Sleep came quickly to Arna, a skill he'd picked up over the years on the run and hiding. However, for extra measure, he flourished his already activated B.Body Blessing, knowing that by doing so he'd be able to get his body to mend itself from the harsh day of practice and work. It was not real rest, but it was enough to keep him alive.

Arna awoke groggy. He sat up slowly surprised that he had woken before his alarm. Rolling back his shoulders, Arna felt good. It was a type of sleep he hadn't had in years. The candles were still bright: no wax, no melting, no smoke, and no real flame.

"Good morning." He yawned to himself. Glancing to the time, he turned off his alarm, before he had to check it again and his heart dropped. He was late to work, let alone morning practice. He leapt from his bed and raced to get ready.

"Why didn't you wake me?"

[*You needed sleep,* Azza said.]

"I have work! I have practice!" He couldn't slack off. He—

[*It's time for the final test,* Xeyaro cut him off.]

The way that Xeyaro said the words resonated deeply in Arna's chest. Right. The last test.

That meant . . . Home.

As in Ven. And his parents and his siblings Ginger and Arco. Aureolin. Phlox. Jasi. *Ebru.* As in *home* and the bed he longed for. As in the one thing he craved more than anything. As in. . . everything he was fighting to protect.

Losing his balance, Arna grasped the counter of his kitchen and stared at the candles. His heart raced and his breath shortened.

Arna thought of his house and the constant smell of cinnamon in the winter. He pictured Ginger's smile, although he supposed she'd not give him that smile when he returned. Then there was his little brother, Arco, beaming at him, expecting greatness. Arna supposed Arco would no longer smile at him too.

How was Ven? Did Ven hate him? Would Jasi be mad when he saw him? Phlox? Aureolin? Would he finally be able to get to know Rosmarinus? Would Ebru hate him too?

His gut twisted in a deep-seated fear. Years ago, it had threatened to swallow him whole in his moments of weakness—telling him he was nothing, worthless, that they hated him—only unlike then, he could not ignore it. His Ch.Insight could do little to stop the panic that erupted.

The last test meant he was that much closer to being forced to face them. They could reject him. They probably hated him. And as much as he wanted to see them, the memory made him sick.

Breathe. Breathe.

He wasn't going home yet.

[*You have perfected the variations of those before you, perfecting your own variation is the final task,* Lumak explained with a yawn.]

Final task? Already? What about the last test? "But I cannot. . . ."

[*No, you cannot pick up a fan,* Xeyaro then added solemnly, *We can't fix that yet.*]

[*Nothing is perfect,* Zaynir chirped happily, repeating back the words from the night before.]

Arna struggled to control himself. His breath shallowed with the passing moment. Fear raced through his body, as he choked back the real question he wanted to ask. His Ch.Insight worked harder than it ever had.

Instead, he asked, "What do I have to do for the test?"

He was tired of tests, but it was all for training for the day it mattered. There were too many factors that could go wrong, and he had to be prepared for all of them.

[*It's a simple one,* Azza giggled.]

"And I'd be a fool to believe you. You're the God of *chaos* Azza," Arna snarked trying not to *think*. He opened and closed his hand, counting and breathing.

[*It's simple in theory,* Lumak sighed.]

Arna believed Lumak, the God of truth. "And what is the *test*?"

[*You know it already. The final question,* Xeyaro answered.]

What? But he wasn't supposed to get the final question until right before he danced? Wasn't that what they said? It would be a choice, the last one he'd ever make before he died.

[*To pick mortality is to pick the Gods. To pick the Gods is to pick mortality,* Pokk recited the Rapture Scripture, one of the shared scriptures in all of the religious texts worldwide. *The day you decide which you will choose, is the day you have the chance to ascend. Mortality or the Gods.*]

Arna heaved. There again were the twisted messages that sent Arna on the journey to begin with. The Gods had not cared when he was fifteen. They told him what to do and expected him to abide by it. He'd misunderstood, and learned that later, but ultimately if he wanted to be the Chosen Child, he had no choice. Not then and not now. If he wanted it, the one thing he'd been working towards and destroyed everything for, the one thing that could keep them alive, then he had to listen.

Finally, the Ch.Insight worked and the panic faded a bit, enough for him to steady himself.

If the Gods said it was time for another test, that meant it was time to leave. They'd send him somewhere new to complete it. What did he need to bring? His dance clothes and practice tools? The ribbons? Wrist weights?

[*You bring only that which you need for your new life,* Azza said.]

Twelve years' worth of life to be left aside as he stepped into his new self, Saint Aubergine 15.2. He'd left it behind before, he could do it again.

He would sell his computer. It was terrible to begin with and not worth much, but he'd be able to get a better one with a good job. How much time would it take for him to wipe his computer? He could take the memory and leave the rest for scrap parts. He would have to buy new clothes; it was better to just toss the ones he had. He could send all his dance tools, pictures and scrapbooks to his holding box in Ixis before rerouting it to his new home when he settled. He'd sell the furniture.

Would that be enough to get him to where he'd need to go? He didn't want to touch his funds from his work as CrimsonFlesh online; that money needed to be used for his variation.

That left him needing to carry his music notes, a few of his necessary fake IDs, dance notes, and his fake practice fans. Those were the only things he could bring with him and could be hidden on his person. Arna forced himself to the counter and grabbed his planner and a pen. He opened it and checked that the Alis files had uploaded before he shut it down.

"Explain."

Why was it given early? What was he meant to do?

[*Mortals or the Gods?* Lumak asked. *The test is the choice.*]

[Before you can answer you must know three things. One, you must know the true question we ask. Two, you must know the weight and cost of your choice. Three, you must be willing to accept the choice even if you are wrong, Zaynir continued.]

[When you Understand, a petal will disappear. And only when all three petals are gone, can you make a choice. Then you will dance, Azza said]

The moment that they said the words, Arna's wrist burned. Gasping, a mark appeared on his left wrist, atop his constellation birthmark, shaped like a lotus with three petals. A mark of Zaynir? No. . . The petal shape changed as he moved to different flowers: lily, tulip, lavender, orchid, rose. The mark was ever changing, in shape while the size and number of petals remained the same: three.

"This is it then?"

[The final test with the final task. Both, Xeyaro answered.]

The moment of truth.

[If you pass, you will finish the dances, They said in unison.]

[If you fail, you know the consequences, Xeyaro said.]

Arna nodded. Arna had caused the Splintering at fifteen and in doing so the God's connection to the world was broken. They had lost power over the last twelve years, and this was the final year that they could hold on for. If he failed, he died, and the Gods died. Blessings would disappear and everything would end in a mess of fire, collapsed cities, and thunder.

The world would die.

Everyone would die.

Arna had practiced every day for twelve years to maintain their connection with him and what little they had to the world. There would be no one to fix it for him. There would be no one to save the day. Either he survived long enough to dance all twenty-seven dances, and everyone was saved, or he didn't. Either way, he would die in the end. But his life meant nothing. Everyone else's did.

Arna's hands began to bleed where his nails dug into his palms. The scriptures, the holy texts, his exile. . . It was all for that day, three months away.

"Is this like the others? I will get no answers?"

[Ask as many questions as you like, They said in unison.]

[But we can't answer them all, Lumak said.]

[Like all the tests before, Pokk agreed.]

"I must make the choice for myself." And their answers might influence his decision.

[What do you want to be, Arna? Zaynir asked.]

[The choice is yours to make, Azza sighed.]

Mortals or the Gods? The question struck a pivotal memory in Arna's life. He'd only heard the words before, *that* night. He thought of the willow tree in the center of his house in Xeysis and the voice in the moonlight. He was there again, suffocating and unable to breathe after lying to Ebru.

He shook in the memory of the question. And the voice, the voice that had not been theirs, haunted his thoughts. Their voices in chorus usually sounded ominous but the one in his memory was like the cusp of a dream before a blooming storm. It was confident, terrifying, and so familiar.

What if you can only choose one?

He did not have an answer then, but he knew that he needed to find one now.

Kill it. Bury it. He flourished his Ch.Insight in a way he'd never done before, drinking the power like a poisonous drug.

This was his one chance to make things right.

"What was the vote Ixxzal?"

[*Near unanimous,* Ixxzal finally spoke.]

"Do you believe in me?"

[*After all this time, you're considering giving up?* Ixxzal asked.]

"No."

Incarnadine Vivicent looked at himself in the black computer screen.

This was just another test, and just another task.

Nothing had changed. He'd make the right choice. He'd finish his dances. He'd save the world.

[*Then prove it,* Ixxzal said.]

[*Because we are putting every faith, we have into you.*]

One last task. One last test.

"Where am I going?" Arna asked. The new mark on Arna's wrist was cool to the touch.

[*We already told you, silly,* Azza giggled.]

[*It's time to go **home**,* Xeyaro said.]

All at once gravity came crashing down around him.

The first six dances focus on Knowledge. What is knowledge? What we know? Yes. But it is also what
we *don't* know: the gaps in the world that we strive to fill.
Knowledge is a memorial to both.

— On the Knowledge of the Gods section of The Twenty-Seven Dances.

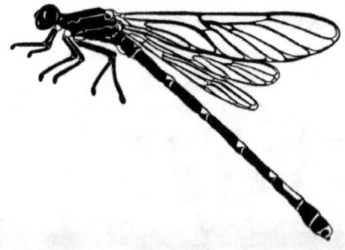

Dance 2

Practice

Incarnadine

"What are you waiting for? Jump."
"I could die."
"Yes. That is why you must try. Are you not willing to risk everything for this? Did you not already prove that?"

15 Poan
100 Days Left
On a Train from Azis to Zaydiel

When Arna was little, he loved storms. Within the cities, they were rarely more than a downpour of rain and a bit of wild wind. He admired the rolling clouds that were real instead of false like the sky. He loved dancing in them and wished for them each season. In Zaydiel and Ixis the storms were worse than those of Xeysis, but Arna had loved those all the same. Arna loved city storms until he was twenty-two.

The train windows were purple, the buzz of the electricity and Blessings were being bombarded with winds and acid rain from true storms.

"All passengers, prepare for submersion." The intercom warned them. Traveling beneath the earth, while safer, affected the speed of the trains greatly. For a short time, Arna stared out wanting anything but to think. In the clouds were the faces of his family. Every truth he held close to his heart threatened to explode. He clenched his fists tight and focused on the clouds.

Real storms, the ones that weren't manufactured by the cities in order to maintain a semblance of changing climate and plant control, were terrifying. The regular ones had winds that could rip plants apart, and rains that could flood and wash away a person, pelting so hard that it ripped the skin. The lightning was stark white and hot, unpredictable and capable of turning the land outside the city into plains of fire.

There was not much that grew outside of the cities anymore. The storms made that impossible.

"Diving," The intercom warned, and Arna stared out of the window more intently.

Arna ran his hands over his body, knowing every inch, every scar, every mark and burn that had never fully healed. Normal storms outside the cities were terrifying, but the superstorms were the end of all. The mixture of Blessings and technology protected the cities. Without them, the superstorms would destroy everything.

The screens changed to advertisements for spas in Zaydiel and as much as Arna tried to change them back, he could not. There were people smiling and laughing then there were images of Phlox's new drama: *Envious.*

[*Visualize,* Zaynir demanded.]

The train sank into the ground, away from the superstorm outside his window.

[*There is no reason for you to see. You know,* Azza teased.]

Arna sank into his seat. His body was itching to move. He had not skipped a single day of training in almost a decade, until this one. Plus, he was on a train, and even if it were on the ground, he did not trust it.

[*Stop moping,* Ixxzal was annoyed.]

"I'm not moping."

[*Clearly,* Ixxzal retorted.]

If the Gods could roll their eyes Arna had no doubt that Ixxzal would roll every one that they had. Arna sighed. He tapped in the air activating the holograms and turned on the sound for Azza's favorite drama. Phlox smiled before him in the three dimensional capture and when she began crying, he sighed. She was a good actress, but her cry only reminded him that he needed to protect her.

All at once everything came crashing back: every thought he forced away moments ago.

failurefailurefailurefailurefailurefailurefailurefailurefailurefailurefailurefailurefailure

Arna flipped through the channels much to Azza's protest until he landed on the documentary channel, that was discussing the history of Zaydiel. He'd had his Ch.Insight up and activated since he got on the train, but it was not working to keep his thoughts clear. Arna had been on the train for too long.

Train travel was far slower than transporters, but Arna refused to travel by transporter. Trains ran daily between the cities, but only in one direction either to or from. Most cities were only connected by a single line for trade. At one time there had been many trains with multiple lines from one city to another. After the Splintering, most of the rails between the cities fell apart.

Arna itched to move. He was nearly certain he was the only traveler on the train, which meant no one would see him. However, he'd snuck on which made it dangerous to walk around. He could not get caught and he could only keep his abilities flourished for so long.

[*Arna, this is boring,* Zaynir complained.]

[*Please change it. Please. Go back,* Azza whined.]

Zaydiel took shape in the images and he ignored the voices of the Gods. He tried to think of anything other than his shaking hands due to being on a train, the sound of the storms above the ground, his memories, and what he had to do.

diediediediediediedie

His Ch.Insight was unable to clear the panic. He turned the focus to what he had absolutely no control over and was the only one that motivated him: the storms.

He recited the facts to himself while clenching his hands and squeezing eyes tight.

When Ilex danced, beginning the Fifth Variance, he had started the technological revolution that started the cities, which were built as a direct response to the superstorms. War and mortal made weapons had destroyed most of the atmosphere before Ilex. Technology and the misuse of Blessings had wrecked the ecosystems. Taboos provided no obstacle.

The superstorms were nothing special to begin with, much like normal storms, but they quickly transformed into catastrophic events: ripping apart homes and drowning coastlines. By the time they became a corroding poison that not even Blessings could stop, Mortals were in the cities.

Historians claimed that mortals attempted to manipulate the divine energy of the Gods and it backfired and caused the storms. Scientists assumed that the combination of science and Blessings had created an adverse effect, a sort of backlash that created an unlivable world.

In some ways it was true, that the superstorms grew worse because of how mortals had poisoned the planet. The complete truth was worse.

(Saffron caused the Shattering.)

Focus. He flourished his CH.Insight Blessing more, until his head ached.

He would not be Saffron. He would be like Ilex.

Ilex solved what he could after Saffron caused the Shattering and thus the storms, but Arna had to solve the rest. For it was Arna who Splintered the bridge that Ilex had made and divorced the Gods and mortals once again.

All of civilization lived within the petals of one of the six flower cities, strategically placed across the continent so that if one fell the others wouldn't. What had once been hundreds of countries, were condensed down to six super city-states operating in harmony. Or as much harmony as they permitted each other.

After the Splintering, that harmony had been tested. Not only were the Gods getting weaker, but Blessings were, and when Blessings disappeared, all the technology built and powered by it would disappear. The entirety of the super cities were based on the reliance on Blessings. Without them the cities would collapse and those who managed to escape the collapsing cities would be left to face the storms.

The idea made Arna shiver.

The image cut off. The room went silent.

[*Don't focus on the storms, respond,* Pokk suggested.]

"Sorry," Arna was not sure how much energy Pokk must have used to do it, but they should not be acting in that way at all. Their powers were like an hourglass, and every time they used their powers to manipulate the world, the sand fell through the glass instead of landing on the other side.

Arna sighed, taking out his black journal and started to write.

In order to fix the Splintering, and more so the Shattering, Arna had to fix the contract between the mortals and the Gods. In order to do that he had to finish his variation and dance it. And in order to dance he had to answer the question they gave him.

"Mortals or the Gods?" Arna asked them.

[*Yes,* Pokk snorted, *What other question could there be?*]

His written words were a blurry mess of questions and doubts.

diediediediediediedie

The holograms reappeared. *Envious* started to play and once more there was Phlox, her bronzed brown face and mint eyes close up. Her hair was a pitch black, pulled into a soft bun as she smiled softly at the audience and Arna's heart leapt.

"I love you," she said.

His Phlox spoke to him. She was the girl who had stood behind him the toes down whenever he wanted to do something crazy, and Jasi told them they might die. Him, her, and Jasi were a trio against the world.

[*Soon,* Zaynir gasped. *Visualize.*]

Seeing Phlox gave Arna the motivation he needed to focus. He would complete his variation, for her. He needed to protect her and all of his family. His Ch.Insight Blessing raced its power through his veins.

He shoved down his fears, sealed them tight and forgot them like he did the scars on his body. All the while he held his left hand clenched, blood trickling through his fingers.

17 Poan
98 Days Left
Zaydiel

Arna stood in line looking up into the false sky of the swirling lotus. Unlike the other cities where their false skies were a faint shift of blue, creating the image of the sky, Zaydiel was filled with clouds. Today, in the petal where he stood, the clouds were wispy, free and white. Past them, further up towards the center of the city, there were thicker-grayed clouds. The city sparkled through the clouds up above in all the shades of blue: Zaynir's color.

Advertisements hung in the sky with Rosmarinus' face everywhere. The city loved him because of the charity fund he'd provided that helped thousands in Zaydiel. Rosmarinus was the embodiment of Zaynir in legend: calm and serene. Everything unlike the Zaynir that Arna knew who complained and cried all the time.

Rosmarinus made Arna think of Jasi. He had grown up never really knowing Rosmarinus well despite him being Jasi's twin, but he'd collected hundreds of stories online in regret. Rosmarinus was the polar opposite from Jasi, from what Arna could tell, and he'd never fully have the chance to get to know him.

The headlines above spoke of Rosmarinus' world tour for the Blessing Charity project which was dedicated to raising money for all those injured due to the sudden loss of their Blessings. He was not the creator of the project but based on the totals reported, he was bringing in a record number donations through his charity work and appearances.

Wind rushed through the city, pulling the low hanging clouds around Arna's feet past him and through the streets that appeared more like floating paths and bridges than they did actual stone. The engineering feat in Zaydiel was fascinating. Almost everything was floating in some way, allowing the clouds and wind to go under buildings and through them. The city of chimes whistled as the air soared past, creating songs.

"There is no god but The One True God!" One Truth Church members screamed at those in line.

Unfortunately, the wind carried voices just as well as it carried songs.

Zaydiel was pretty, with rivers that floated through and around some streets, dancing with the clouds closer to the ground, unlike in Azis where the water floated in the sky. If Arna really wanted to, he'd could walk in the tiny streams.

The city of the birds was filled with swarms that called melodies in the sky. Magnificent large tech-birds in all shades of blue flew, personally transporting people and things. Tiny hummingbird messenger bots delivered letters and packages. Tiny crystals floated about refracting prismatic light and filling the sky in rainbows.

> Rosy: Whistling Falls incoming.
> Alis: You finally got it?
> Rosy: Of course.

"All other Gods are false! Only the One True God is real!" The members yelled.

[*Azza, can you shut them up?* Ixxzal asked.]

[*I have an idea,* Azza giggled.]

Out of nowhere a large wind pushed the members over, with it clouds swirled about them and the members started coughing. Arna pressed his lips together to try to keep himself from laughing. The One Truth Church wore all black, as if co-opting the color of the Chosen.

Years before the Splintering, most of the world did not believe in the Gods. For years the churches across the world had shrunk. The progress of science had proven that magic was all around and part of the universe as molecules were and the stars. Most people chose fact and science over mysticism and divine. They saw their Blessings as the natural order and disregarded all else.

However, when Arna caused the Splintering, something changed. The One Truth Church, who believed in all powerful and wrathful God that was not one of the six, rose. People flocked to it, because clearly Blessings were not simply an aspect of nature like science suggested, but how could the Gods have abandoned them?

[*People need something to believe in to combat fear,* Xeyaro said.]

The One Truth and Harmonious Six offered that: a hope that penance and something new could change the world instead of believing in prophecies. Arna had no love for either church, as a member of the Church of the Apostle, as all Vivicents were.

The Church of the Apostle was dedicated to finding and protecting the next Apostle while preaching that the Gods were equal. They were not a large church as compared to The Church of the Harmonious Six that worshiped the six Gods as equals but did not believe in the prophecies of the Chosen. Long ago the two had been one before they had split.

"The worship of false idols and false Gods caused the Splintering! The One True God shall punish all those who do not believe! Punish all those who wish to become that which they should not."

Arna was disgusted by the fliers they handed out that depicted the symbolic flowers of the Six as the One True God's iconography.

"Incarnadine Vivicent faked the prophecy of the false Gods, and the One True God is angry!"

Arna stepped away from the voice and into the church of the Harmonious Six that was filling with people who were eager to learn the first section of The Twenty-Seven. Past those with lockets of vervain and pendants of holly, Arna stepped through the crowds to the closest corner he could find and hide.

The walls were covered in words and symbols.

There were a thousand stories that Arna knew about the Gods, that he had memorized forwards and backwards.

On one wall: the song of Ixxzal, the loner who all the other Gods ignored. There were depictions of the love story of Xeyaro and Lumak. The lines about the animosity of Azza and Lumak were large and sprawling. The origin of mortals and Zaynir's birth were told in lovely stained glass.

The church was filled with their appearances, not mortal, but dancing in color and depictions of what they controlled.

Pokk, the God of the sun—gold, orange, yellow—of wrath and war, peace and tranquility, technology, pestilence, hatred, knowledge, change, fire and cats. They were denoted by the orchid.

Zaynir, the God of the Clouds and the lotus, was the master wind, mortals, the sky, connections, birds, the home, souls and emotions, children, and the family. Their colors were aqua, sky blue, and navy.

Azza was the God the moon, of death and life, chaos and creation, of water, the oceans, of the hunt, loyalty, happiness, destruction, lilies, and fish. They were forest green, lime, and red.

Xeyaro the God of Arts and nature, was the rose: mint, silver, and white. They were the patron of love, food and wine, the harvest, trust, the seasons, storms, the body, the senses, and dogs.

Lumak the god of balance and the lavender flower was violet, indigo, and mauve. They controlled snakes, scales, justice, laws, lies, the truth, friendship, fate, retribution, of stories, and the earth.

Ixxzal was the God of the unknown and all magic. They were mostly depicted by tulips: bronze, smoke gray, or pink. They were the master of stars, deer, insects, shadows, gravity, space and time, illusions, fear, miracles, and hope.

Arna found a place to stand, behind a pillar. He kept his eyes low, and hood over his head to obscure his features.

"Ginger will not be teaching today," someone said in a hushed voice to another bystander.

Arna's heart sank. He'd stood in line for hours in an attempt to mentally prepare himself for his homecoming. It was the closest he'd ever allowed himself to get to any of them. This had been his way to try to placate his thoughts before everything came crashing down. Instead, he was crushed with the weight of the things he wanted to forget, without reprieve.

"There are five variations!" The instructor from Xeysis was some person that Arna did not recognize. As the lesson began, Arna grew increasingly irritated that it was not sister.

"The original, Twin fans, Roots and Ends, and Holly!" The man skipped over Blue Rose Fears entirely.

Arna bristled at the slight. The Blue Rose Fears variation was the one he had chosen when he caused the Splintering. It had always been his favorite. It was the most complex and difficult. It was his major dance inspiration for his own variation. For it to be skipped meant the man was directly attempting to erase Arna's mistake.

As the man began to teach the dances, he held the fans awkwardly.

He needs to adjust his grip.

[*It's sloppy,* Zaynir agreed.]

The man held the fans tight, muscles too taut. If he did that for the whole dance, his arms would grow tired. The fans were heavy, and while the first six dances were easy enough for most citizens to learn, most people could not dance them without lots of practice and good exercise and muscle. Children learned them as exercises in school for a reason. They exhausted the body.

How Arna wished to go up there and to do it himself, to feel the soft wood under his hands and be weighed down by the fabric.

No. He could not.

For a painful hour Arna watched the man struggle to pull and swing the fans around, snapping them open and shut as he was supposed to. The cloth continued to get caught nor did it flourish in the right way. Arna wanted to groan but kept his mouth shut. Internally he criticized with Lumak, Ixxzal, and Azza pointing out all the inconsistencies and issues.

[*If it were Ginger. . .* Azza complained.]

It would have never been taught this badly. His sister was far better than this.

"Each section of the Dances is danced by one person. They dance a total of six songs before another person dances the next six. Worship is never danced!" The man shouted things that the whole crowd already knew but ate it up with gasps of awe. "For the last three dances always result in death if danced badly."

It was a lie. Only the twenty-sixth dance resulted in death. Twenty-five was just too taxing for most people to dance and required a Child who was the peak of their capability, to perform. His father had danced Dance Twenty-Five for the last twelve years, in penance for Arna, and he wasn't dead.

Yet the man did not flinch in the blatant lie.

[*It's more of an exaggeration,* Lumak supplied the reason the taboo was not invoked.]

Arna shrugged.

"As we approach Apostle Week!" The man shouted. Arna was unable to hold back the groan. Why couldn't the man talk normally? "There will be six days of celebrations instead of one. Not simply a New Dawn Day but a whole New Dawn week!"

It's called Apostle Week for a reason, you fool. New Dawn Day was just the last day of the year. The celebrations didn't change the name of the week. It was *called* Apostle Week because it was a celebration. It only came every thirty-six years, when they added six more days to the year to realign their calendar with the sun. Each day had a specific name for a reason.

[*My ears are bleeding. Let's leave,* Ixxzal lamented despite not having ears.]

"And the dancing of Ceremony of Chaos will last four hours!"

With that Arna turned to leave. Everyone knew that the Ceremony of Chaos took three hours excluding worship, due to the breaks between the sections where the emcee would talk about the next dancer, the history of the variation they chose, and gave a brief overview of the importance of the section they danced. The actual dance time was less than two hours excluding those breaks. Arna's variation fluctuated around an hour and a half.

"The Ceremony of Chaos is the most important event in the world."

The words gave Arna pause because it was true. Since the Splintering it was the one thing the cities could agree on: the dancing of the Twenty-Seven during the Ceremony of Chaos were the most important event in the world. It only took centuries for them to agree. The Ceremony was the final event of the celebrations on New Dawn Day.

Arna clenched his hand and activated his Ch.Insight Blessing.

[*The sweet shop should be open,* Xeyaro suggested the sweet shop on the forth petal that made cakes that tasted like emotions.]

Arna hesitated but left without another word. When he got home, he'd be able to fix everything.

19 Poan
96 Days Left
Podiel

The city of the sun was filled with people, jumping about in their boots that allowed them to glide through the sky, and across floating platforms that continued to move through the air. There were rings of districts in the center of the orchid, woven with the skyrail. The skyscrapers were like the stamen of an orchid rising up and up into impossible heights, in the center, surrounding the inner religious district. Tens of spheres and disks floated in the sky, for full residential communities and colleges.

Tiny cats, large cats, massive sky's cats, were all over watching as cameras, intercoms, delivery bots, and transportation. There were robotic cats the same size as a house cat; they could talk. Years ago this had confused Arna when he'd asked a real cat for instructions and it had not responded, briskly walking away. Cats the size of ancient beasts stalked through the city on patrol.

People wore skintight clothing in Podiel, due to the movement. Aureolin was in ads across the sky modeling the newest tech and clothes. The colors were vibrant, akin to burning fire, that made their bodies almost appear as rays of light or smoke and fire as they moved. Some even wore fashion that moved and grew, made of gears and wires and metal replicating synapses and ripples. Colors bounced across their outfits like it was speaking to itself and as two people passed each other the color rippled across their clothes in an unspoken conversation.

The chaos in Podiel was akin to that in Ixis and Azis in that everything was always moving. Only unlike the other two, everything moved like clockwork and extreme precision and repeated daily. The newest technology was on full display in every shop, advertisement that people blasted through, and the machines that they use. Aureolin's voice bounced across the streets.

Arna had to be extra careful not to interact with the busy streets as people used their Blessings and technology in tandem, as the whole city was interconnected through the movement. Like trees in a forest, they were in constant communication of who they passed and who they interacted with.

Arna was an oddity in his thin black jacket and black pants, the jacket was a poor man's attempt to blend in as it was a few seasons too old. He used his brother's name in jacket's virtual log to avoid suspicion.

Arna rubbed the mark on his left wrist above his constellation birthmark.

The people of Podiel were covered in tattoos that shifted and moved in his augmentations, but it was just an illusion created by technology and specific tattoo patterns. His flower mark appeared the same way, but it was burning cold against the tips of his fingers. Only vows appeared on the body like moving tattoos without augmentation technology, and they had a temperature.

Arna rubbed it, trying to make his way through the crowds to the old home he hoped still existed. It would protect him for the few nights he was in the city, waiting for the next train to Ixis.

Arna's feet were heavy against the gravity that was adjusted to the hover tech and boots that everyone else wore.

He trudged on, eyes low.

There was a scream and Arna paused. Blessings flourished, Arna searched for the sound, heart pounding, ears ringing.

Screams on a train.

Crashing to the ground.

jumpjumpjumpjumpjumpjump

"Help him! Please!"

A child was on the ground struggling to breathe.

"He told a secret!" The girl cried. She was like Aureolin, screaming and wrathful. When Arna had broken taboos as a kid, she had always been the one to tattle, and the girl looked just like her.

Arna paused, staring at the boy who could be no more than twelve. Ixxzal's greatest taboo was telling secrets. Yet, despite the cost of breaking one of the greatest taboos, the child would not die. It would only be a warning.

[*Power comes at a cost*, Pokk said, uncaring at the scene.]

A fan dropping from his hands.

Screams, echoing across blackened fields.

runrunrunrunrunrunrun

Each God had their own set of taboos, but they were so numerous that most people did not know them all. Millions broke little taboos every day. Xeyaro had taboos about killing plants or dropping art equipment, but plants died and sometimes paint spilt. Most times nothing major happened unless a one of the two greatest taboos were crossed for a God. They had more authority in their cities, and it had made Arna more apprehensive.

Cearly the kid did not know that they were real. Who would?

Most people did not take them as seriously, since the Splintering, because the Gods couldn't hear them anyway. Without the connection the Gods could not give Blessings to the new generation of children, despite how much everyone prayed. Most people thought the taboos were the same: impossible to be enforced.

The taboos, however, were a byproduct of the contract to give powers to the mortals. Mortals could only have divinity, Blessings, because the taboos existed to keep them from burning their souls away in the power. Without the taboos, the divinity would devour the souls of mortals in seconds. It was the counterbalance, even if everyone hated them. Even though the Blessings were disappearing, the taboos still existed.

For Lumak the greatest taboo were lies and breaking contracts. For Zaynir it was apathy and torture. Yet a white lie to save someone is different than a blatant one. Killing a five-hundred-year-old tree is different than killing a sprout unknowingly.

[*Arna, keep walking*, Lumak pressed.]

Arna could not move. He could only see himself, hear his own screams. The boy became him in that moment, gasping and clutching for breath. Arna's pulse beat against his fingers like fluttering bird wings.

Non-blessed mortals breaking a God's greatest taboo could result in death, but the God's powers were dwindling, and it was a kid. No kid would be killed for an infraction, Arna hadn't been even when he'd done far worse.

I'm going to be just like Saffron...

Arna's heart raced. He squeezed his hands tight.

All he could see was himself, in the boy. Struggling to breathe when he was young.

Dropping a fan.

Telling a secret.

Screams.

Death.

[Arna!]

The most major of offenses for breaking taboos always resulted in dangerous outcomes. Usually injury, although Arna got more electrical shocks than anything. Breaking a contracted promise to avoid a taboo was worse.

Arna had broken the greatest taboo of all by dropping a Ceremony fan while he was dancing during the Ceremony of Chaos.

painpainpainpainpainpainpain

his fault

S   P   L   I   N   T   E   R

Just like that Arna was cursed. One decision, and everything had broken apart. And now everyone was losing Blessings. He no longer could touch a fan without losing a Blessing and...

He had to pick them up to properly dance his variation. Without the fans, the contract could not be reestablished.

Arna squeezed his eyes tight and flourished his Ch.Insight Blessing. *Kill it.*

[Keep walking, Ixxzal ordered.]

But Arna would fix it. He'd burn the fan he dropped. He would dance. His mistake would not be another death sentence to everyone around him. He had to.

Ignore it. Bury it. I'm fine.

As the child sat up, crying and gasping for breath, Arna slipped into the crowd. He didn't breathe until he shut the door to the cobweb invested house he'd once lived in, years ago. Arna refused to leave again until it was night, when no children would be out, and no screams would sound.

21 Poan
94 Days Left
Ixis

Arna stood shaded by the pillars of the room and blended into the darkness as the shadows danced. Unlike actual dancing, the shadows were cut from paper and using light they danced across the walls with the use of Blessings to tell stories of the history of the world. Getting a ticket into the Shadow

House, the top Shadow and Dance troupe in Ixis, had been a miracle: one that Ixxzal had a hand in giving him.

He'd always wanted to see the group before he died, and this was his last chance to do so.

On the walls was the story of the ancient dance houses played. It began with Watsonia, the second Chosen, who had been from a family dedicated to dance and sharing the knowledge of the dances created by Raven, the first. Vervain the Blythe came from an ancestor family who retained their knowledge. Her family was notably famous for separating the dances from a single person dancing twenty-four to four people dancing the four sections.

The dancers spun in shadows, weaving elements into the display. They transformed what should have been simple black against the wall into texture. As the bodies moved through time, the shadows became crisper and clearer.

The dance arrived at Sable, then Ilex and the Luster family. The Luster family of the Third Variance were the ones who discovered the importance of A.Reverence in the dances. Ilex taught a total of eighteen children who created the families that existed in the modern age.

Arna's fingers traced the mark on the back of his neck, as his family was portrayed. It was shaped like a snake, at the top of the spine, below the head and on the back of the neck.

Carnine Vivicent, Obsidian Hue, and Ash Platinum took the stage as shadows. They were three of the infamous eighteen students, and their bond formed a vow between their three houses. It was to be an eternal partnership: to protect each other in war, health, and all plights, unless one house could result in the direct fall of another. In time the other families of the eighteen students fell. The Vivicent family stood tall with the Hue and Platinum family backing them. A snake formed between them, a vow was made.

The dances continued and Arna squeeze his hands together, praying for something, even when the outcome was predetermined.

They trained all the children who came to them to dance with the same ferocity and care, regardless of name. Arna's father always said the Vivicents did so because they wanted to spread the dances without prejudice. But Arna knew it was because it inspired loyalty.

People clapped as the group triumphed and became a powerhouse and then the lights flickered again. The shadows danced of his ancestor and all Arna could think of was Ebru, the sweet doe eyed boy with large glasses and pitch black hair that he shared two vows with. The boy who was currently in the clutches of the Shadone family.

Vows were meant to be kept. Breaking a vow broke the greatest taboo for Ixxzal and the second greatest for Lumak. It was what made vows so dangerous, breaking a vow meant crossing two Gods, and often resulted in death. Arna had set one on himself at the age of ten.

He promised never to lie to a single person and had thought nothing of it until it was too late. He did not often think of the vow, had no reason to in the last twelve years since he'd last seen Ebru Hue, but as the shadows danced, it was all he could think of. The small boy with black hair the color of the night sky, who stared at him in mirrors and shared the spiral on Arna's chest: the mark of their vow.

The lights shimmered as real dancers took the stage to continue the story along with the shadows that spun across the room in a faded strangeness. They had moved past crisp clarity into a vague hyper-realism, illusion that melded between three dimensional and mist.

Arna clenched his hand.

Everyone knew this part of the story. A Platinum family member betrayed the other two out of greed. He gave secrets to the Shadone family, that nearly killed every member of the Hue family. The dancer portraying Cinnabar Platinum crumpled to the floor dramatically, gasping for air and Arna's body shook. All he could remember is when he had almost died from lying to Ebru.

The shadow dancing went on to depict the bond between the house of Hue and the house of Vivicent, but Arna could no longer remain. *Breathe.*

Arna's hands were quickly healing from where they bled and his Ch.Insight Blessing was activated.

He left the hall wanting nothing more than to forget everything he'd seen but Ebru was loved in Ixis.

Ebru was like the towering skyscrapers twisting into each other, creating false floors above and below him. Every time that Arna thought he knew what floor he was on, he'd take an elevator up or down and be on the same floor, but clearly higher or lower. A maze, a mess, infrastructure growing and weaving into itself across the city with no end or beginning. The skyway ran through buildings tumbled down gardens and flew below. Ebru's pictures were everywhere. The Prince of Dance was adored in Ixis. His false smile lit up a holoscreen as he presented some product that Arna did not care to purchase. This Ebru's hair was stark white, it made him look strange.

Despite Arna having seen Ebru in this form for years—the man had bleached his hair mere months after Arna had run away—it was wrong. Ebru's eyes were the color of raven's wings, his hair the color of the night sky. He wasn't supposed to look like a washed out mirage in the distance, devoid of color.

His face and Arco's face were everywhere. Arco was on billboards, it was Arna's own face but younger and harder—angrier. Arco looked like a storm in the body of a mortal: terrifying.

Seeing them, Arna realized that he did not have copies of some posters and quickly searched online for stores where he could buy them for his collection.

Ixis was shaped like a Tulip with skyscrapers that stretched upwards more than most of the other cities, besides Ludiel. The residential petals were connected via the skyrail and the swirling twisting bridges of metal and plants. Everything was overgrown, entrenched in vines and ivy, and masked in a deep haze of fog. There was little visibility in the Tulip not that Arna cared, it was the most like home outside of Xeysis and he was able to hide the best here.

The towering city was where floors moved and changed. The stores opened at random times and there was no consistency. The plants grew unmanaged, and the seasons and weather flipped in seconds. There were insects of all shapes and sizes walking about all robotic. Moths flying high, beetles out for delivery, spiders climbing about through the mists. Massive gemstone-multieyed creatures staring and scurrying off. Every so often there were large deer, stags with massive antlers or doe with large eyes. Arna was never able to get close to them before they vanished into the smoke.

The citizens wore all gray and pink, dressed like clouds, dressed like stars, dressed in materials that flowed in nearly impossible ways. Some appeared to float on their own: moving and spinning. All were made through a series of optical illusions in the weaving and the ways that wires held the pieces together. Many people wore masks to combat the smoke and to see clearer in the illusions. They had their hoods up, blending in with the environment. The only other city that breathed the same way that Xeysis did was Ixis, and in it Arna was able to breathe as well.

The perpetual city of night that, when it saw the day, was covered in a haze of light, like looking through a mirage. Usually dark, with glittering gems throughout the pathways and skies that both glowed in solar light and bioluminescent pink. The smoky, hazy city was where time and space converged. Where pathways lead to the unknown. Where gravity changed by the hour and sometimes people flew through the sky like magic.

Meandering through the city, Arna thought of his family: his brother, sister, mother and father. He thought of the few ancient families that existed: Shadone, Hue, Vivicent. His thoughts wandered into dangerous territory where it was not meant to go.

Once, the six of them—his sister Ginger, Phlox, Aureolin, Ebru, Ven, and Arna—were called the Golden Generation of Dancers. They had been his everything. Now Arna's everything was six candles in his bag, surrounded by eight different religious holy books that Arna had memorized, and the box of his news clippings, pictures, and posters that he'd sent to the Vivicent manor.

Arna pulled his hood further over his head and entered a shop he knew intimately. It was where he used the buy the posters in the past. Finding the ones he was interested in, printed as postcards for adoring fans of the world's best dancers, Arna paid and left. He glanced at one of his brothers and then lingered on the one for Ebru. It was irritating how handsome Ebru had gotten.

Ebru. Arna wondered how he was. Alabaster, Ebru's father, was a well-known choreographer and could have taken a job anywhere. Yet he chose the Shadones. Arna was not sure how it did not trigger the Vivicent-Hue vow, but something had to have happened for them to go the Vivicent's enemy and for it not to destroy him. The Shadones were the Vivicent's longest standing rivalry, and even a baby knew how hostile they were against each other.

Soft Ebru would have been eaten alive. He was one of Zaffre's *best* students and Alabaster was Zaffre's best *friend*. Although based on the interviews and images around the world: Ebru, the soft boy, was gone. Another thing destroyed by Arna's hands.

Arna's mobile buzzed. Startled, Arna shoved both postcards into his bag, swearing to add them into their proper folders when he got home and had access to all his things he'd sent to be delivered.

> Alis: For Incandescent, should I ask Bluebell or Cyan
>   for vocals?
> Rosy: Are those your only options?
> Alis: Who did you have in mind?
> Rosy: Depends on the lyrics. Part A or B.
> Alis: We wanted Cinth for A, remember?
> Rosy: Right. . . Well. . . Did we get the sample?
> Alis: Not yet.
> Rosy: We're behind as it is. . .
> Rosy: Bluebell is the best pair with Cinth, but she can't
>   meet a deadline.

Arna wandered through Ixis, wondering if he'd run into the Alis. If Alis lived anywhere, Arna thought it would be Ixis. Maybe he was the random person on the street who just turned the corner. Maybe he was someone that Arna knew in his past.

> Alis: You're one to talk.
> Rosy: I only miss deadlines because it's ambitious and we
>   are looking for select sounds that only I can record.
>   Have I failed you otherwise?
> Alis: No.
> Rosy: Exactly. I'll take your apology on a silver platter.
> Alis: Ha. No.
> Rosy: Photos of your plants?

Arna first looked at the photos of the plants, smiling at each one. With even breathing Arna tried to focus on the lyrics, but all he could think of was Ebru. He was going to be *pissed*. Beyond anyone else, Ebru was going to hate him for what he did. They'd grown up rivals. He'd narrowly beat out

Ebru to dance Powers that faithful night of the Splintering. Then Arna had broken the world while he watched.

The vow they made at ten was one to never lie, and the thought of trying to avoid Ebru's questioning made Arna's throat begin to swell. No one could know everything, it was not like they could help him anyway. He would have to avoid Ebru.

[*You can ask for help,* Zaynir corrected.]

Arna ignored them.

```
Alis: Apology accepted?
Rosy: I'll always accept your apologies.
Rosy: Look at my babies. . . They're so big.
Alis: They're my babies.
Rosy: I didn't realize we'd gotten divorced.
Alis: I saw a comment that said it might nice for us to
      see other people.
Rosy: You break my heart.
Alis: Check the lyrics. I changed things.
```

Arna began to read the lyrics as the approaching bus slowed to a halt. Announcements rang over the speaker and as Arna messaged back, he checked that he had everything. Before he could enter, others exited in a flurry of movements. Members of different churches took to the streets.

"The Splintering will resume! Twelve years of waiting are over!" Members of the Church of Harmonious Six were yelling. Arna hid behind a building to watch. The members were dressed in all white, as was customary, and handing out flyers.

"Only salvation can save you!"

"I hope Incarnadine Vivicent is rotting in a shallow grave!" Someone yelled.

"The true God is the One God!" Someone else yelled.

"If he's not already dead, I'll kill him myself," Another person said kicking the priest who tried to hand them a flyer. Arna did not move, as the men laughed and then walked off, not without stomping over all the flyers the priest once held. As soon as they were gone, the priest stood and wiped himself off.

[*This is extremely annoying,* Azza sighed.]

[*Stay focused, Arna,* Lumak reminded him.]

Arna sighed and checked his Blessings. They were still flourishing and active. No one would notice him, lest of all the church members who wanted to control him.

The One Truth Church members walked on trying to scare citizens into submission as they passed. When Arna had last been in the city, the Church of Ixis had been at the forefront feeding the poor, helping the sick, mustering members to fill in jobs for the government to assist with the infrastructure failure. Now they were scraps trying to get by, and the Harmonious Six was losing hold of Ixis as well. Prayers, he'd heard on the news, did not help to save the failing Blessings. The prayers did not reach the Gods anymore.

He began wandering again, in a halfhearted attempt to find Alis in the city of smoke and wonder.

```
Rosy: "Your eyes are the prayer that guide me home."
Rosy: Well, well Alis. I didn't know you loved me.
Alis: ???
Alis: You're the one who wrote the lyrics.
Alis: You love me.
```

Rosy: My statement stands.

Rosy: We got Cinth's vocals?

Alis: As soon as I get it, I'll send it to you.

Arna vanished within the city to visit the places he loved, one last time. Deeply, secretly, without a word aloud, Arna prayed that he'd meet Alis, even if he had to see him from afar.

23 Poan
92 Days Left
Ludiel

Arna hated Ludiel with a burning passion. While Arna had lingered in Ixis for three days, knowing he had to move on but dreading leaving, Arna wanted nothing more than to exit Ludiel's city limits. He was forced to stay for three in Ludiel until the only train to Xeysis left the next day. He hated everything about Ludiel: the smell of it, the look of it, the sound of it. The memorial holograms of the train crash when he was eighteen were still big and wide across the orderly city.

Everything was symmetrical, with towering buildings that mirrored each other across the entire lavender, reaching for the sky. Everything was planned, every district identical and covered in scales. Long slithering technology shaped like sky snakes and dragons rushed through the sky in a too orderly manner. Towering buildings shaped like mountains and valleys, and gemstones were too perfect. The plants were too uniform and the false sky too crisp.

Or maybe he simply hated being there and that judgement clouded his view of the city.

All the same, Arna approached the chestnut forest, the only place in the city he liked, where care for the city was scarce. He traveled deep within. It was the one forest where the trees were not perfectly symmetrical, and it almost felt like Ixis and Xeysis despite how orderly the trees were planted. He climbed over roots and pulled himself into the branches, wanting to sleep there for the night as he awaited his train.

Only when he was sure he was alone, did he stop using his Blessings. Arna was exhausted, but no one could see him until he got back home. He had been flourishing his Blessings on and off consistently since he left Azis. Activating a Blessing took energy, but it was like turning on a light, capitalizing on internal energy and its natural flow. Flourishing was like blowing out the bulb until it sparked. It was dangerous to do for most people, but Arna had been trained to keep it up for prolonged periods. It was easier to do when he was calm, but Arna had learned to flourish his abilities under any condition. It was how he'd stay alive.

He pulled the white and black journals from his bag. White for places he wanted to dance, places he wanted to go, things he wanted to do when he had finally danced and saved the world. The black was his dance notes, on everything about his variation dances.

[*How are you?* Xeyaro asked.]

"I feel like I want to die," Arna admitted. He then killed the truth and squeezed his eyes and hands tight until it was forgotten.

[*Arna. . .* Xeyaro attempted to sooth.]

"Thanks, Xey," Arna sighed leaning closer to the tree as if they were there with him. He breathed tight and ignored the world.

He switched focus between digital images he'd drawn on the train from Ixis when it was too bumpy to draw by hand, and the ones in the book: trying to decide the best pattern for his variation fans. There were three variations with one fan and two that used two fans. In the variations where there was one fan, the fabric was either dyed or embroidered to use the primary color and secondary color for its corresponding God. For the variations that used two, both fans were the same color, usually identical, save in the later dances where the patterns would become more intricate.

Arna was going to alternate between one and two fans. He had decided it when he was ten, and had stuck to the idea for years, but the logistics of it were a nightmare. If he were home, his dad would have known what to do. Arna missed his father.

One day, after everything was over, he hoped that he could build fans with his father again. Running the Vivicent manor, being a fan maker, dancing for a lifetime: how he wished for it.

Arna's eyes wandered and he pulled up the internet.

Blessings Disappearing: No need to fear.

Each year as we approach the Ceremony of Chaos, the world is overcome in fear that all the Blessings are disappearing. The fact is that this is not true. The Blessings always fluctuate, and people who have "lost" them before, will have them returned after. . .

Arna flipped through articles. Between those talking about the non-Blessed—Children who never received Blessings in the last twelve years—and those who lost their existing Blessings, slowly but surely all Blessings were vanishing.

New School Policies: The Future of Non-Blessing Based Education

Schools are struggling to restructure their lessons, as the specialist education based around Blessings is no longer viable. Districts have proposed new alternatives to. . .

Podiel Districts in Power Reserve

The Uncertain Future with the Non-Blessed

Do not Panic: What do if Your Blessing Disappears

Hospitals Under Caution: Non-Blessed No Longer Can be Bealed by Blessings?

Non-Blessed and Blessing based Technology: Alternatives for your non-Blessed Child

Non-Blessed and Blessing made Food: Considerations to Avoid Reactions and Allergies

The whole world was based on Blessings: their technology, their science, their cities were built on it. There were reports of deaths, of mass loss of Blessings, and while everyone acted like it was the same as it had been since the Splintering, but it was worse. This time the Blessings wouldn't come back after the Ceremony of Chaos was danced. This time it would be permanent.

Even without the superstorms civilization was on the ledge of collapse from their dependency on Blessings. When everything from food to travel to the air they breathed was managed and controlled by Blessings, there was no way they could go without them. Their world was dying.

Panic bubbled in Arna's chest.

It's okay. It had to be okay. He was going to succeed. Everyone would live. He'd save them. He used his Ch.Insight to calm his fear away.

[*You will succeed,* Xeyaro said.]

In theory, Arna had his variation figured out. He wanted to create a world where Blessings did not have the same weight as they did currently.

Amaryllis Ink At it Again

What Can Sarcoline Do Without the Blessing for Dance?

Phlox a Mess on the Screen, Proof that A.Reverence is only for Dance

Eburnean Hue: The Only Golden Generation Child Who Understands A.Reverence

He wanted to liberate mortals from their limited view of their potential. He was willing to sacrifice himself for the dream. After all, his family deserved to be free.

The names for the Blessings never changed, across the variation, despite the ways they could be used, shifting across time. Since all Blessings manifested differently for the person, Arna was not surprised that no one noticed the shift. Someone with Un.Mirrors in the Second Variance and in the Fourth Variance might have the same ability, but the basis of the Second Variance was the Twin Fans and the Fourth was Roots and Ends.

Blessings in the second were centered on development, and one in the fourth were centered on memory. The way a person's Blessing develops was unique for each mortal. Two people could have the same Blessing and it will manifest differently. Two people might have different Blessings that acted the same way.

Yet, despite the fact that no two Blessings manifested the same way. The world was dead set on making choices on what was and was not the proper use of Blessings.

Blessings and You: the Proper Way to Use your Blessings

Blessing Mastery

Top Ten People Who Use Their Blessings Incorrectly and it Curses the World.

Arna closed out the feed.

In concept, he knew what he wanted. In practice, he was stuck. He had an idea of what he wanted for his fans but not a complete idea. He had a concept for his outfit, but he wasn't sure it would work. The only thing he was sure of was the message and the name.

The dances started with The Original which was called The Original because The Twenty-Seven Dances of Worship for the Appreciation, Adoration, and Understanding of the Six Gods, was too long. Each dance was named from there, taking into consideration the full name and the slight change to the name itself. All of the dances had obnoxiously long names and short nicknames: Original, Twin Fans, Blue Rose Fears, Roots and Ends, and Holly.

The Holly variation was the only one named for its creator. It's true name had been lost to the annuls of history. Some had proposed nicknames—Dimness Horizon, or Of Horrors and Monsters, or A Blessing Beneath, or Master of the Stars—but with too many theories, there were no facts.

[*Visualize,* Zaynir insisted.]

Arna sat in the tree uncertain of what to do. Thinking of the Blessings, of how they were disappearing, of the storms, and of his own dances, set his heart racing at unhealthy speeds. Yet he could not stop. Arna squeezed his hands.

[*Dance,* Pokk ordered.]

Arna rolled out of the tree, not wanting to argue and knowing that Pokk was right.

He jumped from the tree, landing on the roots and tested his balance. The wind blew through the trees, creating a snapping in the way that the branches moved, and Arna danced what he had of his variation already.

Each step was messy, misunderstood. The idea was there but something was wrong, and he couldn't figure out what it was that he was missing. Unlike what he was used to, the Gods did not tell him to stop and start over.

"What is wrong with me?" Arna asked them.

[*You will keep S.Mirrors and A.Reverence. They will be enough to save you,* Lumak said instead.]

Yes, that was the issue.

He wasn't strong enough. He was going to lose Blessings while he danced.

He knew the order like he knew the scars on his own body. S.Mirrors and A.Reverence had to be the two he kept, as they were the only two that had the chance at keeping him alive long enough for him to finish twenty-seven.

But Arna didn't know how to build the contract. He didn't know how to answer the question they gave him. He needed to complete his variation, and he didn't know how to do that either.

Arna sat once again in the tree, unable to get himself to keep dancing. His mobile buzzed and Arna sighed.

Alis: I think I have a new plan for Incandescent.

Alis explained the song and Arna's heart began to settle and inspiration bloomed. Alis wasn't a Child of music. He did not have the A.Song Blessing.

Is Alis Ven? The thought came unbidden, and Arna choked. He tried to erase it, but it transformed. *Is he Jasi? Rosmarinus?*

Arna stared up at the skies of Ludiel. It was impossible to ignore his family now. He had tried and tried over the last week, to ignore everything and incidents kept propping up that forced him to remember everything he thought he'd killed.

In just a few days, he'd have to confront it all and he wasn't ready. He had to convince himself that his return meant nothing. That despite twelve years, they'd welcome him with wide and open arms, because that was who they'd been before.

His mother and father were once the most cheerful of people. Uncle Alabaster was the kindest man he'd ever met. Rosmarinus, he never knew but he would. Jasi was his best friend who was daring and mischievous. He was the only person Arna trusted with everything.

He'd see the Golden Generation again. He'd see Phlox whose eyes were more aqua than mint and was a crybaby. She was more loyal than anyone. Almost no one believed she was meant to be a dancer at all. Ginger was chaos incarnate, loud and unashamed. She was always creating new ideas, spinning surprises and pranks. Aureolin was spiteful like fire and the lead instigator of their group. She was quick to destroy anything that hurt the Golden Generation, and Arna had always been a bit afraid of her.

Ebru. . . his rival and the one person Arna was certain saw him better than Ven. Ven was the person that Arna had once loved most in the world: who would accept him without question. Arna hated thinking of Ven the most because of how much he had hurt them.

Then there was Arco, who smiled like a rose. His little brother had looked at him once like he was the whole world. The others would accept him, love him, be there as if nothing had happened at all. But Arco was changed, and Arna was terrified of seeing him, of seeing the disappointment that Arna caused. . .

Kill it. Bury it. Arna clenched his hands, but nothing was working.

Arna turned on his music. To Arna, Alis was everything. Ivumalis' songs were like dreams, and when he listened to them his mind stilled. He returned to clarity.

He did not have time for fears, only the facts.

He needed to get back to Xeysis, complete his variation, dance, and nothing else mattered. Everything would go back to the way it was before he left. He would succeed in completing his variation without fail. Then he'd die and the world would be saved. They'd thank him for it.

The second six dances are about Appreciation, not love. They are an expansion of the known. Appreciation shows us the history of the world, our connection to the Gods, and mortality's existence. Appreciation is not dependent on kindness. One can be bitter but appreciate the good actions of another.

— On the Appreciation of the Gods section of The Twenty-Seven Dances.

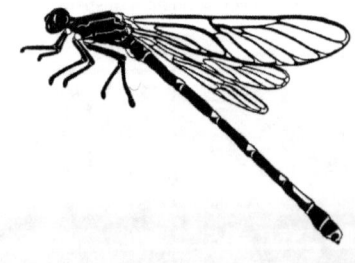

Dance 3

Morality

Incarnadine

27 Poan

88 Days Left

"New homes don't bother me so much anymore."
"One day they might."
"Is that the day you send me home?"
"It is."

Xeysis bloomed on the horizon like a rose. The city's outer districts stretched towards the sky and curled in on itself. Like all six of the mortal cities, Xeysis was designed to embody the ideology and will of a single God, their chosen God. Xeysis was of Xeyaro.

All of the cities were beautiful. Despite their horrific origin, they were splendid marvels of mortal ingenuity and peace. Each was a kingdom in their own right. Yet, Arna was partial to Xeysis. Unlike the other cities, Xeysis was the home of the arts and nature. Something was always blooming or being created within her walls. Life was always shimmering.

Each city was charming, but none had been home. Ixis, was as stunning as it was confusing, with dead ends and one-way roads that went nowhere: it was all questions and no answers. Zaydiel was too bright and colorful, too connected. It was a city with *no* secrets, setting Arna on edge the entire time he had lived there. Podiel was too technological, too advanced, too far removed from nature for Arna, and too interconnected with the people. There was little privacy.

Azis was manageable to live in, despite how chaotic it was at all time, with a government that made no sense and twisted changes to the architecture as the city was entirely floating and changing constantly. Ludiel was too had orderly, too planned, not a grain of sand out of place. Living in Ludiel for three years had been a mistake.

Arna lived for two years in most of the other cities, visiting parts of the world by foot when required to by the Gods, never staying in one place for long. Never growing roots. Never saying he belonged. He'd seen the world, and in that he'd only longed for Xeysis.

Xeysis had the liveliness of Zaydiel and the complexity of Ixis, but it was fully ingrained in nature. Plants wove into the architecture and green spanned every mile of the city. Xeysis was an immersive garden where people lived, and the arts flourished. In each other city, he always tried to find glimpses of the rose, and now after days of travel by train, he was finally almost there.

He remembered those petals lined in living districts and shopping centers. He knew its smell and the way the streets would feel under his feet. When it was in the midst of a storm, the city would close up tight with its outer layers acting as a reinforced shield of technology and magic woven together. Otherwise, she was large and blooming wide. From afar, in the cameras that the train provided, Arna had sworn Xeysis glowed, but up close it was only the sun refracting off the Blessing shields.

Seeing Xeysis was like stepping into a skin he had not worn for years and all at once it was more *real*. He'd see his mother. She'd kiss and hug him and stuff him full of sweets again. His father would be there, to dance with him, to see him, and Arna was terrified of his wrath. The Golden Generation. Jasi. They'd all he there, and Ven. . . What would their reunion look like? Would Ven hate him? He would not blame Ven for hating him.

Panic drilled its way through his veins, mixing with his constant anxiety about the end of times.

The Gods chatted about him, and he ignored everything. They laughed to themselves, and he laughed half-heartedly with them. As the train approached, Arna messaged Alis, trying to calm his heart with thoughts that could keep him focused. He pushed the brewing storm of thoughts out of his mind.

    `Alis: They don't work, do they?`

Arna clicked on the vocal track once more and listened. It was raw but it was good. *Incandescent* was a song that took sounds from all over the world: rare ones that Arna had collected for Alis over the year. It was intended to be something transcendent and Cinth's voice was perfect for it.

    `Rosy: No, I think they do. It's the right amount of`
        `breathiness that we need.`
    `Alis: Which means we need a powerhouse for B.`
    `Rosy: So. . . Bluebell?`
    `Rosy: We're screwed.`
    `Rosy: Say goodbye to being on time.`
    `Alis: I'll figure something out.`

In a perfect world, Arna and Alis would be able to be together to finish the song. They'd find each other, Arna would kiss him.

[*Are you visualizing?* Zaynir asked, cutting through the music.]

"Yes," Arna switched to his notes on his variation. He would make a world that was worth it to everyone. In it Alis would find solace even if Arna was not there. He could not break Alis' heart with who he really was.

Arna clenched his fist tighter, burying all other negativity.

[*What do you think Incarnadine?* Ixxzal asked. *Everything you remember?*]

It was as beautiful as he hoped. It was everything he feared.

With each of the other cities, he had to hide himself by pretending to be someone else. Yet here he was, a single backpack, and most of the possessions to his name on his person. His black variation notebook was slipped back into his inner jacket pocket. In one hand he held a water bottle and in the other he held his remaining fake fan snapping it open and shut.

After emptying his bank account into a money chip, he had bought three sets of clothes, one set he wore. He was clean shaven and for once, he had no chapped lips. Other than his long locs that he kept tied back and hidden beneath his hood, he changed himself into the older version of the boy who disappeared at fifteen. Anyone would recognize him, and after years of being ignored and needing to be forgotten for his safety, his heart was racing.

Incarnadine Vivicent.

His real passport was in his bag, but it was expired. He hoped that the fake one would get him into the city. It was old and worn from constant fixing but looking at it reminded him of what was at risk. He missed the couple from the house with the silver door, who had made the IDs for him. He could not let those he loved die like they had.

[*Get ready,* Pokk said.]

[*He could keep up his Blessings in his sleep,* Ixxzal yawned. *There is nothing interesting about this.*]

[*We are here Arna. You can do this!* Azza cheered.]

He'd gotten through the train ride unnoticed, but he could not slip up. Even if his Blessings could get him through security and no one doubted his alibi, his plan hinged on getting home first.

He had to get home *first* so that his family could protect him.

He repeated the mantra, so he would not get distracted.

Get home first. Get home *first*. Get *home* first.

Despite the numerous doubts he had, Arna was certain they'd still loved him. If they weren't home, he'd sneak in through the back window that his mother always kept open. If she had locked it, he'd break in. And if they refused to love him. . .

Arna shook his head. *No.* They would. He needed to believe that they hadn't given up on him. Twelve years to the day he claimed himself as Chosen he needed to dance. Not a day more or else the Gods would disappear, and the current world would cease to exist. The Chosen prophecy was drilled into the memory of all Vivicents.

He swallowed back the internal screams telling him to disappear again, as the train came to a stop. With a jolt, people scrambled to get off the train; Arna followed until he stepped on to the platform and froze. The thought of disappearing mixed with the fear in his veins. There were so many people, and everything was so changed.

[*Things change, keep going,* Pokk mocked.]

[*Isn't it lovely?* Zaynir swooned.]

[*Didn't we tell you to be quiet?* Ixxzal snapped. *Don't overwhelm him more.*]

Everything was updated, from the neon signs to the platform tiles. Mints, polished whites, and silvers shined around him. The citizens were dressed in clothes reminiscent of ivy, webs, and moths: structured, glittering, colorful and plush fabrics. There were individuals holding the latest mobile holophones and flying bots zooming around with mail and luggage. The advertisements loaded into his retinal augmentation, flooding his sight with recommendations for travel, emergency contacts to upload to his mobile and news reports. He dismissed them all by focusing on the mute option.

As he did, everything was suddenly realer than it had been moments before.

The thought of seeing his family petrified him. It would not be through interviews or magazines and photographs. He'd see them in person.

He'd watched the world convulse when he disappeared. He'd seen his father cry, and his mother break down. He'd seen how his sister and brother fought to grow up in a world that hated them. He'd watched the fall of the Vivicent family.

[*Trust me. It's time to go home now,* Ixxzal said.]

[*I thought you said be quiet,* Zaynir sneered, mocking.]

[*Remember not to speak aloud,* Lumak reminded.]

Yes. The Gods had told him to go *home,* and thus he was headed into the grief. Trying to right himself he thought of Ixxzal, the God of the unknown, stars, and fear. If he could face his death head on, he could easily face his family.

Arna started listening to Serenity's Lament.

Silence is not an absence, but a reminder of what you have. Alis once told him. Arna let his thoughts disappear and he calmed himself reciting Alis' speech. He'd had the manifesto for Serenity's Lament memorized.

```
Rosy: Will be hard to reach for a while.
Alis: You're moving right?
Rosy: Yeah
Alis: Good luck
```

`Rosy: Thanks. I'm going to need it.`

Feigning confidence, Arna got off the train and flourished his Blessings by taking a breath and focusing on igniting them like a flame in his soul: Fa.Mirrors with E.Insight and C.Stillness. He wove them together and held it steady. He'd disappear without vanishing. No one would notice him as anything but ordinary, so long as did not make any sudden moves. As long as he acted casually an UnBlessing immigration officer would not stop him to question him or attempt to block his abilities.

He'd learned that when he was seventeen. When he'd arrived at Ludiel, the world had been in too much chaos to notice him but arriving in Podiel had taught him better. It was a mistake not to be proactive.

Now twenty-seven, he easily finessed the system.

Tired, he could not continue the high level flourishing for long: less than two hours. Yet, since most people could only flourish their abilities for minutes at a time—more if they were dancers, but not by much—no one would think too much about him.

Transporters were the preferred method of transportation. People often traveled between the cities. Moving about the cities for work, sport, or show was common enough. However, Arna could not use them. The teleportation required that all Blessings were inactive or else a person could not be moved by the technology. There were no Immigration stalls at the transporters, as the transporters verified individuals through Blessing and facial recognition. If Arna wanted to hide it until he was home, it meant he had to have his abilities flourishing, but if he did so the machine could never transport him.

Thus, Arna traveled by train, despite it taking longer and hating every second of it.

The immigration stalls for train passengers had three immigration officers each. One was a user with UnAbilities, specialized in negating abilities so that identities could be verified by machines. Arna could easily fool the machines and avoid UnAbilities. The UnAbility user was identifiable by their gray and white uniform where the others wore sharp and crisp white uniforms with purple accents and silver bars representing their rank.

Squeezing his hands closed and opening them again, Arna lowered his eyes and tried to disappear into the crowd: hand open, closed, open, closed. When Arna got to the Immigration Officer's stall, he did his best to stand unsuspecting. He answered her questions as fast as he could, without being suspicious. He held himself still as electricity coursed through him shocking him as he broke taboo after taboo. The pain was nothing compared to what it felt like to touch a fan. A shiver ran down Arna's spine and it took everything, he had to appear unphased. He controlled his breathing.

This is nothing. Lumak supports this. But even if the Gods supported it, they could not change the contract and punishments for taboos.

One officer scanned him, another tried to negate his abilities, and the last attempted to see through his facades. He avoided them skillfully without any one of the three noticing.

"May the God's light never fade," The security guard said to him as they let him pass. After verifying his fake identity, Arna was berated by a mixture of relief and distress. A part of him had hoped they'd recognize him.

He struggled to contain the smile on his face, trying to keep a straight look as to not draw attention. Through the doors of the immigration quarter, Arna moved towards the train platforms that would lead them to the city, or to wherever else he wanted to go. He checked the train schedule on the screens overhead.

[There was distant chatter as if broken up by static.]

Arna had noticed weeks ago that when he was surrounded by mortals, the Gods sounded more distant as if there were interference. While it bothered him, he could still hear them bouncing about in the speakers. As long as he could hear them, he had not failed, there was still time for him to prove that he was the Chosen.

Even when he didn't feel like he was nor that he deserved to be.

No. Kill it.

While the Gods debated amongst themselves, Arna's thoughts were his own. He knew he was supposed to go *home*. It was the correct move. But the moment he saw the trains, the numbers, the familiarity of it all, the rational thought was erased by the overwhelming and debilitating paralysis. A crazed drive in his heart overwhelmed him and his thoughts began to spiral.

There was no bus route. He had to take the skyrail.

nonononononono.

No. Kill it. He could ride a train. It was the safest mode of transportation in the city. He could. Everything else was unimportant.

Mantra forgotten and ticket bought, Arna moved towards the platform to wait for the train. For a moment he stopped flourishing his Blessings, wanting to take in the surroundings without his head threatening to kill him from the pressure of his abilities.

The moment his ears stopped buzzing and his eyes focused, he was able to balance himself and take in the city.

Despite the changes, the station was the same as the last time he'd been there. People moved about in their busy lives, families with children here for vacation, students for school, church acolytes walking and reciting scriptures, musicians, workers, people of all types. They were dressed in clothes that were reminiscent to flowers and trees. Their faces were unimportant, but the energy was intoxicating. Wisteria, the rose, the fresh moss, and morning dew were on the light breeze that carried itself through the terminal.

They may have changed their clothes. The details might be refined and new. Technology might have gotten more advanced, but it was home. Xeysis' soul remained the same.

"Arco, I thought I told you to meet me at my office?" The voice startled him. He had gone so long only talking to people when absolutely necessary—work, shops, excuses—that he was not prepared for the person who walked up to him. Worse, the voice had addressed him, and Arna recognized it. It was older, deeper, but the inflection was the exact same as the one who had whispered to Arna in the dark when Arna had been scared of the voices.

Arna caught a glimpse of the colors of a high-ranking immigration officer—silver and purple, woven to appear like lavender grew off the sleeves—and his blood ran cold. Dressed in all indigo with mauve scales dusting the cuffs, lining his pants, shimmering as he moved, the person approached.

Before Arna was the embodiment of Arna's childhood: a thousand nights of laughter, standing on swings wanting to fly, racing down hallways, struggling with academy lessons, secrets about Gods and love, promises to be best friends forever. Jasi was taller after twelve years, with a goatee and swept-back hair. His birthmark, across his nose and cheeks, was light against his otherwise dark skin.

Arna had not seen Jasi in person for years, but Jasi appeared balanced in all the ways that Arna could never be. He held himself with confidence that Arna had once long ago. His violet eyes were obscured a bit by his glasses.

The last time the Arna had seen a Child in person, he'd been standing on the Weeping Stage blinded by stage lights. All Children had eyes the color of the patron God who selected them. In Jasi's case, his eyes were that of Lumak. Arna, who was Chosen, had brown eyes like majority of society.

[*To be Chosen by all is to be Chosen by none.* The God of Balance, Lumak's figure, shimmered behind Jasi. *We only love our Children.*]

Yes, Children are loved as they are Blessed, Saint Aubergine 1.7. I know. The implication was not lost on Arna. He did not need their love.

[*You're not the only one who can quote scriptures,* Lumak teased.]

[There was a chorus of laughter from Lumak and Pokk.]

How can he see me?

[*You got sloppy,* Ixxzal said.]

Arna resisted rolling his eyes. It had been a risk to stop flourishing his Blessings, but the Gods must have done something to make this meeting happen. Or maybe it was the fluctuating contract even affecting fate. He hoped not, it was not another consideration he needed to have when he was guaranteed to lose Blessings.

Why is he here? Why was he an immigration officer? He could have been anything. He was a *Child.*

[*He took a job,* Ixxzal said.]

Be serious.

[*He stayed in hopes you'd return, so we gave him to you,* Zaynir said like a distant breeze.]

Jasi. . . Arna's heart ached. He did everything for Arna even now?

[*There would be no challenge, no choice, if you were not forced to choose. Not forced to act,* Ixxzal answered.]

Why does it sound like you are enjoying this?

[*They are, but they're right.* Lumak's voice was broken up more, almost like chirps.]

[*Prove to me that my faith in you isn't for nothing,* Ixxzal said.]

"Don't give me that look. . ." Jasi stopped talking and his expression dropped into absolute terror. Arna rarely made eye contact with people, out of fear of being recognized. Most saw his brown eyes and thought him mundane. Jasi was not most people. "Inca—"

"Quiet." Arna used the full force of his Blessings.

Damn Azza, what if someone heard?

[Lumak's laughter bounced in speakers.]

There was a long moment where Jasi's face turned pink and then returned to a normal color. He stood with wide eyes and unspoken words that Arna could only predict. Jasi's eyes darted around, and Arna counted to six before releasing his Blessings.

"You're here?" Jasi said, wiping at his eyes and flicking away the tears. The next gaze startled Arna, as if he were no one, as if Arna no longer mattered. Arna stomach ached as if he had been kicked in the gut.

"Apparently." Arna heard the breathless cracking in his voice and tried to rectify it by wiping away his own tears that stung at the corner of his eyes.

"What do you mean, apparently?" Jasi's eyes narrowed, and the words quivered at the end in the way that meant he was irritated.

"It's a long story."

[There was a filled silence. The Gods were discussing.]

"Arna, Arna, Arna," The voice was deep and filled with a bit of humor that made Arna's entire body freeze. Slowly he turned and faced his mirror. Arco stood, hands in his pockets wearing crisp black, with long sleeves like dragonfly wings, and pants adorned in the iridescent dragonfly scale motifs. Arco was dressed in the way that Arna once had dressed: fashionable, bright, carefree. Arco smiled big, lovingly, hopeful and sure.

"What?" Arna asked in awe of his brother.

"You. . ." Arco's smile faded. He stared at Arna for a long moment and the memory of the smile became a grimace. "Somethings wrong. . ."

The last Arna saw Arco, he had been ten, tiny, and filled with bountiful energy. The Arco before Arna was an adult, tall, and radiating silence. His eyes held a heart shattering pain. His body tensed up, shoulders rising, eyebrows furrowing, rippling in visible anger as he glared Arna's way.

Arna was staring in a mirror. They had the same thick eyebrows, dark skin, and sharp noses. Arco's chin was defined and without any stubble. They reflected different lives: one sheltered and polished, the other a mess of failed expectations. This man was not the same one that had once worshiped him, and there was nothing Arna was going to be able to do to fix that.

Ignore it. Arna clenched his hand. Jasi still looked at him. . .

Jasione stared at Arna in mixed horror and anguish. Something in the look, made Arna's soul scream. It was supposed to be the *same*. Jasione wasn't supposed to look at him like that. It was supposed to be. . . He broke. . . He was. . .

Kill it. Kill it. Smile.

Arna smiled lightly as if he did not care. Because he didn't. Even if things weren't perfectly the same it was okay.

[*Time changes all.* Pokk laughed.]

Despite the rudeness, Pokk was right. It was childish of Arna to believe for a moment everything would be exactly the same. Reassessing, Arna focused. Nothing changed. Nothing would affect him.

Cut it all out and make the divide. Not friends. Not anymore. Strangers.

"Nothing's wrong," Arna said. "I need to get home before anyone sees me."

Sarcoline glared sharper: eyes narrow and furious. What made Sarcoline so angry?

"I don't accept that," Sarcoline said, harshly.

"Sarcoline." Jasione warned.

"He's not being. . . He. . . I. . . It's today but something is wrong," Sarcoline said choking on the words.

[*Time changes all,* Xeyaro disagreed.]

Everyone believed that Arna was the Chosen Child before he left. He told his father and Jasione about the voices. Everyone at the Vivicent studio acted like he was. The Cardinals had known about the voices after Arna had been found conversing with shadows next to Everlit Candles, but the legitimacy was still put it into question and doubt. After all, everyone knew the Chosen Child prophecy, they had to be hesitant to accept it, his father said. The Chosen Child could only reveal so much about their experience, and if they were wrong the Church would be the laughingstock of the world.

"Arco, go get us tickets for the train back home," Jasione said the words so smoothly that Arna almost thought he misheard. Home? Didn't Jasione have to work? Jasione blocked Arna from the view of others, lips pressed into a thin line. Lavender lights flickered behind him.

As Sarcoline huffed and walked away, Arna hesitated. Jasione would be able to get the truth out of him, and Arna wanted to tell him. Alis, Arna's current best friend, knew everything on who Arna wanted to be, but none of his past. Jasione knew everything on who Arna was and would accept him even now. That was the problem.

Do not take me from him again.

[*That is up to you,* Lumak threatened Arna. *You know what you risk if you don't do as we ask.*]

Red blood. Tears and terror. Screams.

[*Why will you risk dancing?* Lumak asked.]

"Are you okay?" Jasione asked.

"I didn't expect to see—" Arna smiled brightly, keeping his emotions down, and forgotten.

"Anyone. You didn't expect to see anyone, and you just waltzed back in. It's why Arco is angry. He's been waiting for you."

What?

"He predicted today would be the day your returned, and I have no idea how he was right," The hostility in Jasione's voice cut like knives. "What if the priests caught you?"

Sarcoline had predicted his arrival? How?

"There are worst things that could happen." Arna shrugged. He doubted they could catch him. He'd run away from enough before.

Jasione had been his exclusive friend and not a part of the Golden Generation. Now they were strangers. Jasione was the one who he had shared all his secrets with. Jasione was the one who he had sworn to tell everything to. Jasione had known everything about Arna: the voices, the visions, the fears. Even Ven didn't know everything. Jasione did. Jasione knew about Arna's first kiss with Ven, about Arna's first date with Ven, about Arna's first time with Ven.

Ven.

He shook the memory of Ven from his mind. Ven would be in the city. It was okay, Ven would forgive him because they were each other's everything. Ven would understand even in Jasione did not.

"What is your next move as the Chosen Child? How do I help you?" Jasione asked him again. At one time Arna had told him everything but now, Arna could not.

"Don't ask me that question." Arna hoped his story telling was as good as he planned.

"Have the Gods forbidden you from speaking now?"

Arna waited for the Gods to tell him what to do.

[*Tell him,* Azza suggested.]

[*Just don't lie,* Lumak warned.]

"I dropped a fan, Jasi. I'm facing my penance." He paused. "But I'm trying to be, what I was trained to be."

Jasione's body grew rigid. Arna heard the sharp intake of breath and then the hesitation on Jasione's voice when he asked, "Can you fix it?"

"I am going to try."

They stopped talking.

[*Try?* Ixxzal snapped. *Might as well have told him no.*]

It doesn't matter if I am or not. He didn't have a choice and neither did they. He was the only connection they had. *I don't become the Chosen until I dance, right?*

[*Right,* Xeyaro answered with a light voice.]

They couldn't know the truth, not the full truth. If they knew that Arna was an imposter, that he had broken the world for the *chance* to be the Chosen, they'd never forgive him. But it didn't matter if he was or wasn't. It didn't matter if he wanted to be or didn't. It didn't matter if he believed he was worthy or not. He had to become the Chosen.

The world could not end.

[*What's the point in hiding it?* Ixxzal snapped.]

I don't want to disappoint them again.

[*You can't hide anymore,* Pokk warned.]

Arna took a deep breathe, furious but understanding. He said nothing as Jasione, typed at his phone furiously and they waited for Sarcoline to return.

I need to keep this a secret.

[Intercoms buzzed and storms rumbled far off in the distance.]

[*We will help you keep what needs to be secret,* Xeyaro said after a moment.]

[*But remember Arna,* Ixxzal added. *You cannot reveal what is already known.*]

The Gods disappeared to the chatter of the station, leaving Arna in the silence that had engulfed him and Jasione. This silence was the soft voices of those on the platform, the lightest sound of wind, and the Ivumalis music playing of the speaker. It was peaceful and calming: familiar.

Be comfortable within silence, Rosy.

When Arna had been a kid, silence had driven him nuts. He'd wanted to fill every moment. Being away, meeting Alis, had taught him to read the silence, to understand that it was as important as sound. There was an importance in silences, Arna had learned.

It is the story told in moments where sound cannot reach.

Silence was not an absence but a breath of clarity. When the Gods were yelling at each other, silence was the soft hum of their voices and the shadows that danced. When he was feeling lost and alone, it was the artificial breeze and the birds and the artificial rain, reminding him that he lived. Silence was not the absence of sound but the space where more existed than words could describe. In them he had found comfort. In them he found the reflection of the person he'd once hoped he could be, even if he could never be that perfect again.

Jasione was struggling, and, perhaps, processing his thoughts.

"Alright, here," Sarcoline said, reappearing with a blank expression betraying no emotion. "Let's go."

There was no way for Arna to escape. Facing his death in the form of two doors, Arna followed the two towards a train, and into an empty car, that started out of the station. It spiraled up towards the sixth petal, sixth district, where the Vivicent manor lay waiting.

Arna sat with his back towards the window and eyes leveled anywhere than across from himself. He clenched his hands tight. He was going to be alright.

Distant screams.

Distant Fire.

He activated his Ch.Insight. He was fine.

Jasione was distracted by his mobile, while Sarcoline glared at Arna, arms crossed and seething.

He's watching me.

[*Yes,* Azza, God of Chaos, laughed.]

I can't do this. I can't face them all. Each passing moment made that fact clearer.

[*You can,* Xeyaro urged him.]

Why because you trained me for this? This is cruel.

[*Trust in us,* Pokk said. *Trust in us.*]

[*No,* Zaynir the God of Souls corrected, *Don't believe in us.
Believe in yourself.*]

But how was he supposed to fix this? Things were supposed to be okay.

[*A conversation is never one sided,* Lumak offered, *Just talk to them.*]

Arna was not sure how that was supposed to fix the relationship and make things back to the way they were, but he tried anyway.

"Who are you messaging?" Arna asked Jasione trying not to be sick at the moving train and the screams echoing in his ears.

"Family," Sarcoline answered for Jasione. "Which you failed to message. We got your boxes, they're in your room. But I suppose you knew that since you sent it from Azis."

Arna nodded slightly. They did not get off the train as it stopped at the business district or the arts district.

Silence filled the air again as Arna unfortunately looked out the window. Fear was replaced by a unfathomable awe as he saw his home from midair. Xeysis was one massive spiral of a biome. Deserts turning to temperate forests turning to jungles and wetlands and plains. Entire patches of the city were dedicated to different environments and the animals that lived there. Sprawling forests lined the six petals, filled with massive trees where homes were placed, around, on, and within.

There were apartment complexes that were dense forests, built within the insides of metal trees. There were homes that hung across bridges, in branches, atop the leaves. There were entire sections of the city that lived within the petals, beneath the roots, where the light they lived by was the bioluminescent glow of white, green, and blue.

In the center of the rose were three circles. The outer business district was filled with towering skyscrapers built in the shape of music notes, trees, and flowers. Some were shaped as animals and the elements. There were branches between them made of glass, as walkways, and glowing in flower petal shaped lights and advertisements. The government center was shaped as a volcano. The embassy was shaped as a waterfall with wind swirling about it: each city had their own floor. The second ring was the dancer's circle: with far smaller buildings. From above it appeared like a grass lawn, with large stalks and buildings shaped like fallen leaves. The Dance House, where the DHS lived and the dancers were tested and auditioned, was shaped like a fan. The Legacy Heritage Foundation building was shaped like an eye.

And in the center of the city, like all cities, was the third circle, marked by six towering dark candles: the religious circle. Towards the center were six rings: the outer circle of candles, tens of church buildings, an open vast space, a circle of free standing stages and buildings, three cathedrals and the temple, and the empty center.

Birds flew and animals roamed freely, with the most dangerous confined to specific regions. There were metal chrome trees floating throughout the sky, their roots, spread throughout the air creating messages of time and weather reports for the city. Islands floated in center and the skyrail webbed around them. They were filled with rare species, their zoos, and greenhouses.

The farming districts on the lower petals could not be seen from the train, although a good portion of the city sustained itself off of the food grown from the plants that lined every empty patch of ground, and the massive greenhouse in the center of the sky. It was shaped like a floating glass rose, towards the top of the city, closest to the petals of metal.

"How are preparations for the Ceremony and celebrations going?" Arna asked, trying to change the conversation away from hostility.

Peeking through the forests, in the biomes, were stadiums dedicated to performances. There were massive, towering structures of the Gods, sculptures of ancient figures of the past: all the Chosen. By them were effigy's of their Saints: those the Chosen had sanctified in their lifetime and chosen to be their closest support. Arna would never have any, for by the time he was officially Chosen he'd be dead.

There were spiraling pink and gray arches and green and red water ways, emulating those of the other cities. Arna could see the Cloud Steps, a structure that was built to emulate Zaynir was on the first petal. It resonated with every movement atop the steps, creating a song as more people walked across it.

"Well enough," Jasione said. "Your father said everything is ahead of schedule, for once."

His father had danced the twenty-fifth dance for the last twelve years, in hopes that the Gods would forgive Arna's mistake. Arna had watched each year, in a public square or on his computer, listening to the prayers and acting as the only medium between Gods and mortals. What had once been a special event, a once-in-a-duodecennial special position of high prestige, had become a repentance for a sin that Arna could not erase.

There was nothing to forgive. The Gods had asked Arna to break the world. He made the choice to do it.

[*And we take the blame,* Xeyaro said.]

"Why were you hiding?" Sarcoline asked. Words had formulated between them that had to be voiced. All at once Arna was shaken back to the train, as it rocked. He gripped the seat. Arna's scars were visible under his collar and along his arms.

Run!

"Arna?"

Breathe. The train was not in danger. He was fine.

"Do you blame me?" Arna asked as his smile dropped, unable to maintain it as the memories threatened to consume him. He focused on honesty instead.

"What are you—" Jasione's eyes went wide.

"Are you ready?" Sarcoline cut Jasione off.

"I could only come back now." It was the truth. Arna was not sure what else he could say. For he was not ready. His variation was a complete mess, and each passing moment made Arna realize he had more to do.

"You can tell me. I understand," Jasione pleaded with him. He leaned forward from where he sat across from Arna. "I—"

"Can you dance with fans?" Once again Sarcoline cut Jasione off.

"I disrespected them by dropping that fan, you know what that means," Arna answered, unsure how to take their prodding. They both were angry and concerned? Why?

"The Splintering was your fault, yes," Sarcoline rolled his eyes, "We know. How will you get the Blessings back?"

Arna said nothing ignoring the panic in his chest and letting the silence fill the car. The train jumped a bit as it changed tracks, and Arna's fingers dug into the seat cushion.

Screams.

Did they know that the Blessings were disappearing for good and not just for a few days like the previous years?

Leave! Jump! Run!

Based on Sarcoline's expression the answer was no.

fallingfallingfalling.

Be able to exist *within silence*.

"He's freaking out Arco," Jasione hissed.

"Because of the train! Not my questions."

"How do you know?"

Arna breathed deeply, using his Ch.Insight more in order to clear away everything. He could do this. If he couldn't sit on a train without having a meltdown, how could he fix anything else?

I'm fine.

If Sarcoline wanted to know Arna's plan, then he could not give it. It would only make them panic and stress. He did not need that.

"The Blessings will be fixed when all is healed," Arna said, pulling his hands from the seat and closing them into fists. His fingernails dug into his palms, but his hands were hidden as he relaxed back and crossed his arms.

Sarcoline nodded and leaned back, unconvinced. He asked, "Where were you?"

"I went to Ludiel first for three years, then Ixis for three, Podiel, Zaydiel, and last Azis, all for two."

"Can you tell me what happened?" Jasione asked, finally able to get a full question out. "On that night. . .?"

"It's funny to see your entire life on holoscreens and news reports," Arna answered instead. "It doesn't feel like your life."

I am fine.

There had been three couples who assisted him: silver house, silver door, silver lawn. All had died because of Blessing issues. Arna had sworn off all lasting connection until Alis. Even now Alis wasn't truly real, perhaps because Arna knew they would never meet. The Gods had forbidden him to reveal himself and for a while he'd convinced himself that keeping Alis at a distance kept him alive. He had thought for a long time that the Gods had caused the incidents, as they took the blame for them. When the Blessings continued to falter, break, and weaken, Arna understood it was not them. It was him.

His exile did mean he had to hide himself, and they forbade hims from revealing himself. But it was to protect him. The Gods never killed anyone for him, they only tried to keep him alive. When he had nearly been killed at twenty-one by a Zylite Priest who was impassioned, he'd learned the truth when he had to save himself. The electrical fire? The disease? The train? The Gods were forcibly disconnected from mortals, where the most they could do was provide their energy to give him strength.

"I worked odd jobs and never stayed in one place for too long," Arna explained.

"No. . . I meant. . ." Jasione said but then stopped, realizing what Arna had done: wide eyed and confused. Arna had always been too honest with him in the past. The best way to protect them was for them not to know the full truth. It would kill them.

"I'm home," Arna smiled at them both, bright as if everything was okay.

Arna's hands felt warm and sticky. He activated his B.Body Blessing for good measure as he carved into the palms of his hands deeper.

"You're in Xeysis," Sarcoline disagreed. "Not home."

"I don't know what I can say to make it right, but I'm back now." Arna faced Jasione, looking disappointment in the face and accepted it. He'd disappoint a lot more people with his lack of answers. "I'm here. But I cannot give you more than that. There are many secrets I must keep. You know the prophecy."

He hoped that would be enough to keep them off his back. He needed space to complete everything, and he couldn't complete everything if he was getting more questions.

"Arna. . ." Jasione sounded as if he'd been betrayed. There was the cracking on his voice that Arna was sure meant that Jasione was on the verge of tears. "Are you dancing this year? You can tell us what's wrong."

"You know the prophecy Jasione. 'I am, but a vessel for the Gods, as we all are. Blessed by those who see their beauty.'" Arna said the prayer tepidly. "And so, it was. And so, it shall be."

Sacroline scoffed and Jasione's looked away. Why were they doubting him? What had happened? The rest of the train ride was filled with a tense silence, discordant and prickling at Arna's skin.

A large willow with leaves the color of crimson and snow, cascaded sparkles of light. Large silver branches swung in the wind revealing the house they protected. The house was three stories, mint and ancient, and wrapped around the willow tree in a complete circle. Holly and vervain lined the walls, masked by the willow branches. The tree called Arna closer to its domain. Green dust and dew drops fell as it wept for his arrival.

Arna moved past the memories assaulting him as he approached the mahogany front doors and heard the familiar chime that signaled, they'd opened. The floors were ancient willow, long single panels.

Inside was a void, which was not to say it was abandoned—not like many of the houses and complexes he'd found himself living in over the years. Nor was it empty, as the family who lived within was home. It was devoid of the prestige from his youth: yesterday's flowers, three-year-old paintings, dust, and the lack of shoes. There were no apparent visitors traversing the halls. That, too, was his fault. This disarray had befallen his family after he feigned death and disappeared.

Arna followed Jasione and Sarcoline into the house. The Vivicent family once had security, maids and staff who called to greet them upon entering, but no longer. The main entrance hall was not long but the short walk went on as if it spanned miles. Slipping out of his shoes, Arna hesitated to step inside further.

Panic spiked in Arna's chest. He was going to be fully perceived in a way he hadn't for years. He knew what was to come. Everyone would know. They'd all question him. He—

[*We will not. You must face this*, Pokk answered.]

[*Exactly. Pokk's right.* Ixxzal chuckled.]

[*I do not need your approval. But it's nice to have your support for once.*]

[*Don't get used to it.*]

Jasione walked forward first. "Are you ready?"

There was movement somewhere upstairs.

"No," Arna admitted.

He shut the door behind him and walked down the hall to the main reception lobby. Ancient portraits of the Vivicent family head lined the walls, dating back centuries. Hanging lights like rose petals glowed a soft white. A massive lobby space for guests to gather greeted Arna.

The house held three floors all circular with a hollow center where the family gardens sat with a massive willow. The top floor was exclusively for bedrooms. The second held the living and entertaining space. The bottom was exclusively used for dance with multiple practice rooms of all sizes and storage closets. There were no virtual ads, no holoprojections, and no sponsor names on the walls.

To the left of the main lobby was the reception desk with a white board. To the right was the grand staircase leading up to the ballroom above. Before him was a long wall of security nanotech hidden from view, giving the appearance of no wall at all. The pillars that supported the upper floors were made of glass.

Arna walked to the glass and paused, looking back to Jasione who nodded. Arna raced down the hall past the reception desk and towards his private practice room where the door was locked. Dropping his hand as if it had been burned, he leaned his head against the doorway. After a moment, he peered through the glass window wall to see inside where there were mirrors on all sides of the room. The glass could be made one-way, two-way, or opaque for privacy from the inside.

"They locked it after you left," Jasione called from the lobby. With heavy feet, Arna walked back. The reservation board behind the reception desk was framed by dried holly and vervain. It had a total of three neon mint names: Sarcoline, Gingerline, and Zaffre. There was a room assigned to each name, but no times, indicating they could use the rooms at any time. Arna's family had fallen so far that they had no other students. It was worse than what he found online.

"Where is Aureolin?" Arna asked Jasione.

"She left two years ago, officially. She comes by with her dance team sometimes, but she's no longer a part of the studio," Sarcoline said, leaning against the desk. "It wasn't announced publicly."

Not like when Ven said they'd go to archery or when Phlox decided to focus on acting. The Hues had left years ago in a storm of publicity. The Hues had hurt the most, even now it made Arna's chest burn. Arna had grown up with Eburnean and their fathers had grown up like brothers.

Many of Zaffre's former students had left at that time as well. One by one Arna had seen all of the announcements of big names moving to different studios around Xeysis, none had made a name for themselves. He had hoped Aureolin had stayed. Sadly, it was nothing but a dream.

Just another thing that was not the same.

"Stalling won't solve anything," Sarcoline said.

Sarcoline walked down the hall away from the grand staircase to the second on the other side of the house: the smaller unassuming, hidden one, used for the family. It led directly to the living room and gave easy access to the living quarters of the second and third floor. Sarcoline pressed his hand to a door, and it slid open revealing the staircase.

All of the staircases, other than the grand ballroom staircase and the one to the third floor from the living room, were hidden behind walls. All the staircases were made of ancient wood and concealed by glass, as if one was walking through a tree. The far side wall of the staircase Sarcoline selected, was made entirely of one way glass. Forcing himself forward, Arna took each step slow.

His father's hand made fans lined the walls. They were nothing particularly special to the unassuming eye, but Arna knew the story of each, as well as what they meant to his father.

"Are they all up there?" Arna asked him.

"Ginger will join us after therapy, but yes. . ." Jasione said as he went up without Arna.

"Jasi! Arco!"

Close to the top of the staircase Arna almost fell backwards. His mother's voice sounded so. . . tired. Time compressed around him. Sarcoline glanced back and opened his mouth but quickly shut it, before continuing onward without Arna who froze in place.

[*Your journey is over,* Xeyaro threatened him. *Face this.*]

"Arco where is Arna? Why didn't he message us? Why are there reports that he was seen at the station?" Wenge, Arna's mother's voice asked. His heart broke hearing her call out his name. He blinked back the tears and steadied his breathing on the stairs.

Time flickered and bent, unraveling and changing. How long had he stood there for? He was not sure. Jasione and Sarcoline were gone.

"Incarnadine?" Arna spun to face below him where his younger sister, Gingerline, stood. Her hair was pulled back to a ponytail of box braids on the top of her head. Her dark skin sparkled in a layer of sweat. She was older, prettier. No, perhaps his sister was the most beautiful person he had met before, and yet she was withdrawn, cold under the surface. She wore all black and her mint eyes were bright. "That can't be right."

She blinked at him three times: confusion, awe, terror. When she reached for him, it was with shaking fingers. She traced his face and pulled her hand back with a ferocity that left Arna with the lightest of scratches on his face.

"Ginger. . . " He stumbled over the word.

"You're real? You're back? You're home?" She spoke quickly, her words toppling over each other. She sized him up and recoiled.

"Yes."

All at once she was reeling, stumbling back on the stairs. Tears were at her eyes and Arna grabbed her so she would not fall.

"You're not a ghost?" she cried.

"No." What had happened to her to think that she was hallucinating? Tears spilled from her eyes as she rose her hand to hit him and then was stopped by Jasione who had returned down the stairs.

"Why?" she choked out. "Why didn't you warn us?"

Arna assumed she meant twelve-years prior. Even then, Arna was not sure. If he had been a better Chosen, he would have been smart enough to realize the puzzle in the God's words. He should have. And instead, he'd hurt them all.

Without an answer all that left was silence: the resounding cry of Gingerline.

Jasione pulled Gingerline into his embrace and motioned for Arna to go up the stairs.

"Why were you downstairs?" Jasione called to her, holding her.

"I wanted to do therapy in my dance room," she cried, clinging to him.

Falling over the stairs, Arna raced away. There was a thud right as Arna reached the door. Jasione comforted Gingerline in the stairway as she screamed out in sobs. They leaned against the glass window drenched in dark green light.

His sister, who had once been full of vibrance and energy, was sullen and shaking. His sister had once been the one to ask him for bedtime stories and to teach him new pop song dances. She had dreamed of making clothes and had him be her model. Gingerline had been the moon in his life—in all of their lives. Yet her brilliance had been stolen from her, siphoned by Arna.

"Go," Jasione repeated as he rubbed her back with crescent shaped movements.

Guilty, Arna opened the door to the second floor.

In the living room, his mother stood with father, Zaffre, and Sarcoline.

His mother's hair had grayed, and her silver eyes and cheeks looked hollow, making her look closer to her seventies rather than her fifties. No sleep could cure the exhaustion that seeped off her sagged body.

She was already crying, hands crossed over her chest as she tried to stand on her own. She wore dark green like an evergreen tree's leaves—at least six seasons old.

"Incarnadine." Arna's father looked older as well with gray hairs in his curls and beard. He was fit as he had to be for the dances, but the weariness was palpable in his voice. He had the same dark skin and dimples that Arna had. He too wore a color close to black, albeit his was gray, old and worn. "I would have picked you up."

What had happened? It wasn't supposed to be this way. Why were they looking at him as if he weren't real?

"We got him," Sarcoline said as Arna said, "I did not want to bother you."

Arna winced as Sarcoline shot him a glare and took a steadied breath trying to figure out what to do. His parents were clearly overwhelmed. His mother was crying. His father looked pale. His sister was sobbing in the stairwell, her cries echoing across the floor.

He thought his former surrogate guardians and their deaths. He thought of the angry priests and citizens who wished for his death online, at church sermons, and in the streets. *The Gods take souls ready to return to Them, from suffering to eternal joy and peace.* Saint Maroon 17.3.

[*Arna. . .* Lumak, God of Justice, sighed.]

Panic bubbled.

His name as a question. The immediate electrical fire that followed. The Gods threatened him. Do not contact anyone, stay anonymous.

He had been so angry, and tried to lash out, doing everything and anything he could to break the contract. He rebelled and called the Gods horrible names and blamed them for everything.

But they were using too much power to keep him safe from those who wanted to hurt him.

The Gods were not the reason the Blessings were fading,

nor did they cause the deaths around him.

The Gods had only been trying to fix his mistakes.

The Gods had only been trying to protect him.

failurefailurefailurefailurefailurefailure

If he had been a better Chosen, they never would have needed to. For years he had been hidden in plain sight trying to do right by them, doing what was required to make it to the day he could dance. Being recognized by his parents, seen by any of them, made him want to vomit.

[*Breathe!* Ixxzal yelled. *Breathe!*]

Not like this, please. It wasn't supposed to be like this. They weren't supposed to be angry. They weren't supposed to be crying. It wasn't supposed to be the way it was. He was never supposed to see them again. They were meant to remain portraits in his memory.

He couldn't do this.

Their pain was the pain of the world directed into his soul. It weeded out his guilt. It dug up every fear that he buried and made him face it.

They always knew he'd had to leave. They always knew he'd come back. But he was supposed to come back and save them, not face them and their wrath and emotions and accept it. It was a weight he could not shoulder, not when he had to stop the apocalypse.

Because he could have done things differently. He could have been better. He—

[*All you can do is ask for forgiveness,* Xeyaro whispered.]

Arna squeezed his fists and looking down. *Kill it.* His Ch.Insight was flourished.

He would not be afraid. He needed to be the Chosen Child, and that person could not fail.

"Arna," Aureolin's voice sounded.

Slowly he searched for her. Past the family portraits without his face, decorations he did not recognize, and furniture that was old and falling apart. She sat near the window in a chair under a hanging fan: the first fan his father ever made.

Drenched in sunlight was Aureolin with her spiralling curls and a crown of yellow orchids. She tapped her long fingernails on the chair as she sipped tea with the other hand. She had little makeup on save the orange flower petals painted like freckles across her cheeks. As a little girl, Aureolin had been averse to dresses and skirts but adored bright colors, animals, and flowers. Long gone was the girl who used to make maps to hunt treasure. In her place was a young woman who wore a monotone brown pantsuit, well-tailored and, like her expression, controlled.

Aureolin, like Gingerline and Zaffre, had eyes the color of dance: mint. Seeing her made Arna tense more. Aureolin wasn't on the board for the studio, but he had to assume she was still friends with Gingerline. They'd been inseparable. Seeing her was like facing daylight after a long night. She once radiated fire, dangerous and easy to explode, but now she was power, sitting without a concern and with no wrath.

Aureolin cracked a smile at him, "Welcome back."

A sigh escaped his lips. "I'm home."

What is Power? It is our Blessings. It is our capability for growth. Gods cannot change. They are stagnant beings, perfect and infallible. Mortals *can* change. Gods are not the only ones who hold power over the world.

— On the Powers of the Gods section of The Twenty-Seven Dances.

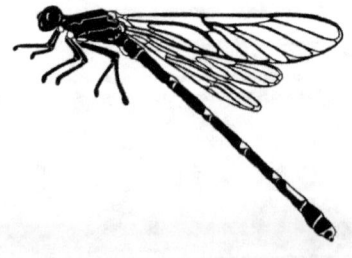

Dance 4

Conclusion

Incarnadine

28 Poan

87 Days Left

"I can't do this anymore."
"You made a choice, Arna."
"I don't care. I don't want this anymore. Please, just let me go home."
"Please Arna. You made a choice and now you're the only one who can."
"I'm tired."
"Just trust us a little more."
"You're the only ones I can trust."

Arna sat in the Vincent manor living room surrounded. The room buzzed in life as people moved about the entirety of Arna's home, rearranging things and preparing different rooms, all so that they could test him. His father had alerted the authorities an hour after he arrived home. No one had wanted him to, but Arna insisted, lest they be berated for hiding Arna when he was discovered. Since there were reports of his sighting, it was easier to come clean earlier than later. He was technically a wanted fugitive, after all.

Cardinals from One Truth, Harmonious Six, and the Church of Xeya, descended with government officials and politicians.

"What does this mean for—"

"There is no historical precedent of —"

"What do we do about—"

"The Gods—" "There are no Gods! Only one." "The Apostle—" "A new Variance—" "How do we control the media?"

"We need to have a press briefing to —"

"The less they know the better."

"There will be riots—" "— the ramifications. We must consider—" "Who should—"

Their voices were a cacophony spiraling about him, as more individuals arrived, and fights broke out. Arna could not follow one single conversation.

"Where were you? How did you hide?" An official asked him, sitting in front of him with pen and paper. Arna glanced to his father who nodded. The words clung from his lips like a promise. Exposing them, revealing every lie he'd told over twelve years, was like unraveling himself. With them went the constant tension of lightning in his veins, the taboo finally appeased. He'd revealed the truth finally.

Finally.

"The first family I stayed with—" Arna explained, listlessly.

The questions came without reprieve.

Where were you? How did you disappear? How long were you in each city? How did you survive? Who did you work for? Why were you there? Why did you not come home? Why did you not contact anyone?

He spoke for an hour, answering every question he could, until every official was accounted for. Some watched him as if he were the messiah there to save their souls and most looked at if he were the end of times in mortal form.

He squeezed his fists, nails digging into his skin, wishing he could disappear. It had been so long since he'd had so many eyes on him. He'd grown used to being ignored. What if he went mad from all the attention?

"Next, we need to confirm your identity."

Before Arna could ask what they meant, he was being poked and prodded like a test subject on a lab table instead of a living, breathing person. They took his blood and his hair, his skin and saliva. He was asked to strip so they could checked his body. He let it all happen willingly.

"Is this a vow?" someone asked pointing at the mark on his wrist over his S.Mirrors constellation.

"No."

They wrote the words 'vow on wrist' in their paperwork anyway.

"What about these scars?"

The ones on his arms, his legs, his back, everywhere. He was littered with scars like they were roads on some ancient map.

"Practice," he said.

"Practicing for what?"

Surviving.

Arna did not answer.

Then came the questions he'd asked himself and the Gods for years. Why *did* you do it? Why did you do *it*? Why did *you* do it? Why? Why? Why was he the Chosen Child?

After hours, Arna was exhausted. Sitting in the living room, the most that Arna could do was focus on the portraits of the walls that surrounded him an attempt not to completely snap as the questions were asked.

There were little pictures of him. One of him as a baby in his parents arms when he'd had his Blessing Revelation Ceremony. Another of him, Gingerline and Sarcoline as children, sitting next together. The last a portrait of him was one at fifteen, smiling bright, behind the decades old couch, hanging above the six unlit candles on the family alter.

The others were not of him.

There were more pictures of the other people. Eburnean was a child in his practice uniform smiling brightly with Aureolin and Ven. Ven and Jasione were laughing in another. Eburnean stood with his father, mimicking his father's expression. Alabaster and Zaffre were in many: as students, as boys, as men, teaching, laughing, at Zaffre and Wenge's wedding. Phlox smiled bright on stage, surrounded by flowers and the whole family.

Sarcoline appeared in various ages and places across the city. Gingerline was in one holding her fans and awards. There were graduation photos and family portraits. Jasione was in many pictures from the day he got his job to one of him kissing Gingerline's cheek. Rosmarinus was on the walls holding awards, and with Jasione, with Sarcoline, with Gingerline, with their family in the family portraits. Rosmarinus stood in the place Arna vacated. It was as if Rosmarinus had completely stepped into his life.

Arna wished he could be jealous. Yet, he was not.

This is good.

It meant that he'd hurt them less when he danced and died. The sturdier they were without him, the better it would be.

"Incarnadine," someone called to him. "Why are you refusing to answer even these simple questions?"

Perhaps because they were not so simple?

Arna glanced from the photos to the enforcement officer. He examined them silently before he returned his focus to a family portrait of Zaffre, Wenge, Rosmarinus, Jasione, Gingerline, and Sarcoline huddled together in a professional shot. His eyes then drifted to his father's first fan.

Zaffre stepped in when Arna refused to answer. "That's enough questions."

"He hasn't—" The Enforcement Officer protested.

"Let the boy rest," Cardinal Black, head of the Church of the Harmonious Six, agreed. "Can't you see that he cannot answer you?"

Seeing Cardinal Black made Arna suspect that the reports of the growth to the Church of the Harmonious Six in Xeysis were understated. They'd recruited in all the cities, but Cardinal White should have been here. He'd always believed Arna. The Church of the Apostle used to hold more power in the city than either the Harmonious Six or the Church of Xeya.

Had the Harmonious Six taken over control of Xeysis? Better than the One Truth, he supposed.

The Church of the Apostle was as hated as Arna was, since he'd caused the candles to go out. He'd hoped that Cardinal White would maintain hold over Xeysis, but Arna was nor surprised. Nothing was going the way he pictured.

Worse, while there had been clear lines between the church and state for centuries, Arna had watched the churches extend their power over the duodecennial. They controlled most of the power, although the governments insisted that the elections were fair. Seeing Cardinal Black, Arna knew: he had control.

"His lack of cooperation could be considered—" the Enforcement Officer proceeded.

"Enough." The Governor of Xeysis instructed his subordinate to step down. "He will answer in time."

"He will answer when he can," Zaffre urged the others away so that Wenge could take her spot next to Arna and fuss over him.

"He disappeared for years, Zaffre."

"A false prophet," The Leader of the One Truth said. "You are faking the prophecy. This is not real."

Arna swallowed, knowing it was, some part true. He was acting the prophecy out at the God's insistence.

"He is the true Chosen Child," Zaffre said but no one else in the room was particularly convinced.

"Don't listen to them," his mother said directing his focus to her. "You're home."

"Yes. He's home," Sarcoline glowered from the corner, sitting next to Jasione, Gingerline, and Aureolin. Gingerline was no longer sobbing, but she had not stopped crying. Aureolin had tea and cakes for the two of them, which Gingerline ate slow.

"It's amazing," Aureolin tried to lighten the mood. "It's amazing, Arco."

"Right." Arna wanted to ask her about where she danced. Did she visit often? Why did she leave the studio? How was her family? Were her sisters doing well in school? Was her mother better after her surgery—the surgery she'd had two days after the Splintering. . . Perhaps it was best for him not to say a thing at all.

"Yes, I told you he'd be back," Sarcoline spat but not at Arna at the others in the room, as if vocalizing the words for them. "But you are fucking hiding something Arna."

"Arco! Language," their father chastised him from across the room.

"He is an imposter." The Cardinal of One Truth insisted.

"What does this mean for the Ceremony of Chaos?" Someone asked the Governor of Xeysis. His eyes squinted into an irritated look.

Accourding to Arco procedures were already underway for the festivities at the end of the year. Usually, the celebrations were only one day: New Dawn Day. The Ceremony of Chaos was the last event of the year. Xeysis as the last city to experience the new year, was the one to host the ceremony. This year, for Apostle Week, there would be a week of celebrations, performances, and sports games. The weeks leading up to the celebrations were filled with other events: competitions, showcases, and festivals.

For all of Xeyan there were nonstop events. Arna supposed that with his arrival a few of the events were called into question: the auditions for who would dance which section of the Twenty-Seven, most notably.

"Nothing changes," Zaffre said, walking over.

"If the boy is the *Chosen*," The Governor spat back. The word was said as if it were dirty. "Then isn't he *dancing*?"

Arna went to speak.

[A flurry of birds sounded.]

Arna stopped. What was wrong? The lights were flickering, and no one noticed.

[*Your choice cannot be influenced by anyone*, Pokk screamed in rage.]

Did that mean he could not tell anyone he was dancing? Why?

[*Only you can make the choice*, Lumak said. *Do not let them affect you.*]

Arna bit his tongue.

"Aren't you?" The man asked.

Arna said nothing.

"An imposter!" The One Truth member shouted. "He's *lying*."

There was a tension in the room, between those who believed that he was the Chosen and those who refused to accept that he was.

"Worried now?" Arco asked. "Why don't you fuck off with your theories that he's a liar? He's back now. He's dancing."

Sarcoline refused to look at Arna, instead he seethed at everyone and no one at once.

"Yes. The Golden Generation is back together." The Governor of Xeysis glared at Arna.

Arna thought of the six of them: Ven, Eburnean, Gingerline, Aureolin, Phlox, and Arna. They were the six Children of Xeyaro all in what was considered the Golden Generation. Most Generations, for Children of the Gods, spanned a duodecennial with years between the births of members: only two or three Children maximum per Blessing focus. Every member of the Golden Generation was born between the span of two years, each with A.Reverence for dance and there were six of them in total. It was unheard of to have so many Children with the same Blessing focus in close proximity. Arna believed it to be because of him, not that he'd ever voice it.

Arna's mother reached for him, holding his hand tight, as if he'd disappear at any moment. She rubbed her thumbs over his palm where he'd left scars from years of curling his fists close.

"Mom. Stop."

Arna pushed her hands away. She cooed but said nothing. Her silver eyes, the indication of her N.Reverence and status as a Child of Xeyaro, were glistening with tears that would not fall every time he pushed her away.

"Why did you drop the fan, Arna? Tell them what you *saw*. You did everything because you were told too. Right?" Sarcoline asked and then jolted, glaring at Gingerline. "Don't kick me."

"Arco, stop antagonizing everyone," she said. When Gingerline looked to Arna for the first time in hours, Arna wanted to run away. The look was short because she started crying again. Once more Jasione rubbed her back and whispered to her.

"Twelve years." Wenge kissed Arna's head. "You've grown so much. And look at you. You've become so handsome, like I knew you would."

"Yes. Twelve years," The One Truth Cardinal mocked. "What a coincidence."

With the words the noise in the room stopped. Arna dropped his eyes to the floor.

"Prophecy," Zaffre insisted.

It was Zaffre who had told Arna about the Chosen Child and what it meant to be Chosen. Zaffre had taught the Golden Generation the Dances. He had taught them about the past five Chosen Children, their variations and how they changed the world. Arna had always loved his father's stories, as Zaffre had spent his whole life dedicated to the dances.

And into the night the Chosen shall disappear. To journey and discover the path for mortals and all life upon the earth, the Chosen will give themselves to the Gods completely. They shall only return when enlightened and ready to impart their wisdom upon the masses.

The Omniscient Sextant Enchiridion was the same across all the old religions and was the text that was the basis for everything they knew about the Gods, Blessings, and the Chosen. The word for it was different depending on the religion but the essence was the same.

Varying years, always a duodecennial or more, the Chosen Child was always exiled away from family and all they knew. In that time, they were to perfect their variation of The Dances along with mastering the others that existed. Arna mastered all the other variations. Now he had to dance his own.

Zaffre taught Arna every religious text. He had taken Arna to church, to lectures, and to studies. He'd lectured Arna religiously, because he had believed Arna when Arna said he heard voices.

Barring the fact that his eyes were brown instead of black, Arna was similar to the legends. He had access to all the Blessings, based on the Blessing Revelation Ceremony. He claimed to hear the Gods, which was the worst kept secret of their family as most everyone knew. He was not a Child of the Gods, not loved but Chosen. Although Ven had often said they were the same thing.

Arna shook his head. *No*, don't think of Ven.

"Arna *is* the Chosen." Sarcoline insisted. "Right Arna?"

Arna continued to stare at his hands, wanting to disappear. How many of them still believed in full? How many of them thought he was faking it? Without Arna's word, without his variation on The Dances, there was no proof. And even if he gave proof. . .

Arna slowly looked at his brother and watched in real time as his brother's heart shattered. Arna tried to say yes, but the words were caught in his throat, because it was a *lie*. He was not the Chosen. He wasn't until he answered the question, mortals or the Gods, and danced. Answer the question wrong and he died due to the ceremony killing him. Answer the question right and he became the Chosen only then, as he danced dance twenty-six.

The room was silent waiting for Arna's answer that never came.

"But. . ." Gingerline insisted.

Arna tried again and his throat burned. Not from a vow, but his own inability. He was going to be sick.

Everything will end.

Then what?

[Distant static was broken up by singing birds.]

"We're ready!" A Legacy Heritage Foundation Official called from the doorway to the hall. The Legacy Heritage Foundation—who kept a record of all Blessings—would be the last to verify that Arna was in fact Incarnadine Vivicent.

It was unlike when he got retested each year. The expressions were far grimmer as he walked forward. The Blessing Revelation Ceremony was meant to be a beautiful moment of pride.

Instead he was a pig being led to slaughter.

diediediediediediediediediediediedie.

Focus. He tried to cling to any thought save what was about to happen and used his Ch.Insight to clear the panic.

In the past, the ceremonies were done by the priests and Cardinals, not the Foundation. In ancient times, relics were placed before the unblessed one at a time, changing candles and colors for each God, until all their Blessings showed themselves.

The Legacy Heritage Foundation was founded in 4 VVVVV, and from there it became a bureaucracy of numbers and records. It was only in the last century that the sensors were developed to measurer the luminance and opacity of the light when it shined, before it was still the Foundation members who had to be trained to see and record the numbers properly. Due to the machines, however, it was harder for test results to be faked.

The light that Arna created had to be real, it could not be an illusion.

[*Can you—* Azza's voice cut in. *Arna! Can—*]

"No," Arna whispered.

"What?" His mother asked and Arna's heart leapt. He'd spoken aloud again. Everyone was staring at him, as if it were an admission response to Ginger's question.

[*It doesn't matter if he can hear us, he knows what to do. We've trained for this,* Ixxzal said.]

I can hear you now...

[*Not for long. We're going to use a lot of energy,* Xeyaro said. *But trust us. We've prepared for this.*]

"Arna... Are you the chosen?" His sister grabbed his sleeve. "You are... right?"

"He is," Sarcoline insisted.

Arna looked at them all. He could not say he was nor that he wasn't. But he could prove it in the only other way he could.

You are sure it will work?

[There was no answer.]

A pang hit Arna's chest, threatening to blossom into a panic. He clenched his hands tight and ignored it. He knew better than to ask, that was why they didn't answer. Obviously.

Years of practice, planning, and preparation led to this moment. The Gods had made him practice, for the retest even when they insisted he would not return home soon. He'd assumed they did it to desensitize him to the loss not that he'd actually be tested. No one could know he lost a Blessing.

Hope, they called it. The Chosen Child could not be weak.

Although, he'd also assumed he'd only return the day before he danced, and there was no way to test Blessings after a person died.

Arna got up from where he sat, pushed past the officials and disbelievers who did not trust him and headed down the hall not waiting for anyone. He walked through the grand dining room, with the huge mahogany table set for fifty, and into the spacious grand ballroom.

The Vivicent manor ballroom was not the largest ballroom in a manor, that belonged the Hue family's ballroom, but it was large enough to hold close to a hundred guests. Long ago, when Arna was a child, and the Vivicent manor hosted parties regularly, Arna was dazzled by the room with its towering ceiling and branch shaped arches. The floating chandeliers were shaped like roses. The walls were painted in depictions of the Vivicent history. There were willow floors and willow branch shaped nanotech that floated about to create private conversation circles when called.

Now it was bare. The floors had been cleared out, the chandeliers were off and large machinery and tech took the majority of the space. They blinked and buzzed in the corner of the room, ready to pick up the glow that was registered as he did the ritual.

The ballroom was set up with six identical sand circles with a candle of three colors placed in the center. Six relics were placed along each circle: a fan for Song, the mask for Mirrors, the candle for Reverence, the flower for Body, the book for Insight, and the sundial for Stillness. Each of the relics were black so that they glowed in the colors of the Gods. The candle in the center of each circle was the God's specific Everlit candle, unlit as the they no longer could be ignited by anyone other than Arna. The names of the Gods were written on the floor in sand.

They'd see all his Blessings as soon as he began.

Arna's heart raced. A single number imprinted itself on his memory and he started to breathe sharp. For years he had listened to the Gods about how many Blessings he had left. He counted them daily. But, the idea of seeing it frightened him. It was an indication of every step closer he was to his death.

What if they were wrong?

What if he didn't have enough to survive?

What if it was all for naught because he'd lost more Blessings than he thought—he had forty-two fans to pick up when he danced. The margin of what remained was tiny, between living and dying even if he succeeded.

[*Focus!* Ixxzal shouted from another room, through glass.]

A bowl was held before Arna along with a knife. Looking up slowly at the Legacy Heritage ambassador, Arna let himself settle into the moment. He had to trust the Gods, so he gave all fear to them and took a deep breath.

All anxiety disappeared from Arna's body as he took the knife. Clarity and certainty grasped at him. He *had* practiced this. He *was* prepared for it.

Cutting the tips of his fingers, Arna placed his hands in the bowl of holy water and dyed the water red. He removed his hands and was ushered forward away from his mother.

"Let me go with him," she begged.

Her arms circled him in a hug, putting him at ease.

Together his mother and he kneeled before the circle, her hands on his shoulders. Before him the bloodied water was splashed across the sand.

Children were usually tested in private rooms with only their parents, the Foundation testers and a priest. They were tested at twelve months old and then retested at twelve years. Arna had been taken to the LHF building after he was baptized at the church and immediately taken back to the church after the tests, to be retested. Arna was certain he was the most retested mortal in the world. They tested him every year on his birthday from that day to the year he ran away.

[*You know what to do,* The Gods instructed in unison.]

Arna flourished all the abilities he had, letting them settle before there was the chorus of chimes signaling the Gods were ready.

His vision fractured. All sound resonated within his bones. He could taste emotions. He could breathe colors. There was a long moment of silence, where he accepted the world and let it exist through him. This silence was full and rich, vibrant and daunting. When the chimes turned to birds turned to the thunder of storms, Arna began. He placed his fingertips to the outline.

Through the haze, Arna watched as the first circle, Azza's circle, glowed bright: all six relics swirling in two colors of equal intensity. The brighter the relic shined, the luminance, the more powerful a Blessing. A Blessing's potential could not be changed. A low luminance meant a lesser capability, even with practice and the growth that can be achieved. Usually, a person could only expand their luminance by ten percent.

Blessings could never disappear, even if they weren't trained, their luminance simply dropped.

The highest luminance recorded was what a Child showed on their patron God, and it was always the same number: 666. It was called the focus Blessing and the upper limit for all luminance records.

Arna was taken aback for the smallest of moments before he pulled his hand back and breathed sharply. Arna clenched his hands together as he scrambled away from the circle.

It worked.

[　There was no answer.　]

For Blessings there were prefixes indicating which of the two sets of powers one could have associated with a Relic. As the Chosen Child Arna had most of the Blessings and had worked with them for years. Seeing them activate and show themselves in a visual form made him lighter.

Refusing to look at the eyes of anyone in the room, Arna moved to the second circle. There were six circles, six relics, and two prefixes for each God. Each God had a total of twelve Blessings they could give and there were a total of seventy-two that existed. Arna recited the prefixes. Azza had Ch. and Cr. Ixxzal had Un. and Fa. Lumak had B. and J. Pokk had K. and G. Zaynir had S. and E.

Amplification abilities started with Fa. Nullifying abilities started with Un. He had abilities to protect his body and abilities to protect his mind and spirit. One by one he moved from circle to circle focusing on the sensors that beeped behind him. They tracked the opaqueness of the color and the intensity of the light. All of Arna's Blessings were registered.

The weight of each Blessing settled heavily on his bones. Keeping complete control over his movement and the powers that the Blessings bestowed, Arna did as he was taught: hoping that no one noticed anything other than the glowing lights.

The common sentiment in the world was that a single God only Blessed once. That one could only have an Un or a Fa ability and not both. The average person received three abilities. Children had six, including one that shined brighter than all others: their gift from their God that claimed them.

As long as the Gods succeeded, everything would be recorded as it was when he was fifteen, the last time he'd been tested. Equal luminance and opacity for each ability, except one circle.

In the Circle of Xeyaro, his A.Reverence Blessing glowed brighter than all the others. Uncle Alabaster and his father had always said that A. Reverence was the most important. For a long time, Arna believed it because they were dancers, and it was their focus Blessing. All other Children said that their focus blessing was the most important.

The truth was A.Reverence was a gateway, the key to the contract. It was the guidance needed to dance Understanding without a fight, and without struggle. It was the way that mortals were able to maintain the connection. A.Reverence created dancers and dancers danced to keep the contract strong.

"'And they said, upon you we ask for reverence,'" Arna said to the circle bowing to it.

Every time he'd practiced the ceremony in the past, he said the words and they flowed out of his mouth before he could stop them.

"'In the form of twenty-seven dances given each year on the solstice, so that the bond between us may be strengthened and continued.' And so, it was. And so, it shall be."

Arna blanched, suddenly aware of the ballroom and the eyes on him. His heart began to race.

How deeply was that practice ingrained into him that he forgot where he was? What if he did it again? What if he messed up during the Ceremony of Chaos and stopped because he thought it was a practice? He could not stop and start again like practice. He'd need to fix that habit, quickly. He could not mess up. He needed to be able to dance all the way though without such an incoherent idea.

[The Gods were laughing.]

"This can't be real," someone whispered when he completed the test.

Arna tensed. People had tried to fake their results, but it was impossible to do without risk of retaliation by the Gods. If someone tried to claim that he falsified it, that he was a liar. . .

No. Arna was fine. Panic would not take him again. *Bury it.*

They could say he faked it; it would not matter. Even if they hated him. Even if they called him a heretic, or tried to vilify him, he had to dance. Their opinions meant nothing.

Besides, his control was better than that.

Ignore them. Disappear. Disappear. They will stop looking and then he'd be able to finally complete the mission.

[*Good job,* Zaynir praised him.]

[*Don't disappear. We succeeded. . .* Azza said listless, softer, and distant.]

[*Don't back down,* Lumak begged.]

Arna turned to the crowd looking over all those who gaped at him. Jasione stood holding Gingerline who was dry eyed. Sarcoline was smiling wildly. Zaffre was praying and Wenge was being pulled back by Aureolin. They were the only ones who looked at him with any sort of happiness. The others in the room had expressions of dread: sunken faces and haunted eyes. The room was filled with a sharp hush.

"No one has registered a Blessing in years," Cardinal Black broke the silence.

What? Since when? He hadn't seen any rumor about it online. How far were they controlling the narrative? Arna glanced amongst the others.

"Not even those with *established* Blessings. When they try, they begin to lose access to the Blessing they tested." The Governor's eyes accused Arna of crimes that were Arna's to bear. He was their ghost, their terror, and the end of an era with little time to react. He was the upheaval of their status quo. The hate in the Governor's eyes was undisguised. "I suppose this means a new Variance?"

[*It sure does!* Azza was drowned in tears, sobbing.]

[*Not yet,* Pokk disagreed. *Soon.*]

Clattered speech filled the room in anxiety as people spoke over each other. An unease spread, that Arna knew well. For once he was not the only one in a state of constant panic. He forced the feeling back and ignored it, like a constant thudding drum in his spine. He'd learned to live with it for years, they could too.

[*We need to rest, but we are here if you need us,* Xeyaro said.]

How much energy did you use?

[*Don't worry about us,* Ixxzal said.]

How much?

[no answer   ]

"Arna?" His father said. Most of those in the room were watching him, waiting for an answer he did not give. His head began to pound.

Arna opened and closed his hands. His heart thudded in his chest, and he willed it to still. *Please.* "Am I done?"

"Yes," Zaffre said and Wenge grabbed Arna again. Arna quickly deactivated all of his Blessings before she began to heal him with her own. The room jumped into motion. The Governor talked to his officials and phone calls were made. Others approached Arna as his vision began to swim and his ears rang.

"Arna!"

"Incarnadine, why don't you—?"

"Incarnadine, you should—"

"Get out of my house." Zaffre's voice was like hot smoke spreading through the air, suffocating any protests until they vanished down the grand staircase. They left their machinery and computers behind.

"Zaffre," The Governor protested.

"We can talk tomorrow. Out," Zaffre said shooing him down the staircase as well. Wenge placed herself between Arna and all those in the room who wanted Arna. She protected him from their pressure and expectations where he should have been able to protect himself.

Sarcoline, Jasione, Aureolin, and Gingerline chased Zaffre down the stairs to assist, leaving Arna with his mother in the ballroom.

Wenge turned to him once they were alone. It sounded as if she spoke through a bubble. "Dad will get your new identification card for you."

"And my passport?" He asked while she examined him again. Her fingers lightly dusted his cheekbones and his hairline, but her eyes examined his face as if he were a sculpture that she'd never seen.

"I could have—"

"I know." She hugged him tight. "You're home."

They sat alone, his mother refusing to let him go, holding him tight, until his body relaxed, and he let himself cry. Being in her arms broke him. He had not been comforted in years. With her he was a teenager again, crying as he was on the run. The candles had just gone out and he didn't know what he had done.

She sang him lullabies like she had when he was a boy until his mind went blank.

"The City Managerial Office will send us his LHF ID, City ID, and passport by the end of the week." Zaffre's voice sounded distant. "The cities are setting up a special World Government Task Force to 'handle' this. I don't know what they mean by that."

"And the news?" Wenge asked. Arna faintly recognized that he was lying on his mother's lap. When had he fallen asleep? His head ached.

"We will have a full media silence for at least a few days, but a few people already saw him," Zaffre said. "I've called Cardial White and Alabaster. We're going to use the Hue's house sale to block some of the news."

"What else?"

"There will be a mandatory guard on the house. They will be watching his every move. I talked them out of the majority of the consequences they considered."

"No fines?"

"Not this time."

Fines? When had their family been fined? Why?

"I think they're too shocked to really consider the weight of his return. They'll probably tell us more consequences as things go forward, but for now he is to be kept under strict watch."

Arna bristled at the idea. He could not be confined.

"We'll deal with it when the time comes. He's had to do so much on his own for so long," Wenge said. "We need to plan his Coming of Age. I doubt he celebrated."

"Not until after the Celebrations. It's already three years too late. What's another few months? Rosmarinus will be back, and he can help you plan. Arna also needs rest. A party will not. . ."

"We don't want more people watching. I know."

A hand touch his head. "How is he?"

"I'm awake." Arna pushed himself upright away from both of them. "Am I the most hated or the most wanted person in the world?"

"Both," Zaffre answered with a frown. "However, we are taking care of it."

"What fines did they charge you when I left?"

Zaffre's eyes darkened. "We were fined because you committed a taboo on stage, citing that we had incited a riot. They tried to level terrorism charges at us due to the disruption caused when you ran, but those were dropped. There is not much more they can take from us."

Which explained the state of the house. How much money did they still have? Were they going into the vaults? The ancient Vivicent money was not supposed to be touched unless in an emergency—that was what he'd been taught. Although, perhaps this was such an emergency.

"What about the Hue's house?"

"It's being sold."

Arna vaguely remembered it being sold years ago, but he did not remember who bought it.

"Again? To who?" Arna asked.

Zaffre shook his head, unwilling to give more information. Fine, Arna would find the information online.

"What else?" Arna asked. "People are going to gossip. Everyone will be watching. What else?"

Arna calculated what to do, where to go without being seen, how he'd avoid wandering eyes as he finished his variation. Could he stay at the house and work? Would that be stifling? Would the others try to pry? How many secrets did he need to keep?

"You'll be scrutinized. Yes," Zaffre agreed. "But nothing else. They don't know how to punish you. There isn't a precedent and. . ."

He needed to save them. He was the only one who possibly could and with the Blessing failures worldwide, they couldn't confine him too much, in fear that he actually could succeed. Perhaps Cardinal Black having a control over the city would work in his favor, so long as he was on the man's good side. Religion always worked in his favor, and this was not just a government issue, but a religious one. Arna could work with that.

Arna's heart accelerated again, vision fuzzy. What if he failed before he could get to the Celebrations?

[*You are home. You will be safe.* Lumak was there, protective and certain. *Calm. Calm.*]

Arna wanted to snap back, but he tightened his grip instead of falling for the instinct. Twelve years of hiding and running would not be so easily mitigated but it would not consume him either.

He struggled not to stare at the Gods who had reappeared around him and his parents. All six of them sat, shimmering, like flickering sunlight behind clouds. When his father's eyes darted around to check for others, Arna was caught staring into space.

[Little birds chirped and debated with the breeze.]

"What do you need from us?" Zaffre asked taking Wenge's hand instead of asking what Arna saw. "We will get it for you."

[*They missed you,* Azza said, placing what would be their hands on Wenge's shoulders.]

"Stop," Arna hissed. His mother's eyes went wide, and she bit her lip.

[*You're around others. You've grown lax,* Azza giggled.]

[*Stop causing problems Azza,* Pokk said.]

Arna knew better than to talk to the Gods where others could hear. He knew better than to react to their appearances.

[*I give him three days. The whole world will know he can see us,* Azza teased sadly.]

[*Three days is being generous.* Ixxzal laughed with Azza.]

[*Both of you!* Pokk snapped.]

Arna focused on their voices, avoiding his father's eyes, and took deep breaths. Arna had never failed a test. He would not now. Lives were on the line.

"I mean..." Arna gathered himself. "I just..."

"We won't confine you. Do what you need to do to dance," Zaffre said the words through his teeth. Arna caught a glimpse of his mother nodding along.

[*See. No need to worry,* Lumak praised himself.]

[*Set up our shrine,* Zaynir whined. *You have not prayed today. They're only acting like this because we're feeling faint.*]

From using energy to support him. *I will soon.*

His father continued talking, but the room began to rock as if Arna were on a boat.

[*There it is,* Ixxzal sighed.]

[*Get to bed, you're going to pass out again,* Pokk warned.]

All of the voices were echoing back and forth. His vision was spotty. It took everything he had to focus. This was nothing, he tried to tell himself, just flourish sickness from overuse of his Blessings. He'd kept standing through worse.

"Were you listening?" Zaffre startled Arna.

"Yes. I was listening," Arna sighed. He had no clue what his father had been saying to him. "Can I go to my room?"

His father's eyebrows creased and then he sighed. There was a long silence between them before Zaffre led Arna upstairs. They passed by the kitchen where Jasione was cooking and past Sarcoline that was going over paperwork.

Like a family.

Arna kept silent despite the number of questions he had. There were limits to what he could say without his father extrapolating information. Besides, it took everything he had to keep his head high and act as if nothing was wrong. He wanted to vomit from the motion sickness and migraine.

Zaffre opened a door to a room that looked like it hadn't been touched in years.

"Arna." Zaffre placed his hand on Arna's shoulder. "Is something wrong?"

Arna looked down and hesitated. He was seeing stars and his father's voice was split in three speaking at once. However it was staring at his father that made Arna truly ill. He was not sure why, but his father's eyes held the most hope and it made Arna sick to his stomach. His father was right, Arna was dancing to be the Chosen, yet why was it so hard to look at him?

"Arna?"

Arna's stomach lurched.

"I'm okay." He convinced himself. He would not burden his family with the truth.

Arna walked away from his father's hands before shutting and locking the door.

"We dance so that the bond between Gods and mortals may be continued now into the future. We're here for you Arna."

Arna squeezed his fists tight until he bled and shoved the emotions down. Only when he was okay and the migraine did not pound as hard, did he breathe. Only when everything was fine and he no longer cared about dying, did he move.

Arna went about closing the curtains on his window leaving himself in total darkness. His backpack was on his bed. From it, he drew out his Everlit Candles, the flower altars, and scarf to place them. He set them up on his desk. As the last existing link between the Gods and mortals, Arna prayed that the connection would be reestablished. He prayed that he would finish his variations. He prayed that the world would be restored, and that all was not lost.

[*We hear you,* They whispered to him in unison.]

The candles lit up.

A breath of ease left him as he stared up at the ceiling of his room, constellations were painted across it like a map to a life he could never live. Darkness soon consumed him.

When Arna awoke it was still not morning, and darkness continued to fill his window that was open. He did not remember opening it. The light of his candles flickered. Without prompting Arna got up. For years he'd maintained a strict and rigorous schedule of practices and training for his body. For a few days he'd slipped up while traveling, but being back home meant he would not. He was itching to continue now that travel was not an issue. However, practice could wait till morning.

[*It's time,* Ixxzal said.]

He had something more important to do.

Throwing on running pants and a hooded cloak, Arna slipped from his room, down the hall, and out the door into the crisp night air. The petals above were closed making the rose ripple in light as if it too were breathing.

He breathed out sharply, turned up his music and began to jog. He headed towards where the Cathedral of the Harmonious Six was located in the Religious Circle. Blessings active, Arna ran for a bit and stretched before continuing to run again. Three buses later, Arna was close to the center of the rose, near the Religious circle and the Weeping Stage. His heart beat rapidly for the stage, but it was not time. He turned to the Cathedral of the Harmonious Six instead.

[*It's there*, Pokk insisted.]

Inside choruses sang above him, accompanied by an orchestra. The tiles were lined in alternating color, one for each God: mint, bronze, aqua, gold, green, and violet. On the polished marble pillars the wax candles above dripped down in long chains.

There was a soft shuffle of footsteps: priests who were stalking the halls. The cathedral was like a nest, with a swarm of priests, bishops, archbishops, and the Cardinal, their Queen, somewhere. They were active this early morning, no doubt because of Arna's release. Their haste and confusion would allow him to slip in easily.

There were more people in the cathedral than Arna had anticipated, including citizens praying.

[*People need to believe in something*, Pokk said.]

"You should thank me. I got people to believe in you again."

[*Silence*, Ixxzal warned.]

Arna rolled his eyes and looked both ways. *This way?*

[*Yes. Keep your head down now. Don't be seen*, Lumak instructed.]

Don't be seen. The word echoed as if it were said aloud, bouncing off the corridor and leading him to a wooden door. With quick hands, Arna broke the Blessing seal on the door and made his way into the labyrinth library underneath the main cathedral.

Where?

[*In the First Variance*, Pokk started.]

Arna groaned. He had to find it himself. What Blessing would help him find it? Insight. Which Insight?

[*Our Chosen, Raven, created art and performance*, Pokk lectured.
*They invented the dances, music, instruments, the Ceremony of
Chaos—*]

And the Celebrations. I know. K.Insight to search. Fa.Insight to enhance it? Arna tried activating the abilities. Seven paths appeared and he huffed to himself.

"Is someone there?" A voice called and Arna started walking, following the closest path. He activated E.Stillness to hide his tracks.

[*In the Second Variance*, Pokk continued.]

Is this necessary?

[*Yes*, the other Gods replied.]

Fine. This was just another high stress, pressure-reaction training. All he had to do was ignore the distraction, although that did not make it any less annoying.

[*Watsonia spread the dances and created the statues of our likeness*,
Pokk lectured. *She created the Harmonious Six religion, which
later fractured into seven. The modern Harmonious Six and
the six additional Churches were dedicated to us as individuals.
Later came the Church of the Apostle, dedicated for the Chosen.*]

Arna activated another three Blessings: his hearing expanded. There were twenty-nine people in the labyrinth. They were easy enough to evade. He wanted to avoid Flourishing all his abilities until he had to. A half night's rest had helped him recover but only so far.

[*Vervain solidified the world*, Pokk said in admiration.]

[*She was my favorite, if I'm to be honest*, Azza giggled.]

[*They're all your favorite*, Lumak mocked.]

[*You have a favorite too*, Azza said.]

[*We pick no favorites*, Lumak said.]

[*When the God of Truth, lies. It's fine?* Ixxzal asked.]

Impossible to ignore them, Arna joined. *Pokk loves Raven. Zaynir loves Watsonia. Azza adores Vervain. Lumak is partial to Sable. Xeyaro talks the most about Ilex. And Ixxzal favors. . .*

Saffron. Saffron. Saffron.

Arna grimaced. He could *not* be like Saffron.

A book clattered to the ground.

[*Careful!* Ixxzal snapped.]

Arna froze. The book lay on the ground before him, where the row of shelves met another.

[*Vervain was perfect in many ways*, Zaynir lamented. *But Watsonia—*]

[*Did you know that Vervain—* Azza started when Pokk hushed them.]

[*Vervain established the foundation for what you now call the cities and brought the world to the modern age*, Pokk went on. *It was because of her that Sable was able create the age of discovery. He helped preserve historical records, found Raven's statues, and established the practice of all citizens learning the dances. But—*]

Arna waited for the Priest to pick it up and move along, but the man lingered, glancing at the shelves.

Do not turn.

[*Vanish*, Ixxzal ordered.]

[*—the Fourth Variance was filled with strife, wars, plagues. With discovery came greed and with greed came destruction*, Pokk said.]

The Priest walked into Arna's row as if summoned by the Gods. Eyes down, Arna forced all of his Blessings to activate and flourish. The world began to spin, and his head ached. He counted: one.

The man did not see him. Arna sighed and slipped around him.

Two.

[*Ilex was born at the beginning of the Ever War, the last war that mortal kind ever had. Millions died. Entire cities were wiped off the map. No mortal is certain of the exact length of the Fourth Variance due to these wars destroying so many records*, Pokk's voice droned on.]

Another man approached.

Three.

[*Ilex wanted to save the world and to stop the wars. He succeeded and stopped most of the wars. He gave humanity a path to evade the superstorms.*]

Four.

The man walked by.

Five.

The steps drifted off into the distance.

Six.

[Ilex was a storyteller, and he gave the people hope. He transformed Vervain's cities into the modern flower cities of today. The Ever War ended only after all the cities were constructed, hundreds of years after his death. The contracts signed between them have lasted to this day, Pokk said dreamy.]

Seven.

It came at once, the sensation that he was used to. At first his stomach curled, bile rose in his throat, and stars danced across his eyes.

Eight.

There was nothing to see, only to feel, like a thousand ants digging at his skin, crawling through his veins, gnawing at his bones.

[You can withstand this. It's nothing for what you'll feel when you lose a Blessing, Ixxzal said.]

Nine.

It were as if he were exsanguinated, the blood dripping from his fingertips and crystalizing on the floor.

Ten.

Push through. Push through. Arna huffed, squeezing his hands tight. He wanted to scream.

Eleven.

Then there was everything and nothing. Arna was not alive. He had never been alive. He was the breath between the earth and the sky. The space between all words spoken and unspoken.

Twelve.

Clarity.

Arna blinked open his eyes and the sensations of pain passed into a faint memory. Four counts in. Four counts out, Arna breathed and steadied himself. The pain from the flourishing disappeared, and he settled into the over driven power.

[Keep moving, Ixxzal ordered.]

Arna blinked twice and nodded.

In the years of training his Blessings, it was always painful at first to flourish them all in succession. Just like Mastery, the more abilities that one has, the more difficult it will be to Master them all and the more difficult it was to flourish them together. For someone with six, it took them three times longer than someone with two, or twice as long as someone with three. Someone with twelve took double the time to master and flourish as someone with six.

When Uncle Alabaster first taught the process and the meditation exercises to practice activation, it had taken Arna forever to get the hang of doing it. Flourishing his abilities was multitudes more painful for him than others. Years ago, he had been crippled by the pain unable to move for days. Through training, however, the pain only lasted six seconds and then it was gone. He could keep them up for a few hours without the return of the pain and consequence. He could flourish three times a day, before he needed to sleep and replenish.

So long as one Blessing was active, he wouldn't face the pain of the initial flourish again. Unfortunately, he'd gone to bed raw, without a single one. He now had to pay the consequences.

Arna focused on the task at hand: another training placed in the back of his mind. He would need to train in the next few weeks to keep his Blessing flourished for at least three hours. When he danced, he'd be using all his Blessings to their full potential as he lost them one by one. He could not falter then, and he could not now.

Additionally, he needed to train his reaction response, cutting off his Blessings and facing the flourish pain could help. He would have to dance through the pain perfectly. It was how the Gods trained him in the past.

[*The contract between Gods and mortals grants us one mortal to be our scion. We bestow Blessings, you provide prayers. We protect you, and your wishes keep us alive. The contract between us cannot be changed or revoked. It can only be renewed and reestablished*, Pokk finally completed.]

What came first mortals or the Gods? He asked sarcastically.

[*We exist because you exist. You exist because we do*, Lumak answered.]

Arna started down the labyrinth again. *You missed Saffron.*

[*Move*, Ixxzal ordered.]

Arna turned a corner with his heartbeat in his ears. His breath was cold and his fingertips raw. The air was thick as if he were moving through pudding. Fear crept its way through him, like a phantom memory of the pain he was to face.

Arna narrowed the paths from two to one. Turning the corner he found the glass case, glowing bright, surrounded by priests who were ignoring it.

[*Get it*, Ixxzal ordered.]

Arna focused on a song: Serenity's Lament.

Be comfortable with silence, Rosy.

Be able to exist within silence.

It is serenity.

It is the story told in moments where sound cannot reach.

Arna pushed over a bookshelf and the shelves toppled over one after another, sending the priests scurrying. Alarm bells sounded and voices started shouting. Arna slipped through the bodies unnoticed and unseen.

Breathe in, one two three four.

Breathe out, five six seven eight.

He would not be found unless he wanted to be.

[*This is the basis for the whole contract. The pinnacle of all taboos*, Pokk said.]

We only think of it after it has passed: when it has come and gone.

Which came first, dancers who danced with fans or The Dances? Many scholars said that fan dances sprung up across the world because of The Dances and their popularity, and that they developed further over the millennia into different styles and forms. Others argued that they existed before, and that Raven had simply been a fan dancer who determined it was the best way to express worship. With the lack of written records and oral accounts of the time before the First Dance and the beginning of the contract, no one could say for certain.

We long for it. We hide from it.

We try to fill it when it is not void.

The Gods told Arna that dance was picked because of its storytelling potential. Stories could be passed orally, but those told visually held more power. Raven picked it was the only form of art they were proficient in. The other Chosen were gifted in other arts, but they followed suit because it was the establishment of the contract and created the best results. Watsonia had tried song but found it lacking. Sable had tried carving. Dance was the only form that bent itself to the divinity, and the Gods demanded that they dance. So, they danced, with fans.

The moments we do not hear, are not lost.

It is there in our imaginations, in our hopes, in our dreams.

It is the proof, the support, the essence of what matters.

Fans helped to weave the story in multiple ways that added a layer of complexity to the dances. There were six bones welded together in each fan creating the skeleton, representing the six gods. Each was inscribed with prayers and wishes of the Chosen for the new world. The fabric was picked to create dimension. Fans represented divinity, represented reverence, represented the Gods themselves. Outside of dance they were symbolic of the Gods, people wore them as pins, used them in weddings, were extra careful never to drop them. Fans provided a breeze to alleviate heat, weather was provided by the Gods. Fans could be used to defend oneself, just as Blessings were.

Many mortals discussed the true form of the Gods, what they looked like. Many artists tried to depict them. But to Arna, the Gods were fans.

[*Don't hesitate,* Ixxzal said.]

Silence is not an absence but a reminder of what you have.

Arna stepped before the crystal box, seeing the fan he made at fifteen. It was the one he dropped during the eighteenth dance that splintered the world. It was the only fan he'd ever made that still existed. The rest had burned for his mistake.

Arna's hands tingled in longing. His breathing was short. Looking at one close, he could almost hear the crisp sound. The fabric was so soft like it was made of clouds and as smooth as scales. The scent of fabric glue wafted. How Arna wanted to hold it.

Terror seized him.

[*Only when we renew the contract can we remove the taboo from you,* Azza said. *Until then, you are cursed. Pick it up.*]

He'd done this before. Too many times before, and each time it was no different.

Training. This is training. So that when he danced, the pain did not destroy him.

[*Yes.* Zaynir was quiet.]

He needed thirty Blessings to survive the ascension, without risk.

[*Less than eighteen and you'll die,* Azza said.]

Which left a twelve Blessing gap. He repeated the order in which they took the Blessings, the order they'd drilled into him when he was young. Losing each Blessing was a calculated risk. Each loss made his survival all the more difficult. It became a game of luck, perseverance, and capability.

Training. He was fine. He could do it.

[*We will shield Ven from the pain, now that you're closer, they will feel it more,* Zaynir warned him.]

He was there again, standing on the train gripping it for life as the train tumbled to the ground after an electrical surge negated the Blessings on the rails.

Jump, they had said then.

[*Pick up the fan,* Ixxzal ordered again.]

Arna hesitated, his hand shaking. He wanted to, oh how he wanted to. Yet. . .

painpainpainpainpainpain

He'd lost the first when he was seventeen. That day was scored into his skin.

He'd wanted to go home. He wanted out of being Chosen. The couple with the silver door had found him yelling at nothing. Arna had begged the couple for fans, and they had gotten them for him. He'd touched them and—

Solid white. Chill. People yelling for him to come back.

He lost the next at twenty-one and another at twenty-five.

He could not miss a step. He could not make another mistake like the Splintering. He would not be like Saffron and fail.

Saffron. . .

[*Take it*, Ixxzal said, less demanding.]

What was his variation called?

[*Arna, this is not the time*, Ixxzal complained.]

You never talk about him! What was his variation called?

The original. Twin Fans. Blue Rose Fears. Roots and Ends. Holly. Each variation had a name which meant Saffron's did too.

Just tell me. I can't be like him. I need to know.

[*Why do you think we call it the Shattering?* Pokk asked. *He broke the connection of mortals and Gods and warped the contract. You needn't compare yourself to him.*]

But Arna had done that too. *Was it called Shatter?*

[*Arna, you can't risk being seen*, Zaynir protested.]

Was it?

[*No*, Xeyaro said, *That was not the reflection he wanted to show the world.*]

[*Move, Arna*, Lumak said.]

Mirror?

[*Mirage*, Ixxzal said finally. *He wanted to break the phantom memories of the world.*]

He'd done the opposite and left a curse instead. It was the curse that Arna had to break.

I can't be like him.

He did not wait for the Gods to support him. Arna grabbed his fan. It was like coming home, familiar and safe. The weight in his hand was a thousand kisses to the forehead and being tucked in at night. It was his father teaching him step by step how to properly carve the frame.

Then a bone chill.

It tainted him, rushing through his hand along his entire body. A sob broke his lips. He lurched, wanting to scream as the chill turned into a freeze turned into a burn. His bones were liquified, and everything,

all

, went white.

[*Move*, Ixxzal said.]

I can't.

In the pain was an igniting sunrise, a burst of divine power that linked him closer to the Gods. Every time he ever lost a Blessing, he was closer to the Gods, and they were closer to the mortal realm. No amount of insistence could convince him that their pushing him to take the fans was not in part vindictive or at least greedy. He renewed their life at the cost of his own. Each time he lost a Blessing through the fans, the taboos did not take the power, they did.

> [*Follow my voice*, Azza said like a trusted friend. *You know your powers. Focus on the ones you have left.*]

He did as told.

He hated them, the Gods. They had stolen everything from him, but he had stolen everything from them. They hated him as well. They'd push him to the brink of collapse, but it was there on the edge that he became the person who could meet their expectations.

He'd do whatever it took to fix what he broke. He'd choose them every step of the way. He'd choose them over his family, his friends, the love of his life. Time and time again, if that was what it took.

For he had to hope in that person who was able to withstand it. he believed in the person who snuck out of the labyrinth and cathedral without being seen and without dropping the fan. For one day he'd be under the spotlights again. On that day he would dance, and that person would have to be able to withstand the world's end. It would be a pressure like none he'd ever faced before.

The eighteenth fan burned in a park trashcan, until only ash remained.

And when we understand this all, we will be able to step into the Gods' minds and into their world. We shall see ourselves as they see us. We shall know ourselves as they know us. To truly understand why the variations exist we must understand what they are trying to say.

— On the Understanding of the Gods section of The Twenty-Seven Dances.

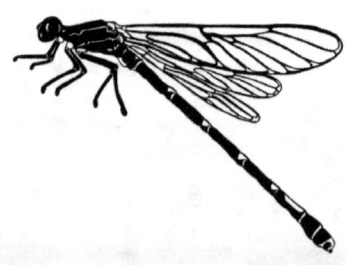

Dance 5

Strife

Incarnadine

29 Poan

86 Days Left

"The Dances are not so simple."
"I don't know anything else."
"One day you will. For now, you master the others."

After his first practice back at home, using his dance clothes that had taken time to get downstairs, Arna planned his travel through Xeysis. There were more supplies to get than he'd hoped: new fabric, a computer, carving tools, wood paint, fabric paint, needles, thread, wood, hammers. There were too many things that he'd need to buy, and not enough time to do it before news leaked of his arrival.

Alis messaged him.

> Alis: When will you send me the last chimes?
> Rosy: Tonight. I just got home.

Alis' video call lit up the air in front of Arna and he grimaced.

> Rosy: Can't. Why do you keep calling?
> Alis: I just want to hear your voice.

Alis had never been curious about his voice before. Why was he now?

> Rosy: Once my move is over, and everything is settled we
>   can have a long chat.
> Rosy: Okay?
> Alis: Sure. . . I'm glad you're alive at least.
> Rosy: You doubt me?
> Alis: Why should I believe you? Bluebell says you're a
>   catfish.

Arna ground his teeth at the mention of Bluebell. He would need to set her straight. Alis was his and he'd never pick her. Maybe...

Arna shook his head. It was better not to get involved too deeply.

> Rosy: Because I've never lied to you.
> Alis: That I believe.

There was movement from downstairs, finally after what felt like forever since he returned from the Cathedral. Pausing, Arna looked to his bedroom door before he walked to the wall next to it. He traced a line from star to star across the wall until he found the loose board on his wooden walls. Prying it back he found a bag covered in twelve years' worth of dust, undisturbed. No one had searched for it because no one had known to look.

He found the yards of opalescent fabric: beautiful, light, exactly what he needed. Arna scoured every inch, checking for holes, age, or damage. It was nearly perfect, except for in a few places where it had frayed from the initial cut. There was enough for the first layer of the ceremonial clothes. He would have to get the second color, an oil slick black that shimmered in the same way as this opal white. Inside the bag were the spools of ribbon he had made for the specific Gods: one spool for each God.

Arna flipped through his most finalized designs checking if he needed more.

Inside the bag were fabric scissors, old thread, pins, a heat gun, and old designs from before the exile: naïve drawings with little practice. There was also an additional money chip, kept safe so he could buy the next bit of supplies in secret. He'd never let anyone know he was building the stash, creating the project. Now the secret was key to his success.

Folding everything carefully, Arna checked off the remaining items in his notebook and made notes on the condition of the fabric.

"Arna," His mother's voice came from the door. "Are you awake?"

Arna was a whirlwind of motion, hiding everything. He checked his privacy settings for his room by tapping at the wall. He set it to 'do not enter,' unless it was his biometrics, with no exceptions. The room flashed purple, and only when he was certain no one would be able to get in, he opened the door and squinted into the daylight. Wenge stood in the hallway with a soft smile on her lips, a bit startled that he had answered.

"Why is your room so dark?" she asked him. The only light was from the candles, which he moved to block.

"Habit. I always had black out curtains at home. . ." He bit his tongue realizing what he had said. She frowned.

"This is your home, Arna," she reminded him quickly, sternly, like correcting a child.

"I know." He had never thought he'd call those apartments and hideouts *home*, but they had been somewhere safe. "I'll be down soon."

"Jasi said you need to go shopping?"

"I do."

He thanked the Gods—who chortled and accepted the thanks with glee—that he'd had the foresight to message Jasione. He needed to deposit the money chips he had on him. He'd been able to open a new bank account and link the account to his mobile the day before. Thank Lumak, the online banking allowed him to do most of the work without being seen.

[*You're welcome*, Azza accepted.]

Yes. Thank Azza. Master of chaos.

[Azza laughed.]

[*Azza was close to superseding us and making your life difficult*, Zaynir said.]

You would have made me go in?

[*It would have been funny*, Azza said.]

Azza! Arna fought back a disgruntled laugh. Thinking about it was humorous in theory, knowing how annoyed he'd have been. Depositing money chips could be done in minutes without being noticed, opening a whole account meant talking to someone.

"Jasi will be back from work soon." Wenge placed her hand on the door. Her eyes glanced inside, then to him, and she nodded. She did not press.

[*You know she knows. You can tell her. You can trust her to help you*, Ixxzal said in a low voice.]

Arna began to recite scriptures. *Temptation is a terror: the unknown captivating and consuming the soul*. Parable of Greed, from the Church of Xeya's holy book.

[The Gods groaned.]

"I'll leave this box for you. It was delivered this morning," she said.

"Thank you. I'll be down in a moment."

When his mother's footsteps disappeared down the hall, he opened the door fully, grabbed the last box, and turned on his lights. The box contained the last of his scrapbooks sent from Azis. The walls of his room were lined with religious art of the Gods and their iconography. He shuddered.

"I was so embarrassing," He complained rubbing his face with the palm of his hands, groaning at his childish vigor.

[*It was endearing*, Lumak said as the others laughed.]

Arna placed the box on his bed with the others. He quickly said a prayer, and the candles went out. After placing the covered case in the wall, hoping it would protect them, he opened his curtains and began removing the art. The color of the willow and her leaves, silver and red light, cascaded in.

"How much do you think I can sell it for?" He asked once he gathered the religious art.

[*Wait until you're official. It will go for a fortune*, Pokk suggested.]

Arna laughed and placed it aside; he then opened the box. Inside were the images he'd carefully picked to keep and the scrapbooks of his friends and family. He kept the scrapbooks in the box and removed the loose pictures, deciding what to put on his walls. For years he kept his walls lined with their faces to remind him. Although seeing their faces now, in the glamorized photoshoots, and knowing he'd have to face them all. . . He placed them all back in the box.

Notifications popped up in the air.

```
Alis: Are you sure everything's okay?
Rosy: Just stress. I swear.
Alis: Moving was that bad?
Rosy: Terrible
Rosy: I feel like I never should have come back.
Alis: Back?
Rosy: I can't explain yet.
Rosy: But I will
Alis: I'm here. You can always call me.
Rosy: I know.
```

[*Nervous?* Zaynir asked.]

"No." Everything would be fine.

[*Be yourself,* Zaynir said. *You must reweave yourself into their lives.*]

Arna used his Ch.Insight to strengthen his resolve and found a gaping hole. *Right.*

He readjusted around the space. After years of losing his Blessings, he'd learned how to move without them. It would take time and he'd continuously try to use it over the next few weeks, but he'd manage. He always did.

[*They're here*, Pokk said.]

Arna looked out his window and below to the family garden of bushes and flowers. A small stream ran next to a stone path, leading to the base of the trunk of the tree where there was an elaborate rock garden. At the edges were six moon doors, situated at the base of the six staircases, leading one from the house into the garden. Lush and serene, the garden welcomed him.

Above, the city sparkled behind the false sky, towering past the willow's swaying branches. Even in the day, the center was as dark as night. The sound of voices echoed from somewhere in the house.

Tossing on new clothes, Arna placed his dance journal inside his inner pocket, and checked his room once more to make sure everything was safe. With his backpack and money chips in hand, he left the room. The hallway itself was bright in natural light from the windows that peered to the garden. Every door that Arna passed had no name. At one time, tens of people had lived in Vivicent Manor. Now it was only six.

The air was fresh and dry, filled with roses, cinnamon, and ancient wood. The lights in the hall were soft white. His footsteps were silent. There were voices as he walked down the stairs to the living room.

"We're going to have to let him do what he wants," Zaffre said sternly.

Arna stopped walking and listened.

"What if he gets hurt?" Gingerline complained.

"If we coddle him, he might flee. He's skittish as it is. Whatever he faced out there. . . This Arna is not the one we knew."

"He's hiding something," Sarcoline hissed.

"You were the most excited. . ." Gingerline complained.

"He is *hiding* something," Sarcoline insisted. "If I can just figure it out, we—"

"Arco, stop. We don't know that," Zaffre disagreed. "He has been on the run for twelve years, of course he's apprehensive and evasive. He had to survive."

"You didn't believe me when I said he'd get back before the celebrations! Why can't you just *listen* to me?" Sarcoline snapped. "Besides look at mom! She's not okay with this. Ginger has already had two panic attacks. We have to find out what he's hiding so we can be better prepared."

How his brother was so confident in the truth that Arna thought he'd hidden well, Arna was unsure. He made a mental note to act more convincingly around Sarcoline. No one could know what he was hiding. It was his burden to bare.

"We are prepared. This is everything we expected," Zaffre's voice rose in frustration.

"No, I did, and I promise you, he's hiding something." Sarcoline said, voice low and irritated. "What if something happened. What if he's not. . ."

"Stop!" Zaffre shouted. "He. Is. He is."

"If your father says we have to let him have space, then we must," Wenge spoke in a voice that was far from calm, angry herself.

"Why? So, he can disappear again?" Sarcoline asked, venomously.

"Arco. You *know* why he disappeared," Zaffre snapped back.

"Yes, but there is *something*. He hasn't said anything we didn't already know. But what if he dropped the fan and ran away because he *lost* his chance at being Chosen. For all we know, he could have been trying to force it by doing what was necessary in hopes that the Gods will come back. You hear what the others say. The world did not Splinter when other Chosen rose to power. They believe he failed. We need the truth from him."

There was a silence in the room. A glass broke.

"You don't know him!" Gingerline screamed. "He wouldn't just abandon us unless it was on purpose!"

"I do know him!" Sarcoline screamed back. "He is hiding something! I don't trust him!"

"You *loved* him!" Gingerline shrieked as if Sarcoline had said something that was not actively true. Arna had no issue with his brother not trusting him. He'd been gone for too long for any of them to trust him.

"Then he left us with this *mess*. Everyone left, Ginger. Everyone. Even Ebru and Uncle Alabaster," Sarcoline's voice calmed to a chilling degree, "We need the truth."

The name Alabaster had Arna remembering slow counts of morning practice. Eburnean standing with him, yawning and glaring through mirrors at Arna who glared back.

"Alabaster left because being here was a threat to his family," Zaffre corrected. "He still loves you."

"Just because Uncle Alabaster and Ebru come over on the holidays, does not mean they didn't leave us. They were forced to because of *him*," Sarcoline went on. "And you want me to just accept whatever he says? No. The rest of the world won't. We need something tangible so we can prove to the world that he did not just destroy it because he wanted to."

Arna's body was melting. Because he. . . Arna shook the thought away. Now was not the time. Arna plastered a smile to his face and took a few deep breaths. One, two, three, four: in.

"If he's the Chosen Child, then you *know* that's unfair to him," Jasione said.

"We need proof," Sarcoline groaned.

Five, six, seven, eight: out.

"His Blessing test should be proof enough," Gingerline scoffed.

Arna started to move again.

"All of the other Chosen Children lived in a time with no internet." It was a voice that Arna did not know, high pitched and airy. It made him freeze. Who. . .? She continued to speak. "Don't you think that if he is Chosen, he has to be all the more careful, Coco? Maybe there is a part of the process that we, regular mortals, aren't allowed to know?"

"Perhaps," Sarcoline's voice was so soft that Arna nearly did not hear it.

"He won't say anything?" The next voice had Arna's heart up in his throat as his S. Mirrors Blessing activated against his will. All at once there was a presence of another beside him, with him, near him. He could pinpoint their exact place and the fluctuation in their emotions as they rejected the sensation of being linked.

Ven.

Ven had the most beautiful eyes. Mint, like all of Xeyaro's children, but Ven's were different. Grey and mint, swirling about themselves, glimmering in hope and adventure. Ven always had the softest voice. It made people listen to them; the sort of voice that soothed the soul and opened the mind. Ven had been the voice of reason when Arna and Eburnean fought, when Phlox was crying, when Gingerline was complaining. Ven had the softest lips that Arna had ever kissed.

Ven gave the gentlest of touches, the kind that led someone towards their fullest potential, a support that was there to fall back to for safety. Ven was Arna's everything.

"I can get him to talk," Ven went on, soft and contained.

"He wouldn't talk to *me*," Jasione disagreed. "Besides, do you even want to talk to him?"

"Ven could use their abilities," the unfamiliar voice offered.

"Arna has been on the run for twelve years. He would have mastered how to navigate his Blessings." Ven probably was shaking their head based on the exasperation in their voice.

Arna wished to tell them that no, he was not skilled in all his gifts. He could use all his abilities together, but the mastery of his Blessings on an individual basis had never been his first priority.

"I would not be able to get it out of him unless he was willing. Although, I could convince him."

"But do you *want* to," Jasione repeated.

"No," Ven answered. "I won't force him."

"Great. No one can do anything," Sarcoline retorted.

"Arco. Stop." There was a pause as Zaffre cut the discussion off. "Keep an eye on him but give him space. We won't let him out of our sights if we can help it. Many people are going to want to hurt him because he is the Chosen Child."

"Then why can't he just say that? If he just said, 'look I was doing this for the Gods,' everyone would forgive him. Why do we have to play a game of what-ifs? We can't protect him like this," Sarcoline said.

Arna did not need them to protect him. He had to protect them. He alone would dance. He alone.

Arna shook his head. No. They could not get involved.

"He might not be able to say anything until he dances again," Jasione suggested. "What are we going to do about the ceremony?"

Arna finished the trek down the stairs before anyone could answer. He made his presence, loud and known, ceasing all further conversation as he entered through the doorway. The living room was bright from the sunlight through the windows and filled with people. Waffles and juice sat on the table, forgotten. The large open space that was living room, family dining, and view into the kitchen, was filled with a somber energy.

The first person he noted was the new girl. She was pretty in pink, with a light pastel jacket and skirt. She had long almond shaped nails painted pink and with white crystals. She had a camera hanging around her neck on a pink lanyard. On the ground there was a pink and white bag, with a white umbrella. Her wavy hair was a stark black. Her skin glowed a deep brown in the morning light, but it was her eyes that stood out. They were peach blossom shaped and the color aqua: a Child of Zaynir.

Before him was the face of a woman he often saw on the news and across the internet, the most hated Child in the world: Amaryllis Ink. She smiled.

Jasione sat next to Gingerline and Sarcoline who leaned back in his chair scowling at Arna. Wenge whimpered and looked to Zaffre who nodded. It took all her energy to look at Arna without reaching over to hug him. They were giving him space, giving him freedom to move. He was thankful.

Then there was Ven.

Ven had short brown hair with large looping curls and pale brown skin. They wore long, light, baggy clothes made of organic materials because synthetic made Ven's skin itch. The clothes were symmetrical, as they preferred balance. They chose cremes and soft purples, never dark colors, which made Ven look sickly. Ven had long eyes lashes that highlighted their eyes.

Ven's eyes.

They were familiar and perfect.

Ven's name was there in the back of his throat, scratching to get out. Ven was a million moments wrapped into one existence. Ven was the five months of meandering about unable to convince himself to ask them out, despite knowing that Ven already felt the same way. Ven was seven hundred twenty-eight days of an official forever, until midnight had struck, and they had been forced to separate. Ven was the sweet breath of morning air. They were the chaste kiss goodnight, the congratulatory hugs when Arna succeeded. The memory of Ven was woven into Arna's very existence.

Ven was there, sitting before Arna, in the flesh and fully formed. This was not a dream. It was real. In twelve years, Arna learned to want little. Yet the disaster that he was, wanted to please Ven more than even the Gods. His Ven was older, wiser, more perfect than he had any memory before.

"Arna." Jasione looked to Arna, stepping forward.

"Yeah?" He blinked, cutting off his blank stare directed at Ven.

[Distant birds were gossiping.]

"Are you ready to go?" Jasione snapped Arna back into the moment, back into his truth. Once more he was dedicated to the Gods and the mission, they had given him.

[*It's cute*, Lumak's voice cut through, weak.]

[*No, it's foolish*, Ixxzal disagreed.]

"Yeah. I have my list." Arna answered, glancing at Ven again, hoping to feel. . . something else.

[*Just because you want—*]

[Once again, their voices were caught in interference.]

"I've set up new accounts for you." Zaffre walked up to Arna handing him a card holder with three cards. "Don't use it all."

"I won't." Arna had difficulties taking the cards as his father would not let go. Arna held his eyes on Ven, until he was forced to confront the sadness that his father expressed: drooping eyes and a distraught smile. Zaffre was afraid. Arna whispered, "I won't disappear."

"How much did you hear?" Sarcoline asked.

Arna ignored him and looked to Ven. "Pervenche."

"That's my name." Ven spoke with a tinge of anger. A wave of surprise overtook Arna, followed by frustration and despair. "Incarnadine. Your S.Mirrors is active. Stop. Your anxiety is stressing me out."

Within seconds Arna was incomplete and ungrounded as he cut their connection. He quickly calmed his heart but no one seemed to pay heed to the words.

"I watched your archery online," Arna said softly, not sure how to broach Ven's fury. Ven had stopped dancing eight years ago to start archery and Arna had tried to watch every competition. When he could not, he'd asked Alis from a replay; Alis watched them all.

"I'm Amaryllis." The girl in pink placed herself between Ven and Arna, claiming Arna's attention for herself. "It's a pleasure to meet you."

"Amaryllis. . ." He stared at the girl who caused international terror each time she posted a photo. "It's a pleasure to meet you."

She was the one girl who lived Incarnate Dreams in the flesh, just as his brother did. She was one of his smaller muses, not that he'd expected to meet her. She was the girl who said she did not care for what her Blessings were supposed to mean. . . As Arna met her eyes, his world was solidifying. The dance began to form in his heart as steps that he thought he could piece together. Everything would be—

Ven let Amaryllis touch them. Ven, who hated being touched by everyone without explicit consent. Amaryllis wrapped her arm around Ven's arm and in an instant the one last hope that Arna held, shattered. Reality set in.

Alis always said that Blessings *should* matter little, but they meant too much. It was why society had nearly collapsed without them and was destined to disappear if they vanished. Arna had always thought he understood Alis and agreed. Blessings should not matter that much. He'd sworn to rely on them as little as he could. Alis had called him foolish. Now, Arna understood that despite saying it, he had still put too much faith in his own Blessing.

[*Heartmates does not mean love*, Zaynir, God of Emotions and Souls, reminded him. *A chance is given. The recipients decide. It's a* **choice.**]

Arna bristled, grabbing his wrist were his constellation birthmark laid. Only one Blessings made a mark on the body like a vow: S.Mirrors, always dressed as a matching constellation on two bodies on the left wrist. S.Mirrors was just like every other test the Gods gave him: a chance at a choice. S.Mirrors gave him a person who was his equal and perfect for him, someone who would love him unconditionally because their souls were linked.

They didn't *have* to be romantic or sexual or anything but platonic; yet they would be life partners, traveling together in all challenges.

> [*He thought they'd be together forever,* Azza said dejected.]
>
> [*It is not his fault that people push S.Mirrors to be lovers. It is the expectation,* Lumak reminded Azza, almost more calloused than normal.]

You gave me this.

The God's voices were changing, but he could not understand why.

> [*We presented you the possibility,* Xeyaro disagreed. *And gave you someone to ground you.*]

"Are you okay?" Amaryllis asked Arna.

Arna's emotions threatened to bubble and lash out. He tried to still his mind and found the gap again. Frustrated, he patched it together with other Blessings, but it would not fill.

failurefailurefailurefailurefailurefailure

Plastering a smile to his face, clenching his left fist tightly around his bag, and killing the thoughts, Arna was fine. They were all strangers. And that was okay.

Seeing Pervenche with Amaryllis made Arna realize he'd never fully pictured himself with anyone else. He had never fully allowed himself that option. He had kissed a girl under the moonlight in Ixis and had a fling with a boy in Podiel. There had been many others, however none of them had known him. He had hidden who he was to keep them safe, and anything more than a fling and the Gods would have forbidden him from seeing them again. The only person he'd allowed himself had been Alis. . .

For years he'd thought and hoped that Pervenche was Alis. Yet, Alis was someone else, someone who would never have the connection to Arna that Pervenche did.

Pervenche had picked Amaryllis in Arna's absence. Arna picked Alis.

Arna was empty. He had made the choice to listen to the Gods and life had gone on without him. He'd been childish and let himself hope that things would return to the way they were. He knew better than to do that. Everyone had moved on, and he was not supposed to have returned until the day of his dances. Everything was a mess.

He reached for his mobile in his pocket and refrained. He could not turn to Alis. Not then. Not yet.

Amaryllis continued to stand looking at him expectantly.

"Yes," Arna said as nicely as he could. Something twitched in Pervenche's otherwise flat expression. Before Pervenche could address it, Arna looked to Jasione. "Are they coming with us?"

"Ven could only stop by this morning to see you. I thought it best for you to see them before the rest of the world knows. Ebru got a heads up too, but he is too focused on other things."

"You're going shopping?" Amaryllis asked.

"Yes," Arna said. The worst part was that he already liked Amaryllis. Something about her set him with ease. He could not hate her when he'd been the one to ruin his relationship with Pervenche. He could not hate her when she was the embodiment of his dream. He needed to let the past go, but he was unwilling.

He said, "I need to buy new. . . things. You know?"

"Yes. Of *course,* you are avoiding the answer," Sarcoline said exasperated from the back.

"I haven't mastered my Blessings, by the way," Arna said steering the conversation away from himself.

"You haven't?" Pervenche asked.

"Technically, I only have one mastered."

The one that mattered he could use to what the Gods considered mastery: A.Reverence. Otherwise, Arna was only mastered all at once, flourished, or in dance. While activating a Blessing was like snapping a finger, muscle memory once learned, he could not use them all. He was horrendous with the majority of his Blessings on their own, save the most useful ones, which was down to one less.

"I have combination work mastered but not the individual abilities."

Still, a duodecennial of work with all his Blessings was nothing to scoff at: there were too many. A person became stronger with practice, and Arna was confident in his skill. He'd been able to sneak through the cathedral the night before and that wasn't due to luck.

"I don't have much time today," Jasione sighed. He waved his hand back and forth, trying to end the conversation. "We should get going."

With a nod, Arna started towards the door, noticing how Pervenche and Amaryllis wished his family the best and left with him. Jasione went over his schedule twice.

"We have to be home in two hours," Jasione insisted.

He had meetings that night with the government officials on Zaffre and Arna's behalf.

Arna accidentally met Pervenche's eyes again. Pervenche had a million unasked questions, and a barrier between them so the S.Mirrors would not activate again. Arna hurried to focus elsewhere.

"You've lived in every city?" Amaryllis broke the silence between them all as soon as they left the house walking towards the rail station. "Which one was your favorite?"

The ever present anxiety in his spine thudded without a drug to numb it.

everyonewilldieeveryonewilldieeveryonewilldie
anditwillbeyourfault

Arna's emptiness spread and threatened to consume him. He squeezed his hand, smiled, and ignored it. The new cocktail of Blessings was a patch but not perfect. But he would be fine, and it would be enough. He flourished them further.

"Xeysis is and will always be my favorite. It's the prettiest and. . ." He said, jubilant and bright. He was fine.

"Everyone knows Xeysis is the best city for Children of Xeyaro. The other cities were built to please the Children of the Gods. I've heard the labyrinth of Ixis is a marvel."

Remorse filled Arna's chest: how he wanted to go back.

"Archways that lead to blank walls. Doors hidden in the cracks. Painted alleys and wells that look so real you fall for them. Dead end streets that you swore were not dead ends the day before. Paths that open sometimes. Windows that close randomly. The only thing consistent in the city was the rail schedule, although locations for the entrances always shifted. Never the same place twice, and yet everywhere would be serviced at some point."

He wished he'd been able to stay for longer.

"That sounds magical," Amaryllis breathed out.

Before he had ran away from home, the only people Arna had ever known to move to new cities to live were Children. Most people did not move. Each city had its own unique culture and language. Without a Blessing to speak other languages, it was hard to adapt. Children, however, moved to the city of their patron, as that city was often better for them in all ways.

Jasione should have gone to Ludiel. It was expected of him as one of the three Children born in the last four duodecennial with the B.Reverence Blessing focus. Instead he stayed in Xeysis.

"It was annoying for deliveries," Arna said, remembering his former job. He used to complain about it all the time to Alis.

What little negative energy and mixed feelings disappeared when Arna thought of Alis. He may have been a fish out of water with his family and friends, but he had Alis. Even if Alis could not know everything. . . He could rely on him for support.

Arna took out his mobile and messaged Alis.

> Rosy: I need you.
> Alis: I'm here.
> Alis: What's wrong?
> Rosy: I can't explain.
> Alis: I'm here for when you can.
> Rosy: Just knowing you are, is enough.

"We need to get going now, Amaryllis," Pervenche spoke up.

"Time to go?" She looked to Pervenche, then back to Arna. "It was a pleasure, truly."

"The pleasure is mine."

Amaryllis took Pervenche's arm, covering them both with her umbrella from the sun. Amaryllis' eyes bore into Arna, seeing all the secrets in him, unraveling him. In her other hand she typed in the air.

Leaves sparkled in their wake, taking to the air and hovering like soft clouds. The world around Arna began to dim, from clouds overhead. Jasione continued to stand in the sun, but Arna was consumed by shadows. Like Amaryllis, Arna checked his messages.

> Alis: Let me know if I can help.
> Alis: Otherwise. I have something that could distract
>   you.

The message was followed by a link to a picture of birds.

> Alis: It's almost time.
> Rosy: Never expected you to be blood thirsty.
> Alis: We get one shot.
> Alis: I can't miss recording their call.

Arna blinked at the image again. Alis was in Xeysis? The bird was only native to Xeysis. . . The sky brightened leaving Arna's skin warm in the light.

"Amaryllis' brother is eleven." Jasione spoke without warning, nervous almost. Arna looked from his phone to the scene ahead, as Pervenche and Amaryllis turned a corner. The little love in his heart that remained for Pervenche went with them. "When he was eight, he broke a taboo."

"Which one?" Arna asked slipping his hand from his neck and masking his uneven breathing and focusing on the moment at hand.

"He plucked the wrong plant and. . ." Jasione sighed. "The best doctors couldn't help him. Not fully. He lost a leg. He gets treatments regularly for it and the augmentation he was given."

Arna ruined everything for the world. There was nothing he could say. The headlines after he left had been clear:

Non-Blessed? Cursed After the Splintering.

He was the reason those children died; all because he had not completed his last dance twelve years ago. On the eighteenth dance with six seconds left in the song, the fans had slipped from his fingers.

Six seconds had destroyed the world.

He had made himself the only tether for the Gods in those six seconds. The world could have been lost forever if he died. Yet, he had survived, still survived, and had to survive to the day when he danced. He could still fix it.

[*You will*, Pokk said.]

[*Ilex created the path forward. You can do this*, Xeyaro agreed.]

I know. Years ago, Arna had tried to research the other Chosen, to learn more about them for his quest. What he had learned was little more than he'd learned growing up. It was as if they suddenly appeared in history, when they danced.

The before was given through the stories told between mortals and saints: scarce and incomplete. There was nothing about the supposed contract that he was supposed to fix.

Most of his other knowledge came from the Gods themselves, and they were biased.

[*Fix your relationships first*, Xeyaro insisted, *You must.*]

"As long as he's alive, that's what matters," Arna spoke out loud to Jasione. He could not just fix the relationships. He saw how leaving broke them. Death would be worse. Not again. He could not get any closer than this. He asked, "How long have they been together? Ven and Amaryllis."

"Two years. Although, they've known each far longer." Jasione paused as if debating what to say. If he thought Arna's silence strange, he did not comment, nor did he have an expression that clued Arna into what he was thinking. "They met at some archery competition that Arco took her to and were friends from that point on. Got together because they understood each other."

"Oh?"

"She lost her Heartmate in the train crash in Ludiel and Ven lost you," Jasione said, and Arna's heart was in his ears. He stopped walking.

Screams. Lights flickering. Surrogate parents begging him to leave.

Jump, the Gods had said.

everyonewilldieeveryonewilldieeveryonewilldie
anditwillbeyourfault

The thudding of the thoughts was not disappearing. *This is the new normal.* After every loss, things were difficult to address what he lost. He'd adapt.

He was fine.

Arna walked in silence. Instead of hiding the thoughts, he faced them with rationality.

How many people had he killed? Vervain the Blythe never would have. Ilex never would have.

[*Ilex was an idiot*, Ixxzal hissed.]

[*You didn't break the world, Arna. That was us*, Zaynir said as Azza and Ixxzal bickered in voices not heard but felt like the turbulence of a storm.]

I know.

Even if he completed the dance, so long as he chose the path of exile, the candles would have gone out one day. However, it was supposed to have been the night he danced his variation. Him invoking a taboo during the Ceremony as the potential Chosen had caused the Splintering; he had corrupted the divine energy.

[*Not corrupted*, Zaynir insisted, *Disrupted.*]

[*The contract still stands*, Xeyaro agreed. *As long as the Bond stands, we can complete the reset.*]

They called it the reset and reprieve. The moment he started dancing his variation the new Blessings would begin. Each Variance had different Blessings and he got to shape them. The candles going out and the breaking of the connection was essential to the God's reestablishing themselves.

But it was supposed to be this year. For two hours max.

Jasione shook his head. "You really have changed."

"It's been twelve years," Arna said the words more for himself, than Jasione. *Twelve years.* He'd missed twelve years. If he had been smarter, it never would have happened. He would have put the fan down.

[*You were scared,* Zaynir said.]

[*The issue is that Ilex created the modern age, and thus the ramifications of the reprieve are now greater,* Xeyaro said, *If he had not caused the technological revolution, your mistake wouldn't have caused so many issues. We should have prepared for it.*]

It was still his fault.

[*But it's not your fault,* Xeyaro's voice cracked as if it were on the radio. *It's ours, like Saffron was.*]

The name Saffron made Arna shake. They rarely mentioned Saffron outside of their disdain for him. When they did, he asked them about him first. They never brought him up first. He was the one mistake the God's were trying to fix.

[*Their deaths are on us, not you. We gave you the order. You followed,* Lumak reminded him.]

Arna disagreed.

[*Do not forsake us,* Xeyaro warned him as if the static had never been there at all.]

I won't. He had worked for year to fulfill their dream. It was everything he worked for, and even if he was the cause of the mess. . . he wanted to do it. The dance mattered to him.

"I suppose you won't kill me if I told you that I'm dating your sister, then?" Jasione said quickly breaking the lingering silence between them.

"Ginger?" That was why Jasione was still in Xeysis? Because of Ginger?

Laughter bubbled in his throat. It was not for his own family or even Arna's. It was for Gingerline of all people? Heat spread to Arna's eyes, and he blinked back the water that formed. He had missed so much. . .

"Yes, Gingerline. I wasn't aware you had another sister," Jasione joked.

"I thought you and Aureolin. . ."

"Absolutely not. We're friends."

"Do you talk to them all?"

"We. . . I still keep in contact with all of them, even Ebru."

Fear coursed it's way though Arna's veins. If anyone resented Arna the most, Arna had little doubt it was Eburnean. If anyone changed, Eburnean had. Arna had seen it.

Arna's notifications rang.

```
Alis: You sure you're, okay?
Rosy: Better now.
Alis: You sure?
```

```
Rosy: I'll explain later.
Alis: okay
```

"Did you date anyone?" Jasione asked. Arna smiled, seeing the effort that Jasione was giving. If Jasione wanted to step into the role of best friend again, Arna could not stop him.

"A few people. Mostly flings. All sorts of people, of all sorts of points in their lives. I couldn't do much, because of who I am," While it was true, it felt like a lie. Incomplete. Wary, he said the full truth unsure how the name would come up otherwise. "Then there was Alis. Although, we never dated more than. . . online."

In some ways despite joking that they were married and officially claiming each other as spouses to their fandom, it wasn't real. They didn't know each other.

"Alis?"

"We've never met in person or even talked to each other really." Arna had never even heard Alis' voice. "We still message. He's. . ."

Arna stopped talking the moment Jasione's face froze with a smile. Jasione's stride was rigid and forced. Arna switched the conversation immediately.

"So. . . you told them all that I'm back?"

"Ebru said he's busy. Phlox said she was happy you returned. She's in Azis for a movie. Rus will be home after his world tour next month. . ." Jasione paused before his voice dropped. "You talked to someone, but you couldn't message us?"

"I could message him because he didn't know who I was." Arna hesitated and tried to change the awkward tension between them with a joke from the past. "Does Phlox still think of you as her missing heartmate?"

"Phlox has no other friends. Save Ebru, and he's not a friend to anyone." Jasione shrugged as the train rolled in and they got inside a bus, much to Arna's prayers. "We don't have much time for shopping and your father has asked me to buy you lots of clothes in the shortest time possible."

"What? Are my current ones too shabby for the family?" He wished he hadn't said it the moment he had. He thought of his mother and sister dressed in clothes that were old and out of style.

"You came with almost nothing, Arna. Yet, you shipped boxes to the house filled with who knows what. What are you hiding?"

Arna tried to smile but could not. When Jasione cocked an eyebrow, Arna knew Jasione had not had prior confirmation until that moment. Arna had exposed himself. Once more the thudding in his spine reared its head.

Just the end of the world.

No. Kill it. Bury it.
"I left my old life behind."

Xeysis was different and strange, with entire architecture and new forest apartment complexes near his home that Arna did not know. The streets and walls of buildings were not littered in art. There was color from the buildings themselves but none of the soul. She smelt different, felt different, sounded different. Twelve years prior the streets were littered in art created by people who crafted it at night and walked away. It changed, grew, expanded daily with people capitalizing off of other's creativity and making it their own, a group project into storytelling and creation. Now it was slate, devoid of life in, metal, cool.

Twelve years ago, the streets around his home were filled with floating vendors offering food and drinks, cooking on the streets handing out their specialties for free to try to entice people to their shops in other districts far away. Now the air smelled of flowers and trees and rain, but not a hint more.

Twelve years ago, there was sound everywhere. Now the most Arna heard was from advertisements and the light drifting of speakers that was almost too soft to hear. Whereas it would have been a cacophony, of consistent dancing bodies, singing voices, laughter, and cheer. People still moved, still were happy but were slow as if mourning.

Arna walked away from his neighborhood.

He had changed, at Jasione's behest, into a white and mint ensemble: new, but not flashy. He wore similar attire to the general citizens of Xeysis, with long sleeves, only he was reminiscent to a willow tree. The rest of the clothes they bought would be delivered for him. Jasione had went to buy groceries and helped Zaffre with some sort of paperwork, like the son Arna no longer was.

Arna did not pay much attention to anything before afternoon practice. And after, he avoided his father, got dressed, and headed out past the forest of branches and leaves, and off into the world.

On his mobile, Arna ordered a computer to be sent to his house. He double checked that the software was compatible with the new model and read his messages to Alis. There was not much, as Alis was busy. He walked listening to Alis' music and activated his Blessings for a disguise.

Slowly the city returned to the familiarity of his youth, albeit changed. He avoided flying bikes, and people running through the sky on their Blessing powered flower carpets made of nanotech. Some people traveled by mechanical birds, and the streets were lined with animals of all sorts. People billowed around him dressed like flowers: bulbs, stems, leaves, and the petals. They were designed in all different flowing arrays, both mimicking the look and replicating the feel.

One Truth Church members wandered the streets screaming about how people needed to repent and turn. Harmonious Six members passed out flyers for help with school. Other voices filled the streets offering free food from too few traveling street cars. Children ran about, singing songs Arna vaguely recognized.

It was all so familiar and all so strange. The streets were relined and old stones that were once badly laid were gone. The street signs were repaired. Alleys he once knew, no longer existed. He was turned around in his home city, that had not waited for him. Twice he got lost on streets he thought he remembered. Three times he took the wrong bus. He was distracted by trees that had grown too large. There were entire residential blocks that had disappeared. People still walked, offering each other help. Buildings were covered in flowers. The streets were still lined in towering plants with massive leaves that blotted out parts of the sky and the false sun. Yet, he searched for the familiarity in the city he once loved and could not find it.

It too was a stranger to him.

Despite this the fabric store was not difficult to find, tucked away in an alcove that he once traveled by as a kid. The store had a tiny door, painted bronze and pink. The sign hung low decorated in rose petals and tulips. Aster Fabrics was unassuming, and unpopular, but Arna swore they stocked and created the *best* fabrics in the city.

He did not need to hide himself making the clothes; standard orders made it near impossible for him to craft them without asking for assistance. He had ordered fabric years ago to the shop.

"Welcome. What are you looking for?"

"There should be bolts for a Mr. Hemlock," Arna answered as he approached the desk. "To be signed for by Carnine?"

Arna had met Mr. Hemlock, a well-known producer of mass market fans, when he had worked as a delivery boy in Ludiel. He had his factories in every city. Arna had gotten the man's signature and practiced it until he had been daring enough to order the fabric. Arna pulled out the card with his identification from those years. The picture was newer, but the ID was the same: Carnine Hue.

The worker stared at Arna for a long time. Scissors in his hand, mouth agape, eyes wide. Arna did not know what to do when another man walked out. He was older, ancient almost and gave Arna a twice over before saying.

"Get the bolts, boy."

The young man rushed to the back and the older man followed disregarding Arna completely.

Arna waited. He'd ordered the fabric to be made five years ago. It had cost him a fortune, what little he managed to make from his odd jobs over the years. He'd always feared the shop would contact Mr. Hemlock through the official channels and not the email that Arna had used. When he had been ordered back to Xeysis, he'd informed them of the new pickup request, and they'd given him a finish date.

Today he was able to look at the fabric with his own eyes, even if it hadn't been cut and sewn into the proper shape for the fan's fabric.

He was lucky they hadn't asked more questions, but he was not sure how long the luck would last.

Arna made his way to the counter, where multiple bolts of fabric were brought out and placed in a cart. He ran his hand over the fabrics, each a different color, weight, and appearance.

In the end, fan weights, fabric weights, and fabric color and design, were variable across variations. The fan fabric had been the first detail he decided. Then he chose which dances had one fan and which had two before he created the steps. He sketched what designs he would give to those with one versus two all before he'd started anything else.

There were six weight classifications for the fabrics: airy, light, standard, dense, heavy, and irregular. The standard fabric was the original weight used in both the Original and Twin Fans dances and what all others were weights were based on.

Airy fabrics were light and floated like feathers. They were three times lighter than standard. Light were durable and heavier but still billowed when pulled. It was half of the weight of the standard fabric. Dense twice the weight of standard. The fabric was wind resistant and created drag. The heavy fabrics were the heaviest at three times the weight of standard. They were extremely unwieldy and often too much for a dancer to hold in one hand without Blessings. Irregular weights were fabrics that transitioned from a light fabric to dense. They created dramatic movements when pulled, due to the different weight balance. Irregular weight fabrics were only used in three dances across all the variations.

There were three appearances that the fabric could take. Sheer fabrics could be seen through. Opaque were rich in color. Shiny fabrics was a catch all term for any fabric that shimmered, as they were only introduced in the Holly variation, due to technological changes.

Before him was the array of decisions he made. The fabric was dyed and woven with exquisite skill. They were uncut but wonderfully made, and expertly designed better than the sketches he had sent over. Would his ceremonial garb come close to it in detail and beauty? Two years at the tailors had seemed enough before, but now it was like trying to navigate across the ocean in a tiny boat. It was not enough. Nor was his two years at the cobbler or the music studio. Arna's hand shook. He had learned as much as he could, but that made him woefully inadequate at best.

It will be enough.

[*We didn't prepare you for nothing,* Ixxzal said.]

[*Ixxzal!* Xeyaro snapped.]

[*He's being. . .* Ixxzal sighed. *Fine, you take care of this.*]

[*I am,* Xeyaro said harshly. *Ignore him. We would not lead you astray.*]

Arna did his best to believe her.

"Incarnadine Vivicent." The old man smiled at Arna. "These fabrics are for. . . your dances?"

Arna slowly nodded. "How long will you need to cut them into the right form and finish the remaining embroidery?

"A few more weeks. We will message you." the shop keeper said smiled, handsomely. His voice was low like the swell of a storm, controlled and proud. "What other fabric do you need?"

"What?"

Someone else entered the shop and Arna jumped. He quickly pulled his hood over his head.

The shopkeeper gave a lie, shoving the bolts back into the cart. "This is obviously for the Celebrations. Zaffre said he'd rework a new set of Ceremony fans this year."

The man flinched at the lie, but it was not so great to cause injury, and he was protecting Arna, which Arna thanked. It was well known that the different variations' ceremonial fans used for the Ceremony of Chaos had to be repaired each year. Some years whole sets of fans had to be replaced and retired. Anyone who looked at the amount of fabric before Arna would know that it was for new fans, enough for all the dances, none of which followed the standard design of any of the preexisting variations.

The woman who entered after Arna hovered about the shop and Arna eyed her, trying not to be noticed, heart racing. He had avoided people, not wanting to alert anyone to his presence and make his travel more difficult.

"And I suppose you would need material to work the fan's boning as well?" The Shopkeeper said pulling open a back cabinet full of options. The structural support of the fan was the one step he managed to forget, as he was not able to make the fans by hand. He had assumed his factory of choice would have the supports but seeing what the that the shop keeper presented made Arna disregard other options.

"I do." Arna nodded. He took a piece of paper on the table and began detailing the weights that he needed and the types of boning he was required. Longing ached in his hands to hold a fan, but he clenched them tight, focusing instead on the pain that touching a fan caused him.

As he finished listing the weights he thought about the fabric in his wall. "Do you take quick turnaround commissions?"

"Yes."

Arna's hand hovered over the embroidery. "How long did this take?"

"The proper fabric always takes years to temper and embroider, at least for the desired effect that *Mr. Hemlock* specified." They must have verified the order and had it denied.

He had gone forward with it despite that? The shop keeper winked at Arna. "You bought a similar opal fabric from me years ago, Mr. Hue."

Ah. His name had given him away. There were too many Hues, the name was common enough. Arna had hoped it wouldn't be tied back to the famous Hue family.

Arna fumbled at his next words, flustered that he'd been seen through so easily. "And if there was already a fabric tempered to an age?"

"Not more than a month."

Enough time for him to get the fabric back and be able to make his clothes. "Do you have oil slick fabric?"

"Not of the appropriate age. . ."

"It must be as new as possible." For that had been his dilemma. He had feared that his opalescent fabric would have been lost to time, leaving him with the necessity to rethink his design. With it, and the new oil slick fabric, he'd combine new and old. Painted and embroidered. Classical form to the new.

"Then. . ." The shop keeper directed Arna around the shop. There was a sister fabric to his opalescent cloth next to the oil slick one. Next to each other they looked lovely, but he had the gut feeling that with his aged fabric, the black fabric would look better.

"Fabric like this, a whole bolt. How much would it take to get it embroidered?" Arna asked.

"Do you have the designs?"

"I do." He pulled out his black notebook from his pocket and ripped out the pages that had his sloppy designs on them.

"With the designs and story, no more than six weeks. We may have to check for progress, however." The shop keeper looked at the sketch, "I see you have not gotten better at drawing."

Arna laughed with the man and nodded. Although, he had gotten better.

"I can do six weeks," he said even when six weeks was pushing the deadline. He needed at least a month to work on the sewing and then the final detailing. The celebrations for the new year were less than three months away. He hadn't built a fan in years.

His fingers itched to move. He wanted to pull the fabric taut himself. He wanted to bind the boning and hold them in his hands when he was done.

No.

He could ask his father, but. . . *No.*

Even if he could not handle them himself, he could do it on his own. He was the Chosen, he needed to be able to do that much at least. His badge for Mr. Hemlock's factories probably still worked.

[nothing.   ]

Arna paid for the fabric and embroidery services. He summoned a car to take him home, rather than taking the bus. It was a luxury, and would take more time, but he had the money now.

Once home, Arna grabbed the keys his old dance room, as opposed to the new one he used for morning and afternoon practice.

Inside reeked of musk and stale air. There was a thick layer of dust on the floors and mirror. Shutting the door behind him and changing the privacy settings so only he could answer, Arna changed the glass to opaque so far that it blacked out the light from the outside. He walked the perimeter of the room and ran his fingers across the dance bar coughing as the dust went flying. The room was once his, Pervenche, and Ebru's private studio that they rotated between for practices. Arna wanted it back.

Arna got to work cleaning, knowing it would take time.

By the time the room was spotless, the sun had set, and Arna made his way to dinner. There was little conversation, which allowed Arna to excuse himself. After prayers, Arna waited until the house fell silent by sorting and hanging his new clothes. He set up his new computer and looked over everything else he needed to get done. Keeping his breath calm and Blessings up, he kept himself from getting overwhelmed. When the night grew late, Arna made his move to return downstairs. He gathered all the things in his walls and carried them out of his room.

"I don't like not knowing where he is." His mom spoke to his father as he passed their room.

"He will do it whether we want him to or not. At least this way, he won't feel as if he has to hide everything," Zaffre said to her in a warm voice.

"I just got him back," Wenge whispered. "I can't lose him again."

"We won't."

With silent footsteps Arna passed by, his fingers digging into the palm of his hand. Lungs tight, Arna did not manage to calm his breathing until he was back in his practice room. After placing the supplies in the loose floorboards of his dance room, he threw himself into the practice for his variation. Arna forced himself to face what a disaster it was.

Grimacing, Arna glared at the mirrors. Ebru would have chastised him for being so terrible. He needed to finish the dance. But he couldn't figure it out. If he couldn't finish the dance. . . he didn't have a chance at succeeding. . . What would the world even look like if he couldn't do this simple task?

[*Are you visualizing?* Zaynir asked.]

Zaynir was right. He needed to visualize it better. He focused on his basics and recited the lessons one by one on how to make a variation.

When he returned to his room hours later, he was pissed and no further than where he started. Furious, he started working on his new computer instead, installing software, and accessing the old memory drive. All he could see was himself in the black screen.

All he could think was: *Saffron.*

The Gods had not wanted to start the apocalypse. Mortals had done that themselves. But the Gods were trying to stop the apocalypse.

He could not be like Saffron and cause them to fail.

Then we Worship. We lose ourselves and worship it all, as a cumulation of everything. The twenty-seventh dance may be the easiest, but it is the most important. The twenty-fifth shows us what the world could be. The twenty-sixth makes the dancer face death. Worship shows us possibility of a greater future; the future the Gods believe in and that we as mortals will, too.

— On the Worship of the Gods section of The Twenty-Seven Dances.

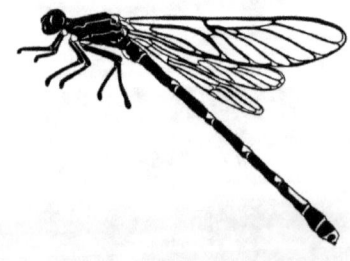

Dance 6

Horror

Incarnadine

35 Poan

80 Days Left

"Again."
"I can't."
"Again."
"I can't."
"Again."
He stood up despite the pain because some part of him still loved it.

Arna moved about his dance room in the dark, black out curtains on the window so that he was certain no one could see him from outside despite the opaque glass. Six candles, set into the alter of the room, and his computer, playing his variation music, provided the only light. Grimacing, Arna stopped dancing and wrote notes in his journal for reworking the harmonies. If he could have Alis' assistance in refining, he had faith that it would be perfect, but that was a delicate line he could not cross.

The flicker of the Gods watched him, speaking to themselves. His dance practices with them were far less structured at the Vivicent studio. He was still training each day to keep up with what was required of his body: weight training, cardio, full body work outs, stringent eating patterns. But. . . Before returning, they'd asked him to dance three times a day. Since he'd gotten home, the number had reduced to none required. Arna continued his hellish schedule regardless, as if he were still in Azis. He had to keep in shape.

Even if nothing could go back to normal, he had to try to keep himself going. Keep the routine, ignore everything else. It didn't matter if things did not return to the way things were. He didn't need to fix his relationships, he needed to finish the dances, so the world didn't get destroyed. Superfluous feelings of isolation, a strange drifting loss, did not matter. Even if it was hard, even if the Gods weren't committed to it anymore, he needed the structure.

But no matter how much he tried he could not figure out how to fill the gaps in his variation.

The first day he was home he had ignored it, due to the stress, but after trying three times today he no longer could. His variation was lacking something. Even as he got steadier in what he planned, in the moves he had practiced and detailed in his black journal. When he danced them side by side, back to back from Blue Rose Fears, it was obvious.

The Gods did not have to say anything. They dances were still too hollow, lacking, and he could not figure out why.

The God's voices were in the distance broken up: a bit like static, a bit like a skipping record. The chimes and chirps in the sounds were more present than the actual words themselves. Usually when they wanted to conceal themselves, they'd do so, but there was an unsettling feeling in Arna's gut that the connection was unraveling.

"What's happening?" Arna asked. "Why is my dance broken?"

[*You returned home,* Zaynir said. *You must visualize. You will solve the issue.*]

"Are you sure?" Arna pressed. "You trained me to do this. I should be able to. . . But I can't. . ."

[*We do not require you to weave the fabric on your own, or to create
your materials,* Pokk answered succinctly and calm, for once.
Support is needed in order to succeed.]

[*When creating your variation's core, no mortal may help you.
Tools are permitted otherwise; assistance is always allowed,*
Azza sang softly like a lover singing their partner off to war.]

[*Something cannot be revealed if it is already known,* Ixxzal's
voice drifted far beyond the mirrors.]

[*It is only your death dance that has to be done alone without the
hand of assistance,* Lumak added. *Not even we can help you
with the dances. Only you can make the choice.*]

They couldn't help him.

Knowing it was one thing, hearing it from the Gods, crushed him. The Gods were not all knowing, and they were putting their faith in him, and it terrified them. It was like a weight wrapped around his heart and was tossed into a lake to sink. If he broke the world again. . . Arna was afraid he'd vomit and tried to swallow the feeling back.

"Why are they broken?"

[There was no answer.]

Hand open. Hand closed. He steadied himself, shoving the thought far away. He'd push past this as he had time and time before. He would not fail like Saffron. He'd dance. He'd become their Chosen.

[*You are already our Chosen,* Xeyaro said.]

"Not yet." Not until he danced. Until then, there was still a chance he could mess up. "Mortals or the Gods? Right?"

[*Yes,* Pokk answered, *But Xeyaro is correct.*]

But he wasn't because they hadn't picked him. He picked them. It had been *his* choice to try to be the Chosen and he was dealing with the ramifications of that choice. They all were.

[*How about you focus on something else?* Zaynir asked, *How will
you reconnect with your loved ones?*]

His friends? Arna shook his head. He did not have time for family or aspirations. No. He could not be distracted. Arna focused on the fans instead. If his dances and music were hollow, at least he could finish the other aspects: clothes and fans. Nothing had changed for them. Nothing, he tried to convince himself even though he had the sinking suspicion things were wrong with them too.

He ached for the fans, and instead of pushing it away he transformed the desire into goals. He planned out his heist into the factory.

Arna needed to get into the Xeysis Hemlock fan factory and use the machines to make the fans for him. Arna hated Mr. Hemlock. Despite specializing in mass market fans, Mr. Hemlock dreamed of making performance fans. The Twenty-Seven Dance fans were special tools created for worship. To use a machine for something crafted for prayer? It was near heresy.

Yet the man tried, and his factory in Xeysis was the only one that had the Celebration Machine: capable to creating performance ready fans.

Arna was disgusted at the idea of using the factory, but he had no choice. He couldn't make them by hand because he couldn't *touch* a fan. If he had not broken the taboo. . . If he had not misunderstood and refused to dance instead, he'd have been able to make them himself.

Mr. Hemlock's machine-made performance fans had yet to withstand the test of time and could not hold up when a Child of Xeyaro used them to dance the Twenty-Seven. They fell apart after one attempt, and thus none were considered true successes. The task of maintaining and building the variation fans for the Ceremony of Chaos had remained with the best of the fan masters, and the world's only grandmaster: Zaffre Vivicent.

Luckily, while the fans made at the factory could not withstand the test of time, they could survive a single dance and that was all that Arna needed. Creating was not the same as touching. The curse should not affect him. He'd just need to find a way to get them home.

Once again, he was sinking. Dread spiraled through him and threatened to drive him mad.

Everythingwillendeverythingwillendeverythingwillend

Breath in, Arna discarded his emotions. They didn't matter. He had more important things to do than to *feel*. Arna breathed out and opened the calendar on his computer. When was the best time to go make the fans? Soon, but on a night when the factory was not in use. Writing a tentative date in his calendar, Arna briefly looked up to the mirrors.

He had shoes, the mask, and the ceremonial garb to make, but not the space. With music, he could be in his soundproofed dance room. With the fans, he would go to a factory. Everything else had to be hidden.

"Right?"

[   ]

He *would* need to hide the process of making everything. He could get their assistance with the materials, but he had to make it all himself or through the use of tools. Showing the world would reveal himself.

"Right?"

[silence   ]

"Please answer me."

[*We are debating*, Pokk said.]

"About what?"

[*Guidance disagreements*, Lumak said, angered.]
[*Don't worry. We are here*, Xeyaro said. Their voice drifted off
across the mirrors like a rolling breeze.]

Arna could not doubt them. Doubt lead to the possibility to rejecting the Gods. He'd learned at sixteen, that there was three ways to stop being the Chosen: to forsake the Gods, to fail their tests, or to make the wrong choice in the end. While failing their tests had been impossible, as they guided him through and ensured he always succeeded, forsaking them had always been a concern.

The moment he truly did not believe they existed, the connection was severed. The moment he rejected wanting to be Chosen, it was over. Whether it was in a panic, conscious or not, Arna had to be wary. For if he forsook them, he'd cut himself off as their tether. They would die and their Blessings would vanish. While the end of the year, the tether would be cut regardless of his actions—unless he danced and succeeded that was—to do it before hand was still a possibility of creating an early apocalypse.

everythingwillendeverythingwillendeverythingwillend

He would and could not.

With a sigh, Arna collapsed back, started the music on his computer again, and thought of Alis' calming songs. The residual levels of panic at the idea of death and the anger at heresy flickered away.

Checking his mobile messages Arna's whole body froze.

```
Alis: Rosy
Alis: Please
Alis: He did it again. I think I have a bruise on my back
      and honestly, I'm not sure what to do.
Alis: Oh Gods. It looks bad.
Alis: Luckily, it doesn't hurt.
Alis: Yet.
Alis: I refused to do the song. The Boss is threatening
      to kick me out again.
```

Alis once told Arna that his father's contract specified who could live in their house. If Alis said no, he would have no home. The boss controlled every aspect of their lives.

```
Alis: I can't tell dad what happened.
Alis: Rosy
Alis: What do I do? Do I make it? But I don't want to
      do it.
Alis: I hate them.
Alis: But I don't have anywhere to go.
Alis: I don't have anywhere to go.
Alis: I need you.
```

Arna checked the time on the messages. It had been hours ago. He'd been caught up in practice and developing his variation. Tense, and with shaking fingers, Arna typed.

```
Rosy: I'm here.
```

There would be no response. Alis was asleep at this time, usually. Arna was lightheaded. He'd never missed an incident like this before. How had he missed it? His augmentations were working. The sound was on. What had happened? Arna's hands shook as he waited for a response.

No. He's asleep. He's okay. He's asleep. He's...

```
Alis: Rosy
Rosy: I'm here.
Rosy: Let me know what I can do.
Alis: Can you answer a call?
```

Arna hesitated. Before he could answer the messages rolled in.

```
Alis: No. It's okay.
Alis: Forget I asked. I know you're busy.
Alis: I just wish you were here.
```

All at once Arna was unable to breathe.

The dance of death, the heresy of making machine fans, the pressure of returning home. Every emotion that he'd swallowed down and ignored exploded outwards.

Screams, the darkness, the sleepless night.

He was once again on the train in freefall. He would not escape this time.

Grasping his mobile, Arna tried to tell himself that Alis was not angry, but that was a folly. What if Alis *died* because Arna got distracted? There was nothing that Arna could do. He didn't know where Alis was. There was no way he could save him. There was no way for Arna to save himself. No way for him to save the world.

As the bile rose in Arna's throat and the tears burned his eyes, like he had woken from a slumber.

The dream broke against his skin as he was faced with reality. Bronze light swirled around him until it rushed into his soul; realization dawned the need to implement changes to his dance. Even in the worst of situations, Alis inspired him.

[*Arna, are you visualizing?* Zaynir was there.]

Arna felt as if arms wrapped around him as a hug and he began to breath with an eight-count rhythm. The candles snapped in in time. There were no words he could register, but a strange humming that went through him. All six of them were there with him.

"Yes." Arna finally got himself back in control.

[*You can't fix what you broke, until you fix what you broke,* Azza offered weakly.]

It *almost* seemed like they didn't believe in him either. However, the Gods, for everything they were, had unwavering faith in him. He may have loathed them at points, but their trust in him kept him going. So long as they believed in him, he could do it. He could dance.

Coughing, Arna wiped his tears. Hand open. Hand closed. His nails dug into his palm.

He'd dance the full Ceremony of Chaos—all twenty-seven dances—and everything would be done. He *would* survive. Then he'd have his family. He'd have his friends again after he saved the world. The tests would be over. He'd find Alis and save him. He was good enough to do it. He would do it. He would not make another mistake. He'd be good enough to survive. He would be. He had to be.

Arna choked on his breath. Clearing his mind of all unnecessary thoughts he focused on what he had to make. He had little times for dreams of life when death was the only option left. He needed to succeed at the cost of himself. Even if he did not sleep the last week, he'd get his variation completed.

It was a long time later when he finally left the practice room. When Arna closed his programs, he was exhausted: his arms heavy and back sore. It was a different type of heaviness from his usual practice, however, there was an all-new pressure on him, one that he could not shake.

The sun had risen when Arna left his studio. His mother was in the garden in the center of their house.

Tiny robots shaped like animals pruned the hedges and watered the plants. She appeared younger in her sundress, a soft green inspired by limes. Her Blessings swirled around her in the form of tiny crystalline bubbles as she sang and enhanced the plants.

Although Arna was used to seeing her in a suit, it was nice to see her in a bright color. Wenge had been a conservationist and city planner when he was younger. She'd continued the job until Sarcoline was born, where she turned to the management of the Vivicent estate.

"The wisteria is blue today," Arna called out to her as she stopped one song and the bubbles popped into a mist of silver shimmering down and touching the plants covering them in a light dusting of dew. The plants glowed and they all bowed and swayed.

She stopped moving and looked back to him with a giggle. "It did not work when your father tried it and it will not work from you."

Arna smiled back. The story was, years ago, Zaffre had wooed her through his knowledge of botany. His mother had little care for the Vivicents and their dancing at the time. Even at the height of the Vivicent family, when hundreds walked the halls, tended the plants, and took lessons, there were those who wished to stay away.

His mother had not wanted to be involved, and Zaffre had tried to sweep her off her feet anyway.

"I should let him know. He thinks it did," Arna teased her.

"I did not join the ancient Vivicent house, Foundational Pillar of the Dance World and Master Crafthouse of Celebration Fans because it was blessed by all the churches or its prestige." His mother used her city planner voice, even and deeper than her normal speaking voice before switching back. She smiled. "I joined it because your father was handsome."

"And rich." Arna shrugged, walking to the end of the hall, standing above the garden.

"I needed some backing in this new city." She winked and waved him over. "Don't just watch, help me."

When Arna was young, they had gardeners who worked weekly. Now, it was only her tending to the garden. He jumped down into the flower beds, and the nanotech formed creating a barrier between him and the flowers, keeping him elevated above the path. He walked to his mother and began to work with her, helping the plants by checking their status in his augmentations and singing with his mother.

"You are much better now, who taught you?" She asked him, smiling as he sang.

Alis. But he could not say that. Alis had not formally trained him, but they had used Arna's voice as a sample in songs before, not that Alis had known that.

The two spoke about the plants. He told her of his time outside the cities, and what he had done in the last twelve years. All the while he avoided her gaze.

She kissed his head, suddenly. "I love you regardless. I left my family at sixteen. I might call them every week, but I've never gone back. At least you came home."

"Do you miss them?" He asked her. She never talked about her parents. Although he understood why.

"I will never fully understand them. I'm a Child of Xeyaro," she answered, focused on nature rather than art like Arna's father or his siblings. Her silver eyes, reflected her N.Reverence. "My family were of Lumak. I am not like them."

While in Ludiel he had tried to get help through her family without them knowing who he was. He had tried to send them letters, which burned, and go to their family home, but got lost. He later learned through interviews that they would have sold him out. They hated him.

Quietly, he helped her pick flowers for the vases upstairs.

"Is your freedom enough?" She broached the subject quietly.

Arna paused. The petals of the lily he held were bright red and soft. When he handed it to her, he said, "I know it must be hard."

"I don't want to let you go out there." She clipped some dead leaves. Arna finally looked up at her: tears were streaming down her face. "If I could, you'd be six again and I'd hold you tight and never let the world see you ever again, but I can't do that."

He leaned forward wiping her tears and leaving slight smudges of dirt in their place. She smiled softly, not turning to meet his eye as if she knew he'd look away. Keeping her gaze was intimidating, he didn't want to disappoint her again.

"We have to let you do what you have to do. I just got you back, you must forgive me for not wanting to let you go. Forgive us both. Your father is doing everything he can for you. You were his favorite."

His mother wiped her eyes and took a deep breath to hum again, resonating her Blessings across the garden, closing the wounds caused by them pruning and picking flowers.

"Parents aren't supposed to have favorites," Arna choked on his bubbling emotions.

His mother's fingertips caressed the side of his face and stole the rain from his eyes that had not yet dropped.

"We don't. But he saw so much in you, that losing you... Losing you, we lost a part of ourselves." She held him tightly, wrapping her arms around him and squeezing. "But time cannot be forgiven. What we must do is travel together now that our paths have intersected again." She kissed his cheeks. "We have you back, and that means that we get to learn of the person you are now."

Now? All he wanted was things to be the way they were.

"You are changed, Arna," his mother said, as if reading his thoughts. "When you were a teenager, you were loud, quick to anger, and boisterous. The world was yours to control. But you are not that person. You are reserved, withheld. You guard yourself in such a manner that has come from being on your own for years. You take care of yourself and ask for little. I can't hear your footsteps anymore."

(But was that really him?)

(When he fixed everything, would he be that person?)

(When there were no secrets, who was he?)

[*Are you visualizing?* Zaynir's voice was a chime on the wind, a song once remembered.]

A thought began to form but it was burst in seconds as Arna shook it away. He could not think of a future, not when he would not have one.

"And you will grow still, now that you are home." She placed her hand on his. "Who you become is up to you, only you."

"I missed you." He hugged her this time. "I love you so much. I've always loved you."

"Your father and I love you. The Gods love you."

Rationality reminded him that only Children were loved. But, perhaps, if he was able to be the Chosen that they wanted... maybe... maybe they'd forgive him for making the choice that nearly killed them.

"There is nothing to forgive. You were where you had to be, and you are home now. I am happy you are home, it's all I wanted. It is not us that you need validation from." His mother whispered into his hair, hugging him tight. He was not sure what she meant.

Arna ran into Sacroline outside the stairs headed to the second floor. Sarcoline was fully dressed in a black ensemble that shimmered in the light with the lines of dragonfly veins. He was holding a backpack.

"Where are you going?"

Did he not have morning practice?

"School," Sarcoline said with a tone that said: *didn't you know that?*

"What?"

Arna tried to remember what day of the week it was and found himself at a loss. Since when was his brother in school anyway? Hadn't he finished his mandatory education?

"Unlike you and Ginger, I'm not a Child of God. Remember?" Sarcoline answered his brown eyes blinking in hostility.

"At university?" Arna tested the word. Not many people went. It was not necessary, they followed the path their Blessings determined. Although Arna supposed it could make sense for Sarcoline. Yet. . .

"Yes." Sarcoline snarked back. "I study Dance History."

Dance history? Not business? That made no sense.

"But you. . ."

"I what?"

Most Vivicents did not go to university. There was no need for them to. They learned what they needed at home, usually finance and management. If Sarcoline was in school, it would only be to learn those things. He was either to be a dance instructor or run the household. There were no other jobs for him.

The Vivicent family was a *dance* family and one of the pivotal religious families upholding and supporting the Celebrations. Their history went over centuries all the way to Vervain the Blythe. They were the last true dance family to exist other than the Shadones. It was their family's duty to oversee the Twenty-Seven Dances, as it had been for centuries before them and after. Vivicents were the best dance family in the world with at least one A.Reverence Child each generation: the nature of which was consistently questioned by authorities. Their family was gifted by the Gods in dance.

And Sarcoline was a good dancer. He had mastered the first eighteen of the dances, in three variations; Arna checked the mastery test site each month to confirm. He'd had been in enough arguments with people on his burner accounts supporting Sarcoline. It was not unheard of, but it was outstanding talent for someone who was not a Child of Xeyaro. Sarcoline was a certified judge for Powers. That was enough for him to be able to have a job teaching the Twenty-Seven without a degree. All primary school children learned the first six dances of the first variation. Why was he in university?

"You know three—"

"That doesn't matter," Sarcoline cut him off. "The DHS doesn't want me. They changed the rules so that I must have mastered *all*. I can't teach or test until then."

The DHS—Dancers of the Harmonious Six, a collective of Children who tested all dancers—decided the four dancers who would dance the four sections of the Twenty-Seven during the Ceremony of Chaos. Usually, younger dancers danced the first two sections while older dancers fought over the second two. The DHS handled all affairs for the Twenty-Seven, from management of the Ceremony of Chaos to community outreach for the Xeysis government.

To be a general member of the DHS, one must have completed and mastered two to three variations through Powers. These individuals could become teachers of the Twenty-Seven Dances. Advanced members completed two to three variations through Understanding. Senior members completed all variations through Understanding. As only A.Reverence Children usually mastered all variations through Understanding, there were not very many senior members. Most generations of A.Reverence only have two or three Children. They needed many teachers to accommodate.

Why would the DHS change the rule? When?

Knowing Zaffre, Sarcoline was already learning the last two variations. Or, perhaps, he already perfected a fourth and had yet to test for mastery. All the same, Sarcoline was a Vivicent. People may have hated them, but they gave results for the Twenty-Seven and no one could deny it.

"Why?"

Sarcoline shook his head, "Why do you care?"

"Because. . ." Arna was not sure how to explain. He closed his eyes and tried to formulate the thought.

"Not everyone wants me," Sarcoline with a blank face. "Because I have no A.Reverence, they thought it best that I prove my worth. An exception, lucky me."

Sarcoline was an amazing dancer. Not Blessed but brilliant all the same, and Arna was certain that was scarier. Without his Blessing. . . Arna was not sure he'd ever be as good of a dancer as Sarcoline or Eburnean. Sarcoline was at the disadvantage due to the lack of the A.Reverence Blessing. If the DHS had changed their rules for their honorary members and initiates, it meant that they did not want any nonChildren joining. It was rare for outsiders to join to begin with but Sarcoline. . . Sarcoline was a Vivicent, and he was a fantastic dancer.

Did that scare them?

"What section of dance history do you specify in?" Arna changed the conversation and tried to ignore his brother's glare. Arna did not pity his brother. Sarcoline, who loved dance more than anything, did not need it. If Arna were in his shoes, he'd hate them all.

There had been a time where Arna had, where he'd wished. . . *No.* He could not wish to give up his status as Chosen. He had already made a choice and he'd already had enough emotions regarding it that day.

A faint whisper on the breeze rolled over his shoulder, in confirmation.

"Third Variance." Sarcoline spoke in a slow monotonous voice, placing his hands in his pockets. His cheeks were a bit redder than usual. Eyes wide, Arna almost laughed at his brother who was trying to be nonchalant. Sarcoline went on, as if his excitement was not showing. "The origin of modern culture, the turning point in civilization. It took three Variances to get to where we are now."

"Two." They were currently in the fifth Variance. "We—"

"Three," Sarcoline corrected; his eyes ablaze. This was a plea, an olive branch between them being extended. One confirmation could bridge them together again.

"Two."

Dismay replaced hope in Sarcoline's gaze. Sarcoline started to back up to walk away.

"If you ever want to talk about the cities, I can answer some questions."

"Some." Sarcoline snorted.

"I mean it, Arco." Arna stepped forward trying to get the olive branch back, one he did not deserve.

"Don't act like my brother now, Arna. You haven't been here. We are strangers and I don't have to *like* you." Sarcoline's voice was the wrath of a thousand burning branches. Arna stopped moving.

"No, you don't," Arna said. "But I would like if we got along."

"Tell us what you're hiding and maybe we can be."

"I've told you," Arna tried again. Sarcoline glared at Arna, pursed his lips, and swung a bag over his shoulder. Arna tried to reach for him. "Arco. . ."

"Don't bother."

He walked past Arna, shouting to the house that he was leaving. Sarcoline was gone: a haze of residual resentment washed over Arna. He should have been there to support Sarcoline. Trudging his way upstairs, Arna struggled with the vitriol.

"He doesn't hate you," Gingerline spoke from the kitchen. Arna looked towards her in the other doorway. She was dressed in dark green with crescent moon shaped leaves running along the sleeves. It was more color he'd seen on her in recent days. "He only is angry because he believes in you. He believes as much as father and Jasi. He doesn't like that people are doubting you."

Jasi. . . The last time he'd seen Jasione, he was cleaning the house and making calls to fix the broken air conditioner.

"I thought it was hopeful thinking, for years. It was easier to believe that you'd died. We all saw you drop the fan, and you disappeared without a word... It made more sense. Then dad had—" She shook her head.

"By the time he was himself again, he began to try to convince us. I hadn't believed him. I didn't want to get our hopes up. I only pretended to believe because it made dad 'dad' again. Then Jasi messaged us saying that you came home... I believe you are the Chosen, Arna. I do, but why is it that you are pushing us all away? Is Arco, right? Is something wrong?"

Arna clenched his fists wishing to disappear, but her eyes continued to hold him in place. His entire body was tight and tense, unable to look away. "I can't tell you."

"Because you are, and you have been silenced by the Gods? Or because you aren't? I think Arco is afraid that you aren't, and you are just trying hard to pretend that you are and that you won't tell anyone the truth." She scoffed, "So many people told us that: told dad that he was crazy, told us that our family was better off dead, that you were better off dead, for what you did."

"I—"

[A chorus of urgent bells rang for the truth.]

"—I'm sorry." Saying it did not bother him as much as he hoped, even as her eyes faded. He was both an imposter and the Chosen Child at once.

"If it's any consolation, he also hates me. And Jasi most days. And mom and dad. The only person he likes is Rus. . ." She nodded to the staircase; her voice strained. She drank her smoothie slowly. Arna tried to look away but couldn't. She was so haggard, so withdrawn, underweight and tired.

How much did she practice and push herself to keep up with Eburnean?

"He has no Blessing." Arna understood the resentment. He'd always been jealous of his sister's eyes. Mint and formerly, unwavering. Zaffre, Gingerline, Jasione, and Wenge were all Children. Rosmarinus was the only one who wasn't. Arna was not surprised Sarcoline liked him best, there had to be a relationship built on kindred spirits.

A pit grew in Arna's chest. Rosmarinus and Sarcoline were in dozens of pictures across the wall. His baby brother who had worshiped him and idolized him more than anyone replaced him. . . Arna squeezed his fist tight and buried the emotion away.

"But he's a good dancer," Gingerline agreed with a vicious tongue, almost as if she were marking her territory. Good, not great. Not a Child of the Gods. He would not master Understanding in any of the variations. He would never breech the realm of the Children. It was a sudden sense of anger that Arna had not expected and from the way that Gingerline covered her mouth, gasping with wide eyes, Arna suspected she didn't expect either. The seconds of the clock ticked away.

"What were you doing downstairs?" Gingerline tried again, clenching her arms, avoiding what she said. Arna was at a loss. "Ginger are you. . ."

"In a dance room that you blacked out the window for?" She avoided further. "Were you dancing?"

It was obvious that Sarcoline and Gingerline's relationship was not the best and it was Arna's fault. But there was nothing he could do to fix it.

"Do you remember that final group dance we did that year?" Gingerline asked instead, grabbing his attention again. There was a lightness to her voice as she put her smoothie down on the table and walked over hesitantly.

Arna did remember it: the flashing lights and the swing music. The bass from the song still thudded in Arna's memory as a reminder of innocence. He remembered standing under the hot lights excited to dance The Power of the Gods section of the dances next: dances thirteen through eighteen. Time had been running a little late, but it would be no issue. Ending after midnight would be no big deal, they did it all the time. The six of the Gold Generation had danced together, and Sarcoline had loved watching it. He had told Arna that one day he'd dance with them, that he'd be as good as them, even without a Blessing.

Sarcoline at least kept his promises.

"I remember it."

What he remembered most from the dance was not the dance itself; it was the figures in the crowd. The Gods flickered in the light and shadows, beckoning him to speak to them. He left backstage, away from his excited brother, saying he was going to get a snack. He found himself behind the stands, under the setting sun and with the figures of the Gods in near tangible form, more perfect than ever before.

They gave him the order and the quest began.

She nodded, moving on with the small talk. "What did you do while on the run?"

"Hiding. Doing jobs to survive and learn trades," Arna answered. "Then I came home."

"And dancing?"

"I can't touch fans," Arna admitted before he could stop himself. Arna tried to keep the reaction of his foolishness off his face. How could he *tell* her? She simply could not know what that meant.

"Which is not to say you didn't dance. Which is to say that you *have* been dancing?" Somehow, she missed the admission and was instead smiling joyfully wide.

Arna was not sure what to say to her because there was no way he could deny it. When he was fifteen, he had mastered two full variations through Understanding. He had been learning a third. Gingerline was not stupid. Arna had been a fanatic for the dances and would have rather *died* than never dance again. Arna could dance all twenty-seven dances in all five variations while sleeping if he were so inclined.

Even without an answer, her expression shifted to that of surprise. She then smiled bright and asked with a cheerful voice, "Were you going to go back to your room?"

"Why?"

He needed to work on his variation music, but her expression suggested another option.

"Come with me. I need some help with my stretches for my morning practice."

She walked past him to the stairs and back downstairs.

For a moment Arna contemplated going upstairs and ignoring her. It would have been the correct move. He glanced to the fan hangind near the window. His feet moved on their own, taking him down the stairs, unable to reject her. It was as if the whole world bent around him, guiding him after her.

[*Trust us. Trust her,* Azza whispered.]

Arna did not care if it were the Gods leading him forward then. He didn't want to isolate her more. He didn't want to hurt her more. He could not. Not like he had hurt Sarcoline. For a moment, feelings won.

Gingerline opened the door to her practice room, and he followed. He placed his laptop down on the ground as she messed with the settings of the room to adjust the lighting and set up the stereo. When done she stood before him in the mirror, motioning him over to where she had her practice fans hanging.

The practice fans were similar to the ceremonial fans in all but color. Where the practice fans were solid, the ceremonial fans were highly detailed. Both had the correct weight fan-boning and fabric.

The weight of the boning and fabric changed for each dance across Variations, depending on the image the creator wanted to shape. Different variations had different rules. The Holly variation had the heaviest fans. The Original was the standard. Twin Fans replicated the original, but with two fans, while Roots and Ends played around with weight distribution. Blue Rose Fears had the lightest fans. The fans could open, close, and locked so they could be tossed. There were opaque fabrics, shiny ones, and sheer.

Her practice fans, all five variation sets, were beautiful and well used. They were new enough that they had to have been given to her recently that year. It was Zaffre's handiwork and Arna wished to examine it. He curled his fingers into tight fists, knowing he could not touch.

"Dad made them," she said. "My old sets were too worn."

"They're beautiful." He wished he could touch them. His fingers itched at the thought but then he reminded himself of the pain that came from touching them, and the desire vanished.

"Performance fans have to be made by the heart, so they are made by hand. It's one true path to the Gods," she quoted their father as her hand hovered over the fans. "Father is the best in the world."

Arna did not disagree with her. There was a reason that Zaffre checked all the Ceremony of Chaos fans before the event. He was the world's only Fan Grandmaster. Gingerline looked up to Arna.

"You were good too," she said.

Little the skill did him now that he could not touch fans. "I wasn't that good."

There had been news articles and photoshoots when he completed his first fans. His father had guided him through the whole process, although Arna had done it all himself. The Gods had been so proud. Zaffre had been so proud. The DHS approved them. All the Cardinals had blessed them.

A New Era of Fan Makers? A Possible Grandmaster in the Making?

All Churches Support Incarnadine's Fans. A New Era of Religious Peace on the Horizon.

The DHS had burned the fans after his disappearance, hoping to purify the befallen sin caused by their creator, save the one he burned nights before. The Cardinals had prayed on their knees for weeks. The only set of fans he had ever made: erased, forever. He had spent a year on the six Blue Rose Fears fans, making sure they were perfect. Burning them solved nothing for the Splintering. No one cared.

Gingerline practiced the Holly variation as Arna sat in the room. She held the fans lightly in her hands, and as she danced the sequence for Appreciation all he could think of was the teacher that replaced her in Zaydiel. She was far better. Her movements were controlled. The Twenty-Seven used the fans to weave a story, the Blessings to shape the world, and the body to dance a sequence that was easy to follow.

She stepped around the room, arms swinging wide, fan fabric flowing and then holding shape as she used her A.Reverence to control the image that they took. She spun, hands light, snapping the fans open and shut to create ripples in the fabric. She spiraled the fans, stepped through the dance with such ease and grace that by the time she was done, there was only a thin line of sweat on her forehead.

Through it all, all Arna could see was the tool that was her body. Her muscles strained in her arms with the fans. Her face twitched each time she made a slight shift in her weight that was incorrectly calculated. She only danced three dances, and yet she was heavy with breaths after. The dances were laborious, because to accurately portray them, one had to give their all at all times, and a bit of magic was needed. Any task that required too much pressure of the Blessings, while exerting physical effort took its toll. It was why performers only danced one section of the dances at the performances, otherwise it was too exhausting.

Unlike the idiot dancer in Zaydiel, her technique was flawless.

Gingerline turned to him, warmed up. "Alright. Let's dance."

"I can't touch a fan."

"I don't want you to touch a fan." She turned from her fans to her stereo, putting on a song. It was not any of the five variations' music.

"They didn't take your gift for dance, right?"

"No."

"So, you can dance." She insisted, smile wide, joy spreading through her tone.

[*Dance!* Azza cheered in agreement.]

"You want me to dance. Nothing special. Not the Twenty-Seven. Just. . ." Arna stood up, weighing his options. This wasn't necessarily a distraction, and it wasn't like it could hurt her. . .

"Yes. Regular dancing." His sister spun towards him and then stood by his side. "Do you know this dance?"

He shook his head. She laughed, skipped to the center of the room and then began to teach him. The song was familiar. Had he heard it somewhere online?

"Five, six, ba-da, Ha! Ta-ta-ta." She added sounds to the count that corresponded to the movements that she was doing, and he couldn't help but laugh. She taught just like their father did. It was something they shared: sometimes moves couldn't be described with words alone. Sounds often got thoughts across better.

Arms instinctually activated his A.Reverence Blessing. The counts resounded in his head. Checking his dance shoes, he shifted in his weight and tested their flexibility. After tying up his hair, he rolled back his shoulders, completely engrossed in the dance his sister was showing him. The song soon ended, and she stood unphased by the exercise.

"If you can't do something this easy, then what can I expect of you?" She taunted him.

"I haven't danced like this since you knew me last." He'd only done the variations. He did not dance to pop songs. He did not dance for fun. Nor did he choreograph for fun. He'd left that all behind in Xeysis.

It wanted him back.

Was it okay for him to take it?

[*It's okay! Trust Ginger,* Azza insisted.]

"It's fine. Come now."

She pressed the song to start over and took her spot next to him. As the song began, he let himself dive into the memory of what she had just showed him. Counting aloud, she began with the words themselves and Arna fell into the beat of it. Together they danced in unison, and her counts drifted away.

Smile on her lips they moved together, Arna matching her, adjusting based on what he had seen before. He typically needed more than one attempt to memorize the moves of a dance, even with his Blessing, but the song was easy enough. Was this a song he knew from before?

Giggling, she changed the move and suddenly he understood. The pop group, Maple Rain, had put out the single years ago, at the height of their popularity, when he was fourteen. Eburnean had decided that they would learn the dance and Arna had complained then. For team building in preparation of the Celebrations, Eburnean declared.

The six of them spent hours perfecting it until they were, arguably, better than the original group. Children of Xeyaro who specialized in dance rarely were allowed the freedom to dance for fun. Everything, for them, circled the Twenty-Seven. It was unfair, otherwise, to everyone else; Eburnean always said it was unfair to them.

Seeing her dance one of the other group member's parts had him laughing at himself. He had done it begrudgingly back then, complaining to Jasione the entire time. Jasione had told him that it would be fun if Arna just let himself enjoy it. Instead of focusing on a destiny that he was not sure he had, Jasione had told him to accept it. A pang of regret resonated in his chest.

"Do you remember it?" she asked him.

"I do." He was a bit embarrassed that he'd forgotten. His sister's face lit up in the mirror as the song continued. Together they danced their two separate parts. Arna relied on the past, refining his moves a bit more and falling into the steps as a phantom memory.

Without missing a beat his sister changed the song; his body reacted to it. And the next, and the next, moving in the memory of sweat and joy. White lights lit up silver mirrors and refracted an illusion of a million memories around them.

One by one, his sister led him through the era he left behind. There were the times she'd dragged him to learn dances with her and Eburnean. There were the dances Pervenche wanted to learn and dances that Aureolin declared a cultural necessity to memorize. Gingerline was having him relive the moments when they were allowed to be people, not competitors. These were the songs of his childhood from when they were friends first.

His father had been right to put them together. They were rivals, but also friends, and had created a bond that united them together, even in separation. Letting his soul fall into it, he laughed out loud. He had not had this much fun dancing in such a long time. The world was blinding in joy, almost like he was on the precipice of an understanding, almost like things were the way they were meant to be.

As he waited for his sister to change the song again, the door opened. His father stood in the doorway silhouetted by white light, breathless.

"Are you okay?" his sister asked Zaffre.

"Teach him something he wouldn't know," his father instructed her.

"Why?" Arna asked. The inspiration disappeared, shattering into pieces he could not put back together. His father walked up to them, replacing his shoes, and shutting the door, not saying a word. He walked directly up to Arna grasping Arna's arm, and Arna understood then. His dance muscles were still taunt, defined, powerful, and they were showing. He had the body of a well-trained dancer, who had never taken a day off in twelve years.

His father wanted to see him dance, to get hope of what Arna's variation may look like.

He refused to jerk his arm away, but he did not acknowledge it. Arna avoided the gaze of his father, looking anywhere else. Zaffre dropped Arna's arm and walked away to the back of the room. Gingerline began her lesson.

Arna's heart fluttered. He had a purpose for being home, one he could not forget. He could not simply have fun. He could not forget everything he was working towards. If he wanted his sister to keep smiling. . . for his father to find peace. . .

[*Why are you worried?* Lumak asked confused.]

[*This farce is tiresome,* Pokk sighed. *Just fix this already Arna.*]

[*There's only so many ways we can explain. He'll understand in time,* Ixxzal said. *He's not an idiot even if he's acting like one right now.*]

Arna took a deep breath, squeezed his hands and relaxed. Arna ignored his father's intensity.

"Arna," Gingerline called to him. He needed to leave the room, but he could not. Her eyes were wide with love and anticipation.

Could he have this. . . For a moment? It was not as if he wasn't making progress. It was okay to relax a little right?

[*You can dance with her. You must,* Azza's voice was a bit more distant, but it was filled with a vigor and life that had recently been missing.]

Okay then. Focusing on his sister, he debated on waiting and repeating when she told him to or letting himself copy as she was teaching it. Choosing the later, he mimicked her, moving through the song quickly.

"Do you want to practice?" she asked him.

"No," he mulled over the thought. Who was he trying to fool? All those in the room knew he did not need it repeated.

Arna danced once the music started, glancing at his sister to make sure he had the timing right, but figuring out the rhythm on his own. A.Reverence flourished, the magic flowed telling him what he was supposed to do and when. Arna's Blessings were always the strongest when he danced.

Huffing out, Arna peered at his father, who stood cross armed, through the mirror. There was a glare in his eyes that told Arna to follow him. With a slight groan, Arna followed his father out of the room, through the moon door, and down into the gardens that were the center of their house.

"Stand there," his father ordered. Arna stood in the middle of the path looking towards the flower beds, identifying all the plants he pruned earlier that morning, when he heard, "Catch."

Hand up, eyes forward, Arna caught a weighted disk. When practicing fan spin tosses, they would use the weighted disks, to perfect rotation and torque without the fear of dropping a fan. Until one could use the disks perfectly, they were not permitted to dance with the practice fans. Unclasping the bag, Arna pulled out the two disks of the twenty-six weights of the Holly variation: the heaviest known variation fans.

"What do you want me to do with these?" Knowing that there was no way he could fake it being too heavy after having easily caught the bag containing both disks with one hand.

"Dad?" Gingerline asked.

"Do you need us to prepare the Ceremony for you, Arna?" his father asked him. There was a pain in Zaffre's voice that made Arna step back twice, an ache for the truth. It became Arna's, and he shoved the disks back into their bag.

He needed to avoid his father. It was why he tried each day to do everything in his power not to see him. He did not want to imagine his father sobbing over his body after he finished dancing. He did not need to. . .

everythingeverythingeverything

Dancing with Gingerline was a mistake. It was time wasted that he could have spent trying to figure out the answer to the question. Time he could have spent finishing his variation. Time he could have spent trying to find a way to stay alive.

Arna's heart caught in his throat.

He hadn't thought of trying to stay alive in years. It was fundamentally impossible. Yet, here he was wishing for it?

(the fault was his alone.)

"Toss them," his father instructed him.

There was absolutely no way he could. There were twelve ways for an individual to be certified as a master of the Dances in any variation. Arna had them memorized as he had the sound of his breathe. He couldn't throw the disks as much as he couldn't wish to live. As much as he wanted to be seen, wanted to try, to attempt the dances, he had to use fans and because of that he'd die.

Longing filled his chest for the soft fans, and his desire to hold them without pain.

No.

He'd killed the hope and stuffed it away where it never saw the day. He was going to die, and he accepted that.

He threw the disks to the ground and Gingerline gasped. They were never supposed to touch the real ground, only in practice rooms that were clean. A scowl formed on his father's face.

Arna needed to go and center himself. He needed to remember what was at risk, and not be consumed by it. He most certainly could not get closer to them, not more than he had to.

"Stop asking me. I will *never* be the Incarnadine that you remember." Turning from his father Arna, waved to his sister. "I'm headed out."

[*Arna what are you doing?* Lumak asked only when Arna left the house.]

[*Arna, trust me. Please. Go Back,* Ixxzal said, almost worried.]

Arna tried to think of anything else other than the possible disgusting thought of wanting another dream. He had made his choice. He lost the chance to live when he chose to drop the fan all those years ago. He didn't have to drop it. He chose to drop it. He chose to put everything on being the Chosen and now he had to deal with the consequences. He focused on his dances, his death, and the superstorms that would destroy the world.

He focused on Saffron.

Mortals had been on the brink of extinction when Ilex danced. Ilex had been able to save the mortals by providing them with more powerful Blessings than before, but even it was not enough to survive the storms Saffron had caused.

Ilex had been a child when the Shattering happened. He had been watching in the audience, to be selected as the next Chosen if Saffron failed. He had been the only survivor of the chaos when Saffron shattered his soul.

[*It was fractured. It did not disappear into nothing,* Zaynir disputed.]

Zaynir always said they were trying to fix the damage that had been done to Saffron's soul, the world, and the Gods. Like Arna, Saffron had wrecked more than his own life. His greed had started the apocalypse.

[*Don't do this Arna. Go back,* Pokk said.]
[*I have an idea! We can still fix this,* Azza said.]
[*Not another mess, Azza!* Lumak snapped.]
[*Just listen to me this time,* Azza argued.]

"Mortals or the Gods?" Arna asked them when their debate started to disappear.

[*What?* Zaynir asked.]

"Mortals or the Gods?" Arna repeated. "That's the test, right? That's why you put him in that room, right?"

[*Mortality or the Gods,* they repeated in unison.]

"You or him? I will pick you." Because by picking them, he had a chance of rectifying all his greed and pride. He had the chance to make up for his choice. He had been such a foolish child thinking he was special, thinking he was chosen. He had no right to dream anymore. His dreams only destroyed things.

He needed to sacrifice himself for the dreams of mortals and the lives of the Gods that he'd nearly erased.

[*Answer not accepted,* they called in unison.]

[*You must understand what we are asking,* Xeyaro's whisper drifted away.]

Arna ignored it.

It was another test with no easy answer. Which meant that Arna was going to be pushed further, and he was okay with that. He would do it.

He would dance on his own. He would finish his dances alone.

He'd find a way to make his fans, because he was just as alone as he had been in Azis. Returning did not change that.

He was okay.

Who cared if they hated him a little longer? He didn't.

Who cared if they resented him more? He did not.

He did not need things to go back to the way things were. He did not need to fix things between them. He didn't need it to succeed. He only needed himself and the Gods. He could only trust himself. He would save the world and he would finally give the world the retribution they desired for all that he had stolen. His death would be his final penance.

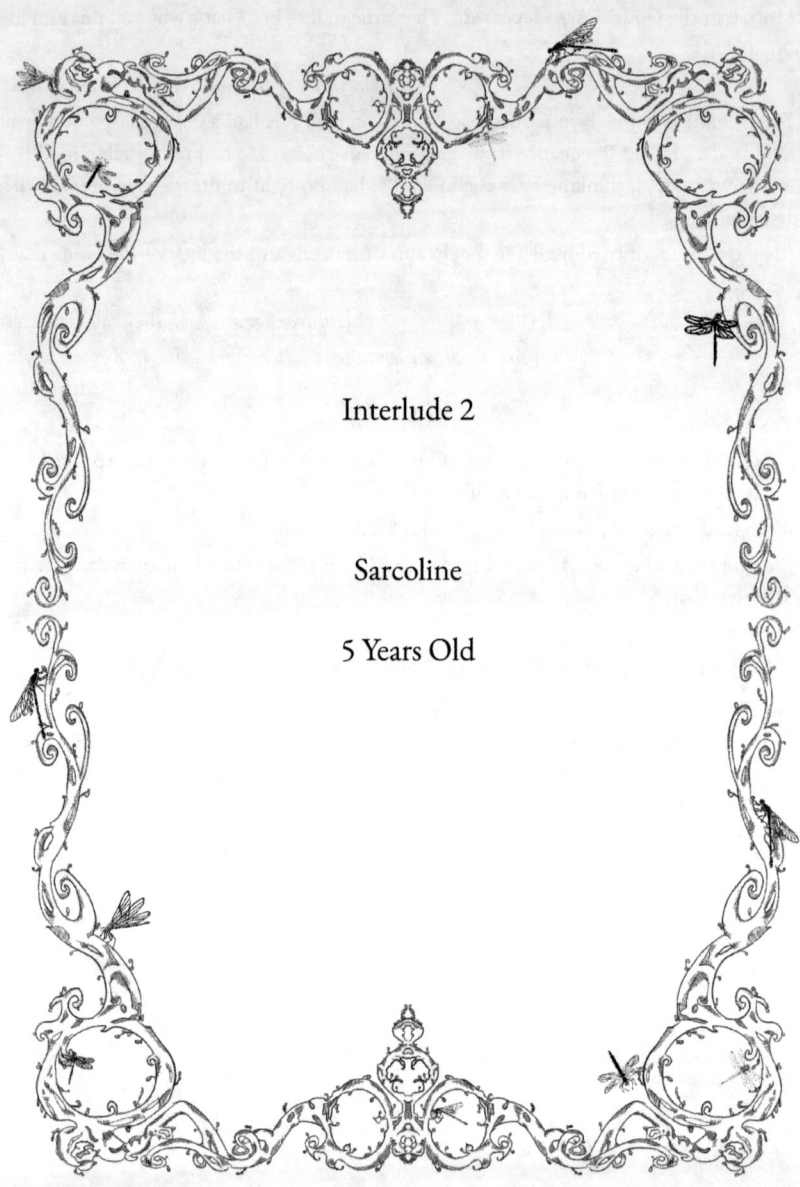

Interlude 2

Sarcoline

5 Years Old

Arco stood next to his brother, clinging to his shirt as they approached Jasi in front of the swing set. Ebru stood waiting with a deep set frown, which was scary because Ebru was always smiling, and Arco didn't like seeing him mad. When Arna stopped walking, Arco cowered behind his brother, terrified that they would get into another fight.

Both Arna and Ebru stood with their arms crossed. Arco clung to his brother unsure what to do. Should he get the adults? He hated when they fought. They were his favorite people in the whole world, and he was happier when they were both playing with him. It had been forever since they all played together, Arna was always fighting with Ebru now.

Arco shivered in his jacket, too light in the spring night air. The city lights overhead were sparkling like the stars Arco had seen in movies. There was one movie that Arco saw where two people kissed under the starlight at a park surrounded by trees, and the others had all gagged saying it was gross. Arco could not help but think that the situation was almost similar. The trees were tall, the sky was dark, it wasn't a fully empty park, but Ebru and Arna were just as angry at each other as the people in the movie had been.

Ven stood behind Ebru whispering to Ebru who shrugged them off. Arco tugged on Arna's arm.

"Hush now Arco," Arna told his brother.

"Why is he here?" Ebru asked and Arco jumped to hide behind Arna further. Tears rose to his eyes. Why was Ebru so *mad?*

"He followed," Arna said, "Arco." Arco looked up startled. His brother pointed. "Stand next to Jasi."

Hesitant, Arco did as he was told. He raced over and hid behind Jasi instead and as he did, Ebru did not glare at him but sent him a soft smile and Arco felt a bit better.

"He's a baby," Ebru warned Arna. "He'll tattle."

Arco stood up straighter. He wouldn't!

"He won't. Will you Arco?" Arna asked him, smiling. Arco shook his head. He wouldn't! He really wouldn't.

"I'm sorry that I'm late!" Phlox called out. She was tiny, huffing, and looking between them all frightened. Arco was confused? Had she escaped the care home? Didn't they have locks on her door so she couldn't? Their father was talking to their mother about that this morning, and how they were trying to get Phlox to live at the manor instead.

As she stepped into the light, Arco flinched. Her hair was shaved off.

"Who touched your hair?" Ebru snarled.

"The house mother cut it. She said long hair doesn't suit a boy. . ." Phlox whispered. Phlox' care home family was a strange family. They followed Pokk, but Arco didn't understand why they insisted that Phlox was a boy. She was clearly a girl.

"Dad will yell at the association. This will be enough to prove you need to live with us. I think my mom might have hair regrowth serums," Arna said, hugging her. Phlox nodded biting her lips. "They're wrong, Pokk's order does not dictate a lack of mistakes. Azza causes chaos."

"They don't believe Azza exists," Phlox said.

"They should move to Podiel if they're going to be so dedicated to Pokk," Ebru snapped, and Arco almost jumped at the hostility. "How did they fall for the cult anyway?"

"I don't know," Phlox said. "Why am I here?"

"Wait. You didn't tell her?" Ebru asked.

"Phlox, me and Ebru are going to make a vow. You're my second." Arna said. Arco's heart leapt at the word vow. He didn't know much about vows, but their father said they never were supposed to make one. They were super dangerous, and he was told that he could never make one or else bad things could happen.

"What if she says no?" Ven said. "You have no second."

"Phlox is my best friend," Arna said.

"What if she tattles?"

"Phlox is loyal."

"I will do it," she said stepping next to Arna, mirroring Ven. "What are you vowing?"

"Jasi," Arna said directing all attention to Jasi, who jumped. Arco nearly fell from the sudden movement as he stumbled back. He hurried to balance himself and held Jasi's hand. Jasi, looked down at him and nodded. Jasi was shaking. Why? Was the vow really that bad?

"State your. . . uh . . Grievances," Jasi said, voice shaking. Arco squeezed Jasi's hand. Should he stop this?

"I am here because Arna is a liar," Ebru said looking at Arna again.

"I'm not a liar," Arna disagreed.

Liar? Arna never lied.

"You claim that you're the Chosen Child," Ebru said with a deep irritation in his voice. "You might be, but you don't actually *hear* their voices. That's impossible."

"But he is. . ." Arco complained. Jasi shook his head and Arco understood. He wasn't supposed to talk.

"'By their will, the Chosen will come bearing gifts and without the eyes of a Child.'" Arna pointed at his eyes as he recited the scriptures. "'In desolation, the Chosen shall give mortals solace.' And so, it was. And so, it shall be."

"Right!" Phlox agreed with Arna. When Ebru glared at her she squeaked.

"Jasi," Ven whined. "Don't let them argue."

"Right." Jasi let go of Arco's hand and stepped forward offering his hands to Arna and Ebru. "Arna. Ebru. We are here today, not because of what was said, but because you want to make an oath. No. . . a *vow*. To never lie to each other again?"

"Are we supposed to do this? The adults won't like it." Phlox asked.

Ebru glared at Phlox and Arco started to shake. This was dangerous. The adults wouldn't agree at all. He needed to stop it, but how?

Arna handed his hand to Jasi and Ebru did as well.

"State your names," Jasi sighed. "Oh, wait! I, Jasione Jade, open this. . . concord and. . . uh. . . facilitate this vow as Child of Lumak and orator of. . . peace. Uh. . . Now state your names."

"Eburnean Hue."

"Incarnadine Vivicent."

"Seconds? Name yourselves." Jasi looked to the two.

"Pervenche Cosmos."

"Ph-Phlox Ruby."

Arco *knew* he needed to do something, but his little legs were ice. He was nothing to them, and as his brother glanced at him, he wanted nothing more than to support his brother. He stood, a witness to the ceremony, framed like the love movie, but so much scarier.

"Eburnean Hue. Repeat after me. I, say your name, vow to Lumak and all the Gods. . ." Jasi let go of their hands, pulled out notes from his pocket, read them and said, "to swear to tell the truth and nothing but the truth to Incarnadine Vivicent, so long as I live."

"I, Eburnean Hue, vow to Lumak and all the Gods to tell the truth and nothing but the truth, to Incarnadine Vivicent, so long as I live."

"Arna."

"I, Incarnadine Vivicent, vow to the Lumak and all the Gods to tell the truth and nothing but the truth, to Eburnean Hue, so long as I live."

"Repeat after me. I swear to uphold this vow at the cost of my life. May Lumak judge me righteously."

"I swear to uphold this vow at the cost of my life. May Lumak judge me righteously," Arna and Ebru spoke in unison. The two were only looking at each other and as much as Arco tried to get his brother's attention, Arna didn't notice him.

"Then as the proceeding judge, under the witness of Ven and Phlox, I. . .Jasione Jade, validate this vow. No more lies."

Nothing happened. The wind did not change. The lights did not flicker. There was no appearance of a mark, in a big show of light, like Arco heard in the stories about all the great vows. Ebru grimaced and Arna looked elated.

"It worked," Arna said, pulling off his jacket and shirt to show the mark on his chest. It was a spiral shape, a shade lighter than Arna's dark skin, right above his heart in the center of his chest. It was smaller than Arco expected, the size of a small rose petal, and he heard that the great vows had larger marks.

"Put on your shirt Arna." Ven sighed.

"Look," Arna said. "It worked. Now we can't lie."

"Arna!" Ginger was yelling. At her voice, Arna shoved his shirt back over his head. At the entrance to the park stood Ginger and Aureolin. Ginger yelled, "I'm telling dad!"

"No you won't!" Ebru yelled but the girls started running.

"No! Ginger!" Arna screamed after her.

Arna started running. The others followed him, and Arco hurried after, trying to keep up. They were all faster than Arco, running down the street and leaving him behind. Arco was pushed by the wind and by the time he arrived, Arco's brother was standing under the willow tree in the center of the house. The others were gone.

"I do know the cost," Arna said to no one.

Arco breathed heavily and did his best to hide.

"That I can't lie to him," Arna continued.

His brother was talking to the Gods! What were they saying? Did they see him?

"Incarnadine!" Their father yelled from upstairs. His brother hesitated for a moment, before he turned and raced towards the stairs. He then slid to a halt.

"Arco?" He asked.

"Arna." Arco moved from where he hid behind the desk.

"Come," Arna said picking up Arco who was still breathing heavily from the running. "You ran very fast."

Arco nodded and laid his head on his brother's shoulder. "Is dad angry?"

"Very," Arna laughed as if nothing was wrong.

"Did you do something bad?"

"No."

Arco believed him. Arna wouldn't be laughing if he did.

Arco turned to look at his parents as Arna stepped into the living room. His father was mad. Uncle Alabaster and Arco's mother were speaking. The Golden Generation sat on the ground, along with Jasi, with their heads down.

"Put Arco down," his father demanded.

"No," Arco said clinging to Arna.

"Sit." Their father sighed exasperated.

Arna sat and Arco sat on his lap, held by the person he loved most in the entire world. His big brother who was his biggest idol, and most important person held him tight. Arco buried his head into his brother's shoulder afraid to let go.

"Ginger. Is what you say true?" Arna's father asked. "That they did something?"

"Yes," Ginger said.

"What?"

No one spoke. Arco peaked out a bit to look at his father. When he did, his father was staring directly at him.

"Arco what did they do?" His father asked, and Arco gasped, holding Arna tightly. He shook his head. Arco did not want to tattle. He was only allowed to be there because he wasn't a tattletale.

"We made a vow," Arna admitted, rubbing Arco's head. The boy calmed down into the touch.

"What?" Their father asked breathless and then addressed Jasi, "Tell me what they said. Exactly."

Jasi repeated it.

"It should be okay," Uncle Alabaster put his hand on Arco's father's shoulder. "That's not enough for a complete vow."

But it was enough and everyone at the park knew. Arco saw the mark. It was a real vow.

"We should hope. He's a Child of Lumak, it could be as simple as a few words." Arco's father rubbed his temples. "Can you two take the others home? Not Phlox. She is staying with us. Phlox you can go to your room. Ginger take Arco upstairs, I need to talk to your brother and Ebru, alone."

Arco did not want to leave but Arna whispered for him to go, and reluctantly Arco let go of his hero. He took Ginger's hand and headed up the stairs. Phlox chased after them chatting to Ginger who ignored her with an upturned nose. His sister was so annoying sometimes. Arna loved Phlox, he didn't know why Ginger didn't.

Ginger put Arco into his bed.

"Why did you tell?" Arco asked her.

"Because he did something bad. You should have stopped him," Ginger told him with a voice that made Arco mad. She was making him feel bad or trying to.

"Why?" He asked.

"Because he could die." Ginger said low and scary. "Vows mean death."

Arco started to cry and as his sister shut his door with a slam. He didn't want his brother to die. But his brother said to trust him and Arco trusted Arna more than anyone in the world.

Arco awoke in the middle of the night, hungry. His eyes hurt from crying. Without much thought Arco walked to Arna's room. Arna's was bed empty. Confused, Arco turned to Ebru's room and went inside.

"Ebru," Arco shook Ebru who was sleeping. "I'm hungry."

"Go away Arco," Ebru swatted his hand.

"I'm hungry."

"Go ask Arna," Ebru rolled over and moved away. Arco climbed onto the bed with some struggle and pushed Ebru more.

"He's not in his room."

Ebru sat up suddenly. Arco plopped back on the bed.

"Where did he go?"

"I don't know."

Arco had not looked.

"He's going to get into trouble. What if he gets kidnapped again? We need to find him. Did you check the house?" Ebru hurried out of his bed, grabbing Arco's hand and throwing jackets on them both. Ebru's jacket was too big for him, but Ebru didn't seem to care.

"No. . ." Arco said, scared. "Isn't he dancing?"

Ebru blinked as if he had not considered it, despite that Arna practiced more than anyone. Arco's brother often practiced late at night when no one was watching.

"Right," Ebru did not remove the jacket. "I'll get you a snack and we can check if he's dancing. Then I need to practice."

Ebru hated practicing late, but he did not want Arna to be better. Arco nodded and squeezed Ebru's hand and in the much-too-big jacket, the two headed downstairs. As they approached the kitchen, they heard a voice.

"I could die. Cake or Brownie?"

Ebru stopped walking.

"I can't do neither, I'm hungry. I'll have both," Arna said irritated.

Who was his brother talking to?

"No?"

Ebru slowly moved them both closer to the kitchen door. Arco's heart leapt in his chest. Was he going to be able to see the Gods? His brother was Chosen, but could he show them to others?

"Between mortals and Gods?" Arna asked very confused, voice breathless.

Ebru whispered something under his breath. Ebru gave Arco a nod, and Arco nodded back despite not knowing what they were nodding about.

"Both?" Arna asked. There was a brief pause. "Then. . ."

Ebru breathed in deep and stepped into the room with Arco.

"Who are you talking to?" Ebru asked squeezing Arco's hand. They were going to get his brother to finally admit the truth. Finally.

"No one."

His brother reached for his throat unable to breathe. He was gasping for air, tumbling to the ground.

"Arna?"

Ebru let go of Arco's hand and groaned in pain. Arco stood, in the midst of the chaos: his brother collapsed on the floor and gasping for air while Ebru clenched his chest in phantom agony.

Arco raced to his brother, who was on his back with unfocused eyes, unable to breathe. Arco grabbed his brother's hands to keep him from scratching himself to death. Tears streamed down Arco face.

"Breathe Arna, breathe!" Arco screamed. Ebru was screaming too, crying for help.

This was a vow, Arco understood. But why? Why did the Gods have to take his brother away? Wasn't his brother their Chosen?

The lights were thrown on and Zaffre took Arna from Arco's arms.

"Arna breathe!" Zaffre yelled. Soon Wenge was soon next to Arco, yelling and using her abilities to heal Arna. Ginger pulled Arco back from the others, towards Phlox. They both were sobbing. They got him to Uncle Alabaster.

Ebru was collapsed on the ground shaking next to his father. He cried Arna's name and reached his hand out towards Arna's limp body. Everyone looked haunted. Arco's father's expression was that of the worst distress and pain that Arco had ever seen.

"Arna! Breathe!" Arco cried with his father as Arna's eyes fluttered.

Please, Arco prayed, *Don't take him, Ixxzal. I want my brother. I need my brother. Please. Please. Give me this.*

Arna breathed out in a large gasp. Arco started to sob in relief. He broke free of Ginger and raced over, past his father and grabbed Arna. His tears drenched his brother as he clung to Arna who was gasping for air. Even their mother couldn't pull him away. Then Ebru was on them both sobbing as well.

Arco was forced to let go as Ebru got closer. Arco tried to make his brother look at him. Instead Arna was focused on Ebru's eyes. Ebru held Arna's face cupped in his hands as Arna hugged him lightly. The two were inseparable.

Gravity condenced around them as everyone forgot Arco was there. Their parents fussed over the two, as did Ginger and Phlox. Arco backed up, into the shaodws, watching from afar.

"It shouldn't have worked," Uncle Alabaster said.

"Jasi oversaw it. He is Lumak's Child. It didn't matter what was said as long as it was a vow," Arco's father disagreed.

Their vow caused this. Ginger was right, Arco should have stopped them. He should have done something. His brother almost died, and it was his fault.

He should have been the one to stop it. He had to be the one to stop it next time. He had to protect his brother just like his brother protected him. He needed to. He had to.

In the dark of the night under the eyes of all the Gods and his parents, Arco vowed to himself.

His side burned in the thunder of a thousand storms, and he did not speak a word.

the APPRECIATION of

Do not remove yourself when you dance. There is a story you are meant to portray. However, your soul and personality should still remain; it is how you Understand.

— On a dancer's personal touch.

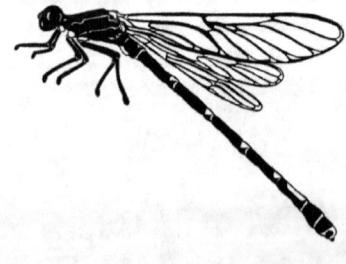

Dance 7

Enmity

Incarnadine

35 Poan

80 Days Left

"Friends? And what happens when you leave the city next year?'
"I leave the city next year?"
"Do you have time for such distractions?"
"No. . ."

Arna stood on the tip of the outermost rose petal of Xeysis. He'd come to this spot many times in his life, but the last time he'd been there—the time that stood out in his memory as he stared off into the dark—was the year that he decided to ask Pervenche out. He was thirteen and had been debating it for five months. He *knew* that Pervenche liked him back like a shining beacon. It was ever present in their bond.

Now any and all connection was warded off from the incessant anxiety and panic. Arna could ignore it, but he did not want Pervenche to have to do it themselves.

theendtheendtheendtheendtheendtheend

S.Mirrors was the most special of all Blessings because it linked two souls together. While all pairs had different outcomes, they always shared a mark: a constellation on their left wrist. It was the only Blessing that functioned the same regardless of person, as a bond, and was the rarest to receive. However, S.Mirrors did not mean love. It meant understanding. S.Mirrors allowed one to understand their partner as they would understand themselves when faced with a mirror, they reflected each other.

imgoingtodieiimgoingtodieimgoingtodie

Pervenche liked him back then, as certainly as Pervenche was furious at him now. Lightly touching the constellation under his flower vow mark, Arna sighed. Back then he had meandered for so long, until Pervenche called him out and he finally gathered up the courage to ask the question. Now Arna would not be so foolish. He'd had too many one nights, single chances, non-commitment flings not to know that his heart no longer remained with Pervenche. Most of him had moved on a decade ago, the last lingering part had died as soon as he saw Pervenche with Amaryllis.

And now, he could no longer deny it. No amount of online jokes and fake marriages could be laughed away. Not anymore. Without the mirage of Pervenche to hide it, Arna had to confront it. His heart was with Alis fully and Alis could not take it.

He was going to die anyway.

Arna leaned against the guardrail, chin in the crook of his elbow. The railing was meant to keep people from jumping below, to the overlapped petals. Up here, the petals appeared close enough to make the distance safely.

He reached out with his left hand, and for a moment he was near certain he could touch the other side if he just leaned a bit closer.

The moment someone tried, however, they would fall. They were not actually as close as it appeared, and gravity on the petals was Blessing manufactured: an illusion to maintain the image of a rose from the inside. It was all an illusion, the sky, the gravity, all Blessing created to allow the city to curl up on itself in the shape it took.

But if he tried and fell, would he be able to catch himself? Would he be able to fly again? Or would Ixxzal take him in terror?

The lights of the business district and the void center were above him. The train web glowed, powered by the intricate Blessings and technicians who supported it. Birds were flying with flowers petals through the city in a spiral of light and artificial wind, manufactured by technology to create the illusion of moving stars. There were flickering lights of the closest cable cars on their Blessing powered lines. The skybuses flew about, on the Celestial Highway, with their Blessing powered engines. The whole world was opened up to him, in the dark flickering false sky.

Below, from where he stood, the outside world was visible through the small places where the rose petals did not touch. The city had curled up to protect its inhabitants from the storm that night. The winds berated and scarred the metal, threatening to rip it apart. A thin mist of moisture rose in the form of steam. The rumble of thunder shook but did not sound.

Xeysis would hold. So long as the city was closed, it could not be destroyed. So long as the Blessings worked, Xeysis would not fall.

The storm outside was a miasma of gray and bright silver lightning. Flickering Blessing defenses rippled in waves. The softest rumble of the thunder rolled through his bones. Beyond the clouds, he imagined, there were millions, billions, of stars sparkling in the night sky.

Usually, it was one of the most beautiful locations in all of Xeysis.

keepmovingkeepmovingkeepmoving

The Gods were dying because of him and his want for a dream. Perhaps if he had come to this spot instead of making a rash decision on the stage, he would have been better off.

Perhaps, the Gods would not be flickering out about to die.

There were thousands of stories, told through different churches in different ways. Their wrath, their cruelty, their power was mangled into mere threads of rationality. Their distinct personalities twisted into obscure and intangible forms. They were perfect, infallible, and so complex that his child mind had never fully been able to understand the deeper reasoning behind many of their stories.

And while at a time they were still delusional that they would survive, acting in ways similar and still far too human. . . Now their fear was palpable to Arna, where they were no longer themselves but something more mortal. They were like scared children, bickering and huddled together. They were shells of their former selves.

They were terrified of dying.

runningoutoftimerunningoutoftimerunningoutoftime

Arna groaned and leaned back, both hands on the railing. He placed his head against the cool metal and tried to calm down. He squeezed the railing tight, and it squeaked: loose and threatening to fall. He'd let it take him.

[*Arna,* Ixxzal warned, a deeper truth threatening to consume.]

He reminded himself: he couldn't die yet.

Complete his variation.

Answer the question.

Accept divinity.

Divinity. . . He'd come to the spot to clear his head but standing there he thought of Blessings. He thought of horror instead.

hisnamewasSaffronandhefailed

Saffron was the Chosen before Ilex.

Unlike most other failures where the chosen died instantaneously, upon reaching the twenty-sixth dance, Saffron survived through the twenty-sixth dance: dying before completing twenty-seven.

Arna hated Saffron because they were too similar.

He'd picked up clues over the years. Saffron liked seafood like he did. Saffron liked the color pink like he did. Saffron had a partner who he worshiped like the sun, and they died in the Shattering.

Arna would not know he made the correct choice for certain until he danced, and if he chose wrong, he'd die. If he messed up his count and lost one too many Blessings before he danced, he'd die. If his variations as not good enough, he'd die. It was part of the reason that despite them telling him to start over and over again, that Arna could not be angry with the Gods. He had to be perfect.

Even if he succeeded by getting through all the dances, he'd die.

But Saffron had been perfect, and Saffron rejected his Divinity despite picking the correct answer. In many ways, Arna was more terrified of the prospect of rejecting Divinity than making the wrong choice. For it meant that if he rejected it, that he had made the correct one, and *still* managed to fail. He'd die in the end for nothing.

Saffron died because he rejected Divinity, and in doing so the superstorms were created as a backlash of the contract between the Gods and mortals being broken. The balance between Divine and mortal was *shattered*.

Pokk said that he rejected Divinity on purpose, nearly erasing them. Lumak said that they had pushed him before he was ready, and the lack of preparation shattered the equilibrium. Azza said he wished to become a God and join them out of some foolish belief that he could. Zaynir agreed but said he wanted to save the world that was in a constant state of war. Xeyaro said that when they woke, they did not remember what happened, and they had been drained. That it didn't matter why he did it, because, ultimately, they had failed.

Ixxzal said Saffron rejected Divinity by accident and, in doing so, was caught up in the energy: bending the laws of reality without their consent. This always confused Arna.

Arna never asked Ixxzal to clarify, in fear of what it would mean to know the one accident that the God of the Unknown claimed. To the God where everything was fate or a choice, how could they claim such a thing? It made Arna want to fall off the side of the petal, just contemplating it.

likeSaffronlikeSaffronlikeSaffron

Arna had always been horrified of the concept. The ancient question consistently threatened to destroy Arna. How did one accidentally do it? Arna could understand how it was done on purpose. It was another thing Arna had to be worried about.

What if he did it right and he messed up on accident in the process?

It was the one answer that they could not give him. He was not sure if it was because they did not know or it was because they did not want him to know in fear of him doing the same thing. Arna was terrified of being the same. To work so hard. To do everything right. To still *fail*.

likeSaffronlikeSaffronlikeSaffron

And worse: to fail by *accident*, by something he couldn't even control.

keepmovingkeepmovingkeepmoving

And now he had to fix the Splintering. He had to fix Saffron's Shattering.

He was going to die anyway.

Arna was okay with dying so long as he died after dancing the twenty-seventh dance. Arna was okay with dying so long as the Gods and the mortals were saved, and his one catastrophic mistake was fixed.

He was okay with dying so long as he had a say in when and how and why. But for him to do everything right and still fail by *accident.* . .

(Every struggle would have been for nothing.)

Arna clenched his fists twice as he held his breathe.

Kill the thoughts. Ignore the feelings. They did not matter. He did not matter.

He didn't need to see his dream come to fruition so long as it meant that he was able to fix the consequences of him dancing it. His reckless, foolish, selfish choice, had left everyone in the state they were in. He owed them his death for making the choice to chase a dream.

runningoutoftimerunningoutoftimerunningoutoftime

However, his death was only worth something if he succeeded. It only meant something if he stayed focused on his goals on what he had to do. He'd build a world for all of them, one where they could chase their dreams openly, without scorn and without fear. He'd give them the future he had once so desperately wished for himself—the one he destroyed everything for. He would give them the penance and retribution. He owed it to the world.

He *would* succeed.

theendtheendtheendtheendtheendtheend

The softest whistles of the wind rushed by him—true wind that had broken free from the Blessing wards—as a sound he'd never heard before: high pitched, soft, and almost like a giggle and a scream had been mixed. For a moment he wished he'd brought his recording equipment.

And, then all he thought of was Alis: recording sounds with Alis, traveling the world with Alis, showing Alis the real stars. Alis acted as if he'd never even seen fake stars in his life. He was cooped up and caged in his home by his father. Alis. . .

Arna managed to pull his mobile from his pocket with his bleeding hands, Blessings running rampant as he activated them to heal. The crescent moons on his palms closed, but the blood remained under his fingernails.

> Rosy: I miss you.

Arna needed his best friend even if Alis possibly hated him too. He wanted it even if Alis could not see him. He reached for it even if Alis would never meet him. For a moment, he needed the solace.

> Alis: Good.
> Rosy: Do you miss me?
> Alis: I'm alone.
> Alis: Of course I do.

For a moment reading the words stung. For a moment Arna wished to tell him something: that he'd call, that he'd be there, that they could meet. None of it could happen, so Arna forced the feeling into the box and clenched his fist tight. He gave the only thing he ever could.

> Rosy: I'm here

There was no response for a moment and then Arna's eyes lit up in the image of a video call incoming. Alis, attempting to call him again. Arna's heart raced as he stared at the call. *I could answer.* It would be simple. He could do it, and ruin everything, but then at least Alis would know.

But he couldn't do that to Alis. There was a reason that despite having been in contact for years that they'd never called each other. There was a reason that they only ever sent pictures from the waist down. It was easier this way. It was better this way. A person without a face would save Alis a world of heart break, rather than knowing who Arna was before Arna died.

Arna rejected the call.

> Rosy: I'm sorry, I can't. I love you.

```
Alis: You never can.
Alis: Sometimes I wonder if you're even real. If this
     isn't some sophisticated program lying to me.
Rosy: I'm real.
Rosy: And I'm here.
Rosy: I just can't answer.
```

Please. Please accept it. Please let it be. Arna waited on baited breathe. Would this finally be the last straw? Would this rejected call be the final time Alis tried?

```
Alis: I love you, too.
```

At the response, Arna could breathe.

It was wrong. He was the worst person alive, for all he had done, let alone clinging to someone that did not know his truth. He was worse, allowing Alis to say he loved him, when Arna refused to show his face. But without Alis, Arna was unsure if he would be able to motivate himself to complete the variation at all. Arna needed him, like he needed air in his lungs.

```
Rosy: Tell me what's wrong
Alis: I don't want to be hated by him.
```

Arna's lips curl up at the words. Alis ranted about his father and his father's Boss. As Alis typed, Arna let himself heal. The messages before him lined up with the forming scars across his palms. He locked away the fear and anger and all the other emotions he had, and he settled himself into thinking of Incarnate Dreams.

He would build a world that Alis wanted to live in. A world where he was free, even if Arna was not in it with him.

Arna finally relaxed when Alis sent an image. Large and painful, Alis' skin was purple and blue along his lower back. Anger bubbled in the back of Arna' throat. It was *massive*. Oh, how Arna would destroy the Boss when he finally met him.

[*Are you visualizing?* Zaynir's voice was on the giggling wind.]

Arna forced himself to relax and snap his thoughts back to Incarnate Dreams. *Think of the dance that can set him free.* That was productive, not thinking of something he couldn't do. *No.*

He visualized the steps and what he had to do. He asked himself the question:

(Mortals or the Gods?)

The Gods had left him alone for the most part, which meant they were debating. What exactly did they want from him? What *exactly* was this test?

"So, you *were* here." Pervenche's voice startled Arna.

Pervenche stood, in a shirt with sleeves cut mostly short and with strands of fabric that flowed outwards on the sides. Like floating petals on the wind, they drifted from where Pervenche stood with their arms crossed, long skirt on, and irritated look on their face.

```
Rosy: Gotta go. Keep venting.
Alis: It's fine I have something to do anyway.
```

Arna sucked in a hiss. There was something about the words that made Arna know he'd really let Alis down. However, he couldn't fix it. Not now. Especially with eyes glaring him down.

Placing the mobile in his pocket, Arna prepared himself.

Pervenche was dressed in shades of white and lavender, with patterns like that of gemstone veins in a cave. The clothes were more Zaydiel than Xeysis: like soft clouds, nearly floating instead of rigid in structure that was currently in style. Their eyes were filled with irritation, but relief. Pervenche had come here because they suspected this was where Arna would go.

Only this time, instead of the location screaming romance, with Pervenche about to question Arna about his feelings. . . Instead of it being the place where their relationship started. . . Arna was faced with wrath of a vengeful nature, a spiraling S.Mirrors activation that told Arna that he had fucked up. Everything between them had been fractured and dissolved years ago.

Why was Arna still here? Usually, he couldn't keep still without going crazy.

[Distant flowers rooted him in place.]

"Are they looking for me?" Arna asked, his voice quiet. Had he always sounded so insecure? Or was it the location and the fact that Pervenche was staring at him like a stranger?

"Ginger was afraid you'd disappeared again." Pervenche walked up, grabbing Arna's jacket and pulling him away from the edge. "You scared her. Why? Because you were angry? Why are you so anxious? What is wrong!"

Arna stumbled away from the edge, without much of a fight but as soon as he was far enough away, he forced Pervenche to stop touching him. He peeled Pervenche's hands off his jacket and let the hand fall. The two stood closer than they had before, but far apart all the same. An illusory cavern opened between them as the park lights flickered and the air stilled.

"Why are you here?"

Arna ignored the sensations only he could feel. It was just their S.Mirrors, making him react and see and feel things that weren't real. Pervenche's anger slowly disappeared and vanished into a ghost as their S.Mirrors deactivated.

Must have used it to find me. He hadn't even noticed his own activate. It was the issue of the Blessing. Both partners could activate and control the other's connection. Bristling at the thought, Arna ignored it and clenched his fist. He needed the anchor, even if it made him uncomfortable to know someone else could control one of his abilities so readily.

"Jasi has us all looking for you," Pervenche answered, fury building visibly on their face. Mouth twisting into a frown, shoulders tightening. They yelled. "Do you even realize how much Ginger is panicking? Do you care?"

Arna recoiled, trying to move away but Pervenche would not let him. They steped into Arna's path repeatedly. Arna needed an out. How could he get out? He did not want to confront this right now.

"And your mother, Arna. Your mother has a weak heart. You can't just disappear. You can't just. . ." Pervenche's voice cracked.

Arna's eyes darted across the path, choosing to ignore Pervenche, and to simply flee. Disappear and hide as he had every time any real person had physically confronted him in years.

"I was going to go back." Arna ducked his head in aversion, knowing Pervenche's eyes bore down on him. "Why did you come here?"

"You always came here when you were angry or confused or thinking," Pervenche said, with a hiss. They then snarked, "You are a sneak now and a damn good one. I assume it's how you survived for twelve years without anyone knowing who you were. But to me, you *are* predictable."

They were right, but Arna refused to admit it. He found a path out and started to plot his escape, lowering his center of gravity. "I didn't mean to come here."

"I just wish you had warned me you'd do this." They stepped back, leaving the path open so that Arna could run, if he chose. It was a dare. "Then maybe I would have said no to dating you."

Arna's attention snapped to Pervenche, taking in their sorrow in full. Pervenche stood, arms crossed, eyes locked on Arna, and disappointment bleeding across their frown and glare.

Arna's heartbeat wildly in his chest, emotions springing up. Fury, frustration, sorrow, and betrayal threatened to explode. He grimaced, bit back the scream that was there building, and clenched his fists.

How could Pervenche say something like that? He'd tried to contact them, and each message was deleted. He had tried to comment, to see the accounts blocked. For years he had cried about it and raged. The Gods had been cruel at times to keep him safe and a part of him resented them for it.

Pervenche stood motionless. A quick glance drenched Arna in chill. They were trying to get a rise out of Arna, to see emotions that he could not control. Cutting it all out, Arna did his best to steady himself and clear his thoughts. Hands open. Hands closed. Nails digging into his skin.

"You hurt me more than I think you will ever know," Pervenche went on, breathing slowly and eyes narrowing watching everything Arna did. "By choosing them, you decided to forgo the rest of us."

Arna winced.

"Is the game the same? Acting like the Chosen Child? Making the impossible happen with a clear disregard for the rest of us? We *know* you are the Chosen, Arna! We know the prophecy too!" Pervenche shook their head, taking a deep breath. They turned from Arna, taking more breaths before speaking again. "Something happened and now you won't tell us anything what it is. Why did you drop the fan? Is Arco, right?"

Arna squeezed his hand tight.

"Are you really forcing it because you fucked up? You really wanted it so much that you chose them over us, after you lost the chance?" Pervenche added, slowly and simmering with anger, seething in the tone like a fire ready to burst.

What? Did Pervenche think that Arna was an imposter?

[*You are not an imposter,* Zaynir's voice swept around. The God of Emotions was thriving.]

Arna tried to reach for Pervenche and Pervenche snapped back with their S.Mirrors, activating Arna's in the process. Arna felt the pain and sorrow, and the figment of hope. Pervenche cut the connection seconds later. Pervenche was pushing for answers that the others couldn't get.

[*Keep going,* Azza whispered. The God of Chaos and Creation was blooming.]

"You know me," Arna begged, the words sounding worse than he meant. But Arna was not a liar, not to them.

He was not sure why the Gods wanted him to reach out, but something about Pervenche coming so close to the truth without knowing the truth. . . He wanted to admit that yes, he had left them. No, he was not forced. Yes, he was trying to be Chosen, just because he wanted to be. But then what? Where would their hope go? He would have done everything because he was selfish.

"Yes. Just like you. I know the exact number of days before you broke up with me, by running away and not. Letting. Me. Know." There was hostility there, in the sarcasm and wit. Years' worth of torment and healing that was coming undone each moment that they continued to stand there speaking.

"You wouldn't have said no," Arna said so low he almost didn't hear his own voice.

"And you shouldn't have disappeared," Pervenche snapped, viciously.

What would have happened if he had ignored the Gods that night? He should have. He shouldn't have made the choice.

"I—" Electricity gripped his heart, but he held steady without faltering.

"Are you about to lie? Lumak be damned. Do the taboos not affect you?" Pervenche screamed, horrified. "Why must you always do this? When will you pick us, over this obsession with Gods. The same Gods who have abandoned us!"

This is just a test, he repeated thrice. He tried to steady his breathing. Tried to throw the thoughts away and ignore them. Tried to hurt himself until the pain overcame all other worries in his mind but none of it worked.

everythingeverythingeverything

[*Talk to Ven, Arna,* Azza sobbed, loudly and viciously like a swelling tide.]

theendtheendtheendtheendtheendtheend

[*Are you going to tell them the truth or keep quiet?* Pokk asked, softly, calm like a sunset.]

(It was all his fault.)

[*What will you do, darling?* Zaynir asked, the distant smile of spotlight.]

"I—" Arna did not know what to say.

How could he fix this? How could he fix everything? If he were just better, he'd already have the answer and. . .

All he heard was screams.

Somewhere in the distance a woman was crying. Somewhere in distant cities children were losing their legs after breaking taboos. Somewhere in distant future societal collapse was imminent.

"Yes. Arna, darling. When will you stop?" A new voice asked with a sardonic giggle tacked on to the end. High pitched and so soft that it demanded attention.

There at the edge of the field, beyond Pervenche and walking up the hill between the trees, were two figures.

Phlox was dressed in rich, soft blue luscious silks, extravagant as they draped around her shoulders like a cascading waterfall. The fabric rippled, however, not like water at the shore, but wind over the grass. Reminiscent of a forget-me-not, in shade, the bottom of her skirt was a series of similar flowers waving and spinning as she moved. It glittered so lightly under the lights by which she walked, a bounce in her step and chin held high.

The Phlox of Arna's memory was a skittish child, shy and nervous. His best friend was afraid of everything and always crying or whining. This woman was a powerful actress, certain of herself. Her makeup was done in elaborate and deadly precision: sharp eyebrows and eye liner, lipstick a brilliant shade of red. She was a fatality. Phlox had eyes the darkest mint shade of the Golden Generation; the dark green in her eyes, a reminder of Azza who had also loved her. Her hair was dyed red, the color of fire, and contrasted with her rich complexion. She had a lightness about her movement, gliding across the path like a graceful swan.

Next to her was Eburnean.

For a moment Pervenche and Phlox disappeared. All Arna saw was the current Prince of Dance. With shoulder length bleached white hair, Eburnean Hue approached almost like a mirage in the fog. When Arna thought of Eburnean, he thought of the small black-haired boy who had always been a powerful dancer. He had been a kid with a scowl and sharp words. Eburnean may have been rough, but he had been the softest and cutest of the Golden Generation, with pinchable cheeks and a pout that made adults smile.

Eburnean had lost his childhood, refined by a group of people who hated him. His eyes were no longer doe-like, but were narrow and sharp. They were glass crystals filled by a mint abyss of resentment and negativity. His skin was no longer milky and soft, but like a defined diamond blade. Eburnean was a machine in the body of a mortal, walking with his hands in his pockets.

His outfit was reminiscent of sharp metal, rigid and inflexible. It was gray and bronze, contrasting daringly with his hair. It was floral in the way a mushroom was, with nanotech causing a light show to sparkle in the fabric like glittering stars as he walked.

Arna was pulled apart at the seams, reducing him to a mess. The fight was ripped from him, and all that remained was Arna's hope. He had hoped to give them all back what he had taken from them. Eburnean was a reminder of all that Arna lost and all that could be gained.

Arna wanted them back in his life. He wanted his friends and his family. He didn't want to keep fighting them all and pushing them away. Even if it was better for them that way. He didn't want them to suffer more because of him. Eburnean was the personification of all the ways they suffered because of Arna.

For a moment the world was a blank canvas and in it Eburnean was a rediscovered dream.

"Arna." Phlox's voice was a soliloquy, taking the spotlight. It drew Arna in and dared him not to fall too far. Just above a whisper, she held all the power that came from a louder voice. Phlox commanded them to listen. "You have grown up. He's grown up, hasn't he Ven?"

Pervenche backed away from Arna as the two walked closer. "Where is Jasi?"

"On his way." Eburnean's voice was deep—deeper than Arna expected. It was like the swell of a melody, reaching for a harmony, but finding none. It was powerful enough to sustain itself, even if it desired to transform into something more. Arna was chilled. He'd heard the sound a thousand times in videos and songs and live streams, but never in person. In person it sounded so lost. Eburnean glanced to his mobile before he focused on Arna.

Eburnean's eyes traveled over Arna long and slow, Arna was exposed by the look, as if he were naked or worse, being undressed here in the middle of public. The man stepped into the light and Arna could take in every curve of his face, the proportions of his body, seeing it in person rather than a thousand pictures online.

Fuck, he's hot. Arna swallowed. Eburnean's silhouette was Arna's ideal, the body of a dancer: sturdy, strong, lithe. Online images, advertisements, and music videos did not do him justice. Eburnean in person was ethereal. This man was more his type than Arna ever wanted to admit when he was on the run. Yet for some reason this damned day had him admitting things to himself which were better off suffocated and buried in the back of his mind.

"For someone dead, you look very much alive," Eburnean said finally, finally, making eye contact.

He hates you, Arna reminded himself. If it were anyone else, Arna may have jumped at the chance to sleep with him once. This was not that chance, and Eburnean was the last person on the planet who'd ever want to fuck him.

"I—" Arna's throat constricted. This would be dangerous. This time: one mistake meant death. No questions about it.

"No," Eburnean cut him off with a smile. Arna's entire being shook. The smile was almost sweet, with a touch of softness and adoration. Eburnean's voice was a song, a litany of love and called for Arna to listen. "We don't lie to each other. Isn't that what we swore?"

If Eburnean continued to stare at Arna with the eyes that were half lidded, seductive and sure of himself, Arna would have another problem other than a death sentence. He tried to think of Alis instead. Only Alis had no face. Alis only had half a body, one that was transposed with the one that was currently before him. Alis may have been the one he was in love with, but *damn* was he attracted to Eburnean. And every moment he'd tried to ignore the fact over the last ten years was slapped in his face.

"Why are you here now?" Arna took the offensive instead, head held high and unwavering. If he could not run, then he could not back down. Still, he avoided Ebru's eyes.

"I was on a shoot until today," Phlox answered, lightly like she was dancing through the words.

"I didn't care to see you before," Eburnean said with the hostility that Arna had expected. Eburnean shifted on his feet. He said to Pervenche, "I'm surprised you did."

"I wanted to see," Pervenche responded. "Nothing more."

"Sure. . ." Eburnean reached for Arna's shoulder. Arna saw it coming and his heart raced. Instinct took over and Arna knocked his hand away before Eburnean make contact. "Fast reflexes. I suppose you have been practicing while on your mission."

Arna backed up, needing to flee again. He had been cornered before by angry people who wanted him dead and. . .

Eburnean stepped forward, hands slipping from his pockets and Arna's eyes rested on them, staring at the long fingers and just thinking. . . Oh. *Oh no*. Tens of moments, over ten years, washed over Arna in a second. Things he had long forgotten, because he had been too angry to remember them after they happened, and later too busy running for his life to really contemplate.

Eburnean stepped forward and despite knowing he should run, Arna was rooted in place in anticipation of what Eburnean would do next.

"You dance with the Shadones?" Arna instigated Eburnean into anger, wanting the response he thought Eburnean would give. He could not fall into Ebru's pace. Yet, he was pushing for the worst anyway.

"You cared so much that you paid attention to me?" he mocked Arna. One step closer. "Oh Arna, how kind of you."

"I paid attention. It's hard not to when it was on every news outlet across the world."

Arna watched Eburnean's hands, waiting for them to rise again.

"You left and poor Ginger and I had to do it all ourselves. Do you know what they said to us?" Eburnean's voice was soft, but the words cut Arna's heart to shreds.

"Ebru," Pervenche warned.

Eburnean cut deeper. "'You aren't good enough.'"

Eburnean stepped before Arna, favoring one side. Arna was not sure other people would tell, but Eburnean would never shift his center of mass unless there was a reason. Something was wrong. Eburnean, however, acted as if all was well, laughing, "'You are the reason he left. You are dead to us. You—'"

"Ebru!" Pervenche snapped.

The Children of Xeyaro were in the media but their personal lives were much a mystery. All Arna knew about them was what he saw online in the forms, in articles, and in the tabloids.

Arna could not imagine what had happened. Eburnean was right. He should have been there instead of chasing a dream that no one wanted him to chase.

"Why do you think Ven left? Phlox? Aureolin?" Eburnean ignored Pervenche.

"Now, Ebru. I love acting more than dance, you know that," Phlox laughed.

How horrible had it been at the Shadones? Did they hurt him? How far did they scrutinize him? Finally Eburnean lifted his hand and Arna was certain his soul was moving with it.

"Nothing we could do could fix what you broke and then you decided to waltz back here, as if *nothing* happened." Eburnean lifted Arna's chin with his fingertips. Arna met the wrath head on. Their eyes locked. They were close. Eburnean's words were frosted javelins. "If I had not slipped in the audition, you would have never danced Powers. None of this would have happened if I hadn't *fucked* up."

How many people had told Eburnean that? How many times had it been used to carve him apart? Eburnean laughed without the depth and lightness that came from humor, squeezing at Arna's heart.

"You should hate me." Arna scoured for an answer in Eburnean's eyes and found one that he had not expected: sorrow instead of loathing. "But you do not?"

"Hate you? No. How can I hate someone who ruined me? Apathy is better for you."

Eburnean pulled Arna's chin closer. Their noses were almost brushing. They stood in silence for a moment, close enough that Arna could feel Eburnean's breath, refusing to blink.

Eburnean had a nasty way of taunting, when they were young: pushing Arna to the brink of insanity. He always used to force Arna to confront issues and his own insecurities, by getting too close into Arna's personal space and then playing it off as if he'd been innocent the entire time. As the master of all things uncomfortable and flirtation, Eburnean was close because he wanted to break Arna. However, Arna had faced far worse than anything Eburnean could do to him. Eburnean was little more than a foggy mirror, and Arna had faced clearer memories that reflected his death.

Eburnean's mischievous eyes flickered once more. When Arna was younger, he grew furious every time Eburnean got too close into his space. He had been such an innocent boy wanting to keep himself at a proper distance and do everything by the book. Twelve years later, Arna did not so much as knock Eburnean's hand away. Instead, he leaned into it and smiled. Startled Eburnean pulled back and Arna caught his hand. Arna's vow mark prominent on display.

"You wouldn't risk angering Zaynir," Arna joked, pulling his arm back. Eburnean caught him that time, thumb brushing across the flower mark. Eburnean looked at it and then back up to Arna, clear confusion in his gaze before it was hidden away in a flirtatious smile.

"Gained a spine?"

Eburnean ran his thumb over it again.

"I've gained a lot more," Arna said.

Two could play Eburnean's game. When he was a kid, he refused to play, but Alis taught him well, and he could control Eburnean's incessant flirting.

Arna said, softly, "Keep touching me like that, and I could *show* you."

Eburnean blinked, clearly blindsided by the comment, "Show me?"

"What it's like to truly hate someone," Arna said stepping forward, back into Eburnean's space. He retreated and Arna chuckled, "I could make you scream my name until you loathed the sound."

Eburnean blinked twice and then his face went red. Phlox started cackling and Arna won.

"Trying to flirt with me now that you lost your chance at Ven?" Eburnean's voice was not nearly as confident as it was before.

"I like to keep my options open," Arna said, leaning back when Pervenche separated them both. Eburnean jumped back before Pervenche could touch him, landing on his left foot and quickly shifting to the right again. It was a small movement but moving as such meant he had an injury.

Eburnean chuckled, playing it off. "Defending him? After he left you?"

"Don't antagonize me. I'm not going to let you get into a fight with either of us. Stop the fake flirting and tell me why you're here."

Pervenche was clearly tense as they stood before Arna, arms open keeping Arna from view. Arna wanted to reach out and soothe them but stopped himself.

"Who said I wanted to fight? I was looking for him just as you were. Ginger messaged everyone." Eburnean stepped back as Phlox giggled madly.

"You are being rude, Ebru." Phlox winked at Arna. Arna's skin crawled, Phlox was like his sister. Her flirtations made him itch in disgust. Phlox said, "Rumor has it that Arna is pining for Ven again, gave him love eyes and everything."

Arna could not see Pervenche's face, but Eburnean could and Arna could see Eburnean. There was a satisfied look of smugness that graced Eburnean's face.

Eburnean asked with a twisted smile once more. "Oh? It's true? Strange. I vaguely remember you flirting with me minutes ago, Arna. That fickle then? Move on that quickly? Or am I just that alluring that you can't keep your hands off?"

Arna widened his smile and tilted his head, daring Eburnean to say more. Eburnean's mint eyes widened.

"I have Amaryllis." Pervenche answered and put a bit more distance between themselves and Arna.

"Last I heard, that wasn't necessarily true," Eburnean ignored Arna in full.

Pervenche stumbled back and snapped at Phlox. "Phlox I told you that in secret!"

"I don't fear Gods that don't exist," Phlox said, and Arna wondered how big of a retaliation she had received. She looked unaffected.

"Why you trust her to keep her mouth shut, I'm not sure," Eburnean teased her. "You can't trust her with any secrets."

"You do," Pervenche said simmering in anger.

"That's because Phlox is loyal," Eburnean said the words Arna once said years ago about Phlox.

"I was just trying to get you two to talk," Phlox pouted, "You're best friends after all."

"Not anymore," Eburnean and Pervenche said at once and Arna recoiled.

Arna was inclined to stare at the shadows on the ground below.

[*Face this,* Zaynir disagreed.]

Arna forced himself to confront Eburnean again and squeezed his hands tight.

"What a beautiful mess. I suppose that's what they mean by it being a choice," Eburnean mocked further. "Just because you have a heartmate doesn't mean you have to pick them. Must be exhausting."

Pervenche glanced back at Arna who met their eyes. There were unspoken words: *support me.*

"Lovers? No." Arna stepped to stand beside Pervenche. "But lifelines. We will always support each other. Our S.Mirrors makes us *heartmates.*" Arna did not like the word. "If anything, you should wish you had one. Maybe then you would have a heart."

"Who needs a heart?" Eburnean shrugged. "It's just another organ that can kill you."

[*How is this helping Azza?* Lumak, God of Balance, asked from across the petals little more than a whisper of a thought.]

[*It will work,* Azza, God of Chaos, insisted.]

[*I will step in before this makes it worse,* Lumak said.]

[*It will work. Ebru is here,* Ixxzal, God of starlight, twinkled and glowed.]

"What are you talking about?" Arna asked the Gods.

When Eburnean started laughing, Arna blushed. He'd said it aloud. Trying to quickly backtrack, he lost focus on where the God's voices came from as they bounced around him like the lightning beyond the rose.

"Enough of your jokes, Ebru!" Jasione yelled as he came into view on the path. With him were others. All dressed in their best. "You don't need to be cruel because the world hurt you."

"If I'm not cruel, then what would I be?" Eburnean turned back to the five others who arrived. Amaryllis rushed past towards them to Pervenche who gave her soft eyes: ones once directed Arna's way, long ago.

Strangely Arna's stomach did twist, but not in jealousy of their relationship. Instead all he could think of was Alis, and white, and a wish for a life that he could not have.

Jasione walked past Eburnean to Arna, standing at his side. There was a different relief with having Jasione at his side, like they were kids again facing Eburnean's pranks in the park. With Gingerline and Aureolin, the Golden Generation was together for the first time since The Splintering. Sarcoline sauntered up, hands in his pockets and looking pissed.

They stood in a circle: Eburnean, Phlox, Sarcoline, Amaryllis, Pervenche, Arna, Jasione, Gingerline, and Aureolin. All of them in a specific color: gray, blue, white, pink, violet, black, indigo, red, and orange.

A storm brewed between them, swirling, glowing in the moonlight like the sun: a delicate scale threatening to tip over into chaos. The leaves around them rustled. A single dragonfly flew through their group dancing around each one of them before disappearing into the night.

"What a party," Eburnean said after a long silence. "When was the last time we gathered like this?" Eburnean answered his own rhetorical question. "What was it? Right before Arna went on and—"

"Shut it," Gingerline snapped with ferocity Arna had not seen in her since he'd returned.

As if he was reliving it, Arna was there. All six of them in the same circle, with their hands linked, giving him support. Eburnean wished him to break all the bones. Gingerline was squealing and jumping up and down, tears in their eyes.

[*You wished to be the best*, Zaynir, God of Souls, sighed.]

Aureolin promised that she checked his fans. Jasione called from the curtains, next to the stage manager, reciting how much time there was until midnight.

[*Focus on the moment Arna*, Pokk, God of Change, urged.]

Phlox questioned why Arna had felt the need to be so rushed. Pervenche kissed him on the cheek.

[*You don't need to be the best*, Xeyaro, God of Dance, reminded, like a lullaby.]

Arna slipped into reality once more. It was not a coincidence. Mortality or the Gods. Six to pick over six: his friends or the Gods. Each of those around him were dressed in one of the God's colors. Each of them demanded his attention.

"Maybe you should have broken my leg, like you threatened," Arna joked with Eburnean.

"I should have." Eburnean's smile twisted.

"We need to get you home." Jasione shook his head. "The longer we are out, the more people will notice."

There was a strange way that they hovered near each other, like strangers but somehow closer. *They're still friends.* In some way and some shape, they viewed each other as friends despite the time they grew apart. All of them, at heart, still thought of themselves as a group. Arna had created a void between them, one they'd been unable to fill. How much had they tried to?

Amaryllis turned with a snap to face the ledge. Sarcoline whipped around with her and dropped low. They all looked over and Arna tried to search for what she heard. There was a rustling in the leaves, the soft chortle of streams and rivers as the Gods discussed somewhere: nothing that Arna noticed out of the ordinary.

"You should know that paparazzi follow Ebru and I like the plague," Phlox giggled.

"We are screwed," Aureolin groaned. "That'll be all over the internet by the morning."

"The morning?" Amaryllis asked. "It's probably already online. I heard the shutter of an RLX81. And. . ." She pointed to the other petals. "There are more there. The whole world already knows."

"So much for the media hold," Jasione groaned.

"Great. Just great," Sarcoline kicked at the dirt. "What is the best way home Am?"

"Thinking now. Sending you a map," Amaryllis said with her hands moving in the air.

"Well, I suppose it will create quite the stir," Eburnean said with a pout, far from the innocent one he had when he was younger. This one was taunting, threatening. "Think of the headline: the Golden Generation together once again."

"Are you really seeing this as a joke?" Gingerline snapped.

"It's all a joke, Ginger. Everything's been a joke since Arna decided to become the Chosen Child. We've always been understudy to his vendetta to destroy the world." Eburnean glared at Arna.

"Enough. Let's go home. There is little to talk about here." Pervenche stepped ahead, ignoring them all.

"Ven. . ."

They motioned everyone to follow when there was shouting. Arna's name.

"Incarnadine!"

Arna did not recognize the voice, but the moment he saw the sea of robes his palms were warm and sticky.

There were many levels of power and status in all of the churches. Despite this, Arna could identify the church of the Harmonious Six far too intimately. They held the Omniscient Sextant Enchiridion as canon in a malicious sense, taking and ignoring aspects a well. They were always dressed in the colors of the Gods.

[*Azza!* Lumak screamed.]

[*He's trained for this,* Ixxzal said, *Stop coddling him.*]

Those that approached on the hill all wore solid colors. There were no Cardinals, but there were Archbishops with priests to assist the crowd of believers that had formed. Arna's hairs stood on edge. They looked crazed and the last time he ran into a hoard of zealots from a religion, they tried to kill him.

As much as he wanted to die, he could not do that until after he danced. His Blessings for danger were screaming at him, telling him that there were those in the crowd that wished him harm.

[*It* will *work,* Azza said.]

He could escape on his own. Jumping from a petal to the next would be dangerous, but he probably could survive it. But what about the others? And what if he didn't survive? No. . . He couldn't risk something stupid. He needed to be smarter. Could he avoid them? Run? Disappear? Would flourishing his abilities let him disappear with this many eyes on him?

"How predictable." Eburnean stepped ahead, cutting off the crowd. All of Arna's thoughts slowed. "You hear: Incarnadine. You come running."

"Move aside, Eburnean," The Archbishop of the Harmonious Six, dressed in white for Xeyaro, ordered.

"No." Eburnean held his ground. Enthralled, Arna's thoughts for escape started to disappear. Could Eburnean get them out of this? How much power did he hold? Eburnean said, "You are interfering in DHS business."

"Incarnadine is not—"

"DHS. Business," Eburnean repeated. "Now. All of you."

He lifted a hand and waved it side to side. The sea of people parted. Eburnean began walking, Phlox trailing after him. Jasione and Sarcoline grabbed Arna and pulled him after Phlox, as Pervenche trailed behind with the others. Gingerline and Aureolin flanked Arna on either side, surrounding him so that the others could not touch him. Tens of voices called out to him.

"Incarnadine."

"Incarnadine."

"Incarnadine."

He avoided all eyes. He did not need to see to know. They saw him a heretic. Wanted to prove he was nothing. His heart raced. His gut was twisting in confusion from wanting to trust those around him and trusting what the Gods had drilled into him for years. He could not trust others. He could only rely on himself. The world was spinning. The noise was getting too loud. He needed. . .

Silence.

Fuck it. Arna did the one thing he knew would work. He recited scriptures.

"'And silence erupted from the crowd as the heavens bathed the First in holy light. The Gods' Blessing descended and all Mortals were gifted,'" Arna quoted from the Binding Origin Parable from the Book of Dances of the Omniscient Sextant Enchiridion.

Eburnean stopped walking and turned back to him. All of the voices around him stopped calling. Arna continued to dig his nails into his palms, wanting to disappear but wanting them to shut up more.

Be comfortable with silence, Rosy. Alis' words were there for Arna, guiding him forward. All pressure disappeared. *Be able to* **exist** *within silence. It is serenity. It is the story told in moments where sound cannot reach.*

Arna had always had a difficulty with silences when he was a kid. He'd use the space to quote from the holy books, trying to fill it at all costs. His home had always been filled with chatter, with laughter, with so much noise that when Arna was alone those first few weeks, he'd almost been driven mad. The Gods talked to him, but even they left him in silence and alone often enough.

We only think of it after it has passed when it has come and gone. We long for it. We hide from it.

Alis had been the one to help him through it, and even if Alis was not there, Alis could still help him.

"'The Gods said in words not heard by any, save the First. 'You shall be our voice for all mortals who need guidance. You shall show them the way.'"

We try to fill it when it is not void.

Arna paused. Eburnean faced him completely. Phlox glanced over her shoulder to him. All of the eyes were on him, waiting on bated breath for him to finish.

The moments we do not hear are not lost. It is there in our imaginations, in our hopes, in our dreams.

"And so, it was. And so, it shall be."

It is the proof, the support, the essence of what matters.

Arna let the silence fill the void that his words left in their wake. With it came peace. Arna then began to walk again, before anyone could comprehend his distraction.

Silence is not an absence but a reminder of what you have.

"They are going to think that was an oracle," Jasione warned him when he caught up. Sarcoline was cackling, and Amaryllis hissing at him to stop.

"But you saw him. . ." Sarcoline laughed. "They're idiots."

"Any person with a brain would know he was quoting it on purpose to get them to stop talking," Eburnean disagreed.

"Was it on purpose?" Pervenche tested.

"Yes," Arna said.

Let them think what they wanted. The Gods thought them morons, all of them.

[*Not all of them,* Zaynir disagreed.]

[*Most of them,* Azza agreed.]

[*No. All of them,* Ixxzal, agreed with Arna.]

[*I told you it would work,* Azza cheered.]

[*That is yet to be seen. This might be temporary,* Lumak groaned.]

[*Something has changed,* Pokk hushed them.]

Arna was going to ask the Pokk what he meant when Gingerline asked. "Why use that quote?"

"Because he was telling them to shut up," Eburnean said, knowing Arna. He knew the holy texts as well as Arna did. Arna often quoted them at him. "Incarnadine has always used the holy texts when words have failed. Right?"

Arna grimaced at himself. He had been such a fanatic as a child, using the holy texts as his backing for everything. He was embarrassed to think of it. Standing in front of Eburnean lecturing him with the words righteously, when Eburnean just wanted to play. Telling Gingerline to stop crying about spilled ice cream. He'd used it at the worst time, and at the "right" time for the Bishops and Archbishops to love him more.

"Don't mention it." Arna shook his head. Once more Arna thought of his bedroom and the religious iconography stuffed under his bed.

"Oh. Arna is embarrassed," Phlox called him out. "Cute."

Arna wanted to defend himself and say he didn't. But it was a lie, and he couldn't lie to or around Eburnean. Instead, he shook his head.

"Then, at least one good thing came from your exile: humility." Eburnean used the word and Arna glanced to him. Eburnean walked to the side looking up towards the center of the city. No one used exile, save Arna. Others called it a pilgrimage. Why?

"Two. Our little Arna has grown into a gorgeous storybook hero. Chiseled, refined, beautiful. . ." Phlox winked at Arna. There was a brief moment where Arna froze glancing about the others who avoided his gaze. "Don't look at me like that. We are all thinking it. Ven, did you know this would happen?"

"Phlox," Aureolin warned her. "Stop."

Arna looked at Pervenche who was avoiding him the most. Amaryllis looked exasperated and gave Arna her a soft smile of comfort.

"Right Ebru?" Phlox said to Eburnean. She eyed Arna up and down twice, then smirked as Eburnean's eyes slowly traveled over Arna again. Chills ran down Arna's spine as their eyes met. There was something there, masked behind the haze of whatever illusion Eburnean was crafting. Eburnean went to say something when his face paled.

He tapped at the sky.

"Yes?" Ebru answered a call. "No. I'm. . . Yes. Yes. I know but I—" Eburnean flinched. "I'm on my way now."

"Dad?" Phlox asked when he hung up.

"The news has already spread." Eburnean shook his head. "The Master is not happy. Apparently, no one told him."

"Master?" Arna repeated. When Eburnean shot Arna a glare, Arna realized he'd accidentally said the words aloud. "Do you mean Cyclamen Shadone? He's—"

Had Eburnean recognized the man as his official dance master? Was Arna wrong? Had they always treated him well? Had he decided to change alliances himself?

"Bye, Arna. Let's not do this again," Eburnean said as he walked away.

Phlox chased after him, sending kisses their way. She then tried to wrap her arm around Eburnean's left side. He reached for her, twirled her around and she landed on his right. Giggling she sent them another wink and dragged him away.

"That's strange," Arna said.

"He's always that dramatic," Aureolin said. "It's to make a point."

What? Did no one else realize he was injured?

"We need to get Arna home." Jasione picked up the pace.

Arna followed him, towards where a hover car was parked, wondering how it was that the others had not noticed Eburnean's injury. Pervenche had been Eburnean's best friend for years and the others were dancers. Or was Eburnean just. . . like that? Worse than before. Acting at all times so they never knew what was real?

Sitting in the car, Arna watched as Pervenche, Aureolin, and Amaryllis said their goodbyes. They were not going back to the Vivicent's, either. Gingerline spoke with Jasione in a low voice as they got into the vehicle. Sarcoline sat silently. Private transportation like hover cars, were expensive and Arna had a feeling that his family did not have the money for this car. He hoped it was Jasione's, however the unsettling sinking feeling told him it was borrowed. How much more money had they wasted on him?

Arna stared at his palm, healed thanks to his body Blessings and covered in blood that was sparkling like star dust. What little remained that was not sticky or dry had run down his wrist, circling the flower mark.

Silence is not an absence, but a reminder of what you have.

Arna sighed.

There was no more running and hiding. He was going to have to decide, and in order to do that, he needed to know the cost and the consequences. His friends and family or the Gods? He understood the Gods, but his family. . .

What were their lives like after he vanished? What had they faced? What were they like now? He wanted to *know*. Once upon a time, they had been friends, as close as siblings. Now, they were strangers.

[*What do you want?* Zaynir asked.]

If he wanted answers, he was going to have to put effort into understanding their lives now just as the Gods wanted. Test or not, it mattered little; it was personal. There was no going back, only forward.

The Original was the first, but does that mean it is the best?
Or was it simply the first turning point in history?

— On the first variation.

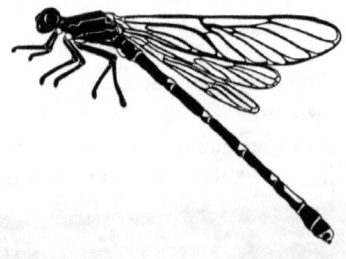

Dance 8

Despair

Incarnadine

7 Ixan

71 Days Left

"The choice was always yours."
"But you made me. . ."
"Did we?"

In the week after the pictures had spread, Arna had not left the house once. Gingerline had convinced Arna to give her his contact information and then had given it to everyone else, much to his dismay. There were messages in his notifications that he ignored. He refused to message them back, let alone read what they sent. Instead, Arna did what he always did, and lurked online.

CrimsonFlesh had always been the top moderator for the Ivumalis comment section and discussion forms. When Alis ranted and complained about the comments, when they got him down, Rosy was there to cheer him up. Arna was an expert at digging and internet fights. He was an expert at using the keyboard to find everything he wanted to see. Arna had scoured the internet for every bad comment, for every bad review, and read them all so that he could refute them when Alis said them about himself.

A part of Arna had always been waiting for the day when he'd have to face it himself.

The official statement, confirming Arna's identity, was released after the world was aflame in conspiracy.

Incarnadine Spotted

Golden Generation Together Again

Golden Generation, Twelve Years Later: First Look

What Do We Do Now?

Incarnadine Vivicent: Harold of the End or Apostle for a New Beginning?

The Vivicents Were Hiding Him The Whole Time!?

How Zaffre Vivicent Failed Us All

Incarnadine EXPOSED

Pervenche and Incarnadine: Is Xeysis Favorite

Couple Getting Back Together?

Amaryllis Ink Distraught: Pervenche Going Back to Incarnadine

Eburnean Hue: Relegated to the Back Stage Again

Things Heat Up in the Dance World: Incarnadine Returns

Is This The End?

Arna flipped through the message boards, laying on the floor of his private dance studio. He'd watched the released security footage at the Xeysis train station and seen leaked photographs of himself in other cities over the years. There were thousands trying to piece together where and when he had been in locations. Arna doubted that it would take them long to do so. Or the official story would be released and then everyone would know.

Arna was not sure why the government officials had taken so long to officially report on his return, but now their hand was forced.

Arna looked at the comments below the picture of him and Pervenche who grasped his jacket and was yelling.

- ► What do you think they're yelling about?
- ► I love them!
- ► Looks like the news is fake. Figures. They hate each other.
    - ► No! I love Blooming! Amaryllis and Pervenche forever.
        - ► No. Pervenche deserves so much better than that liar too.

Arna looked back to the picture. He downloaded it with the flick of an eye, saving it to the folder with seventy others. Most of the images were of Pervenche gripping Arna's jacket from different angles. Arna used his mobile to click on another when his retinal augmentation refused to listen.

At the time, he had not noticed the love in Pervenche's eyes. Pervenche still loved him, wanted to love him. It was not romantic, but it was a love, something deep and platonic. They were still family. Arna could tell, but the pain was visible and all encompassing, too. Sorrow etched deep into their expression as they yelled.

[*Make them fall in love with you again,* Zaynir suggested.]

"And how does one do that?" Besides he didn't want to. He didn't deserve their love.

[*You don't,* Ixxzal said.]

[*Ixxzal!* Zaynir snapped.]

[*I didn't agree with you then, and I don't now,* Ixxzal said. *You know my choice and I stand by it.*]

Arna did not have to ignore them as their bickering turned to raindrops. He continued to save pictures. Arna's mobile had once been filled with photos of scenery or pictures for Alis, exclusively. In the last few hours, he saved over a hundred photos of his friends and family. He'd read thousands of messages and discussion board posts about them all.

Jasione.

- ► Gods, who is this hottie?
- ► Is that Rosmarinus?
    - ► The swimmer? No. That's his twin. Jasione, I think?
        - ► He's also Incarnadine's best friend.
            - ► So, he's trash too. Got it.
    - ► No, it's not, but I've heard Rosmarinus is just as bad.
        - ► Yeah, his teammates hate him
            - ► He picked the Vivicents. Of course, they do.
- ► Lumak should have picked his Children better.
    - ► One is always a failure.

Gingerline.

- ► Once again Gingerline manages to disappoint us all.
    - ► She didn't have to do much. She's been worthless since the beginning.
- ► I can't believe that she's the heir to the Vivicent family.
    - ► Sarcoline still has a chance.
        - ► Anyone would be better than her.
- ► I said it once. I'll say it again. Gingerline is the WORST of the Golden Generation. I don't know why she tries.
- ► I never think the Vivicent family could get worse than Incarnadine, then I remember that Gingerline exists.
- ► Gingerline is a good person. She helps the poor and feeds the sick.
    - ► Yeah, because she has no other skills.
    - ► Maybe she should stop dancing and do something that she's actually good at: helping others where no one can see.

Sarcoline.

- ► Sarcoline better have punched Incarnadine in the face.
- ► Zaffre really is a fucked father if he raised three failures.
- ► At least Sarcoline can dance, the other two would be nothing without their Blessings.
    - ► I think that Incarnadine is faking his Blessings.

Arna flipped back to the news articles. Jasione had not been on the internet much until that week, at least not in the capacity like the Golden Generation.

Rosmarinus, despite his generally good image online, was being ripped apart. His teammates had to come out with a statement saying they did not, in fact, hate him.

Gingerline and Aureolin had thousands more posts and articles slamming them. Pervenche and Phlox's management teams had put out statements to keep much of the backlash away. Whoever was on Amaryllis' press relations team, was horrible at their job.

Who Could Ever Be Friends with Amaryllis Ink?

Step Down Amaryllis, Public Enemy #1 Has
Returned

Why You May Hate Amaryllis and Why You Should
Hate Incarnadine More

Another Family Destroyed!

Amaryllis Ink Proving She Does Not Care For
the Sanctity of the Arts

Artist? Maybe a Conartist

Top Ten Pictures We Love to Hate and Ten We
Hate that We Love

Sarcoline's fans had pushed posts to the top, dragging the others and promoting him.

Sarcoline Are You Okay?

We Are Waiting for Sarcoline to Show Us True
Anger

Ten Times Sarcoline was Better than Incarnadine

The Best of Sarcoline

Sarcoline Rage Compilation

Sarcoline's Best Looks

There was a shuffling of feet in the room over, with muffled voices.

"—If you had—"

"He's not going to talk to you—"

"The Gods need us to protect him!"

Arna found a new photo of him with Eburnean, where Eburnean was lifting his chin. Where Arna was leaning close to him head tilted daring Eburnean to flee. Arna saved the photos and read the article. He was tempted to log onto his burner accounts to argue but paused when he thought of Alis. He'd promised Alis to stop arguing online and Alis knew how to identify his burner accounts. There was a bigger risk of being caught as Arna, now more than it ever.

Eburnean Hue At It Once Again.
*Since he dyed his hair at eighteen, Eburnean has
continued to bleach away our expectations. The Prince of*

Dance has stunned crowds, wooed audiences, sold out a stadium tour, acted as our most beloved academic, and most recently became the youngest small council member for the DHS. Just when we thought there was little more he could do to surprise us, he once again upstaged himself.

Last week Eburnean was found flirting with the heretic Incarnadine Vivicent. In a move that we should have seen coming and yet no one expected. . .

Arna searched Eburnean's name. There were more than ten thousand search results: images, videos, dance compilations, rude comment compilations, tabloids, and articles of praise. There were videos of his time with the boy band group that were being brought back up. There were listings of the movies and television shows he was in. Arna had already seen every video, show, and movie. Eburnean had the most search results out of them all.

The HUE Manor is Up for Sale: Eburnean and Alabaster's Thoughts

Bad Boy Eburnean Back For Good?

The Mysterious Son of Alabaster Strikes

Zaffre's Best Student?

The Shadone's Not-So-Secret Weapon

Ten Reasons We Love Eburnean And Ten Reasons He'd Never Love Us

Ten Reasons Why Your Father Would Never Let You Date Eburnean (And Why We Want To)

Eburnean vs Sarcoline: Who is The Better Dancer?

Eburnean Hue: Monster or Miracle?

Eburnean Hue: The Greatest Dancer of All Time?

Arna read everyone article twice. He found videos of Eburnean dancing in all the six cities and a few international parks. There were hundreds of interviews. Eburnean had done everything and anything to please the world.

Over the years he had followed Eburnean the most out of everyone.

Although, now Arna was confronted that he did it was because he was attracted to Eburnean rather than the self-serving reason of trying to make sure his rival was okay. He really shouldn't have saved as many pictures of Eburnean as he had.

Arna empathized with Eburnean. In some ways more than his brother. The internet made him dangerous, and then relished when he met their demands for horror.

Yet no matter how hard Eburnean tried to be great, even he was not good enough.

- ► He should give up acting. He's terrible.
- ► His voice makes my ears bleed.
- ► When is his new song coming out? It's been years.
- ► This picture isn't too bad when you forget that he's the reason the Splintering happened.
  - ► Imagine dancing for twelve years to make up for a mistake and still being this dramatic. He should be humble that we've forgiven him.

For the good and bad that came with the title, Eburnean was the greatest. Eburnean was a better dancer than Arna; he'd know that for years.

[*We did not pick Ebru,* Xeyaro said as they always did.]

"Why?"

Eburnean was the best, better than Zaffre who was undisputed before. The only person who could compare to Eburnean in raw talent for dance was Sarcoline. Sarcoline first took to the stage of Powers at fifteen, the same age as Arna. When Arna did it, he'd surpassed his father's record as the youngest ever to dance Powers by a year. Sarcoline did it without the A.Reverence Blessing. Eburnean should have been able to do it at fourteen but had not auditioned because he wanted to compete with Arna.

Arna was only good because he had all the Gods supporting him.

[*I did not pick Arco. We did not pick Ebru,* Xeyaro answered. *Talent does not mean Blessing. Some are better with their Blessings than others and some have talents that are not tied to their Blessings. Remember Incarnate Dreams.*]

"Yes."

Incarnate Dreams.

Years ago, when he had last asked the question, Xeyaro had given him the same answer and it had been the spark for his variation. Xeyaro had not picked Sarcoline despite his motivation, drive, and talent in dance. The Gods had not offered Eburnean to be their Chosen.

Still, Arna was the genius of geniuses, only *because* of all of his Blessings. Without them, without A.Reverence, he was nothing. Eburnean had made himself the best because he had to prove himself. Arna searched his own name and immediately closed the tab. He opened it again and turned over on his stomach.

It was some odd hours later when he finally logged off of his new burner accounts, thoroughly pleased with the arguments he'd won online. Arna hoped the satisfaction could help him with his variation. With great difficulty, Arna turned his attention back to Incarnate Dreams. Before him, on his computer, was a travesty. Despite the work he put in, since coming home everything was wrong. The music was hollow. The steps he'd refined were worthless. The fan motion was incomprehensible, lacking.

What had happened?

Immediately his notifications lit up and the messages rolled in.

```
Alis: You alive?
Alis: Hey
Alis: I need you.
Alis: I fucked up again.
Alis: I can't do this anymore.
Alis: I don't want to stay here. I can't stay here.
Alis: I don't know what to do.
Alis: He hates me.
Alis: They all hate me.
```

Arna started to respond and jolted to stop. Alis needed his best friend, but Arna could not respond. His fingers would not move. Articles and comments about himself replayed in his head.

Worthless. Terrible. Better off dead.

Self-doubt spun in his head. His chest began to give in, and his breathing shortened. It would be better for Alis if Arna stopped talking to him. It was better for Alis if he had someone else to rely on instead of a living corpse.

Arna looked back to his music, trying to figure out what to do.

Focus on this.

Not on the thoughts. Not on the comments. Guilt circled, reminding him why it was that Alis told him to stop the online warfare. The satisfaction transformed to abasement transformed into loathing.

He'd never complete his variation,

fix the world,

be there for Alis when Alis needed him.

The notifications continued.

[*Talk to Alis,* Ixxzal said.]

"I need to focus on this." Arna did not believe what he said. He couldn't breathe. Couldn't think. Couldn't. . .

theendtheendtheendtheend

[*Ignoring him will not help you,* Lumak said.]

"Why can't I just do this. Tell me what I'm doing wrong!" Arna begged. It would solve all the problems. If they just told him, he could do it and fix it and he would dance. He would.

[*This is necessary for your success*, Pokk disagreed.]

"What do you mean?"

They had never told him anything.

"What am I supposed to do to fix this? They hate me? I hate me. How do I fix this?"

How could he stop the pain? Stop them from hating him. Let himself breathe.

[*We cannot tell you how to do it,* Azza whimpered.]

He thought of Eburnean glaring at him. Alis was freaking out and needed him.

What did they want from him? It was not like things could go back to the way they were. He couldn't just be in their lives. There was no way for him to survive even if he wanted them.

[*Are you visualizing?* Zaynir asked instead.]

"Why do you always ask that?"

[Zaynir giggled and their voice swelled with confidence, *I want to confirm that you're making progress with your future.*]

Arna swallowed a retort, knowing he'd get nowhere with them when they were being purposely obscure.

[*Maybe fixing your relationships will give you the inspiration to best visualize what you want,* Zaynir suggested.]

"I have so many other things I have to do," Arna said and peeked at his mobile again. Alis was there again, buzzing and notifications popping up before his eyes.

[*Don't avoid them,* Ixxzal said.]

diediediediediediediediediediediediediediediediediediediediediediediediediediediediediedie

(It was all his fault.)

runandhiderunandhiderunandhide

He clenched his fists tight and swallowed the panic back.

No. He was doing it again. He was fine.

He could not have a breakdown. He was okay.

He was capable to doing everything. He killed it, shoved it back, bit back the vomit, and gulped in the air like he was dying.

Focus on Alis. Just like Ixxzal said. On anything else.

```
Alis: I can't keep doing this.
Alis: But I have to. I can't expect handouts. The world
      isn't just going to give me things because I think
      I deserve it.
Alis: They're all depending on me.
Alis: If I don't, who will?
Alis: Rosy.
Alis: Rosy?
```

Arna did not want to avoid Alis, but the fear was still in his throat that he'd disappoint Alis.

[*If not now, then when?* Ixxzal asked.]

Ixxzal was right. He needed Alis to finish his variation. He couldn't let Alis go. Not yet. Not until the end. Until the end he could not disappoint him.

```
Rosy: I'm here.
Rosy: Sorry. Busy.
Alis: You're always busy.
Alis: What's different now?
Alis: You can tell me.
Alis: What's going on?
```

Everything. Arna stood up, facing the mirrors. In it, was himself harrowed and tired. Trying so hard not to collapse under the weight of the world.

```
Rosy: I'm sorry.
Alis: You keep saying that.
Alis: What does it fix?
Alis: Actions are more important. You know you can tell
      me.
Alis: You can trust me.
```

You can trust me.

A spark of inspiration flashed before Arna in the flickering lights. Was this a part of it? Getting closer, having to repair what was broken so when he picked the Gods again, he knew exactly what he was picking?

The lights dimmed almost out.

He hadn't known the extent of his choice at fifteen. If he had known, he doubted that he would have agreed especially not if he knew what he did at twenty-seven.

[*You can only move forward.* Zaynir's voice sounded pained. *We can only move forward.*]

He could make it to the Ceremony of Chaos. The Gods wouldn't let him fail. And even if the rest of the world hated him, they would always support him.

theendofeverythingtheendofeverythingtheendofeverything

Focus.

Arna swallowed back every negative thought. He left them to fester. If he ignored them long enough, they'd go away.

"I suppose it's not so bad being the most universally loved and hated. Maybe I should ask Ebru for some pointers," Arna gathered himself.

[*Repair the relationships,* Azza persisted.]

[*Deal the wound that has grown,* Pokk insisted.]

I was planning on it. Arna would find a way to get his family to stop doubting him without hurting them and giving them false hope. He would not rip himself away from them, but they were the only support he had.

And. . . A hopeful thought sparked.

Arna would find Alis and take him from his family. And he'd ask his family to take care of Alis before the storm. Alis would never forgive him, no, but at least Arna would know he was safe. He could die easily that way.

Arna pulled open the door of his dance studio meeting the crisp midmorning light. The house was leveled with a stark silence, stale as the air that filtered through the house, gradually beginning to warm as the summer sun grew brighter. Artificial seasons, although Arna knew nothing else, gave just enough to cause changes but not enough to cause discomfort. Just enough to change the aesthetics of parts of the city each month but not enough to be a logistical nightmare. As the most southern city in the world, however, Xeysis was experiencing an artificial summer as opposed to the artificial winter in the north.

With this in mind, and the arts district announcement for extreme heat, Arna dressed for the day with much regret. The nice jacket that Jasione had bought him, was beautiful but he'd be hot. It was too heavy a suit for the warm summers of Xeysis. He slowly buttoned the cuffs and faced himself in the mirror: the most put together he had been in years. Shimmering white of the jacket with hummingbird small feathers along the sleeves that moved on their own and glittered in the light.

He locked his room as he tried to clear his mind of all thoughts.

[*Don't be afraid.* Azza cheered solemnly. *You are enough!*]

Azza always cheered him on. Always supported and believed in him. They may have been a trickster and teased him, but they were like a sibling, there to annoy but love deeply. Arna sighed. Their voice had been softer and more melancholic as of late. He chalked it up to anguish of the oncoming deadline, even when the voice reminded him of Gingerline.

"Let's go. We need to go," Gingerline said from the staircase, waiting for him. She too, had a deeply melancholic voice, slow and scared.

"Sorry." Arna stepped up next to her. She was dressed in a long flowing dark green trench coat, the color of Azza. Beneath it was a long silver silk dress with knit flowers of the darkest shades of blues and green and purples. The flowers were completely hand knit from the looks of it, soft, and not something he'd seen before. Was it a new designer?

For a moment she simply stared at him before she offered a sad smile. It turned a bit brighter as she shifted on her feet but not much. "Don't worry. I get them too. After a while, I promise it won't hurt anymore."

What?

She hurried down the stairs towards the hall outside and he stumbled after her, confused. What did she mean? Arna tried to reach for his sister, but she continued to slip out of his reach, weaving her way through doorways and out into the yard.

"Ginger what?"

"The hate mail, right? I'll tell dad some slipped through somehow," she said rushing up to their father. Arna's head rang as his sister said things to their father and their father's expression turned grim as he nodded.

Hate mail? His sister thought he got hate mail? No. She knew *he* got hate mail. Already? And they were stopping it? *Why didn't you tell me*.

[*Find it yourself,* Lumak said.]

Like Gingerline, Arna's parents stood in silver and gray. His father in a silver suit, crisp and clean with a long gray jacket in his arms. His mother wore a rose shaped white dress. Sarcoline flattened the white suit that he wore, cuffs and sleeves lined in mint, dragonfly pin at the collar holding his tie in place. For a moment, had Arna not known himself to be the Chosen, he had thought it was his brother. Here Arna stood in a mix-match of colors, without a dragonfly in sight, but his brother fit the part. He wore the colors of Xeyaro, embraced the symbol of the Chosen.

Do you regret not Blessing Arco? Arna asked. His brother was what picture books and sacred texts said the Chosen Child should be: pristine, perfect, untouchable.

[*You are our Chosen and Arco is a brilliant dancer,* Ixxzal said.]

[*His legacy lies elsewhere,* Xeyaro added.]

"What?" Sarcoline snapped when Arna stared into space for too long.

"Please keep your temper Arco. The cameras will be on us the moment we leave," Zaffre sounded more tired than Arna last heard. When was the last time he'd actively been in the same space as his father since his father tested him? This may have been the first time that they'd been in the same place for longer than thirty seconds and even now Arna wanted to bolt.

Without much of another word, Jasione arrived and gave a crisp nod to Zaffre. Guards followed him into the yard. The men were government agents, wellness guards for the city to keep the peace, not private security to protect the house. The once tense emotions on his family's faces turned invisible. It was as if they all put on masks. Gingerline and his parents began smiling, Sarcoline had a blank face. Together, they were ushered to the private hover car, flashing lights brightened all around him.

"You should have died!"

"Why now!"

"Praise be the Gods who have offered us salvation."

"My brother is dead because of you!"

"My sister is dead because of you!"

Dead because of you. People were screaming. Priests and guards lined the street and yard, keeping anyone from getting too close. There were people with signs protesting him. *Imprison Incarnadine now. International Criminal Incarnadine Vivicent.*

Jasione pushed them into the car and Arna wanted to disappear. Gingerline sat next to Jasione, holding his hand, and leaning against him. Sarcoline sat glaring out the window, and their parents discussed in hushed voices.

Arna tried not to look back, but his fingers scanned the web for more of the protests. Videos popped up. There were open letters to the government.

"When do we talk to the world government task force?" Arna asked his father.

No one responded.

> [*Don't worry, darling, they can't get you,* Zaynir's voice was confident, certain.]

Arna wanted to believe them, and he shut his eyes tight.

The car itself was spacious, enough for the whole family, and was the property of the Xeysis government. It hovered over the streets and flew at the second story level high above the people who walked below. It was shaped like a sphere, with metal plating inspired by seeds. Holographic projections made it appear like a dandelion seed floating through the sky.

It did not take much time for them to get to the Celestial Highway: a large expanse of floating metallic and glass petals. It twsited through the sky, radiated its own gravity, and sparked in lightning. It was a river meandering through the skyrail.

The highway system for private transportation was far less expansive than the public transportation. It also required a fee to use, regulated by the government. Very few people had private hover cars, less could rent them due to their cost. Sky streets were made for floating gondolas for goods, cable cars for short travel, and hover buses for longer. Skybuses were used exclusively between petals and great distances in the petal, taking the Celestial highway. They were Arna's only alternative to the trains before.

Private cars had to meander around neighborhoods and to one of the few onramps that existed. The Celestial Highway ran parallel to many of the rail lines. Once on, it was a straight shot to the entertainment district and the recording studio where they were filming the interview.

"They hate me that much?" Arna asked again as soon as they were on the highway. The little talk that was there in the car stopped.

"Ignore them," Zaffre ordered.

"They want me in imprisoned?"

No one was imprisoned unless they were the worst offenders and had hurt too many people. Usually, the taboos were punishment enough for offenders who hurt others, as murder and lying were two of the greatest taboos in the world. Most people were put through rehabilitation to be helped, but imprisonment meant confinement.

"No. No baby, that won't happen," Wenge said, shaking her head and turning in her seat, reaching out to take Arna's hand. She squeezed it.

"Yes," Sarcoline said, and Arna looked at him, not letting go of his mother. "They hate you and believe it's your fault for all the Blessing catastrophes. Did you think that everyone was like the fanatics who fled to the churches to pray their pain away? No. They want you captured, imprisoned, and tried for the crimes they say you committed by dropping the fan."

[*It's not your fault the blame lies with us,* Xeyaro said.]

Arna had a hard time believing that.

"We won't let them," Gingerline insisted, a bit more fight in her voice than earlier that morning.

"They have no case," Jasione offered. "The Splintering was an accident, and no one could have predicted it would happen."

Still, their family had been fined without just cause.

Arna looked down at the crescent moon scars on his left hand and squeezed tight, closing his eyes. They all truly hated him. He dropped his mother's hand and squeezed the right one too, harder.

"Twenty-six million, seven thousand, eighty two people dead because of the direct effects of the lack of Blessings, since the Splintering," Arna said, and the car went silent again. "Trust me. I know it's my fault."

"It's not," Sarcoline said, and Arna looked up to meet Sarcoline's glare. "Their protests are nonsense. You couldn't have known what would happen. And they're only mad because you're the only one they can physically direct their anger towards. They should be angry at the city governments who haven't found solutions. The anger is misplaced."

It wasn't, but before he could respond the car pulled onto a street lined with people. Believers, protesters, concerned citizens. People yelling, with signs. Showing support. Showing their anger. Their words a shouting cacophony as the car slowly pulled into the lot of the studio where he'd be interviewed.

Imprison Incarnadine. Incarnadine is our Savior. Incarnadine I love you. You Should Kill Yourself.

"A farce all of this. I know Cyclamen had a hand in this. What if the guards aren't there?" Zaffre said, worried to Wenge.

Arna was not sure how it was the Cyclamen had control over city affairs. Potentially because of his status as the ten time Philanthropist of the Year? Or maybe he held more power than Arna suspected.

"Ignore him. He can't do much. Remember it's all politics," she reminded him, hand on Zaffre's shoulder and squeezing. "But they can't take away the name and legacy of the Vivicents even if they try."

"It's why we called for the Cardinal, we already knew that Cider was in Cyclamen's pocket," Jasione cut into their conversation. "Rus warned us."

"Luckily," Sarcoline mumbled to himself.

The car stopped in a lot where a congregation of people from the Church of the Harmonious Six stood waiting with guards provided by the Cider, Governor of Xeysis. There were eight Bishops, one Archbishop, and Cardinal Black. All members wore pendants around their neck: vervain and holly.

Tiny cameras whirled around them as they got out, trying to get in his face and far too close. Jasione and Gingerline swiped at them, sending them back into the air or crashing into the ground.

Off in the distance there were priests and bishops of other religions. Arna could see members of the One Truth religion. Unlike the Xeysis Harmonious Six members who wore long robes with spiraling fabric that twisted about them like a cyclone, the Xeysis One Truth priests wore suits of black and white, with sleeves with no adornments and straight legged pants that were flat in color. The uniform was the ugliest thing Arna had ever seen, plain and simple.

The guards were dressed in all silver with purple and gold embellishments, for justice and war. They stood with full faced masks, domed around their head, reflecting all the light. All of their skin covered with batons in their hands, tasers at their side, and no other weapons. All guards in Xeysis had either Fa. or Un. Blessings. Most cities had guards with the same Blessings and training to use them to a startling efficiency in order to maintain order. One guard, the leader of the group, had a gun at his waist: a class-zero weapon.

There was no standing military in any of the six cities. There was no need for guns since the wars in the Fourth Variance. It was a government highly controlled tool that never left the high security facilities without a reason. The gun meant violence was expected. It meant they'd be willing to kill if necessary.

"We have been expecting you," Cardinal Black's voice boomed.

"You got the Church of the Harmonious Six to help us?" Sarcoline groaned as he stepped out of the car.

"I needed someone other than just the city to guard us. Cardinal White did not have the personnel." The resentment in Zaffre's words scraped at Arna's skin.

The crowds filled with people, screaming. Their signs were glowing, as if begging him to notice them. *You should be dead.* Paparazzi and civilians filled the area with flashing cameras and microphones. The City guards surrounded the building, tens of them monitoring every entrance and exit. *You should be dead.* Arna stared ahead to the Archbishop. He did not know her name, but her eyes were filled a mixture of apprehension and adoration.

diediediediediediedie

Once everyone was placed to defend him, they began walking.

"You should be the one dead Incarnadine!"

They walked into the crowd who yelled with signs. Arna trudged forward, slowly, as if in sludge. He curled in on himself, shoulders hunching and chin lowering.

[*Don't,* Pokk warned him.]

Arna stopped himself from activating his Blessings, which would have erased his presence.

[*You need to be seen,* Pokk went on.]

[*You used to love the limelight,* Azza chastised him.]

That was years ago. Back when he hadn't had to hide. Back when people were allowed to know who he was. Back when. . . they loved him. Now they. . . and he could not even blame them. Did he even deserve to be Chosen?

[*We gave* you *the choice,* Lumak said, sternly.]

[*Face this,* Ixxzal urged.]

"Go back into hiding!" Someone yelled.

"I can't do this," Arna whispered to the Gods.

[*Ignore them. Head up. You've faced storms. You can face this,* Ixxzal's words were harsh.]

[*Your family is with you,* Zaynir said. *Trust them to support you.*]

A light hand landed on Arna's shoulder.

"Music helps me," Gingerline said handing him her headphones. She stepped to Arna's other side, flanking him with Zaffre.

"Thanks." Connecting them to his mobile, he searched Ivumalis' name and selected his favorite song seeking a reprieve. Not all silence was soundless; it was tranquility and balance. Soon, the melody of Serenity's Lament was all that mattered.

Arna rolled his shoulders back, lifting his chin. Gingerline kept her hand on his arm, supporting him as the Gods said she would. He relaxed. The Gods could not force mortals to act. They could inspire and suggest through thoughts and dreams, but the way mortals reacted was their own.

Gingerline was there with him. They all were. Was it alright to accept the help?

(It did not have to be done alone.)

Arna walked, focusing on the sound of their footsteps until all the noise in the world drifted away. In the void there was an answer: a gift explained by Alis. The blue lines of rails above were a promise. The spotting of the artificial sun as it refracted across glass, and shadows that bloomed into infinities were a cherished love. Heartbeats like the sturdy flapping dragonfly wings supported him. Feathers drifting and falling, close enough to touch, were safety. Soft breaths that turned into waves, slow and methodical, were protection. The music was soft in his ears, soothing his soul.

Hands open. Hands closed. Hands open.

He was standing in the wastes of the lands discarded by mortals. He was standing in the dark looking up in awe and terror at the storms that could destroy everything. He was standing when the world went quiet, when thunder rolled and threatened to consume all sound for thousands of miles: a single melody conducting the cacophony. He was powerful from dancing in them. He was powerful enough to withstand them. A bit of screaming, a few million eyes on him: it was nothing.

He was trained for this.

Another hand landed on Arna's back. Cardinal Black walked alongside Arna, saying words that Arna chose not to hear nor acknowledge. He swam in the eternity of absence, disregarding all else. Silence was his soft embrace and dearest friend.

Zaffre pulled Arna away and placed himself between Cardinal and Apostle. Their conversation continued behind the melody in his ears.

"Don't touch him."

"We came as you asked, Zaffre. We can leave all the same."

"He is not yours."

"As the lead Cardinal of this city, his security is my top priority."

"Stop arguing. They can hear us," Wenge reminded them.

Arna walked faster, wanting to get into the studio that seemed forever away. He heard whispers praying to Xeyaro, as if by saying them, Arna would grant their wishes. One person reached to touch his sleeve but was stopped by Jasione. His family was there with him. Lowering his gaze he trusted them, thinking of Alis and the way he'd left things.

[*Talk to him.* A soft urging of exploding stars.]

Arna did.

```
Rosy: I wish I could tell you.
Rosy: But I can't
Rosy: I can't have you hating me too.
```

There was no response.

In his periphery Gingerline was staring. He slipped his mobile back into his pocket, her eyes following the form. Then her eyes darted away, and she bit her lip. What had he done wrong now? He. . .

Hands open. Hands closed. The soft lament of serenity telling Rosy that he was safe. Alis' first love song to him.

Hands open. He could not bleed now.

Arna shook his head of the thought. He could not understand what he did to make his sister upset. Not now. Now was for Incarnate Dreams and all the hopes he wanted to give to the world.

He thought of his variation, and options for the songs—visualizing it—as they walked through the front doors and halls. Alis' music in his ears, his dances for the future in his heart, Arna was at peace.

While there were many news stations and channels in Xeysis, they stood in the government-controlled recording studio meant for secure interviews and reports given that effected the city as a whole. It was not large, but safe enough to be protected and monitored. There were more guards inside lining the entrances and exits.

Arna was pushed ahead by Jasione as Zaffre stopped to talk to Cardinal Black. The church members did not follow them past the line of guards into the studio where tens of people watched. Cameras and camera crews sat on floating platforms as Blessing controlled remote cameras buzzed about. Holograms changed in the air, giving images of the commercials, and views from the lenses so that everyone could see how the 3D capture would look. Wenge walked up to the host and producer, bowing in apology as Arna looked to his sister. He gave her the headphones back.

"Better?" she asked.

"No," Arna admitted. He was not sure why he did.

"It will be one day." She smiled, bright like the crescent moon over a river.

"It shouldn't," he told her, taking her for a hug. "I'll make it stop, Ginger. I will."

"I want to believe you." Her tone was reminiscent of the one he heard himself use when the Gods told him he deserved to be Chosen: a level of unwillingness but wanting it more than anything.

For once, she avoided his eyes and said, "I'm going to help mom," before racing off.

Jasione followed her.

Face to face with the cameras before him, Arna's skin crawled. There were hundreds of the protestors waiting outside. Thousands of the church zealots around the world were hoping for him to reveal himself an imposter. Millions of people needed to see him. Not even turning his eyes to the ground and activating his Blessings would make him disappear from their memory. He was already there, already seen.

[*You don't need to hide,* Lumak told him.]

For years, it had been his best way to survive, to assure that those around him lived. It was a habit, that Arna had long given into. He didn't deserve—

[*Don't finish that thought,* Ixxzal cut in.]
[*Trust in us. Trust in them,* Lumak added.]

Could he?

"It's not too bad," Sarcoline said.

His brother was at his side, in part protecting him, in part—Arna hoped—extending another olive branch. Sarcoline said nothing, hands in his pockets, relaxed and confident as he stood shoulder to shoulder with Arna. Arna straighten up next to him, feeling safer next to Sarcoline, despite Sarcoline being five years younger. How the times had changed from the young boy who used to crawl into his bed after nightmares, and hold his sleeve as he walked, scared Arna would disappear.

There were tens of conversations around him. Gingerline and Jasione were checking the 3D holocapture cameras and talking with the crew with disarming smiles. Wenge had made her way to what Arna suspected was their lawyer. The host was waving, and his father was arguing with Cardinal Black.

"We can handle his security better."

"He is my son!"

I want to go home. He could not say it. It was too selfish. They all wanted to go home.

"He's real," someone whispered close enough for Arna to hear.

Arna refrained from turning back, but there were more. A cascade of voices made comments around him.

"Told you he's not a ghost."

"I can't believe he showed his face."

"It's like seeing double."

"No. Sarcoline is far more handsome."

"Afraid of getting caught up?" Sarcoline asked forcing Arna to focus on someone other than those talking about him.

Arna looked at his brother, confused. Had he missed a conversation? Sarcoline cocked an eyebrow at Arna and Arna was not sure what he meant.

Arna responded anyway. "For someone as smart as you, I'd think you'd realize I can't be afraid."

The Gods needed him to be strong. And if he were perhaps stronger, he would be able to do what they asked without pretending.

"Responsibility weighs heavily on you," Sarcoline said before chuckling. "And yet, you still choose to shoulder it all."

There was a brief moment where Sarcoline's expression shifted, brow furrowed, on the brink of some thought that he shook away.

"What. . . " Arna asked as Sarcoline slid his hand out of his pocket tapped at the air.

Sarcoline tried to share a file with him. When had he changed his settings to allow for people to send him things unprompted? Somewhere a giggling bounced through the room like a stream in a distant city and Arna rolled his eyes.

He accepted the file. A list appeared before him of names, ages, and dates.

"Homework?" Arna asked, scanning through the list and using his mobile to scroll down.

"What would you know about that? You dropped out as a teenager." The teasing was almost an attack.

"Is it, or isn't it?" Arna glanced to Sarcoline who was looking rather grim.

"It's a research project on all those who have mastered Blue Rose Fears, and their ages as well as their experiences with understanding and mastering the dances," Sarcoline said turning towards the room again, as if wanting to avoid Arna's interrogation. Arna did not miss, however, how his brother grew stiffer. He was fractured in a way that Arna could not place.

"Were they all Children?" Arna flipped through the pages looking through the charts ignoring the world around him as he stared at the files. Arna changed the opacity settings on his augmentations so that the rest of the world vanished, and the files almost appeared like they were real before him, with no shadows of people walking behind.

Sarcoline sighed and then quietly answered, "No."

"Interesting. Who?" Arna scanned the names looking for ones he may know.

"You don't know?" Sarcoline's gasp was genuine. "But. . ."

"No. I never cared to research if nonChildren had mastered variations." There had to be many of them. Arna found the chart that compared the number of Children who had mastered to nonChildren.

"When looking at the data for all the different variations. NonChildren have mastered Understanding in one variation a total of nineteen times. In recorded history at least."

"Not so special then?" Arna teased Sarcoline, turning the opacity back down to ten percent.

"I never claimed that I was." Sarcoline shifted his weight the way Arna did when he was nervous.

"How old were they?" That was the question that mattered more in the end. Children always mastered quickly. Even the best took at least thirty years to master all five variations: like himself, his father, or Eburnean. Gingerline and Aureolin were close behind.

Most Children were fully mastered through Understanding before they were forty. One day Pervenche and Phlox would be expected to finish their mastery tests in the dances they had yet to complete. There was a certain expectation for Children.

[*In the years with less variations, students often took longer. They had to find masters to teach them,* Pokk spoke up. *Even with A.Reverence there is a need for some guidance.*]

I know. Children still needed teachers.

[Pokk laughed.]

"A lifetime," Sarcoline answered Arna. "Understanding is not so easily broached by those who do not have the A.Reverence Blessing. Figures that having to use your own natural abilities instead of magic makes things more difficult."

Sarcoline sent Arna another document and Arna opened it to see another graph.

"Most completed the first by thirty, through dedicated study of the single variation. The second would come when they had spent equal time."

"And did they lose their mastery in the first variation?" Arna zoomed in on the graph and the numbers. Over a million samples in the data set? How much time had this project taken?

"Yes. Most did," Sarcoline admitted.

Which was also part of the issue. The A.Reverence Blessing helped to keep the variations separate in the mind. The Twenty-Seven Dances to the Gods were woven with magic, intricacies, and so much lore, that too keep it all straight. . . It would be like memorizing a new language that had never been discovered. A.Reverence made the dancer naturally multilingual. And while mastery could not be lost once it was achieved, A.Reverence was the only tool to get there.

"Most but not all?" Arna repeated.

"Those that didn't, had one thing in common."

"And what is that?"

"They took longer to master. Forty to fifty years of age, but they mastered two through Understanding." Without prompting, Sarcoline went on, "Additionally, they mastered more than two variations through Powers."

Like Sarcoline.

There was a short silence between the two of them.

Sacroline shifted, fractured and vulnerable, making a wish that Arna could hear but not answer. Sarcoline wanted Understanding.

"There is not much about them in history." Sarcoline said and Arna closed the files. "Only one existed in the time of the Third Variance. The second and third were in the Fourth Variance. The fourth in the Fifth Variance."

Sarcoline sighed. "The woman that I'm writing my paper on is Hazel Reed. She mastered Blue Rose Fears and Twin Fans."

"Both are danced with two fans." Arna nodded. "You can do it too."

"I— Yeah. . . " There was something else Sarcoline wanted to say.

"What?"

"I'm not sure I can do it. They dedicated everything to it. Traveling the world. Their jobs? Everything. And for what?"

Arna froze. "They traveled?"

"What?" Sarcoline turned to him concerned.

"The world. They traveled the world?" Arna repeated and reached for his brother. A thought from late nights, something he'd asked the Gods for years. A concept left unanswered and unproved. Etched into notebooks: *Understanding for nonChildren? How? To be like the Chosen?*

"Yes, both close to when they mastered." Sarcoline stepped closer, eyes wide, searching for the truth.

Arna was *right*. All things were interconnected. Maybe nonChildren dancers had to travel, just as the Chosen did, to find Understanding. Maybe there was a way to reach Understanding without A.Reverence.

"Why?" Sarcoline asked hurriedly. Arna contemplated how to answer when their conversation was cut short.

"Incarnadine! How are you?" The interview host stepped up.

Arna engaged in the mindless small talk with the host as he thought to himself. *Why didn't you tell me about those dancers?*

[*The world doesn't care about them*, Xeyaro answered in haste.]

Arna did. If he could prove a new way to advance in dance, without the use of A.Reverence. . . It was the basis of his variation. This was the hope he wanted to give the world.

(Defiance.)

[*When your entire life can be dictated on what you are better at, people tend not to go against that*, Pokk continued. *They choose to do what they are gifted in, even if their interests lie elsewhere.*]

[*And those like your brother are often shunned by their communities or have to pretend to be what they are not*, Lumak simply added.]

[*Everyone makes their choice*, Azza went on. *And that choice makes history.*]

Why gift people with skills that they do not want? He asked them. *Why make Blessings so important?*

[*How does one become a Child?* Lumak asked instead.]

You become a Child by getting your respect.

[*Yes, but no mortal-soul will be a Child twice in a row*, Pokk said.]

[*A Child's patron will determine their main Blessing and then we will confer and debate each other's gifts. If we believe someone is being biased, we will step in*, Zaynir sighed deeply.]

And each God has their own criteria for picking a Child and picking Blessings to give to regular mortals. I know.

[*All souls have a history*, Zaynir explained. *Each life shapes a soul differently. I try to sooth lingering feelings and resentment before the next life, but sometimes there are emotions even I can't tame. Some regrets must be faced.*]

Thus, the Gods gifted Blessings they believed would heal that damage.

[*We gift you with what we believe you need. The only ones who we have ever asked to follow our path are the Children,* Xeyaro said. *Yet, all have a choice.*]

[*Like your friend Jasione. He clings to dance despite being a Child of Lumak and knowing he could do so much more,* Ixxzal agreed.]

Pain rippled through Arna. Jasione. . .

[*We blessed Sarcoline the specific skills that we believed best for him in his life. His path is his own,* Xeyaro told Arna. *With his R.Reverence and K.Insight your brother could be an excellent historian. With his Un.Song he could be an excellent official unable to be manipulated by other abilities. His E.Stillness allows him to calm himself and those around him. He has what he needs, nothing more.*]

This information was everything for Incarnate Dreams. He was going to make sure they didn't matter.

He wanted to give people the chance to be anything. All things were interconnected. . .

The expectation threatened to suffocate Arna. Once again, his variation was at the forefront of his thought, forming and shifting before him.

Arna glanced back to his brother, not listening to the host anyway. Sarcoline had only ever wanted to dance and yet the Gods had not picked that life for him. Or was its society that had not picked that path for him?

Blessings matter too much, Alis had said, **but that's why people dream.**

(Sarcoline was Incarnate Dreams.)

"Understand?" the host asked him.

"Yeah." Arna looked back; he had not heard a word.

"You're certain about the pictures Arna?" Sarcoline asked.

Unsure of what Sarcoline meant by pictures, Arna nodded anyway. Whatever they could show him could not shock him. He'd seen and caused too much horror as it was. "It's fine."

"Great! Follow me." The host motioned for him to follow when a notification popped up. Arna nearly tripped over his feet as he read the message.

        Alis: I will never hate you.

The weight on his shoulders vanished and the anticipation for the day's events returned to a simmer. He was nervous, yes, but he had Alis. He may even have Sarcoline. He might have his family. He could get through this interview.

After handing his phone over to his mother, Arna followed the host to the stage and took his seat before the camera. A few more words were said, nothing from the Gods who had gone silent. The crew busied themselves around him. Arna's family gathered, standing apart. Sarcoline had his arms crossed, standing far from Gingerline who said something to him. He shot her a glare, and she shared in his hostility.

Arna had known the two were in contention, but they'd been quick to hide it around him and others. Even now, they quickly mended their act by creating a frigid wall between themselves.

Jasione stood with Gingerline as Zaffre and Wenge stood watching Arna. Zaffre looked worried about the interview, staring at the host and crew. Wenge was concerned for Arna, her silver eyes not leaving his form.

The studio was called to silence. Gingerline smiled at him and pointed at her mouth. Arna smiled back and turned back to the host ready to face his demise. Then the cameras started to blink.

I can do this.

[*It's just like any other interview,* Zaynir agreed.]

Arna had done tens of them before.

"Incarnadine Vivicent," The host cheered. "Rumor has it you are alive."

"I would hope the rumor to be true or else I'd be pretty confused about how I am sitting here," Arna chuckled.

She laughed. "Where have you been hiding, Incarnadine? The world has missed your humor."

Was it still his humor? Most of his childhood interviews had been showing off and talking about what he was working on. People praising him for his progression in the dances. Had he ever talked about himself?

"Here and there," Arna answered. "Around the world."

"They say you've lived in each of the cities."

"I have," Arna relaxed into the seat, trying not to let his nerves show.

She feigned a gasp. "The culture shock must have been huge."

"You learn to get used to it. Each city has its own individual story and energy. Once you know it, you know how to survive and to thrive," Arna let his tone stay confident. Hide all his insecurities, be what they needed him to be.

"And survive you have. For twelve years. On your own!"

"It was not too bad." Arna shrugged.

"Yes." She nodded. "You shocked us all, disappearing like that. Right off the stage, as if you had been spirited away. The whole world was watching!" She sighed dramatically. "And Incarnadine. The world needs to know. *Everyone* wants to know: what did you see that night?"

Before him was a picture of his expression from the infamous moment he stopped. He was there again, on that stage looking out. Behind Sarcoline there was the shimmer of the figures shaped like people. Ixxzal loomed tall. Xeyaro had been waving to him as Pokk stood arms crossed. Zaynir had been looking up to the clock tower. Azza was dancing with Arco, in the crowd, as Lumak told him to run.

There was silence. The music slowed and trickled away. Arna could picture the clock tower's time and the flicker of the candles in the distance. Dread coursed through his veins again: there was no time.

He had to make a choice then and there.

runrunrunrunrunrun

"Incarnadine?" The host snapped him from the memory.

"I. . . I do not remember," Arna answered.

What had made him stare out in absolute terror? Was it the Gods? The flickering candles? The clock tower? The realization that he would have to drop his fans while dancing? Did it matter what had caused him to make the expression?

(He made the choice.)

"It is terrible."

She nodded and the picture changed. Arna's fingertips dug into his palm as he stared at the image of the fan on the stage floor, and his sullen expression at fifteen. It was the last image captured of him before he left. The terror had turned to sorrow and desolation all at once; Arna suddenly remembered what made him make both faces.

imgoingtodieimgoingtodieimafailure

He shook his head off the memory. No. Not right now.

"Incarnadine?" The host asked again. "Are you okay?"

"Sorry." Arna turned from the images on the screen. "I—"

His mother clung to his father. His sister had her hands over her mouth and Jasione was grimacing. Sarcoline looked. . . Was that the same face that Arna had? The same distress? It looked the way he'd seen in mirrors, his brother was reflecting the horror of Arna's memories.

"I know that's not the answer anyone wants, but it's the only answer I have." Arna looked back to the host, steadying his breathing with eight counts.

He controlled his expression, tried to smile, and failed. The memories had painted themselves across his expression and response. He'd been prepped, and guided through what would be said, and still. . . He had not expected his own emotional response.

[*Your emotions are valid,* Zaynir, God of Emotions, comforted.]

[*You are safe. We are with you,* Xeyaro reminded him.]

"What made you decide to come home?"

Arna hesitated. Then he settled into it, smirked and let his confidence bleed even if it were false. The false sky was still beautiful to someone who never saw the real one.

"It was time to come home. I was tired and I could."

Her expression twitched with that. There was an implication that he did not intend, accented by the gasp that rushed through the room. A glance to the priests and Cardinal Black told him that they took it as a sign from The Gods. From what Arna could see, others in the room took it as a confession of his duplicity, that he was a fake, giving him glares and whispering. Whether or not he was the Chosen Child was up for debate. Prophecy or not, everyone rejected change.

He wanted to care but found it impossible. After remembering what he saw that night twelve years ago that made him freeze and create such a look of shock, he didn't care.

No. Never again.

Unlike the others, his family looked relieved. They believed him and that was enough. Their belief kept him alive.

This time they'd be proud.

For the first time in years, as the interview questions continued, Arna's heart began to sway. And for a moment, even if he was not the Chosen the Gods wanted. . . or the best choice. . . he wanted to be the Chosen Child.

For them.

The second variation came after the first, in a way to refine it and to make it better.
Is it wrong to want to make a better world than the one before you?
Is it wrong to seek change?

— On the second variation

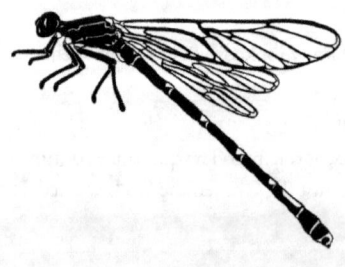

Dance 9

Dissonance

Incarnadine

12 Ixan

66 Days Left

"That was close."
"Next time you won't let it be."
"Next time I won't let it be."

Arna sat on his bed carving the ceremonial mask. During the Ceremony of Chaos, it was worn strapped to the head, the placement changed depending on the variation. Where the ceremonial clothes and shoes were to be made by hand, he'd gotten assistance with tools and supplies. The mask had been all on him, finding the willow wood, tempering it, and working it into shape. He was only happy that it did not have to look good because it would probably be destroyed after he danced.

His mask was supposed to look like it was smiling, but it looked like it was pouting instead. The carved markings in the wood were too deep. It was supposed to represent all the Gods, with antlers of a deer for Ixxzal. Somehow the antlers looked more like teeth, and all together it was possibly one of the ugliest things he'd ever made. His sketches were no better.

He sat in the low light with his tools, his back against his bed. The longer he stared at the mask, the more wrong it became. Something was off other than how ugly it was. Perhaps it was due to it being incomplete, without paint. Yet. . . Arna shook his head.

It would not be another aspect that he was stuck on. He had to be finished with one part. Frustrated, Arna tossed the tools to his bed and screamed out internally.

[*That won't help,* Pokk sighed.]

"How do I fix this?"

[*We've already told you,* Azza complained. *So many times.*]

Then why was it all still hollow noise: a discordant mess of intentions with no real direction?

saffronsaffronsaffron

[Silence.]

"It would be nice if you could be less cryptic." Arna sassed.

[*It wouldn't be fun then,* Ixxzal snarked back.]

Asshole. He screamed again.

[*Think Arna. Visualize the future you want and create it,* Zaynir said, tired and listless.]

Yes. Yes. Arna pulled himself out of his bed, said a prayer, and his room was drenched in darkness. Removing his black out curtains, he peered outside to the crowds that still stood, all without yelling. The chants had died away sometime in the night, or perhaps they thought he could not hear him, so they were not trying. Hiding everything away, Arna changed into something more suitable: a jacket and trousers that would let him blend in with the crowds. He grabbed a few loose papers, his headphones, and his white journal.

Arna tried to keep himself from exploding as he headed out of his room.

What he needed was a change in scenery to practice, and he had a few ideas in his journal about where to go. As he walked down the stairs of the sleeping house, Arna did not expect to find anyone. Despite this, Sarcoline sat at the kitchen eating a sandwich with a blank expression as Arna walked into the living room. He faced their father's first fan.

The first fan was the one both Sarcoline and Arna had been taught with, when they'd learned to build fans. Their father had slowly walked them through the stitching and the carved marks. Arna still remembered tracing his fingers along fabric while being told why each mistake was okay.

Fans are a bridge between the soul and divinity, his father always said. *They are tangible prayers in the hands of mortals.*

Sarcoline eyes were sad: haunted and tired. He was on the verge of breaking down from the looks of it. He stared absently until he turned his focus to Arna. There was a brief moment where time stopped and the two met as equals, with secrets laid bare. The image was quickly erased by confidence, as Sarcoline banished his emotions away.

Their eyes locked.

"Do you ever sleep?" Sarcoline asked.

"No," Arna admitted.

He'd gone years with less than four hours of sleep. Besides he had too much to do in too little time, and he was consistently three steps behind each night despite the progress he made the day before. He was trying to play catch up to the near perfection he had before he left, and instead he was certain his variation was a mess that needed to be rebuilt from scratch.

Rebuilt this close to the date? Arna seethed at his own incompetence.

"Sorry for disturbing—" Arna started an apology. Before he thought, *Wait, why is he awake?* "Why are you—"

"Don't worry about it," Sarcoline cut him off. "Where are you going?"

"I—" Arna was not entirely sure where he was going.

"Nope." Sarcoline cut him off again. "I don't want to hear things that are laced in lies."

The bitterness caught Arna off guard. Sarcoline snorted as he continued to eat.

"Go off. Disappear. Lock yourself in your room. I don't care, but don't say you're sorry, because you aren't. You aren't sorry for running. You aren't sorry for returning without a word. You aren't." Sarcoline wove him off, eating his sandwich slowly, as if Arna was nothing more than a nuisance.

He was right. Arna was not sorry, he couldn't be. He hated that he had done it. And he hated that he hurt millions and was the cause of their deaths. He hated himself so much, and Sarcoline's vitriol only touched the surface.

Arna started back on towards his dance studio.

"Was it worth it?" Sarcoline asked before Arna could head downstairs further.

"What?" Arna stopped.

"Leaving."

"I am where I need to be." Arna said, unsure what was true or not. He turned back to Sarcoline who was slowly finishing his sandwich and leaned forward to stare at Arna.

"I suppose you were." Sarcoline grumbled and stood. He ignored Arna, passed him, and he headed down the stairs to the practice rooms. Arna hesitated and then followed after him. The two walked in silence towards the counter, as Sarcoline grabbed his keys and tossed Arna his.

"Thanks." Arna said. "Why are you practicing this early?"

Sarcoline stopped walking and slowly turned to Arna, "Have you really not been paying attention?"

"To?" Arna asked. There was a long moment where the two just examined each other.

Sarcoline was fuming. Possibly in pressure of wanting Arna to admit to things. Partially out of anger from being abandoned. If the news articles and discussion boards were right, then there was also the pressure too. Sarcoline had to be perfect.

Arna accepted it all.

They all deserved to be angry at him.

Sarcoline glared, with such vitriol that the lights around them began to spark in flashes. How Sarcoline did not notice the blinding popping, had Arna wanting to yell at the Gods for sending him such visions.

Finally, Sarcoline shook his head. Once again, he began to walk, and Arna hesitated. The popping stopped. Shaking his head, he headed towards his own studio door.

[*Follow him,* Ixxzal suggested.]

Arna's hand hovered at unlocking his door, glancing back at Sarcoline. The Gods had their favorites and Arna had his. Out of all the Gods, there were two opinions that weighed the most heavily for him: Xeyaro and Ixxzal. Following Ixxzal's suggestion, Arna walked to Sarcoline's practice room and opened the door. Inside, Sarcoline took the Blue Rose Fears variation fans off his practice rack for dance eighteen.

"Excuse me?" Sarcoline asked as Arna stepped inside.

"You're practicing Blue Rose Fears?" Arna asked.

"I did not invite you in," Sarcoline said. Arna did not respond.

Be comfortable in silence.

Sarcoline bristled for a long few minutes before rolling his shoulders back and glaring up at the ceiling. Seeing that his brother was not protesting, Arna walked fully into the room.

"I'm being tested in a month for mastery in Twin Fans by the DHS," Sarcoline finally broke the silence when it grew near unbearable.

"But you're practicing Blue Rose Fears." Arna repeated, insisting that Sarcoline admitted the truth. Why had he picked up fan eighteen instead of thirteen? Why the cusp song into Understanding instead of the one that started Powers?

"No one other than me dances it anymore, no one teaches it or tests in it unless they're a Golden Generation trying to master all five. Did you know that?" Sarcoline snapped back, deflecting from the answer.

Deflated, Arna nodded. The world hated Blue Rose Fears because of him. Sarcoline was neither smug nor satisfied by Arna's reaction.

"It was your favorite."

"Yes," Arna admitted.

Holly was a close second, but Eburnean loved Holly. Roots and Ends was Gingerline's favorite although Blue Rose Fears suited her more. Zaffre preferred the Original and Twin Fans. Arna had wanted to be original in his choice years ago when he picked a favorite. No one loved Blue Rose Fears back then. Everyone hated Blue Rose Fears now.

"Father doesn't want me dancing it," Sarcoline said. "No one does."

But Arco danced it for Powers every year, as he had since he was fifteen.

[*He looked just like you, and the commentators drove you mad because of how much they were booing him off the stage. Remember?* Pokk said softly, like a garden growing in summer sunlight.]

He was there again, like it was yesterday. It was all anyone could talk about: Sarcoline succeeded in getting the audition over Gingerline with Blue Rose Fears. It was the first time he saw his brother's face in years, a near perfect replica of his own. Sarcoline had looked so brave and so scared at the same time. The fear had long been replaced by visible anger, from the way Sarcoline's muscles were tense and his eyebrow twitched.

The small boy lifted his fan on the night of the Celebrations, glared at the audience, and danced his heart out. They had thrown things at him, knowing that if they hurt him that he'd have to leave the stage. He was not a Child who could use their Blessings to dance seamlessly. Worse, he looked like Arna. Sarcoline had performed perfectly, regardless.

"Original, Blue Rose Fears, Roots and Ends. You still need to finish Holly and Twin Fans through Powers, and you'll have them all."

While it was not impossible, it was strange for a dancer who was not Blessed by Xeyaro to learn all the variations through Powers. It was a lot of work and took too much time. However, Sarcoline was a Vivicent, and the Vivicents were the best dance family in the world. There was a reason they held so much power for so long. Their dancers were the best.

"The current five, yes," Sarcoline corrected. "I am testing for Twin Fans next month."

"How long until you finish Holly?" Arna asked ignoring him. Sarcoline did not answer, and it was all the answer Arna needed. "You're mastered already?"

"Father approved me. Who else can judge me, save him and Ebru? The official test is a joke," Sarcoline scoffed.

"Are you testing in both?" Arna asked.

"No. People don't take kindly to nonChildren passing two mastery tests in a single day. I learned that lesson, I'll pass Holly next year," Sarcoline said. Arna did not remember reading about any sort of controversy when Sarcoline tested and succeeded in both Roots and Ends and the Original variation when he was eighteen.

"So, you are practicing for the auditions?" Arna asked and Sarcoline froze.

"Why? Are you going to stop them?"

Arna's heart leapt. This was a bad idea. He should go. A chorus of chimes rooted him in spot, and the lights flickered overhead, directing Arna's eyes to a specific set of fans. The Blue Rose Fears Understanding fans looked worn. His brother held the eighteenth fans. The fans of the last dance before Understanding.

"You're practicing Understanding?" Arna asked, turning the conversation around.

"How. . ."

His brother's eyes were wide, startled and like a deer in the midst of Ixis at night.

Arna's heart started to race. His brother was mastered through Powers in *five* dances. His brother was attempting to master Blue Rose Fears in *Understanding*. He wasn't a Child. It was unheard of. Variation notes, music, ideas, came to him in a flash. The Gods *knew,* but never told Arna.

Arna needed Sarcoline to show the world what he could do.

[*Incarnate Dreams,* Pokk agreed.]

Yes. It was Incarnate Dreams. He was a direct threat to the culture around the Twenty-Seven Dances. If Sarcoline, a man without the A.Reverence Blessing could reach Understanding. . . Was it truly possible?

[*He'll need to do far more than any Child. If he wishes to,* Azza said, affectionately.]

It was not a no. That meant it was possible. That meant that the one act that people *insisted* could only be achieved with a specific Blessing, did not need to be. If Sarcoline could prove that one did not need A.Reverence to complete the dances through twenty-four, what would that mean for the world?

No Blessing would be tethered any longer. Any Blessing could be used for anything.

(Defiance.)

sacrificesacrificesacrificesacrificesacrificesacrifice

"Test in both," Arna said breathless. His brother was so close to Incarnate Dreams, living it rather than simply being a muse for Arna. This was unfathomably great. It was proof Arna was right.

"What?" Sarcoline gaped at him. "I can't. Last time. . . That's asking for drama."

"Just wait for when you prove mastery in Understanding," Arna joked. His heart was racing at the thought.

"I can't." There was terror in the words and misery in Sarcoline's eyes despite his blank expression.

"But you've tried." Arna's mind was spinning, his Blessings wanted to activate. Music was sounding. The variation was formulating.

"Yes but. . ." Sarcoline shook his head, unconvinced.

"How far are you?" Anticipation rose in his blood. How *good* was his brother? How far was he? How close were they? How long would it take? If Arna could help his brother reach Understanding now. . . No, it would potentially take too much time. He'd have to do it after Arna danced, but after. . . Sarcoline could reach it after.

Sarcoline bit his lip. "I can't master nineteen."

"In Blue Rose Fears?" Arna stepped forward wanting to test his brother, wanting to see him dance it.

"Original. Twin Fans. Roots and Ends. Holly. None of them. I just. . ."

"But you think you can with Blue Rose Fears," Arna said feeling, *knowing.*

It would be Blue Rose Fears. There was no one in the world who Understood the variations better than Arna. Azza had told him everything about it in their ravings about Vervain. Arna could feel the dance the way that Azza said the Gods could feel the dances. He *knew.*

Sarcoline grabbed his fans tight, a distressed laugh caught in the back of his throat. He said more to himself than Arna, "Why does this always happen to me?"

"What?" Arna asked.

"Nothing. Leave. I have to practice." Sarcoline shook his head and pointed the fan towards the door shutting it with a snap and waving Arna out. Arna ignored him.

"Vervain the Blythe created Blue Rose Fears after twenty-seven years of effort."

Arna began the lecture, as it had been told to him tens of times in dark solitary rooms. The might of creation wrapped itself around him, as if Azza was there with him, standing and speaking through him.

"Vervain the Blythe was cast from her clan to die after she was infected with a deadly plague. In all that time, her mother saved her life and she worked to get back her strength. For twelve years she traveled, injured but learning. This is the root of Blue Rose Fears."

Sarcoline gaped at him.

"The dance shows the worst in mortality. The worst of mortals and Gods. The terrors that people choose to shy away from. It is the most layered of the dances. Holly's variation is happier in its complexity compared to the unfathomable deepness of Blue Rose Fears."

"Arna."

"Blue Rose Fears makes you face yourself, and your closest secrets. You have to go to a horrid place to Understand it."

"Arna!"

"Named after the Blue Roses that saved her life, the dance digs deep into fear and shows so much wonder after."

"Are you done?"

"Dancers have avoided it through all of history, not just now," Arna said all in one breath.

His hands were itching to help Sarcoline hold the fans properly. How would it feel to help guide his brother? Even if he could not hold the fan himself. This would be the closest he got in years to being able to control them.

"Twin Fans is more avoided, historically," Sarcoline disagreed, stepping back.

"Twin Fans is simpler, slower, and a beautiful show. Most choose the Original over it or one of the flashier two fan dances," Arna stepped closer again.

Why was Sarcoline so adamant about distancing himself from Arna? Arna was just trying to help him.

"Like Holly." Sarcoline nodded. "Elegant and complex, Holly shows the perfection as a commentary on the horrors of the world. I know."

"Holly is the opposite of Blue Rose Fears, Arco. Holly shows you beauty to make you question it, to think about what could be done better, and how to be better," Arna lectured, standing in the center of the room and motioning Sarcoline to stand next to him. "If you have Blue Rose Fears done, Holly should be done within the year."

"It won't," Sarcoline disagreed, placing the fans back on the rack. "Besides, Blue Rose Fears shows mortality's strengths and beauty despite the deep and complex horrors. They're not full opposites."

"All the same you can do it. You, the man who has researched the starting of the cities, Xeysis as your cradle, guided by Vervain herself, can understand Blue Rose Fears." Arna was frustrated.

What was his brother doing? He could help if Sarcoline would just stop being so stubborn. He had to know Arna could help.

"What will that give me?" Sarcoline asked, sitting on the floor instead and glaring up at Arna. "Nothing. It can't fix anything. Xeyaro won't love me."

"Understanding can change everything."

And Xeyaro's was not partial to Blue Rose Fears.

[*I am,* Xeyaro protested.]

Really? You mention a different Chosen far more.

[There was laughter like the sound of chimes.]

Everything was interconnected with the Gods and Understanding was about recognizing that complexity.

"Understanding?" Sarcoline repeated before growling, "That's rich. What? You want to rub it in my face that much?"

"Contrary to popular belief, mastering Understanding is the easiest of the processes in the long run. Either you get it, or you don't. It is as simple as mastering the steps. You have to understand the dances and the creator in order to reach Understanding. Once you master nineteen you will master twenty, within hours." Arna walked up to his brother and stared down.

"Weeks," Sarcoline corrected, leaning back on his hands and tilting his head in indignation towards Arna. As if he was looking for a fight.

"Hours," Arna insisted rolling his eyes and not engaging in the anger.

It had taken Arna days to master the dances upon mastering the first, but something told Arna that Sarcoline would be different.

"Even Ebru took days to master all the Understanding dances in a variation after mastering the first," Sarcoline looked towards the door, anywhere but Arna's eyes. Frustrated, Arna wanted to make his brother even angrier if it meant he'd look at him and listen.

Arna sighed dropping down to squat in front of Sarcoline. "And you are a good dancer."

Sarcoline's face changed to disbelief, head snapping back in attention to meet Arna's gaze. Arna had seen the articles. Everyone called Sarcoline a great dancer in mockery or a good dancer in scorn. Arna meant it. He believed in Sarcoline's skill, and Sarcoline had heard.

"You don't mean that," Sarcoline murmured, eyebrows creasing in concern.

"I do."

Any non-A.Reverence Child who could complete the Powers of the Gods section of the Dances were considered a Great Dancer by most of society. Most nonChildren only ever mastered one of the variations through Powers.

Sarcoline had mastered all five that existed through Powers.

Could Sarcoline master Understanding for all the dances? Sarcoline was not a Child. No one other than Children mastered all the variations in Understanding. It just wasn't done. However. . . Arna placed his bets on three, Holly, Blue Rose Fears, and Incarnate Dreams. That was how good Sarcoline was. Blind faith was overwhelming him, but he did not doubt the feeling.

[*Follow it,* Zaynir agreed.]

For the first time since being back, Arna wanted to do it without their prodding. Despite everything, Arna loved dance and Sarcoline. . . he loved dance too.

"You say that as if you've seen me dance." Sarcoline stated, shaking his head, standing and walking past Arna. He clicked on something in the air, and music began to play in the studio. He began to stretch as if Arna was not there at all.

"The whole world has watched you dance. You and father are the only two who have never lost their position in the Celebrations. You've been dancing Powers in Blue Rose Fears since you were fifteen. No one knows it better than you." Arna stopped the music, with a wave of his hand, glaring at the holostereo and back at Sarcoline. "You know the steps."

"It was *your* dance," Sarcoline turned over his shoulder, expression blank as if Arna no longer mattered. "The rest of the world might be afraid of it, but dad would not teach me. Because it was *yours.*" Sarcoline then said to himself more than Arna, "Even when it was my favorite too."

As Sarcoline returned to facing the mirror, his expression flickered. A longing rather than spite, on full display before he noticed that Arna was watching him in the mirror and his emotions vanished.

He wants it, Arna lived the look in Sarcoline's eyes. It was the same one he'd given himself in the mirror: the drive to succeed in Understanding no matter what.

Long ago Xeyaro had told him that the journey to mastery comes to each dancer in its own way. *Does he need to be like me?*

[*Like you?* Pokk asked.]

A pilgrimage? Is that the secret for nonChildren and those without A.Reverence to achieve Understanding? Arna needed to know if his conjecture was right.

[*The Chosen must go on the journey to discover what is not yet known,* Pokk asked. *Your Blessings cannot provide you guidance for that which does not exist.*]

All Chosen had to go to experience the world despite having A.Reverence. Usually, A.Reverence allowed a Child to understand the Dances the way the creator intended them, with the complexities. It took time: practice with a teacher who Understood and mastery over their Blessing. A.Reverence was designed to give them insight to things that were near impossible to comprehend for other mortals. And Sarcoline was not like Children; he was like Arna.

Arna had Understood the existing five variations easily thanks to A.Reverence, but in order to make something new he had to delve into the unknown. He had been guided by the Gods, but it was not magical. They could not force him to recognize anything. He had to learn it, reach for it, and shape it within himself. Sarcoline did not have A.Reverence. He would not get assistance from the divine to comprehend. But he could do it. It would just take time. He needed to experience the world, face the unknown, see the truth of possibility. If Sarcoline wanted to Understand, he was going to have to be guided.

[*Will you guide him?* Xeyaro asked.]

Could he?

dontbelikeSaffrondontbelikeSaffron

"And yet you think I can master Understanding in a few hours?" Sarcoline scoffed.

"A few hours after you master nineteen, yes. This is amazing. You can—" Arna hesitated.

Sarcoline's eyes were blazing, and his cheeks were red. Arna had seen the look on himself enough times in mirrors to know that Sarcoline was embarrassed. Backing up, Arna gave him space. Unspoken conversations fell against the floor.

Arna had the path forward, why wouldn't Sarcoline listen?

[Hypocrisy is a funny thing.]

Arna was right, but Sarcoline was not ready to hear it.

It was time for Arna to leave and thus he headed to the door.

[*Those who are not our Children, have destinies that they can pick for themselves. Anything is possible for him. It is why we did not Bless him. Possibility,* Lumak said, zealously.]

Those who were Children were chosen for a path, a destiny, following their God. The path could change forms, but they'd always serve their God in the end. Sarcoline was free of that and given the possibility to become anything.

That was why he was a good dancer.

When Arna left his own studio hours later, Sarcoline was nowhere to be found. He found his sister sitting in her own dance room.

"Where is Arco?" Arna asked.

"Shopping. I think?"

Arna nodded. He could talk to Sarcoline later that night. There was an energy in Arna's bones that had not been there in weeks. It was the precipice of an understanding. If he had to start over from scratch on his variation, then he needed to do it thoroughly. Every time he had in the past, he started with the subject, the theory, and in order to refine that: he needed to explore. In most cities, he placed himself into the shoes of those who lived there. It was how he found all his dream dance spots. It was the way to Understand.

"Where are you going?" Gingerline called after him.

"I'm going to talk to Ven," Arna lied, the shock coursed through his body so strong that he should have flinched, but he bit it back with a laugh.

It was nothing compared to the pain of losing a Blessing or choking from lying to Eburnean.

"Are you really?" Gingerline chased after him.

"I'll be back. Okay? Trust me," he said, and she stopped running. When she nodded Arna activated all his Blessings for hiding and vanished from sight.

Headphones on, Ivumalis music blasting, Arna slipped past the protesters and guards too easily. They were not expecting him to leave through the front door alone, nor were they prepared for him to use his flourished Blessings. He walked through the crowds without touching a person, eyes held on the ground until he pushed through them all and moved down the street. He let his visualizations guide him forward. The city was his to take, and his to relearn.

His phone buzzed.

> Alis: To my surprise. Bluebell sent her samples.
> Rosy: What

Alis sent a link to the samples, private so only Arna could listen. As he did, the world appeared in a new way, and he let himself explore what he had been keeping back. The song itself was an Ivumalis song, deeply layered. It was also a song for him, almost a guiding light. It was nearly perfected, missing a few sounds and the final touches of both voices but it was raw and real.

> Rosy: Our best choice to date
> Alis: I cannot believe she got it to us on time.

Walking without a goal and messaging Alis. Arna was more certain of himself than he had been in weeks.

> Rosy: A blessing truly. My prayers were answered.
> Alis: Yeah. . .
> Rosy: What?

Alis sent an image to Arna and Arna stopped walking to read it.

> Bluebell: Your husband will kill me if I'm late again
> Ivumalis: He won't. He's harmless.
> Bluebell: I'm not going to test that theory.

Arna laughed.

> Alis: Please don't tell me you threatened her.
> Rosy: She's in love with you. I had to stake my claim.
> Alis: You have no claim.
> Alis: Despite what everyone thinks.

Arna smirked at the teasing.

> Rosy: Should I remind you?
> Alis: Please do

Arna went leaned against a building, standing in the shadows, flipping through the album of dirty photos he'd taken but never sent Alis before. He clicked one and sent it, smug.

That should rile him up.

whoishewhoishewhoishe

What if Alis was someone he already knew? He was certainly not Pervenche or Jasione. But what if he was—

"Arna?" Aureolin called out to him, freezing him in his tracks.

Arna jumped, grasping his mobile and glancing about, heart racing.

She couldn't have seen what he was doing. Only he could, that was the benefit of the augmentations, yet his heart raced.

She was standing outside a restaurant, across the walkway, dressed with a crown of orange flowers in her hair. Her brown dress was loose and shaped like a oversized mushroom, with folds that moved as she walked over.

The strangers she left behind looked around confused.

How did she see him?

[*You got sloppy,* Pokk laughed in tandem with Aureolin, their voices mixing.]

He had a feeling they were the reason he was seen. Resigned frustration started to mutate into resentment. Every time he'd seen her since he got back, she was always silent and staring at him, as if she could see through him. He did not want to talk to Aureolin in fear of her Un.Mirrors, that had the possibility of being able to do just that.

"Why are you alone?" Aureolin groaned grabbing him by the arm and dragging him in a different direction.

"Not so rough," Arna hissed looking back to the group of girls she had been with. Other friends?

"Escape at night. Or do it in the morning. Do not do it in the middle of the day." She started down the street, with a harsh bite to the end of her words.

"It is the morning," Arna disagreed looking to the sky, unsure where the sun was in the false blue.

"It's the middle of the day."

Had he lost that much time? He searched beyond the blue to the glittering city masked in haze. Based on the color it was a bit whiter, like the middle of the day. Time was harder to establish in a city that was different petal to petal. He had not expected to get so lost in thought.

She sighed, letting him go. "What are you doing?"

"How's the dance group? That's who those girls were, right? You've been together for five years?"

Aureolin smiled but did not call him on ignoring her question. She never did. Aureolin of the past had a way of reading people and their intentions. However, this Aureolin was strange. The old her would have demanded he answer until he did.

"They're amazing: my sisters. I'll introduce them to you sometime."

Arna nodded. He didn't know much about Aureolin's group, other than it was a dance group that also doubled as a pop group, sometimes. There were seven of them and she was the group leader. He had never found a song with Aureolin singing in it, which made him doubt that the whole group was involved in the music part.

"Why did you leave the studio?" Arna asked.

Why was she not becoming a raging inferno like the past? How was she so calm and collected? Had time really changed her that much?

"It became... unbearable." She had a problem saying the words, a worse topic than the previous one.

Arna thought of empty rooms, chatter-less halls, dance-less studios. Vivicent manor was lifeless.

"I'm just happy you're back," she said, placing her arm on his, "But now, let's get you home because there are people that are less happy."

They walked in silence and as much as Arna thought she would press him, she did not. They were strangers walking together and Arna did not try to fix it. A chasm had opened up between him and all the Golden Generation, caused by his own hands.

Later.

After he saved the world, he could ask her more about her life and her great-grandmother and all the things he missed.

(After?)

buthewasgoingtodiediediediediedie

saffronsaffronsaffronitwasanaccident

Inspiration slipped through his fingers and faded into ash.

When they got to the Vivicent manor she gave the guards a salute and pushed him into the house, rushing away to her dance practice. He waited a few more minutes before walking back out, saluting the guards, and disappearing again. They did not move to stop him.

He returned to his mission. Arna headed in the opposite direction of Aureolin. He had to find inspiration again.

In a haze, Arna walked, losing track of time and place once more. The city was beginning to cave in on him, curving in and making him want to flee. It was all new, all different: filled with winding confusing paths, without the familiar smells and sights. The streets were lined in chaotic and violent, angry art. The people around him sang sad love songs and songs of death.

Despite the Ivumalis music ringing in his ears, he was suffocated and confined. Why was something so familiar, so different? How come he couldn't find its rhythm as he had in the other cities? He'd been in Xeysis for weeks.

He thought of his variation, stuck again, no matter how he tried to brute force it. The little inspiration he had before was gone. He tried to search for it by retracing his steps before he saw Aureolin and failed. There was too much chaos in his life around him. Everyone wanted him to fix things instead of focusing on the dances. The dances were where his focus needed to be. He could only fix what he broke if he fixed the world first.

The faces of his family and friends circled his mind. What did they want? What did he want with them? Why had the Gods sent them back to them early? What part of being with them answered the question and what happened after he danced? With him and them?

[*You need this,* Zaynir told him. *Keep visualizing.*]

Something felt like ignoring his dance that he was supposed to visualize and practice, thanks to Zaynir's insistence. It was finding a patch of grass, sprawling out, and watching the sky. Above him were living districts on other rose petals, where other small shops, schools, and communities prospered. He thought of the people who lived in the houses and their lives. He thought of his friends, of his family, of Alis.

Something felt like wanting to cry at how nothing was the same despite how desperately he wanted it to be. Something felt like wanting to scream at his family to just accept him. Something felt like wanting everything to return to the way it was, but it never could because he ruined it and there was no way to fix it. The months would be treacherous.

Finally, Arna looked at his mobile as it buzzed.

```
Alis: Hey. You're not responding.
Alis: Did something happen?
Rosy: Something happened yeah. . .
Alis: Are you okay?
Rosy: Did you like what I sent?
```

```
Alis: Don't distract now. What's going on?
Rosy: I'm just nervous. I'm about to do something that
      is going to make a lot of people angry.
Alis: Why?
Rosy: I'm the only one who can fix this. I have to do it.
Alis: Fix what
```

There was a long moment where Arna was frustrated, unsure how to answer.

```
Alis: If it helps. . .
Alis: I'm also the only one who can fix things over here.
Rosy: What? What happened to you?
```

Alis was typing, before the next set of messages rolled in all at once.

```
Alis: Don't worry.
Alis: I'll explain one day.
Alis: Sorry. I have to go.
```

Arna read over the messages multiple times trying to process them as the sun above him disappeared. There, hovering above him, scowl on his lips, was Eburnean. Of all the people he had expected to find him, it had not been Eburnean. The wind spiraled around Eburnean as the bronzed light of the fading day warmed his otherwise pale skin.

"Yes?" Arna placed his mobile down and glared.

"Why are you out here?" Eburnean crouched down, hands in his pockets. He wore a long shirt and flared shorts, his calves exposed, and Arna did everything not to stare at them.

"Why are you here?" Arna asked, keeping his eyes on Eburnean's eyes.

"Charming. I had thought your cockiness was because you were freaked. Turns out it's just the way you are. Somethings haven't changed."

Eburnean's eyes darted in the air, before returning his focus to Arna specifically.

"Why are you out here? You don't live on this petal." Arna asked.

"And neither do you. But surprisingly, for some reason. I had a feeling you'd be here." Eburnean smiled softly, his voice like a melody almost as if he were serenading Arna.

"What? Were you searching for me?" Arna clenched his fists and kept his eyes locked despite how close Eburnean was getting. Despite how much he wanted to. . . Arna smirked and leaned closer. "Keep talking like that and I'll think you *care*."

Eburnean, began to kneel, placing his hand on the ground beside Arna's head and meeting Arna halfway, "If I were following you, you'd never know."

"You'd have fun doing it too," Arna reached up to place a hand behind Eburnean's neck, tracing the vow mark that was hidden. He tilted his head daring Eburnean to go further.

"Seeing you squirm is what I live for," Eburnean's breath tickled Arna's ear and then he backed away. As he did, Arna saw Pervenche, standing staring at the both of them. What? Arna sat up rapidly. Pervenche could not have seen that. Arna choked down the embarrassment seeing the smug smile on Eburnean's lips. He won this round.

"You owe me Arna. Don't make a scene the next time I see you." Eburnean backed away, standing, and starting off.

"I owe you nothing," Arna yelled after him, heart racing and irritation freeing itself to cool his head and body. Ignore the provocation.

"You owe me the world," Eburnean said winking, and walking past Pervenche. He said a few things to Pervenche before leaving. There was a long momentary pause, before Arna sighed.

"I don't understand him."

Arna scratched his head and folded his legs unsure how to address the awkwardness. He doubted Pervenche wanted to speak with him.

"None of us do." Pervenche shook their head. "But he's always been like this since we were young: acting like he's in love with you. If he isn't trying to kiss you to rile us all up, is he even Ebru?" Pervenche laughed at their own comment before their tone changed to a more serious one. "He is just like that. . . pushing us away."

Pervenche grimaced and Arna chose not to ask. Something had gone down between them that could not be easily solved. Pervenche's face was devoid of anger. They appeared more tired if anything.

"Ginger messaged the group. Aureolin said she delivered you home, but Ginger said she could not find you. I told her you were with me so she wouldn't spiral. Don't make me lie for you. It might not kill me, but it does still hurt."

Arna frowned. He never thought of them as anything more than jolts. . . but perhaps that was because he had faced worse.

"You didn't have to."

"You know I will."

Arna searched behind Pervenche for Amaryllis.

"She's not here," Pervenche said, stepping closer. Wind flowed through the cutouts in their indigo top, making it billow and flutter like butterfly wings.

Their eyes were locked on each other. Arna was not sure what to say. He didn't want to date Pervenche again, but staring up at them, he wanted to know them. For a split second he wanted to be their friend again, for real, and understand what they were going through.

S.Mirrors was his anchor, but it did not mean they had to be lovers.

But he wanted them to be friends. The silence filled with a thousand words he wish he could say. *I want to talk to you. I want to know you again.* He wanted to be in Pervenche's life again.

[*Are you visualizing?* Zaynir asked.]

Arna grimaced. According to the tabloids, Pervenche no longer lived at home. Pervenche always swore they would. Their stepmother hated them. Their stepfather was a lazy man who used them for clout.

Arna was not the same fifteen year old boy and Pervenche was not the same person either. They had grown magnitudes apart, and the depth of that change faced Arna in all its glory. For a second, Arna was at a loss of what to do. Pervenche had found him, and they couldn't even talk.

"You love her?" Arna asked them, breaking the silence first.

"I do. Did you ever love anyone else?" Pervenche asked with a small voice, offering their hand to Arna who sat in the shadows, isolated from the world.

Love? Arna blinked. Serenity's Lament played in his head and Arna's heart fluttered. Alis. . .

[*Yes,* Ixxzal smugly agreed.]

When Arna fell in love with Pervenche, it was like plunging into a lake headfirst: consuming and all at once. His love for Alis was different. It was the rising tide brushing over his feet as he stood on the sands of the coast.

For years he had tried to ignore it bubbling and threatening to sweep him away, and by the time he fully accepted it, all he could do was submerge himself further and deeper. He loved Alis, deeply, and irrevocably. Yet, it was never supposed to work. They didn't even know each other.

Arna's heart ached.

Alis would never love him once he knew that Rosy was Incarnadine Vivicent.

[*How do you know?* Ixxzal asked.]

[*Let them talk,* Lumak chastised.]

[*Stop interfering. We agreed to give him space,* Zaynir insisted.]

[Distant chimes swelled to the softest of songs.]

"You did?" Pervenche asked, eyes widening.

Arna wore a half smile, not wanting to admit it.

Someone gasped. "Incarnadine Vivicent?"

Fuck. Arna jumped to his feet.

"Damn Azza," Arna cursed, searching for the source of his name. Tens of people were staring at them.

[Azza roared like an wave.]

Without another word, Pervenche and Arna started running. *Where to go?* Arna flourished his already active Blessings but as he did, Pervenche took the lead.

[*Follow them,* Lumak ordered.]

They led Arna on through the park towards the streets and through the streets past the tenement apartments and shops all the way to the freestanding community housing. Unlike the private communities, where the Vivicents lived, Arna was more at home running through the rows of buildings where vines with drying clothes draped between rooftops, and ivy crawled up the walls to different apartment windows.

Blessing activated, Pervenche jumped up and over a wall. Arna hopped after them, running up the wall and flipping over it. As he landed, Pervenche hopped over another. Arna chased Pervenche through backyard gardens, across walls, up balconies, and over rooftops.

"You've done this before?" Arna asked.

"Amaryllis likes to do free running in her spare time. For photography," Pervenche answered jumping down and rolling.

In the skyscape the light faded from the rose petals that reflected the darkening cerulean sky above.

"This way."

Pervenche led him to a back alley and then to a garden behind a two-story private home. Roses trailed up the back of the house towards the large red roof. Holly and vervain grew along the sides. A trellis of wisteria and lights covered a patio of beautiful white stone.

Pervenche said nothing as they led Arna through the garden. Amaryllis grew in towering bushes, creating a labyrinth. Small rivers flowed through the plants, and there was a tiny micro forests near the pathways. There was a lake of lotuses and paths of lilies, roses, tulips, orchids, and lavender. Dragonflies and butterflies danced through the garden.

Pervenche's hand glided across the plants, moving them out of the way so they could move to the door. As a child, Pervenche killed everything they touched, which was why Wenge kept them out of the Vivicent garden. Tough, dependable, honest, that had been Pervenche. Pervenche was like summer rain, chilly at first and comfortable in time.

"You chose to run instead of fighting?" Pervenche asked plucking a violet, shaking their hand from the slight jolt they had to have felt from breaking a taboo.

"Fighting would get me nowhere."

When Arna was a kid, he fought those who angered him. Had Arna been that person, he would have acted against them and stood his ground taunting them. He had once been too confident for his own good. This Arna was more comfortable keeping his eyes down, and his voice back. It was better to disappear than to be seen.

"Stay here until you think it's safe." Pervenche opened the door. "Amaryllis!"

Arna's heart thudded in his chest. This was Amaryllis' house? He slowly entered into the house with Pervenche. As Arna walked in, all the air in his body escaped him. They entered into a kitchen lined with open cabinets and herbs that spilled over the shelves. They were white wood with hand painted flowers. A small wooden table sat with a pot of still steaming tea. Ivy and vines, flowers of all kinds, lined the walls, the floors, a greenhouse of exotic and beautiful plants.

"I brought Arna," Pervenche said walking in.

Beyond the hanging pots and ivy there were paintings and photographs. There were images of mountain ranges Arna had only seen online and cities he remembered like it was yesterday. There were places that Arna had always wished to dance, in high definition and color. Created in oil, charcoal, and acrylic, there were canvased prints of all sizes. Recently hand developed photographs hung along clothes lines crossing everywhere. They were scattered on the floor and piled in corners. There were canvases and pictures everywhere and anywhere that there was space. The air was tinted in the memory of flowers and sweet fruits.

In the middle of the room was Amaryllis, hair tied up and photographs in hand as she hung them to dry.

[Distant bells and birds sang.]

"He's going to stay here for a bit. People are chasing him," Pervenche said. They slid the violet behind her ear. She nodded. They said, "I have Archery."

They then turned to Arna. "Tomorrow 9pm, meet at my range, we can talk and catch up on what we missed over the years."

Arna nodded listlessly, as if stuck in a dream. Pervenche left out the front door, shutting it behind them. Arna and Amaryllis were left alone. His eyes darted to anywhere he could look that was not at her. On the wall he found a portrait of an old woman: ancient in her bones, blind in the eyes, dark brown skin, slick straight black hair. She looked wise beyond her years.

"That's Chamomile. She was my teacher. This was her studio before she died," Amaryllis said walking up to him.

Arna looked at the art everywhere, another piece caught his eye and his breath hitched again.

Chamomile was an artist whose paintings were considered to be some of the most expensive paintings in the world. There was little known about her online, other than excellent photographs of her work, which Arna suspected were taken by Amaryllis.

"Was she a Child?"

"No. She was just a woman who had seen the world and has tried to replicate it to no avail."

Arna approached the painting. It depicted Arna dancing when he was a child, standing on the stage with his fans bright in the sky and eyes looking up with such a haunted look in them.

"These are good," Arna said in awe. A look around the room told Arna that she had lived a lush life: traveling the world and seeing things he could not fathom. Her art was a passion.

"Yes," Amaryllis said, resigned. "She is not a Child, but I have been able to sell many. Pity that people only appreciate her art now that she's gone. She was brilliant, or I suppose. . . only good."

Arna flinched at the word. How could such a positive word be used to hurt so many people?

[*It should be changed,* Pokk, God of Change, agreed.]

[*Are you visualizing?* Zaynir, God of Emotions, asked.]

"This painting is called The Moment," Amaryllis said.

[*She's watching you,* Lumak suggested.]

Arna internally groaned. He finally looked at Amaryllis who tilted her head, examining him without a word. She then motioned him to follow, and he did so.

"I've had this studio for three years since she left it for me. Coco said you're restless at home, and Ginger doesn't want you to disappear. If you like, you can come here if you want to get away. Everyone else does," Amaryllis said leading him up the stairs to other rooms.

"That's my dark room, don't go in there. That's my office. This is storage, but you can use this one," she said opening a room that had a desk and walls filled with portraits of flowers and nature still life photography.

"Make yourself at home. I'll be downstairs hanging pictures."

Without another word she left him behind and headed down the stairs with a skip in her step. For a moment, Arna was unsure what to do, when he caught sight of the room that she pointed out as her office, the door slightly ajar. From where he stood, he could see inside.

Hands open. Hands closed.

Curious, a chorus of bells led him forward, and he pushed the door open further.

Hands opened.

Tentatively he stepped in, eyes widening and heart stopping. Photography lined the wall in all sizes. Sarcoline was dancing in the snow. Sarcoline was dancing on The Stage. Sarcoline was smiling. Sarcoline was with Ven. There were paintings too. Sarcoline was sleeping in flowers. Sarcoline was sitting at a table with one knee up and half asleep.

Each had a name: The Dancer in the Forest, The Dancer on Stage, The Dancer with Friends, The Dancer Sleeping.

There was a painting of a boy, spinning in the garden of flowers, a smile on his face and tears in his eyes. There were scratches on his cheeks and bruises on his arms. His head was bandaged and there was a trace of blood in the white. His clothes were a mess, but he was alive. The image was full of vibrance and energy and love: love for the art of it.

The Dancer.

"He was both of our muse, me and Chamomile," Amaryllis said from behind Arna. He jumped.

"I'm sorry."

"Tea?" She placed the mug in his hand and smiled. "He's Ven's muse too. Coco's drive to succeed pushes us all to do greater things. Ven was the one who designed the space. Do you like it?"

Arna was not sure what to say. What he said was certainly not correct, "He was crying in the garden."

"Dancing." Amaryllis corrected. "It was the second day we met. He had gotten a rough beating by some older boys. He came here with me. She gave us green tea and chocolate. It does not heal all, but it helped."

"When you met?" How long had they known her? There was nothing online about her and Sarcoline being friends.

"I found him lost, as most folk are." Amaryllis said and Arna almost was certain she was talking about him.

"Why. . ." Arna was not sure what he was asking. Not sure she could answer.

"Most people hate Coco because he dares, to say things people don't like. Dares to do things that people want him to stop. People take their anger out on the wrong people all the time, and he was playing a dangerous game, dancing when the whole world told him stop," Amaryllis shrugged. "But now he never has to stop."

Arna blinked.

"You're back. Now, Arna. Drink your tea. Don't let it get cold," And as suddenly as she appeared, she turned again to leave.

When Arna arrived home it was much later, and Arna had missed his first afternoon practice since returning to Xeysis. He was off kilter, as if his entire orbit had been fractured. Amaryllis had not said another word to him as he sat in the upstairs room alone. Nor when he left. His emotions were a mess, a whiplash of inspiration that was causing a discordance in his body. His hands were an aching mess, albeit not bloodied.

[*It's time to begin again,* Lumak pressed.]

[*Visualize,* Zaynir repeated.]

Arna stumbled into the hall to find his entire family and Jasione standing, talking to Sarcoline. There were bags on the floor at his feet. He was dressed in a mint jacket and perhaps the best dragonfly inspired clothes that Arna had seen: iridescent and flowing like wings that were swirling in a rainbow of colors with each movement. Sarcoline was fashionable, but Arna could not help but wonder where Sarcoline got the money for his clothes. The Vivicents clearly did not have the funds, and he said he didn't have a job.

Was he a brand ambassador? Zaffre and Arna used to be years ago. He was not the best in his fashion knowledge, but he would have known if their family had sponsors. Based on their family's state, the answer should have been none. Who would sponsor them now?

"Where are you going?" Arna asked.

"He's going to Podiel?" Jasione spoke the statement as a question.

Sarcoline cocked an eyebrow at Arna as the whole room looked at him. *Have you really not been paying attention?* Arna's cheeks burned as he remembered Sarcoline's question from the morning. No. He had not been.

"Be safe," Wenge told Sarcoline.

"I will, mom. There will be extra security." Sarcoline pushed her off.

"You don't have to go," Zaffre told him.

"We spent the money, dad. I can't waste it. Rus worked too hard for it." Sarcoline shook his head. "I'm going."

Arna looked between all those in the room and then towards his brother. None of them had said a thing to him.

[*He has the wanderlust. I can feel it,* Ixxzal whispered.]

Arna stood, staring at his brother, the lights in the hallway flickering as no one else noticed. Ixxzal was all around him. Xeyaro's hums bounced across the floors. The world slowed and the Gods appeared like figures in the mist, not human but something between birds and flowers, creatures perched all around. On the floor was Ixxzal as an all gray raven staring up at Arna.

"Arna?" Gingerline asked.

"I'll be back next week," Sarcoline reminded them.

[*I don't think he wants to,* Pokk urged.]

Understanding required a journey and guidance.

[*Visualize,* Zaynir persisted.]

Arna thought of the paintings and pictures from all over the world. He thought of the boy who danced wherever he could. The Dancer, they called him. But he was not a Child, so he needed help. Arna hesitated, his hands shaking.

"Arna?" Gingerline repeated.

[*Will you guide him?* Xeyaro asked.]

Arna breathed out, sliding his white journal out of his inner pocket and walking up to Sarcoline. He was not sure this would work. He was not even sure that it mattered or if he could be a good guide. He was certain that this did not make up for the time that was lost. It did not change anything between them, but. . . Incarnate Dreams was about possibilities.

Arna walked up to Sarcoline and handed him the book. "Be back before your mastery test."

Even if he missed his mastery tests, there were ten other ways for him to be certified outside of testing days. Understanding mattered more than the official tests, no matter how long it took.

Sarcoline said nothing as he took the notebook. He flipped open the journal and froze as he read. Arna had taken time to color coordinate and tab each page. He had maps within on how to find locations. Every place he wanted to visit when he had time, was within.

"Forgo the tourist spots. Go to these. There is this shop in Ludiel that is to die for. Order their floral mocha cake, and then go to the back, trust me," Arna said, voice shaking. "In Ixis, everyone says to stop at the third door. Don't stop at the third door. You have to go to the wing staircase. Just keep walking and I swear you will find it. Trust me."

Arna could remember the exact pathway to the magical hanging gardens famous in Ixis and nearly impossible to find.

He said, "I know you don't believe me. But *this* is the way. . . Trust me."

Sarcoline gripped the journal tightly.

"Understand the city as the citizens do. Learn it. Feel it. Dance," Arna took his brother's hands, squeezing them. Hoping Sarcoline would believe him.

Sarcoline chewed at the bottom of his lip before saying, "Contact Ebru. He doesn't hate you as much as he pretends, he does. He hates you, don't get me wrong, but not as much as he says. He's been through a lot."

Caught off guard, Arna looked over his brother again. Sarcoline avoided his gaze, and shook Arna off of him, stepping back. Was Sarcoline giving him advice? But. . . Arna thought of what Amaryllis told him about those who hated Sarcoline.

If Eburnean was willing to make enemies to survive, it would make sense for Sarcoline to make himself the villain so others could thrive.

"As you have been," Arna said thinking of the blue lily garden and the Justice Square at midnight under the new moon. Arna hoped that Sarcoline would do all the things Arna never could, and dance freely without fear. Sarcoline had to, for him.

"Ven will be the hardest." Sarcoline looked to his watch. "You need more than forgiveness from Ven."

"I know that." *Tomorrow at 9pm.*

"Since when were you so forgiving yourself?" Gingerline cut in.

"I'm not." Sarcoline shrugged, placing the white journal in his bag. "He's a liar."

"I'm not," Arna protested.

"Sure. Tell that to Lumak," Sarcoline cracked a genuine smile at Arna. Jasione chuckled and Arna snorted at the comment.

[Lumak, God of Laws, cackled.]

"This won't fix things Arna. But I will consider what you said." Sarcoline turned to the door. "I have to go."

As Sarcoline left, Arna prayed. *Please let this be the right thing.*

There was not a sound. The birds disappeared. Arna was left alone in the hall with Serenity's Lament. The mists in his mind began to clear and for a moment all he wanted to do was dance.

What is fear? What is hope?
Why do we focus on the bleak, the horror, the ends?
There is so much beauty in everything, so long as we choose to see it.
But you must choose to see it.

— On the third variation.

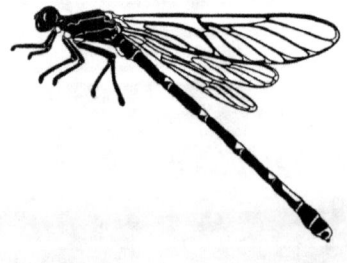

Dance 10

Turmoil

Incarnadine

19 Ixan

59 Days Left

"This new city makes me feel wrong."
"You have a job interview in fifteen minutes."
"I know. Do you think they'll notice I'm an outsider?"
"No one has noticed before. Keep your head down, and they won't see you now."

Arna sipped on his drink as he waited at the cafe. He was dressed in the best of the best: silver and white reminiscent of dragonflies and gemstones in its design and pattern. He wore sunglasses, despite the setting sun, while waiting with Aureolin for Jasione to get off work. She was dressed in an all-white ensemble, reminiscent to orchid petals and wings of butterflies with soft gold running through to add definition. She had a crown of white flowers in her hair, speckled with red, yellow, green, and gold.

The world around them was quiet, despite how busy it was. It was a condensed moment where his anxiety was threatening to make him explode.

It was the annual Ceremony of Chaos Benefit Banquet, marking the beginning of the DHS' preparation season for the Ceremony. Arna was expected to act as an upstanding member of society, per his position and his family name. As usual, he was late. As usual, he didn't want to go—although this year that was because of those he'd have to see and not the event itself. All the Governors of the Cities and all the Cardinals and Archbishops were attending. People who were richer than should be allowed and celebrities from all over the world would be there.

All eyes would be on him.

theyregoingtofindoutthetruth

imposterimposterimposter

imgoingtodiediediediediedie

Gingerline was supposed to meet them, but she was also running late.

Aureolin hung up the call and sighed softly.

"Are we meeting him there?"

Wenge and Zaffre had left early in the morning and Jasione had not arrived on time to pick up Arna, so Arna had left on his own to meet Aureolin.

"Jasione is picking up Gingerline. She was panicking after her session." Aureolin threw her bag over her shoulder.

"Panicking?" Again?

Arna chased after Aureolin as she tapped her card to pay for their snacks and drinks.

"Does that happen often?"

"Often enough. When Sarcoline doesn't go to events with her, she panics," Aureolin explained sipping at her tea. "They defend each other."

Sarcoline had yet to arrive home.

"I thought they hated each other."

"Their relationship is strained, but they don't hate each other. They rely on each other a lot," Aureolin shrugged. "The only thing that she is confident in is dance. Much of it comes from the bullying in school."

Somehow the bullying did not surprise him. Some of Ginger's comments and actions had suggested it was a consideration. Everyone was ruined by him in ways he was consistently unraveling.

"She's two years younger than us; I didn't catch it in time," Aureolin said swirling her drink. Emotions did not spread to her voice as she spoke in a deadpan tone. "She told Sarcoline one day while he was practicing, and he forced her to tell me. Rus and I stopped it."

"Was it because of me?" Arna asked, needing to know.

"You need to stop blaming yourself. Not everything that changed was bad. Ven got out of their house. Phlox started acting and she's brilliant. Rus and Jasi moved in with your family and finally got a family that could love them the way they needed. I found my sisters. I wouldn't give up my sisters for anything." Aureolin pointed them in the direction of the rails. "For some of us, the Golden Generation was suffocating. We loved each other but the pressure from the world? As if we stopped dancing it would stop turning? Unbearable."

"But for Ebru and Ginger, they remained." And the rest of Arna's family? They *were* ruined.

"They got the worst of it, that's for sure. Still, it's not your fault. When Alabaster left the Vivicent studio, Ebru changed. He became. . ."

The wind rushed between the two of them as Aureolin could not continue. She shook her head.

"Phlox begged him to go back to the Vivicent studio, but he did not listen, said that he and his father could not. . ." Aureolin tilted her head up looking towards the top of the rose, words dying on her lips.

"Aureolin?"

(Was this too his fault?)

sacrificesacrificesacrificesacrificesacrificesacrifice

Arna's fingers dug into his left palm, and he killed the emotions.

He did not have time to freak out. He barely had time to rework his variation daily, despite getting nowhere when he did.

"Look. . . And, I am quoting Phlox here, he said, 'They may try to eat me alive, but I am scarier than they are. They can't hurt me.'"

"That's horrible." The sentence was vaguely familiar, not that Arna could place why.

"It's only him and his dad. I don't know much about it, but they were either going to lose everything or fight to survive. Neither Alabaster nor Ebru wanted to leave your father, but your father couldn't pay them without students. They lost the house for a variety of political reasons that I'm not exactly certain on. Now the house is getting sold again. Things happened. Don't take the blame for things you cannot control." She shrugged, scanning her pass for the rail.

"Can we take the skybus?"

She shot him a look but said nothing, leading him towards the express bus to the center of town. They waited in silence, Arna's thudding heart in his spine, and the spinning words echoing in his ears.

"Arco said you hate trains."

"I do."

She nodded and the two of them boarded the bus.

"They'll be there tonight, you know. Alabaster and Ebru."

"I know." Arna followed after her with little to say otherwise. "Almost everyone will be."

"Yes, everyone that is anyone in the dance world will be there," Aureolin said with a bit of snark.

Sarcoline wouldn't be there, Arna wanted to say. Although, he had not gotten an invitation at all. He refrained from saying anything about his brother because Aureolin's hands were shaking.

She was terrified as he was. The whole Golden Generation in the same place. The pressure of the world watching them, expecting them to fail. Expecting everything of them. Arna could imagine the pressure was intense, but he did not much care for it. There was nothing that anyone could expect of him that he did not already expect of himself.

runningoutoftimerunningoutoftimerunningoutoftime

"I know."

"Nervous?" Aureolin asked.

"No." Arna attempted to calm himself by focusing on what he'd have to do that night.

The Benefit Banquet signaled the countdown to the Celebrations. He did not have much time left to finalize his variation.

runningoutoftimerunningoutoftimerunningoutoftime

I'm fine. Kill it.

Hand closed. Hand opened. Hand closed, tighter than before. Arna released all the tension he had and suffocated the rest and buried it deep.

"Smiles, remember? Smiles." Aureolin sang to herself, and Arna mimicked her smiles as the bus headed deeper into the city. When they were kids it had been a game between Golden Generation: perfect their fake smile even when they were uncomfortable and debate who did it best later.

"You hate it," Arna laughed.

"Pretty much. But my sisters will be there! You'll finally meet them. They've been asking all about you." Aureolin smiled truly, returning to a radiant star. "You'll love them, or I'd hope you will."

About the bus people were sneaking glances at the both of them.

"Don't stare back. It gives them motivation to say something," Aureolin warned him with a nudge. "It's a shame that Arco won't be there. He always takes most of the stares."

"How?" Arna relaxed a bit at his brother's name again.

"Always does something to wreck himself. Last year he got drunk, and no one is entirely sure how. The year before he challenged Ebru to a dance off. The year before that—"

"He embarrasses himself?" Arna was surprised. His uptight brother did not seem like the type.

"It takes the attention off the rest of us. Between him being a mess and Rus charming the room. . . It used to be the only time we were all in one room together, you know? And when we are together? They'd think of you. He took the edge off. Rus made them forget us." Aureolin twirled her cup, spinning the liquid three times before saying, "They won't be there. They should be."

"Rus is in Ludiel right now and Arco should be in Ixis," Arna nodded, thinking of the last update their family had been given.

"So, I heard. Podiel to Ixis. Then Azis?" She only then looked at him. "Then Zaydiel, and Ludiel after." She held out her mobile. "Ginger said he told your mother that he'll be back the day before his mastery tests. *Next month.* He's pushing his luck."

He met her gaze and shrugged. It couldn't be a risk, not when no one expected anything of him.

"He'll be here. Don't worry."

"Jasi said you told him to do it. Why?"

"I didn't think he'd listen," Arna admitted.

Yet finding out that Sarcoline had, made him pray harder that his brother would succeed.

Each night he did so, speaking the wish to the Gods who were busy trying to avoid his other prayer on getting answers on how to finish his variation. They could multitask.

"But he'll do more of it in the future. I wouldn't be surprised if he tried living in each city for some time."

She cocked her head asking the question of why.

"Intuition. He wasn't meant to stay in one place for too long." Arna changed the conversation to the first thing he could think of. "Is Amaryllis going to be there?"

"Yes," Aureolin stood as they approached their stop. "She's selling paintings for charity. She used to try to sell her photography, but no one bought it."

"Paintings?" Arna pondered. Whose? He had a hard time believing that the world's best photographer would start painting.

"Tha artist Chamomile," Aureolin said as she stepped off the bus.

Arna's heart leapt. Of course, it was Chamomile. He really needed to sleep if he couldn't have made that connection himself.

"She donates the money to charity for hospitals with kids who don't have Blessings, I think," Aureolin said tapping the air, "I could ask her if you want."

Arna shook his head. Aureolin nodded, messing with her hair to make sure it laid right. The flowers bloomed. He followed suit when she tossed her empty teacup in the bin for glass recycling.

runrunrunrunrunrun

The two walked in silence to the next bus like marching to Arna's death. Aureolin's hand wove in front of her at times, but otherwise she stared ahead, and sent messages in secret.

Running out of time.

The familiar thrum returned as the world began to pale around him. The point between dusk and night was littered with lights that did not turn on and others that were sepia. The universe condensed around him. His heart raced.

theendtheendtheendtheendtheendtheend

All Arna could focus on was of how fucked his variation was and Alis.

Alis.

Arna glanced to his inbox at the corner of his vision, and it opened to no new messages. Alis' messages had been oddly sparse in the last week. Alis was preoccupied with something, and no amount of messages could get Arna an answer. They were just 'i miss you' and 'i'm okay' over and over. Something between them was slipping away.

hatehatehatehatehate

lefthimalonewhenheneededsomeone

He was fine with it. He accepted it. He expected it.

Arna rubbed his left hand with his thumb, willing the marks to close and needing the blood to disappear. He'd have to wash his hands before he met anyone. He had to be perfect.

"Rus said he's sending his best wishes," Aureolin sighed. "And good luck."

Arna nodded, shoving his hands into his pockets.

"He didn't replace you, you know," Aureolin said and stilled like time right before death.

Heart thudding in his ears. Thoughts threatening to part his lips and vomit over the ground, he swallowed, painfully.

runningoutoftimerunningoutoftimerunningoutoftime

Arna breathed in sharply and forced it all back, eyes focused on the then and now. He had to get through the party and once it was done he could get back to work. If he had to, for the sake of progress, he wouldn't sleep that night either. He was fine.

"I know you didn't know him. None of us did. But he didn't. He always made that very clear."

"I know. . ." Arna was not sure he believed himself.

"He was always not one of us. With his own friends, that weren't us. I honestly didn't even know Jasi had a twin until they both moved into the Vivicent manor," she sighed. "I do feel bad for him. He's always so quiet, and I heard a rumor that while his teammates like him, they're not close. He is only ever doing Philanthropy work or at the Vivicent manor when he's not practicing or competing. They said they don't know him very well."

Arna thought of the brown eyed man whose face is all over the world. Why was he trying so hard to be everywhere? Why was he giving so much up for Arna's family?

"He's one of us," Aureolin said as if it answered any questions. More to herself than Arna.

Arna spent the remainder of the time on the buses trying to distract himself with Alis. Why was Alis busy? Why was he slipping away, despite how much effort Arna was putting into keeping up their relationship? Why was it falling apart just like his variation was?

By the time Arna followed Aureolin into the religious district with heavy feet, his mind was clear, and all his emotions were buried away. He was breathing easily and the ever present thrumming in his bones was settled to an ignorable level.

The city lights were shining like a million stars above them, and wax candles lit the path, dripping their rainbow of colors onto the cobblestones. They walked into the Temple of Xeyaro, bypassing the line outside. They showed no identification and were asked for none. Giving their jackets to the coat check, Arna kept his black journal close.

He could not lose it.

Massive screens showcasing the guests and cameras flying around, filled the air. People were dressed in the finest clothes Arna had seen in years. Everyone wore white or silver. Most were draped in lush fabrics created by hours of dedicated hand stitching and embroidery. Some even wore teal gemstones that swirled internally with a smoky white mist and flashes of black.

True stormstones were marked by the smoky glow and mined outside the cities while lab-grown stones glowed clear and bright. Opulence hung off the bodies of those in the room with a disregard for the workers who risked their lives for the stones.

To Arna, the stone may as well have been crimson.

Speakers played soft tunes that Arna could not name. Despite being called a banquet, little food was served. All vegan appetizers, intricately designed like works of art, were served on floating silver trays. The rare dishes were devoid of most scents and instead contained the harsh stench of roses. All the drinks were multicolored and sparkling, with ice and jelly within.

The Temple was a large hexagon, with rising pillars shaped as trees and made of white marble. The ceiling of the flat roof depicted hundreds of different ecosystems of the outside world before it had been destroyed. There was a map of the world's only continent etched into the tiles at their feet, glowing with six lights for each city. It was Blessing touched with a sun and moon atop the image, showing their progress in the sky. Part of the floors were darker than the others, mimicking where the world was night and where it was day.

Along the walls were faceless portraits, stained glass, and sculptures of the Chosen and their Saints. The Saints were always powerful, always gifted with strange gifts before other mortals, and always the closest to the Gods after the Chosen. The Saints, if ever depicted, were always with their Chosen who sanctified them, not that Arna knew how to do that. The Gods were as cryptic about the process as they were about the contract. Not that Arna needed to know, he'd never have any.

The banquet was held in the center of the Temple, surrounding the massive statue of Xeyaro.

[*Watsonia's art is breathtaking*, Zaynir sighed, lovingly.]

Each of the cities had statues of their patron God, and like Xeysis, they were usually held within the Temple dedicated to that God in the center of the city. Made in the Second Variance by the Watsonia, creator of the Twin Fans variation, the statues were relics of a time in the ancient past. Before they were rediscovered in the Fourth Variance, they had been believed to be myth.

[The Gods were like chimes bouncing across the speakers and flashing across the screens.]

Like all the statues, the statue of Xeyaro was the best representation of Xeyaro's voice. It was a collection of feelings rather than a form that represented a mortal: a motherly figure with a rose for a head and skin like that of a tree. It was carved of granite, with gemstones of all kinds and painted tiles depicting scenes of artists with mountains, rivers, and oceans. All the Chosen before Arna created art with lasting impact, other than their dances, after they completed their variation.

Sometimes Arna wondered what he would have made if he were given the chance and the odds of his survival were in his favor. He also knew better than to wish.

[*Don't worry about visualizing for now. Focus on the event*, Zaynir said like broken static.]

[*We will not be able to say much*, Pokk agreed.]

"These are my sisters." Aureolin led him to a set of women and girls aged sixteen to fifty. She introduced them by name and the wide variety of faces greeted him by smile. Three were from the pop dance group that he could not remember the name of.

"Pleasure."

Small talk began and they ate appetizers. When the girls began talking amongst themselves, leaving Arna behind in context, Arna took in the venue searching for familiar faces. There were hundreds of eyes watching him. The stares containing the weight of a thousand worlds bore down at him, crushing and cracking his resolve.

failurefailurefailure

saffronsaffronsaffronsaffronsaffronsaffron

I'm fine. He would not be like Saffron. He could not be like Saffron. He would not make a mistake he would be perfect.

theendtheendtheend

everyonewasgoingtodieanditwasgoingtobehisfault

Arna rushed to the bathroom with a flimsy excuse and washed his hands under the cold water, rubbing away the crusted blood.

The rushing water transformed into static. The music in the halls contorted into a cacophony of screams. Arna's face in the mirror warped into a pretty little flower with six purple petals and three red stigmas that were also a spice.

The open crescent moons on his hands ran crimson. He focused on his B.Body Blessing needing the wounds to heal, why wouldn't it heal?

(Why was he incapable of finishing his variation?)

Why did he only destroy things?

[In chaos there is creation.]

[What is silence?]

Alis.

He messaged him, just needing something to hold on to.

Please answer.

```
Rosy: Save me
Alis: From?
Rosy: This event. People are staring.
Alis: Flash them a smile to imply you're available and
    when they approach, tell them you're taken.
Rosy: By you?
Alis: Who else?
Alis: You're mine.
Alis: Don't forget it.
```

Arna laughed.

[Fear dashed away with an Ivumalis song.]

The wounds on Arna's hands knit themselves back together. The scars were deep and white, incorrectly healed but no longer bleeding.

He was okay.

```
Rosy: Gods, I love you.
Alis: I love you too.
Alis: You'll be okay. I know you will.
Rosy: What are you up to?
```

A tap at the shoulder startled him. Arna blinked away the messages, hiding his mobile even when no one else could see. Arna nodded to the man, left back to the hall and searched for Aureolin.

"A delicacy from Ixis," the Governor of Xeysis said before Arna could make it back to her. He had a man at his side who Arna had never met.

"Incarnadine. This is Mr. Thyme, the head of the World Government Council's Chosen Task Force."

In Lumak's lectures he'd managed to pay attention to, Arna understood the fundamentals in how the city's functioned. Since humanity had moved to the six cities, the world effectively only had six countries. The World Government Council was their collective of representatives elected and appointed by the city leaders to control relations between the six cities. They also managed conservation efforts of the lands they left, as Lumak and Xeyaro often harped when Arna complained that the WGC did nothing.

"Pleasure." Arna shook the man's greasy hand and secretly wiped it off on the back of his pants. "What can I do for you gentleman?"

"Well..." The Governor motioned for Arna to walk further with him. "We were discussing what is to come with your new Variance."

[*Tread carefully,* Ixxzal warned like thunder through an old recording.]

"Regarding?" Arna asked unsure what Ixxzal meant but pushed his body weight forward onto the balls of his feet, and made sure his knees never locked.

"Is it possible—" Mr. Thyme looked from the Governor to Arna. "—to wait another year?"

"What?" *No.*

"The infrastructure is not prepared. We are already struggling with the consequences of the Splintering and society will need time to prepare for a new Variance. The market will not be able to take it. People will lose their life savings," Mr. Thyme said glaring at Arna, anger curling in his words as the glare grew stronger by the moment. "We must consider the upcoming elections as well."

Xeysis was controlled by a council who balanced power with the City Governor. They oversaw the general city progress, while petals had their own governments with smaller regions, zones, sectors, districts, and wards. Everyone was supposed to be elected, but Arna had a feeling, more than ever, it was not the case.

"What?" Arna said in a low voice. "You want to make money off of a new Variance?"

"No. We must maintain order," the man disagreed. "This childish little dream that you insist on pursuing despite it not being true is—"

"If you don't think I'm the Chosen then why does it matter if I dance?" Arna glared at the man.

"Incarnadine." The Governor smiled halfway. "You must understand. We must account for all scenarios including—"

"I was not aware you could tell me what or what not to do."

Both the men's expressions shook a bit. The Gods laughed, which was enough for Arna to breathe out in relief.

"We are asking for a bit of time. Just a year," the Governor tried again.

"That is something I cannot give you. Now—"

"The Chosen Task Force can tell you what to do Incarnadine," Mr. Thyme cut him off. "It is our job. We are here to protect the world from your hubris which you have made it clear you are deadset on pursuing. There are world changing aspects that you cannot possibly fathom."

Arna bristled.

theendtheendtheend

No one *but* Arna knew the "world changing aspects." He kept them all blissfully unaware for their own safety. They were lucky he wasn't screaming from the top of his lungs that the world was ending and create ceaseless havoc. He let them continue to spread their propaganda that this year was just like all the others.

Even when the Blessings were being lost at an unprecedented pace.

Even when there was global technological failure.

Even when the cities were being battered by more superstorms than any recorded year.

[Fluttering panic erupted.]

The ONLY one who understood the impact was Arna and he delt with it daily.

Constantly.

Every hour of every day.

[Winds unlike storms cried for clarity and silence.]

How D A R E he —

A hand was placed upon Arna's shoulder.

"You must excuse us gentlemen," Cardinal Black said.

"We will talk more. We will have weekly meetings about your. . . decisions," Mr. Thyme said.

With every ounce of his soul, Arna was certain the man didn't believe him. He looked at Arna like he was an imposter faking everything and did not have the proof. It was the same look as the protestors outside his house, not that Arna cared. He hated the man.

"Were those rats trying to get you to wait?" Cardinal Black sighed, pushing Arna on ahead. "Xeyaro's wisdom tells us that we need not a world of money, but one in which society functions in unison and harmony as nature intended."

Is that what you say?

[*Close enough.* Xeyaro was amused.]

Arna coughed from the laughter that bubbled in his chest. The levity helped to contain his temper. He searched for further escape.

Everyone around him was a predator ready to strike.

"They are only trying to guarantee their reelection campaigns." Cardinal Black sighed even more dramatically, prompting Arna for a response that he did not give.

Arna's eyes narrowed. Cardinal Black never believed him as a kid. He had no reason to trust the man now, no matter what he wanted.

"What do you want?" Arna asked him.

"Merely for your assistance," the man said rubbing Arna's shoulder and Arna pulled away. The Churches had an ethics board to check the city's powers in order to stop them from violating taboos, but they were meant to have little control in policy and law.

"I'm not helping you make Xeysis into a theocracy," Arna disagreed, not certain it was the man's goal, but knowing that he was fighting the One Truth Church for supreme power. The One Truth Church was, luckily, not involved in the proceedings of the night from what Arna could tell.

The Cardinal's smile did not waver.

"It already is, isn't it?" Arna asked with dread.

[*It's close,* Pokk, God of Knowledge, and Lumak, God of Laws, said in unison.]

"We have done what was needed for the Xeysis," Cardinal Black said with a dramatic flair at the end. "The One Truth Church is threatening to destroy everything. We are lucky that my church could keep them from disturbing tonight's proceedings which they demanded were halted, claiming the Ceremony of Chaos is heresy."

Arna glared on ahead as the man tried to hand him appetizers which he refused to take.

"You see the men who run and hide behind money. Xeysis needed strong leadership in these trying times." Cardinal Black was shorter than Arna was, but he was imposing and insisting that Arna take the plate of food. "In the hundred years since the Contract of Lucidity was signed, the six cities have not had war."

The superstorms made it difficult to have war, but the last armed conflict had been a hundred years ago.

Arna reluctantly took the food but did not eat.

"We are not living in the Fourth Variance where we have to worry about that," Arna said.

"Mortals will fight over anything. I simply ask for a guarantee so I may prepare."

"What have you done?" Arna asked.

After the Contract of Lucidity, the churches had one instance of true control in Xeysis: on the night of the Ceremony of Chaos. In order to ensure that the contract with the Gods and Mortals was maintained, a single church given control over the barriers for the night only. No technology or Blessings could interfere with the ceremony. When Arna last danced it was the Church of the Apostle, and Cardinal White. Since then it had been Cardinal Black.

[*Unfortunately, it is needed,* Pokk hissed.]

[*Sending help,* Xeyaro said.]

"You used the Contract provision stating the Church can take control in religious emergencies as a loophole, didn't you?" Arna gaped at him. Had it not been closed off? Had they just been letting the man get away with whatever he wanted for years?

"If the Splintering does not constitute an emergency? What does?" Cardinal Black's smile dropped. A threat was in his eyes as if saying that Arna needed to comply.

Arna caught the eye of a person who hovered in and out of his periphery. Seeing him put Arna at ease in the way a lullaby put a child to sleep. Arna let out all the resentment and frustration, fear and anxiety in a single breath. His shoulders relaxed as Cardinal White, the leader of the Church of the Apostle, mouthed: *do you need help?* Arna nodded.

"Now, Arna. We should discuss when you dance—" Cardinal Black began to say.

In seconds Cardinal White was there.

"We should discuss it," a deep voice said. Cardinal White was taller, older, domineering as the eldest Cardinal in the world. Despite being a hundred eight, he stood strong and muscular, with his beard long and eyes full of wisdom.

Cardinal White shot him a look that said, *we'll talk later.* For now, Cardinal White would do as was his job and what he'd always vowed Arna he'd do: protect him.

Arna took the chance to slip away, meandering through a crowd until he was surrounded. People asked him questions of all types, and he fielded them with recited scriptures.

"Now, Mr. Vivicent," A man with a glean in his eye approached. "Are you in need of assistance?"

The truth was that Arna was not overwhelmed, not since Cardinal White started shadowing him. He never got too close but was within distance that he could step in if Arna needed him. Just like when Arna was a child, the Cardinal let Arna do as he wanted. He never coddled Arna, simply supported him.

Besides citing scripture was second nature to Arna at this point and the Gods were laughing and egging him on in the distance at his expert use of the holy word. He had annoyed them for years; the priests were like kittens in comparison. He did, however, want to know why this man offered help.

"Mr. Hemlock," Arna greeted him.

The man was dressed in all mint, with his long hair tied back into a bun and his goatee sharp and freshly cut. His skin was a dark brown, and he stood at the same height as Arna. The man had met Arna a few times when Arna was at his factories in other cities, but luckily it had no impact. Mr. Hemlock did not seem to remember it now.

"I did not expect to see you here," Arna said. After three failed attempts to prove he could make a suitable performance fan by machine, Arna was surprised he was invited.

The man was not a fan master, where Arna's father was. He had been an apprentice but left before mastering the craft. Mr. Hemlock claimed that mortal error could ruin the fans and thus made it his life's mission to find a way with technology to make them. It was impossible for him to reach lasting success, after all the techniques needed were not something a machine could replicate.

"Have you succeeded?"

The man smiled something far from kind.

Arna smiled back wider.

The man grimaced and said, "Progress is the way of the Fifth Variance. This is the logical next step."

Arna's eyes darted searching for a way out, not wanting to debate theory of fan making with a man who gave up the craft for commodity. Not when it was the one thing Arna longed for.

Those around Arna, however, took the bait and started talking theoretical concepts of fan making and the progress of art without soul.

Beyond the crowd were more Governors with their own financial advisors lying in wait.

"Arna." Amaryllis' arm looped around his. "I heard Ginger was sick."

[Distant birds chirped in victory.]

"Sorry. I— Please excuse me." Arna let himself get dragged off by Amaryllis. She was dressed in a white tulip dress that was designed with soft gray and white layered tulle. With Amaryllis at his arm, the crowd parted for them, like a path through the darkest woods.

"Snakes, all of them. Did they tell you that society is on the verge of financial collapse or technological collapse?" Amaryllis laughed under her breath. Arna chuckled with her.

"Both."

(both were true.)

Kill it. Bury it.

Instead of closing his hands, Arna held them together. His right thumb traced the marks on his left hand. They were healed, but not.

(How could he fix what he broke?)

"A new Variance means everything changes and they're quaking. They don't know what to expect." She viciously smirked at those who turned their gaze and ignored them. "I think you should see something."

The sea of stares became an island of two.

At the silent auction five of Chamomile's paintings were on display. There were many names lined under her paintings with numbers that made Arna check twice.

"Amazing, isn't it?" she asked. "No one even knows who she is, but each year the numbers keep growing."

Arna blinked at the sum. This would certainly help children in hospitals.

"Her art is. . ." Arna agreed, awestruck.

"Good?" Amaryllis asked?

Arna winced at the wasy she said it as an insult. Chamomile was so much more than that.

"You really don't mean 'good' as an insult."

"I never mean it as an insult," Arna said.

"Everyone else does." Amaryllis grimaced. "Why does one have to be a Child to be great? Why are nonChildren only ever good? Why can't they be amazing? Superb? A genius?"

"Genius is reserved for Children." Arna reminded her, the words stale on his tongue.

"Why?" She turned to him, eyes relaxed but mind clearly spinning as she tapped her fingers on her arms, short nails painted white. "I'm a Child, but I could never paint like this."

Arna had the stifling belief that no matter how much he tried, he would never be able to either.

"So, why? Why do we only call them good? It's a compliment, yes, but most times it's not. Why is it as an insult if it's the only word we allow them?"

It was how Children put others in their place. They were good, but not good enough.

"Being good is about emotion," she contined. "It's the feeling created. Anyone can be good, is that the problem? Anyone can make feelings from nothing? Why does that matter?"

"They are great."

"No. Great is reserved for money. It's fame. It's people deciding you're worth something because *they* say you're worth something and *they* tell your friends your worth something. Being great is the way the world views us. They don't care about us, our art, what we've done. They only care about convincing others to buy us and sell us and use us."

She ranted with no anger. Her aqua eyes sparkled like the clearest sky. Arna was unsure what she was getting at, and unsure how to help her.

"Being good is about how those who matter see you. It's about how you see yourself. No amount of greatness can make you good. If you can't captivate others, if you can't inspire one person. . . No amount of greatness can make a person a legend. So why is *good* an insult? It means you matter to someone." Amaryllis said softly, her voice like the swirling litany of dreams.

Arna stood reeling and processing. Accepting and agreeing. She was right.

Why was good so bad?

"I wish we didn't have to decide a thing like that. I wish we allowed for people to be whatever they wanted, instead of pushing them through roles they believe we fit into."

Incarnate Dreams.

She was speaking about Incarnate Dreams.

For the first time since he met her, before him was the girl he'd called muse. She was the same one from the protest videos and the online interviews. This was Amaryllis Ink, the photographer the world hated. This was the girl who was so good at what she did despite not being a Child of Xeyaro.

"Coco should be considered a—"

"Don't say that here," he cut her off. She twisted uncomfortable beside him. But she was right. Sarcoline should be considered a genius.

"Just because he isn't someone 'important' in their eyes. He says he doesn't care but. . ." she bristled, and her eyes darted to those behind Arna with a fury that was Arna's own.

Sarcoline was both a lucky nobody and their most cherished tool. He was a face they liked to forget, and someone who inspired great hope in the masses each year. Without him dancing, Arna was certain there would be mass panic. People had grown to rely on him even while they lashed out with vitriol and poisonous hatred.

"And we can't call him what he is because of how people will react knowing their positions are questioned. Isn't that unfair?" Amaryllis asked, turning her attention once more to Arna, dropping her arms and smiling sadly.

"Of course, it's unfair."

But what if Sarcoline could be considered a genius? What if after Arna danced, Sarcoline could fully be accepted for what he was? What if Amaryllis could be a photographer without fear?

[*Yes*, Azza cheered. *A variation changes everything.*]

A warmth bloomed in his chest from the sweet litany that led to epiphany.

Hope was his variation's center. He thought he add it fully into his variation, but *this* was what was missing. For weeks he'd been stuck because he somehow had erased the hope? Why? How could he add it back?

How could he ensure that his dance embodied hope fully? What did it truly mean to make dreams a reality? What did he have to do to make a world where hope mattered more than sacrifice?

[silence.]

What was he supposed to do? What would that future look like?

[*Are you visualizing?* Zaynir asked.]

"It's frustrating." Amaryllis looked to the paintings again. "I met this girl who was working as a florist. She's a legal master—trust me, I've asked her for too many things I felt embarrassed to ask Jasione about—and she's not a Child. She is blessed in plants, so says everyone. But when you look at her Blessings, it could also be childcare, or. . . "

Arna pieced it together. "Care of a city."

"Legal care. Depending on how she worked it." Amaryllis hesitated a second before she said the next words softly, "Ebru's A.Reverence manifests as dance, but Phlox's? Ven's? Does A.Reverence *have* to be dance focused? We imposed that law but is that what the Gods intended?"

No.

Arna did not need the Gods' answer to know that. People pushed for them to dance because they had A.Reverence, but the Blessing was more than that. It was for all performance, the pinnacle of performance.

[*The only one who needs it is.* . . Pokk tested.]

Me.

It and S.Mirrors were the only two Blessings he had to have to complete his variation dance twenty-six.

"I just want people to be able to choose. I think that would be nice," Amaryllis spoke almost at a whisper.

"Me too."

The two stood in silence staring at the paintings. Hands open. Hands closed.

Hands opened.

How could he add back in hope? What did that look like? What was he missing?

soclosesoclosesoclosesoclosesoclosesoclose

"Did you speak with Ven?" She jumped into a new conversation almost too suddenly. The look in her eye said it had been on her mind for a while and based on the fact that she knew of the S.Mirrors, Arna had expected it.

The threads of epiphany broke, waiting for the stars to align one more.

onelasttimeonelasttimeonelasttime

"Yes. . ." Arna admitted, although the talk had not been memorable.

He shook away his anxiety that was beginning to thud again.

"There are things that were never healed between you two and as much as Ven wants to move on, until that is laid aside, they can't." She looked at him. "I would know."

Arna wanted to ask how they met. He wanted to know why they were together. There was a pain to her voice that told him that she had been hurt. Had she sought comfort? Had Pervenche supported her?

"You are the same age as Ginger, no?" Arna asked instead.

She shook her head. "A year younger."

"Do you go to school at Arco's University?"

"Yeah. We went to Secondary Academy together." She smiled as bright as a thousand suns and raced through her next words without a breath. "I watch out for him, don't worry. Ginger asked me to, although I knew him first out of everyone. He's my best friend in the whole world. We met when I was fifteen. Did you know that? He introduced me to everyone else.

"I was actually talking to him earlier today and he asked me to save you, if needed. Coco's such a sweetheart always looking out for people. I swear, he acts like he's tough but he's really just a possessive cat: looking out for those he loves. Which he does. Love you, that is. Coco might not say it, and he's still real angry, but I think he'll forgive you soon.

"He had hoped I'd be a good friend for Ginger, since she had none. We became quick friends and I'm actually wearing the dress that she made for me. I love it. I'm just sorry I wasn't there to look out for her before, you know? We only met after she went through. . ." She took a breath, did a double take at Arna, and then laughed. "Sorry. I met. . . I met Ven through him."

No friends? Best friends? Arna had a hundred questions but only one thing to say. "I wish I could have been here too."

"You were off," Amaryllis said without accusation. Her smile turned into a knowing look. "A decision was made, and you were not here. We can't go back and fix that now. All we can do is—"

"Arna! Amaryllis!" Phlox wrapped her arms around the both of them. "This artist. I must know more. Tell me that *you* must know more."

"Yes. I've told you. Her name is Chamomile Gladiolus," Amaryllis answered. Whatever conversation and information Arna was hoping to learn was cut short. Amaryllis face twisted into disappointment and irritation.

"Wonderful, brilliant, beautiful. I must have one." Phlox threw down an absurd number on an auction paper that was never going to be topped. "Charity, for the children. It will be great for the press." Phlox leaned against Arna. "Amaryllis, doll, I believe I saw Ven searching for you. They look like a fish out of water. Please go assist."

It was an order, stated, as Phlox pressed all her weight atop of Arna. Amaryllis gave a dark laugh under her breath and walked off after giving Arna a hug and promising to talk to him later. Phlox thrust a glass of wine into Arna's hands.

"And let me guess. Ebru is searching for me?" Arna stared at the burgundy liquid. In the reflection his eyes brown eyes were black. But it wasn't possible, until he danced and officially was Chosen. "I don't drink."

It messed with his Blessings and made it so that he could not distinguish between living voices and the Gods.

"Can't be at a party without wine, love." Phlox winked at him before looping her arm through his. She was dressed in a glittering silver dress with veins of deep green and neon blue, reflecting against each other almost as if the colors themselves were moving. "And yes, he is but I do not intend to lead you to his clutches. Not yet. I must protect you."

"Why send Amaryllis away then?"

"She's a smart girl. She knew I did not want to talk to her," Phlox said with disdain.

"Why?" Arna asked, half paying attention and checking his mobile again.

Alis had not responded.

> Rosy: Alis?
>
> Rosy: Are you okay?

"I hate her. We have artistic differences," Phlox answered with a quick swirl of her wine glass. "One bad photoshoot can tell you everything you need to know about a photographer."

"Bad?"

Impossible. He knew her art and she had tens of awards.

"Atrocious. Horrible. They were the worst photos I've ever seen of myself. And you would not believe it!" Phlox dramatically sighed. She leaned into his arms, and he had to support her whole body weight. "The magazine *still* published them. My manager had to sue them and yet the pictures are still there online. I swear she uploaded them herself. She says she did not, but I know she'd bitter about me disavowing her."

Amaryllis did not strike Arna as the vindictive type. He'd have to ask later.

"That's unfortunate."

His phone rang.

> Alis: Stop messaging me.
>
> Rosy: What happened?
>
> Alis: Stop messaging me.

Something was wrong.

> Rosy: Carnations are dying?

"Dreadfully so." Phlox sipped her wine. "She's a fox in sheep's clothing. Be wary. She'll trick you, charm you, and leave you wanting to support her because she's so *sweet* and *kind*. It's all a ploy."

"Sounds like you are jealous."

It was not the character Amaryllis had shown him and he was inclined to believe what he saw.

"And she already has you." Phlox winked at him.

Arna sighed half focused. "What did the pictures look like?"

> Alis: Carnations? Are you crazy? Stop talking to me. I
>   don't know who you are and you're suffocating me. If
>   you actually care about my music, you will leave me
>   alone. Stop spreading poisonous rumors.

Years ago, when they had first started talking, Alis had warned Arna that because of the contract, the Boss had access to his messages at times. They'd established a code for when the Boss was reading the messages that Alis typed. They, Alis and Rosy, were Carnation. 'Poisonous rumors' meant there was an outsider viewing.

Alis was about to go dark and was warning Arna that he'd do everything he could to ensure they'd be able to talk again.

> Rosy: What are you even talking about?
>
> Alis: I'll give you one last chance before I block you.
>
> Rosy: Then do it.

"Arna, are you listening?"

"What?" Arna looked up once more. She was watching him with a controlled and even expression. He said, "Sorry."

"Girlfriend?" She laughed when Arna's cheeks flushed. "I knew you were a heart breaker."

"No. He's not."

Arna sent one last message that bounced. He'd been blocked, but Alis would message him again when he was safe. What kind of man has that much power over another adult? Just what did the Boss hold over Alis and his father?

"It matters not," Phlox wove it off. "I saved you from her clutches and now you must entertain me."

"I will do my best." Arna glanced back searching for anyone to save him.

"You hurt me by searching for a way out." She released his arm and faced him.

"I was not—" the lie stung his tongue.

"Ah." She placed her finger against his lips. "I know you, Incarnadine. Don't forget that I was your first kiss."

"I'd rather not remember that." Arna frowned at the memory. It had been when they were twelve. The mood had been right and Eburnean said that practice was important in all things. Phlox had agreed to help Arna practice.

Phlox giggled as she dropped her hand from him.

"I told you; I know you. Enough to know that you are struggling with all of this." There was a pain in her voice, a betrayal. Did she think he'd turn to her?

"I'm sorry."

"Apologies?" She brought her fingers to her lips as she smiled. "I accept."

Arna blinked at her.

"What you say or do is of little consequence to me. It matters not. I don't care. I am not like the others."

It sounded like a lie.

"I am not like Ebru or Ven, who you do need to worry about. Ebru cut all of us out of his life when he moved studios. I just *couldn't* understand anymore because I was not dancing. And Ven? Ven cut us all out when they went to archery. That one, perhaps, smarted worse," Phlox grumbled sipping her wine and glaring at the paintings.

"I apologize," he said again.

"You already did," she said without the mirage and the sing song voice, plainly and with a glare shot in his direction.

"I can't say it enough."

She pondered a moment. "For the lies or for leaving?"

"Neither? Both?" He was not sure.

"And there is a truth. You needn't worry, I will tell none. For I have none to tell." The words were not hostile or vicious, but such a truth that Arna did not need Lumak to confirm them.

He had thought that Jasione had been joking about their separation. Phlox had been an orphan, raised by her grandparents. But they had died, too—when she was five. She had lived with the city care, as the Vivicent Manor 'wasn't a suitable place for a child to live' according to the child services department, despite the fact that four other children did. She, Jasione, and Arna had been inseprable for years. She would have aged out of the care home at eighteen.

Eburnean and Pervenche were one thing, but Jasione? Without him. . .

"You lost everything," Arna said fully trying to fathom how bad it had been.

"Oh, heavens no. I have acting. It is *everything* I have wanted. I simply did not realize that choosing it would leave me without anyone." She began laughing.

"You have friends there?"

"I have my acting friends. However, there is a dichotomy. Me versus them. You know how it is. NonChildren don't want to be seen with me. I mean, you did break the world and I was friends with you. The other Children of Xeyaro? I have A.Reverence, they do not. I am a 'dancer,' as they always so rudely reminded me. But at least *I'm* still within my God's domain unlike *some* people." She rolled her eyes and immediately started cackling. "Take into consider my inclination to Azza? They hate me. It's entertaining."

soclosesoclosesoclosesoclosesoclosesoclose

"That's. . ."

"I needn't get condolences." Her voice dropped into a dark cadence before she chirped back into the lofty elegance of before. "You are back, which means the group is back together. Regardless of what we want, any of us, we are going to be forced into proximity. And no matter what any of them say, fifteen years of friendship cannot be erased so easily."

Arna wanted to say it was true, but they were all different, changed. He was not sure it would ever be the same.

(Why was he sent back early?)

"And there is Ginger." Phlox rolled her eyes. "She is going to call to you, and you are going to go." Arna turned his head and saw no one.

"Again, searching for an out. How you hurt me, Incarnadine," Phlox said woefully. Before Arna could apologize, her thousand layer mask fell apart. Her eyes were glistened in tears that would never fall and her lips quivered. She was haunted.

(Why was he sent back early?)

Then it was gone. Erased. Confident Phlox had returned, vulnerability gone. "You needn't worry, no one ever notices when they hurt me. I won't hate you for it, it's expected."

"Arna!" Gingerline called out to him.

"And there is the call." Phlox placed a kiss on his cheek before turning and walking away.

In seconds the others rushed him. He rubbed his cheek wondering if it had been an act or her real emotions. Gingerline, Jasione, Pervenche, Amaryllis, and Aureolin surrounded him with wide eyes.

"She kissed you?" Gingerline gaped.

"Yeah." Arna dropped his hand and Gingerline shrieked in frustration. Pervenche glared at the kiss mark and Jasione shook his head. Aureolin and Amaryllis fell into a giggling fit at the sight of it. By the time they sat him down, Gingerline had begun to wipe his cheek raw with a handkerchief. He did not let go of his wine glass, and cradled it with both hands.

Gingerline was dressed in muted silver, with wave like pleats and folds. She wore a silver lily in her hair. Jasione was in a suit of white with lavender petals sleeves. Pervenche was dressed in a symmetrical long sleeve ensemble of soft, flowing white and silver fabrics that worked beautifully with Amaryllis' dress. All eyes were on them, as they sat and talked about what had happened before. Jasione swore not to let Arna out of his sight again.

"The DHS shall speak in two minutes," the emcee announced as Pervenche and Amaryllis walked off to get water.

"What sort of lipstick does she use? It's not coming off." Gingerline scrubbed at his face.

"What did she want?" Aureolin asked.

"Just to talk. Saving me, she said, from Amaryllis," Arna then whispered. "Why does she hate Amaryllis?"

"You know Temptation Magazine?" Aureolin asked. "It would have been years ago. There was a cover shoot for Phlox."

Arna had a copy. He had copies of all the magazines that talked about it after.

Golden or Porcelain? Will Phlox Break?

A Good Actress or an Illusion?

When Blessings No Longer Matter: The Phlox Problem

Dancers Should Stick to Dance

PHLOX EXPOSED: You Must See This

Golden Star or Diva?

He had picked up a copy of the magazine because Phlox had been on the cover: vulnerable, tangible, real. Phlox had been depicted without her carefully constructed mosaic of answers, without her mask. It was true, beautiful, and exposed. She hid so much, just like he did.

He looked it up online, surprised that he'd missed that Amaryllis took the photos.

The comments on the message boards from the time were not so kind.

> ► God. I knew she was fake.
>   > ► She should go back to dancing.
>   > ► I should have given her shitty acting more credit. She had us all fooled.
> ► When will the world realize what good acting is? Phlox needs to go back to dancing so we can have our art again.
> ► Is it just me or is Phlox really ugly?
>   > ► I knew it. No amount of makeup can make someone pretty.
> ► I'm happy she's suffering.

Did Phlox read the comments? Arna could almost picture Phlox in silk sheets, curled up in the dark, reading them all.

"Amaryllis did that shoot," Gingerline went on. "She'd done some other magazines before, but it was her first major one. She was nineteen. Phlox helped her get the gig, as a favor to me. And then Amaryllis gave the world something Phlox never wanted to show them. I've never been able to apologize."

No wonder Phlox hated Amaryllis. It was too real.

"You don't need to," Aureolin told her.

"Amaryllis is a Child of Zaynir, but it manifested in photography. No one wanted to give her a chance." Gingerline bit at her lip, tears at her eyes.

Amaryllis was wading into waters that many would claim she had no right to break. She had stepped into the arts without being Xeyaro's Child. The risk was substantial; and why Arna had gravitated to her to begin with.

The thought made Arna laugh.

Reasonably, Amaryllis, as a Child, was a genius; but she was also only *good* because it wasn't in her God's realm of control. No wonder she saw Phlox. No wonder she cared for Sarcoline, Pervenche, and Chamomile.

"She's *good*," Arna stated. The others solemnly nodded as Gingerline continued to rub his cheek raw.

"It's smearing," Gingerline complained.

"No one will know it's the lipstick now. Good job," Aureolin laughed.

"They're beginning." Jasione turned their attention to the stairs as the DHS gathered. Zaffre and Eburnean stood at the front with Alabaster, his father, and Cyclamen Shadone. Cyclamen Shadone was short, with a full beard, pale skin, and mint eyes. He may have been considered handsome. Arna didn't know. He hated him.

Arna's father stood to the side, without the power he once had. Cyclamen stood in the center, and began a prayer in extreme religious fanaticism, that made Arna wince in embarrassment. Alabaster looked tired and stern; odd for the man who had always been lopsided smiles in Arna's past.

Every DHS member was dressed in white, with vibrant mint eyes, save Cyclamen who had a rich purple pin as the current head of the committee. The pin should have been silver, but it too had changed as if to say that Lumak blessed Cyclamen's placement.

[*I do not*, Lumak huffed.]

I know.

Cyclamen Shadone said the Prayer of Benevolence with the whole room chiming in at the end, their attention fully enraptured.

"We praise the Gods and their wisdom," Cyclamen spoke after the prayer. "In their wisdom we have been given guidance regarding this years' Celebrations and Ceremony of Chaos. To speak this year, I present Eburnean Hue."

Eburnean stepped forward, notes in hand. His white suit was crisp but made him like a ghost, an illusion of a person in power. He rolled his shoulders back and then smiled speaking in a clear voice.

"As everyone knows, this year is Apostle year. The Celebrations will take place during all six days of Apostle Week. As such, each city will have their own specialized day, with main shows and events happening on their assigned day. Information will be up on the website. Please note that this means that there will be more visitors than usual, as all six cities have agreed to open up the transporters for free for the whole week."

Apostle Week, a week of six extra days not on the regular calendar, came once every thirty-six years and helped reset their time keeping to the seasons.

Eburnean went on, "Next, the auditions, for those wishing to dance in the Ceremony of Chaos, will be two weeks before the Ceremony. For those wishing to perform at all other time slots, there will be an audition in five weeks hence. Fans for the dances will be checked and repaired by Zaffre Vivicent. Vendors and installations will be decided on a first come, first served basis. The annual play will hold its auditions next week. All sports leagues are required to sign up by next week to guarantee space."

Eburnean droned on like a metronome, no personality.

Amaryllis and Pervenche made their way back with Phlox and her make up remover in tow. She sat smiling and removed the stain from Arna's face in two strokes.

"The Golden Generation—" Eburnean's voice turned all attention in their party to the stage. "—will have a dance. One of the positions for the group dances will be given to them."

It was, perhaps, the worst moment to see them. Gingerline and Phlox wiping off his cheek. Jasione looking exasperated. Aureolin laughing with Amaryllis as Pervenche glared at Phlox. They all looked to Eburnean who waved to them, knowing how off-guard he had taken them. Eburnean passed off the microphone and descended from the stairs towards them.

"Azza be damned," Jasione said.

[Birds sang with her.]

"I don't have the time for new dance practices," Aureolin muttered under her breath. Alabaster took the microphone and finished the announcements.

"I have a movie and I have to get into the annual stage play." Phlox sat next to Arna dramatically, laying her head on his shoulder. "I will have less than three weeks to prepare."

"You are Children of Xeyaro." Amaryllis reminded them. "It doesn't need to be a masterpiece. It's a statement, an act of war. You just have to exceed expectations."

War?

"How is this. . ." Arna asked.

"After you left, many people began protesting. They weren't happy with what happened and blamed your dad." Jasione explained to Arna in a low voice. "They wanted a return on investment from the taxpayer money they'd used to support Vivicent Studio. Which, was impossible."

All of the Golden Generation had been taught as a group in the Vivicent Studio by Zaffre and Alabaster. The Shadone studio and a few others, said that it was an unfair monopoly and that they would never get individual styles. However, the Vivicent family used their legacy as a way to refute it.

Besides, the Shadone family had wanted to destroy the Vivicents for generations. It had been clear that the accusations were another way for the Shadones to undermine the Vivicents. Just as it was clear now, with Cyclamen smiling their way.

"They are constantly pitting us against each other to prove that your father's methods were wrong, that he had wasted the money," Aureolin explained. "It's all an effort to destroy your family."

"By the Shadones?" He asked glaring at Cyclamen.

"Everyone." They all said at once, including Phlox.

"Why?"

"Some people think the Vivicents have had it good for too long. Others wanted to exploit all Children and make them all government wards and are using your dad as an example. A few think that by taking your father down, they can control us and ensure that no one gets the bright idea they could be Chosen, ever again," Phlox answered. "Of course, we believe you. But they don't."

All the eyes on the room were leveled at them.

Gingerline shook her head. "It still has to be good. We have a standard."

"A standard of one upping ourselves each year," Pervenche groaned as Eburnean approached. "They want to prove that we never should have been trained together to begin with. That our harmony was all a lie. They've been spreading the rumors for years. This is their final push to prove it."

"And they'll be right. We are a mess," Phlox said. "We haven't danced together since that night."

"We can't be a mess, Phlox."

"Well, that will depend on you all, won't it?"

The hesitation amongst the group was laced with fear and panic, so much so Arna swore he could taste it.

"I know your schedules," Eburnean told them when he was close enough. "I have already personally selected practice times for us all. Starting after the shoot." He smirked at Phlox who snorted and leaned on Arna further. "I have also gone ahead and added practice rooms for the two of you—Phlox, Ven—so you can get back up to standard. Or at least something suitable."

Eburnean had worded it to goad them.

Out of all the Golden Generation only Eburnean and Arna were masters in all five variations through Understanding. Gingerline was a master in four and not yet a Senior member of the DHS. Aureolin, Ven, and Phlox had only mastered two. While Aureolin at least had the luxury of her dance group, Arna wondered when Ven and Phlox had last danced.

Eburnean drew closer to Arna until they faced each other. He stepped between Arna's legs, his hand snaking behind Arna's neck just as Arna had done to him days before. Arna held the wine glass in his hands close to his lap as Eburnean's thumbs traced the snake vow on the back of Arna's neck. He lifted his chin to look up at Eburnean.

"And me?" Arna asked as they got too close in front of too many people and cameras.

"You?" Eburnean laughed quietly. "You can do what you want. Isn't that what you've always done?"

Eburnean then backed up just a bit, using the same hand's thumb to trace Arna's cheek, where Phlox's kiss once stained. There was a softness to his eyes, something in there, as he stared at Arna, that Arna could see. It was not a hesitation but a calculation.

An act of war.

There was no way that Eburnean did not know that the DHS was using this as a sign that they were broken and as an operation to take down the Vivicents. Even if Eburnean had defected, Eburnean had always been loyal.

In the softness, right as the vicious blade returned and Eburnean faced the real world once more, Eburnean was trying to prove that the Golden Generation were just as strong as they had been before. They may have been fractured, but the rest of the world would see them as united, as if nothing between them had changed.

itstimeitstimeitstimedontrunoutoftime

"Now, Phlox, dear, accompany me. We have people to talk to." Eburnean turned from him.

She groaned and took his hand. Before she left, she said to Arna under her breath, "Stop isolating yourself and trust us. They will forgive you if you forgive yourself."

closecloseclosecloseclose

Once again, Phlox kissed Arna's cheek, the other side this time. Gingerline stuttered a protest. Phlox laughed. Arna sat listless as Eburnean and Phlox walked away, leaving them with nothing more.

It all was a show: it had always been a show. Eburnean was the master of ceremonies; he held them all in his palm. Eburnean made himself into the enemy that they had to defeat. He had made them a real team again.

(How did he add hope back in?)

Arna downed the wine from the glass still in his hands. It was lukewarm and bitter. His eyes flickered black.

All things grow and change, are born and die.
Only the Gods do not change.
We as mortals will, and that gives us power:
the power to shape the world and to be anything.

— On the fourth variation.

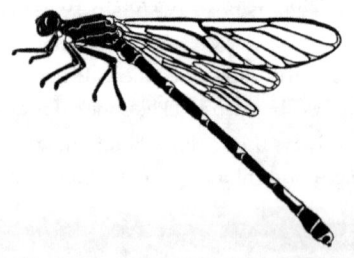

Dance 11

Ignorance

Incarnadine

31 Ixan

47 Days Left

"Are you sure you want to?"
"I'm never sure these days, but I like him."
"Then trust him."

The thing about the music for the variations was that it always changed. No two variations were the same, despite having the same basic melody retold in different styles and notes. Each took and adapted the variation to embody the message that the Chosen wished to instill.

The Original was considered classic, ancient, untouchable. Twin Fans had serene and tranquil music. Blue Rose Fears was horrifying but beautiful. Roots and Ends was empowering but hollow. Holly was the catchiest and most modern. Arna had to make something that both reflected his era and was a guide for the future. The variation that would define the new Variance.

Before returning home, he had thought he knew. He thought he understood what he wanted. He had perfected each song, but perfection was like glass: it was easily shattered with scrutiny. Arna thought he'd known what it would sound like, look like, but with each change in his life, each tweak his Variance was further and further away. He had somehow destroyed the essence while trying to fix everything.

(What is hope?)

After his inspiration with Amaryllis, he knew to add hope back in everything, but he only came away with crumbling dreams. Whether it was the music, the choreography, his clothes that he had not even begun to touch. Everything should have tumbled into place.

Somehow, he was lost more than before. Again and again, he tried: nothing worked.

[What is silence?]

He needed Alis.

Ivumalis had been the one to teach Arna how to make music. Alis had been the one to get him this far, without hearing a chord. Because Alis was his inspiration, his Muse. Alis, was always the most important. Alis. . . was the reason he'd made it so far.

    Rosy: Alis?

No response.

Alis would know what to do. Alis would understand how to find the flaws even if Arna didn't explain everything. Alis had listened to Arna for years. Alis had talked him off the edge more than once. Alis had told Arna that he was worth something even when the world did not see him, even when the silence overwhelmed him. Alis had been the one to believe in Arna when the rest of the world did not.

Arna needed Alis to finish his variation.

Arna's mobile buzzed.

    Ginger: Are you at home?

Not Alis.

After days of begging, Arna had finally relented and messaged her. She kept track of him at all times now, which made him regret it.

```
Arna: Yes.
Ginger: Where?
Arna: Bedroom.
Ginger: I just got home. I'm going to take a nap. Where
    are mom and dad?
Arna: Out.
Arna: Sleep well.
```

Arna flipped through his contacts. Arna had ten numbers in his mobile, none of whom could help him. None of whom he'd even contacted after Gingerline sent him the information. It felt like a betrayal to Alis to message them. Although Arna had never had Alis' number, and instead messaged him over an app with their usernames. His world was no longer just the Gods and Alis. Could Alis sense that?

[Distant storms disagreed.]

Arna stared at the posters on his wall, that had overtaken the religious iconography that he'd put back up as a reminder of his status as Chosen. Not a single one was Alis. He ached for a person he only saw half of, who he only knew in bits and pieces, who did not know who he was.

For years he'd searched for Alis in the faces of passersby and begged to false stars that they'd give him a sign. Who was Alis? Arna did not know. He'd stopped trying to put a face to the name as soon as he got home. Alis was not Pervenche nor Jasione. Alis was not Aureolin, Phlox, or Amaryllis. Alis was certainly not Gingerline or Sarcoline. Alis was not Rosmarinus. Alis was—

Arna's mobile buzzed before he registered the words that appeared as a notification. Back into the messaging app, Arna read the words again.

```
Alis: Yes?
```

Arna gave a long sigh originating from somewhere deep in his soul. The overwhelming relief made his hands shake, and the fully healed wounds in his palms ached. With delicate fingers he typed back and hoped that it was not a mistake.

```
Rosy: Are you back?
Alis: Yes
Rosy: You left me alone for weeks.
Alis: I was busy fixing my mistake.
Rosy: Are you okay?
Alis: The house is being sold again despite how much I've
    tried to stop it.
```

House? Since when was Alis' house being sold again? Why hadn't he told Arna.

```
Alis: I've been recruited into things I can't get out of.
Alis: With the new year it's. . . a lot. You know how my
    father gets.
Rosy: But I can talk to you?
Alis: When I'm not. . . at work. I have to be more
    careful.
Rosy: I'm sorry for messaging you when you're at work.
Alis: If you keep saying those words, they'll stop having
    meaning.
Rosy: Are you okay?
```

Alis: Stressed, I guess. Nothing new.

Rosy: I won't leave you.

Alis: We won't have a choice if they force me.

Alis: But I'm fine for now.

For some reason, Arna believed him.

Alis: Incandescent is a mess and driving me mad. I have
    to completely redo it.

Rosy: Can I help?

Alis: Not unless you can steal me away like a knight from
    the stories.

Rosy: Whatever you need.

Alis: You'll never be here.

Arna looked to the words twice.

Rosy: Alis?

Alis continued to type for minutes: deleting and rewriting and deleting again. Arna collapsed back.

Alis: Words are cheap Rosy.

Alis: And I can't keep believing in a dream.

Alis: Pretend I didn't say anything.

Multiple messages were deleted one after another.

Alis: I gotta go.

Arna tried to get him back, but Alis did not respond. Arna blew up the chat until a notice popped up that Alis had blocked him again.

"He hates me." The words sank into his chest and then out through his eyes. He blinked away the haze. His whole body began to shake as he forced himself to sit up. He had no direction for his Variance. Without Alis, there was no new Variance.

[*Then meet him?* Ixxzal offered.]

"I can't." Alis hated him now, but what of when Alis knew that Rosy was Arna? No. There would be no reconciliation. The only ones who loved Arna were the ones who loved him before the Splintering. He'd been able to hold on to Alis for as long as he could, but this was it.

It was impossible to love someone he'd never met. Alis had given up on him.

[*You need to see him.* Azza was restless. *There is not much time.*]

Don't you think I know that? Arna snapped.

[*It doesn't have to be this hard!* Lumak shouted.]

If you just gave me straight answers, I'd be done!

[*Arna we tried, you won't listen.* Zaynir cried.]

This would all be far more pleasant if you shut up.

[*What else are we doing?* Pokk asked.]

Arna's stomach lurched and a somber wave consumed the slight frustration he had before.

Was it difficult for them to speak? They were there when he needed them. But they more often said nothing. He thought they were letting him wallow and fail. They only spoke when he was with his friends and family.

When was the last time they'd watched one of his morning practices? The last time they'd watched an evening one? When was the last time they gave guidance?

"Berate me into doing this," Arna demanded.

[*You want us to force you into your Variance?* Ixxzal asked.]

"Yes."

[*You know it does not work like that*, Ixxzal snapped back.]

Arna threw his laptop shut, pissed. It had taken him years to decide on his theme, still more to know a direction to take. All the work, for nothing. All because he came home, and he didn't know how to do anything anymore.

[*Just see him.*]

"I can't see him when I don't know who he is, and he won't tell me where he is." There was no way to find Alis. And if he did, then what? Use him to make a new Variance? Was that all that their relationship amounted to? Was that all it had ever been?

Arna's heart was breaking.

With his mobile, Arna made his way to his practice room without extinguishing his candles in his room. *Let them burn.* When he got to the practice room, he said no prayer to ignite the candles before the mirrors. He needed the darkness, away from the Gods. He left the blackout curtain open and faced himself in the mirror.

His reflection was the shell of a person.

[*What is Incarnate Dreams?* Xeyaro asked, standing beside him.]

"I left the candles burning so you'd leave me alone."

[*Only I am here*, they said.]

Xeyaro's hand moved his arm and lifted him up into the opening stance of his variation. They were there as the softest breeze in spring: nostalgia and fleeting warmth.

[*Tell me. What is Incarnate Dreams?*]

"Dreams in mortal form," Arna relented.

[*And what are dreams if not hopes and prayers? If not questions and answers? If not passion and sorrow? You want your dance to be like dreams, but dreams are what you mortals have when you sleep. Fleeting, powerful, lasting, longing.*]

I know.

[*How can you make them physical when you have not experienced the true depth of them?*]

"This is a nightmare." Arna paused, looking at the form of Xeyaro that became more like a mortal, uncanny and unsettling.

It was all a nightmare. His life. The world. If he didn't succeed, then. . .

saffronsaffronsaffronsaffronsaffronsaffron

He didn't want to be another mistake.

[*A nightmare is just another form of a dream. You will wake all the same.* Their hands glided across the silver mirrors and shivering skin. *You know how the story will end.*]

"I don't know how to get there," Arna said as his body was guided into the last stance of his twenty-seventh dance.

[*You do. Shape it to your intention.*]

Visualization, Zaynir's warping voice was less a memory and more an ingrained reaction flowing through Arna's blood. If he was going to create his variations, he had to get out of this paralysis.

notgoodenoughnotgoodenoughnotgoodenough

"I'm not good enough," He admitted to himself more than them.

The weight of saying the words made him implode.

He heaved, and it drained from him. Xeyaro kept him standing as the sobs racked his body and he finally let it go, no longer buried.

[*We always ask for more of our Chosen than any of our Children.*]

Arna's chin was lifted by Xeyaro's hands, much like Zaffre used to when he was a child. Their fingers like roots of some plant, digging into his skin and along his bones, making him sturdier as the God filled him with peace.

His tears were dried.

[*Start from the beginning. We will start as many times as we need.*]

notenoughtimenotenoughtimenotenoughtime

New Dawn Day, Apostle Week's Day of Dreams, was nearly a month away.

[*As long as you believe, we have time to start again. As long as you have not made your choice, we can try anew.*]

They had not abandoned him, and he could not forsake them.

[*What is at the core of a variation? What questions?*]

"What do I want to tell the world?" The question he'd been asked when he'd first began. "How do I want to change the world?" Arna focused on himself. "I thought I knew."

[*You think you know many things,* Pokk spoke next, an apparition in the back with the others. *But mortals do not know all. Your dances have to withstand time and scrutiny. The former iterations were amazing dances, but they were. . .*]

"Not perfect." Glass sparkled. Glass shined. Glass broke. Perfection was fickle and subjective. He did not need flawless greatness.

No.

To be amongst his predecessors, he needed to be remembered.

He stared at himself in the mirror surrounded by six shadows. Raven, cool and collected, had created the original dances. Watsonia, vibrant and bright, had made Twin Fans. Vervain had been dedicated. Sable had been refined. Ilex had fought to save the world that Saffron broke. Saffron was a distant accident that Arna was terrified of replicating.

Arna knew so much about each one of them, stories told to him by the Gods. Yet, it felt like he knew little about them at all.

"Why me?" Arna asked again, not expecting an answer. He never got an answer.

[*The Chosen can be anyone so long as we think you capable of changing the world,* Lumak said the words that were always said.]

While the prophecy laid out in the Omniscient Sextant Enchiridion was clear, the rules for becoming the Chosen were vague at best. Arna never fully understood why the Gods had offered him the chance.

"In our current life, between the ages of twelve and twenty-four," Arna said.

They could be selected anytime between their second official Blessing Cleansing Ceremony to when they became official adults.

"Why did you pick me so early?"

He had first started hearing them and seeing them as fragments when he was six.

[*Because we knew early,* Azza said.]

"Why? What did I do?" How was he special? "Why did you give it to me?"

Tenacity like Pokk always said? Passion like Lumak said? Because he was motivated as Azza insisted? Because he could adapt as Zaynir often reminded him? Because he wanted it enough that Xeyaro thought to consider him?

They always gave different vague reasons, and the one he could trust never did.

[*It's because you weren't special*, Ixxzal said.]

Arna's breath caught in his throat. Ixxzal was answering?

[*But I knew that you could be. If given the chance, you would not let it go.*]

"What did I do in my past life to make you so certain?"

[*You know we can't tell you that Arna*, Zaynir chastised with a laugh.]

[*Nothing*, Ixxzal said as Zaynir spoke. *But I'm the God of the Unknown. I know. It's the only condition. You must not let it go.*]

The answer was more than he ever should have received. It was the fact that they all avoided to say. It was the worst possible answer, as it confirmed all the worst things Arna thought about himself. He was nothing. He had done nothing but destroy everything.

There were no special conditions, any sort of checklist he had to meet. It was just a desire? A guess? How could something so world changing be determined on such a simple. . . chance? What if he chose wrong? They couldn't go to another person and offer it to them? What if he didn't do everything they asked? It was all a risk.

hewasgoingtodiebecausehewasanimposter

runrunrunrunrunrunrun

[*It's the same risk you took chasing me,* Ixxzal reminded.]

Chasing Ixxzal was chasing a dream. He dropped his fan in faith of them. They picked him for the same reason?

If Ixxzal thought that Arna could fix what Saffron broke, that which Ilex could not finish, Arna wanted to believe in that. They all thought that Arna could erase the Splintering and the Shattering, even when he had never proven to them that he could.

whywhywhywhywhywhy

[silence.   ]

Their unwavering faith in him should have been suffocating. Instead, he was a man who had tasted air for the first time in his life.

Arna's image in the reflection changed to Sarcoline. His brother looked less like him than he believed at first, with a sharper chin and lighter skin. But he was just like Arna: driven, needing, loving dance more than anyone. He was The Dancer, just a boy in a garden refusing to stop doing what he loved: bleeding and crying and dancing. He was just a boy fighting the universe when everyone told him to stop.

He was a little boy staring up at candles making a wish, that one day he'd dance on the Weeping Stage, that one day he'd be better than everyone.

[*Incarnate Dreams*, the six Gods said together.]

"I'm not an imposter." He told himself, needing to say it, needing to believe it.

He wanted to see what they saw.

[*Incarnate Dreams was a seed long before you met Alis*, Xeyaro said.]

Arna stood face to face with the Gods, as they had stood on the night of the Splintering. They were there, behind him in the mirror, and thus also before him. He was standing in place of himself and Sarcoline at the same time.

Incarnate Dreams was as much Sarcoline as it was Alis.

Completing the variation would be the proof that Sarcoline would need. It would get Arna his forgiveness. Arna would use his variation in order to create a world where that little boy could be considered great without scorn.

His variation would finally, set him free. Where he could become more than Incarnadine Vivicent: Apostle, Heretic, Imposter.

[*Do it for Alis*. Xeyaro flickered like a candle about to go out. *Do it for Arco. Do it for—*]

There was a knock at the door. The figures vanished. "Yes?"

Gingerline opened the door and walked in. The light silhouetted her figure making her glow almost green, like the color of the leaves of the willow tree behind her. "Were you dancing?"

"Why are you awake?"

Had he missed too much time again? He blinked at the light.

"I had a nightmare." She shuffled on her feet.

He looked her over twice, concerned, and approached her. "Are you okay?"

"It was nothing new." She smiled at him soft. "Are you okay?"

"I'm okay." He nodded. Looking back at himself, he meant it with every fiber of his being. "You want to dance?"

"Sure. Let's dance. We need to get you into shape," she giggled before walking into the room. She had her dance shoes with her: prepared. She became flustered when she noticed him staring at the shoes. "I thought. . . You weren't in your room."

"It's okay."

He connected to his stereo through his augmentations and started *Twice Not* by Ivumalis.

Alis would reach out to him again. Alis always did. As long as he was alive, he could make their relationship tangible. The Gods wanted him to meet Alis, which meant there had to be a chance Alis would never fully hate him. He had to believe it.

"Oh. I love this song!" Gingerline swayed to the beat.

"Me too." Arna stood next to her. "Try this."

Arna then began to show Gingerline the steps to what he had choreographed in his head years ago. He'd never had the time to see it danced until that moment. It was lightness, airiness, dreamy. She caught on quick.

The two danced for hours, through the backlog of ideas that Arna kept locked away. With each new Ivumalis song, was Arna's variation. He could picture himself dancing, the clothes specifically. Like the first droplets before the storm, Arna was almost there.

"Personal Incarnadine choreography to an Ivu song? I must be dreaming." Aureolin's voice came from the door as the song ended and Arna was sketching in his journal the designs for his ceremonial clothes. She tossed them both waters. "I was looking for you both."

"Sorry." Gingerline laughed as she caught the water. "Are we going to be late?"

"You probably want to get changed," Aureolin teased.

Gingerline squealed and raced out of the room. Arna continued his sketch and looked it over twice. It was ugly but it would work for what he needed to do. After all, only he needed to see it.

He thought of what he wanted to do with his mask and flipped the page to start a new sketch with the idea.

"Where are you going?" Arna asked as he sat down to sketch the crude drawing into his notebook, grimacing at how bad it looked. At least only he needed to see it.

"Ginger and Jasione have a date. I'm playing third wheel in case someone tries to interfere," Aureolin said without approaching.

"Does that happen?" Arna looked up, snapping his black book shut.

Aureolin shrugged. "I didn't know you knew Ivu."

"Everyone knows Ivu." Arna hated the way the word tasted. Alis was a better name, but Alis was Arna's exclusive nickname to use. Arna refused to share. "I've been following him since the beginning."

"What?" Aureolin blinked before falling into a fit of laughter. "Turns out that all of us have been listening to his music. One degree of separation this whole time."

"Everyone?" Arna repeated? As in their group had been listening to him make music online the whole time?

"Arco found him, freaked out, and told Amaryllis. He loves Ivu and introduced him to us all. I know that Phlox listens to Ivu, and I've seen Ebru looking at the songs before at auditions."

"Wow. This whole time..."

Aureolin beamed with excitement but did not walk into the studio. She wore brown and tans, with a cape over her shoulder. She wore tall heels with gold sunflowers etched into them. In her hand was a travel mug with steaming tea. She had gold flowers in her hair.

"Your hair looks nice. You wear a lot of flower crowns. Do you make them?"

"Yea. Phlox said that..." Aureolin pouted. "I like them. Everyone likes them, not just Phlox. But I think they suit me."

"Phlox likes them," Arna said Phlox's name carefully and Aureolin shot him a glare.

He laughed. *I'm right.*

"She thinks I need to be more feminine. She and Amaryllis are enough for the lot of us." There was a touch of almost jealousy on her voice. "They should just be friends already."

"They should be," he teased her.

"Enough about her. I don't want to think about her," Aureolin said, defensively.

"Do you often?" Arna pressed, with a knowing smile.

Aureolin pretended not to hear him. A light flush dusted across her light brown skin. "I hear you and Ven talked. Was it good? Are you better now? I know that they are strong headed but... You know? It's Ven."

She continued to talk, and Arna could see how hurt she was beneath. Once again, Arna said the words, "I'm—" *words are cheap.*

"Sorry?" Aureolin's smile dropped. "Why do you feel like you need to say that to me?"

Until it worked. Until things went back to the way they were.

It would never be achieved.

[No one debated. No one way. No one there.]

Arna said, "I don't know. I feel like I'll be apologizing my whole life."

"You will be. But you don't need to apologize to us Arna. You just need to be with us."

Arna blinked, uncertain of what to say. Be with them? But that would mean he'd have to put them at risk of being hurt again. He couldn't do that to them... He... wasn't going to survive...

Arna thought of his fans and a distant dream he'd once had to create a new type of fan boning. Something light that could withstand the heaviest pressures. A support system that could carry the weight without looking like it should be able to.

Arna pondered the impossibility. If he did that, then he'd. . . He'd need help.

Help?

[A new dawn broke within.]

The Gods always made it clear that the Chosen never did everything alone. The only thing they had to do was dance alone and take on the pressure of Divinity alone. But the taking of Divinity was a completely internal process; the way the universe lashed out as it descended into the physical plain was an external one. External aspects were a consequence, assistance with the tools was a consideration, help was allowed. They were not a part of the test. The choice he made was: mortals or the Gods. The dance was the proof of that choice.

He was allowed to ask for help on everything but his choice. They had told him he could ask for help time and time again. They had practically screamed it at him, and he thought they were being cryptic. This was why he was home.

The Gods wanted him to reconnect with his family for help.

[Distant elements burst and combined.]

Arna clenched his hands tight. He couldn't put that pressure on his family. He couldn't ask them for help, tell them the truth, and then still die on them. The chances were slim to none that they'd be able to anything to actually assist.

No. He couldn't be that cruel. Not again.

As if reading his discomfort Aureolin spoke. "Enough about them and apologies. Let's talk Ivu. Did you know that Ivumalis could have been the composer for our group dance?"

What? All of Arna's worries vanished.

"They asked him?" Arna asked.

Why didn't Alis tell him that? Working with the DHS was a privilege and honor. Was Alis that dead set on keeping his anonymity? Or had he told him? Did Arna miss that message?

"Rumor has it that they did," Aureolin smiled.

"Phlox?" Arna asked. She was the source of all rumors.

"No. Your father." Aureolin laughed genuine and loud, bubbly and bright. It was like when they were kids. "He gossips like a teenager when it comes to the DHS."

"They didn't get him?"

"Apparently not. Although I'm not surprised, Ivu only ever takes song requests from Crimson." Aureolin said with a shrug.

Hearing his username made his heart skip a beat. He was famous online. His name was listed in credits and descriptions as a collaborator or the requestor of songs. Hearing his username out loud, however, was strange.

Aureolin did not notice his reaction and went on, "Cyclamen Shadone must have been furious."

"Why?" Why would he care?

"Apparently, he was mad enough to suggest it." Aureolin looked behind her, hearing something Arna did not.

"I'm here!" Jasione yelled from the lobby.

"She's getting changed. She was dancing!" Aureolin yelled back. She then looked to Arna again. "And he was mad enough to get Ebru to make the music."

Since when could Eburnean make music?

Slowly standing, Arna tried to piece together his thoughts as Aureolin motioned him to follow. Stepping into his hall slippers, Arna left his dance shoes behind. "Ebru's doing the music?"

The name felt wrong. The idea felt wrong. It was familiar but wrong. Why?

"That's what he said, Phlox told me." She paused thinking for a moment. "Apparently, he can compose music? Basics, or something."

"And that's good enough for Cyclamen?" Arna wasn't sure that could ever be good enough for the man unless there was more to it.

"It's war remember? He wants it to fail. He wants to prove that your father made the wrong choice in keeping us all together," Aureolin sighed and walked over to the front.

"We were still rivals," He reminded her.

"They think we should have only been rivals. That it was our unity that caused you to seek to stand out." She shook her head.

"We were born together," Arna said what his father told them years ago.

"And thus, belong together," Aureolin nodded, continuing the quote. The Vivicent motto for the Golden Generation had been drilled into them every practice, every day, for years. They could be angry, but they had to love each other. They could be competitive, but they were friends. They were united. Always.

"Only by dancing together can we grow to greater heights," They said together.

They had always danced in one song together during the Celebrations in order to reinforce their teamwork when the rest of the world wanted them to tear out each other's throats. This year it was being used against them.

"The Gods do not want competition. They want beautiful dancing," Arna finished.

[The Gods hummed in agreement.]

"It's always been strange that there are six of us." Aureolin sighed when Jasione called out to them. "Have you ever wondered why?"

"No." Arna said honestly when it hit him like the electricity of breaking a taboo.

He *did* know.

For me?

"Isn't it strange?" Aureolin went on.

[*You needed help*, Zaynir said.]
[*You have a lot more to fix than your predecessors, although we did not expect the Splintering*, Pokk admitted.]

"It's never happened before in recorded history," Aureolin went on.

You made them all Children for me? Just to help him?

[*Not all of them. Arco isn't a Child*, Azza sang.]

"Why now?" Aureolin asked.

[*Usually, we allow for a bit more freedom, yes. But not for this. For this we needed to know that you would have the support necessary to succeed with healing the Shattering*, Pokk continued.]

Arna struggled to keep his breathing even.

[*We're just giving up all our secrets today*, Lumak groaned.]

He needed them to fix the Splintering? Needed them heal the Shattering?

The Gods had sent him home, to reconnect with his family. They kept pushing him to do so. *No. . .*

[*Ixxzy started it*, Azza joked. *Pokk is more than willing to help.*]

"Arna?"

They needed him to betray their love again? To die for them? Truly? In a way they could not stop this time?

hewasgoingtodiehewasgoingtodiehewasgoingtodie

[*We collected the best souls possible, who would not need to ask. Who would* know, Ixxzal, the God of Secrets, ignored them.]

Arna did not press on the implications of the statement. He could not ask them to risk their lives for him. It was better for them to stay away. He could not sacrifice them like he had to himself. But. . . What if they could help him? What if they accepted his truth? What if they were his way at staying alive?

What if they could be his Saints?

[Alive. A life. Survive.]

His heart thudded in his chest. Arna had been so certain that he'd die for so long, so distressed by the thought, he never let himself think of an after, dream of a future.

But what if?

"Because we need each other. Because we understand each other better than anyone else," Arna said breathless, his hands laying limp at his sides.

"You think?" Aureolin asked. "It was destiny not chance?"

"In my experience, the two come hand in hand."

They were not opposites, but the same thing glowing in different lights.

(A choice to make.)

(A risk to take.)

But could he do that?

Hands open. Hands closed. Arna did not squeeze.

The two walked into the reception hall where Jasione stood waiting. He was dressed in soft purples with sparkles, draped sleeves of a cloak and long pants that were almost sheer. His eyes trailed over Aureolin. "You're wearing that?"

"It's your date."

Jasione was about to speak when Gingerline rushed into the hall, dressed in a brighter green than Arna had seen her in since he'd come back home. The color of fresh picked limes, the dress bounced in ripples as she moved, wings lined her back and trailed to the floor as her hair was twisted up atop her head, braids framing her face. Her dress was like Jasione's, glittering in moon dust.

"I'm sorry. I'm sorry. Are you ready?" She asked.

"Yes." Jasione kissed her forehead and looked back to Arna. "Don't leave the house."

"I make no promises." Besides, the guards never cared if he left or not. They were there for appearances.

"Arna and I were dancing to Ivu's music and lost track of time." Gingerline deflected for Arna.

"We should go. Phlox will be waiting." Jasione sighed, defeated by the both of them.

"Phlox?" Arna asked.

"Aureolin's date," Gingerline smiled. Arna shot Aureolin a wide smile.

"It's not a date," Aureolin stuttered. "We are both watching you both. Phlox wants to be friends again and I don't trust it."

Sure, Arna mouthed at her. Her eyes widened and she tilted her head with a tense smile: a clear threat for him to shut up.

Jasione shook his head. "You talk to Phlox the most out of all of us."

"Ebru talks to her more. Besides all it is bragging, telling me what she's doing." Jasione and Gingerline shared a look, and Aureolin stammered on, "Besides, Phlox *likes* Amaryllis."

"No. Phlox hates Amaryllis," Jasione corrected.

"Amaryllis said they talked," Gingerline reminded them.

"Thin line between the two. And we aren't going on a date." Aureolin shook her head. "Now we are late, we need to go." She pushed them out the door, past the guards. Arna followed them into the yard, standing under the swaying willow branches. The sun was fading away from the weekly simulated rain that kept the plants healthy and alive.

"Wait!" Gingerline raced back and hugged Arna. She then whispered: "If it's any consolation, Arna. I think we are all imposters in some way. None of us are good enough, we only have to be good and that is enough."

She then stepped away and waved, leaving him with his mouth hanging open. She heard him talking to the Gods?

goodenoughgoodenoughgoodenough

Arna's hands opened.

The three headed to the rails and Arna turned to head back inside but chose not. Inside was empty and held no truths for him to follow. The guards looked at him with resentful eyes and radiated danger. Still in his slippers, Arna walked off towards Amaryllis' studio and then fell off the beaten path, directed by the wind as he processed what he'd learned. The Gods wanted him to trust his family.

It would hurt them more to ask for help than keeping them at a distance and dying without another word. Right? He couldn't give them false hope of his survival. He couldn't lie to them either.

Yet. . .

The future laid in wait.

He could dance with Gingerline at any time of the day. He could speak with Aureolin more and watch her group dances as live performances. He could finally see Phlox's movies live and attend a premiere. He could go to Pervenche's formal archery competitions. He could accept Rosmarinus and travel the world with Jasione. He could. . . Eburnean. . . Eburnean was clear in Arna's memory, leaning over him close enough to kiss, speaking harsh but flirtatious words.

Arna covered his hands over his face completely disgusted and ashamed of himself. How could he be crushing on Eburnean at a time like this? How could his emotions be this fickle? Guilt spiraled through Arna as he thought of Eburnean first before Alis; Alis who had been there for him through everything. He loved Alis. . . He needed to find Alis. And. . .

Alis was the one he avoided out of fear of rejection. Arna stopped walking.

If he had his family and their support. If he truly had it all. . . He could have Alis. If he survived, he could love Alis. He could be with Alis. He could finally, finally, touch him and not fear. Arna would never have to hide from him again. It didn't matter if it took time to convince him that Arna was not the worst person in the world.

If Arna lived. He had time.

Arna's heart clenched. But the odds were too great it was impossible. Even if everything went right, he'd already lost Blessings.

The Gods always told him that his death wasn't a guarantee if they prepared enough, but he knew that was their way of comfort. He'd run the numbers himself. He'd checked every option. There was no way for him to live after he completed the twenty-seventh dance.

No. He could not risk it. He could not put that pressure on them.

Not even if he wanted it more than anything.

[*No! Visualize,* Zaynir pleaded.]

Arna tried.

Wandering the streets, Arna made his way to the business circle, where all the big businesses and shops in the center of the city were. While there were small family-owned stores and schools on all the petals, as well as large petal centers for commerce and business, the business circle was filled the most profitable and world renown brands.

The district was celebrating the beginning of Xeysis fashion week. People were dressed in all the best from designers from the other cities. While other cities had their own fashion scenes, they were less celebrated, because Children of Arts and fashion belonged to Xeyaro.

Thus, Xeysis fashion week took the other Gods into consideration and made designs with the other cities in mind. There were some designers who specialized in Ludiel and others in Podiel designs. Everyone around him was dressed in clothes reminiscent of the natural world: flowers and leaves, stars and gems, butterflies and moths. Hand dyed colors moved together, creating a prismatic array. Light bounced through clothes as they whirled and moved.

Arna did not need to keep to the shadows as he walked. Most people were too absorbed in the fashion shows on the streets and the falling rose petals from overhead. There were screens everywhere, with consolidated audio that could only be heard as one walked through certain bubbles illuminated by colored circles on the ground. Robotic dog vendors walked around with samples on their backs.

People drank a variety of white drinks, some sparkling, some moving like smoke, and others nearly gelatin in totality. All the food was silver, tomatoes dipped in silver glitter, chocolate cast with a silver sheen. Warm scents—cinnamon, nutmeg, smoke from a fire—filled the air like summer.

Everyone was enthralled with the show.

As Arna walked, he found Phlox's face on the big screen of a building, showing off her clothes in an interview. Aureolin, Gingerline, and Jasione were nearby from what Arna could see as the frame tightened up on Phlox's face.

Cardinal White was on another screen. Arna had not talked to the man, despite the times he'd reached out. Without needing confirmation, Arna suspected it was either because there were too many things to do for the church, or because Cardinal White was being pressured by Cardinal Black. Regardless of the reason, Arna paid it no heed. The man would always support him, and when it was time, they'd meet and talk. He didn't have time to worry about it.

theendtheendtheend

Arna's mobile buzzed.

Alis: You think I don't know you when I see you?

What? Arna's heart began to race. Was it finally happening? Was this the end?

theendtheendtheend

Crashing emotions swelled up about him, like waves consuming all that they touched.

Alis: I thought you promised me you deleted the accounts.

The images Alis sent next were a series of screenshots of Arna's burner account messaging people on forums for Sarcoline and Eburnean.

theendtheendtheend

Rosy: I'm defending people.
Rosy: Besides, they're new accounts.
Alis: Old or new. It's not good for you.
Alis: Have you been reading our hate boards again too?

Arna paused, unsure what to say. He didn't want to lie. It was a burning at his chest that would *kill* him if he if tried.

Alis: You aren't responding but I know you're there.
Alis: How many accounts do you have that I don't know about?
Rosy: Someone has to defend us.
Alis: We defend us, by being a united front.
Alis: As partners. We're partners, remember?
Alis: Getting into online fights only feeds your insecurities.
Alis: Please

Arna was not relieved at seeing the fact that Alis did not know who he was. If anything, there was a bitter disappointment. All he could see were the lies, in all the screen shots. It was the same lies that he'd given Alis: in everything he'd ever said.

Rosy: I'll delete the accounts.
Alis: I want proof this time.
Rosy: My word isn't enough?

There was a long moment where Alis was typing, before the next set of messages arrived.

Alis: You're my everything.
Alis: I won't let you destroy yourself.

Arna reread the messages over and over again.

Alis: I have to block you again. Send proof.

Arna held the mobile close to his chest and heaved. Discordant songs flowed through him. The dances that had been so close were again so far.

Why did it seem that he was just messing everything up? Why was it that there was no way for him to fix any of this?

Did he really have to rely on his family, break his family again? Was there no other way?

"Yeah. No. I'm headed to them now." Amaryllis' voice made Arna jump. Pervenche was not with her. A mobile call? "No. Not yet. Ven messaged me that transportation is running late. They'll be here as soon as they can. Yeah. . . Yeah. . . No! Really? You can't say that."

She had stopped walking, staring up at the screen with Phlox's face.

"I promise you! Sar-co-line. I promise. Me and Phlox? We're going to be fine. . . No! I promise you. No! She. . . She's— She's on a date with Aureolin. I promise." She laughed. "Yes— I wouldn't pick *Phlox*." Amaryllis groaned. "Okay. You're right. Phlox is cute and she— What?— You're the one who said she was cute!"

Amaryllis started walking again, and Arna hesitated on reaching out to her again. He did not want to ruin her call with Sarcoline, but he was embarrassed at having heard her conversation with his brother. It was a breach of confidence in his book.

By the time he decided to call out to her, she had run off and he was forced to follow.

"Okay. Okay. Yeah. . . Yeah. I love you, too, Coco. You go, dance. . . Dance. I'll talk to you later, okay?. . . Yes. . . Yes. . . I'll send pictures. No. I don't want to take them. Work was *killer* today." She laughed again. "Okay. . . Yeah. . . Yeah. . . Go— Bye— Bye—Bye—Love you. Bye. . . Yeah. Bye. . . Love you, too, Coco."

"Incarnadine?" Someone asked as he passed them, trying to catch up to Amaryllis. Ignorant of his own situation, Arna was surrounded by those who saw him. He'd been so focused on Amaryllis he'd forgotten to keep himself protected with his flourished Blessings.

"Found you!" Amaryllis suddenly pulled on Arna. "Come on!" Arna was dragged away before the scene could get worse. "Can you use your Blessings to make us disappear?"

Without being told twice, Arna did so, and the two ran. She wore a long pink and white dress, that fluttered as she ran. Glitter sparked off of it in the shape of rose petals disappearing into the air like smoke.

"Sorry," Arna apologized to her when she stopped and looked around.

"I didn't expect to see you here," she said staring at his slippers.

"I heard you talking to Arco." Arna was vaguely aware he should be embarrassed, dressed in shorts, a hoodie and slippers looking like he should be at home instead of at the biggest fashion show in the world.

"Oh!" she gasped, looking back up at him. "He said to tell his family he loves them."

"I didn't mean to listen."

"I have nothing to hide." She began to sprint again.

Arna let her lead him through the crowd and to the others, who had finished their interview. Phlox was dressed in the latest by some designer that he'd never heard of. She was like a hurricane, dressed in a variety of shades of blue that twisted about her body in a vortex of impossible design, defying gravity.

"Arna!" Phlox cheered. Jasione paled and Gingerline's eyes grew wide. Pervenche stood with them in an indigo outfit that flattered their pale skin. They were almost a bit distant in their nod to Amaryllis. Had something happened? What was going on?

"I told you to stay home," Jasione said to Arna before he could think too deeply about Ven and Amaryllis.

"He's already here." Phlox took Arna's other arm. "This means we're all here."

"Arco's not here." Amaryllis let go of Arna and hurried to Pervenche.

"Right." Phlox gave Arna a kiss on the cheek and then let him go. "Ebru also isn't coming either. He's *practicing*."

"He's always practicing." Aureolin shook her head. Phlox skipped over to her side. Aureolin eyed Phlox as Phlox fixed Aureolin's hair. "What do we do now?"

"We should get drinks," Phlox offered. "We have time before the next show."

"I'm not planning on staying," said Arna.

He had only come to the event to try to find inspiration and that wasn't working out like he wanted. Not when he didn't have Alis. Not when he couldn't put them under the pressure he was carrying.

Phlox led them along anyway.

"Guess what we found out," Gingerline said when they were far enough away.

"What?" Amaryllis asked.

"Arna listens to Ivumalis too!"

All eyes were on him. He did not look away.

"Really?" Phlox beamed.

"That. . . makes sense," Pervenche nodded.

"One degree of separation this whole time. We could have been messaging him in the comments," Gingerline laughed.

"Arco is going to love this," Amaryllis said messaging on her mobile.

"What's your favorite song?" Phlox asked.

"*Serenity's Lament*," Arna answered and then quoted Alis. "Silence is not an absence but a reminder of what you have."

It was his favorite song that Alis had written for him.

The others hummed and eyed him carefully.

"I would have expected something more upbeat," Phlox admitted.

"Its' beautiful," Aureolin said. She smiled bright like the sun. "Mine is *Meetings at Eternity*."

"*Eighth Day*," Pervenche said as the scales of their indigo jacket shined in the changing light.

"I love *A Mystery of Trees*," Phlox added, bouncing on her heels. Her cloud dress swayed as she did. Arna laughed.

"What?" Aureolin asked.

"Nothing. I'm just amazed how vast your tastes are."

The others laughed with him.

His friend's favorite songs were the same as the Gods'? The Gods and his friends were more alike than he had expected. It was common to see the Gods in people since the Gods touched everything. Maybe this was what it meant to be a Saint: this familiarity.

But it was also different. At the beginning of his exile, the Gods had come to him in the figures of his friends in an effort to cheer him up. Maybe they picked the songs to connect him to them.

"Mine is, *Glass Eyes*," Jasione went on. "Rus loves *Forever Me*."

"*Masquerade Rivers*," Gingerline said. Above her the artificial moon was rising, and Arna's heart skipped a beat.

"Mine is *Spring Roses* but Arco loves *Twice Not*." Amaryllis smiled at Arna. With her smile Arna was struck, looking at all of his friends thrice more.

"What is Ebru's?" Arna asked, the words dry on his tongue.

"*Not Again*," Phlox said when no one else did. It was Ixxzal's favorite song. Once was fair, twice was a coincidence, three was funny, but all of them?

helphelphelphelphelphelp

"You're certain?" Gingerline asked her.

"He never admits it, but it's the one he listens to the most."

"That doesn't count. Wasn't that the song Crimson wrote for Ivu?"

"Ivu finished it," Arna said half-heartedly.

It was the first song he ever completed on his own that Alis had refined before uploading online. Alis had said to put it on his own channel, but Arna had insisted it went on the Ivumalis channel under his name. Alis had still made it clear that Rosy had created it.

The group got in line for drinks.

"I never took Ebru for the romantic. That's *the* Carnation love song." Gingerline gossiped.

It was the first time he'd heard his and Alis' pairing name out of someone else's mouth. Arna had fought long and hard over the years to ensure that when referring to their pair, their couple, that people only ever referred to them as Carnation instead of Crimvu, which still made him cringe in disgust. As soon as Alis wrote his first love song for Rosy, *Serenity's Lament*, Arna had been in the comments fighting for Carnation.

Alis never cared, and Arna assumed that was because Alis agreed.

Did you pick your favorite songs to be the same as theirs on purpose? Just to make me feel better?

To make him feel closer to them? To trust them? To rely on them? To make them Saints?

[*There are no accidents,* Ixxzal said.]

(Could he rely on them?)

(Was he allowed to live?)

"I sometimes wonder what sort of person Ivu is," Amaryllis said. "All of the Carnation love songs seem a bit. . ."

"Star crossed?" Phlox offered and Amaryllis nodded. "I bet you they have heartmates who are different people. Somehow they met online and fell in love. It would be heartbreaking. If the Gods did exist, they *would* be that cruel."

"The Gods do exist Phlox," Gingerline complained.

"Gods are nothing more than a lie created by our ancient ancestors to keep us in line. The Omniscient Sextant Enchiridion was made to keep us from destroying ourselves in using our Blessings," Phlox said, sweetly. "The Gods only exist because people believe they exist. They're only what we make them into, that doesn't actually make them real."

Arna was shocked. Phlox had always been very anti-God, due to the homes she grew up in, but the words, despite being blatant heresy, did not sting.

The Gods exist because people exist.

Without one the other wouldn't survive.

It was the nature of the contract and the magic between them.

[*There are no accidents,* Ixxzal said.]

"He's the most famous composer in the world," Jasione said, ignoring Phlox and talking to Amaryllis. "Yet, he hides himself and rarely talks in forums. He's probably a recluse."

Alis never admitted nor accepted it. He thought that his secrecy and anonymity were the only reason people liked him.

In the distance an Ivumalis song began to play.

They ordered their drinks to go and began to wait.

"We should ask Crimson," Phlox laughed typing in the air. "He answers most of time."

"Neither he nor Ivu have responded to messages in months. They're working on a project." Gingerline shook her head, then giggled. "I bet you it's going to be another epic."

"Or maybe they finally got married, for real this time." Phlox winked. Arna had to fight himself from flushing at the words.

Despite having joked about it many times of over the last year, it was impossible to consider.

But if he lived, he could marry Alis if he wanted, so long as Alis said yes.

Arna's hear fluttered.

[Distant laughter roared like a fragmented memory in the mist.]

Stay calm. Stay calm.

"I bet Ivu's really nice," Amaryllis went on with a dreamy voice and a big sigh. "His music is so pure and filled with emotions. Nice. . . but hurting."

"Hurting?" Phlox scoffed. "Really, you can *hear* that?"

"Phlox be nice," Aureolin chastised her.

"I agree," Arna defended Amaryllis. She was right, and Alis was hurting. "His music always has a reflection of pain in it. I wouldn't be surprised if his life was a mess at times."

"Another genius with issues. Great. The world does not need another Ebru," Aureolin sighed.

Eburnean?

Heat rose in Arna's chest and rushed through his veins.

[Perfection is rose-colored glass.]

"I tried finding out if he was a Child, and I can't find anyone with A.Song that fits the correct age," Phlox gossiped.

Eburnean? And Cyclamen and. . ?

"He could be lying about his age," Jasione offered.

Eburnean.

The image of his smile was plastered in Arna's brain. He was on billboards and neon signs, on posters and in movies. His voice sang songs across the internet and radio.

But Arna had never heard Alis' real voice. Nor had he ever seen his face.

"Even then, all the A.Song Children can't be Ivu. I checked." She turned and went to the counter to get their order.

Arna pictured Eburnean's ankles. He'd been injured on the same side Alis had been.

Think. Think.

They only ever sent pictures from the waist down, but not ever above. Arna did it because he could not show his vow mark on his chest. Alis couldn't show. . .

"Then that makes him like us," Pervenche said to Phlox when she returned. "Blessing hopping."

"We can't be certain he's a Child," Gingerline offered.

"He's a Child." Everyone else said at once, save Arna who was stuck on the name: Eburnean.

The Ivumalis song grew louder and louder.

Jasione shook his head. "Regardless of who he is, he's talented. And he has a reason to hide himself."

No.

Alis was hiding himself, because he had not wanted anyone to find out: to save money to escape the Boss. He didn't want to worry his father more. Then his father found his secret. Later the Boss learned—

The heat in Arna's veins spread into a roaring fire.

"Ebru should be here." Phlox passed out the drinks. "It's weird that just five of the Golden Generation are together."

Arna thought of Eburnean standing too close, lifting Arna's chin, eyes locked, a diamond masked in layers of fog and mists. He thought of Alis messaging him late at night wishing Arna to find him.

"He's *practicing*," Aureolin reminded her.

"That's his code for that he pissed off the Shadones and instead of facing their wrath he's staying late."

"Did they hurt him again?" Arna asked as the images aligned.

His entire world began to shake. The winds were louder. The sky was heavier. The weather was changing rapidly.

Everyone turned to stare at him confused. Then their eyes turned to the sky. The weather was actually changing, not just Arna imagining it.

"What?" Pervenche asked, shaking their head and waving their hand to activate a nanotech umbrella. Tiny bots flew through the air to cover them all. "When did they. . .?"

"Weeks ago." Amaryllis nodded. "When you all met up the first time. Right?"

"Yeah." Arna looked to Phlox. "Did they?"

Thousands of text messages were before him. Every image made sense when compared in memory. Every interaction suddenly lined up. Everything he had tried to ignore, slapped him in the face. *Oh. . . Gods.*

[Distant static broke up the Ivumalis song.]

"They hurt him?" Pervenche's voice cracked. Then they glared at Phlox. "I thought you were being hyperbolic."

"No. I meant it," Phlox whispered.

Everyone looked at her with varying degrees of horror. Was Arna the only one who had assumed that Ebru had been hurt?

"You didn't know?" Arna asked them.

The Gods had *known*. It was why they told him to keep pressing and to find Alis.

[do you see   do you feel   do you know   what do you   ]

"He always said he was fine, and Alabaster said that no one touched him," Ginger explained. "We just assumed that Phlox was being dramatic."

"He doesn't tell me everything, and he rarely says that he's hurt. When he is, he says he did it to himself. I don't think his father knows." Phlox squirmed under their eyes, her voice turning in on itself no longer confident.

"How can Alabaster not know?" Arna hissed. "Ebru is in a viper's den there. The Shadone's want Vivicent blood and Ebru might not be related to us, but the Hues have supported the Vivicents since Ilex. I can't believe it. How naive. . . no. How could Alabaster miss it?"

"Uncle Alabaster. . ." Gingerline tried to find an excuse.

"No. Don't say it. If Ebru is hiding it from him, it's still not Ebru's fault. His father might be busy but that is no excuse to neglect—" Arna stopped talking and dropped his tea.

All at once Arna understood something else that he had been wanting to ignore. For the first time in months, he had not thought of the end of the world. He had not thought of dying. He had been laughing, enjoying his time. He'd been flushed. He'd experienced sorrow and rage.

He had been *living*.

Living meant them. Living meant reconnecting. Living meant. . . Alis. Meant Eburnean.

"Arna. . ." Gingerline called.

Arna's attention snapped up and his eyes met Amaryllis who was the only one not smiling. Her eyes were on his, seeing his soul.

"Sorry I. . . I. . ."

closeclosecloseclosecloseclose

"I need to go home."

timetimetimetimetimetime

He needed to confirm but not here. If he was right. . .

"What? No. I'm sorry. . ." Gingerline reached for him, but Jasione stopped her.

"What?" Arna looked at them all. "What? No. It's not your fault it's. . . No. I'm not angry about you not realizing. We just. . . We. . . Need to help Ebru."

Because he was Alis.

helphelphelphelphelphelphelp

Arna covered his mouth again. "I need to go."

Amaryllis squinted, unconvinced.

"Arna." Phlox tried to stop him and Aureolin stopped her.

"Are you okay?" Aureolin asked.

"Yeah. I am. I just. . . You guys have fun. I. . . I didn't intend to bring down the mood like this, but I just had an epiphany and. . ."

All at once, every single one of their faces changed. What had been desolation and confusion, turned to strange surprise. Every single one of them had misunderstood him, that it had to do with the dances they assumed he was creating. In a way, they were correct. But they were also wrong, and he had no way of explaining.

"I'm going to go. Okay? You all. . . I'll see you at home." He then hurried to leave, casting his Blessings over himself to vanish.

With single focus, Arna ran home.

Two names circled into his head, creating a fuller picture by the moment.

Bronzed lights of the city mixed with a dark gray haze of moisture in the air. A soft pink hue danced across the sky. The rail lines overhead were digital synapses connecting people across distances.

Raindrops began to fall.

But when you turn away from horrors, be sure not to forget them.
When we pretend they are not there, we cannot fix them.
Choosing to see beauty is not forgetting the horror exists.
With as much progress as we have, we must not forget that which can destroy us.

— On the fifth variation.

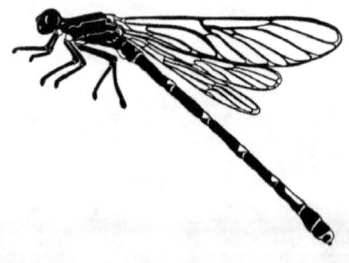

Dance 12

Cacophony

Incarnadine

36 Ixan

42 Days Left

"What are you going to be making with this?"
"My variation – "
"Not good enough. Start again."
"How many more times?"
"Until you can visualize the future you want and can achieve it."

When he was little, Arna loved the light of the stage.

He liked the way that the theatre was always colder than the outside world. While he should have worn a jacket, the chill air was a relief as soon as he finished dancing. The bodies on the stage created a heat that would envelop him in sweltering blanket. That was why he liked the Weeping Stage. It was always cool, because of the open air.

Arna loved the sound of applause, the rumbling that filled a room and reverberated across walls. He loved the way that cheers could implant itself upon his memory, for all time. He thrived off of the adoration of others and fed off their notice, or he had once. Arna had long starved himself of devotion through isolation.

Then there were the lights and the way that they beat down on him. They were bright, much too bright to look into—not that it stopped them from daring each other to do it. Like the sun, the lights poured down on him, adding layer and layer of heat in unfiltered and focused light. He had loved the lights like a moth loved fire.

However, fire wasn't always warm.

Arna fed the letters in his hands to the Everlit candles, and the cold blue flames transformed the paper into glittering white smoke. After Gingerline mentioned them, Arna had started looking for them. Each morning, he checked the mail before his parents awoke to find them in droves. Reading them, he found what he had expected: cruel words. Each day that he burned them, the words stung more.

> You're such a colossal failure at life. Even if you spent the next six hundred generations trying to reconcile your mistake, you would not be able to unfuck this.

> Even if the best part of you hadn't dribbled down your mother's legs, you'd still be a disappointment. Kill yourself.

> Hundreds of Vivicent generations and bloodlines led to you. What a disappointment. It would be a blessing for us all if you disappeared.

> Imagine the shame your ancestors must feel to know that their hard work has led to you.

Even killing yourself at this point wouldn't make amends.

Arna rubbed his hands to remove the chalky residue, looking at himself one last time in the mirror above the candles. His fade was clean, his eyebrows sharp. He had his father's chin. His mother's nose. His sister's smile. His brother's eyes. When the world saw him, they would see his family. Arna took a deep breath and sighed turning to face his room.

Arna was furious as he sat in his room, a collage of religious iconography back up, in tandem with the photos and posters of all those in his life. The two were woven together, akin to the way it was in Amaryllis' studio. Hundreds of pictures were pinned to the walls, overlapping each other, feeding into a rainbow all surrounding him. The past echoed, reminding him of what he was fighting for.

His eyes were on Eburnean, flipping off the camera of a reporter, stern glare, and light circles under his eyes from lack of sleep.

[*Arna,* Pokk spoke in a hushed tone.]

"Shut up." Arna glared at the walls, staring at the way Eburnean's cheek bones were shaped, and the narrow of his collar. He pulled up the pictures again, presenting them to himself in his augmentations.

Eburnean in bathing suit photoshoots, Alis' legs as he sat at his desk. The same.

The shadow? The same.

The backstory? The same.

[*Arna please,* Pokk pleaded.]

"You lied to me," Arna flipped to the messages he'd screen shot and compared them to the headlines he'd found. He noted all the injuries disguised as accidents. They were all things he would have noticed if he had been paying closer attention, but he only ever searched for his family's and friend's triumphs not the scandals.

In the corner of his augmentations, the notification number was rising. They were messages he refused to look at, from Alis and potentially others. He could not risk reading them.

[*Incarnadine,* Azza pressed, trying to keep the peace.]

"This entire time Ixxzal?" Arna demanded.

[*Yes, this whole time,* Ixxzal snapped back.]

This was why they said just to talk to Alis.

Just go find Alis.

Arna knew exactly where Eburnean was. He always had.

"I thought you said I couldn't talk to anyone." Arna snarked back.

[*It was anonymous,* Ixxzal sighed deeply, the sound shattered the room and skies above.]

Or was it that he couldn't talk to anyone because it could affect his decision? That it would keep him from being driven. They'd only given him Alis once he turned twenty, when he was at his lowest point. For seven years they had talked. Three years were anonymous and restrained. Four they spoke like best friends, three of which Arna was in love with Alis. The last two? Flirting openly. And the most recent one. . . they acted like a couple.

Alis was in love with him, had been in love with him longer than Arna loved Alis.

Eburnean didn't know who he was, because if he had, he wouldn't have acted as blatantly flirtatious in front of everyone. Which meant that if Arna told him. . .

Arna placed his head in his hands.

He had *promised* Alis that he'd save him. He'd sworn to himself that he'd find Alis if he ever knew how to. But if he went to get Eburnean, there would be no way he'd let him go. Even now he wanted to rush to the Shadone' studio, wanted to grab Eburnean and steal him away. But. . .

I'm going to die.

[*Arna, trust me,* Ixxzal implored.]

Arna hated moments like this. Because he did trust the Gods. But what they were asking him to do was cruel.

Repair his relationships.

helphelphelphelphelphelp

Succeed or. . .

theendtheendtheend

He had to dance, and. . .

diediediediediedie

What other option did he have?

Arna's palms itched but he did not clench his hands, instead he grabbed his jacket and got off his bed.

The house was closing in on him. He needed to be anywhere else but there. Leaving his room, with the candles still burning, Arna started towards the one place he'd been itching to go but feared.

There was the remnant of smoke in the kitchen, as Arna entered the second floor, fresh and stale at the same time. Arna paused amongst the chairs of the living room. The kitchen lights were off, but the smell wafted from within, and the late night moon's glow lit up the room. Once again Arna was a child, who had made a vow and did not know the weight of it.

The sink of the kitchen was filled with ash and a few scraps of paper that his mother's fire had failed to destroy. *Die. Kill. Better off.* They were letters that Arna had failed to retrieve first.

Arna's stomach constricted at the thought of his mother reading them. He turned on the tap washing the hate away. Crystal waters blurred the lines, but they could not be erased.

"Get rid of this," Arna demanded.

[*Arna, just trust me,* Ixxzal sighed.]

"What's the point in being able to rupture reality if you won't do it when I ask?" Arna snapped.

They could do something as simple as this without too much risk.

"Please. Can you get rid of this?"

Ixxzal said nothing but a soft breeze rushed through the room.

[*Visualize Arna, darling, visualize,* Zaynir begged.]

Arna wished to punch a wall. However, breaking his hand over the Gods wasn't worth it now. It hadn't been worth it the first time he'd done it either. Besides, he was asking the God to expend more power for something so frivolous. In hindsight, Arna was embarrassed asking.

Arna left the house, slipping past the guards, with his Blessings active and flourished, head down and hands in his pockets.

[*Be careful Arna,* Azza warned him like a too clingy sister.]

The air spiraled around Arna as he walked in the dark, deep into the night.

Eburnean was Alis, the fact was an obvious as the superstorms would destroy the world and Arna would die after he finished dancing the dances.

Arna wanted Eburnean anyway.

He wanted to hold him. He wanted to cherish him for the few weeks they had left. He wanted everything he had always assumed he'd never get.

And worse, he wanted to believe in a future where he could possibly have it.

It was frighteningly selfish and Arna couldn't get himself to care.

He walked down the streets. They twisted and curved, were unfamiliar and strange, leading nowhere, leading somewhere away from anything he'd ever known.

> [*Arna what can we do to help you?* Pokk asked, the dying sun flickering to ash.]

The light of his Blessing formed five paths, glowing bright, glowing strong, leading to the center of the rose and Arna did not follow any of them. He opted for a path he'd never been down and squeezed his eyes tight.

"Humor me," Arna said opening his eyes again and shutting down his Blessings, standing cold in the summer night, cloak over his head and alone on the street.

> [*How?* Lumak's voice was a crumbling cliff.]

"Knowledge is the foundation," Arna recited.

The first six dances were the stories of mortals and Gods together, the relationship and dynamic. It was an overview of all known history in six dances, which made it exceedingly complex because Arna had millennia to cover. The worst part was that Arna had to filter the history through the lens of what he wanted for the future.

> [*What?* Lumak's voice quaked.]

"The path forward. Not the future, but a future I envision within the steps. It must be precise *and*?" He prompted the Gods.

> [*It must be fluid,* Ixxzal finished.]

Arna had heard the lecture a hundred times over the duodecennial. Each time they told him to start again, he had burned his previous plans and started back from the beginning.

Back to basics.

> [   ]

The Knowledge dances were technically easy. Taught to all citizens across the world, they were accessible to all.

> [*Appreciation of the Gods is the next section, dances seven through twelve,* Pokk started, hesitant but accepting. *It is here where common folk no longer dance.*]

Arna breathed deeply at the words, relaxing.

Appreciation, the second section was about expanding the relationships between mortals and the Gods. It was the section that dove into how the Gods and mortals affected each other and where the message of his dances fully took root.

"I show the expanded relationship between the Gods and mortals." Arna then mocked Pokk's voice: stern, fiery, impassioned and strict, "We will not approve unless we find it acceptable."

> [*Arna. . . We're sorry,* Pokk apologized.]

Arna refrained from rolling his eyes.

"Powers is where the message and story form," Arna went on.

The streetlights were out, the only light was that of the city overhead. There was no false moon this night, the sky was clear of all haze and distraction.

Powers of the Gods, the third section was the last section that nonChildren could dance. It was all about Blessings. It was the link that bound mortals to Gods and vice versa. It was the essence of the contract between Gods and Mortals. It was where he paved the way and started to define his future.

It was also where the variations deviated, as each variation created a new contract. Arna's was particularly difficult because he had to fix the Splintering *and* the Shattering. His own mistake and. . . Saffron's.

"When I dance it, you and I will rewrite the contract between mortals and Gods. The new era of Blessings will begin. It must be solid and strong," Arna recited.

[*Your message becomes our anchor.* Xeyaro's voice was a hushed tree in a forest with no one to hear it fall.]

Each dance had a single word center that the rest of the dance revolved around.

[*Worship, development, hope, memory, change.* Azza was the weeping moon, nowhere to be seen.]

"Hope." It had been his center from the day he began.

But he was the antithesis of hope. His variation was predicated on fear. His variation began because he chased a dream and destroyed everything trying to achieve it.

How could he fix that? No amount of help from his friends and family could fix that.

"The variations continue because both Gods and mortals change," Arna said. "We need you as you need us. New variations allow for new bonds between us."

[*Without us, you all would die. Without you, we would disappear. The moment we are forgotten, you all will cease to exist.* Ixxzal was the ominous mirage looming and powerful.]

"Azza, Lumak, Zaynir, Pokk, Ixxzal, Xeyaro," It was the order that the first three sections repeated in. He had built his fans around the order, as had those who came before him. "It changes for Understanding."

Understanding, the forth section, could only ever be danced by the Children of Xeyaro due to the need for A.Reverence. The dances were needed each year in order to maintain and reinforce the contract. A.Reverence gave the dancers the ability to *understand* the contract between the Mortals and Gods, even if they could not change or fix it.

Without Understanding the contact could be neither maintained nor reinforced. It would not be fulfilled.

For Arna, Understanding was where the contract flourished and where the message of the dances came to fruition.

"Blessed are those gifted by Xeyaro who maintain our connection to the Gods," Arna recited.

But he questioned the logic that someone could only master Understanding if they had A.Reverence. He had for years and it was why he'd sent his brother off on the foolhardy mission. If anyone could do it, Arna thought his brother could, but the Gods insisted that in order to reach Understanding one needed guidance. . .

Guidance?

A shadow danced across the street in the flash of white and silver light.

"Arco," Arna said, knowing that his brother was not there, but feeling it in his chest.

[*Define Incarnate Dreams,* Ixxzal suggested.]

Shaking his head, he went on with the lecture as they always did, "One must have mastered all eighteen dances—Knowledge, Appreciation, and Powers—before trying to move on."

For the first three sections, so long as one mastered one dance they could skip up to master the next difficulty of the same God. A person who mastered dance one could work on and learn dance seven before mastering dance two. However, in order to master nineteen, one had to master all eighteen before. To master twenty, the nineteen prior.

(what did it mean to dream?)

"Understanding combines the stories, the relationships, the old and the new Blessings, my message, everything." Arna stopped walking and stared up at the dark center of the rose.

Understanding was the reflection of modern society, morality, nature, time, space, and the future he wished.

The future...

[To Understand is to understand us and the way we think, for the briefest of moments. Zaynir was the last breath that left the lungs before death.]

All of the Twenty-Seven Dances variations were, in essence, completely distinct. The tempo of a song, pacing, and step order could be shifted, adapted, or changed. They used different instrumentals. The fans were different as were the outfits. The only thing that was consistent from variation to variation was the principals of the canon: teach the history, reconnect the Gods to mortals, and push for a new world order. There were always twenty-seven dances that resulted in Divinity, all danced with fans, all accepted by the Gods.

Worship and memory.

The first and fourth variations were based on new beginnings. The original connected everyone together. It established practices and implanted the Gods into memory. The fourth variation, Roots and Ends, was the most historical intensive of the variations, revolving around advancement of civilization. It showcased the beginnings and endings of eras. It revealed society and how it crumbled. It was named for the rise and fall of history. It was the most accurate portrayal of the ancient past that their world had.

He'd had to read a myriad of history books to understand aspects of the depth. In many accounts that he read, it was the most important dance due to what it recorded. It was a frustrating dance as he had to portray accurate history while flourish all his Blessings. He always wanted to pass out after dancing it.

Development and change.

Two and five were linked as well. The Twin Fans variation reestablished the world and reestablished the contract. Watsonia proved that Raven was not a single case, that there would be more, and laid the groundwork for it.

Meanwhile the Holly variation dove into hypocrisy. It showed the beauty of the world while contrasting it with the atrocities that mortals, have created. It was a social commentary designed to evoke an ill feeling of desperation, sorrow, and guilt in all who watch, in order to cause change.

Holly was the second most complex dance of the five variations. It asked you to see the horror behind the beauty and to change it, calling the viewer to grow and to be better. He liked it for the number of spins he did with his fans, but the seventeenth dance always tripped him up as the steps were the reverse of Blue Rose Fears.

Holly was one of Arna's roots of inspiration for his own variation. It was Ilex's dance that saved the world from the storms, or at least created a reprieve, in which mortals could flee.

Ilex had done something with his dances that Arna had to replicate.

Hope.

"Blue Rose Fears." Arna finally started walking again.

[*Blue Rose Fears,* Xeyaro repeated.]

Blue Rose Fears was Arna's favorite. It was the dance he danced when he caused the Splintering. It was the first he mastered in all five sections. It was the basis for his own variation, as it was his mirror. Like it, he was basing his variation in hope.

"Blue Rose Fears is the dance of horrors," Arna said more to himself than the others. "Where Holly disgusts people as time progresses, Blue Rose Fears starts with the negativity and turns it into beauty. Blue Rose Fears was named after the Blue Roses that saved Vervain the Blythe's life and the fears that the dance inspires in the viewer. It asks you to see the beauty beyond the horror of the world and to strive for something greater."

Some said that Blue Rose Fears was the most complex variation as such it was typically the last taught to students, the last mastered by dancers, and the last Understood. To Arna it was perfect. It was the most intuitive of the dances for him: moves connected the way they were supposed to.

[*And what is Incarnate Dreams?* Ixxzal asked.]

Incarnate Dreams was—

Arna wanted to create something like Blue Rose Fears in complexity, in part because it was penance, in part out of adoration. He also did not want to be similar to Holly, despite the fact that they were two halves of the same coin.

"Worship, is the last section, three dances all given special names," Arna said, voice low as he stepped towards the bus station. No one was around him to hear.

Twenty-four of the twenty-seven dances had to be performed each year, with the twenty-fifth usually being danced every duodecennial. The twenty-fifth dance was a special dance that only could be done by the most skilled of dancers, the pressure and intensity of the dances too great for most. As the twenty-six and twenty-seventh could only be considered complete when danced together in succession, it was impossible. Regular mortals could not survive twenty-six. It was where he'd reach Divinity.

[*What is the cost?* Lumak asked.]

"For twenty-five, the loss of ego. You lose yourself, your identity, your sense of self, to become a God," Arna sighed, finally they were catching on.

The city lights were blinding, a nightlife awake and alive in the center of the Rose. Arna got onto an empty bus and leaned against the seat as it tumbled through the sky. He counted the districts, like they were stars.

[*Twenty-six?*]

"The loss of body." Arna shivered. The Dance of Destruction.

It was the most dangerous of all the dances. Most who attempted it were elders, as any attempt resulted in death. Some claimed it superstition, yet no one tempted it till they were old enough that the strain of the dance could kill them. People never danced it with fans unless they were prepared to risk everything.

There was more to the truth.

"A dancer who dances the twenty-six leaves the mortal plane, and in doing so, they ascend only to descend."

Divinity itself was a pressure, something immeasurable Pokk said. It grew from the soul and changed mortal body into the half Divine from the inside out. The physical and material world reacted to it like magnetism. As a result, there were always accidents that occurred—falling lights, burning stages, flying knives, stray arrows—long before the dancer could reach the end of twenty-six and Divinity fully rooted in the body. Without the necessary Blessings to withstand the divine change, the body disintegrated.

This was where Arna was to die based on his choice. The Gods always said that when he danced, they'd be able to do nothing but watch. Either he'd fail or succeed.

If he made the right choice he could die due to the loss of his Blessings or the universe trying to cut him down before he could take it all. There was nothing they could do to stop him. Those were his insurmountable odds.

If he made the wrong choice then he lost all his Blessings at once.

Mortals or the Gods was the final question he had to answer. If he answered correctly, he would become Chosen and keep all his Blessings. If answered incorrectly, he'd lose all his Blessings except six. Divinity would kill him, or the world would, hopefully painlessly.

> [*Only those we may permit, our Chosen, can dance it. Mortals cannot bend the divine easily.* Lumak sounded exasperated. *It must be someone we trust.*]

The Gods needed the mortals prayers for sustenance. In order to ensure the mortals did not forsake the Gods, the Gods often searched for the Chosen to reestablish the contract. All the time, thousands of times a year, individuals failed over and over and over again, for reasons Arna never understood.

"And if they pick up a fan to try again, they die," Arna said.

Up above were the residential petals curling over in the black sky. This Xeysis was strange to him. It was not his home before he'd had Incarnate Dreams. Before he came back. He didn't know the city, didn't know her inhabitants. He was. . .

> [*Arna?* Lumak asked.]

The Gods also hated when mortals risked their lives for something they could not hope to succeed at. A person needed to have at least thirty Blessings, and a specific combination of abilities, to potentially survive the Dance of Destruction. Since most mortals had less than five there was no hope for them.

Only the Chosen Child, with all of the Blessings available, could survive dancing the Dance of Destruction with fans, but there was no physical proof only stories and what the Gods told him. And Arna had dropped a fan.

> [*We can only revoke the taboo on you once you reestablish the contract and declare the new Variance.* Xeyaro had a tone of remorse for the taboos they had established with the original bonding.]

Dropping a fan was the greatest of all sins, and the cost was to lose the very thing that could keep him alive. He'd lost four Blessings over the years in training. The thought of it made him sick, imagining the pain. Arna *only* had to pick up forty-two fans, but the repeated pain from losing the Blessings could possibly stop his heart. Any less than eighteen and he was mush from the pressure of Divinity's descent, because his Blessings would not be powerful enough. All the while the pressure of Divinity would eat away at him as the physical world did as well.

The margin of error was so minuscule that he did not bother thinking of survival after he danced and healed the Splintering and the Shattering. It wasn't possible. There was no spark of energy, no connection strong enough to survive it.

> [*We will take from you what is unnecessary for you to complete the dances,* Xeyaro said, voice shaking.]

Arna was the only one who could save the world, alone. It was him or no one. There was no second chance.

imposterimposterimposterimposterimposter

He'd done everything at fifteen because he thought he had been Chosen. He may have had the Blessings. He had the dark eyes. He may have done the practice and training. He may have heard their voices and seen them by his side, but it was all a series of tests preparing him for Divinity. He was not their Chosen yet, no matter what the stories and scriptures said. Failure was a possibility until the very end.

[*Twenty-Seven?* Xeyaro asked.]

"The Dance of Destiny." Arna looked to the artificial sky searching for their images in the wisps of artificial clouds. There were none and the bus stopped.

"One must complete twenty-six before twenty-seven, for it to be considered complete. It is where the contract is woven and signed."

The descent of divinity occurred during twenty-six and matured in twenty-seven. Divinity created the tear in the veil between Gods and mortals and the maturity of Divinity, the acceptance of it, allowed the contract to be respun.

It was why they had him dance twenty-seven after twenty-six, each time he practiced. The two had to be done together in tandem. It was why mortals could dance twenty-seven with fans with no consequence but never master it: it technically wasn't a completed dance on its own.

[*A loss of ego, then body, and then mind,* Ixxzal reminded him. *Twenty-seven may be the least technical, but you will give everything to the world and to us. You will not remember dancing it.*]

The twenty-seventh dance was the apotheosis.

"I will do it," Arna swore to them.

Hand open, Hand closed. Arna squeezed tight and held his breathe. He killed the fear. He killed his worry and buried it deep. It did not matter. It was the only chance he had to save the world.

Yet. . .

Alis.

As Arna got off the train in the business center, an Ivumalis song was playing in the station. They had given him Pervenche as an anchor, but they'd given him Eburnean as one too.

He couldn't even protect Alis. He couldn't even fix his family.

How was he supposed to make it right? How was he supposed to fix everything when he couldn't even picture the dances he wanted to dance? When no matter how much he pushed and focused and did everything for the sake of the dances, he wasn't able to make any progress?

He was regressing. He was failing.

everyonewilldieeveryonewilldieeveryonewilldie

How could he fix it? How could he save them? How could he do it without hurting them more and using them and relying on them and—

[*Arna.* The voice of a storm in mortal form.]

Arna's head snapped up.

Ixxzal?

[*Arna.* Calling further, father, away. Away.]

"Is there another choice?" Arna begged for an answer.

They did not respond.

Because at the root of it all, at the worst of the truths, was that the Gods, while they believed that he would try, they too did not believe he would live either.

The only way to get to the Stage was either from the immigration station or from the business district by walking to it. Headphones on, Ivumalis music on loop: *Serenity's Lament* would not leave his thoughts. He always turned to Ivumalis songs when his mind was close to breaking. Yet, all he could see was Eburnean everywhere. All he could feel was the pain of the choice he had to make.

I'm going to die.

Everything was his fault.

[*Arna.*]

Arna began to follow the voice. He did not care where the Gods would lead him, so long as it was somewhere, somewhere where he would get clarity.

Arna made his wat to the center of the business circle. Billboards flashed and glowed. Commercials played on his augmentations. Holograms of people selling things and store hours glowed brightly. Despite the time of night. People were shopping and laughing.

The towering skyscrapers were hundreds of stories tall, with bridges between them, like trees in a forest. They were covered in plants. The streets were lined in towering trees that, if it weren't for their positioning, would have been so tall that the skyscrapers could not be seen beyond them. They lined the street in a rows, leading towards Dancer Square.

[*It's time, Arna*, Ixxzal was the mysterious glimmer of flashing lights, *Do you believe in me?*]

Arna walked through Dancer's Square, watching as people moved. Dancer's Square was alive despite the time of night. Dancer's Square was surrounded by a multitude of dance studios and dance supply shops. The Legacy Heritage Foundation building sat on one end with The Dance House—where dancers were tested for mastery of The Twenty-Seven Dances, and the auditions were held for the Ceremony of Chaos—on the other side. The traffic moved in a way to avoid either location.

"Come on, Honeysuckle," Arna heard through his headphones.

A mother pulled her small daughter towards the LHF building. The little girl did not struggle until the wind picked up her hat and blew it to Arna's feet. The little blonde girl, with large round brown eyes and scared skin along her hands and arms, looked back. Arna raced after the mother, handing it towards the little girl before the mother snatched the hat away and glared daggers at him. She picked up her daughter and walked faster to the building.

Despite the time, they entered.

The busy bodies tumbled around him, leaving him isolated in a sphere of his own making. Pressured on all sides, it continued to crush him. Sound died. Light died. Everything died and he was consumed whole. His breath was swallowed by some unyielding creature that threatened to devourer him too.

A cacophony. A vortex. A jumbling mess of thoughts and feelings and the incessant panic that would never go away and struggled, struggled, struggled, to cling until he faded to.

Nothing.

But.

Silence.

Everything faded. Everything stopped. It was just Arna alone.

[breathe.]

"Arna?"

Yes?

"Arna?"

Turning rapidly, Arna sputtered out a series of apologies towards Amaryllis who was standing behind him with camera in her hand. She was dressed in an ugly orange jumpsuit, staring at him with large all-seeing owl eyes. She tilted her head side to side, eyes narrowing.

"Are you on duty for work?" He asked her trying to avoide her gaze.

"I'm off soon." She had bags under her eyes, clearly sleep deprived. Last, he had seen her, she had not looked so despondent. "I need to talk to you."

"What?"

"Stay here. I'll be right back."

She hurried to the LHF building. Arna was at a loss, yet he waited, feeling as if the whole weight of the world kept him from moving forward. When she returned, minutes later in soft pinks and creams with a white backpack, Arna followed her. Without a word, they journeyed onwards.

In silence there was distant arguing, like muffled cries that Arna tried to parse together.

[*Trust me,* Ixxzal said.]

[*This is impossible, She'll scare him,* Lumak argued.]

[*Amaryllis is perfect,* Zaynir disagreed.]

[*Focus on her. Not us,* Xeyaro said loudly.]

Amaryllis turned down an alley way, through a gate and into a back garden, with terraces and lines of glass wisteria flowers tumbling everywhere, like they were growing down from the sky. The city lights sparkled through the petals, creating an array of mystical movement as they swayed. Arna walked through the hanging forest of flowers, trying to catch her but she disappeared.

"This reminds me of the alley of mirrors," Arna called to her. In Azis there had been a whole alley system of walls covered in mirrors that created a labyrinth. He'd once been caught for hours and—this was a perfect place for dancing.

Backing up to take in the whole forest, he could not find his way out. Where had they entered from? He was surrounded. He spun and spun, searching and never finding. He stopped and stared out, lost, alone. So very alone.

"Here."

Amaryllis stood on the other side, smiling at him from behind her camera, snapping photos of him—perhaps the entire time.

"Why are we—"

"Ven and I broke up," she said flatly, surprising Arna.

"What?" he asked, his lips dry and his stomach turning. He reached out with his S.Mirrors and felt tremendous sorrow. When? Arna searched Amaryllis' eyes for answers. He had not seen it coming. They'd been so happy days ago.

"Sometimes you are with people when you need to be, but as you grow, you don't grow together. You grow apart and want different things." She gracefully moved the flowers around her, light fingers pushing them apart.

She said with a dreamlike quality to her voice, "They were everything I ever dreamed of, when my last relationship had destroyed me, when I was rejected time and time again. When all I heard was no, Ven said yes. They asked what I wanted. They asked what I loved, wanted to be. I became a photographer when others said not to cross the line. They got me to listen to myself."

She locked Arna in a trance, unable to continue forward. She was half in the light of the sparkling sky and half masked by the shadowed petals. "We both lost our heartmates. Mine in the Ludiel train crash."

Arna winced.

SCREAMS.

Fire.

runrunrunrunrunrun

"Leave."

"And they had lost you. They had become as destructive, in and out of relationships and homes. Cutting out anything and everything that reminded them of you. Self-destructing internally even when they said they were fine. And we found each other. First as friends, then as something more."

She disappeared in the shadows.

"When Jasi said that you were back—"

Her voice came from behind him. Startled he spun and found her staring at him from the other side. How?

"—Ven had not wanted to go to see you. I thought that I would be left again. I was fully prepared to hate you, to be jealous of you. . ." Her face was empty, vulnerable, lost, exposed. She wanted him to see her. "Then you saw them, and I saw you. I saw you the same way that I see everyone. The raw and unfiltered you."

"You didn't have to break up with Ven because. . ."

"I know. You don't love each other. That is not why we made our choice."

"Then why?" Arna asked confused. They were in love. They were so happy.

"Why do you want to die Arna?"

The words pulled at his heart, ripped it from his chest and smashed it to the ground.

> [*Arna*, The voice in the moonlight said, soft, detached. *What if you can only choose one thing? What if you can't choose both?*]

"How. . ." His voice shook as he asked her. He did everything to hide it, but. . .

"You're like me. You're like Arco," She laughed, placing her hand on his shoulder and smiling softly. "We all might think you are the Chosen Child, but the rest of the world doesn't want you to be. You're like me and him: an imposter."

She stepped forward and he backed up. Her image bounced across the glass, and he swore that her eyes started glowing. She saw everything he wanted to hide.

"The others say they would die for it, but they won't. That's why they don't understand us. But unlike me and Arco, you will die. And strangely, despite being so obsessed with it, so *selfless* as to give up everything in the world. . . there is an emptiness. It's not selflessness. It's self-sacrificial. You won't die for it because you love it. You would because you think you deserve it."

Arna stopped breathing.

"I am a mirror. People avoid me when they can. Because I see you."

He did not know how to answer her nor what any of this meant.

"Ven doesn't understand me," she said with no anger or sadness, as if it were a truth as old as time. "They love archery but it's different from the way I *need* photography. It's my soul. It's my everything. Through it I can be. I exist."

"So, you broke up." Arna tested the words, unsure if he believed them.

"They were what I wanted and needed at the time, but I've used Ven as my crutch for my entire adult life. They've used me as their shield. They need to learn who they want to be and find the passion that makes them soar. And I need to stand up, learn who I am, and love her on my own."

"I never wanted. . ." Arna's skin tingled in warning at the lie that was about to slip through.

She hushed him, and lifted his chin with her light fingers. Then with quick hands she snapped a photo, flipped the camera around and showed him his face. He was enlightened and distraught, a mess of grace and haunted complexity.

"Sometimes people mistake selfishness for selflessness," she said. "I don't want an apology from you, Arna. Not for my heartmate who died. Not for my brother who was hurt. Not for the years I spent in pain. I don't need one. I want you to take what you want."

Why. . . Why was she doing this?

There was a long silence as Amaryllis walked around the flowers. She flipped through photos, intently. "What do you want to be Arna?"

What did he want to be? It didn't matter what he wanted. He had to save the world.

"And what are you willing to live for?" She leaned in and said lightly, like a dragonfly grazing the waters of a lake.

To live for?

"Everyone always talks about dying. But no Arna. We are artists. We breathe and thus we create," Amaryllis said. "Would you be the Chosen Child if you were not picked? Would you still want to be Chosen?"

But he. . . He wasn't the Chosen at all and. . .

Arna was there again, at fifteen, standing behind the Weeping Stage talking to the Gods, receiving the task.

He was eighteen frightened and determined: never again.

He wanted to be the Chosen Child more than anything back then. But what of now?

Arna stopped breathing. An abundance of desire grew inside him, scratching at his skin. Demanding to be heard.

Incarnate Dreams was about following passions. It was about hope. It was a dream from someone else that he'd be following for so long: the him, as a child. It was the desire he'd held from the time he first saw the Gods. It was his deepest wish to succeed even if he didn't live, because he wanted them to thrive. However, it was there, scratching at him: screaming.

"Who will you be after?" She asked.

[*Are you visualizing?* drifted on the wind.]

Lightning struck.

The question was not about thinking of his dances, the world, or their lives. It was not about fixing his relationships or saving his family. At its root, it was about him. It was about what he wanted. It was about his future.

"I. . . I don't know." Arna admitted. The two stood staring at each other as wind rippled through the flower forest. Amaryllis looked at her camera.

"We all explore who we are and what we want. I'm not sure we ever stop." Amaryllis concealed herself behind the flowers and vanished. Chasing after her, Arna found himself alone.

"Go after what you want, Arna." Amaryllis' voice echoed from multiple directions.

Arna turned trying to find her, trying to understand how she was able to warp the space with her Blessings. "I don't know what I want."

"You don't know who you are, either. That hasn't stopped you."

Then she was gone. He felt it in his skin. He tasted it in the air. Her presence around him had vanished. Releasing the breath from deep in his chest, Arna rocked back on his heels looking to the sky. It glittered and glowed.

Mortals or the Gods. Arna waited. There was no response. "Is it a question on who I want to be?"

It was a question of what he'd live for. It was a question on what he'd fight for.

Chimes sang in the distance, but Arna could not understand the words.

For the first time Arna was able to feel the weight of the world after he danced. He was able to see it. Was that what Zaynir meant by visualizing? Not the dance itself, but the world after he danced. It was about what *he* wanted, and *his* future.

I am a mirror. She had said and Arna was exposed once more. There had been so much that she had said. So much she had thrown at him all at once and why? *Self-sacrificial.*

Arna hated himself. He had known that for so long. It was his fault everything happened. But. . .

There was a mist of a dream, the consideration of a thought. It was his variation dancing before him the crystal flowers, almost tangible. If he just reached out—

[silence   ]

Arna ran past the six hundred foot tall candles that surrounded the Religious circle. The six of them formed a circle and used to glow in the very center of the city. He raced through the churches, past the vast empty fields, around the Cathedrals and the Temple, and towards the center.

When he finally arrived at the Weeping Stage it was as it always had been and would be. It was not tall, nor large by any means. It had no roof, just a set of wooden beams that held lights and speakers and the curtains. The backstage was covered by walls and a roof, but the stage itself was not. The back of the Weeping Stage was a massive fan made of wood and no fabric, emulating the fans of the dances.

The Weeping Stage was simple, with hardwood floors painted black, and curtains of black velvet. On the back wall there was a glass display case for the five original ceremonial garbs of the Chosen Children, and the original fans for the twenty-fifth, twenty-sixth, and twenty-seventh dances of each of the five variations. They were only kept there during the Celebrations and Ceremony of Chaos and were otherwise housed in specialty accommodations by the Church of the Apostle.

The grass before it was completely empty.

The Weeping Stage was where the Twenty-Seven Dances were danced each year during the Celebrations of the New Year during the Ceremony of Chaos on the Day of New Dawn. It was the only place they were to be danced, and the most sacred spot in the entire world. Said to be where Ilex danced to save the world after the Shattering, The Weeping Stage was untouched by technology: handcrafted, hand painted, and hand maintained.

Gazing upon it, he heard the music of that year. He could feel the spinning of the fans in his hand as he danced the eighteenth dance.

Resolved, Arna walked on the Weeping Stage. He balanced on the edge before turning inward measuring the width, depth, and length with his footsteps.

[*Do you understand?* Xeyaro asked.]

"Remember when I stole the shoes of Vervain the Blithe?" Arna asked instead kneeling down to the wood and checked the stage for dust.

[*My church was not happy,* Xeyaro said, confused.]

It was a national emergency. The city was a mess for days as they tried to find the shoes and then Arna waltzed into the Cathedral of the Apostle and handed them over. He'd gotten a slap on the wrist but there was not much that they could do. He told them that the Gods told him to take them.

It was his first real test. It made him laugh that much of his life had been about stealing. At one time Arna had used his position, his name, to get out of everything. The thought of doing that now, made him blanche.

Arna stopped walking. He searched for something, anything.

Arna could remember the Splintering as it had been carved into his bones.

The crowd sat in an awed silence as he danced the variation of his choice. He'd been frustrated because the interlude before the Dances had taken too long. He begged for them to remove the interludes between the sections, but he'd been denied. Arna had known he was not going to complete the songs before the clock struck midnight.

"'And they shall have eyes the color of the deepest night, loved by none.'" Arna recited to himself.

He traced his face with his hands. In the center of his palms were crescent moon scars, puckered and wanting to heal properly.

That night he had danced, continuously glancing up to the clock on the distant building. He had less than a minute left when he first saw the Gods in the audience. Practice had drilled itself into him, to be perfect until the end, thus he acted as if he had not. Yet, the offer rang in his head over and over again. He could not hold a fan if he wanted to be the Chosen Child.

The only thing he'd ever wanted was to be the Chosen Child.

"'And they shall have the Blessings, picked by all.'" Arna closed his eyes and then faced the field. He flourished his Blessings, letting the pain consume him until all that was left was clarity and bliss.

To this day he could still see it. The audience filled to the brim of people chanting his name. He remembered the love, the adoration, the pride within him. It was a dark night, but he could see the clock on the Temple of Xeyaro. Backstage the Golden Generation were watching with expectant eyes as he was the first of their generation to dance Powers. Then there was Sarcoline.

Sarcoline stood in the center of the audience, watching him with large eyes. Shadows danced around him, figures of the Gods in the form of whips and shadows like both people and animals. Xeyaro had features of a large leaf wolf. Pokk was an angry cat, arguing with Xeyaro. Azza was a type of deep sea creature with glowing eyes and swimming about. Zaynir was an owl, dancing with Azza. Lumak was a towering snake with no eyes, spinning Sarcoline when the boy asked. Ixxzal had antlers and spindly legs and wings.

They were speaking to him. They were motioning to him, pointing up, at the clock, at him, at Sarcoline. And Arna had danced. He danced and danced and didn't care that the time was running out until, the shadows began to shift. They began to coalesce around Sarcoline and dance with him. Lumak warned Arna the time was coming to an end and all Arna could see was Sarcoline.

Sarcoline's face as if it were burned into his memory: the elation, the love, the eyes that said *I want to be just like you*.

In that moment he had known that he'd not only change his own life, but all of Sarcoline's dreams. Worse, he'd break them both.

The Gods telling him he could not touch a fan past midnight, had been one of the few unanimous decisions they made. Arna had been the one to misunderstand and drop the fan.

If he had been better, he would have stopped and put it down. If he had been smarter, he'd have convinced the staff to skip his introduction so he could finish before midnight. If he had been less egotistical, Arna would have given up and never dropped the fan to begin with. He would have never severed the connection between Gods and mortals unintentionally. He would have given up being the Chosen Child. He would have never caused the Splintering.

He would have let Sarcoline have the choice instead.

He had six seconds left in the song, two large moves to go, and instead of finishing Arna opened his hands at midnight. The toll of the bell snapped the world awake. The Everlit candles snuffed out the moment the fan clattered to the stage floor, casting the world into eternal darkness.

There was a blackout across the whole city and screams resounded from the audience as they tried to figure out what was going on. The winds picked up, a storm blooming in the center of the rose. Then there were different screams: true horror. They were screaming in a way that Arna could never forget, as the world saw that the Everlit Candles no longer shined.

For the first time in history.

[It happens every time.]

He had prayed, **what now?**

Screams. Screams. Screams.

The Gods told him. **Now. . . run.**

"'And they shall disappear for twelve years, to understand, to gain guidance, and create a new truth'" Arna's words were soft, and his body lighter, as he stood toes hanging off the edge.

Later he learned that the candles and lights had gone out across the world all at once and the Blessings were stopped. What was called the Splintering happened the moment that the fan had clattered to the ground, and he had run.

Screams. Screams. Screams.

The faint whisper turned into echoes. He ran.

There were prayers and questions. People begged for forgiveness. He ran.

They said the rapture had come; the end had begun. People stood in the streets listlessly, in disbelief, unaware that the world continued to spin. He ran.

There was silence. Silence from the lack of care. Silence from the dread. Silence. Suffocating silence. Horrifying, terrible—

Silence is not a void, Alis had once said.

Arna clenched his fists tight, carving into the scars that were never fully healed.

[*Arna.* The voice a bygone echo on the breeze. A child stunned by a vow.]

Arna faced the empty field and the Apostle Cathedral's clock. There was no one there. He had been alone for so long and it was all he knew. But the Gods didn't want him to be alone anymore.

They wanted him to visualize his future.

Because he had never truly been alone. He'd always had them, the Gods reflecting his family. They were in the wind, and in the rhythms of the world. They were in his friends' voices and all mortals' eyes. They were everywhere and nowhere all at once, in mirrors and light and shadows.

His heart ached and he heaved.

Tears spilled from his eyes in a way they had not in years. There had been a time that Arna thought the Gods false. He had screamed and cursed them.

Arna no longer resented them.

They were trying to survive. They were trying to protect the mortals. They were trying to keep him alive.

alivealivealivealivealivealive

"'And they shall dance,'" Arna said words choking in his throat.

The Splintering was a split-second decision. He had been given a choice and he had chosen without knowing the weight of what the decision meant. Arna, twelve years later, would have never made it, knowing the consequences. Once again, Arna had an option for a vow, and this time Arna understood what was at risk.

"'And when divinity descends, their dance shall renew our bond,'" Arna finished the prophecy.

But who would he dance for?

He had given everything up to make things right. He told himself he had to push forward because it was the only way. No one knew the pressure of expectation more than he did. No one knew the cost better than he did.

What do you want to live for?

[*Arna*, Ixxzal said softly, as if standing there in the field.]

Amaryllis' words circled. Who did he want to be after he danced? What did he want to do? Who did he want to become?

Arna had often forgone dreaming of the future for himself after the dances because he thought of it as a distraction. It had been so easy before. All he had to do was survive each day. Short goals. Short plans. The end goal had always been a far-off, impossible thing. Because he would die.

[   ]

What do you want to live for?

He had wanted nothing for so many years because it gave him hope. However how could he make Incarnate Dreams if he did not dream? How could he give the world hope if he had no faith himself?

[*You cannot fix what you broke unless. . .* a melody. A song.]

It is not worth it.

He was not good enough.

(But. . . What if. . .)

(He was allowed.)

[Not all wishes were vocal. Not all wishes were known.]

[All wishes were heard.]

He had thought he had a billion reasons to die, to sacrifice himself for them. But no. He needed a billion reasons to live. He had to find his Understanding. But in order to find his Understanding he needed his family.

He needed their help. He needed their love. He needed to believe in a future with them.

Live.

He wanted to see the world. He wanted to finish the bucket list with Jasione. He wanted to bring Eburnean and Alabaster back to the Vivicent studio. He wanted to be best friends with Phlox again. He wanted to garden with his mother. He wanted to dance with Gingerline and Sarcoline. He wanted to have Saints and make up stories.

He wanted to make fans with his father. He wanted to hold a fan again without pain, without suffering.

He wanted it to just be a fan.

[*Arna*, Ixxzal called.]

"How do I live?" Arna asked them. He stared out at Ixxzal who stood eight feet tall, masked in shadows, the embodiment of fear.

[*You just do. You accept the consequences that it won't be perfect, but
it will be new,* Ixxzal explained.]

Arna stopped breathing. He let go of the hands he was clenching. Red lines dripped from his hands, expelling the poison in his veins.

Serenity's Lament echoed in his mind, a promise he planned to keep.

Thirty.

Forty-two.

Die.

Not statistically likely.

Alis and Arco and Amaryllis: three people who consistently did what they loved despite the fact that technically they "did not have" the Blessings for the art. They did it anyway and did not care. Why not them? Why not him?

In a world where being great was a fickle destiny,

what did it mean to be only good?

[It was enough to simply exist.]

He still hated himself for breaking the world all for the sake of chasing his dream. But, maybe, just maybe, he could try to fight to see the world he aimed to create. Maybe he could defy the odds.

Who will you be after?

No more running. Jump first ask questions later.
Take the chance.

The Chosen could have been anyone in the world. He had reached for it and grabbed it because *he* wanted it.

[*We didn't choose them. We picked you,* Ixxzal reminded him.]

Perhaps it was foolish. Perhaps he'd regret it. Perhaps he'd hurt them all more and worse than he ever intended.

Hands open. Hands closed. Hands open, so he could let himself heal.

How did one embody dreams in the flesh?

Dreams were not stagnant.

They were belligerent things:

clawing and fighting
to exist without judgement.

"I want this," Arna said more certain than he had ever been of anything.

This was the way to Incarnate Dreams.

He was going to get his family back. He was going to do whatever it took to finish his variation. He was going to hope and believe and attempt to defy fate. He was going to get the man he loved.

He was going to try and live.

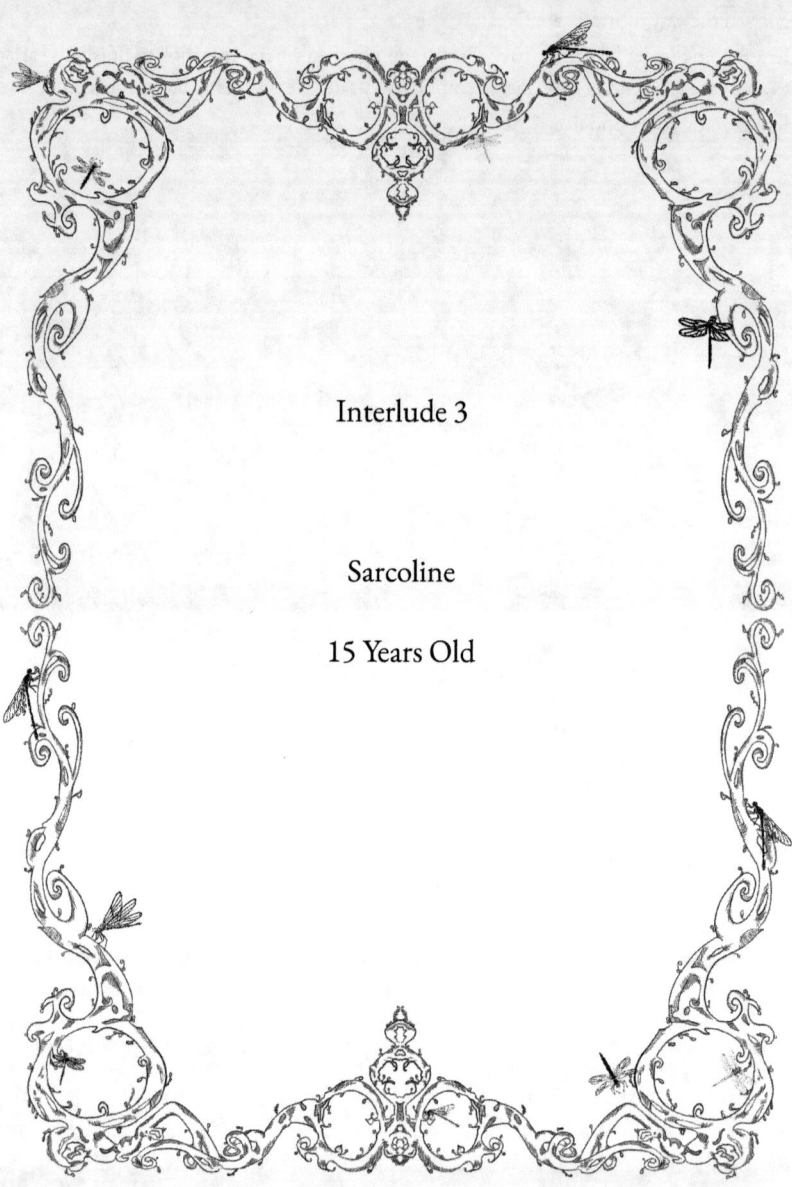

Interlude 3

Sarcoline

15 Years Old

The hall was filled with cameras and reporters. Hundreds of competitors from all over the world were ready to audition. Arco stood in a white tracksuit, chin up, glowering at those who wanted to intimidate them. His mother, too, was dressed in her best billowing, white clothes with accents of mint. Jasi was dressed in white and deep purples, walking alongside them. His father and sister were listening to music, ignoring the world around them. For the first time all year, they were in the same room together, and they had not said a word.

Arco swallowed hard. The Vivicent family had arrived, and with it a hushed set of whispers. There were snippets of conversations, gossip about their family, hushed stories about how the Hues had left the studio. People anticipated the fall of their whole family. Many talked about Arna, and his supposed fake Blessings, using Arna's name like a slur. Cameras and drones flew about, capturing everything for audiences around the world. Advertisements filled his augmentations: ones that were made for the auditions and were not there for the dance tests days prior.

Reporters bombarded them, and Wenge fielded them like an expert, sending them aside, as Jasi led them to sign in. Arco followed after his father and sister, to sign his name under the sections of dances he was auditioning for. He was handed his wrist band, and his father helped him put it on.

Arco was left on his own then: Zaffre going to DHS members to discuss, and his sister to taunt Ebru.

For a moment it was almost as if they were a family and not on the brink of collapse. It was as if his father wasn't drunk most days. It was as if Jasi wasn't on a personal quest to break every taboo possible. It was as if Ginger wasn't withdrawn and different and wouldn't tell him why. It was as if his mother hadn't lost every job she applied for.

It was all a façade and Arco was alone in the sea of people who hated him.

"Arco." Amaryllis's voice startled him, looping her arms around his shoulders.

He turned. "You should be in school."

"I've never paid attention to the auditions, how does this work?" she asked, blatantly avoiding his statement.

She was dressed in all white. Startled he took her in and had her turn. She had slowly started adding white into her wardrobe, but this was the first time he ever saw her in the color exclusively.

"Like it?"

"Yes."

She tilted her head and he sighed. If she made the choice, it was not like he could convince her of another. He motioned for her to follow, and they walked to the seats as he explained.

"All competitors have wristbands. The color dictates the section we're auditioning for: white for Knowledge, silver for Appreciation, white and mint for Powers, Mint for Understanding, and all three colors for Worship."

"Only your dad has the Worship bracelet," Amaryllis said, pointing at him across the room.

"It's his retribution and repentance. No one else will compete with him," Arco said with a shrug. All the eyes in the room were on him. He had cut his hair short, so he didn't look like his brother. It hadn't mattered because when they saw him, they only saw Arna, no matter what he tried.

"Repentance for what?" she asked with a sweet innocence that had to be faked.

Arco shot her a look. She had to know. She blinked back at him a bit caught off guard, and then controlled her expression nodding slowly.

"You're dancing Powers?" Amaryllis asked instead, busying herself with his collar and dusting off his shoulders. "You only tested for mastery. . ."

"Last month? Don't worry. No one expects me to win." He hated it. His sister would get Powers and Ebru would get Understanding.

Arco continued to explain, not wanting to lean on her but accepting the comfort she brought. Her light hands distracted him from the other eyes. Her aqua ones said, *only you matter right now.*

He said, "Once I'm called back, I will be placed with the others for Powers. We will be called by name, and I can't miss my name, or forfeit. If I mess up, I fail."

"And then they score you?" She wiped his face with her fingers before she turned and sat straight, knocking her shoulder into his on purpose. Reluctantly, as if lulled like an anchor to the bottom of the sea, he rested his head on her shoulder. He was too tall to do it while standing, now that he was beginning to pass her in height. However, sitting they were on equal footing.

"All the judges do a score for the competitor, and then they do a ranking as they watch us dance. Once it's all done, the system compares the scores and makes a ranking per judge based on the scores they gave. The judges compare the scores they gave against the ranking they made while watching performances. And then once they approve their new ranking, all the judges personal rankings are compared and combined to a personal master ranking," Arco said, relaxing and closing his eyes.

"Scores are forgotten?" She took his hands in hers and laid her head atop of his.

"No. All scores are aggregated, and the system makes a list ranking based on all aggregate scores. The full personal listing and aggregate score rankings are compared, and the judges talk and decide. Scores and rankings are then given to us individually in our DHS passport record. Onle the top two final choices are publically announced." Arco breathed deeply, closing his eyes and letting the world slip away in the melody of her heartbeat.

While it was not unheard of, it was rare for someone to audition in multiple sections. The committee never allowed a dancer to be the primary dancer in two dances and a dancer was chosen once. They said they'd never allow a dancer to be primary and understudy, to allow for new talent to rise. Although it was precedent, not a rule, one could understudy in two dances.

"How are you scored?"

"There are six categories: technique, style, artistry, knowledge, awe, and understanding."

Technique was measured by the technical mastery of a dancer. Style was measured by how well the dancers added their personal take into the messaging of the dance. Artistry was measured by how graceful they were. Knowledge was measured based on the dancer's knowledge of the dances themselves. Awe was measured based on how well they used their Blessings to work with the dances themselves to create a surreal magic to the moves. Understanding was measured by how they allowed the audience to access the story and how clear they made it become.

All scored out of twelve. They were the six scores that would make or break his audition.

"Hello everyone," Arco's father's voice sounded over the microphone. At the sound, Arco jolted up but did not let go of Amaryllis' hands. His heart fluttered like crazy, and she squeezed him, refusing to let go. Zaffre went over the very same rules that Arco had told to Amaryllis.

"'To the God of dance, we seek guidance and hope. Guide us in our struggles and our lives, as we weave stories and speak color into the world. . .'" His father quoted. He rarely heard his father's voice these days. He was always locked in his room.

His mother and father slept apart these days. It was almost like when Arna first left, but instead of them crying because Arna was gone, his mother cried because their family was being torn apart. Zaffre couldn't keep himself together from the constant pressure and pain he experienced each year dancing twenty-five. They had no students. Everyone hated them.

Yet his father stood, sober for the first time in weeks. His eyes were masked in a lie of confidence. He was the shadow of the man Arco had known as a child.

Zaffre recited, "'Yesterday, we danced. Tomorrow, we will dance again. Today, we shall dance for you, and all the Gods beside you. May you see us. May this please you. Be with the Gods. May the Gods' light never fade.' And so, it was. And so, it shall be."

Arco's father walked back, and without much of a wait, the Understanding dancers were called back. Arco's heart started racing even faster. He squeezed his hands together and focused on the ground. Usually, he had three rounds of dances to wait through before he was called. His father, as the only Worship dancer, would get his spot without much contention.

"Your dad looks better," Amaryllis said trying to distract him.

"He's worse each day. Rus doesn't know what to do anymore," Arco admitted. Rus was trying to keep them all together. He was the best older brother that Arco could ask for, but he wasn't Arna.

Rus' twin, Jasi, was breaking too. He was getting into trouble even if no one else noticed. Jasi had come home smelling of fire the same night there was an arson attack on the paper bridge in the first petal. Somehow he was breaking laws without breaking them. Maybe trying to feel something? Acro didn't know.

"He looks just like him," someone said.

Or maybe it was him. Maybe he was the reason.

His father couldn't look him in the eye. His mother teared up. Jasi avoided him most days. Ginger was always so angry when he danced in his brother's studio. Rus was the only one who was kind to him.

Arna was fifteen when he first got Powers. He was the best of his generation. Everyone would know that Arco was trying to be just like him. The only dance variation that Arco knew through Powers was Blue Rose Fears. He should have danced Appreciation this year. He shouldn't have auditioned for Powers. Now everyone was staring at him like he was a catastrophe.

Why was he so prideful to say it was Powers or nothing? He wished Rus was there instead of working.

"You're okay," she whispered to him, her lips against his ear. He turned and covered his ear with a flush. She giggled and smiled. There was a loud thud as the first dancer exited with no wristband, running away and crying. Arco's heart thudded.

There was a seating section designated at the front of the room for where successful competitors would sit and wait. Those who passed, sat. Those who failed were free to leave. Some failures could occur at the very end, some at the beginning. Only a few passed.

"I want this," Arco admitted to Amaryllis. It was the one thing he'd been hiding for too long.

"Then take it," she told him, words becoming serious.

"No one will want me to have it," he said low, squeezing her hands. No one wanted him to be like his brother. But *he* wanted to be like his brother.

"I do," she said, and he slowly looked up. Their eyes locked and he believed her. She always wanted what he wanted. He always did everything for her.

One by one, all the Understanding dancers finished. Based on the small smile on Ebru's lips from where he sat, it was clear had made no mistakes. A perfect Ebru always won. The official judgement period began, and Arco wanted to puke.

"Tell me," Amaryllis said to him, pulling him closer until their foreheads touched.

"I am scared," he admitted, closing his eyes and needing this. He needed her to see him. Even when he wanted to be like his brother, he did not want to replace his brother. He simply wanted to be as good. He just wanted to dance.

"You're the best dancer I know."

But he was not a genius. He was just good. He would never be as great as them. He admitted his fear. "I can't do this."

"Then do it for me." She released his hands and cupped his face with hers.

Arco snapped his eyes open and pulled back. The two of them were alone in the seats. At the moment they were the only ones in the world. They were surrounded by snow and ice, the white floors growing frosted, like where they first met.

"You dance. I get to take your photos. For us."

She demanded it of him, there was not an ounce of sympathy or condolences in her eyes. She was a fire ready to destroy the world. She would never rest until he danced. This was what they promised. This was their unspoken vow.

He nodded and swallowed. What did it matter if no one else wanted him to have the dance? What did it matter he was dancing the most hated variation and was the only one to do it. So what? Amaryllis would stand by his side no matter what and he wanted to dance.

He wanted Powers.

This was what they were living for.

Please, he prayed to the Gods. *Give me this.*

"Powers of the Gods!" the woman with the pink sign called and Arco jumped to his feet. Amaryllis squeezed his hand one more time and finally released him. His fear, his anger, and his dissonance settled like falling snow. It melted and was replaced by the same raging fire within Amaryllis.

"You look good in white," he said.

She smiled, just as confident and radiant. "Dance for yourself, Arco. Win."

"I always do."

Sarcoline walked through the corridor, seeing his sister up ahead, leading the line as the incumbent. They were put in alphabetical order, Arco sat in the very last chair, but his sister sat in the first. Her name was called and before she walked into the doors, she glanced back to him. He nodded at her, and she nodded back.

One by one the names were said. Arna and his friends used to count, when Arco was younger, and his brother was still there. They'd count the seconds between names.

He could almost hear his brother's voice, *"You have six minutes to prepare. Then you must dance the full section with only six seconds between the individual dances."*

Arco counted. His sister succeeded. Three minutes, next name? Failure. Fifteen minutes? Failure.

"Most people fail. Only a few get through all six dances in a section." His brother's voice echoed in his mind. *"You will always be one of the few. You're a Vivicent. We always pass."*

Arco's eyes snapped open as his name was called. When he rose, he was the last left. Only ghosts accompanied him: his most well-known companions. He slowly stalked towards the door to the testing room, leveling his breath and settling his center of gravity. Each footstep was steadier than the next. Arco pushed the door open and stepped into the room.

Unlike the Mastery Tests, all auditions were in the audition hall. Like the Master Test rooms, the audition hall was two floors. He glanced up to where the judges sat hidden behind a series of mirrored glass. They could see him, but he could not see them. The majority of the walls on his floor were blank, without glass at all. There were no mirrors, only black walls; they held cameras to watch his every move.

He turned to the back wall of the room and spotted the Blue Rose Fears practice dance fans. Quickly and without much thought, Arco began to prepare. Carefully, he selected the fans and set them down on the ground in their Fan Form. He had submitted his variation on the Blue Rose Fears Fan Form weeks ago after his Mastery Test and it had been approved. Unlike the traditional form of a circle for Blue Rose Fears Powers, he set three sets on the left and three on the right, forming two crescents, without touching in the center.

He took a breather and approached the stand where other wristbands were left, all white and mint. He removed his and placed it on the stand before returning to the center of the room.

"Once you reach the center, focus on nothing else but the dances," his brother had once said, and Arco did so. The voice vanished and Arco was physically alone but supported by his memory.

"My name is Sarcoline Vivicent of the Vivicent Studio, DHS ID 867322. I am auditioning for Powers of the Gods. I will be dancing the Blue Rose Variation," Arco said, his voice heavy in his chest like an anchor. *I can do this.*

Arco dropped to one knee, both hands out at his sides.

"How did it go?" Amaryllis asked, as Arco sat in a daze.

"I don't remember," he admitted. He passed, but. . . How had it felt? What did he do? How well had he done? Strangely, despite not knowing, Arco was confident.

"Can I sit here?"

"Technically no."

She did anyway and started going over homework with him to distract him. He let his mind drift away as the dances continued into the day. The two of them continued their homework, getting through all that they had missed at school.

It was a series of hushing noises that made Arco look up.

The DHS members stepped out from the back. Zaffre took the microphone and spoke out to the world. "Thank you all for coming today and for watching from home. We are going to announce the results momentarily. Thank you to all the competitors who danced. Each one of you is special, and a master in your own right. You danced your best. For those of you who failed, we hope to see you next year. For those of you who did pass, know that even if you are not selected, you have the heart for dance. Do not give up."

Arco's heart stopped beating. Amaryllis took his hand.

I want it.

"When called," Cyclamen said, taking the microphone. "Please stand and take your spot."

Arco's ears started to buzz as applause filled the room, and names were called. Understudies and primary dancers began to fill the line for Knowledge and Appreciation. Chatter filled the room, by those who were disinterested in the charade. The same names were called yearly; there was never an upset.

"Powers of the Gods, understudy, dancing Twin Fans variation: Gingerline Vivicent of Xeysis," Cyclamen announced.

"What?" Gingerline stood. Her gasp echoed across the floor.

His sister *lost?*

Arco began to hope for the first time in a long time. Gingerline slowly walked to her spot in the Understudy line. Her face was blank, bleak, and confused. There was a hush that spread through the crowd of questions.

"How did she lose?"

"Who beat her? Ebru isn't auditioning for Powers."

Pictures flashed and soon the whispers became demands, became screams needing answers. People shouted at the DHS.

"Everyone please settle down," Cyclamen said, grimacing and then looking directly at Arco. "We must continue."

Arco's heart leapt.

"Oh, my Gods," Amaryllis whispered, having seen it too.

"Powers of the Gods, primary dancer," Cyclamen said as soon as the room returned to a reasonable level of noise. "Dancing the Blue Rose Fears variation. . ."

Arco sank into his seat. He could hardly believe it. No one danced the Blue Rose Fears variation. He was the only one. The variation name was a harrowing feeling that then filled him with such joy that he was unsure what to do. He squeezed Amaryllis' hand. He got it.

"Sarcoline Vivicent."

The room erupted in silence. His heart was in his ears.

"Go," Amaryllis said to him, a light smile on her lips.

He looked to her, uncertain.

"Go," Amaryllis repeated and Sarcoline jumped to his feet. He raced over to the line, smile on his face. He had done it! He won. All his practice paid off and he—

His sister's face was twisted in abject horror and anger. His father was equally terrified. Cyclamen glared at him. The hall was filled with gaping faces of anguish and disgust. A nightmarish horrific silence consumed and threatened to destroy everyone. No one, not even his mother, was clapping for him. No one excited for him—except Amaryllis who was smiling brightly and taking photos of him.

She was the only one. She was always the only one.

Arco's smile faltered and fell.

None of them wanted him there. None of them wanted him dancing Blue Rose Fears—

No.

No one wanted him dancing at all. This was the place of the Children of Xeyaro.

He would never be as good as them.

Arco became an inferno. He needed to be a fire, unable to be put out and unable to die. Since the candles no longer burned, he would instead. If everyone else wanted him to reject him, he'd become a flame so bright they'd never be able to live without him. He would be visible to all and never back down.

Arco lifted his chin, narrowed his eyes, and slid his hands into his pockets.

Let them hate him. Let them spite him. He earned his spot.

Once upon a time Arco would have danced for them if they let him. He would have died for them. He would have protected them and fought for them and defended them. He'd have been the world's everything, their hope and their faith, if they let him.

But they never would, so he'd dance for himself.

the POWERS of

Every move must be elegant. It is a story you are weaving. It is poetry in motion.
All stories must be edited, and all dance must be refined.

— On practice and the importance of repetition.

Dance 13

Silence

Incarnadine

1 Xeyan

41 Days Left

"I think I'm in love. Zaynir, am I? I don't know. This isn't Ven. This is someone I don't even know. Can that happen?"
"The unknown inspires more than fear."

Be comfortable with silence, Rosy.

The bell for the Shadone studio rang. Arna walked in, taking the room in stride, chin lifted, and eyes ahead. What began as a smile turned into a grimace as the receptionist saw him. There were comments from parents and students; Arna paid them no heed.

Be able to exist within silence.

Unlike the Vivicent studio, the Shadone studio was a large complex where no one lived. Sterile white lights flickered above. The bleached floors were spotless from the constant cleaning crews who stood in the corner of the reception lobby, ready to move at any time. Arna walked up to the white marble desk, ignoring the pointed looks. He was not there for them.

He had taken the morning to gather himself for this. Each passing moment made that composure crumble, and passion bloomed in its place. His heart raced. His hands shook. His mouth was dry in the anticipation of it.

He wanted to squeeze his fists tight but he did not. *Keep calm.*

It is serenity.

"Can I help you?" the receptionist asked.

It is the story told in moments where sound cannot reach.

"Where is Eburnean Hue practicing?" Arna asked, trying to stay in control. He could not let them know how excited he was. He let himself simmer in the emotion and feel it deeply but kept it low and contained.

"Is he expecting you?"

"Yes." The lie did not hurt him.

"He is currently in personal independent study and Mr. Shadone has indicated that he cannot be disturbed."

"What room is he in?" Arna tried again.

We only think of it after it has passed: when it has come and gone.

The Shadones and the Vivicents had been rival studios since the Shadones had entered the dance world generations ago. Arna had grown up believing that their mutual animosity was petty bickering regarding style, form, and teaching practices. It was a bit toxic at times, nothing too unusual, until Cyclamen Shadone took control.

Arna *hated* him.

"I can't let unknown visitors inside," she shook her head and said in a haughty tone.

"He knows who I am. You know who I am."

"Unfortunately, I—"

He didn't have time for this. Arna flourished his Blessings for control. "Give me the number."

"362," her eyes said dazed, before she blinked and gasped. "How dare you!"

Arna walked away from the desk and headed towards the elevator, ignoring her.

We long for it.

Alis once told Arna about how he'd been beaten by a group of fellow students, at the behest of a teacher. The students also hid Alis' things or destroyed them. Alis begged Arna to save him. Alis cried himself to sleep for years. Alis hated his father's Boss.

Alis loved his father. Alis' father was overwhelmed and let too much slip through the cracks. He expected Alis to be strong, because it would only be for a little bit until their family got back on their feet. But a little time turned to forever. Alis was forgotten by his father and thus Arna hated him too.

We hide from it.

Alis tried to tell Arna that it was justified. The Boss withheld checks, collateral to make sure that Alis' father never left. The Boss had been behind Alis' father losing their house. Alis' father signed an illegal contract with The Boss because no one else would take him after his last job.

His father was trying so hard to keep them afloat, and to keep Alis from the worst of the Boss' wrath. Still, Alis' father failed and Alis hid his pain. Alis loved his father, and his father loved him, but it could not save Alis from the situation. Alis might have tried to amend their relationship, but Arna had never agreed.

We try to fill it when it is not void.

Alis described it like a fire. The fire was burning, nothing would ever put it out, and he had to keep going. Alis said he became the flame and smoke itself. Instead, Arna now knew Alis became frosted mist: never tangible, never real. He became a mirage, where no flaws existed. Chilled to perfection, no one could hurt him. He claimed the impossible and tried to become a god.

He became a ghost instead.

The moments we do not hear are not lost. It is there in our imaginations, in our hopes, in our dreams. It is the proof, the support, the essence of what matters.

Ebru was sitting on the floor of his private studio when Arna opened the door. Without invitation, Arna entered, slammed the door shut, and took off his shoes. He locked the door. He stalked over, eyes slowly drawing over Ebru who sat startled. Analyzing the pictures was proof, but seeing Ebru in person was fact.

This was his Alis.

theendtheendtheend

"Arna. How pleasant to see your face." Ebru scowled at him, as if he were expecting a fight. He stood and leaned against the dance bar inviting Arna closer, taunting him.

"You make music," Arna declared examining every inch of Ebru's face. There were no visible scars, but he wore a long sleeve shirt and pants even in his private room. Arna stopped walking the moment he was in front of Ebru.

The statement caught Ebru off guard, but he quickly turned it around. He reached for Arna, sliding his arms over Arna's shoulders, trying to push Arna into the defensive, his usual tactic but this time it would fail.

"Why? You want my services? How charming I. . ." Ebru's words faded into nothing as Arna's smirk grew. It was the exact same humor. The same sarcastic way of speaking.

Silence is not an absence but a reminder of what you have.

"Years ago, you wrote a song." Arna's voice was shaking, his breath shallow. The ever present thudding in his spine became a resounding song in his heart, and for a moment the end of the world was forgotten. "A song about silences called Serenity's Lament. Written for CrimsonFlesh, after he had a breakdown about being forgotten. When everything was too quiet. When I had nothing. The first love song you ever wrote for me."

Ebru's body tightened. His shoulders lifted and his expression was caught between a laugh and panic. He quickly released Arna, backing up and hitting the dance bar, hard.

The image of Alis' profile picture online was an ancient aurora borealis done all in white tones. It was a reference to his name: Eburnean. How had Arna missed it when the similarities were so obvious?

Arna placed his bag on the ground.

nothingwasanaccident

"No." Ebru did a double take, staring at Arna's shadow for a bit too long, then his legs, and slowly moving up until their eyes locked.

"And you told me, when you sent it to me, that I needed to be comfortable with silences," Arna said, placing his hands on the dance bar, trapping Ebru. "Silence is not an absence. It is a reminder of what you have."

"Rosy?" Ebru spoke so lightly that Arna was half sure Ebru said a word.

"Alis." Arna smiled. "I found you."

"There's no way! You were in hiding." Ebru tried to escape but Arna held his grip steady and placed his knee between Ebru's thighs. He was trapped.

"No. We shared pictures, songs, stories. . ."

"We never shared our faces, or above here." Arna let go of the bar and poked Ebru in the stomach, drawing his finger up to tap at the vow mark over the heart that was hidden under Ebru's shirt. "Because you couldn't risk this being seen. And I couldn't risk you knowing who I was."

Ebru took Arna's hand but did not throw it aside. He eyed Arna carefully.

"That's why you never answered my calls. . ."

[Diamond and rose dust, sparkle not lost.]

"I can now." Arna tugged Ebru into a hug.

Ebru was like a corpse in Arna's arms: still and lifeless. When Arna felt Ebru's hands against his back, Arna tightened his hold. This was real. They stood like that for seconds, growing tighter by the moment as if the other would disappear if they let go.

"You can't be Rosy," Ebru said chin on Arna's shoulder, nails clawing into Arna's back.

"I won't let them hurt you again," Arna promised.

The lights started flickering, due to someone being unable to control their Blessings and it wasn't Arna.

"Don't make promises you won't keep."

"I'm here," Arna insisted. Arna swore to himself that this time, he'd keep the promise.

"It's always been you?"

Arna let him go but he did not flee. Ebru leaned against the mirror, arms crossed and not moving from the precarious situation. His words wistful and like the faintest mist. The mirror tried to consume him in the shifting lights, as if he belonged on the other side. Ebru grimaced at Arna.

"This whole time? Did you know?"

"No. I only recently realized it," Arna admitted. "I'm still angry that you blocked me."

"Me? You kept ignoring all my calls and coming up with excuses and—" Ebru snapped, before the realization dawned. "Shit. You were busy with us."

"Yes. You, asshole." Arna laughed from the chest, as if he hadn't in years.

Arna wanted him in every way he could. He wanted to push him up against every surface of the room and kiss him until he was breathless. He wanted to do every single thing he'd ever said in sly messages, hiding behind the knowledge that he couldn't because they didn't know each other. But now they did, yet he could not.

Instead, he backed away from Ebru to give him breathing space, not wanting to go too far too fast. Ebru may not act like it, as confrontational as he was and with how much he liked to play flirt with Arna, but Alis was skittish as a deer. Arna had learned over the seven years that they talked that he needed Ebru to reach out to him first. Otherwise, it could result in Ebru shutting it all down.

Ebru covered his mouth as he laughed with Arna. He began to relax visibly, shoulders dropping, hands no longer shaking. Ebru fell away from the mirror, stepping towards Arna, he was almost corporeal, as the lights stopped flickering.

Arna smiled. "Turns out we could like each other after all."

Ebru's face turned red, his lips curling up. "And here I had nearly convinced myself you only wanted me for my body."

"Me? *Yes, please kiss me until I stop breathing*," Arna repeated the message. "You liked every picture I sent you."

Ebru's face glowed brighter pink but instead of his eyes darting away he glared at him: *Shut up.*

Arna smiled. Good he didn't scream at him to leave. Arna let the message bleed into his expression: *Be good.* Ebru bristled and grimaced but said nothing.

"What possessed you to start calling me?" Arna asked. The calls had only begun that year.

"I wanted to for years, but I was terrified that if you knew who I was then you'd either stop talking to me or you'd become like all the other fans I'd ever met."

"But. . ?"

"I decided it didn't matter. I wanted to know you more," Ebru drew himself closed, curling in on himself away from Arna's reach.

It was strange to be in the same proximity and yet, so far apart. A chill ran down Arna's spine as he thought of how touchy they had been with each other before, when their relationship was a masquerade. How long had they danced around their attraction for each other? The mask of anonymity had completely dissolved whatever illusion either of them had ever been under.

nothingwasanaccident

dontbelikesaffrondontbeliesaffrondontbelikesaffron

"I promised you I'd come find you, and here I am," Arna finally said, wanting to try closing the distance again. His fingernails dusted the crescent moons on his palms.

Ebru rolled his eyes, without the slightest shimmer of tears: controlled, distant and cold.

"You were forced here because of me," Arna said softly, reaching out again and Ebru pulled away shaking his head. Arna did not press.

"Because your father couldn't pay my father. Not because of you," Ebru corrected. "You might have fucked over the world, Arna, but you aren't the one who paid my family's bills."

"It's my fault my father lost his patrons," Arna offered instead, turning his hand over asking for Ebru to take it. In it he revealed all the parts he tried to hide.

theendtheendtheend

"Your father lost his patrons because for the first three years he was a miserable drunk who only danced for the Celebrations. No one wanted to be near him. He lost you and in that he lost himself," Ebru said ignoring the hand.

Arna let it fall back to his side.

What?

"My father kept him together, tried to keep teaching. But my father wasn't good enough. He wasn't Zaffre. Students hadn't gone to your studio for my father; they went for Zaffre," Ebru clenched his arms and glared at the floor not meeting Arna's eye.

"I didn't. . ."

"Of course, you didn't." Ebru laughed in pain. "No one talked about it. Most people thought he had disappeared from the public eye and was practicing at all times to dance twenty-six. Most people thought he was preparing to sacrifice himself for your mistake, not that he was drinking himself into oblivion. Then he and Jasione fell into a fevered stupor swearing you'd be back. He's been sober since."

"Did Ven know?" Arna asked. How had no one mentioned it to him?

"No one knew but family," Ebru answered: meaning Alabaster, Ebru, and Arna's family, including Jasione. "Your family lost everything. The savings vanished. Jasione was a mess, in and out of jail. I bet you didn't know they could jail Children because I sure didn't. But Jasione was dead set to break every law possible. As if doing so would spite Lumak and make the Gods smite him." Ebru shook his head. "Your mom had to raise Arco. Ginger couldn't keep it together and neither could my dad."

Then the Hue's had lost their home. Ebru had lived at the Vivicent's household, as was tradition for the Hues and Vivicents, but the Hue ancestral home had existed since the Vivicent's was first built. It was an open secret that Cyclamen owned it—wanting to protect a cultural artifact was his official reasoning. Ebru had told him that Cyclamen helped someone else buy it and created the illegal contract for Alabaster. Work for the Shadones and, when the house went back up for sale, Cyclamen would help Alabaster buy it back.

"I'm sorry," Arna said, meaning it with every fiber of who he was.

"I don't want to hear it, Rosy. Words are cheap. I want proof."

"Proof." Arna repeated. Yes. He had to give proof. It would not be as easy as simply waltzing back. But he would do it.

"You are alive. You need to dance," Ebru said taking Arna in once again. "Prove to me that our suffering was worth it."

He needed to live, that would be proof enough. Arna squeezed his fists tight but then let them relax. He could do this.

The two of them stood for a long moment, staring at each other. Ebru's eyes locked on the vow mark on Arna's arm, exposed and visible. Then to the scars on Arna's palms, not saying a word. He picked up Arna's left hand, and lightly traced the scars with his fingertips.

"I have practice," Ebru said weakly moments later.

"You are the best Child of our generation. Everyone knows it. You know it." Arna pulled Ebru over to sit. Ebru refused. Arna ignored him and pulled his laptop from his bag, and accessed the speakers of the dance room, guessing the password to be similar to the one that Alis always used. Once he was in, he turned on the laptop and shared access to his screen with Ebru. Before them both, through their augmentations and contacts, the screen appeared.

"If I have any chance of stealing your father's spot at Worship. I can't be. . . whatever this is."

Whatever this is. Arna's heart thudded at the words. Years of emotions cascaded down on him.

theendtheendtheend

dontbelikesaffrondontbeliesaffrondontbelikesaffron

(find the silence.)

Not yet, Arna. Not yet. He had to do it slowly. Patiently. Ebru had to reach out first.

"Yes, you can." Arna opened up the programs. "Because you aren't going to take it from him."

And Arna didn't want Ebru dancing when there was a potential he could be injured. He might have had a healing ability, but it took more time than Arna's did; days instead of hours.

"I've been aiming to take it from him since I got here," Ebru disagreed, and Arna pressed play. The soft sound of a song came from the speakers. Whatever else Ebru may have said was lost. He slid to his knees next to Arna, listening.

"Incandescent?"

"I was working on it, since I realized you stopped. I added some of the sounds that I collected but never gave you. Will this help you finish it?" Arna spoke slowly, shifting closer. When their shoulders touched, ease filled him.

Ebru jolted suddenly as a crash sounded in the song. Arna paused it and looked at Ebru who was staring at him as if he were a ghost.

"You've seen the superstorms. Haven't you?" Ebru asked slowly, without the veil and pretense of being calm. Arna vaguely remembered telling him about the time in the cave. "The thunder was from a storm you said, and I know you went outside the cities. You told me."

He asked with is eyes: *how bad are they?*

Arna had danced in regular storms outside the city many times, in preparation for his final dance. The rain burned the skin, the winds lacerated the body, but he had been able to hold himself steady and in time had mastered dancing all five variations in the conditions. It had taken weeks of sneaking out of the cities over the course of the years. It was necessary, he'd been told. He could not falter when his time to dance arrived.

He had been twenty-two and training within such a storm, when Ixxzal had made him flee. The superstorm turned the clouds red, like chaos. When the silver lightning touched ground, everything for miles went up in flames. It lit up the sky in cackling terror; the air turned to steam then lit aflame. The rain had not been water but acid, melting everything it touched. The little plants that had managed to root themselves were gone in seconds. He'd been inside a cave, but he'd watched as the winds carved the ground and sky in half. He'd flourished his Blessings when the thunder rolled in fear of his insides being liquified.

He had been twenty-six when he finally had to stand within a superstorm for six minutes and dance the twenty-sixth dance of Blue Rose Fears.

saffronsaffronsaffronsaffronsaffronsaffron

"Worse than they say." Arna shrugged ignoring the memory and releasing the tension in his fists. "Don't worry about that."

Ebru uncurled Arna's fingers until Arna's hands laid flat on his thighs. Ebru once more rubbed at the scars, making the pinkness go away.

"I'm here," Arna repeated.

Finally, Ebru nodded and breathed out, relaxing. He nudged Arna over and took the laptop. Arna slid closer to Ebru with one leg propped up, his fingers lightly dusting the tops of Ebru's pants. Ebru smacked his hand away but chuckled as he did, and Arna did not touch him again. He smiled as Ebru worked. The man started messing with the mix, with a dexterity that Arna could not replicate.

The sound changed and Ebru's eyes; they were shining.

Arna had many flings in his life: short relationships and one-night stands. They had never meant anything because the nature of his life meant that they could not. Arna had Pervenche for a moment. However, Arna had Alis for longer. Alis had been Arna's first new crush, and his last new love.

Alis was the one he spent his late nights thinking of and dreaming of. Alis was the one who haunted his thoughts for years even more than the ghosts of those he'd left behind.

"This," Ebru said breathless, "This is. . ."

There was a spark in him of pure unfiltered excitement. Arna's heart flipped seeing it. Twenty-seven songs played in his head, discordant: wanting to be the first to come to fruition.

"Why are you looking at me like that?" Ebru asked.

Arna contemplated it. Knowing the answer. Knowing he shouldn't say it because it may send Ebru running. Yet he wanted to be honest. And he refused to run away, was that not what he promised himself? He just had to do it.

"I've loved you. For three years now," Arna admitted, despite his better judgement. It was too early for the words even if they both knew them to be true.

"You. . . Why do you have to be like this? Can't you keep your mouth shut for once?" Ebru's eyes darted away with flushed cheeks. *Oh?* Maybe it wasn't the wrong choice.

"No. You know I can't." Arna would not let a moment slip through his fingers. He had liked every new song first. He had messaged Alis about new releases. Alis had been his saving grace, and Arna became his. He slid his hand behind Ebru's neck, thumb lightly and tracing the mark of the Hue-Vivicent vow.

"Has Ven forgiven you?" Ebru asked suddenly. There was a pain in Ebru's voice that made Arna's hand freeze.

Arna thought of Ven and how every interaction they'd had was contained. Arna thought of the day they talked to get to know each other again: the rain against the archery targets and the patter that filled the silence that their voices left. They had spoken for hours and agreed to meet again and talked once more but never had. Arna was pretty sure he could recite every aspect of Pervenche's life by memory, by Blessing. They had exposed so much to each other yet. . .

It was not memorable.

"We aren't getting back together," Arna insisted. Lightly tugging at Ebru to look at him. Ebru refused.

"Oh, Rosy. How unfortunate," Ebru said solemnly but there was a hint of joy playfully seeping in.

"You should take the chance," Arna taunted him and asking for a retort. *Please be in love with me the way I think you are.*

"You think I want you?" The words were harsh, yet without the grating that Arna would have expected, instead it was almost shaky. Embarrassment? Fluster? Good. Arna dropped his hand, before Ebru could peel him off.

Ebru pressed play, ignoring the action. He said, "Now, listen with your unsophisticated ears."

The piece had been radically changed. Arna had not thought Ebru had done much, just a few tweaks, but not this. . . Not already.

Alis was good, but this was beyond his imaginings. Ebru clicked a few things, uploading the updated *Incandescent* to their shared file. He muttered things under his breath and tried to move away from Arna.

"I'll work on it more at home. This setup is dismal."

"Can I see the studio?"

Arna wanted to see it in real life. Not just pictures.

"Later. It's a bit tense at home." Ebru shrugged. "Once the Master—"

"He's not your master. Don't call him that," Arna snapped.

Ebru balked. Before Ebru could apologize, Arna shook his head. Arna did not want the apology. He wanted Ebru to stop thinking of himself as being caged.

Ebru tried again, "Cyclamen found out who I was… He demanded a cut because I'm using his house."

"How much money has he taken?"

Ebru shifted further away, shrugging, and telling Arna all he needed to know. Cyclamen tried to take everything, leaving Arna feeling cool and angry.

Ebru glanced up at Arna and then looked back at the laptop: fear present in his eyes.

[The God of the Unknown was a phantom.]

Arna moved closer until their thighs touched. With Ebru, Arna had always been afraid of failure: in everything. They'd been rivals for so long. Yet now, Arna feared a different type of failure. After he had fallen so hard, had hoped so much it began to show. What if he failed to get what he wanted because Ebru didn't truly want him back? Arna lightly traced Ebru's hand and Ebru, startled, looked at him.

Don't let me fall alone, Alis, Arna begged him with his eyes.

Ebru face was flushed, his eyes were uncertain. Ebru needed time to place Rosy and Arna as the same person. Arna had days. Ebru was always the faster one of them to adapt, but he needed time. Despite that Ebru's expression held the answer: *I'm here.*

safesafesafesafesafesafe

"You changed everything I did," Arna said easing Ebru back into their usual conversations.

"You're too classical in your choices," Ebru said, the same lecture he always gave Arna online. "Music is about innovation, Rosy. We have a concept of what we want to say, and then we have to think about and do it in a way that has never been experienced before."

Arna laughed.

Ebru hesitated and then joked, "If you keep holding me back, I might have to find a new partner."

Arna knew the provocation like the back of his hand. It was the invitation for flirtation, and Arna engaged without qualm. "Who else will tolerate your whining? Besides, you wouldn't dare, you enjoy me too much."

"Enjoy what?" Ebru asked, with a flat tone and taunting look, pushing Arna to say it. Arna instead leaned closer to Ebru, their foreheads touching. Their breathing was in synch.

"Neither of us need to be caged anymore," Arna whispered.

Rosy had been free to Alis, but Arna had always been bound. Ebru had to know that. Just as Arna wanted to steal Ebru away from the sterile white cage that he was forced to call home, Arna needed him.

Because he wanted to live, and Ebru could teach him how to defy fate.

[The God of the Unknown was more than accidents.]

Ebru pushed Arna away suddenly, turning to the mirrors once more. Ebru had a funny way of scrunching his lips into a lopsided pout when he was debating on saying something. Every time Ebru did it, he would say something he would regret.

"I loved you for three years," Ebru said finally.

Arna's eyes met Ebru's and they lingered for a moment. Time was a single a feather falling to the floor, a breath away from eternity.

"Only three? I was certain it was longer," Arna teased.

Serenity's Lament was the first love song, and it was what made Arna realize he loved Alis.

Ebru looked away but their legs were still touching. He wasn't running.

"You're an asshole."

"I think you might be projecting."

"Maybe." Ebru dropped his hand shaking his head. There was a brief second where Arna tried to reach out when Ebru jumped up in a fright. Eyes wide and pointing at the time projected before them. The moment was lost. "You need to go. The master of the studio will be here in ten minutes. He's never late. I have to show him my progress."

"Why must I. . ."

There was true fear in Ebru's eyes that was quickly masked. Without another protest, Arna put his things away.

"You know how to contact me."

Ebru nodded and didn't say another word as he stretched out his body preparing for whatever was going to bother him next. Arna quietly left the Shadone studio knowing that his presence would be alerted to all those that cared. As he rounded the corner away, he passed the car that he assumed had to hold Cyclamen Shadone.

Arna hovered around the studio for a few hours, looking over his messages, waiting. It was late afternoon when Alabaster exited the building.

Alabaster had dark eyes and hallowed cheeks. Seeing the man up close confounded Arna. Alabaster had not bothered to reach out to Arna since Arna had returned. Part of him wondered if it were because Cyclamen forbid it. Part of Arna did not care. Knowing what he did about Ebru and Alabaster's relationship had Arna ready to snap, unable to see him as the uncle he'd once been. Ebru was too important to him for Arna to forgive the man.

Alabaster was, however, nearly lifeless. It was as if his soul had been stolen. As Arna approached, the man was confused as if he did not recognize Arna. Arna's anger transformed to frustration and his hate began to stifle itself. Nothing could forgive Alabaster for what he'd done, but if Alabaster did not know, there was only so much that Arna could blame him for.

"Uncle," Arna greeted him, trying to keep his hostility to a minimum.

"Arna." The man smiled, soft and haunted. "What brings you here?" His eyes darted back. Terror was rising. "You shouldn't be here. You. . ."

"Did you know that Ebru—" Arna asked as Ebru walked out. He raced over and pushed himself between the two of them.

"Ebru?" Alabaster turned back to his son. "Why is he. . ."

"He wasn't supposed to be here, but we are leaving. Don't let the Master know we were here." Ebru shot his father a look and the man nodded.

"Go. Go. I'll distract him." Alabaster turned back to the door, and Ebru grabbed Arna, dragging him away.

"Don't tell me you were here all afternoon," Ebru snapped as soon as they were far enough away.

"You didn't message me," Arna said, glancing over his twenty messages he sent.

"I was going to when I got home," Ebru groaned. "Go home."

"No," Arna disagreed. Ebru glared and the two of them had an unspoken argument that Arna ignored, instead saying, "We're going on a date."

"What? We don't. . ."

"If you opened the chat, you would have seen the plans I made," Arna answered, tapping at his temple. Ebru had removable augmentations: contact lenses for his eyes. They did not work as well as implants, but Ebru still should have seen the notification messages.

"I have things to do!" Ebru protested, not particularly well, as he got closer to Arna. He was not running away.

"Obviously not. Do you even go out in the sun?"

Ebru was never tan in Arna's memories, but now his skin was devoid of color at all, almost frozen.

Ebru rolled his eyes in response.

"We should get you some sun. We could do so tomorrow. We might need to make sure you don't burn. The sun does destroy those who consume other's souls, as said Saint Ashe."

Saint Ashe was the famed saint who had broken up religious cults dedicated to stealing and eating those with Zaynir's soul Blessings thinking it would transfer the abilities.

"Arna, no," Ebru laughed at the joke. "Besides, wasn't it that the sun purified, not destroyed?"

Arna shrugged. "Same thing. Pokk was probably ready to smite them all."

[The Sun, through the God of Knowledge and Change, warmed the air even as the clouds took over Xeysis.]

Arna placed his hand on Ebru's head, placing their foreheads together. "You said you wanted a knight to whisk you away."

"I didn't mean a literal knight."

"And I'm not. But I'm here."

letmesaveyouletmesaveyouletmesaveyou

"You're here," Ebru repeated. The words sank to the ground beneath them and swirled into tulips and roses. Ebru said softly after a moment, "I need to protect my father."

"He should be protecting you."

Ebru moved and their eyes met: *he is.*

Not enough. But Arna did not say that. He took Ebru's hand, lacing their fingers together and said, "We have dinner. Let's go."

"Arna." Ebru smacked Arna away. "We aren't. . ."

"You need to eat, and I haven't eaten all day." The words elicited anger from Ebru. Arna went on, "And we need to collect the last song of the twelve-summer bird."

"No. . . It's next week," Ebru corrected, slowly.

"It's tonight."

Arna was certain of it. He'd done his research during the time he was waiting for Ebru. The Blue Larx population, commonly known as the twelve-summer bird, was to die at sunset. Their chicks would hatch on the solstice.

Ebru relented by giving his hand to Arna once more. With a grin Arna held his hand and for a moment the end of the world was forgotten.

After going to Ebru's house to drop off his things and for Ebru to change, they made their way to the restaurant. Once they had ordered, Ebru leaned on his palms, examining Arna from across the table.

Arna cocked an eyebrow, asking him: *what?*

"How much money do you want in the split?"

What?

"*Incandescent.* You collected most of the sounds this time, how much?" Ebru elaborated.

"You don't need to." The payment was always split between the both of them. And hadn't he just admitted to not having anything because of Cyclamen?

"I can pay you back for all the time you spent gathering them," Ebru insisted. "Even if it's my Ceremony money."

Arna rolled his eyes, all dancers who danced for the Ceremony of Chaos got paid. It was their job. They worked the whole year for one day, but compensation was not equal across dances. Worship and Understanding were paid the most. Due to the danger of Worship, despite it being one dance, the two were weighed equally. Powers got paid half of what Understanding and likewise the numbers were halved for Appreciation and Knowledge.

It was all taxpayer money and Arna had a feeling it was part of the reason for the rule changed on who could teach the dances. The city and voters were not happy with all the money they supposedly wasted on the Golden Generation.

"No. Instead, come home to the Vivicents," Arna disagreed. Ebru could return to the Vivicents today and no one could stop him.

"The Ma— Cyclamen would make my life hell. The DHS is in his pocket since your family fell."

Arna grimaced. He had expected as much. He had wondered why the competition for Understanding was between Ebru and Ginger each year. There were other dancers who had not retired, all in the DHS small council, who could compete. But if they were acting at Cyclamen's behest, then that meant that it was a Shadone and Vivicent competition. Cyclamen was using it to ruin the Vivicent studio further. If all the DHS members started competing again there was no guarantee that Ebru, let alone Ginger, would get the spot.

"Besides, I can't hurt my dad like that," Ebru went on, running his finger along the rim of his water glass. "He's locked into the contract."

"You're protecting us still."

Ebru shouldered the blame of everything onto himself just as Arna shouldered the end of the world.

Ebru's eyes snapped up. "I'm not."

"You could leave. Say goodbye to it all and focus on music instead. You can make enough money from it. By dancing, and continuing the competition, you are taking on all the pressure so that they don't have to. You're the reason that my family wasn't completely destroyed."

Arna was certain that if Cyclamen wanted to destroy the Vivicents. Ebru had taken the beatings, the pain, the pressure, and the scrutiny, all for a performance. Cyclamen tried to degrade the Vivicents, but Ebru protected them.

"But I'm back now."

Ebru twisted his fork in his fingers and sighed.

"I will never give up on dance and I won't leave my father," Ebru disagreed. Arna wanted to retort but held his tongue. "I can't give up on him, even if you want me to. . . he's your family too."

"You're more important to me than relations of fathers," Arna admitted, and Ebru grew red again. Before Ebru could say another thing, the waiter arrived with their food. When the waiter left, Arna said, "You're going to have to get used to me saying that I care."

"Zaynir be damned. What did the Gods do to you? You're supposed to quote scriptures, not lay your emotions bare."

Ebru spun his pasta around a few times. Silence overtook their table.

"Alis," Arna tested. "I'm here."

Ebru closed his eyes and nodded slowly. The rest of the dinner passed without a word.

As they approached the forest, Arna began telling Ebru stories of how he had gotten some sounds for *Incandescent*. The Giggling Stream of the Zalial Plains in Podiel had been an excursion he did not want to replicate. The Whistling Falls in the Araxas Hills of Zaydiel were beautiful, but he'd nearly fallen twice. The Claiser Clock in Azis was the most annoying. The Harrowed Halls in Ixis was the hardest to find, and he'd nearly gone crazy in the process. The sound of a thousand voices in Ludiel had been embarrassing to say the least. The sounds of the skyrails had been the most difficult to record, but he did not go into detail.

The storms Ebru had wanted to know more about, so Arna gave him stories of traveling outside the cities and what the air felt like, what it smelt like, and what it tasted like. He never talked about the superstorms.

Ebru didn't ask.

Arna had gathered six sounds from each city, excluding Xeysis. Ebru had gathered those himself.

When they arrived at the Greenwidden Forest on the first petal of Xeysis, the trees were covered in tiny blue birds. Hundreds of other people were in the forest, sitting and watching. Arna sent his sister a message that he was out and would be home later but did not clarify what time. He then shared his location with Ebru, who accepted. The two of them found a secluded spot beneath a tree.

An Ivumalis song, *A Mystery of Trees*, played and as it did, Arna thought of Phlox who fiercely protected Ebru.

"Does Phlox know?" Arna asked as Ebru got his recording equipment ready.

"Know what?" Ebru asked as if he had not heard.

"That you're Ivumalis." Arna elaborated but he had his answer without Ebru needing to shake his head.

He hadn't told anyone unless he was forced. Perhaps Cyclamen and his father were the only two in the world that knew, or perhaps the other Shadone students and staff knew and were using it as blackmail.

Arna was not sure.

"Will you ever tell anyone that you are Ivumalis?"

"No. I don't want to," Ebru said, sternly. "I'm happy being unknown."

As if Ivumalis was unknown. But Arna agreed, he wasn't ready to let the others know. Alis was his secret, and he wanted the safety of having the support, for a bit.

"I can't believe we were talking this whole time. . . on accident." Ebru stumbled over the words that came out of nowhere.

There are no accidents, Alis.

"Are you mad about that?" Arna asked instead.

"No. . . I. . ." Ebru's hands stiffened as he spoke. Arna wanted to jump in, to say that Ebru did not need to explain, but as Ebru struggled more, Arna sat and waited. Past Ebru, on the horizon, the center of Xeysis was dark. Ebru was half covered in shadows, half in the warm light. The differences swirled and glittered across his skin.

The silence consumed the air, until Ebru said, "It's nice knowing that you know. That . . . That someone knows. That. . . you're Rosy."

The last words were said like a prayer, soft and nearly inaudible. It had taken all day, but with the words Ebru finally accepted it, fully. Now Arna could push.

Arna's heartbeat in his chest was methodical and slow. He was no longer alone, Alis was with him. He reached forward, moving Ebru's hair out of his face. Ebru looked up from where he'd pressed record, stunned. Arna's thumb caressed Ebru's cheek and he leaned closer.

Before Arna could kiss Ebru, the chirping turned melodic and all at once the whole forest turned to a single song. Startled, Arna looked up in time with Ebru, dropping his hand. Ebru grabbed it and did not let go.

A swelling melody formed haunting and poetic. The blue birds sang their last song towards the sky, as night took over, their glowing bodies turning brighter like tiny stars ready to explode. Ebru sent a message to Arna:

    This is beautiful.

Ebru was glowing in the bright light, his bleached white hair moving in the breeze. Arna typed his response:

    I'm happy you're Alis.

Ebru read the message and then behind his cool facade, he smiled like fresh winter snow, pure and untouched. Once again, they were a single moment from the feather falling, locked on to each other. One more note and it would all end.

All at once Arna could sense his variation music in his skin.

It was as if no one had lived in the townhouse: white, sterile, not a speck of dust nor an item out of place. It was unlike Alabaster's house from Arna's memories. The Hue Manor had been filled with colorful art, sculptures, and a water feature. It had been built around a chestnut tree. This house was devoid of a soul.

Arna followed Ebru in the dark through the glass house, too simple for one of Xeyaro. Even the hanging garden in the center of house was enclosed, controlled, and filled with beautiful things that were forced to comply. Alabaster was not home, out with Cyclamen doing something either Ebru did not know or did not want to explain.

"No wonder you hate it here," Arna said as their footsteps echoed through the hall.

"Dad hates it here, too. But it's what we have, since we lost the house and Cyclamen has a need for cleanliness."

Cyclamen? Right. Alis said The Boss owned their home and was often there. Ebru led Arna up the stairs and into Ebru's studio.

The walls of Ebru's studio were painted a rich dark green, with deep oak furniture and flooring. Lush plants were in every corner with a trellis across the ceiling. Beyond the initial ambrosial scent was the shadow of petrichor. The greenery surrounded speakers, a standing drum kit, a microphone, and his bed. Petals littered the floor, sparkling as if they were gemstones. There were rounded plants and plump flowers: so many soft-looking, delicate creatures that needed love and attention. Arna knew every plant by name from the years of photographs Ebru had sent.

On the wall past the plants were instruments from all over the world: brass, strings, woodwinds, percussion. There were instruments Arna could name and ones he could not. Ebru could play them all; he often recorded himself.

"How often do you sleep here?" Arna looked at Ebru's sound-proofed closet, home to his speakers, computer, and sound boards. Inside was a folded chair with the name Rosy on it, like Arna had asked of Alis years ago: waiting for him.

"Often enough." Ebru leaned against the wall as Arna looked at the set-up he had talked about for years. It was the newest tech, reinforced with Blessings against moisture. Every bit of it was bronze in color: bronze and gray.

"This is amazing."

"I told you it was." Ebru brushed past him quickly. "Here." He put on one of his songs, letting the music vibrate through the room. "Dad hates it, but it's the best I can do here."

The neighbors also hated it, from the amount of noise complaints Ebru received.

"Why did you insist on coming over?" Ebru asked as his shoulders tightened as his eyes flickered to Arna's. Arna hovered closer, carefully. He lightly moved the sleeves of Ebru's shirt out of the way to check what Cyclamen's students had done. Ebru stopped him. "No."

"Okay." Arna dropped his hands and did not press further.

"Is that the only reason?" Ebru asked, almost sad.

Arna's heart raced. His music was missing something so simple: Ivumalis. Every song he'd ever made was with Ebru. Arna could not do it alone.

I'm allowed to ask for help. The Gods had said it to him long ago, and Arna had discarded it as nonsense. He was going to trust it. It was a leap of faith, but he needed Ebru's talents. He needed the support.

[*Yes,* Ixxzal's voice cut through the fog like a light of understanding.]

"Can I log into my account?" Arna asked, ignoring his uncertainty and reminding himself that he had to take the jump. The only way he could fix things was by going all in.

dontbelikesaffrondontbeliesaffrondontbelikesaffron

Arna squeezed his hands tight before releasing the fear and burying it deep.

"Sure?" Ebru said turning on his computer. As he did, around the physical screen, five other holographic ones appeared in various sizes, all booting up on the augmentations.

Arna mirrored him and both turned to the screen. Ebru's expression was shielded. Arna slid his hand through Ebru's hair moving it away. Ebru flinched at first until their eyes locked. Unwavering eyes met hesitation in the reflection. Ebru bit his lip in debate.

"Tell me, Alis." Arna spoke softly, hand sliding back behind Ebru's neck and pulling him closer. "What's on your mind?"

"I made them hate me. It was the only way they stayed united: if they fought me. They needed a common enemy in their grief." Ebru spoke from the heart, softly leaning on Arna's shoulder. Becoming a tangible being, releasing emotions held deep within. "But if you're here then. . . I'm better off alone, Rosy. But you're here."

"You aren't a monster, Ebru." Arna rested his head on Ebru's and ran his fingers through Ebru's hair. Ebru was melting, finally.

"I don't want to hear that from you."

"Ask Ven, then," Because there was no way Pervenche would ever say Ebru was a monster. They loved him too much.

Ebru's face scrunched up in the screen. He typed in his password, and for a long agonizing minute, he opened up his music software, logged out, and had Arna log on. Arna clicked open his storage and started the download of the file named: For Alis. Ebru said nothing about it.

"You know how they broke my heart, Arna. You broke theirs and they broke mine. I can't. . ."

"But you want Ven back in your life." There were one too many late-night conversations Arna had with Alis, lamenting about the friends he wished he still had and about the best friend he missed. "You can do that."

"I—I can't." Ebru pulled away: intangible once more, pulling the vulnerability back. "I can't hurt myself like that again."

"Ven won't hurt you again. Not like that."

Pervenche cared too much to hurt Ebru again. Why was Ebru shutting him out?

"They'll hurt me. It's always been destiny's plan. What's the point in opening myself up?" Ebru shut down the thought with quick and hash words.

Arna was at a loss hearing Ebru's nihilism for the first time in person. Arna changed the conversation. Perhaps there was another way to get Ebru to see he was worth something.

"Do you want to dance, Ebru?" Arna had never asked the question before. "If you could give it up for music, would you?"

"Never," Ebru said without taking a breath or thinking about it. "I love music so much, but I love dance equally. I can't give either up."

"Then you can choose both Ven and me."

Ebru did not react. Arna briefly glanced to the Ebru beside him, then back to the screen, returning to the refracted image of him. It was as if seeing him through the glass let Arna see Ebru better. In the image Arna saw, there was no sign of the pin-up villain that Ebru portrayed himself as. Instead he was lost, confused, and startled.

"You don't mean that," Ebru said, cracking in the heat of the moment. "Your heart—"

"And you know I'm in love with you," Arna cut him off. Fully turned to him, eyes wide, eyebrows furrowed. Ebru was absolutely incredulous that Arna had said it again, but Arna did not care. "Don't give me that look. I did not spend the better part of the last year trying to convince you to call me your boyfriend and then telling everyone this year that I was your husband for you to give me that look."

Ebru's cheeks were pink again, the tips of his ears bright red. His stark white hair made it more apparent. Ebru tried to say something and was unable, turning back to the screen, where the file was downloading painfully slow.

"It's different now," Ebru tried to deflect but failed. "That's online joking."

"No. It's not," Arna disagreed.

"You could have them back, if you wanted." Ebru slipped his hands from the table to his thighs and curled his hands closed.

"I can also have you. Finally."

Ebru shivered, visibly. He clung to himself, refusing to look at the computer screen or at Arna.

It was clear Ebru was struggling to figure out what to do and to say, when Arna was content with saying nothing at all. Arna turned Ebru's chin to face him. Mint eyes met brown eyes so dark they were almost black.

Neither looked away.

"Is this awkward for you?" Arna asked. "'Be able to exist within the silences.' Remember?"

Music was as much the moment as the pauses and breaks.

"The silences tell a story," Ebru agreed.

He went still for a moment. When Ebru reached out to Arna, Arna pushed closer. Ebru wrapped his arms around Arna and leaned in until Ebru hot breath slipped down Arna's neck. Parched, Arna's heart raced. He knew what to do next, knew that Ebru would reciprocate, and yet Arna was unable.

The unknown inspires more than fear, Zaynir had once told him. But damn Ixxzal, it was not easy to cross the line. He tried to convince himself to jump but was unable, something holding him back: the tremble that rippled down Ebru's spine. Ebru was terrified.

Not yet. He was close but not yet. He let Ebru set the pace.

They sat like that, nearly on top of each other with little noise between them other than their breathing. There was no awkwardness, as Arna had expected. It was comfortable: a strange conversation between them. Arna glanced at the download.

"It's done—" he said as Ebru's lips landed on his, light as a feather. It was so quick that Arna nearly swore he hallucinated it, until he they locked gazes: intense and needing. Ebru was fractured in the light, shimmering, trying to solidify. Arna reached up and pulled him back down. Before their lips could touch, Arna met Ebru's eye: *yes or no?*

"Yes," Ebru said against Arna's lips.

The second kiss was more forceful, hungry, craving and filled with so much anger at the two of them being apart for so many years. It was a thousand stolen moments crashing into one, a symphony that peaked and left Arna reeling and gasping as Ebru pulled away.

"Show me," Ebru said, sitting in his own chair and pulling to the desk.

"You're just going to kiss me and get right to work? Really?" Arna's desire grew and threatened to crush him. He did not care about his variation then, all he wanted was Alis.

"This is for me, Incarnadine." Ebru pointed at the large physical screen. *Show me the depth of your feelings.*

Arna swallowed and nodded. He opened the download and was confronted with all twenty-eight files. The file names were simple: dance one, dance two. The twenty-eighth file was filled with voice memos that he left himself over the years, going over his thought processes and what he wanted for the sound.

"This isn't. . ."

theendtheendtheend

Ebru's hands shook as he gripped the mouse.

"I need your help finishing this." As Arna said the words, it was as if a weight went with it.

theendtheendtheend

"Are you allowed to get my help?" Ebru asked, breathless. Ebru met his gaze, Arna nodded, and something behind his eyes flickered. Ebru leaned back, sleeves back in place. "Easy enough. Send me the files and I'll get it done."

Being in this house, looking at Ebru, made Arna remember Ebru's dream: large house, family, laughter. Ebru would never ask for money from him, not for this, not for anything. He was Rosy, and Alis never asked him to pay, not for any request. But Arna wasn't going to let him do the labor without compensation, for Ebru was saving him in more ways than one.

Arna may not be able to trust him with the end of the world, but he was trusting him with his life. Ebru would help him become better than Saffron.

"You're Family Home is being sold and your money is being tied up by the Shadones, right?" The only money that Alis had was the money he made on commissions. All his money from his appearances as Ebru and dance, were controlled. He'd told Arna hundreds of times that his money was managed by his Boss, which always was highly illegal. The Chosen Child stipend had to be more than enough to buy the home, or at least to get a loan to do so, until Ebru could get his money back.

"What?" Ebru's already too pale expression turned stark. "Why does that matter?"

"Why is Cyclamen selling it?"

Ebru did not hesitate to answer, whether it was because Arna was asking or whether he no longer could keep it in. "He's selling it in order to control my father, to stop him from going back to the Vivicent studio. I was in contact with Cardinal White to have the Church of the Apostle help me buy it. But. . ."

He'd buy it. He had to. "When does it officially go on sale?"

"You can't just buy it."

The two of them held each other in a contest of silence, eyes locked, and faces frowning. Arna asked for Ebru's help, and he was willing to give it. Arna would help him too.

Ebru broke first and said, "After the celebrations. The Church is currently blocking the sale due to the 'uncertain circumstances' that you brought."

He said not another thing as he clicked open the twenty-seventh file and pressed play. The music filled the room, drowning out the uncertain tension that struggled to die. Had Arna pushed too far? He went to say something when Ebru asked, voice filled with a hit of hope, "What is it called?"

"The Incarnation of Dreams Upon the World Variation of the Twenty-Seven Dances of Worship for the Knowledge, Adoration, and Understanding of the Six Gods Danced with Alternating Fans," Arna said in one breath for the first time aloud to anyone other than the Gods.

"Alternating Fans?" Ebru cocked an eyebrow. "Does anyone else know?"

Arna shook his head.

Ebru nodded and opened the first fie, asking, "Shortened is Incarnation?"

"Incarnate Dreams," Arna corrected, heart settling. He was no longer a pot at boiling point. The steam was being released and with it, the pressure. He didn't have to do it on his own anymore.

"I won't Understand it. Is that okay?"

"Listen to track twenty-eight. I add my thoughts as voice notes there and I'll continue to add them. Do you think we have time?"

Ebru pressed his lips together tapped the table a few times and said, "I can make it in time."

Thank Ixxzal's stars, Arna thought relieved. He squeeze his hands tight, until the familiar biting returned and his panic was shoved deep.

Ebru slowly turned back to him, tilting his head and melting from composer to Alis once more. Ebru said nothing as his hand left the keyboard and landed atop Arna's fists. Arna froze. He played with Arna's knuckles for a moment, before turning Arna's hands over, and forcing Arna to open them. He traced his fingers over the bleeding scars.

"No more," he requested, lightly as if Arna would not heed him.

"Okay," Arna said, breathlessly. He swore to himself that he'd stop, even if his panic consumed him. Even if he never forgot the ever looming presence of the end of the world. He would stop.

Slowly, but surely the pressure of the touch intensified, and Arna leaned in.

Don't go. The words were unspoken between them.

Arna laced their fingers together. *I don't want to.*

You're here. Ebru lightly smiled and Arna's brain began to short circuit. He had spent years of staring at this man's photos. He had spent more time talking to him online: talking dirty to him, sweet talking him, and trying to convince him to love Rosy. Finally, Arna caught him.

There was absolutely no hesitation in his actions as he pulled Ebru closer, capturing his lips once more. Tens of flings and moments that were always wrought with skepticism were discarded. Memories of how slow and deliberate he'd been with Ven were forgotten.

This was his Alis. He had imagined this moment for years, with a man without a face. He had screamed this man's name for years, jacking off in corners of a room when he wished that the Gods could not see him. This was his Ebru. They had danced together as teenagers, flirting and fighting, and he had crushed on his image for years without admitting it.

If Arna was going to know Alis, was going to be able to be near him, he was going to have him. He was going to let himself want him and never regret a moment of it.

"Rosy," Ebru gasped between kisses.

"I thought you wanted to see how good I am with my mouth," Arna said kissing Ebru's neck, teasing him and wanting more.

"Are you sure?" Ebru asked. The fear was potent and palpable.

Are you sure you love me? And not...

Arna kissed him again. And again. "I love you Eburnean. Alis. You know me better than I know my own heart."

As Arna said it, he meant it. Everything about it was his deepest and most important truth. Ebru to grabbed him in full, kissing him back with a ferocity that made Arna groan.

"Midnight," Ebru said as Arna was leaning in for more. Two hours was not enough time for all Arna wanted to do. He was not going to rush. Azza be damned if Alabaster returning home was going to stop Arna. Ebru chuckled as if reading Arna's mind.

All was forgotten, as Arna and Ebru left the studio, tumbled onto Ebru's studio bed. Ebru's hands traced Arna's storm scars, saying nothing but letting his fingers dance across the skin. Arna did the same for Ebru's bruises, lightly touching him ensuring that there would be no pain.

Their vow marks, not to lie, were an identical spiral above their hearts. The snake on their necks was an identical promise to protect each other. Arna kissed the marks that were self-inflicted on Ebru's thighs, knowing the story from hours when he'd talked Alis down from over the edge. Ebru kissed the palms of Arna's hands and not once did they look away from each other. They spoke without speaking. They breathed in tandem, dancing as a pair. They were knowing and hearing with only the sound of silence.

In the shadows of the room, the garden of plants sang around them, filling the air with a lullaby of tomorrow. A universe of stars blossomed across the ceiling. A harmony burst between the two of them, quickly, loudly, and then vanishing into the soft hum of miracles.

Each variation is rooted in the emotions of the Chosen who created it. However, your emotions must be considered. They too guide the dance and form. Your version of each variation shall differ because your experiences are wholly your own. Capitalize on it and embrace it.

— On the importance of the self in the dances.

Dance 14

Enlightenment

Incarnadine

3 Xeyan

39 Days Left

"You have learned to silence your mind from us."
"Does that bother you?"
"You are doing well."

At the counter sat the black, oil slick fabric with the embroidery that he had commissioned. It was the softest silk and glistened as Arna moved it examining the pattern. It looked right. It felt right, but he was not sure if it would look good on him.

Did I make the wrong choice?

panicovereverytinychoicewhennooneelsewillnotice

The owner of Aster Fabrics walked away to get the other fabrics that Arna had ordered to be cut and the fan boning. Arna contemplated completely starting over on his designs.

      Alis: No.

Arna paused.

No. He made the right choice, and he couldn't second guess himself, not this late in the game.

theendtheendthe—

Arna ignored the thrumming of the world, that resonated through him. No more, it could not control him. *Pretend it doesn't exist. Make it silence.*

Finally, Arna's cocktail of Blessings to cover for the Ch.Insight gap, transformed into the correct mixture. He drank it in.

It became silent.

      Rosy: We're dating. I can't hide it forever.
      Alis: We have to. No one can know I'm Ivumalis, and it
            makes no sense for you and I to be dating without the
            explanation.
      Rosy: Have you seen us? The fact that we only fucked now
            should be more of a surprise.
      Alis: Please.
      Alis: We can figure out some other way to tell them later.
      Rosy: If that's what you want.

Arna was not sure how he was going to keep if from anyone. He was sneaking off to see Ebru each night. The night before he got home to find his sister sleeping in his room.

No one lectured him. No one demanded to know where he was.

But Arna had a feeling he was going to be getting back in the early hours of the morning a bit too much that they wouldn't question it.

He was also going to miss many of his evening practices. He was going to have to rearrange his schedule to keep up his routine and training. He could not slack off now.

The owner set the folded fabric down for Arna to see. All of his requests, cut to the proper shape and size. Arna's heart skipped a beat and his hands wavered as he hovered them over the fabrics.

"We have one Heavy Opaque ombre, one Heavy Sheer striped, one all colors Airy opaque, and one all colors airy sheer. All have been cut and made per DHS standards for fans, with enough excess to adjust. Customizations have been made to the weave, as you specified," The store owner recited.

Arna lightly held the fabric up to the light. It was the softest material he'd ever felt, durable for what it would be used for. It was beautiful, exactly what he wanted. But something about it, and his plan for it was off.

"And then. . ." The man said pulling out the last three sets of fabric. "Iridescent black fabric of the airy specification." The man moved the fabric so that it shimmered, and Arna was able to see the opalescent hue to it. He drew out the next. "Glitter woven black fabric with black gemstone inlays, hand pressed, of the heavy variety." He showed off the black fabric that glittered due to the weave of the thread including both the stones and the glittering thread. "And finally, the Black fabric combining the two techniques, with a dragonfly pattern created."

The man unfolded the fabric for the twenty-seventh dance. A massive dragonfly appeared before Arna. Whoever had made the piece was excellent at stitching, combining the iridescent pieces, that made up the dragonfly, with the black heavy glitter fabric. As the fabric was moved Arna would be able to simulate the wings moving, with his Blessings.

The fabrics were perfect and yet there was a pain in Arna's gut. Something was wrong, but he could not figure out what it was. Perhaps he was simply nervous for how he intended to make the fans. The process was sacrilegious at best, but it was the only viable option to him.

He supposed, more than that, it was that he wasn't going to be able to touch the fans until the night of the performance. Here was the most beautiful fabric he'd ever seen and held, and he wouldn't be able to do anything with it once it was used. Longing filled his chest.

I want to hold a fan.

Arna clenched his hands and for a second didn't realize he'd done it before he released them quickly. Alis said no more, which meant no more. He needed to be better than it, and find another way to release his stress.

"This is classified as an Irregular weave. As requested, the end that is to be attached to the fan boning is. . . lighter, and the density falls towards the bottom. With this and the sets of fan boning you requested of the heavy quality, that is your total order." The man hesitated. He finally looked up and met Arna's eye. "Will it be done in time?"

Arna finalized the payment. "For the Celebrations? Yes."

Arna had faith in his abilities, even if the final outfit was not the exact craftsmanship that he wanted.

"The excess fabric?" the man asked. "We have enough for another three sets."

"Keep it for now." Arna did not want to take it, and besides, if he took it, no one would know where to find it if he didn't survive the twenty-seventh dance. Leaving it at the shop gave his fans a fighting chance to be recreated. "Thank you for this."

"It's my job. And I believe in you," the man told him, as he helped Arna package it. The individual pieces of fabric were not too heavy on their own but once they were loaded into Arna's bag, it was difficult to lift them without his Blessings activated and flourished. Hauling the fabric and fan boning from Aster Fabrics, Arna tried not to imagine what it would be like to build the fans himself.

He tried not to think of the fabric between his fingers and what it would be like to finally make the one thing he could not touch.

diediediedie—

(make it silence.)

How he longed to touch fans. Most days he ignored it. The memory of the pain was more overwhelming. But for a moment he let himself dream of the day after he danced, when he could make them without fear. He thought of a life where he could do nothing day in and day out but make fans.

It was a short lived dream.

Dreaming of a future in which he lived past his dances, felt strange. It was impractical. And each time he did, the desire to live grew stronger and stronger. The truth of the end of the world clawed at him further and without a proper outlet it was making his hands shake without reprieve.

I'm fine. He clenched his fists without noticing.

Arna sat on the bus surrounded by vacant seats, listening to his Ivumalis playlist on repeat. The few who were there with him, gave him space. Some kids with archery bags were in one corner. Some others read books. Many were on their mobiles, sneaking photos of him as he sat.

Alone.

The world fractured and rearranged itself, folding in and compounding until sound no longer reached him and the breath was stollen from his lungs.

[*You are in pain,* Zaynir spoke seated on the bus.]

Where have you been?

Arna released his fists with a gasp at the pain in his palms. *No more,* he swore once more.

[*Listening.*]

I did the right thing with Ebru... didn't I?

[*Yes.* Ixxzal sounded smug and triumphant.]

[*Asking for help is within your right,* Zaynir seethed.]

Why did they sound so distant? Better yet, why were they fighting? Was there something else they were debating about him doing?

[*Our connection is growing weaker.* Azza sounded scared.]

[*But we are here.* Pokk sounded soft and calm.]

Arna did not respond.

[*What do you want, Arna?* Xeyaro asked him through the radio.]

Is it okay for me to want to live? Arna asked them. It was an impossibility. A deep guilt was settled in his stomach, boiling at the thought. It felt like something Saffron would have wanted.

[*You are our Chosen,* Lumak offered. *We want you to live.*]

Arna sighed out loud exiting the bus and heading to Amaryllis', despite wanting to head home. Arna usually ignored the others' messages, but Amaryllis had messaged him when she never did before.

    Amaryllis: my studio, now.

As he arrived at the house, he found the door unlocked.

"I'm here!" He called as he entered.

Arna walked in and Amaryllis sat in the kitchen wearing a pink pant suit. She was a silhouette behind the myriad of her glorious art. Her hair was up in a messy bun atop her head, and she was drinking a smoothie.

"I wasn't sure you looked at any messages. The others say they text you, but you never answer," Amaryllis said, sipping her drink softly.

"I do." But it was strange. It had felt like a betrayal to Alis: messaging the others. Now that he had Ebru, talking to his family through text was probably a good way to start reconnecting properly.

"I'm adding you to the group chat."

Arna nodded and she pointed to the back.

"They want to talk to you."

"Who?" Arna glanced back. He didn't have time, today was the only day he could go to the factory and. . .

"Whatever it is you have planned. It can wait," Amaryllis told him. "Go."

Arna shrugged and placed his fabric bag down, including the bolt of black fabric for his clothes. She asked no questions.

"Hi Coco—" her voice drifted as she disappeared up the stairs.

The warm light of the fading day left half the garden in shadow. Arna walked along the path, towards the back. Pervenche sat in the back reading a book, engrossed in the words. Fairy lights twinkled in the trellis above as fireflies waltzed in the air.

"Ven. . ." Arna stopped walking. Out of everyone he expected to see, Pervenche was the last one.

Pervenche shut their book after placing a bookmark. "Arna."

"Why are you here?" Arna looked back to the house and then to Ven. "I thought you two. . . Are you. . ?"

"I love her." Pervenche shook their head. "But it was a long time coming."

Arna stepped forward tentatively. He did not wait to be offered before he sat on the bench beside Pervenche. Pervenche sat in the light, Arna in the shadows.

"Why did you call me here?" Arna asked when he was centered and ready to have the conversation. This one would not be like the last. This one was going to change things, and Arna needed to make things right this time.

"Amaryllis sees people," Pervenche answered. "And she told me that we needed to talk, without holding back. So, I want to. Now."

Silence.

The silence between them was awkward, where in the distant past it would have been electric: Arna striving to say something and Pervenche telling him not to. They were always small, quick silences in the past, bookended by kisses and memories. Their shadows inched closer from the magnetism of a shared history. Their realities were pulling apart from the gravity of the same echoing times.

Arna sat for a moment before he recognized a turmoil that was not his own. When the Blessing activated in the past few weeks, it always happened like a jolt. At the archery range, the Blessing had remained dormant as the two had spoken like strangers. This time Pervenche activated and flourished their S.Mirror's Blessing, slowly. Arna felt the pain that Pervenche felt, the anguish and the anger. It was all consuming: hundreds of complex emotions raging. Their face remained still.

Arna broke the silence. "If you hate me, you don't have to talk to me."

That was the issue with S.Mirrors. It linked them together, but what that link was, was up to them. They could be strangers if they so desired, even if the bond tried to pull them closer.

The two faced the garden without looking at each other once, everything that needed to be seen was felt, deeply in Arna's bones.

"I don't hate you, Arna. You made a choice and we both have to live with the consequences." The turmoil grew. "You can't just waltz back into my life like nothing changed."

It was a stab to the heart. "Trust me, I know."

There was another dreadful silence between them. Once more, Arna did not strive to fill the dead space with noise

Pervenche spoke soft, tentative, "You aren't the same person as you were before."

"No. You aren't either," Arna insisted, trying to shape his own emotions to send back. He sent back the understanding, realization, and hope to reconnect.

"You left me all alone. . ."

Pervenche was taking deep breaths in time with Arna; it was time to disconnect. It was the best for the both of them and as he went to forcefully cut it off, the wind blew through the trees and the lights sparkled brighter. He let the Blessing stay active.

[*Talk,* Lumak said.]

But between him and Pervenche words had never been needed. As Pervenche exposed their emotions so completely, Arna did the same. He let the confusion and anxiety wash over him. He let himself feel everything:

The words of hundreds of articles and comments circled in his head.

The hate for himself.

The hate for Mortals.

The hate for the Gods.

The anger, the sorrow, the pain.

The overpowering fear of death and the want to die, but the budding fire that was his desire to live, screaming at him to listen.

The great anxiety he had about Ebru and how others would react.

The want to be loved, the need to be seen.

Then he let himself think of the Weeping Stage and of Amaryllis destroying his soul in the garden of flowers. He relished in it, let the anger consume him. It was not Amaryllis who broke him: she'd revealed the truth.

Pervenche pushed back with their own anxiety. There was a deep, deep sorrow that felt as if the world was breaking. There was happiness, joy, and so much apathy. It twisted into hate, and hate, and hate, and finally: acceptance. There was grief and hope. The all-encompassing sorrow was a solace. The deep resentment was an itch that could never be scratched. The bittersweet love filled Arna in abundance, but it was shattered by a deep betrayal that never fully healed.

Then there was a second betrayal of a different love, this one as painful as the first. Then another breaking but not from betrayal. It as from a truth: it was time to let go. There was a fear to do so, afraid of being lost.

Pervenche was lost, alone, isolated in all the ways that Arna was, but in vastly different ways.

Not a single word was said but Arna understood it all: how they felt when he left and how they finally moved on. There was an anguish due to him returning and a peace from the fact that they could never be the way they were. Neither of them wanted to be.

They had simply grown too far apart, and while they could be anchors to each other, they did not have to be each other's everything.

Arna pulled at Pervenche's good memories, wanting them to feel the warmth even when Arna did not feel it himself. Pulling at emotions could let him know roughly, what Pervenche felt, even if he did not see the exact memory.

Pervenche began to cry. Arna pulled more at every good time, every strong solid feeling he could, unable know what they were. Pervenche's eyes lit up, in joyful sobs and painful smiles. The love and overwhelming heat was so strange and strong that it began to make the air churn. Pervenche continued to cry, but instead of pushing Arna away, they pulled, wanting to soothe Arna as well.

Pervenche smiled at Arna, *I never stopped loving you.*

Arna could read it in their face, in the way they breathed, in every emotion they spun. The love had not died, but it was changed. It was something that was no longer pure, but it was resolved. It was profound and accepting, and deeply platonic. A romantic love was a love that no longer served either of them.

Arna suddenly understood Amaryllis, intrinsically. Pervenche's love for Arna was similar to Arna's love for Pervenche: a weight to keep him from vanishing, but not to control.

[*We gave you what you need,* Lumak said.]

They had given him a tether, that was meant to keep him safe. It was never meant to break. Arna trusted them with his life.

Pervenche pulled at something light that Arna protected from taint.

He was there, standing beneath the clocktower yawning and recording the chimes. He was laughing at jokes told by those whom mortals did not see. He was bantering with Gods who smiled in the dark. He was seeing The Dancer for the first time. He was messaging Alis for the first time, falling in love so thoroughly that it wrecked everything he knew.

He was at the silver house.

At the house with the silver door.

The house with the silver lawn.

His father taught him how to make fans for the first time, weaving the threads one by one, carefully and with praise. This was the first time Arna ever made a fan. He was stepping onto stage feeling them for the last time, wielding the pride of being Chosen.

He was a thousand stars and a million whispers only he heard. He was the overwhelming calm and awe They gave him, even when They annoyed him to the sun and back. He was reading messages and believing them: `I'm here.`

He was enraptured by mint eyes that met his in the mirror.

"I'm in love with Ebru." The words tumbled out, before he could stop them. "Coming back, I thought it would be you again. But. . ."

Pervenche who wore a tightened smile and furrowed brow. There were hordes of emotions that Ven was feeling, and Arna could name each one. The most powerful, the one dominating the others, was confusion.

"I wish I could tell you how it happened but. . ." Arna paused for the smallest of moments not wanting to break what was between them, yet he could not expose Ebru. Ebru had explicitly asked him not to. Instead, he focused on all the emotions of Alis and of Ebru since Arna returned.

The confusion. The heat. The desire. The passion. The need. The connection over years. The way the waves slowly washed to shore and pulled him out to sea until all he could breathe was the depth of the feelings. The billowing winds that were light as a feather. The complex shuddering of reliance despite the unknown.

Pervenche laughed, truly and almost bright. Amusement filled the connection from their side instead of anger. "I used to get so jealous of you two when we were kids. But each time you got close,

I'd feel your emotions and I'd know you were angry. . . But everyone thought Ebru was in love with you. If we didn't know any better, we would have thought you loved him. You ran to each other when you had nightmares or were afraid."

"We lived together." Although Ebru had always been his first choice, even when Jasione was there.

"You constantly took each other's things and got in each other's personal space."

Arna opened his mouth to retort but could not. Pervenche was right. Ebru was not his first choice as an active thought, but he always was watching Ebru, and thinking about him. Had he fallen for Alis because it was Alis, or had he turned to Alis because Alis reminded him of Ebru? Arna found himself foolish for not noticing. They were the exact same. They'd never fully hidden who they were from each other since the beginning.

"Ebru chose me as his best friend. And, back then, the love you felt for me was enough. I was convinced whatever was going on between you two was bullshit, childish nonsense, meant to distract and taunt. Until I saw Ebru break down when he thought he was alone. Months after you left. He was. . ." Pervenche shook their head.

"I always wondered if it were a mistake that I were your heartmate," Pervenche continued. "I told that to your brother once when he was practicing. That it was a mistake. That the Gods should have picked Ebru for you because I was heartbroken, but he was more and. . . Sarcoline reminded me that heartmates is about trust, knowing and reflecting each other. Our hearts can be considered one. So can you and Ebru. Once he and I. . ."

Arna blinked at the anguish as it washed over him more powerful than anything so far.

"Ebru was my best friend, and I hurt him in a way I can never fix," Pervenche said, voice quaking and hands shaking. "I was supposed to anchor you both. Without me, you'd both vanish into the skies. You more so than him. You proved that much. you were my wings. I needed both of you in so many ways and. . ."

"Ven. . ." Arna reached out to them.

"I've felt so stifled," Pervenche growled, with so much internal anger. "As if I'm stuck. And I've been so angry for so long. Amaryllis helped. Archery helped. But I lost you both, and it was only when I was with you that I ever felt like I could do anything. You cannot leave us again Arna. I would never be able to forgive you."

Forgiveness?

"Please. . ." Pervenche's emotions shifted, from deep anger to a stifled fear. Arna responded with every desire he had to live, even when it was not much, even when he was terrified. Saying, *I need you,* to Pervenche whose expression lightened.

"Let me be your wings again," Arna offered, taking Pervenche's hand. He squeezed and Ven squeezed back. Acceptance and forgiveness radiated from Ven, waves of it in the form of trust and support, and love. The scales of balance were reset.

Arna looked on in awe and confusion. Ven smiled softly. *I want to forgive you.*

"Will you let me?" Ven asked softly, squeezing Arna's hand again. "Let me anchor you again."

"But. . ." They did not know each other. Was it truly that easy to fix?

"Just promise never to leave us again. To fight for us. You can't leave him like you left me," Ven insisted, their excitement brewed and tugged at Arna's own. *Jump,* he had told himself. With Ebru he had, because it would be easy: Alis loved him. With Ven he was terrified because there was no reason for Ven to trust him. Not really.

But he was going to do it anyway. Was that not what he swore to himself? "I'm scared Ven."

Arna gave Ven his self-hatred. Ven's eyes twitched.

"Why are you always so anxious? I've felt it more in recent years like an echo sometimes, but since you've been back it's like the thrum of some distant, low bass. It's ever present and always there. What are you so worried about?"

Arna opened his mouth to speak but the words caught in his throat. Not from a taboo or a vow but the fear of it. Ven's expression softened.

"It's okay if you can't tell me yet. I know getting all your secrets will take time. I'll be here when you can."

I'm sorry, Arna said with a squeeze and admitted aloud, "I'm terrified what it would mean if I told you."

"Ixxzal is scary and proud," Ven said. "But they shall always guide you."

[The God of the Unknown was the guiding light home.]

This time they fell into a comfortable silence. Seconds became minutes, mutating into a radiant tranquility. When was the last time the two of them had been together for so long, so comfortably? The quiet between them was a weave of forgotten chapters melding into one.

Ven chuckled, lightly, "You know. . . I've always been a jealous person. You and Ebru. Amaryllis and Arco."

Amaryllis and Sarcoline?

"You haven't seen them together," Ven snorted. "The fact that Amaryllis and I were dating so long is more a testament to me trusting both of them, than how they act."

Arna gave a tentative nod, not sure but believing Ven's words. He'd have to pay more attention to his brother when he got back.

"Amaryllis wasn't my first partner after you, nor will she be my last," Ven sighed, leaning their head against Arna's shoulder. "But in each relationship, I've learned what I don't want."

Arna leaned his head against theirs, relaxing.

"I want someone honest. Kind. Soft spoken like me. I don't like a lot of chatter," Ven laughed, and all Arna could picture was Amaryllis talking away, as well as himself. "Someone who is an athlete too. I think it would help us understand each other. Dancing is one thing, but no one really seems to understand my archery."

Arna was included, but he wanted to try.

"Sounds like the polar opposite of our group."

Ven laughed and Arna joined them. A thumb traced over Arna's wrist, where his constellation birthmark sat. Ven lightly turned Arna's wrist over and traced the lines. They eyed the scars on Arna's palm and ignored them.

"What is this? What did you vow?" Ven asked, tentatively.

"It's not a vow," Arna said but he did not pull his arm back. Ven examined it thoroughly. "It's a test."

[*Visualize,* The God of Souls was a repetitive clock waiting for
the turn of the hour.]

"A test?" Ven's thumb traced the marks.

"Yes." Arna smiled at them. Arna's heart raced as he tried to figure out a conversation to have. *Fix this.*

It was time for him to be honest about it. Even if he could not risk Ven knowing the true consequences, it was at least the proof he could give to Ven that he was trying to fix everything.

[*Mortality or the Gods?* Xeyaro asked.]

"To pick mortality is to pick the Gods. To pick the Gods is to pick mortality," he recited. He held his breath, hoping that Ven would understand.

"Isn't the Harmonious Six' Rapture Scripture is too apocalyptic for the Gods?"

Arna chuckled and shook his head.

"Okay then which translation? Morality as it people or as in dying?" Ven grimaced.

Arna blinked thrice. *What?*

achoiceachoiceachoice

When the Gods asked him, Arna had thought it similar to the Scripture. He had assumed it meant to pick between mortals or the Gods: one over the other. However, the scripture said it was more. It was moonlight through silver, the sun behind clouds, swirling scales, and some distant memory he could almost hear. It was the question they asked him in response when he asked them cake or brownies.

"You picked them over us, and now you have to choose again? How could they be so cruel? You'll pick them every time."

"But. . ." Arna said to himself. *That doesn't make sense.*

"No, you promised me Arna. You can't do that to us. You can't do that to Ebru."

Ven was speaking but Arna was not listening.

He could not pick mortals, not since he had dropped the fan. The Gods were the only choice, just as they always had been. However, by picking the Gods, and surviving, he could get his family back: he got the mortals. He got both. It had been a double phrased statement, he had assumed.

[*Mortality or the Gods?* Zaynir, God of Souls, asked again.]

In the second version of the Rapture Scripture translation, mortality didn't mean people. It meant death. It was a direct reference to the Dance of Destruction. Despite not knowing the truth of the dance, the translation understood that it meant death.

diediediediediedie

Under that translation the question was about divinity. To pick the risk of death was to pick the Gods and reach Divinity. To pick the Gods was to pick a death of his mortality and become Divine.

"Arna?" Ven asked.

He'd never considered it an option before because he assumed he was going to die. Why would the Gods pose him the question, when they recited the logistics of his survival until he wanted to scream? He didn't have a choice in wanting to stay alive: death was the highest probability.

[*Mortals or the Gods?* Lumak, the God of the Justice, asked.]

"Arna?" Ven was more worried, voice louder, calling to him but Arna was not listening.

His hands curled in his laps, nails biting the skin. Blessings failed not from imperfection but chaotic insight.

theendtheendtheendTHEENDTHEENDTHEEND

That meant the question was not about life or death. It was not about choosing Divinity or picking between the Gods or Mortals. It wasn't the Scripture. It was about something else entirely.

[*We've prepared you,* Xeyaro, God of Arts, said.]

[*You have all that you need,* Pokk, God of the Change, said.]

"Arna. . ." Ven peeled Arna's hands apart, forcing him to let go and stain his pants red.

"I. . . I don't know what it means." Arna panicked. He had assumed.

imposterimposterimposter

justlikesaffronjustlikesaffronjustlikesaffron

Suddenly he was eighteen, standing at the top of a moving train, watching the city below him tumble closer. The only way off was to jump to another train. But if he did it, he could die.

He had jumped then. He had always jumped. He always would jump. And he needed to jump here.

What was the question?

[*What if it's both? What if its neither?* Lumak, God of Balance, asked hurried.]

It was choosing between cake and brownies in a dark kitchen. It was telling a lie to his brother and rival, when caught. It was not an acceptance of all. It was a rejection. It was defiance.

dielivedielivedielivesurvive

For the moment he was vulnerable, raw, the most real he'd ever been. Arna's body was crushed under the weight of the question, until it no longer was. Ven helped him, pulling back the pressure until they shook Arna to look at them.

"What is going on?" Ven's eyes were void of emotion as they spoke, calmly. They pulled everything with the S.Mirrors and tugged at Arna's panic, seeking answers Arna could not give.

The assistance was enough for Arna to gather himself once more and get his Blessings back up. He crafted silence and injected it into his veins.

He was fine.

"I won't be a failure," Arna said to the Gods. "Regardless of what it costs me."

[*It is so much more,* Zaynir stated, a zephyr of the east.]

A vow must be understood.

[*There is only one answer,* the Gods said in unison.]

I won't fail you, like Saffron did.

[*He didn't fail us,* Ixxzal said.]

The three marks on Arna's wrist tingled. All three petals shifted.

[*We failed him.*]

He'd heard them before, many a time. Yet, it was the first time that it occurred to Arna that the Gods had watched their friend die when they could do nothing to stop it. They had thought he had succeed.

The Gods didn't want him to die. They wanted him to *live*.

Years of resentment and hate were erased at once.

livelivelivelivelivelive

It was why they sent him home. It was not just to learn how to live again. It was not about regaining his hope, in order to complete his variation. It was not just about dreams.

You think that they have the power to keep me alive as I dance?

[*I hope there is,* The God of fear admitted.]

They had repeated over and over. He alone would dance, but that did not mean he could not have *help*. But how?

[*If there is a way, you'll find it,* the mysterious voice like a storm called from the distant past.]

Arna had to find the path. Resolved thickened, and the barrier between him and panic formed like a medically induced shield.

"But you promised!" Ven snapped Arna's attention back to them.

Why were they freaking out? What had he missed?

"You cannot leave us again Arna, you can't!" Ven was about to cry again. "Don't die for them, Arna. Fight for what you want."

"Ven. . ." Arna grasped his wrist and rubbed the mark, hoping to warm it up before it froze him solid.

Ven said in a hushed voice, looking at him as if it was the first time, they were seeing him. "They can't be—"

"My everything? that's my problem. With everything there is duality. When one thing is my everything, I forget the rest," Arna cut them off.

The words that had led Arna to Understanding Blue Rose Fears, spoken by Ven years ago, were said once more.

Ven's eyes screamed: *please.* Arna was unsure how to explain how they had misunderstood. His anxiety thrummed loud like a drum between them, Ven carrying part of the weight for him. Arna cut it back. Instead, he sent back his desire to live, hoping that the feeling was more powerful than words.

Arna met Ven's eye and did not waver. "I will do whatever it takes to fix this. And I will fight."

The first thing he had to do was fix his relationship. The second step was to find his answer to the question.

But how was he supposed to find the path to survive the twenty-seventh dance, and the loss of the Blessings? The pain itself would overtax his body and the injuries he sustained from the twenty-sixth would bleed him out. No one else could be on stage with him. How could they help him?

He was not sure.

"Arna," Ven said tracing Arna's healing hands. "Please don't hurt yourself like this anymore. I'm here to shoulder it with you."

"I know."

Arna commanded his Blessings to heal and accepted the support. As he sat with Ven for a bit longer, a different thought began to turn in his mind. The love and pain warped and stirred into an ache for that which he could not have.

Fans were made from the heart. They were the most important connection, tethering the Gods to the mortal world. Similarly, Arna's S.Mirrors constellation tethered him, only to another breathing person. S.Mirrors had far more tangible reprecussions.

Built by mortal hands, with prayers for the Gods to listen. Each movement to create them was precise like a dance, but with a needle and thread. Pieces were stitched together and woven around six pieces of bone that created the frame. It was a slow methodical practice that took years of pain and mistakes to perfect. One needed to trust the process and believe in themselves above all.

In traditional teachings, his father told him, fan houses were filled with tens of students, learning, helping, and supporting each other through the process. One just needed to be able to rely on others to make sure the fans were pristine. Only through partnership could one find true guidance. In the Vivicent studio, the Golden Generation had learned to make them together.

Ven continued to shoulder the weight of Arna's remnant anxiety, refusing to let Arna curl his hands back into fists.

Arna's plans for his Incarnate Dreams fans were wrong.

He'd prepared for a certain level of density, but he needed brevity, he needed lightness. He needed a delicate contrast that was impossible. He needed his fans to be like Ven, delicate and yet strong.

They needed to be sturdy and yet like a cloud, drifting in the sky. They had to be complex and yet seemingly something everyone understood.

Arna relied on Ven, fully, allowing their bridge to form in full. Ven gasped out in the pain of what Arna was shouldering but accepted it with eyes that said: *I am not afraid*.

When Arna was younger, before Incarnate Dreams had solidified, he had an idea. There were three different types of fan boning: light, standard, and heavy. The standard weight was made of wood. Made from a Willow soaked in holy water and left to dry under the full moon before the year's end. The tree was holy and light, meant to connect mortals to divinity in a stronger way. Original and Twin fans used it, but Vervain the Blythe had invented the light boning created through actual bone instead of wood.

Whalebone covered in sap from a willow tree and baked in the sun for a fortnight while under continuous prayer until it dried, was considered light. The whale was the largest creature, the supporter of the world, and the spirit of the planet. It was meant to ward away disaster, that riddled her land as well as the land of her successor. Yet, war was different from the horrors that Arna faced, that Ilex faced.

Both the Willow and Whale bone sets were created with the idea of connecting to nature and getting guidance through it. They represented a world where mortals and divinity were in harmony. Such harmony no longer existed.

Ilex crafted the heavy boning, made specifically to withstand the storms that began to tear apart the land. They had to be stronger, denser, and capable of withstanding a pressure of a world that was ruptured, where the spirit of the world were dying. It was the first boning made of metal, and extremely durable and heavy in the hand. It was flexible due to the way the metal was inlayed, like bones on the spine of a mortal. The metal was polished in the juice of crushed willow leaves before the fabric was laid.

The willow was the tree of the Apostle, and Arna had always wondered what it would be like to create boning as light as the whalebone but made of metal and as durable as the heavy boning. Resilient and emulating the motion of willow branches. It was possible with modern technology, but Arna had given up on it quickly. It was much too complex for him to learn to weld.

But, it was necessary. His fans need to be complex, light and durable. If he was going to fix every mistake, he needed it. If he was going to do what Saffron couldn't, he had to find a way. If he was going to pull the world back into stability, his fans had to be able to withstand it.

"I need to go now," Arna said. Time was running short. Ven did not ask where he needed to go. As Arna disconnected their S.Mirrors, he resolved himself.

Ven nodded and sighed out a deep sigh. "You can rely on us Arna. All of us."

Arna smiled softly as he headed back to the front. As he did, he found Amaryllis with her camera. She glanced over to him and tossed him a picture that was still warm from the printer.

The image was almost dreamlike. Was that what he and Ven had looked like? He doubted that it was because it was too ethereal, too well placed almost as if it were drawn instead of photographed. The fireflies danced around them. Arna was cast in shadows and Ven in light but there was a certain harmony and unity to the photo.

A desire to help her rose within Arna. He had to get the world to love her as much as he—no, as they all did. He would get everyone to see the world the way that she did.

"I'm calling it Calm, and I'm adding it to my portfolio for the Celebrations. You can keep that copy."

Arna held the picture close and met her eye.

"You're going to do what you need to, right? You aren't running?" She confirmed but there was a giggle in her voice that said she already knew the answer.

"I'm not. I'm going to find after," Arna was not sure she'd understand in full, but if anyone it could be her.

"We'll be here waiting," She smirked and pointed towards the door, nodding towards it. He hurried out.

With all of his Blessings activated, Arna made his way to Mr. Hemlock's factory. As he walked, he gathered leaves off of willow trees. Plucking them from the long spines and stuffing his pockets full of them. On his mind was trying to find the path towards life, the one the Gods did not know, and his fans.

Are you ready?

[   ]

Strange. . . They had been talking to him earlier.

"The factory should have the capability to make the light metal skeletons. I think. I'm not sure, but if it can, I'm making them."

[   ]

Okay, perhaps they'd used too much energy. That would be okay, the Gods were still with him.

"I need to. It's the right thing to do."

The decision weighed in every muscle of his body. He could picture the dances perfectly. He could see himself with the fans, could imagine the world as it would be after he danced. This was the way forward.

As he walked through town, to the petal with the factory, Arna visualized his dances. He stripped willow trees of their branches and leaves, and gathered additional materials on his way. Focusing on them was the only way he could stay calm. Hands open. Hands closed. His hands stayed open: for Ebru, for Ven.

Make the fans, get home, finish the dances, see a new world. It was the first time he had broken into a facility without them. He could do it.

Are you visualizing? he asked himself. *Yes.*

The music of tiny bells bounced across the pavement when Arna approached the factory. The building was not large, small in comparison to many others. It was shaped painfully like a square, with ivy that grew up the sides of the chrome walls. It stood out like a sore thumb despite being covered in green. No building in Xeysis was shaped like a square; other shapes perhaps, but not something so symmetrical.

It was only as he got there that his gut twisted in disgust for what he was about to do. Fans for the Ceremony of Chaos were supposed to be made by hand. He staggered like taking a knife to the stomach. What if he accidentally touched one once it was finished being made?

Heart racing, Arna stop sharing his location with Ebru. He would not be able to stop Ven from feeling his panic, but he could stop everyone from reacting if the worst case happened.

He shook himself of the thoughts. There would be a way to move the fans without touching them. Hand open. Hand closed. Hands open. Hands closed.

THEENDTHEENDTHE—

Squeeze just enough to kill the panic. Release.

(make it silence.)

Go.

With a deep breath in, he centered himself and stepped through the front gate. It was late enough that there were few guards.

"Hello?" The intercom asked him. "Business hours are over."

"Mr. Hemlock sent me with his latest fabrics," Arna answered, changing his voice with his Blessings. He twisted the rest to compensate for the gaps he was still not fully used to, where an Insight ability once laid. The three other voids were masked well enough.

He opened his bag and showed the camera. "It's a secret."

Mr. Hemlock was known for his secrets. Arna hadn't planned on using his name again, but it was worth the risk.

"You can leave—"

"It's top-secret Ceremonial material. You want me to leave it on the ground? Sacrilegious! Debauchery! Heresy!" Arna did not let them turn him away, he screamed into the microphone demanding to be let in. "I'm supposed to make them tonight!"

"I'll ring you in. You know where you are going?" The man was strangely convinced, which made Arna chuckle. It was the same as when he was a delivery boy for a Hemlock factory, the workers did not much care, and they were used to Mr. Hemlock's more eccentric partners demanding things at all times of the day.

"Yes." Arna had no clue.

As the buzz sounded, Arna opened the door and walked in, looking for the cameras and smiling to them and walking on. He relied on his instinct, Blessings, and the videos he had watched on the factory to make his way to the operating hall.

The Celebration-Machines were towering, tens of feet tall, with folded mechanical parts that was obscured his vision. Most were contained in slick sheet metal, boxed like rectangles that made Arna grimace. There were vague instructions on the machine's conveyor belt with pictures.

Arna used his knowledge Blessings to guide him on how to turn on the machines. After pressing a few buttons, they thundered into motion. The few cameras in the room were not pointed his way, but he made sure to stay out of their sight the best he could.

Arna walked the room, going over every picture and letting his K.Insight do most of the work. Once he was certain he was ready—but who could be certain with machines such as these—Arna took out the materials: fabric, ribbon, binding. In his hands he held the boning he'd paid for but could not use.

Arna searched for the last machine he needed, finding it in the corner. It was a bright white box ten feet tall, with a screen and only a conveyor belt on the side.

He'd seen pictures of it on the internet: the great boning innovator. It was said to make the boning for the fans with a few touches of the buttons and capable of customization.

The DHS had nearly made Mr. Hemlock discard the whole project when he'd announced it two years ago.

The fans have specific qualities and requirements. They cannot be customized, his father had yelled at Mr. Hemlock on an international stream. The Churches had all agreed. The variations needed to be made to specific standards and not deviated. Mr. Hemlock's machine was relegated to making nothing more than props for people to wave around when others danced.

Now, Arna was going to test the man's word. He'd seen many tutorials online as he hate-watched the machine being promoted. He did not know it perfectly, but it did not matter.

Arna tapped on the screen for the machine and reviewed the options. Quickly moving through menu, he selected the material, metal, and the weight class: light. He opened up the preferences and adjusted the design based on what he wanted, and the machine calibrated. It presented him with a suggestion, reminiscent of willow branches. Arna accepted and selected the blessing to be placed on it by the machine. There were three options: leaf coating, sap, and custom. Arna pressed custom, and then selected none. He then pressed send and the machine began to spit out the result.

The boning was completed in a slow, agonizing process, but when the first one appeared it shined. Arna slowly picked up the lightweight boning, that was almost flimsy. He snapped them open and closed. They were not perfect, but they would do. When closed the fan was rigid, but when open and moving, the bones bent like branches. He replicated the process for enough copies for all his dances and got to work.

Taking the fan boning to the floor, Arna pulled out the willow leaves and branches from his bag and took a deep breath. First he ripped the bark apart with his nails, letting himself bleed in the process. His Body Blessings quickly healed him, and he had no blade to do the task properly. His hands were coated in fine particles of bark, crusted blood, and the sap from the branches, that he laid wet side up and place the boning atop of.

After rubbing the leaves in his hands, he began to recite the prayers of fan makers. The Scripture of Creation came from the Omniscient Sextant Enchiridion, book three: The Book of Dances. The prayers were necessary while making fans, and while he did not need to repeat them daily as the fans dried, he did repeat them as the leaves melted against the heat of his hands, turning his hands green, and he rubbed the pigment onto the fans coating them thoroughly.

Once he coated the first, he picked them up with heart ached.

diediediediedie

Hand open. Hand closed. *Ignore it.* Make it

silence.

He breathed deep, released the love for fan making and focused. He could not do the rest himself, no matter how much he wanted to.

He brought the first copy to the machine to make the fans, added it into place with the fabric, ribbon, and binding, and pressed start.

The machines began to move. Arna raced to the end of the conveyor belt to where the first fan appeared five minutes later. It looked sturdy enough, he would never know until he danced with it. It would have to work.

Arna searched for what to do next, his Blessings showing him another button. He pressed it and the fan was sent onward to packaging where it was folded, wrapped, and dropped into a crate. It looked so vulnerable there, and a desire roared within Arna.

touchittouchittouchit

How many Blessings did he have left? Which one would he lose next? Could he really do this? Was it worth it?

[Distant chimes asked him to try anything else.]

Voices spun in the room. Questions circled. Hesitation bloomed into a looming fear.

Pain. Pain. Pain. Pain.

Lessons taught over and over again so he would not falter.

(Don't do it now, be rationale.)

Forty-two. . .

Ven tugged on Arna, stabilizing him.

[Clarity in the fog.]

Arna knew he shouldn't do it. He knew the result if he did. But he also knew that there was a fear within him that he needed to root out. He could not be afraid to touch the fans. He had to accept the consequence, without the Gods yelling at him to do it. He had to prove to himself that he could do it, take the pain, and keep going, without them.

I can do this.

When he lifted the fan, something poured out of him. As if someone had cut his neck at the base of his skull, his brain cascaded out like a waterfall. It was another Blessing gone, just like that. The pain was tolerable, each time better than the last. Or perhaps he had learned to ignore the pain when his Blessings were flourished, for it did not hurt less.

Beyond the pain, however, was the flurry of voices. The Gods screamed at him, and he felt closer, so much closer to them. He could feel their breathing in his lungs. He could see through their eyes. They were weak, like melting snows at the end of winter. Just enough to barely hold on and the connection replenished them. Not in full, but in part: enough to stop them from disappearing in the next few weeks. They had been so close to death and had not told him.

Arna placed the package down, trying not to drop it and make his life worse.

Okay.

It was not so bad; it was just one more Blessing gone. He had enough Blessings for the dances. What was better was it was not as bad as he worried it would be. It wasn't that he was desensitized to it, he doubt he ever would be, but he didn't need the Gods to goad him into it. He could make the choice himself.

Arna rubbed the back of his neck, feeling the distant sensation of worry tugging at his soul. Ven had felt it, he knew they would. Arna sent soothing back and thought of their face, of his determination. He could not let this moment go to waste.

Why didn't you tell me you were that close to disappearing?

[There was no answer.]

Whether it was frustration or exhaustion, Arna was not sure why they remained silent. He also cared little for their lack of a response. Their hands were still within his skin, urging him forward. Later, they would talk.

Arna used his augmentations to mute and block all calls just as Ven's name popped up. He silenced his notifications for messages.

Focus. Focus. Move faster.

He thought of Lumak and Ixxzal pushing him forward: Lumak with orders, Ixxzal with sarcastic comments. Pokk would remind him of the obvious things. Azza would cheer. Zaynir would be worried. Xeyaro would comfort him. They would lecture him if he were particularly distracted.

Arna began reciting scriptures to himself.

Arna repeated the blessing process on all the boning and then after they were done, he loaded them all up into the fan making machines and the fans plopped out the otherside. While they did so, he cleaned up the bark, swept up the floors and cleaned his hands the best he could.

The wait for the last six fans was deathly silent except for the machines.

As the last fan dropped into the crate, Arna twirled the broom in his hand and prepared to push with it. The wheels at the bottom of the crate squeaked in harsh ear-piercing shrieks as he moved to the final machine.

Pushing the crate over and using the broom to lift the crate and pour the packaged fans out, he got everything onto the last conveyor.

He pressed start and the machine packed the fans into three boxes and deposited them into another cart.

Arna turned off the machines and gathered himself. He once more looked to the cameras hoping they had not seen too much.

They'll be erased, he told himself, as Ixxzal always did.

Technology is little more than a gift granted by the Gods for our safety, Saint Maroon said.

Arna moved the packaged boxes on a trolley to the mailroom, where he printed a label for Amaryllis' studio and slapped it on each box. He shoved the trolley into the corner and pushed it over so the boxes mixed with the other packages. There was no way to ensure that the boxes were not checked, but he had faith that Azza was fighting with him. Saying one last prayer, he returned the cart and left.

Leaving the office with less than what he had come with, Arna was confident. In the worst case his plan failed, and he'd have to get someone else to make them, he still had time before the Celebrations. Things would be okay. There was left over fabric he could use at Aster Fabrics.

Arna pulled at his jacket, folded all his bags that he'd used to carry the material into a backpack and flexed his Blessings to see what he lost: a support ability.

He winced. Fa.Mirrors was an ability that allowed him to disappear on the whim while on the move. It had gotten him through security, and through so many of his secret missions. He wouldn't be able to disappear anymore. Was there another combination of Blessings to create the same effect?

He squeezed his hands shut, leveled his breathing, and continued to walk steady as he been trained. It was fine.

makeitsilence.

He thought of Ven's face and was filled with confidence again. All would be well. This was the right thing. And if it was not, he would get help to make it okay.

For now, he needed to get out. Get home. He was singularly focused on Incarnate Dreams as he walked on.

[Watch it! Azza screamed.]

Arna jumped back as a private car pulled into the hanger he was leaving from. He tried to disappear, unable. No matter the times he reached for it, the Fa.Mirrors Blessing was gone. Right.

theendtheend—
(make it) silent.

It was fine. He'd lost Blessings before. All he had to do was use the others. Ignoring the ache, Arna started to weave a new combination of effects with his Blessings. He attempted to get a similar effect to what he lost. It would take him time to fill the gap.

Thanks. Were they back?

[Be careful. Zaynir's sorrow bubbled into nothing.]
[We are recovering. Thank you. Lumak addressed the sacrifice.]

Don't forsake me.

Mr. Hemlock stepped out of the vehicle before Arna. He wore a suit of all gray and his eyes were dark and trained on Arna, mint but not for A.Reverence. His shadow loomed over Arna.

He asked, "What can I do for you Mr. Vivicent?"

Arna should have known the security would call to confirm. Arna grimaced. He had overlooked it. He was lucky that the man had not arrived earlier.

"Nothing."

The answer came across as indigent, but Arna could not be bothered to care.

"Did you like what you saw?" Mr. Hemlock asked, others beginning to get out of the car.

A fight? Arna was not in the mood for a fight, not at this time of the night. Nor did he want to be arrested for trespassing.

Is the footage erased? He was prepared to sprint, but he needed the confirmation.

[   ]

"Why would you think I've been inside?" Arna asked as he stood within the hanger not yet past the gate to the outside. "Although, I would love a tour if you're offering."

There were ten men, easy enough to get by. He could slip past them and so long as he got down the street before they chased him, he would disappear. He's run away from enough men before. One man pulled out what looked like a bat.

"I'm inclined not to believe you, Mr. Vivicent." Mr. Hemlock motioned to the others to get closer. "Not you nor your weasel of a father. Did you come to sabotage my machines?"

Is the footage erased? Arna dropped his center of gravity and relaxed his arms and knees.

"I wouldn't do that."

"Again, I don't believe you," the man growled. The other men began to approach, closing Arna's pathway to escape. "If I find as much as a single bolt out of place, I will sue your father for what little he has left."

There was not much time left. . . *Is the—*

[*Yes!* Ixxzal yelled as if they were just across the street.]

"I swear to you I have not. Now, if you will. . ."

Arna flourished his abilities, focused on everything, and bolted. He spun his Blessings crafting a web over the gaping hole that Fa.Mirrors left. He couldn't find the right combination of Blessings to get the exact effect, so he put everything into running instead.

He sprinted towards one man who was not ready for it, spun around him, stepped onto the hovering car, and launched himself into the street. He raced away, past the gate. Shouts chased after himself. Finally, his Blessings resonated to fill the void. Instead of stepping into the periphery of the world, he willed the shadows of the night around him, slipping into the darkness and becoming no one. He turned the corner and jumped over a wall, headed towards the business circle.

He fell into a cadence as he ran, letting the adrenaline rush push him forward. He laughed loud, his voice echoing in the night. Finally, he was free. Finally, he had taken a massive leap forward. Finally, he was on the right path.

This was the way to Incarnate Dreams.

When he got to the bus, Arna hovered close to the doors, got off on a stop that was not close to his home and continued running. Four more buses later, Arna turned onto the street towards his home. All the lights were on, glowing like a candle in the dark night.

Arna slowed. The guards were standing about without a care.

As Arna stepped inside, voices were yelling upstairs.

"What if he's too injured to move? Ven said it's the worst pain they've felt in their life."

"Where do you think he could be?"

"Do you think someone is trying to kill him?"

"I am searching for him right now, the others are trying to reach him, but no one can."

"What's wrong?" Arna asked as soon as he exited the staircase. His parents were pacing. Jasione was dazed, sitting on the couch and moving his fingers in the air. Gingerline was in pants and a hoodie with boots on and her hair tied up like she was ready for a fight. Everyone looked about as if a ghost had spoken.

He dropped all of his Blessings and all at once they looked at him and stumbled back, surprised.

"You!" Gingerline rushed up to him, tugging at Arna's clothes, pulling him away from the stairs. She lifted his arms searching for injuries, and then moved his neck and chin and turned him around three times. Once he faced her again, she yelled, "Ven said you were hurt!"

"I. . ." Arna did not know how to explain it.

theendtheend—
MAKE IT SILENT.

"I'm fine. No one hurt me. I'll call Ven and let them know."

His family stared at him with open disbelief. His mother collapsed into the couch and Gingerline stepped back glaring at him, unconvinced.

"How did you get here?" Jasione asked, removing his glasses and massaging his temples.

"Took a few buses. I was found loitering outside the Hemlock factory, but don't worry. I didn't do anything wrong. He may yell at you, though." Arna directed the last bit to his father without looking at him wanting to avoid the gaze. He was still not sure how he would approach his father, especially not after learning how despondent he'd become in Arna's disappearance. Arna wasn't ready for that yet. Instead, he focused on the fan near the window.

"You swear?" Jasione asked, elbow on his knees and hands rested under his chin. The room turned eerily silent. They had to suspect by now that Arna was hiding something, but he was not prepared to broach that subject. Not yet.

theendthe—madeintosilence.

"I'm safe," Arna offered instead. He pointed up the stairs. "I'm headed up and. . ."

Before he moved, he opened his augmentations, and pulled out his mobile. He opened back up his location sharing feature, and sent the location to everyone in the room, Ven, and Ebru.

"Now you'll know where I am," Arna offered. "Better?"

"Better," Gingerline said, eyes narrowed, and arms crossed. "But you need to stop hiding things Arna."

"I am working at that, trust me. After twelve years on the run, I'm used to relying only on myself." Arna said and all of those in the room's expressions softened. "But I want to rely on you again. Just give me time?"

Gingerline nodded and with that Arna headed upstairs. He removed the silence on notifications and was bombarded with tens of messages and calls. They were consistent from, what Arna imagined was, the moment he lost his Blessing.

The only person he messaged back individually was Ebru.

```
Rosy: I'm home.
Alis: Ven said you got hurt.
```

Arna checked the group chat and messaged them that he was home. Ven had freaked out. He'd have to apologize.

```
Rosy: It was another Blessing, but I'll be okay.
Alis: Call me.
```

Before Arna could call Ebru, however, he messaged Ven.

```
Arna: I'm home now. Don't worry.
Ven: . . .
Ven: That is the last thing I want to hear from you.
     After I told you NOT to do anything reckless.
Ven: What did you do?
Arna: Made a mistake while handling a fan.
Ven: What?
Ven: But you. . .
Arna: I can't touch a fan, Ven. I broke the taboo.
Ven: But you're the Chosen Child.
Arna: Taboos still apply to me, but I'm okay.
Ven: You've lost them before. . . I've felt it.
Ven: Is that why you're always panicked? Because you'll
     have to pick up fans when you dance? Because it
     always feels like you're dying when you do?
Arna: Promise me you won't tell anyone. It will freak
     them out.
Ven: Can you get them back?
Arna: Only after I complete my variation.
```

Arna's mobile started ringing: Ebru. With an incredulous laugh, Arna laid down on his bed and answered the call. Ebru did not appear before him, choosing an audio call instead of a video one.

"What do you mean 'Blessing'?" Ebru asked as soon as the call connected.

Arna tapped at his mobile. Three tiny nano chips flew from the back and circled Arna. He adjusted the screen recording so that his whole body could be seen by Ebru. It would not be the highest quality video, but it would not matter.

"What are you. . ." Ebru mumbled, as he answered the video call. Ebru's face appeared on Arna's ceiling, wearing his glasses.

"How many have you lost?" Ebru asked as soon as the camera expanded to show him sitting at in his studio at his computer.

"You know the number."

Arna had messaged him about the pain every time it happened, besides the first. Silence filled the other end as Ebru's eyes slowly trailed over him.

"Are you okay?"

"I'm home now."

Ebru contemplated in silence. The image flickered catching Ebru somewhere between real and not.

"You don't believe me?" Arna asked.

"No, I know you're home. I don't think you're okay," Ebru admitted, shimmering. He withheld whatever emotions he may have had from Arna, who grimaced.

it was silent.

The weight of the words sank into him. He'd always wanted to tell someone the truth, to reveal it all. Could he? Finally? Ebru already knew the basics.

"Arna?"

"I lost my first one at seventeen," Arna said. The story tumbled from his lips. Ebru said nothing, his eyes leveled on Arna, pinning him down and letting him settle. This was just telling Alis the whole truth, Alis who always knew almost everything.

As he felt safer, the words fell faster, and pulled every emotions Arna had kept back over the years. His tears began to fall. Noise turned to white, and thoughts drowned and disappeared. The hologram of Ebru shimmered like the scales of a dragonfly.

Dance is a relationship between you and the Gods.
Like all relationships, it has two sides. The Gods are always reaching for us, loving us, wanting us to
succeed. However, if we fail them, we will anger them. Do not forget.

— On the sacred nature of dance.

Dance 15

Peace

Incarnadine

6 Xeyan

36 Days Left

"This studio is run down, horrible. Does anyone even come here anymore?"
"It's a dance studio in a city that does not dance but during the Celebrations."
"I guess that means it's perfect."
"It is. Don't get hurt."

The first group practice arrived with a sense of bewilderment, which was not to say that Arna did not know it was coming—he spoke at length about it with Ebru. Rather, Arna had been dreading it since the invitation arrived.

To Arna's dismay, the day of the first practice, the Vivicent household received the formal handwritten request for their attendance, accompanied by a full practice schedule and the disclosure that the practices would be recorded to share with the public after the event. If they had not been already aware, Ebru letting all of the Golden Generation know through Phlox, they would have missed the date in its entirety by how late the request came. The letter was postdated weeks prior, but Arna was certain the Cyclamen had paid off the mail couriers to withhold the letters until the day of, to make them look bad.

Additionally, Arna was not sure how he was going to handle himself.

```
Alis: I'm nervous.
Rosy: Why?
Alis: How in Ixxzal's damned universe am I supposed to
      look at you?
```

Arna laughed, at least he was not the only one.

```
Rosy: Everyone is expecting you to look as if you're in
      love with me.
Rosy: Since you are, it won't be any different.
Alis: No. They can't know.
```

Arna was not particularly sure why Ebru was so adamant that the others could not know about their relationship, but he did not want to press. There were more important things to worry about.

His variation progress was moving slowly.

His progress for the path to living was at a standstill.

Arna picked at his food, watching as his mother wove a flower crown for herself. It was made of bright pink and purple flowers. The crowns themselves were intricate, but his mother's careful work with her fingers kept him mesmerized. Arna was ten years old again, trying to help her with her garden and flower crowns. She and Zaffre were exceptionally talented at creating art with their hands.

His mother smiled up at him. "If you keep staring like that I will mess up."

"Sorry." Arna tried to eat, unable to do so. Despite the fresh floral scent, the scent of ash and smoke lingered. It made his stomach turn.

You waste of a mortal—

"Don't think of the letters, Arna," his mother said, cutting into his thoughts. Snapping up, he tried to play it off with a smile, but she laughed. "You are just like your sister. I check the mail each morning. I know you've been reading them. Ignore the words. You know they aren't true."

[There was a chorus of bells.]

"The rest of the world in inconsequential." She placed the flower crown down. "Look at me." He did. "The only ones who matter are those who care: Your family. Your friends. The Gods."

Arna nodded, searching for the God's voices. He hadn't heard their voices in what felt like forever, even if it were only the better part of a week. They had yet to explain how they'd almost vanished, and he doubted they had the energy to try.

s i l e n c e

Arna pressed his variations to the forefront of his mind instead of the fear. It was how he saved them. He'd be better than Saffron.

Wenge placed her hand on Arna's shoulder and kissed his temple. "You are loved. We are here for you."

After the train crash, Arna had tried cutting off everything and isolating himself in his appartment. Back then he had never believed himself worthy of love like this. But the Gods had been there for him. His family was here for him now. Through them he'd find his path to survival.

"Thanks mom." Arna checked for messages, then the time. There was no point in eating now: no time left. "Have you heard from Arco?"

"He will be back for his dance test on the 12th. Rosmarinus should be back from his world tour the next day. . ." Wenge stepped back, exasperated. "Just what did you tell that boy?"

"I wanted to give him inspiration," he told her; another secret he'd been keeping.

"Don't give him false hope," Wenge warned him, but smiled and kept weaving.

Arna hoped he had not.

"Where is Ginger? We need to go to practice."

"When you see Mymy after, make sure that you tell her I'll be at the festival today," Wenge said as if she had not heard his question at all.

Arna nodded. His mother had not worked for the government for years, but she always attended the flower festivals. She had once been the dazzling star of the flower world, and Aureolin's great-grandmother adored her.

Gingerline rushed down the stairs out of breath. She was a frazzled mess on the verge of tears, but she straightened herself up. She wore a set of long green dance pants and a cropped red top.

"Eat something before you go," Wenge told Gingerline. She was walking over frigidly, as if her limbs were not moving.

"Nervous?" Arna asked with a chuckle.

"Deadly," Gingerline admitted with a nervous half-smile.

"We have the flower festival after. It will be fun," Arna said, trying to cheer her up. "Besides, Aureolin told me she has a surprise."

"She's competing this year in the annual competition."

Gingerline began to glow, smile large as Arna's and tone jovial with pride. There was a long silence before his mother began laughing.

His mother smiled brighter than them both. "We know who is going to win. I must set up a celebratory dinner for her."

"We won't know if she won until the Celebrations." Gingerline slowly relaxed and began to eat. Their mother's laughter was a soothing lullaby that calmed the fears that even Arna had.

While the third week of Xeyan was the awards week for all art forms, there were two awards given on New Dawn Day: The Monarch of Flowers for the Floral Festival and the Philanthropist of the Year. The Monarch of Flowers won the annual competition at the Floral Festival while the Philanthropist was voted by citizens across the city for who did the most for society. The both would work together in the next year to promote the health of the city and the people within.

"That girl turns everything she touches green, plants and people alike. She has an enviable talent. I promise you, she'll win." His mother winked. "Which means I must prepare. This will be an amazing year. She'll win the title of Monarch. Rus will be the Philanthropist of the Year. Amaryllis will have her art show in the Temple of Xeyaro, she's a shoo-in. Phlox's movie is playing, and she'll be in a stage show. Ven will be in the archery showcase. Jasi is part of the security and planning committee. You all will be dancing together. Arna's home. I must make an amazing dinner."

"For the next day?" Arna asked. For a second Arna let himself hope that he may actually see such a celebration. Crashing panic swept back at him. Before he could clench his hand, he breathed in and pushed the feeling away. He would see the dinner.

She laughed, "Yes. Too many things to do before. I also need to plan your coming of age. That will need to be in Late Zaid. We need time to contact everyone."

Arna took the promise as another thing he'd hold on to and rely on. Their mother sang as she moved through the kitchen setting flowers. Life was flowing through the Vivicent manor, and it felt right.

The two Vivicent siblings and Jasione walked into the studio hall as a united front: the three of them having sworn to protect each other's backs, and keep Arna out of trouble, as they entered the battleground. Arna kept his chin raised and reviewed the landscape. The halls were still stark and lifeless. The fluorescent lights were still painfully bright. The receptionist gave him a cold glare as he smiled.

"This is the worst," Gingerline hissed under her breath. Jasione laughed quietly.

"Hello again." Arna walked up to the receptionist. He signed in. "Where are we today?"

"Room 111," the receptionist frowned more.

"Thanks."

Arna smiled at her before walking away.

"What did you do?" Gingerline asked as she caught up.

"Don't worry about it," Arna said.

"You did something," Jasione pressed.

"Don't worry about it," Arna chuckled under his breath and tried to keep his tension from rising. All eyes were on them.

They rounded the corner towards the room, where Alabaster Hue stood talking with Cyclamen Shadone. When the two saw Arna, they stopped talking and smiled: Cyclamen's vile and Alabaster's real. In Alabaster's eyes was genuine love. He still cared about them, which made Arna sick. He could understand why Ebru wanted to fight for the man and hid so much from him.

"Welcome, welcome. Pity this couldn't be held at your studio." Cyclamen glared at Arna, his purple scarf making his face look far redder than it should be. Arna glared at him, unsure of how to answer or what to say. Alabaster shifted where he stood, eyes on Arna with a slight shake of his head.

Arna wished he did not hate the Shadone family on principal. They should have been allies. Unfortunately, it appeared that ancient grudges filtered through his bones as much as they did for Cyclamen. Arna would not rest until the man was thoroughly destroyed.

He added the man's destruction to his list of things to do.

The promise to himself became a light fluttering that filled him with an abundance of seething hate. That, too, he clung to as a reminder that he had something else to live for.

"A pleasure to work with you," Arna said as nicely as he could, baring his teeth in a false smile that neither seemed to acknowledge. He pushed past them both.

Alabaster wished them the best. "Have a good practice."

"Be with the Gods. May the God's light never fade," Cyclamen prayed, but Arna discarded it with a flick of his hand. He did not need the man's sullied words.

"Thank you." Gingerline was the only one to respond back.

They walked through the doors to the practice room where tens of cameras were poised about with lighting and audio crew members preparing their equipment. There were reporters, other Shadone students, and DHS junior members: a whole entourage and audience to watch their practice. Although DHS Small council members were forbidden, and the Vivicent Studio invitation said they were only allowed one guest per dancer, Cyclamen had filled the room with his people. All of them were probably hoping for the dance's failure.

The others were already changed and stretching as Amaryllis stood fiddling with her camera in a corner. Six Shadone students sat in the back who, based on Alis' descriptions, had to be the ones who had bullied Ebru in the past. Arna ignored them and shed his bag; they did not matter. On the wall there were fans, much as Arna feared. Instead of letting the feeling consume him however, he sauntered up to Ebru.

Focus on the future. One day, when he lived, he and the others would be able to dance whenever they wanted away from prying eyes.

It wasn't good enough to necessarily calm him, but it was enough to distract him while Ebru finished giving instructions. Upon Arna's approach the crew members fled, leaving Arna and Ebru far from prying ears. Ebru's camera-smile dropped as Arna leaned in, domineering.

"What?"

"If I don't antagonize you once, people will think it is strange," Arna said with a sarcastic smile letting the actual humor bubble up inside at how flustered Ebru looked by their proximity.

"Go play family." Ebru crossed his arms and backed up. "I have a dance to teach."

"Sure. Sure." Arna turned on his toes and headed towards Ven who stood reading a book, leaning against a dance rail.

"Why are they all here?" Jasione asked, as soon as Arna, too, rested against the rail.

"Same reason you can be here, Jasi: nondisclosure. They're watching," Ven answered instead.

"What? But there's so many," Gingerline complained.

"The Shadones make the rules. They won't let it be a one to one, like we were told. They want to see us fail," Arna said, eying down every one of the bullies memorizing their faces and wishing the worst upon each of them. He hoped they all lost their Blessings before he danced. He then said to Ven, tilting his head and glaring at the audience. "We won't let that happen, right?"

"Of course not," Ven said snapping their book closed. "We're Vivicents. We never fail a dance."

Ven glanced at Ebru and shot Arna a knowing look followed by a more serious nod.

You were born together, you belong together. The words resonated between the two of them.

Zaffre had reminded them of it time and time again, when they fought and competed. He'd fought tooth and nail for them to train together; they'd fight for eachother.

"No knife, no poison, no accident can make us falter." Aureolin walked over, standing with them. From the day they'd been taught, they were taught as if they were all Vivicent blood, without judgement and without qualm.

Vivicents were resilient. Despite the many assassinations attempts from multiple families, governments, and churches, across the years, they stood strong. Even in the wars of the Fourth Variance, they survived. When the Shattering devastated the world, they pushed forward. When all other families struggled, when all other families disappeared, their family remained.

"A Vivicent is not made by blood, but by practice," Phlox said, hugging Arna from the side, resting her head on his shoulder. It was the closest she'd been since the Banquet and Arna did not shrug her off. He relished the closeness. They were all together again, standing against a common enemy.

The Shadone Family and Vivicents had a grudge as old as the Fifth Variance. For a time, Arna had wondered if he needed to forgive them, asked the Gods if he needed to bridge the gap between the families.

[*Not all things need to be forgiven,* Pokk reminded him.]

Some things were impossible to forgive and bridge. All one could do was move on and process. Arna would never get the forgiveness of the entire world. And that had to be okay. Likewise, he did not need to forgive the Shadone family for what they did, especially after they took the Hues and used them as they liked.

Not for long.

[There was a spiraling black in the mirrors of the room.]

[It cackled. It grinned. It beckoned.]

Only Ebru stood alone, slowly glancing over them all. He was isolated in the middle of the room: torn between the Shadone placed distractions and the Golden Generation. Ebru looked particularly perturbed, and his eyes were leveled on Phlox, who was hugging Arna. Jealousy? Arna laughed.

"Are you okay? You're all brooding," Amaryllis asked as she walked over, dressed in all white. The layers of her skirt were shaped like rose petals.

"Yes," Arna chuckled darkly. This was war.

Amaryllis eyed them with clear eyes, like the lens of a camera, examining them. She finally spoke with an equally dark but jovial tone, picking her side. "I'll be in charge of photography. Jasi, will you help me with music?"

"When do you start?" someone in the back yelled, shattering the otherwise silent room.

"Right! Stretching." Arna took control of practice, stepping out of Phlox's arms and past Ven's side. He made it a show, projecting his voice and being more dramatic than necessary. "I figure we must, if we are planning on actually dancing."

"Yes." Ebru looked away and motioned them to the floor. Everyone filed in.

Arna stepped up close to Ebru and whispered. "Just give me the word."

And I'll keep them all from touching me.

Ebru grew stiff, eyes lingering on Arna through the mirror with tens of unasked questions. Then he gave an answer in the form of a glare: *shut up.*

Arna laughed and turned his attention to the audience who watched with narrowed eyes and deep breaths.

They were sucking not just the air but the joy from the room.

Arna returned his focus to Ebru and cocked an eyebrow. Ebru's mint eyes flickered away.

They began warmups with a single word from Ebru. As they moved together replicating the movements they'd learned together as kids, a strange tension between them formed. Phlox and Gingerline kept hitting each other, too close. Ven and Ebru stood too far apart. Aureolin was the only other competent one and Arna kept forgetting movements. He was so used to practicing on his own, with the God's training regimen, that the old Vivicent ones were like a muscle twitch instead of a memory. They were fighting each other. They didn't trust each other. Or rather. . .

Ebru.

When Ebru began teaching them the group dance, the distance became more palpable. Like the room grew in size from the apprehension. Ebru upheld his mask of falsities, even when being a part of the Golden Generation meant unconditional trust. It was causing a dissonance as he guided them through the movements. The tension became a rot that seeped through the group, causing more chaos and mistakes.

Ebru hated the dance, as was apparent from the way he taught: too quick, without pausing to explain. It wasn't a boring dance; it was a scripted one. It told the story of them coming together again like the world was going to heal. The DHS' propaganda of unity for the world was potent and bleeding in every move. There was little story, mostly the messages of: stop fighting, everything will return to normal, and the world will remain the same as you've always known.

But it couldn't be because Arna was going to change it.

Arna stood at a crossroads, the path laid blatantly before him: fix this or lose all the progress on his variation. At least this time he heeded the signs like neon flashing lights, instead of ignoring them. Unification or fracturing?

"Who choreographed this trash?" Arna stepped forward, his voice cutting the rot from growing further. Jasione quickly stopped the music.

"You hate my work?" Ebru feigned hurt, touching his chest and dropping his voice low.

"You are far better than this, Ebru. You know us," Gingerline supported Arna. "This is pathetic, woefully so."

Ebru shrugged. "I had warned them."

"Who choreographed it?" Ven asked, stepping up to Arna's side, like a second knight for the battle that Arna had called to begin.

"Cyclamen, of course," Ebru said. Gingerline's face drip in terror, eyes darting to the cameras and the microphones. The other members of the Golden Generation looked livid, their tenuous solidarity becoming stronger by the moment.

"Are you trying to get her attacked by the media again?" Ven snapped, stepping past Ebru, like a coil ready to spring into action. "You know what happened last time she said something about him."

"You should have known better," Ebru said as if it were a taunt, but there was the familiar swell of regret in his voice. Ebru was causing the divide on purpose but that did not mean he was going to stop.

Amaryllis snapped a picture of them all.

"You're an asshole, Ebru." Aureolin grabbed Gingerline who was starting to shake.

Ebru shrugged and the room was filled with a palpable silence. It was discordant and messy, irritating and aggravating. Arna was certain that in minutes they were all going to snap.

The audience was silently looking amongst themselves, laughing. Ven was playing with the hem of their clothes. Phlox had wrapped her arms around herself and was rocking slightly. Aureolin held Gingerlne too tightly, as if Gingerline would float away. Gingerline gripped her as tightly, horrified, and reliving some distant memory Arna did not know. Ebru was pulling in, clearly preparing for the strike when it landed.

What was the future Arna wanted? For the Golden Generation to be truly one, once more.

Never again.

He visualized what he wanted, then made it happen.

Arna stepped up. Hands in his pockets and nonchalant. "It doesn't matter who choreographed. It still sucks. I could have done better at twelve years old."

All eyes were on him, including Ebru who opened his mouth as if to say something and closed it immediately. The shock that rushed through the room was electrifying. The mirrors began to shimmer around him, and in them, he could see animals, could hear chimes as they moved. Finally, six figures settled in the back as something between an element and a cat: water, stone, clouds, fire, twirling metal, and wood. Azza, Lumak, Zaynir, Pokk, Ixxzal, and Xeyaro sat in various sizes before the audice, stretching and watching.

Arna glanced back to the others who were frozen stiff, save Phlox who was staring at him and no longer rocking herself.

Phlox is loyal. *Help me.*

As if reading his mind, she sauntered up to Arna's side with her fluffy cashmere coat draped over her shoulders. She crossed her arms, planted her feet and tilted her head.

"No, six years old, darling. This is pathetic," Phlox said, the hesitation in her voice caused her to hiccup on the first few words but as she kept speaking the confidence grew. Soon her voice was alluring, light, and demanding to be heard. "You cannot expect us to embarrass ourselves with this, Ebru."

"You haven't even learned it all," Ebru warned them, eyes darting across the mirror to six locations. "Are you sure you want to judge it so prematurely?"

"Arna. . ." Gingerline warned. "They can hear you. . ."

Alright, Arna thought. He was not afraid of a few cameras, nor was he afraid of a few students. Arna needed to be safer for the others than Cyclamen was terrifying. He could do that. He could be their light. He could be their savior.

"Nothing said in here can leave this room until after the Celebrations, so said the contract, and it is monitored by Lumak," Arna said with complete confidence.

"Lumak does not watch us," Ebru reminded Arna. "There are no candles burning."

"Lumak always watches," Arna said, and the stone cat darted across. With it, the room rumbled and as everyone reacted, Arna was amazed that they felt it, not just him. The God of the Earth had spoken. All eyes landed on Arna in awe.

"Personally, I stopped believing in the Gods long ago. Does that mean I can talk? I'd love to tell everyone about how you and Ebru are officially together. The reporters would eat it up." Phlox joked, ignoring the movement. Arna laughed loudly as the room shook again. All, but Phlox and Arna, stumbled as everything rocked.

"The Gods are fickle," Arna agreed, tilting his head and glaring at the students. "But they're always watching."

A few of the students paled as Arna said the words. Four glared with more hostility, as if they believed they would not be punished for doing what they did.

Perhaps they thought it was Arna fooling them with his Blessings, perhaps they thought it was some sort of city shake from Blessing technology collapse; it did not matter. Arna made a point, and it was beginning to stick.

"Exactly. Who can trust that?" Phlox spun brightly, holding her arms out and her cashmere coat billowed around her in imaginary wind.

"But they're loyal," Arna said, turning back to Ebru who bristled at the words.

"Let's see the full dance," Ven suggested.

Arna whistled at Phlox, the whistle he often used with her when she was outside his window trying to get into the manor when she ran away from home. It meant: *It's me, I'm here.* The smile that graced her face was wide and true. Jasione's head snapped up and his eyes narrowed.

Welcome home, she whistled back. Jasione said nothing.

Amaryllis snapped a photo, and the Golden Generation vacated the main floor to give Ebru space.

Ebru nodded and the music began when Jasione pressed play.

Ebru danced the terrible dance in full for them. For another group it may have been an excellent performance, but it was unworthy of the Golden Generation. It saw them from the outside and not the inside, even when it masqueraded that it did.

The dance suggested they were competitors: vying for recognition to the point of tearing each other down to get it. It ignored their complex dynamic of support and belief in each other's skill. It ignored their unwavering unity.

"No?" Ebru shrugged. "Then I guess we must choreograph it ourselves."

"Is there enough time? With the practice schedule. . ." Aureolin disagreed and stumbled into the answer that Arna had understood from the day they got the schedule with the scraps of offered practices: it was designed for failure.

"Are you saying that because you don't trust us to pull it off? Or are you saying that because you don't want to try?" Ebru asked.

Despite the hostility in his tone, it was clear that Ebru wanted to take the risk. Arna was certain he was not the only one that saw it. Ebru shifted on his feet the way he did when he was a kid and pissed about a situation that he could not control. He may have grown up, but it was quintessential Ebru.

The group was silent at the suggestion. Surprisingly, no one agreed.

Not one of the Golden Generation of them met Arna's eye, and became more divided than they had been moments before. Unwavering unity no longer existed amongst them, and for that, somehow, the terrible dance was true. They were fissured, and while something was trying to grow in the remains, it was consistently being smothered.

What though? Why?

"No? Then we practice," Ebru called them all to order and as they took to the floor, they were cut off. They became budding flowers that would never fully bloom.

The practice for the next three hours was agonizingly painful. They learned the steps, quickly, as was their gift, but everything about it hurt. The way they moved about each other was as if everything that had been momentarily fixed was erased. They were plants pruned too far, trees in a forest cut for no purpose other than greed.

All the while the six cats watched, with glowing eyes and swishing tails, fracturing and misting into nothing. It took them a lot of energy and power to appear before him so visibly. This moment had been important. Solving this group dance, uniting the Golden Generation was necessary for him to succeed, and for him to find the path for them to help him stay alive.

It was going to take effort. If it was easy, it wouldn't have been something the Gods were not certain of.

The golden generation were heaving by the end, glaring at each other, and Gingerline was crying.

"We'll call it there," Ebru suggested, waving them off. His eyes were hollow and glassy.

"Ebru. . ." Arna approached him, wanting to comfort him.

"You have the Flower Festival to attend to, don't you?" Ebru said, and without another word he left.

"Ignore him, we need to go," Aureolin said grabbing Arna's shoulder. "We aren't welcome here."

Arna glanced back at the students and reporters who had seen the failure from the beginning, when Arna had wanted to hope for something new. What was he missing? Why were they so catastrophically wrought?

littlepurpleflowersweretryingtobudandbloom

s   i   l   e   n   c   e

Hide it all so it no longer exists.

How do I do this?

[*Visualize, darling,* Zaynir's voice was hushed with a gasp.]

Zaynir? Were they dying again?

[*We expected this,* Xeyaro said, exhausted.]

What do you mean. . ?

[*What do you want of yourself?*]

I want to be with them.

[*Exactly,* Ixxzal almost sounded proud. *Think of what they need from you.*]

The Gods vanished like pops of lightning, vanished as if there had never been a form at all. *What they need from me. . .*

[   ]

He was going to find out.

Arna did not speak much as he and Aureolin walked from practice. While the others had gone ahead to the festival, Arna specifically traveled with Aureolin to help her prepare.

The stagnation of the group was spinning in his thoughts. What did they need from him in order to fix their group? They were still friends, or at least they all still thought of each other as friends. Arna had seen that the day they all found him at the tip of the rose. He was on fundamentally good terms with the others, even if there was still a bit of distance.

Yet, how was it that he had tried to be strong for them, and even when Phlox helped, they were still scared? Why were they still torn? Ebru had been practically begging them to agree with him to make a new dance, and they still did not do it. Why?

(what is silence?)

As Arna pondered, Aureolin chatted about her dance group. He had not cared enough to learn the names of her "sisters" or what they liked, but Aureolin cared. So, Arna cared just enough to pay attention despite his wandering thoughts.

"Enough of my prattling. What about you?" Aureolin asked him as they walked through the gate into the massive garden before her house that was thriving and blooming in summer flowers. "Did you meet anyone special?"

"Alis," Arna admitted, the name light on his lips, not wanting to out Ebru but not wanting to hide it completely.

Aureolin's house was not too far from the station. The house was a large complex surrounded by rose hedges and apple trees, more a castle than a house. Not that he'd ever say anything, lest someone of the Begonia family heard him. On the opened door there was a wreath of holly and vervain, for good luck. Many houses hung them in preparation for the Celebrations. Her home held five generations and six branches of her families: uncles, aunts, cousins, siblings, grandparents, and her parents.

"Is that why you and Ven aren't. . ." Aureolin smiled gently.

"Time moves on, and I'm happier now." Arna looked up at the big house. Inside, Arna could smell food cooking and hear the sound of laughter. "What do you need help with?"

Aureolin let them inside the house, into the foray where the handcrafted ceramic tiles lined the floor in an array of floral patterns and the walls were handpainted.

"Yes, let me get dressed and—"

"Lila, is that Incarnadine?" an elderly woman's voice said from inside. Aureolin hated the nickname and only let one person use it.

"Yes, Mymy," Aureolin yelled back. "He's coming in for tea."

"Good!" The woman then started shouting other incomprehensible things to others in the house.

"How is she?" Arna asked.

The last Arna had seen the woman she had looked ancient. She was the family's matriarch, and older than most citizens of Xeysis.

"Still kicking."

Aureolin's family was a true, bred-and-bled, family of Xeysis. They always had at least three Children of Xeyaro in a generation. Nature was their calling card and by it they thrived.

"Mymy was called by the Floral Association for this year's Celebration and Floral Festival."

Arna gaped. But she was nearly one-hundred fifty. She shouldn't be working at all.

"As a consultant?"

"Yeah. They swore they'd stop asking her ten years ago after she threw a fit about the petunias but looks like they had a feeling you'd return. This year is perhaps going to be the best blooming season yet. Your mom is helping, too."

"I didn't know that." He now understood why his mother had given him the message for Mymy that morning.

"She can't say no to Mymy," Aureolin laughed, lightly and with an abundance of love. The flowers in the pots around her spun and bloomed wider. "Mymy walked right up to the Vivicent garden, yelled at your mother for wasting her talents, and then dragged her to the Floral Association."

"Don't tell the boy lies." Myrtle Begonia walked into the room with her cane and shaking hands. She was hunched over and had a fight in her eyes that said that they were going to oblige to her or get their ear talked off. The woman flicked her hand and a smaller child handed Arna a cup of tea.

"Chamomile, for the nerves," Myrtle nodded to him. She moved slowly closer, eyeing him. "You look like you could stand to gain a few pounds."

"Mymy!" Aureolin chastized.

"What is Wenge feeding you? I will have a word with that woman. All of her kids, saplings," Myrtle began to rant, poking Arna and grabbing his chin with a bit of force to make him look left and right.

"It's good to see you, too, Mymy." Arna handed Aureolin his tea and gave Myrtle a light hug. "My mom said she'll meet us at the festival."

"No time for sentiment, boy. You have work to do. You've returned home and there are only messes." She gave him a pat on the shoulder. "Come by for dinner and I will hear all your stories."

"Of course, Mymy."

"Now, go. You both need to go to the closing ceremony, no? We'll be down with the family later. You said Wenge will be there. I'll be sure to fix her. You need more food, boy."

Arna could not resist laughing and did so openly as the woman patted him over, making sure that he was not, in fact, skin and bones, but well-toned muscle.

"Well, maybe not. Perhaps you're well fed after all," Mymy eyed him suspiciously, "But I'll keep an eye out."

"Thank you, Mymy," Arna said as Aureolin handed Arna his tea back and pushed him towards the back.

"We'll leave soon. I need to grab a few things." Aureolin called to her great-grandmother as she got them away as fast as she could. Arna glanced over his shoulder to see Myrtle hobbling off with the assistance of one of her great-great-grandchildren.

Arna laughed at Aureolin's clear discomfort. "You know I love Mymy."

"She'll make us late, you can talk to her later." Aureolin shook her head, with a bit of sorrow gracing her otherwise pleasant smile. She was clearly more tense than before: arms crossed, shoulders straighter, eyes locked ahead.

"Where are the others?" Arna asked. The other voices and laughter died in the house. "Your parents?"

"Not everyone is happy you are back, but Mymy made the decision to accept you, so they have to do it," Aureolin said, opening the door to her room. The walls were lined in art both framed and unframed, stacked and hovering atop each other: postcards, insects in frames, mirrors to bounce light off the walls. The whole space was covered in plants.

Seeing all her plants reminded Arna of Ebru. Ebru was aware of Aureolin's love for flowers, but he doubted that she knew of Ebru's. Unlike Ebru's room, her room was filled with exotic flowers, all dried and hanging from the ceiling across the lattice of vines and nanotech swirling lights, mimicking fireflies. The air carried the hint of dried sunflowers and sunlight. Her bed was a massive circle in the corner of the room with a sunflower sheet and the tiled floors were white, lined with gold.

"I'll be back." She rushed off, grabbing clothes and locking herself in her bathroom.

As she changed Arna examined the hanging flowers. He could name some of the flowers but not all of them. Near the wall was a curtain of flowers, woven together and concealing something. Arna pulled the flower-curtains, and they moved attached to a hidden rail above the lattice on the ceiling.

Beyond them was a wall of crowns.

They were layered atop one another, in beautiful arrangements and piles, all of them dried and old: seven sets of eleven and three sets of six. Arna traced the flowers he could not name, in the elaborately designed crowns. The sets all were unique but within each set, the flowers were reminiscent, similar.

"I make them for everyone each year." Aureolin's voice startled him. He had not heard her exit the bathroom. She walked over to him, dressed in an all tan suit.

While Arna had showered and changed at the Shadone studio, he was not dressed nearly as well. He wore white pants and a white shirt, as simple as possible. Everyone wore simple clothes to the Flower Festival, so they could be draped in the colors of the flowers that were given to them.

"That one is you." Aureolin pointed, and Arna gaped, looking up. His eyes darted across the rows, placing a name to each set based on color. The smaller sets were for Amaryllis, Sarcoline, and Rosmarinus: pink and white, black with mint and white, sky blue and aqua.

"Why. . .?" he asked. This whole time?

"I think we all did something to try to remember each other. You don't go through fifteen years of your life just to forget everything all at once. I once told Arco—when he was practicing actually—that I was afraid you all hated me, because when we all fell apart it seemed like everyone expected that I was just okay. I had no reason to be as distressed as everyone else and I thought, for a moment, that maybe none of you ever liked me."

"We did," Arna disagreed hurriedly, needing her to understand that she was as much of one of them as anyone was.

"Arco told me that, too. I had already started making the crowns for you all back then, but talking with him reaffirmed that I was never just an extra, someone that did not matter. He was the one that convinced me to start doing the floral competition." She smiled lovingly at the crowns. "I never felt comfortable—skilled enough—to give the crowns to you guys when we were younger. . ."

"They'll wear them."

She hesitated and then laughed. "Sometimes I think that everyone thinks I don't give them flower crowns because I am egotistical. . . I'm not that confident."

"Then why are we here?" Arna slowly turned to her.

"Because I want you to convince me that I should do it this year anyway," Aureolin said weakly. She glanced at him, arms crossed, and curly hair pinned back to reveal her whole face. She didn't need his convincing. She already had her answer.

Arna smiled lightly and placed his hand on her shoulder. She took a deep breath and gathered the crowns in her arms. As she took them all Arna could see it, his dances: the choreography was cleaner than before but something. . . something was still off. On the wall three crowns were left behind. Lightning struck: *I was afraid you all hated me.*

"I really didn't need your approval," she said.

"No," he agreed, staring at the crowns for Ebru and Sarcoline. Ebru's crown was one of all pink and gray flowers, woven together with branches almost like antlers. The other, Sarcoline's crown, was black leaves with mint and white roses, simple and refined. Rosmarinus was the simplest of all, sky blue roses and aqua leaves, with a thin band of black to hold it together.

Aureolin did not hate Ebru, but Ebru thought she did. Phlox and Jasione were not on good terms. The others assured Arna that Rosmarinus had not replaced him. Sarcoline always fought.

"But it's nice to have support," she said: lighter, happier, excited to go and nearly rushing for the door. "Finish your tea, we have to go."

Every member of the Golden Generation believed the others hated them. It was not Arna that was the problem. He needed to get the Golden Generation back together, to trust each other and to finally believe in each other again. What did they need from him? Faith.

The city of Xeysis had been transformed for the grand Flower Festival.

Flowers were everywhere. The trellises were lined in them. Vines of them were strung between buildings that were bathed in their colors. Floating drones in the air were covered. Everyone wore flower crowns and clothing of all white, airy and light.

"The committee in charge of decoration had their work cut out for them this year." Arna wore his flower crown of lantana, snapdragons, and delphinium.

Metallic cameras disguised as actual flowers hung in the sky, glimmering in the artificial light.

"Was it the same in the other cities?" Aureolin asked. She wore her own crown of sunflowers, coreopsis, red geranium, and hibiscus. In her arms she held the other crowns waiting to be seated on a head.

"The decorating? No. The events? Similar."

Arna pondered. How could he make them all confident in each other again? How could he give them faith?

"None of their flower festivals are like ours," Aureolin laughed.

How did he get them to trust each other? He needed to know where their issues with each other fully stemmed. He knew most, but clearly not all.

Ivy fell off of roofs, twisted into swings for people to sit, into canopies for cover, along bridges where groups could watch and toss out necklaces and rings of flowers. Petals danced in the airs, swirling with bubbles and mists from wind machines. The air wafted with the scent of a thousand flowers, all working in a harmony of notes, expertly placed so that as one walked through the festival there would be no clash of the senses: color, smell, or texture.

The screens that doubled as the windows on the skyscrapers showed only advertisements that were soft and pastel. The soft ambiance of music swelled. *Meetings at Eternity*, set the stage. A soft hum buzzed through the crowd as many sang along.

The windows that could be seen that were not screens, were polished so bright, that they were nearly mirrors, and the thousands of flowers appeared as millions. Flowers hung from the trees. The streetlights were changed to appear like snowdrops, and chalk art lined the streets.

"No. They have different events. While we have the Flower Festival, Food Festival, and Awards Week for our specialty weeks, Azis has Chaos week and Ludiel had Freedom week," Arna explained.

"Freedom week?"

"Most crimes are legal the whole week," Arna said with a hushed voice and wicked smile.

"No," Aureolin gasped.

"Yes," Arna laughed. The lead up for the Celebrations consumed two months. Each week there was a different thing happening in each city. There were graduations, awards, festivals, presentations, and all kinds of events. Due to the ease of the internet, everyone had access to everything, but the Celebrations website presented high quality recaps the week of the Celebrations.

"Lumak allows that?" Aureolin asked, aghast.

[The earth rumbled.]

"No. I'd imagine they hate it. But. . . technically no laws are broken. It's all in the semantics," Arna stepped over the cracks, hands behind his back, breathing in the scent of the flowers. He missed the Flower Festival.

Arna continued on with stories of the other cities when a familiar arm wrapped around him.

"Hello, loves," Phlox said, red flower crown in her hair. "We were waiting for you. What took you so long?"

"Mymy," Arna explained, and she laughed as if it were the most hysterical joke she'd ever heard.

She pulled them through the crowd to where Amaryllis, Ven, Gingerline, Jasione, and Wenge stood waiting. They all wore flower crowns of their own. Arna glanced to Aureolin, who shrugged off Phlox, cheeks tinged red and with clear nervousness from the way she shifted. Arna smirked at her, catching her eye. He mouthed: *you like her.*

Shut up, she glared back.

"I made you crowns," Aureolin said nonchalantly, ignoring Arna as Arna plotted ways to help Phlox ask Aureolin out. It needed to be done with lots of flowers.

"You what?" Gingerline squealed. "No!"

"Here." Aureolin handed them out almost as if she were disinterested.

Gingerline looked to their mother, handing over her crown and taking the one from Aureolin. The others followed. Their chatter about the crowns turned in a discordant song, with no real purpose other than to showcase emotion. Jasione smiled softly to himself. Phlox acted dramatically, making Aureolin place the crown on her head, while Gingerline actually jumped for joy. Amaryllis was soft with hers, touching the petals one by one. Ven tried to find a place to put all the old crowns, before placing the new one on their head and smiling.

The lack of cohesion reminded Arna of the few times that he had done things similar at other past festivals in other cities: trying foods, trying events, because the Gods asked him to.

I miss you.

[Winds over the sea missed him.]

He wished for their chatter and nonsense, even if it drove him crazy. He could imagine Lumak talking about the crowns as Pokk stood silently. Ixxzal would be mocking Arna and bothering him incessantly until Arna relented and teased back. Azza would have pressured him to do more and to say more. Zaynir would have told him to express himself and Xeyaro would have been there the whole time supporting him with a silent smile.

"What's wrong?" Gingerline asked him.

Arna wiped the tears at his eyes, clearing his blurry vision. He shook his head. "I just missed this."

He would go to all the festivals with them. There was an award shows next week where Phlox had to win for acting. The music festival the week after was where Ivumalis' music was going to be presented for award without his face. He *would* see all the festivals next year as well.

[The ticking time reminded him: he was safe.]

"No need to cry." Gingerline hugged him lightly and pulled him into the circle that grew tighter.

Together they were standing in unison, a bit splintered but more harmonized than they had been hours before; all dressed in stark white, pure and open to possibility.

Arna looked around. Petals drifted toward them on the breeze. "We should dance."

"Here?" Ven asked, confused.

"Yes." Arna smiled.

"We'll cause a scene," Gingerline reminded him, shaking her head.

"We already do."

Arna pointed to those who stared at them, blatantly, and those who tried to be discrete. They were already being watched. They had been watched from years and, without Ebru there, Arna hoped he'd be able to find the issues that were present between them.

"Not here. There," Amaryllis said, pointing towards the street where the rain of flowers continuously fell. She held up her camera. "I'll take pictures."

Ven shook their head but sighed with a slight smile at the corners of their lips. "Fine, but not more than five minutes."

"Oh? Nervous?" Phlox teased.

"You aren't?"

"Ebru isn't here to show us up. We're fine."

Phlox began skipping, grabbing both Aureolin and Amaryllis and dragging them off ahead.

Arna followed the girls, tugging a reluctant Ven along with him. They were surrounded by a whirlwind of flowers, standing with a variety of other people, children and adults. The Ivumalis song *Spring Roses* played, and without much effort Arna glanced at Gingerline. Together the two of them started dancing, not waiting for the others to catch on. The dance was easy enough.

Ven was the second to catch on, S.Mirrors active in order to better read and understand Arna. Then was Aureolin who had seen it in part before. Phlox was last, but her excitement and energy transformed the dance. What had once been soothing turned electric and Arna's soul connected.

They were one unit, finally.

He loved them, even now. He had never stopped loving them. Dancing with them was the one place in the world he'd always belonged, and there in the rain of rainbows and flowers, it was the one place he was meant to be.

You were born together, you belong together. The Gods may have given them each other as a chance, Zaffre may have urged them, but in the end, by choice, they had chosen eachother.

The more that he danced, however, the more he noticed the void.

As they stopped dancing, with a fit of santified giggles and tears in their eyes, it was clear: Arna was not the only one who was whole and relieved. He was also not alone in the hyper awareness of what they were missing: Ebru.

Arna looked amongst them one by one, swearing to himself: *Next time...*

Even if it were not perfect. Even if it were rough around the edges and all new. Next time, they would all be together.

"That was brilliant!" Amaryllis raced over. "I have to add these to my portfolio. I think I still have time to revise it."

"Of course, you do," Phlox said, rolling her eyes.

In seconds the unity fractured.

Ven was glaring at Phlox. Aureolin looked uncomfortable. Gingerline glared at Phlox, as well. Amaryllis was a weak link. Phlox hated her. *Okay,* he could fix that.

Jasione walked up to Gingerline and rubbed her back and she smiled at him. Aureolin's eyes traveled from him to Phlox and then away, back to Amaryllis.

Aureolin did not act on her feelings. Jasione was disconnected from Phlox. He could fix that.

"Am, do you think—" Aureolin started.

"Arna," Amaryllis cut her off.

His attention snapped to Amaryllis, who stared at him with an unfathomable expression. It was the one she gave him the night he was with her in the wisteria alley. It was the one she gave him when he first saw her studio. She was seeing him.

"Look harder," she demanded.

"What?" Aureolin asked, but the message was for Arna, so he did. He turned back to his friends. Ven looked at Amaryllis, confused, and then back to Arna. Aureolin avoided Phlox who was complaining. Gingerline and Jasione were in their own world.

Ven had no pair. They'd lost their best friend. Aureolin and Phlox's will-they-won't-they relationship was making no changes, despite what Phlox tried. Why? Because Aureolin was Gingerline's best friend and Amaryllis' friend. Phlox hated Amaryllis, so Aureolin had to keep her at a distance. Gingerline was too focused on anything but herself, which was why Jasione pulled her away consistently. She was too busy trying to make them all friends, that it was hurting her. She was so selfless that she tried not to be selfish. When she was, it fractured the party and hurt her more.

There was a visible gap in peace, with them all so loud and debating each other. There was no counterbalance to calm their emotions. But who could do it?

"It will be difficult, and I am more nervous than anything else," Ebru's voice sounded over the speakers. Immediately, Arna's eyes turned upwards to the screens that were showing his face. He was done up beautifully.

[All diamonds were sharp.]

"But you must be excited to dance with the Golden Generation for the first time in years," the reporter said.

[They were brilliant, dazzling, breathtaking, and impervious to the world.]

"Feeling has nothing to do with it. It is how it is. My excitement is of little consequence. I will dance because I must. We all must," Ebru answered, a clear Shadone-prepared answer seeping through the tone. He smiled without a hint of joy.

[All diamonds feigned perfection.]

Arna looked back to the others who all had looks of mixed emotion. Gingerline held deep seeded anger. Ven only held sorrow. Phlox gazed in horror while Aureolin held shock.

Only Amaryllis stared at Arna.

[All diamonds could break.]

This was why the Golden Generation could not come together, and why it was worse when Ebru was in the room. They didn't know how much they already needed him, and he didn't know how much they all loved him.

What was it that they needed? How did he give them faith?

Sometimes people mistake selfishness for selflessness.

Arna stepped away, flourishing his abilities and stepping into the mix of crowds and petals to vanish. It was difficult at first, filling the void and twisting the Blessings to serve his purpose, but after a few seconds the Blessings slipped into place.

He'd return. They had to go to Aureolin's flower show, but for now, he needed to begin to fix this.

"Hello?" Ebru asked, annoyed. His voice was rough, as if he had been crying.

"You need to tell the others you're Ivumalis," Arna said quickly, certain it needed to be said. His variation played in his mind. Inspiration bloomed at his fingertips. Answers sparked like a path on the ground towards the unknown future.

"They love your music. You need to tell them."

Silence filled the call and Arna breathed with the seconds. Give Ebru time. He would understand.

"I fail to see why what they think matters," Ebru finally spoke, soft and concerned.

"Because it's a part of you. And it deserves to be seen. And I know you don't want Cyclamen to hold it over your head. It doesn't have to be a secret anymore. I'm here."

"No," Ebru said. "It wouldn't change anything, Arna."

"I can't tell them your secret, Ixxzal would kill me," Arna insisted.

"Then don't. I don't understand why it matters," Ebru argued back, irritation rising.

"Because you deserve to have your friends back," Arna said standing against a tree. "We will protect you."

Ebru went silent on the other end of the phone.

(what is silence?)

Arna didn't care. "They'll accept you. And they need to know just how much you've been supporting them. Ivumalis is what linked them together after I broke everything apart."

"You don't mean that," Ebru said, even though neither he nor Arna could lie.

(silence?)

A tumultuous pause filled the air between them before Ebru broke. "Arna. I can't. . ."

"'We search for meaning in the unknown. Give names to that which we do not understand.' I'm tired of running from the unknown, Alis."

He wanted to dance. He wanted to have his life back. He was going to fix this.

"Trust me, okay? I love you," Arna said, not expecting a response. He waited regardless, seconds passed to minutes with Ebru simply breathing on the other end of the line.

"I will come over tonight, before your father gets home. And we can be together and talk about it."

"As soon as the festival is over," Ebru demanded, and Arna laughed. Ebru's then said almost too softly, "I love you, too."

The call ended, and Arna stood blinking into the tree leaves that swayed about him. For a moment their shadows looked like people. The people were dancing. They swung their fans around in the thrill of harmony and cohesion.

One day they would be united. One day they would laugh about this like it was nothing. One day they would tell their children of their trials and tribulations and how much it had not mattered because they always believed in each other.

(He would not be like Saffron.)

In fact, Saffron no longer needed to exist.

littlepurpleflowersfadeintonothing.

Are you visualizing?

The light in the tree leaves asked him as he peered up into the sky, blinding white almost like moonlight: a remembered vow. It was a promise that this time he'd understand before he swore it. This time he would not make that mistake.

Yes, I want to live.

Trust is the foundation of the dances and all in life. Trust in the Gods and in your fans. Trust in the hours of dedication and practice that you have spent on training. Trust your guides, your teachers, and those who support you from the crowd. Without trust, the dances are nothing.

— On trust and the importance of faith

Dance 16

Tranquility

Incarnadine

12 Xeyan

30 Days Left

"You are too laid back."
"I have time."
"You have lessons to learn."
"Lessons you won't teach me."
"Some cannot be taught."

Arna awoke early that morning: the day of Sarcoline's test for mastery. It was the last dance test before the new year. There were usually testing days two times a month, the 12th and 30th, but due to it being the end of the year there was only one. There would be too many people that wanted to test and not enough spots. If his plan was to work, he needed to be at The Dance House first thing.

Arna opened the group chat, scanning individual schedules through his augmentations. Ebru had responded to the surprise of everyone saying he was testing at the end of the day in Holly Worship, dance twenty-five. Aureolin was testing for Blue Rose Fears Understanding, making her the third of the Golden Generation to have mastery in three variations. Sarcoline said he was testing for Powers in Twin Fans.

The chat was flooded with messages asking where Sarcoline had been, and when he was returning. The only people who had heard anything from him in weeks were Amaryllis and Arna's parents.

Arna's phone buzzed.

>   Alis: You owe me.
>   Rosy: Thanks

Arna opened his DHS provided email he had not touched in years and glanced over his dance time slot, approvals given to him by Ebru.

When Ebru had mastered all five variations through Understanding, he had become the youngest dancer to ever do so: certified at age twenty-five. In the following weeks, Ebru had been officially announced as a member of the DHS small council—certified and able to judge all Ceremony of Chaos auditions and all mastery tests—and the internet had gone up in flames. Officially, with his ascension, the Shadone studio held four of the twelve DHS small council seats. It marked the official end of the Vivicent supremacy in the small council. Ebru's position in the council was highly contested and Arna's key to Sarcoline's mastery tests.

In order for Sarcoline to test three times, Arna had needed testing spots. He'd sent in the application last night as soon as he knew for certain Sarcoline would be back in the city. There were only so many testing slots per month and Arna submitting for approval was against the code. Yet, the rules for Children with A.Reverence were a bit fickle, as the DHS wanted to promote them quickly. Only one member of the small council had to approve a late request made by a Child. Ebru had swung his weight around and at first Arna felt guilty until Ebru sent the times.

>   Alis: Use them wisely. Whatever you're planning better
>   be devastating. If it's not, I'll be disappointed.

Arna's gut had never led him wrong. Sarcoline would come back having understood.

Arna sent his two dance times to the chat. The two were far enough apart for Sarcoline to rest in between his first, second, and third test. Arna went to the kitchen and made lunches for Sarcoline and himself. Arna planned to be at the testing facility all day with Sarcoline. The anticipation had him jumping around the kitchen.

"What has you so giddy?" Gingerline asked from the staircase.

Arna tried to act nonchalant. "Arco's coming home today."

Gingerline eyed him, cautious and a bit guarded. "You're the one who told him to go to the other cities."

"I did," Arna agreed. "And he's home just in time." But he would not go home. Sarcoline would go to Amaryllis to calm himself.

"Why did you make two lunches?" Gingerline glanced over the food he was making and pointed at them like they were fake.

"Arco is going to need one," he said, and she did not respond. Slowly he met her eye as he cut sandwiches and she motioned for him to elaborate. "He's testing in Twin Fans and Holly."

"He only has the spot for Twin Fans. He can't unless. . ." She groaned out. "Dad thought you were joking."

"They gave me the spots." Arna smiled wide, letting the knowledge circle around him as a carefully crafted shield.

"And you're giving them to Arco?" Gingerline shrieked. "Do you have any idea what sort of storm that will cause?"

"He'll be the first nonChild in generations to complete all five variations through Powers, I know." Arna shrugged, with a smug smile on his lips.

"He has classes to attend. He's skipped weeks of lessons!" Gingerline protested.

"Maybe he'll pull off a miracle." Arna shrugged putting the lunches in his bag. "I'll meet you at the testing facility. I'm going to do something first."

Gingerline opened her mouth to protest and then shook her head.

"Hey, look at me," he said. "After the tests are over, you and I will hang out, okay? We haven't had the chance to."

Her eyes grew wide, and she nodded vigorously, whatever despondent fury she'd had before, vanished into joy.

Arna gave her a hug and left the house with a bag of Sarcoline's things and the lunches.

When he walked in the door to Amaryllis' studio, Arna was not surprised to find Sarcoline. He had his bag next to him and tea in hand as Amaryllis force fed him breakfast. She loomed over Sarcoline, pinching his cheeks and forcing a piece of cantaloupe between his teeth. The two turned from where they sat in the kitchen on the complete opposite side of the room.

Arna peered back at them through the trellis of hanging pictures. It was a sea of vines: hanging photographs twirling in the air. Through them, across the room Arna found a look of confused disgust on Sarcoline's face.

Amaryllis forced Sarcoline to take the fruit and he shot her a glare as he chewed.

"Since when are you friends?" Sarcoline asked, pointing at Arna. Arna walked through the vines of hanging photographs that spiraled and turned to let him through.

"Since Ven crashed in my garden with him," Amaryllis answered, shoving a bowl with more fruit Sarcoline's way.

"You can't be serious." A full flush spread across Sarcoline's face as Arna approached, he picked at the fruit like a bird. "Am. . . He's. . ."

"My best friend's brother, here to save the day," Amaryllis cheered, placing her hands on Sarcoline's shoulders and squeezed. She then sat at the table picking at the fruit bowl herself.

Sarcoline groaned and Arna took a chair across from him.

"What?" Sarcoline asked as Arna placed down a map of Xeysis and slid it across the table.

Arna once wore Xeysis like his own skin, but since returning home it was foreign. He had neither had time to truly explore it, nor to find places he wanted to dance in that made him feel like he Understood the city. Created by noting the places that had always stood out to him in the past, and with a bit of help from the internet, he created the list. There were tens of marks across the map.

"You have more places to go to," Arna said. "It's up to you if you go or not. I decided to come and give you this and then I'm heading over to The Dance House. I've packed you a lunch, your dance clothes, and indoor shoes."

"Is this your way of finally being my big brother?" Sarcoline hissed, sliding the paper back. "I don't need it. It didn't work." Sarcoline then said with sneer, "I see you took two test slots. How did you get in? Bribery?"

"I asked." Arna took fruit from the bowl on the table. "I'm giving the spot to you. Your planned time is first. The next time that I made is three hours later. The last is at the end of the day, four hours later; the last spot available."

"For me?" Sarcoline scoffed. "You expect too much of me. I told you it didn't work."

"Not yet. Because you haven't learned Xeysis yet." Arna was not sure that it would work at all. Did guidance mean that he needed to be there with his brother? Or was his ghost enough?

"I've lived here my whole life," Sarcoline disagreed.

"It's exactly because you've lived here your whole life that you don't know." Arna pointed to the map. "Aren't you curious if I'm right or not?"

"You're kidding me. This isn't a game, Arna," Sarcoline growled. "Even if, for some Xeyaro-blessed reason, I was able to Understand nineteen, I can't reach mastery in a day unless Azza sees it fit to destroy rationality. For me."

"It'll take you a few hours," Arna insisted.

"Days," Sarcoline snapped.

"We can disagree, but if you keep sitting here, you'll never know," Arna protested, his hope superseding any worry he had. Just as Arna needed to unite the Golden Generation, he needed Sarcoline to reach Understanding. It was the proof he needed for Incarnate Dreams: community and changing the status quo.

Before Sarcoline could snap back, Amaryllis threw a blueberry in his mouth.

"You've already danced here," Amaryllis said tapping at the Cathedral Forest. She then pointed to another: The Sea of Vines. "And here."

Then she tapped another: the Art Bridge, where Xeysis left all the bridges that they removed from the city before they destroyed them. It had been turned into a massive art installation and skatepark. "And here. The others no."

"I can't go to all of these," Sarcoline disagreed.

"Go to these," Amaryllis tapped at three more points.

The Alley of Empty Houses was where people sang in disjointed harmony, calling to each other. Arna had read about it online but had never seen it outside of videos, as they only sang on testing days.

The Fabric Forest was where people left fabric of all types, strung up and tied together. It created a forest of fibers that had been taken over by the nature of Xeysis and supported thousands of plants and animals.

The River of Paper Animals was where people sent folded paper with written wishes down a river that ended at the only waterfall in Xeysis that fell to the outside world. Apparently those near the waterfall swore they could see and hear the animals outside. Although, there were none.

The three spots were all over the city, in wildly different directions. Sarcoline would at most be able to get to one before he had to return to The Dance House for his test.

"Even if I did, I wouldn't be able to. . ." Sarcoline's eyes drifted to the map and in them was a flicker of hope. "Do this."

On his own accord, Sarcoline picked up a strawberry from the bowl and ate it with a grimace. Amaryllis shifted next to him with a smug smile.

"Do it, Sarcoline," Amaryllis said, pushing another strawberry towards him. Sarcoline flinched at his full name. "You did not send me all those videos for nothing."

"But—" He protested, and she lifted the strawberry to his lips and he grimaced.

"He has more faith in you than me. Than you have in yourself," Amaryllis spoke low. "He's going to support you. Take it."

There was an unspoken series of words that were sent between Amaryllis and Sarcoline. He bit the fruit and ate with a frown. Minutes passed in silence.

"My family has always supported me, Am," Sarcoline finally said when the fruit bowl was empty.

"But you are not a Child, and they never hold you to that standard. They never look at us like we belong," Amaryllis said and for a moment Arna was confused. Why would his parents. . . Sarcoline's expression of pain gave Arna clarity. They were talking about society.

"For the first time in our life, someone is holding you to the same impossible standard you set for yourself. Don't back down now." Amaryllis slammed her hand down into the table.

There was a split second where Arna thought to back off. He didn't want to crush Sarcoline forever. He only wanted to support the possibility of the future. This could not be an end all be all moment. Yet, Sarcoline studied the map and with each second, Arna could picture his dance better and better. Arna took the risk.

"If you don't Understand, I might have overestimated you," Arna pressured his brother, leaning in at the table and pushing the map closer to Sarcoline.

Sarcoline's eyes narrowed in competition. Amaryllis laughed.

"So?" Arna asked as Sarcoline jumped up, pulling the map with him. Arna laughed. Sarcoline was going to do it, because Sarcoline wanted it more than anything. Sarcoline left the house with the softest clicks of the door.

"Before we go to the testing house, I want your opinion," Amaryllis said, leaning back in her chair.

"On?" Arna asked, studying her as she pulled her hair up to a bun atop her head.

"Chamomile always left strict orders only to sell a few pieces of her art for charity, never more. Unless I saw a reason," Amaryllis said, nodding to the paintings on the walls. "Every year your family has auctioned her art at their stall to help them raise money."

Arna's heart sank. Since they didn't have students anymore, was this how they'd managed to keep themselves going?

"Between the auction and the vaults, they've managed to get by but this year, I want to sell more," Amaryllis said.

"Why?" Arna asked her.

"The world thinks of us as one thing: the thing that they've determined based on the Blessings we are given," she said pointing to her eyes. "But you want something else. You are giving Arco hope. Hope that if stripped from him could destroy him irrevocably. Yet, you're not afraid."

"He can do it," Arna said, certain. He needed to believe that this could happen, that Incarnate Dreams could be realized.

"I want the world to know Chamomile's name. I want them to wish they'd cherished her when she was alive instead of mocking her for being a painter despite being gifted with Blessings that were not suited for art."

"Not what has been thought to be suited for art," Arna corrected.

Amaryllis cracked a wide smile and leaned closer to him, seeing him, reading him. Her eyes almost looked like they were glowing, and when she blinked Arna understood the message loud and clear.

(what is silence?   )

Let's change the world.

By the time that Arna and Amaryllis got to The Dance House the doors had been opened. The entrance hall was buzzing with those who had arrived, nervous for their tests. Most of the people dancing were adults. There were a few teenagers preparing to be tested. No one was younger than eleven.

On the distant wall, across from the doors, was a line of cabinets surrounded by a congregation of individuals who examined the contents behind the glass. There were five cabinets, one for each variation, with the most recent consecrated version of its performance fans. Each variation was separated by a door to the inner part of the building where studios held classes, and today was where the tests would be held.

Amaryllis walked off to the Vivicent studio seats. Arna signed in, making sure he would keep his spots. Arna, exploiting his ability as a senior studio member, wrote Sarcoline's name down twice on the waitlist: luckily, first to sign in. No one would take him seriously: not when Sarcoline wasn't a Child, and not when Arna was already being considered a joke.

The tests always went faster than predicted, as people often failed quickly, and whether it was the failures or no-shows, Sarcoline would be taken off the waitlist at least twice, as Arna gave up his spots. The rules never changed, not the procedures and certainly not the exceptions to the rules. Today was no different.

The one Arna planned to exploit was the exception to the rule about who could dance when a dancer missed their time slot. When reading a name off the waitlist, a dancer could not retest within two hours of a prior test. In the best-case scenario, no one would lose their spot between the tests and gave Sarcoline enough time. Arna prayed for the best.

[no accidents.   ]

The exception was in place for Children of Xeyaro, to give them time to recover between dances. The DHS never expected anyone to manipulate the waitlist system as Arna was attempting to, as only Children tested in more than one dance a day. They usually made appointments. So long as there were no strange inconsistencies with timing, Sarcoline would get both of Arna's spots and successfully dance for Holly Powers and Blue Rose Fears Understanding.

"Incarnadine Vivicent." Cyclamen Shadone, dressed in all white with a purple shirt, stood behind Arna with his students. Ebru was amongst them, dressed in his mint DHS uniform instead of his dance clothes. While only one DHS small council member was required to sit in on all mastery tests— with five judges in total per test, all of whom were required to be mastered through the dance section—somehow Arna had thought it would be beneath Cyclamen to do so. He had so many other things to do, trying to destroy the Vivicents, that Arna thought he would not care.

"Greetings." Arna bowed to him, forcing a smile and wanting to rip Cyclamen's head off. He stepped aside for them to sign in and Ebru shot Arna a glare telling Arna not to do anything.

"I hear your brother is testing today, and yourself?" Cyclamen asked and Arna bristled.

Ah. He's here for me. Dancers of the same studio could not judge each other for mastery tests. Even if the glow for mastery was clear to all dancers, one still had to prove the act by dancing the variation without mistake. Cyclamen would be hostile about even the smallest of mistakes.

"I am pleased to test you today. 'We greet each other in open arms and thorough contemplation, acknowledging our differences and recognizing similarities,'" Cyclamen quoted, Luminance 18.4. Was that what Arna always sounded like when he quoted texts? Haughty and annoying?

I need to stop doing that.

[Distant laughter dusted the walls like memories not yet conceding to obliteration.]

Cyclamen sized Arna up, comparing him to Ebru. Arna glared back uncertain what was being seen. He cocked his head at the man, ready to fight if he had to.

"I suppose you do look rosy, Rosy," Cyclamen said. Ebru stiffened and Arna's blood rushed to his head. Cyclamen glanced to Ebru before he smiled in a way that made Ebru jolt. Cyclamen must have figured it out by beating it out of Ebru. *I'll kill him.*

[Thunder rolled, yet oceans agreed with drowning.]

Containing himself, Arna attempted to be pleasant. He forced the words out of his mouth. "May the tests be fruitful."

"They will be," the man smiled. Sparks flew between the two of them. Cyclamen was called before he could say more. "I must bid you a farewell for now. I have a test to oversee."

Arna waved as the man walked off trying not to imagine him suffering in a ditch in the middle of nowhere, outside Xeysis.

"Don't antagonize him," Ebru warned Arna, stepping between Cyclamen and Arna to keep Arna from seeing the man.

"If he touches you again, I may not be able to stop myself." Arna glared at the man's back, purposely moving so that he could see. Ebru fought back words as the corners of his mouth ticked up to a smile. He closed his eyes, rubbed his temples, and walked past Arna to sign in. As he did, his fingers lightly dusted Arna's hand and it got Arna's attention. A clandestine touch in the middle of the room where anyone and everyone could see them.

Arna glanced at Ebru's testing position: lead proctor, for half the tests. It was seniority behind Zaffre.

"If that man is pushing you to do this, Alis. . ." Arna said placing his hand on Ebru's shoulder, the most he could do instead of pulling Ebru into a hug and stealing him away from the room.

"He's not. I asked to do it." Ebru pushed Arna away from the sign-in desk to the center of the lobby staring at the chairs that were being filled. Ebru crossed his arms and stood close to Arna, speaking so one else could hear. "Now are you going to tell me why in the world you are testing if you can't touch a fan?"

"He hurt you. Where?" Arna asked instead.

"Don't worry about it."

Arna hesitated to touch Ebru's arm and when he did it was as light as a feather, ensuring that Ebru did not flinch. However, the way he twisted told Arna it was his back. Could he dance like that?

"He found out about Rosy on the night of the Banquet." Ebru jolted back, putting more space between them, albeit not much. He was still leaning on Arna for support, even if they were not physically touching. "He didn't hurt me to find out it was you. He made a guess because we've been spotted together."

"What did he do?" What had Ebru not told him?

"Threatened dad, two days ago." Ebru shook his head. "Dance. Fans. Answer. What is Arco planning?"

Arna glared at Ebru. "You should have told me."

In two days, this had happened? Was this why Ebru had refused to see him the night before? Arna assumed it was because Ebru didn't want to hear another lecture on why the others loved Ivumalis, but this was far worse.

"You can't do anything. Answer." Ebru faced Arna, with a stern look but eyes that were tired.

Arna sighed. He put it aside, for both of their sakes. "Arco will Understand."

Ebru's expression dropped further. His fingers curled around where he held his arms. There was legitimate fear in Ebru's haunted smile. It was the sort of fear that could shatter someone forever. It was fear that invoked so much raw emotion, one couldn't feel anything. No anger. No sorrow. Just numbness and disbelief. His expression was completely blank and hollow.

"He's definitely dancing Twin Fans and Holly today," Arna answered, careful with his words.

"Which did he Understand?" Ebru asked.

Arna shrugged. For the first time in a long time, Arna was sure of himself. The hate mail often criticized him saying that without his Blessings he was nothing. But Sarcoline wasn't nothing. Take away Arna's Blessings and would he still be good? Sarcoline made him believe: yes. Sarcoline made Arna believe that it was not just his A.Reverence that made him able to dance at all. That even without the A.Reverence, Arna could be the Chosen Child.

The idea nagged at him and left a sweet taste in his mouth.

"How comforting." Ebru slid a bit further away from Arna. "Where is he?"

"He won't be here for a bit." Arna looked around. "You might as well go get the testing room ready."

Ebru eyed him and then nodded, leaving Arna's side. Arna found Amaryllis with a set of chairs set up in a circle as opposed to the rows in the majority of the room. The name Vivicent Studio was plastered on a holosign in the air indicating it was their personal waiting section, just as all the major studios had paid for. It was a small, secluded section for them, including a ring on the floor that when crossed created a Blessing barrier to reduce sound, both coming in and going out.

Unlike before, their section was smaller than it once had been, but there were enough chairs for all of them, and more if the Golden Generation ever came back. Large and cushioned like soft roses, instead of the uncomfortable, hovering wooden chairs that were throughout the majority of the room.

Arna sat in the chair that had always been his, once a lifetime ago. He took his laptop out, and began to work on his variation music. Ebru had added himself as a collaborator on the project so that he and Arna could work on it simultaneously. Arna reviewed the most recent changes Ebru had made, making notes and tweaking things as he saw fit. The songs were more complete, almost there.

He hoped the Gods were okay.

[   ]

He was a bit worried, but he continued onward. He had been trained for this, he could do it with or without them.

Every so often Amaryllis would stretch and offer Arna fruit, cheese, or crackers. At first Arna refused, but the hunger became too great, and he agreed. When Amaryllis pulled a blanket out of her bag to hand to Arna, he did not refuse it either. The two shared.

The Dance House was freezing to accommodate the false summer heat that radiated through the city, heightened by the failing Blessings that made it harder to regulate the temperatures. Xeysis, which never got too hot, was sweltering as the city tried to find ways to cool down the tech that moderated the temperatures.

It was about half an hour to Sarcoline's test that Gingerline, Zaffre, and Wenge showed up. Jasione was, unfortunately, at work. Sarcoline still hadn't showed. They arrived at the chairs where Amaryllis and Arna sat working on their laptops in silence.

A tension filled the air as the Vivicents sat, each one noting the lack of Sarcoline's presence. Each pretended it did not bother them. Gingerline sketched too hard in her book. Their mother spoke to Zaffre in a too quick voice. Zaffre glanced to the door three too many times. Amaryllis repeatedly checked the sky, looking for notifications. Arna pulled the blanket up further.

"Sarcoline?" Zaffre asked Arna. Arna looked to the time and shrugged. Sarcoline had to sign in at least fifteen minutes before his first test. The only person who had ever been cocky enough to do it exactly at the last minute had been Arna.

Gingerline stopped sketching and stared at Arna as if her glare alone could make him reveal his secrets. Their father and mother spoke in hushed tones about where Sarcoline was, and when they'd last heard from him.

The doors thudded open, with such a large noise that the whole room went silent. All at once Amaryllis looked up and Arna turned to face the doors behind him. Gingerline smiled. Their parents breathed out, tension turning to a sigh of relief.

Everyone avoided Sarcoline as he entered, whether because of his determination or the aversion to him. Sarcoline was the only dancer that created scorn, palpable envy in others, and apprehension in all. People parted ways for him as Sarcoline stalked in, like a predator ready to kill.

Sarcoline beelined towards them and dropped his bag unceremoniously into Arna's lap. "I'm going to sign in."

The spell was broken as Sarcoline walked off, stretching his arms over his head. Zaffre jogged after him, no doubt about to give a lecture. Arna's eyes did not leave his brother, searching for the glow of Mastery. He did not find it. When Sarcoline returned after signing in and arguing with their father for a few minutes, he knelt down and pulled his indoor dance shoes out of the bag Arna brought. Zaffre followed Sarcoline over.

"I know there are twenty minutes left." Sarcoline snapped at their father. "I'm already warmed up."

"Where were you?" Gingerline asked, beginning her own lecture with a tone that made even Arna groan.

"A park," Sarcoline answered, waving her off and sitting on the floor. "One I didn't know existed. And oddly enough—" Sarcoline glared at Arna, "—I'm no closer."

"You are closer." Arna believed it.

Please help him.

"You put my name down on the waitlist," Sarcoline said, standing up with his shoes and ready to leave.

Arna smiled brightly at him. Sarcoline opened his mouth to say something. The words were lost as Amaryllis reached up, grabbed Sarcoline's hand, and yanked him down next to her. When he crashed into the seat, she grabbed his head with force and put it on her shoulder. Sarcoline squirmed but she did not let him go, eyes focused on her laptop the whole time. Slowly but surely Sarcoline stopped moving, shut his eyes and looked visibly calmer.

"Better?" she asked as soon as he stopped trying to flee. Only then did she let him go.

"I hate you," Sarcoline grumbled.

"I love you, too," Amaryllis said, patting his head and returning to her work with both hands.

"You are doing Holly today?" their father asked, astounded. He sat in the chair next to Sarcoline. "I haven't. . ."

"I know." Sarcoline opened his eyes without a hint of shame. "Arna wants me to."

All the eyes landed on Arna, but nothing was said about it further. Their father started to remind Sarcoline of the audition procedures like where the fans would be located and what to do. He had six minutes between each dance to rest and prepare for the next one. The proctors wanted him to perform them all at a state as close to his peak condition as he could be.

Seconds later Sarcoline stood without a fight from Amaryllis. His name was called on the intercom, and people in the room turned to him. Arna tossed his brother a water. Arco caught it without looking at him and started walking, whistling as he did. People moved away in fear.

"Does he always do that?" Arna asked.

"Yes," Gingerline sighed. Arna recognized sorrow in Gingerline's eyes. There was guilt in his fathers and mother's expressions that turned more solemn.

Silently the family waited, sitting together as the hour began. Once again, Arna opened his laptop, but as time passed he got nothing done. Their father finally broke the silence more than thirty minutes into Sarcoline's test. "Why did you convince him to do Holly?"

"You know he has the glow. He can. . ." Arna started, taking the moment to disengage from fixing his variation. He jumped to his feet, heart in his throat, as he struggled to keep his laptop from tumbling to the floor. Sarcoline walked out of the doors, pissed off.

No one got out early. No one. Not unless they failed. . . But Sarcoline was approved by their father and he had the mastery glow for Twin Fans. Even now Arna could see the wisps of it off of Sarcoline's skin, fading as the high of the dance dissipated. What happened?

"I danced them all through in one go. I saw no reason to wait. It would be how I'd do it for a performance anyway," Sarcoline said, answering their collective question as he got to them. He took a towel from Amaryllis and wiped away his sweat.

"The breaks are an advantage for you," Zaffre chastised him.

"I'm leaving," Sarcoline stated, ignoring their father and grabbing a few things from his bag. He changed to his outdoor shoes. There was a renewed vigor in Sarcoline. Arna's heart began racing, confident. He might wear himself down by the evening, but Sarcoline was going to do it.

"You're going to trust me?" Arna asked him.

"I'm going to believe in a miracle," Sarcoline corrected. He glanced at Amaryllis. "Am. Let's go."

She stood, placing her laptop in her bag, but not putting it on. Instead, she picked up her camera.

"Don't be late this time," Arna warned him.

"I don't plan on it." He turned to leave. Gingerline protested, but he ignored her. Amaryllis waved for her to follow. After a bit of hesitation, Sarcoline nearly at the door, Gingerline chased after them. Zaffre excused himself to go to the back to proctor tests.

"What are you having him do?" Wenge asked as soon as they were gone.

When Arna did not answer, she did not press.

Time progressed quickly. Testers left in small bursts, those who failed often returning at the twenty-minute mark. Aureolin came and went, staying only a few minutes to talk before she hurried off to her group dance practice and unable to stay. At noon Sarcoline came back. His white, rose pants were almost a dusty pink from dancing outside. Arna fed him and Sarcoline promptly fell asleep. No words spoken.

"We went to two places but. . . You had him dancing the variations?" Gingerline asked.

Two? Wait. . . Variations? As in plural? He clarified, "All the variations?"

"Yes?"

Sarcoline was a monster.

Arna had wanted him to focus on one variation, and Sarcoline had been focusing on all five. No wonder he was having difficulties. Was that the problem with not having a Blessing? That they could not separate themselves? Or was. . . What did Sarcoline say? In order for a nonChild to learn two, they had to reach for both at the same time? Was Sarcoline trying to Understand all five at once?

The thought chilled Arna.

At exactly twenty minutes until Arna's time, Amaryllis poked Sarcoline awake. Without a word, he left for a practice room to stretch and get ready. At three minutes until the test, he returned.

"Incarnadine Vivicent," Arna heard his name called. Arna stood and walked to the front desk where the announcer spoke at the microphone.

"I'm withdrawing," he said as he got close enough. Those that could hear him stopped talking. The woman, who was not phased, rolled her eyes.

She took the waitlist from her companion and her eyes went wide. "Sar—Sarcoline Vivicent."

Sarcoline, who had walked up with Arna, nodded and headed to the waiting proctor. Much like the first, Sarcoline walked out of his second test early. Just as angry. Just as crazed.

"You are going to kill yourself." Gingerline said as he got to them. "You did two full sections of the variations."

"I'm fine. It's only Powers." He shook her off, and once more left with Amaryllis. Ignoring the glare of his mother, Arna worked. Inspired by Sarcoline, his fingers tingled as he moved. The smile on his lips threatened to become permanent. He'd fallen through the sky before, but in that moment, he was weightless.

It would work. Everything would fall into place. Arna could taste it as Sarcoline returned with Amaryllis, frustrated but a spark in his eyes.

He's close. Arna stood. "Ready?"

Sarcoline met his gaze and shook his head. Arna motioned for Sarcoline to follow him regardless. There was hint of the glow once more. If he was able to practice. . .

"Sarcoline Vivicent," The name was called over the speakers. Arna froze. *No.*

Sarcoline's expression twisted, as his head snapped to the front of the room where the proctor was waiting. Sarcoline's name was said again, and his heart thudded in his ears. When Sarcoline turned back to Arna, they shared one thought: Sarcoline wasn't ready.

Solemnly, Arna followed Sarcoline to the reception desk cursing his luck.

"Please," a little girl, no more than eleven, cried out at the reception desk. Her long blonde hair was tied up and her brown eyes were the color of freshly turned dirt. Her pale skin was etched in light scars from training in the dances: the clear sign of dancer with no Blessing protection and no proper teaching. She clutched something in her hand. "I can only do it today."

"We already told you. You were too late, there will not be a slot for you today," the woman told her.

"Please." The girl was young. Many looked at her in pity.

"Is she next?" Sarcoline stepped forward to the desk, sullen. "After me?"

"No." The receptionist shook her head. "There are many names before her."

"Let her take it," Sarcoline suggested. "I'll give up my spot."

If they one more hour, then maybe. Maybe they would have. . .

The receptionist scratched out his name and read out the next, ignoring Sarcoline. They were pushed out of the way. The man who was called accepted the spot, dashing the girl's hopes. As the man walked away to be tested, Arna found the girl staring at them.

"Are you okay? Where's your mom?" Arna asked her.

"Not here. This is your fault!" She glared at Arna as she sobbed. She dropped what she was holding to wipe her eyes, revealing an amber-coated saffron pendant necklace. Arna stared at it as she cried. "I know I would have been a Child if you hadn't ruined everything."

Many people wore vervain or holly pendants as good luck and remembrance for Vervain and Ilex. This was his first time seeing a saffron pendant. Saffron was never meant to be remembered by history. *There are no accidents.*

(make it hidden)
itwassilence.

Arna released his closed hands.

"No," Sarcoline stepped in, kneeling down to her. "You can't guarantee that, but you are a dancer now and that means you have another chance another day."

It almost sounded like he was trying to convince himself more than her.

"My mom won't let me. I ran away to do this. If I go home, she'll never let me dance again," the girl cried, falling to the floor in her near silent sobs. Sarcoline soothed her for a minute before he went back to the receptionist and argued with her that the girl be given a spot.

The small girl's voice called to Arna moments later, "I'm sorry."

Arna knelt next to her.

"I got mad and said a bad thing," she said. "Mom says it all the time. She's ashamed of me not having Blessings." The girl wiped her tears and clenched her pendant tight. Her brown eyes were red but determined. "But you aren't the one who convinced the Gods to abandon us, that was their decision. They didn't have to."

They didn't have to. I made them. Arna smiled at her. "Maybe you'll be able to convince them to love us again."

Arna looked back to Sarcoline: the embodiment of proof that Arna could fix things. He stood without breaking, without worrying. As if this set back meant nothing. And in his shoulder's Arna saw a familiar twitch. On his smiling face, Arna saw himself in the mirror.

He stood. Sarcoline's name rested on his lips. When Sarcoline turned to Arna, Arna saw every instance before. He was meeting his brother in Xeysis after twelve years: the dying light. He was listening to his friends talk about how Sarcoline had kept them all together, how he had always been the one they relied on.

[Glass roses sparkle.]

When Sarcoline caught him staring, he began to glower. Silence filled the space between them: distant chirping, thunder, so many bells. He motioned for Arna to follow. Like a ghost, Arna did. Once they dropped the girl off at the Vivicent seats, they walked to find an open practice room. Once they were alone, Sarcoline's rather disdained look turned to betrayal and frustration.

Arna tried to speak but was unable to find the words. They were stricken from his mind as his brother started to implode.

"It's not your fault. I knew it wouldn't work." Sarcoline fought back tears. The ever present spark in his voice, the one filled with passion and hope and vigor, died.

[Glass roses break.]

"I was so frustrated in my Holly variation. I think I put too much hostility into it," Sarcoline laughed, devoid of humor. Sarcoline gripped the dance bar, placing his forehead on the mirror.

"We can get you another chance," Arna offered. He wasn't sure how, but he'd find a way.

"It won't work!" Sarcoline screamed, collapsing against the bar further. "I failed."

Arna's heart ached. What was he to do? Sarcoline could reach it, but it was clear that Sarcoline believed he never would. Their ploy had failed. He would not have another chance that day, and even if he got the chance in the future. . . Arna wanted to see it. Despair filled Arna as he stood behind his brother. Their reflections melding into one.

Arna had only kept pressing, kept fighting, kept believing because he believed that Sarcoline would be his path forward. And now. . ? Now he'd never see it. Now there was no chance it could happen. Everything they'd both fought for was a waste.

In the mirror was the faintest reflection of burning candles: six of them. And between them was a mirage of flowers shaped beings sitting in silence. His eyes were so brown he nearly thought they could be confused for black.

There was a pop, like a metronome. The candles sounded in unison. One, two, three, four. . . And there, enough times that it no longer was a word but a feeling:

[again]

He'd been driven mad for years by the Gods who forced him to build himself up, back to basics each and every time. All to create the foundation for Understanding something that did not yet exist.

[again]

If Sarcoline had to see the world, like Arna had to, then the guiding had to be the same through to the end. Much of Arna's testing had been done blind: him being told things with no direction. Yet, when it came to Understanding, it was always harsh, directed, and cruel.

[again]

Arna began reciting scriptures in his head and leveled his eyes on Sarcoline's back. Arna clenched his fists. Perfection was glass, was not enough. To reach Understanding the one must be more.

Arna did not believe in himself, but he believed in Sarcoline because he had worked for this more than anyone. Sarcoline had wanted it badly enough that he'd faithfully trusted Arna without question. In order to succeed, one had to defy. If there was a path forward, it was through his brother. And even if the rest of the world never saw it, Arna would. Sarcoline would Understand.

Be thorough. The air twisted, it pulled at Arna's Blessings. Sarcoline was close, needing just one more push. Just one more break before the silver and white could fill the gaps and shine.

(Again.)

"It's not easy to Understand," Arna said, calloused and being as rude as he could. "That is why it is only ever accomplished by Children and the best of the best."

Sarcoline stiffened and then spun around from where he stood; tears were streaming down his face. His eyes were filled with so much resentment that it made Arna almost doubt himself. They were the eyes that cursed Arna for being Blessed, that cursed all Children for being Blessed. Arna had seen the same eyes on himself in mirrors, over twelve years, as he was told to stand up and keep going. The difference between destiny and chance was a choice.

Sarcoline voice dripped in venom. "Why did they have to pick *you?* Why does history forget and erase those who... Why is it always you?"

Arna wanted Sarcoline angry, but not to resent him more. Carefully, he directed the anger. "'Upon you we grant Blessings so that you may thrive, and so that our brilliance may shine through you.' The Gods decide what we need."

Sarcoline glared at Arna as if to say, *you don't mean that.* Arna did not believe his brother incapable, much as Sarcoline must have assumed by the quote. Arna let Sarcoline misunderstand.

"I do." The Gods always gave a soul what they needed, and Sacoline could do this.

Sarcoline shattered completely. There were no tears as Sarcoline's faith and trust died. He became a shell of the person he was moments before.

Please work.

"Why must I be forgotten? Why must I be erased? Why will I only ever be *good?*"

The words struck Arna. In that moment he could picture Incarnate Dreams fully. It had been there formulating, manifesting, festering. It had been bits and pieces mosaicked into a whole, but the full art was now before him. Returning home. Facing his past. Meeting those who cared. Visualizing was not about the past, but the future.

Arna wanted to make a world where Blessings no longer mattered. Even after he danced, he wanted to help people push their talents in ways they never thought they could. Now he could see the dance, feel it in his bones, saw it in Sarcoline fully.

For Alis. For Arco.

Arna glared at his brother and his brother collapsed to the floor. There was a visceral sorrow that Sarcoline exuded as his knees thudded down. Sarcoline tried to wipe away at tears that were not there, turning his face red. He was racked with silent sobs, caving in on himself.

Arna knelt down to him.

Sarcoline screamed in silent abject terror, clinging to Arna. The room filled with nothing more than the metronome of popping candles. Arna hugged Sarcoline and squeezed. Sarcoline heaved, until he started cackling and choking on his words.

"I just wanted it so much. I just want it so much." Sarcoline looked up to Arna, tears finally falling. "All I want to do is *dance,* Arna. Everyone keeps telling me to give up. To trade my place for others! Just like I did for that girl. And I always do. I always do it because I know... One day I'll be knocked from my place by someone more talented, more skilled, more perfect than I could ever be. And then I'll be nothing."

Sarcoline laughed again, wildly. "I had hoped, prayed. I never wanted to change the world. I never wanted to make everyone like me, let alone respect me. I know I'll never be special. I just want to dance, Arna. That's all I've ever wanted. I don't want to be a historian. I don't want to work as a researcher or a teacher. I don't want to study things of the past forever. Not if it's without dance."

Sarcoline shook as if he was freezing, laughed as if he were dying. He collapsed in on himself, curling his head between his knees. The lights sparked around them, going out one by one until there was none but the light from the candles, and Sarcoline was about to vanish.

"The Gods only love a few and abandon the rest. I will never be a Child. I'll never have A.Reverence," Sarcoline screamed into the abyss, with a voice so soft it was almost not heard. "What is the point?"

"You exist, Arco. That is enough," Arna called back. "So long as you breathe, you can dream. So long as you dream, you will dance. Your dream is worth something because it matters to you."

There was a long pause where the two orbits collided. The lights flickered back on as if they had never gone out. One set of brown eyes and another that flickered black met. All at once the tension in the room swirled with a haze, and a consistent eight count click. "Again," bounced across the walls in a constant tempo. Six shadows danced.

"I. . ." Sarcoline dropped his sentence. "I Understand."

A shiver ran down Arna's spine. Sarcoline's eyes filled once more, with the same prismatic light. And like every dancer who had mastered one of the Dances before: Sarcoline was glowing the white light of mastery.

Arna's hand shook as he struggled to breathe. Was this how the Gods always felt when they guided him? Only another Master of a section could see the glow, and Sarcoline was beginning to spark blinding white. "Dance it."

Sarcoline nodded, struggling to his feet in apprehension yet determination. Just as he turned to get a set of fans, Gingerline threw herself into the room. "Arna. They called your name!"

Once more, brown eyes met brown eyes, and an unspoken resolution was made. *Later.* Later they would prove it to themselves, but not here. Not now.

Gingerline filled them in as they returned to the main hall. The man who had taken Sarcoline's last chance left early, in a steam of anger at being dismissed according to Gingerline. Arna's stomach twisted in knots of frustration. He had a hard time not hating the man. Sarcoline deserved the spot, even if he had not been ready.

"Incarnadine Vivicent." Arna's name was called as he walked in. Like marching to a funeral, Arna approached the receptionist and withdrew. She nodded, called the next name who did not respond, and the third who withdrew. One after another people withdrew their names from the waitlist until the she said, "Honeysuckle Dawn."

"Yes." The little blonde girl from before jumped up. Before going to proctor, however, she walked up to Arna and gave him her pendant. She said nothing before hurrying off towards the back.

"With that we end today's Mastery Tests. If you'd like to register for next month, please approach the desk in an orderly fashion," The speakers announced their final call, in the familiar A.I. voice.

The sound barriers in the room vanished, indicating that people should leave. The room refused to empty. Some went to sign up, but most others were glued to their seats, eyes held on the doors. Prayers were recited in hushed voices. All results would be announced online at the end of the day, yet no one cared.

"You okay?" Amaryllis asked Sarcoline in a hushed voice when they got to the Vivicent seats. She spoke nearly too quiet to hear. Sarcoline held up two fingers. She placed their heads together at the temple, in comfort. "Well, I'll make smoothies and we can—"

Their words drifted into near silence, as they spoke with their eyes and their messages. The room was filled with a tense hum. A single girl's name was repeated in prayer.

Let her succeed.

When Honeysuckle walked out of the testing hall with Zaffre and Ebru after an hour, she was beaming ear to ear. There were cheers in the room, and she jumped startled by the outcry of those who had been wishing for her success. Cheeks flushed, she clung to an exhausted Zaffre who smiled. Ebru, who walked with them, was pissed. He stalked over, past Honeysuckle and Zaffre, to Sarcoline.

On the displays of the room, the final results were shown, names with new masteries. They would be repeated online on the public website. Arna found the names that mattered.

```
Aureolin Begonia Mastery Certified in
        The Holly Variation (Through Understanding)

Honeysuckle Dawn Mastery Certified in
        The Holly Variation (Through Knowledge)

Eburnean Hue Mastery Certified in
        The Holly Variation (Through Worship)

Sarcoline Vivicent Mastery Certified in
        The Twin Fans Variation (Through Powers)
        The Holly Variation (Through Powers)
```

"You gave up your spot for someone who was only going to fail?" Ebru snapped at Sarcoline as soon as he was close enough. Ebru looked devastated.

"Yes. All so a little girl could dance." Sarcoline shrugged. "I'll try again in another three years."

The little girl in question, came to their side and Arna handed her back her pendant. She looked amongst them all, as if searching for confirmation. Of what, Arna was not sure. She did not ask.

"Which means you have it now," Ebru said in a hushed voice, filled with awe. All eyes in the room turned towards them, listening intently.

Ebru glanced back to the exiting judges and walked away. He hurried over to Cyclamen. Had his competitive nature overtaken him?

Please. Arna wanted to believe in another miracle.

[Smell the saffron and holly.]

"What is he doing?" Amaryllis asked.

No one answered her, and Arna was not sure anyone knew. No one else understood what Sarcoline was trying at first, but as Ebru fought with Cyclamen more, Arna heard his sister gasp. Ebru stood talking for minutes, animated, and pointing at the Vivicents. Quickly, their voices overtook the room, and those who had simply chosen to stay for Honeysuckle started heckling as well.

"Give him the spot!" Someone yelled.

Arna's heart stopped beating. *Please help him.*

[Vervain is a hidden secret, poison and cure.]

Ebru managed to convince Cyclamen and the other judges to walk over. Arna took a deep breathe. Ebru may have given Sarcoline the chance, but Arna needed to secure it. He thought of every possible loophole, exception, and rule.

There were twelve ways to be declared a Master of a section of the tests. One, the primary way, was the official tests, however the additional eleven could be used by a Master outside of official settings. Most people did not know the exceptions existed, and those who did were often embarrassed at the idea of the attempt, for it was harder and it had to be public. Of the eleven ways, only option six was viable:

A dancer, backed by at least one Master in the Section from an official dance house, can request an exception on the day of the tests. At least two Masters backed by a different dance house must agree that the Dancer did not have an appropriate opportunity to attempt the dances earlier in the day. The dancer must have access to all appropriate tools and music at the time of their request.

On the back wall were the performance fans of all the variations, calling to Arna and evoking a strange longing in him.

Per the third rule of fan ownership: all consecrated performance fans belong to Xeysis and the fan maker who created them. All the fans in this room were made by Arna's father.

We can do this.

"Ebru tells me that you gave up your spot so this young lady could dance." Cyclamen's tone almost sounded too pure, in a form of mockery. "She was the first child to pass our tests in twelve years. Giving her your spot was admirable. We must give you our thanks."

"I don't need it," Sarcoline stated quickly.

Cyclamen then smiled at Sarcoline. "I've heard something very interesting, and it intrigues me."

"No." Zaffre disagreed, "He is not—"

"However, while it is unfortunate we cannot give you an exception." Cyclamen cut their father off with a wave of his hand.

"It was the only viable option," Arna stepped in. "Everyone in this room agreed."

"Do you suggest that we give everyone the chance to retest?" Cyclamen laughed.

"Was it or was it not the correct choice?" Arna asked. Cyclamen's brow furrowed, clearly trying to figure out what Arna was suggesting.

Sarcoline and Arna glanced at each other at the same time. Sarcoline was in no position to dance. He'd be lucky if his body made it. He'd done two full sets already that day, and while A.Reverance dancers could do it without a care, Sarcoline was not one of them.

Sacroline dancing as he had that day was already exceedingly dangerous. The weight of the dances and the use of his Blessings could injure him.

If Sarcoline failed, he had to wait another full year before he could pass. With what Sarcoline was attempting, he'd become a laughingstock. It would never be a secret.

Yet. . .

There was a pleading on Sarcoline's face, directed to Arna: *Believe in me.*

Arna smiled: *I do.*

"It was," Cyclamen said, his pride winning in the end.

"Then they did not have the appropriate opportunity," Arna said and all at once the DHS member's faces grew stern. Sarcoline stood close, behind Arna.

"Ginger," Arna called to his sister. "They said that Arco was not give the appropriate opportunity to attempt his dance."

When they were younger, speaking of the rules, they always found it funny that the Master who backed the Dancer did not have to be a judge. They just had to be a Master of the appropriate section.

Their father told them this was because the rule was designed to allow for Dancers, who did not have the backing of larger dance houses and Masters who were consistently better than them, to be able to succeed.

"Is this *your* declaration?" Ebru asked.

"No. It's mine." Gingerline answered, stepping up to Arna's other side.

"What?" Zaffre hissed.

"Well? I have the time to watch, and you're right, Cyclamen, he wasn't given the appropriate opportunity to attempt the dance," Ebru said, declaring his allegiance to the Vivicents in a way Arna had not been sure he'd do in public.

"With that, three have agreed." Sarcoline said, dropping his things to the floor.

There was a brief pause as all the judges around them and the witnesses in the room, parsed what was happening. Cyclamen found humor in it. "We have the judges prepared."

The man was setting Sarcoline up for public failure. Amongst them all, it was unspoken what Sarcoline wanted to attempt. In the man's desire to put Sarcoline in his place, Sarcoline was going to shatter the world.

"Absolutely not," Zaffre disagreed, but Arna was already moving. Quickly he grabbed his father's wrist and dragged him to the glass cabinets where the fans lay waiting. Zaffre said, "If your brother fails, they will play dirty, Arna. We need to back off now."

"Do you underestimate the genius under your roof?" Arna used the word for his brother, the word that was never used for those who were nonChildren. The word was enough for Zaffre to stumble after Arna across the room, knowing that Arna was right.

"You can't use those!" Cyclamen called to them, taunting.

"Under fan use protocol three of the Mastery test rules any fans can be used, so long as they are official property of the dancer or their dance house and have been approved for official use as either performance or practice fans," Arna recited.

"These are performance fans, Arna," Zaffre said pulling his hand back as Arna brought it to the biometric scanner to open.

"Trust us," Sarcoline said stepping up as the intercom system cracked and the music of Blue Rose Fears played. At the desk counter, Amaryllis stood with her hand hovering over a keyboard.

After a second more, Zaffre's hand landed on the glass biometric reader and the glass opened. Arna glanced over the fans, his fingers twitching and aching to touch the fabric and hold their weight. Before he could reach out in his greed, Sarcoline grabbed them and returned towards the center of the room where Gingerline and Ebru had moved the chairs out of the way.

When Sarcoline returned to the center of the room, he laid the fans out per the proper layout for Blue Rose Fears Understanding. He stood still for a moment, and Arna meandered his way to stand before Sarcoline. Like a mirror. When Sarcoline opened his eyes again, they did not leave Arna's face.

Please, Xeyaro, guide him.

> [*A Child he is not.* Xeyaro responded veiled like behind a bubble.
> *I cannot guide him. That was you.*]

Be with him, where I cannot.

> [*We are.* Xeyaro's voice faded away.]

There was another brief moment of silence. Sarcoline then said, steady and low, "My name is Sarcoline Vivicent of the Vivicent Studio, DHS ID 867322. I am testing for Understanding of the Gods. I will be dancing the Blue Rose Fears Variation."

There was a sharp intake of breaths.

Zaffre turned to Arna, desperate, unable to form the words. Arna kept his eyes locked on Sarcoline with silent prayers in his mind. Thousands of questions in the form of invisible daggers were thrown his way as all eyes turned to them. A small hand grabbed his. Honeysuckle, who had not left, clung to Arna staring at Sarcoline in open anticipation. She clutched her pendant.

"You may begin," Ebru's voice called, and the music began, through the speakers, crystal clear and familiar.

Sarcoline's first step was worried, fearful, scared. Then the world came ALIVE.

Sarcoline   g   l   i   d   e   d   across the floor.

All eyes were drawn to the man who twisted about,
with fans in hand and steps ingrained into his soul.

SNAP

An open fan.

TOSS

A collective gasp.
Catching the fan
before it
touched

the floor.

Arna had never seen his brother dance in person before and for a moment he almost lost his own concentration.

Refined like a stone
Polished till it glowed
Pressurized under years of heat
A reminder

(All gemstones needed time to solidify.)
(Sand and dust melded together.)

[All glass could be repaired.]

Rose winds
          t w i s t e d
                    about the room,
                              as the fabric of the fans whipped
about.

Each step was calculated and executed with a precision that could only be done with years of dedicated teaching.

From a technical standpoint, the moves were executed perfectly: the spins on time, the story accurate, and steps percise. However, that was never enough to complete a variation at Understanding. Divinity needed to bleed through, collapse upon the world and twist it.

[Petals on the wind. Roses in the air.]

Sarcoline glowed white nearly silver. For those who could see it, that was. Impossible to ignore, the glow of Mastery seeped off his skin like dew, dripping and creating ripples against the hardwoods that resonated outwards.

(what is a guide?)

[*What is silence?*]

(what is a story?)

Between.

Sarcoline's Understanding of Blue Rose Fears was darker than any variation version Arna knew. Despite the darkness and horror there was so much beauty, so much majesty and brilliance.

The picture was painted of everything Arna ever knew the dance to be.

The depth of it was palpable,
the movements calling the viewer closer.

And a prayer spoken, as Sarcoline stilled.

Step.

Step.

Step.

Step.

Step.

Step.

Sarcoline stood before Arna. Their faces apart by no more than a fan length. The edge of the stage, deviating from proper protocol.

A breath.   A pause.

Sarcoline spun away, whipping the fans with him, a rippling sound filling the room louder than the music itself. A breaking against the brilliant beauty of the music, as he collapsed to the ground without the grace of the first steps. He retained all the control, heaving and staring to the ceiling.

Click.

The fans touched the floor, as they were meant to at the end of the dance. The room was filled with a rippling silence a crescendo of awe. The lights were bright. No one moved, but no one breathed either.

That was, until they had to, and Arna found himself breathing in time with his brother.

When Sarcoline stood and bowed, the trance was broken.

He said with a quivering voice, "Thank you."

His body was shaking, and Arna had little doubt that he was struggling to remain in control without falling.

"Yes!" Amaryllis cheered. She was the only one who had the gall to clap with Arna at first until Honeysuckle quickly followed. The smile that graced Sarcoline's face was that of pure bliss, uncaring that only three people were pleased by the result.

"That's Mastery," Ebru said breathless.

The room became a vortex of voices and movement, as the fans were collected, and others were asked if they wanted to attempt to dance. No one said yes while the judges conferred. Amaryllis was at their side quickly, with their things in her arms.

"I did it, Am," Sarcoline said leaning against her with his full body weight.

"You did," she said with a dark smile, glaring at the judges who confirmed Sarcoline's mastery. A few people typed in the air and Arna had no doubt the whole performance had been recorded.

Good. Arna slipped his arm under his brother's shoulder, ignoring the questions that were asked. They needed to get him home. He did not say it, but Arna heard it in the way that Sarcoline let Arna help him: *Thank you.*

Up above, the display screens changed.

> *Sarcoline Vivicent Mastery Certified in*
> > *The Twin Fans Variation (Through Powers)*
> > *The Holly Variation (Through Powers)*
> > *The Blue Rose Fears Variation (Through Understanding)*

The variations exist because the world is constantly evolving. They mirror a specific time and place. They explain fundamental values of our society. However, mortality is not stagnate. Thus, we always have another variation that will come for us.

There is always more to learn. There will always be more room to grow.

— On why there are five variations.

Dance 17

Hope

Incarnadine

13 Xeyan

29 Days Left

"I want to go home! I want to end this all now! Just let me go!"
"Is that so? You want to go home?"
"Yes."
"No. We will tell you when you are ready to go back."

Sarcoline slept like the dead as the internet imploded in analysis videos, articles, and comments about his leaked mastery videos. At first Arna had been pissed, but then he couldn't care less, because while there were those online who were furious at Sarcoline or scared, most were in awe. Sarcoline dared to do what they dared not, in public. His audacity no longer left people online stunned. Instead. . . They were filled with hope.

> ► If Sarcoline can reach Understanding, then I can become a lawyer!
>> ► Don't be too confident in yourself.
> ► Has this ever been done before?
>> ► Yes, but Sarcoline is the first in a few decades to attempt mastery after testing was technically over.
>>> ► I mean reaching Understanding. He's not a Child.
>>>> ► Oh. No. Never. He's the first.

The first. Arna beamed at the comments.

> ► Arco: Chosen Child?
>> ► I believe it.
>> ► I believe it.
>> ► I believe it.
>> ► Makes more sense than Incarnadine.

Rolling his eyes, Arna closed the forum and started writing movement notes in his variation notebook. Every variation of the dances had a specific fan formation, the formation on the ground that the fans were placed so that a dancer could grab them easily between dances. While dancers could modify it for their own performances with approval, Arna had to create one that was best suited for Incarnate Dreams, that matched the message.

[*He did well,* Xeyaro praised.]

[*I'm so—*]

[*—excite—*]

The God's voices were like distant static: a radio station he could only dial into every so often. It was a sign of the waning connection between mortals and Gods. Arna was trying not to fret about it: to no avail.

He knew where to go, but with the closing deadline he feared he would not be able to make it in time.

He still had so much to do. He needed more help.

Arna sat at the table in the living room writing in his notebook, trying to parse together what the Gods were talking about. As he wrote, it became abundantly clear that it was not worth his time trying to figure out what they were saying. They sounded happy, and Arna assumed that was because Sarcoline passed, *and* because it proved Arna's concept.

Rosmarinus walked in.

Carrying his bags, over his shoulder and in his hands. The two stared at each other in open-faced shock. Rosmarinus had Jasione's face, as his twin. Only Rosmarinus was not a Child. He had brown eyes, brown skin, and dark black hair. He was clean shaven and wore glasses on his nose for his augmentations and sight. Where Jasione was lithe, Rosmarinus was muscular. It was the body of a well-toned swimmer and a professional athlete.

"Arna," Rosmarinus said with a soft voice. He'd always been soft spoken. He had never been a part of the Golden Generation. Nor had he forced his way into the group the way Jasione did.

When Arna and Jasione met, at six years old, Rosmarinus was there. They were playing, watched by their grandfather. Their father had died before they were born in a research expedition outside of Xeysis, when a superstorm appeared without warning. Their died mother when they were four: a Blessing technical malfunction within the petals as she was doing routine checks. Arna had clung to Jasione, claiming him as a friend, and completely disregarded Rosmarinus for years. He regretted it now. Rosmarinus was never around, choosing to stay home with his grandfather instead of being constantly ignored.

"Welcome back," Arna greeted him.

Rosmarinus finished the trek into the room, placed his things down, and sat in a chair in front of Zaffre's first fan. It hung above his head like a crown. Rosmarinus fidgeted with his hands taking a couple of extremely shallow breaths, before clasping his hands together and squeezing them tight.

Strange...

"I know you and I never really got along," Rosmarinus said, finally.

Suddenly, Arna was not surprised by the man's nerves. He too had expected himself to hate the man upon seeing him. He was the one who fully stepped in to take Arna's place as Jasione broke down. He acted as the eldest son, where Arna should have. Yet, Arna held no resentment nor jealousy. Instead, he faced his best friend's brother wondering what it would take to be friends this time. He wanted simply to thank Rosmarinus for all he did, without overwhelming him.

"What? No. I was too self-absorbed," Arna opted for humor instead. Rosmarinus hesitated. *How do I convince him I don't hate him?* The same way he proved it to the others. Arna tried, "I hear you are going for Philanthropist of the Year."

From the charity donations and the events Rosmarinus had attended, it was a clear he was aiming for the title. Rosmarinus was doing a world tour, trying to save everyone and help all those who were without Blessings at a global scale. His face was everywhere in advertisements, trying to get money for the fund that had helped billions of lives.

"Yes. I'm trying to end Cyclamen's ten-year streak," Rosmarinus said, delightfully innocent as if he had not declared to destroy reign of the most beloved man in the world.

" Good." Arna grinned maliciously at the underlying threat and Rosmarinus smiled back.

Above Rosmarinus' head the first fan shined in the light that filtered through the window.

Rosmarinus' smile faltered. "Arna I never—"

"Where's mom?" Sarcoline's sleepy voice echoed from the stairs as he walked down, cutting Rosamrinus off. "Rus?"

Sarcoline rushed in, tackling Rosmarinus in a large hug. Arna was rushed by the waves of jealousy for a moment. Arna focused on the first fan and the memory of careful hands.

Family helps each other.

He respected Rosmarinus for all he gave up and all he'd done. He, too, was a part of their family.

"Mymy's," Arna answered quickly and Sarcoline let go of Rosmarinus, remembering that Arna was in the room.

"Dad?" Sarcoline asked, unperturbed.

"Work." Arna was not told why his father had been called into the DHS so early that morning. Potentially due to Sarcoline? The failing Blessings? Maybe the weather?

Arna did not shut his notebook when Sarcoline sat down. He passed his brother blueberry pancakes that were on the table before him.

"Dad thinks you mastered it while traveling."

"It's better for his heart that he thinks that," Sarcoline said as he began to eat. "It's better for everyone."

He ignored Rosmarinus and Sarcoline who began to talk of Rosmarinus' adventures. Although things still felt off, monumentally, no one addressed it. Rosmarinus accepted the bridge that Arna had made. They'd be a united family again.

"Did you get Understanding on your travels? Where?" Gingerline asked, sitting down on Arna's left, surprising him. She was dressed in a bright green dress with a silver lily pattern.

"Don't worry, Ginger," Sarcoline said, cheery and bright. "You know I won't say."

"You're the worst!" she laughed, unperplexed. She nudged Arna and asked, "What are you working on?"

Arna paused. For a moment he wanted to tell her. His heart leapt in fear: *not yet* but soon. Telling her was different from asking Ebru for help, even when he thought she could help.

I can do this.

Turmoil spiraled through him.

!!!

No more.

He would not ruin this moment with his fear of the end of the world. Instead of digging his nails into his skin, he squeezed his pencil tighter and breathed slowly. His Blessings silenced the rest.

He met her eye, met Sarcoline's, turned back to the book and continued to work without a word. Taking this as an indication that he would not answer, the three continued talking about school and the dances and what Sarcoline saw across the world until the pancakes were gone and their drinks were empty. Rosmarinus excused himself to go upstairs in order to unpack and rest.

"Do you want to dance?" Gingerline offered, and Arna slammed his book shut. Sarcoline and Gingerline jumped.

"Let's go." Arna gave a disarming smile and before they could confirm if he meant it, he went upstairs to change.

When Arna finally returned downstairs, they were both waiting inside his practice room. They sat stretching, giving him expressions of mixed anticipation and apprehension. The desire to dance prickled under his skin. Arna stepped past both of them, still warmed up enough from his morning practice. He threw on an Ivumalis song, turned the speakers on loud, and began.

When the three of them danced, Arna smiled and his eyes were trained to their figures in the reflection. Through mortals, he found the Gods. Through his siblings, he saw himself. Three songs later, Arna sat on the ground laughing as Sarcoline scowled and Gingerline spun in circles.

Slowly, Sarcoline collapsed down next to Arna and Gingerline stopped spinning.

With a giggle she hurried over, sitting next to the two of them. The three stared into the mirrors beathing softly. For a moment they were children again, laughing after a terrible practice. Peace filled Arna. This was his home. He finally had his siblings back.

Arna studied both of his siblings for a long moment, analyzing how both had changed. Gingerline's face was no longer round as a child, but her eyes retained their dash of chaos. His brother's constant grimace framed his face, punctuated by playful grins. There were entire chapters Arna had missed in the twelve years he was gone, but for a moment, in those mirrors, he could read each one.

"Do you like dance, Ginger?" Arna asked, thinking of the girl who used to dream of having her name known to the world, embroidered on cloth, and worn across cities. Was that still her dream or had that changed?

She blinked confused but he locked her down with his eyes, urging her to answer. She did so with a shake of her head. "Of course! I love dance."

"No. I know you love dance. But do you like it?" Was it the way that Sarcoline did, the way that Arna did?

There was a long moment of silence as a new Ivumalis song began to play in the background.

"Of course, I. . ." Gingerline started.

"She was the only one who could dance Understanding," Sarcoline answered instead, speaking over her. "Dad had to do penance. And one dancer per section. He couldn't do Worship and Understanding. I didn't have Understanding, but Powers doesn't make much money. Worship is okay, but students kept leaving and dad wasn't teaching, and—"

"I *like* dancing," Gingerline protested with a pout.

"Would we have lost the house?" Arna asked Sarcoline without letting his eyes leave Gingerline. She breathed in deeply, in six counts, akin to what he sometimes did when he panicked.

"I don't know," Sarcoline admitted. "When Jasi and Rus moved in—after their grandfather died, you know?—Rus started putting all his pay checks to fund the studio, but it wasn't enough. We needed more to keep up the maintenance and tech. He was only sixteen."

Which was to say that Rosmarinus was a major backer of their family's funds even then. He kept their family afloat for years. Arna respected him greatly.

"Rus couldn't do it alone," Gingerline cut in, voice low and angry at being ignored. "You weren't here. That left me. The whole of the DHS is against dad. They listen to Cyclamen. I had to do it, for the family."

For the family. Arna bristled. Chapters of childhood were ripped from them just like he'd torn apart his own. Dreams ruined, and for what? *No more.* Arna said, "Cyclamen is a rat."

"He's not," Gingerline disagreed, snapping her focus back on Arna. Arna wanted to argue, but he let his sister continue. "He donates consistently. He keeps the world in his palm by appearing like a saint. He regularly attends church, and the world loves him. He's everything the Vivicents used to be. He's an apex predator, and we are injured."

The rest of high society wanted to see them fall, even if they never admitted it publicly. Cyclamen used his position, fame, and the lack of faith in the Vivicents to his advantage. It was admirable in some ways. All the same, the man was ruthless and cruel and had hurt Ebru. Arna hated him.

"You were always the best of us, but without you. . . I . . ." Gingerline stumbled over her words.

"Do you like dance, Gingerline?" Arna tried again, this time knowing the answer before she retorted.

"Why do you keep asking that?" she squeaked. "I do!"

Arna thought of a little girl dressed up in bright lime instead of dark greens. She wore red instead of black.

"You don't dress the way you used to." She was always the chaotic child, running about as if guided by Azza herself. For years Phlox, who had eyes so dark they were almost the color of Azza, had said that Gingerline should have been picked instead.

"Black is the color of the Chosen," Gingerline said. "I thought that by wearing it, I could be closer to you. . ." Gingerline's voice faded as she stared. There was a spark behind her eyes as they narrowed. "Oh!" She finally understood. "Yes. . . If I could, I'd be a fashion designer."

He thought of the little girl who used to make them do fashion shows on the weekends, the girl who made her fingers bleed. Her hands were covered in bandages when she presented her first hand-stitched shirt, with frayed edges. The girl who once had a desk covered in sketches, who taught him about materials, who had given him the idea for new fans when she was thirteen years old: presented on a notebook. It was the same idea he used years later.

Over the years, Sarcoline always looked like he was straight off the runway and wore the clothes without a hint of embarrassment. The clothes were good enough to be from a famous designer, but it wasn't one Arna could find online, no matter how hard he searched. As soon as Sarcoline had been born, he had been her doll. As soon as he could walk, she constantly made him walk back and forth in her new clothes.

Gingerline admitted, "Arco is the only one who wears my clothes now. Even though he hates it."

"I don't hate it," Sarcoline corrected with a gruff voice. "Your clothes are good."

"You hate me!" she corrected with a snap.

"And all other clothes are garbage in comparison."

Gingerline glared at Sarcoline. He laughed, bright and loud. After a few seconds her glare was accompanied by a bit of redness at her cheeks.

"You should be a designer," Arna said, breaking them apart with a smile of his own.

Gingerline shook her head and looked away, eyes shifting in nerves. "No one would want my designs."

Arna turned to Sarcoline, who was rolling his eyes so far back, they were only white. When he finally met Arna's gaze, Sarcoline tilted his head in confusion.

. . .

Arna took a few solid breathes. It was time to ask for help.

This was the way to Incarnate Dreams.

"They will," Arna insisted to Gingerline. "I do."

Gingerline's head snapped up at him: startled.

"You will." Arna looked to the ceiling. "Arco can be heir to the family. You don't have to worry about running the Vivicent studio. Arco will. Ancient traditions say the best dancer must take over, doesn't need to be a Child. There have been many of our ancestors who were simply the best choice and not a Child." Albeit only three examples, but it did happen. "And he wants to inherit this place more than anything."

"It's true," Sarcoline agreed. "Rose, Clementine, and Garnet. Besides, Arna is Chosen."

Arna being heir to the Vivicent studio was never an option as the Chosen. Gingerline had always been the apparent, but it was clear that Sarcoline wanted it more.

Gingerline was unconvinced. Instead of trying to force her, Arna started talking about the fashion in other cities. He told her of the sweeping long capes of Zaydiel that mimicked wind, and the droplet dresses of Azis that moved like running water on the body.

She gasped in awe as he described the butterfly wing gowns and starlight inspired outfits of Ixis. She asked about volcanic dresses in Ludiel, and if they were real.

"Fashion always includes flowers here in Xeysis," Gingerline said, almost bored by the idea.

Arna smiled. "And all city specific fashion will include themes of their patron God."

"Why am I even here?" Sarcoline complained.

"Your fault for missing class," Arna and Gingerline said at once. Then they laughed, which made Sarcoline join in. Once again, they were children, without frustration and anger or yelling. Back then the three of them wanted to dance because it brought them together. It was what made them family.

In his sister's smile was the answer to his issues with the Ceremonial clothes, the ones he could not solve.

Gingerline tilted her head, "What's wrong?"

He couldn't continue to keep his sister at a distance, not when she had been the first to reach out to him. She loved him so much that he'd wanted to protect her, but he could see that all she wanted, all she and Sarcoline wanted, was for their family to be whole again.

"I need your help," he admitted to her.

"With?"

[   ]

Arna took a deep breath in and then out, six times. The air was misting and swirling, chimes rang in a chorus of agreement.

[*She's good,* Azza said.]

And that is enough?

[*More,* Azza giggled and spun around the room.]

Arna walked to the loose floorboards in his room, peeling them back and pulling out the fabric, one after another: new oil slick embroidered, old white, and the ribbons he'd collected. He did not look at either of them as he placed the floorboards back. It was only as he placed the materials before Ginger that he finally met the eyes of his siblings.

Sarcoline's mouth hung open. Ginger had a blank face.

Arna pulled out his black notebook and ripped out pages to give to her. "I can give you the designs I've settled on, but my sketches aren't that great. It makes more sense in my head."

Ginger had tears in her eyes.

Sarcoline took the sketches before Ginger could and flipped through them, handing them to Ginger one by one, smile wide on his face and his laugh growing softer and more incredulous. Ginger held them lightly as if cherishing each one.

"Can you help me?" Arna asked her and she nodded vigorously. Within seconds she tightened her grip on the designs and stood.

Arna laughed as Ginger scooped up all the materials and race from the room, kicking off her dance shoes and running away. Sarcoline chased after her and Arna was left alone.

[*What are you waiting for?* Azza breathed.]

Chaos wrapped around him in a hug, clinging to his skin and filling him with fire.

[*Run.*]

Arna ran faster than he ever had before, living the whole way that he did.

Arna stood outside a building: drink in his right hand, sunglasses and hat on, leaning as nonchalantly as he could. Ginger continued to bombard him with questions, sending him better, prettier sketches that he could approve or disapprove. She was quick with each correction he gave, to a point that it was almost terrifying. Each design was better than the last, closer to what he imagined.

All around him the world was a silent montage of life, a breath of quiet where nothing mattered. His Blessings wrapped him in their mirage of shadows and the story of life danced past him. There was no longing. There was no noise. It stalled until it was:

n   o   t   h   i   n   g

Breathe in.

Free hand closed.

Breathe out.

Free hand opened.

Arna checked his mobile when it vibrated again, and the world sprang back into motion.

    `Alis: You had better tell me how he did it.`

    `Rosy: I'd love to, but I love seeing you flustered more.`

Ebru had not messaged him back since the mastery tests. While Arna did call the night before, something was wrong. Ebru insisted there wasn't, but Arna would check in later that night.

He pulled out his fake fan from his pocket and began to work it in his left hand: opened and closed. He hummed to himself, his variation, visualizing what he still needed to do. He'd gotten Sarcoline to Mastery. He'd helped his sister begin to accept a selfish desire. However, the crux of the issue for their group still remained.

"What are you doing?"

Jasione's voice did not startle Arna. He snapped the fake fan shut with a click.

"Hey." Arna smiled. "Your brother is back in town. He got home this morning."

"I know. He came to me first. You aren't supposed to be out alone. You know we can't protect you like this."

"You know I sneak out," Arna laughed, "Don't get all strict with me now."

Jasione's face crumpled. Jasione and his brother were polar opposites. Rosmarinus was like a gentle spring breeze, unfathomable but generally calm. Jasione was an earthquake of rocking emotions and determination. In the past the two stabilized each other, could Rosmarinus do more to stabilize the Golden Generation as a whole? Aureolin considered him one of them, clearly Ginger and Sarcoline did as well.

He'd need to pull Rosmarinus into their group in full.

"What is wrong now?" Arna asked him, placing the thought away for the time and focusing on Jasione.

"More Blessing tech failures and city shutdowns." Jasione shook his head. "This year is worse than last."

It would just keep getting worse, but Arna did not say that. Instead, Arna switched his drink to his left hand and fake fan to his right.

"Why did you call me out here, Arna?" Jasione asked him.

"You're dating my sister," Arna said as an ice breaker. After taking several deep breaths, his heart settled. He was ready for whatever wrath came his way.

Jasione eyed him, mildly disinterested. "That is the brilliant observation that had you calling me out to the center of town? I told you that weeks ago."

Arna never thought he needed Jasione's forgiveness. Like his family, like Aureolin and Phlox, like Ebru, Jasione was another person who accepted things the way they were. It was what he believed, but Jasione was trying to step in for Arna in their group. Instead of being himself, he was trying to be the leader, and struggling because he favored Ginger. He was trying to be the voice of reason.

It was not Jasione. Jasione was an authority, but he was never meant to be a leader or a guide. He was meant to read books in libraries and make plans and schemes. He was good at strategy and tactics, not trying to deal with everyone's emotions all at once.

Or he hadn't been. Arna wasn't sure if Jasione had mastered the skill, but Arna saw that he had been mistaken. Jasione was one of the few people that did need an apology. Because Jasione had done everything for him and his family at the expense of his own dreams.

"Thanks for taking care of her," Arna said. Jasione rolled his eyes. "For taking care of all of them. I know that they suffered."

"They still do. If you stayed where they could watch you, they wouldn't have to worry," Jasione said with a sharp sigh. He was irritated but not expressing the anger, holding it back in a practiced manner.

Ebru said that Jasione was almost imprisoned. He'd broken nearly every law in Xeysis. He had gone off the deep end and Sarcoline corroborated the story. Jasione got their groceries, helped with the bills, lived at their house, and acted as the son Arna never could have been.

"They could stop me," Arna suggested, examining the way that Jasione held himself: stiff, controlled, tired, and withheld.

[*No, they wouldn't,* the Gods retorted.]

"No, they couldn't," Jasione said.

The Jasione he always knew was a bit overconfident and relaxed because the God of Laws and Balance was on his side. This Jasione was not. He was clearly overwhelmed, watching for those who could hurt them. He was searching for a way to escape, to run, to hide: like Arna. Arna was not sure how he did not see it before. This Jasione was afraid of losing everything.

"But again, that's not why you called me out. We could have met at home instead of all the way out here—" Jasione began.

"I'm sorry," Arna cut him off.

Jasione's words died at his throat. He stared at Arna as if he were seeing a wildfire beginning and there was nothing he could do to stop it.

"I never said the words to you. You did everything that I never could. I'm sorry I put that burden on you." Arna needed to give this apology, and he needed to step up, to take the weight off of Jasione finally. Arna had to help him breathe again.

"You did what you had to." Jasione's words were careful, structured, planned, but not honest.

Arna had hurt him in ways he'd never fully know. Despite how much Jasione said that he was forgiven, Arna sensed that there would always be something missing and withheld. Jasione's heart was kept from him, in fear.

"I want you to hear it," Arna insisted. "I am sorry."

A breeze enveloped Arna and Jasione before washing over them and disappearing down the street.

[*Be kind with his heart,* Lumak said, aggrieved.]

Jasione balked, then spoke with leveled speech that did not sit right to Arna. It was just proof of the controlled hand. Jasione smiled like nothing was wrong, but his hands twitched, and his chest heaved like he wanted to scream.

Jasione said, "You did what you had to survive. You were where you were supposed to be."

"You wish I stayed. I should have never gone to Ludiel."

The two stood atop the sturdy ground, as the words knocked them off kilter. It was the admission that Jasione would never voice. He stepped back and took a deep breath, leveling whatever emotion fought to come out.

I need to press more, if he wanted his best friend back.

Jasione searched Arna as if trying to piece together what Arna meant and refusing to see the truth. He shook his head, ignoring what Arna said.

"You came back. . ." The sentence died as Jasione spoke it, his eyes fell to the ground. He was close to falling apart. The grimace at his mouth flinched in anger. The familiar twitch of his shoulders indicated that he was going to explode. How much more longer Jasione keep the anger back?

"I did. You should go to Ludiel," Arna said.

Jasione cocked his head to the side asking another question that Arna ignored. His eyes were wavering, wanting to end the conversation but Arna would not.

Arna needed something real from Jasione or else they'd never move forward. Jasione would always resent what Arna had done, at least a part of him. After all, Arna had left and it was necessary; the anger was a silly feeling that did not matter. It was a convoluted lie that Jasione was clearly fighting to believe even now.

"You already made your choice to stay here, Jasi." Arna meant the nickname, for the first time since he'd returned. It was like greeting an old friend, familiar and serene. "You'll come back. Not because Ginger is here. Not because my family or your family. Not because your friends. Not because of me. You'll come home because Xeysis is your home. Your heart is here."

"Don't tell me you just wanted to talk about traveling advice," Jasi joked instead, trying to diffuse the tension.

Arna pressed on, needing some sort of reaction. Something other than the deflection and the hiding. Something true, raw, uncontrolled. "Some days I'm not sure I deserve your forgive—"

Arna was cut short by Jasi's fist flying towards him, stopping inches from his face.

"Don't you dare finish that," Jasi snarled.

Arna chuckled. "Hitting me would resolve your anger?"

This was the something real he needed. Finally, they could speak without code, without worry, and with all honesty.

He had known Jasi needed justice. In one action Jasi could settle the score, and Arna could pay him back for the years of torment. However, Jasi would have never hurt him. Arna did not flinch for the same reason Jasi started the attack: a conversation. They were both trying to get a reaction out of each other, and they knew each other best.

The two locked eyes and breathed in unison. As the fist hung, all Arna could think of was nightmares. They were always slow, hyper realistic, and could steal a person from a peaceful dream. His variation played out in that moment, dark and disturbing: inspiration for the horror he needed was placed before him. It fell into his grasp as Jasi dropped his hand and shook the tension out of it.

[A chime of victory.]

"You'd never hit me."

Arna kept the inspiration close. He'd have to adjust the music and dance moves, but this was good. He was making progress. He hoped this would help fill the void.

"No. But you want anger from me." Jasi sighed.

"If anyone would be angry at you it would be Ven."

Jasi collapsed against him.

"Once, I was," Jasi said before he hugged Arna and squeezed. "I already got over my anger for you, years ago. I don't need to forgive you for what you did. You came back to us."

Before Jasi could continue Arna jumped in. "Like almost getting locked up?"

Jasi gaped at him, surprised. It was not anywhere on the internet, as if it had been covered up. "Arco told you?"

Arna shook his head. "Ebru."

Jasi blinked surprised. "I didn't realize you two were talking."

"He was also hurt by me, going to the Shadone's. But you nearly destroyed yourself," Arna said, placing his hand on Jasi's shoulder. "I'm home now."

Jasi hesitated for a moment before he laughed. It was filled with sorrow. "Your father couldn't stop me, it was Arco who had to. He was the one who bailed me out, got me to the house, sat me down, and yelled at me telling me to get my act together. That he couldn't lose me too."

"How old?" Arna asked. Arna tossed his empty glass.

"He was seventeen," Jasi admitted.

Arna pictured himself at seventeen, lost and alone, wanting and screaming at the Gods to let him go home, unable to.

"I did not want to listen to him, truth be told, but I was locked at the manor. I could only go places with guards for a year after that," Jasi admitted, a bit embarrassed,

"What changed?" Arna asked.

Sarcoline had said hope and a fervor for believing in Arna. But could that be it?

"Honestly, one day I just woke up and told Arco everything. Found him in his practice room, screamed and yelled at him, telling him everything I'd been holding in and. . ." Jasi shrugged. "Then all I could do was hope. For you. And when you returned, when we were right. . . It proved our faith wasn't for nothing. Don't take that away from me. Please. I won't know what to do."

"I won't take it from you, Jasi. And I'm not asking your forgiveness because I left." Arna hugged Jasi again and squeezed him tight. "I'm back. I'm sorry, it took so long."

Arna worried for a moment if his bones would break from how tightly Jasi squeezed. Hot tears hit Arna's shoulder and Arna tightened his grip. Arna let Jasi cry until the tears stopped.

When Jasi sighed and backed away, they faced eachother as equals once more.

"This is inappropriate, we're in public," Jasi said straightening himself out. He took off his glasses, wiped his eyes, and put them back on. His purple eyes were a bit red but peaceful.

"Phlox always says public is the best place for dramatic displays of affection. It gives people something to talk about."

She said it in a few interviews that he watched over the years.

"That was your first mistake. Phlox can get a person's mind spinning." Jasi chuckled deeply, an adoration there that could not be masked.

"Rude." Phlox's voice sounded from around the corner, appearing before them in shimmering pastel blues, akin to butterfly wings, and a wide brimmed hat. Arna slipped his practice fan away. "I've always adored you, Jasione, but you are far too harsh with me."

"You were claimed by Xeyaro, but your connection to Azza is too great," Jasi mocked her tone. "You know my disdain for the chaos you bring."

[Both Creation and Balance cackled like lightning.]

"Envy sounds so pretty when it comes from you." Phlox kissed them both on their cheeks.

"How long have you been here?" Jasi asked.

"Since before you showed up. I was the one who got drinks with Arna." Phlox smiled brightly at him.

"Why do I need to talk to you?" Jasi asked her.

"Not her. Me," Arna disagreed. Jasi looked back at him. "I called Phlox out, too, but she's early."

"Guilty," Phlox giggled. Arna had a feeling nervous based on the way her eyes darted to and from Jasi. "Now, boys, I'm going to get something else to drink. Do you want anything?"

Jasione and Arna gave her a drink order and she walked away.

"She's constantly giving me a heart attack," Jasi said with an exasperated sigh.

"It's certainly something to get used to," Arna went on. "but I know she wants us to be the invincible trio again."

If Jasi was going to debate that they were not friends or that he did not want it either, he said nothing. These days, from what Arna could tell, Phlox and Jasi got along like water and oil. They were intrinsically built to oppose each other. Yet, neither of them could hate the other. In the chaos of their relationship, they reached balance.

In the past, Jasi and Phlox were like Arna and Ebru, constantly tormenting each other. Whereas Ebru and Arna were vocal, Jasi and Phlox were passive in everything they did, oppositional at all times. Phlox always said they were best friends because they knew each other best. Jasi always said he had to be on his toes so that Phlox did not wreck everything in her dramatic emotions. Arna had a feeling both were true.

The intricacy of their relationship made him think of Ebru. Ebru had always known exactly what Arna was planning before Arna could tell Jasi. Diametrically opposed and allies all the same.

"She ran from us," Jasi finally said. The 'us' sounded a lot like 'me.' Phlox said the others shut her out, but Jasi had stayed. How much of it had been them rejecting her? How much of it had been her rejecting them in order to fit in with the actors who ignored her either way?

"I hurt her," Arna said, but Jasi would know Arna meant all of them.

"Thus, you owe me," Phlox said returning with their drinks. "I deserve to have my friends back. I deserve to have my heartmate back."

She shoved the drinks into their hands.

"We aren't heartmates, Phlox," Jasi disagreed.

"Weird, I think I heard a lie, Arna," Phlox said. "Shouldn't Lumak smite him for that?"

Arna chuckled.

[Earthquakes cackled.]

Jasi shook his head and sipped at his drink with no response. Wind rushed around them.

"You know, Jasi, I also told Arco everything in his dance room," Phlox admitted. "How it felt like I was alone in wanting to save the Golden Generation. How angry I was that I couldn't save all of you. Ven from their family and anguish. You from your self-destruction. Ebru and his shut down. Aureolin and her withdrawal. Ginger and her self-sacrifice. When you were all falling apart, I tried so hard, but no one seemed to notice.

"Nothing I did helped. It made it worse. Then the government wanted to control me, and I felt I was truly alone. No one was coming to save me. But I learned a few years ago that you helped me get out and you were the one who helped me land my first audition. Even if you won't admit you did. I found out through Rosmarinus."

Jasi, who was drinking, choked and coughed, glaring at her.

"That snake," he gasped.

"Your brother is smarter than you are, when it comes to telling me things." She smiled softly at Jasi. "Thank you."

Jasi's cheeks were red from both the choking and his embarrassment of being called out. He looked anywhere but at her. She turned her attention back to Arna. "Now the Golden Generation is united again."

"Almost," Arna corrected. "To do that you need to actually talk to Amaryllis."

It was time. Then they'd get Ebru. Once they were united, he'd be able to finish his dances. The thrumming fire in his bones and the starlight song in his veins, were sending him forward.

"I will not forgive her." Phlox flipped her hair over her shoulder. She spoke with a lazy tone and sipped her drink.

"She took the best photographs you've ever had taken, and you know it," Jasi spoke up with a softness to his tone.

"They were disgusting. Atrocious even. The most despicable things I've ever seen," she said with a whining tone, but there was none of the hostility she'd once had when she told Arna about them.

"They were you and they were beautiful," Jasi added, coaxing her like they were children again and she needed to see reason.

"Exactly." Phlox sipped letting the silence hang. They waited for her to finish drinking and to continue. "It took me years of careful construction to create the image that she shattered in seconds. She showed the world the true me. The one, no one could protect but myself."

[Zaynir and Azza began to bicker.]

[The moon and clouds danced.]

[Aqua and dark green loved deeply.]

"You have us now," Arna reminded her. He could fix this. He believed in himself.

"Now? We are working towards now. Ginger might be speaking to me. Aureolin might finally considering dating me. Ven might finally talk to all of us again. But Ebru only calls me when he needs my pretty face as a date. Dear Jasione, my only heartmate in the whole world, and I are still estranged. And you?"

She said it dramatically, but there was an airy note to it that meant she wasn't serious. She giggled at her own joke.

"Did Amaryllis apologize?" he asked. Maybe he could convince her. . .

"No. She never tried. Because she doesn't need to. She's a Child. Children do what they are good at. It's easier for me to hate her because she is good, than to like her and know that we aren't friends. Or it was. . . " Phlox's mobile rang once, and a smile went wide on her lips. She tilted her head, looking past Jasi and Arna. "Ah. And there she is."

Arna and Jasi looked back; Amaryllis was not there.

"Not behind you. Jasi, Arna and I have a date and you still have work," Phlox said, taking Arna's arm. "We can gather for tea later, Jasi, so we can kiss and make up. But we really must be off."

"Phlox. . ." Jasi said with concern.

"We're best friends, Jasi," she demanded, and he blinked twice before he nodded. She smiled brightly, holding up three fingers like she did as a kid. "Then there is no need for apologies Jasi. We just are. You. Me. Arna."

"The invincible trio," Jasi and Arna said with her together as they had since they were six, hiding from the monsters that plagued her dreams. Phlox smiled wide and Arna laughed with Jasi who was also smiling.

Jasi's mobile rang, cutting the joy short.

"I have to go," Jasi said with a glare into the air. His glasses lit up in color as he picked up the call. "I'll meet you at home for dinner. Phlox, make sure he doesn't get into trouble." Jasi tapped at the headset in his ears and started off. "I'm on my way—"

Jasi paused, looked back, and raised his left wrist up so it crossed his brow. It was a simple movement that could be mistaken for an awkward wave, but Phlox mirrored the move, her left wrist bare of a mark, but her skin sparkled anyway.

Phlox and Arna arrived at the Dancer's Square a half hour later. It was brimming with people and screens showing awards celebrations that were occurring. Phlox expertly wove them both through the crowds towards The Dance House.

Phlox sent Arna a screenshot that was the image of a collection of photographs. "Amaryllis is submitting her final Celebrations portfolio for approval today."

"You follow her account?" And had notifications?

"Of course. On a puppet account, I wouldn't be caught on my own," Phlox said as if she were offended before she winked.

"You want to talk to her now?" That seemed oddly fast, considering her protests earlier.

"I no longer, on principal, need to hate her. You showed me your resolve," she explained. "So, I will accept her friendship again."

"You decided that in the last hour?" Arna thought back to how soft she'd been earlier. Had she decided as soon as she was certain Arna and Jasi were her friends again?

"I decided it when you came home," she explained.

Arna gaped. *What?* But she'd been so adamant that she hated Amaryllis for so long.

Phlox continued, "We can only come back together if we all work at it. Once it was seven of us, but now it's ten. If I want you all, she's a part of the package."

"But. . . You'll forgive her?" He still could not believe it.

"I don't have to forgive her. She hurt me without asking me. However, I can make the choice to still be her friend despite that hurt. One day I might forgive her. I'm not sure. I can't risk anything that means losing you all again. Although, I know she did not mean any malice by it. . . She thought I was beautiful."

The way that Phlox said beautiful had a soft airiness to it, like it was the only time that Phlox ever believed she had been beautiful. She must have felt safe with Amaryllis. Arna believed that Phlox still did.

"Amaryllis!" Phlox called out as they approached the building. Amaryllis was walking with Ven, who was surprisingly with her. Amaryllis spun around with fire in her eyes and fight in her bones. Phlox giggled madly, skipping with Arna, before saying in a sickening sweet voice, "Hello, my love!"

"Why are you here, Phlox?" Ven stepped before Amaryllis, defending her. "It's a bit late for callbacks."

"Don't worry. I'm in the annual play. Today, I'm here to get the decision for the movie I'm in: as the lead actress. The director asked me," Phlox lied.

Arna winced, and she jolted ever so slightly from the shock of the taboo. It was a well-known fact that producers submitted the requests and received the acceptances. It was a flimsy lie at best and Amaryllis clearly did not believe it. Phlox smiled at Ven, letting go of Arna to kiss their face on both sides.

"Hello, Ven. Did you qualify for the archery showcase?"

She then grabbed Arna again, leaning into him.

"I did."

Ven eyed them both, particularly where Phlox held their arms together. They then shot Arna a questioning look: *Since when?* Arna shrugged and offered a smile: *Friends again.* Ven rolled their eyes as if it were obvious and chuckled.

Amaryllis fidgeted, glancing between them, clearly trying to piece together what was happening.

"Is Arco in class?' Phlox asked her, taunting and a bit intimidating.

"Yes. . ." Amaryllis hesitated.

"Then, he can't save you from my wrath." Phlox laughed loudly and a bit like a villain. She walked straight past Ven to Amaryllis, taking her arm, "Come now A-ma-ry-llis. We have things to discuss."

The way Phlox said discuss was particularly creepy and sent chills down Arna's spine, but he did not stop her.

"What do you want, Phlox?" Amaryllis asked her, debating whether or not to shake Phlox off. The apparent desire to flee grew in Amaryllis with each passing second, as she twisted and avoided Phlox's hands.

"Girl talk," Phlox told her, kissing her cheek which caused Amaryllis to completely freeze. "Now, come on. We have submissions to turn in."

She dragged Amaryllis forward, who stumbled and tripped over her own feet.

"Am. . ." Ven said.

"Nope!" Phlox called back.

Amaryllis glanced back telling them with her eyes that she'd be okay. She stabilized herself but was still pulled ahead by Phlox without a fight.

When the two disappeared behind the doors, Ven turned to Arna. "Phlox is going to forgive her?"

"No." Arna was not sure how much they knew. "But she wants to talk."

"Good. Amaryllis doesn't want to be forgiven. She doesn't regret it. She just doesn't want to be hated by someone she cares about," Ven said softly.

"She wants to be friends," Arna agreed, and Ven's expression lit up, incredulous and amazed.

Truly? They asked with their eyes and Arna nodded. Ven laughed, hopeful and light.

"Where should we wait?" Ven asked with a hushed tone, walking closer to Arna.

Arna shrugged and Ven led them over to a copse, using his Blessings to hide the both of them. They sat and talked about the group dance. Arna explained how he was slowly trying to fix the group, so that the dance could work. He explained how he had talked to Jasi finally and told Ginger about his clothes. He revealed how he'd helped Sarcoline reach mastery and was currently helping Phlox and Amaryllis.

"He doesn't hate you," Arna said finally when the topic broached Ebru's name. "I promise."

"He won't respond to me," Ven complained. "No matter how much I message him. I think I'm blocked."

Ven wasn't blocked because Arna saw Ebru check his mobile at night and toss it aside. There was only a few people crazy enough to message Ebru randomly: namely Phlox, Amaryllis, and Ven.

"We'll get your best friend back," Arna assured Ven.

Ven relaxed, "You know, the only reason that I even tell Phlox anything is because Ebru won't respond to me. I know if I tell her, she'll tell him."

Arna blinked. *Seriously?* That was so cryptic.

Ven laughed softly.

"I know. It's wrong." Ven shook their head. "But he responds to her. And it won't hurt her if it's not actually a secret."

"Because he trusts her," Arna understood, thinking back to the night that the whole Golden Generation had met up after Arna's return. Ven was so distressed that Phlox revealed their secret; but had they in fact told her on purpose and acted surprised? Ven shot Arna a knowing smirk and Arna let the mirth fill him, silently.

Perhaps Phlox was not the only actor in their group.

"Phlox is the most loyal out of all of us. God of Creation. God of loyalty." Ven sighed. There was a long moment of silence. "Do you know why he and I got in a fight after you left?"

Arna shook his head.

"We were all distressed. And despite himself Jasi was trying to be strong, keeping us together. However, Ebru locked himself away. I needed him, and I couldn't find him, and when I did, he. . . he was worse off than I was."

Arna thought of the feelings that they'd shared. There had been betrayal that was due to Arna. Then there was the worse betrayal, which he'd assumed was due to Ebru.

"He snapped at me, said he was fine, and became cruel. He turned everyone's focus on him, until he became our enemy," Ven said, playing with their sleeves.

"And everyone was no longer sad?" Arna asked, seeing the way that Ebru still thought it was necessary.

"We were still sad, but we had a target, and he just took it. The anger, the way Ginger screamed and Aureolin ignored him, and Phlox slammed doors and kicked him out. He took Arco being furious and Jasi fighting with him. They got into actual fistfights," Ven said, voice growing despondent.

"Jasi. . . and him. . ?" Arna pictured Jasi. He'd never thought that Jasi would actively get into a physical fight with any of them.

"Fights that Ebru instigated when Jasi had too much pent up stress, and I saw it all happening. I tried to stop him, said he didn't have to do it, and he told me he had to, because no one else was going to be able to unite us." Ven shook their head, seething.

It didn't work. They all left the studio.

"And the worst was when I found him crying and I knew it wasn't because of what he was doing but. . ." Ven bit their lip. Their purple sleeves fluttered in the wind as the false sunlight flickered in the trees, casting them in shadows.

"What?" Arna asked, leaning closer, needing to know what it was that Ven was hiding.

"I can't say. . . It's a secret, an actual one," Ven said shifting in the grass. It was a moment before they said with a soft voice, determined, "It doesn't matter now. Ebru can tell you when you finally convince him that he doesn't have to be the villain anymore."

[The God of Secrets was disappointed.]

He would. He was close. He just needed to prove to Ebru that he could trust them and that he could be soft with everyone again. After all, none of them hated Ebru. They were just furious at what he had to become, in the same way they were angry at what they had to do to survive.

"We're the Golden Generation," Arna offered. *We belong together.*

"Arna!" Phlox's voice cut through the air, startling them both. Her Blessings with Amaryllis' cut through Arna's masked shadows.

The girls walked towards them with a wave. Amaryllis looked softer. Phlox looked brighter. Whatever had been said between them had mended some bridges. Phlox let go of Amaryllis's arm, who was reluctant to part. Phlox took Amaryllis' hand instead.

She said, "Since I know you are all *dying* for the result, I must declare us friends. You can give me the applause I deserve for being so magnanimous."

No one said anything and Arna cocked an eyebrow towards Amaryllis, who sighed.

"We are friends again, I suppose." Amaryllis side-eyed him with a smirk. "No forgiveness, no apologies. Moving on despite it. . ."

"Congrats, Amaryllis," Arna said instead, and Amaryllis laughed as Phlox stuttered. Phlox collapsed to her knees, shook Arna, and tried to convince them that it was her idea.

Arna and Amaryllis walked into her studio, with Arna's new supplies for a mask in hand. He had the old one, carved by hand since he'd been in the city, but after his conversation with Phlox and Amaryllis, it was wrong. He needed to start over.

"Coco says you are having Ginger make your clothes?" Amaryllis asked as she turned on the lights. It was clean, no photographs hanging on the walls. The whole downstairs was open. Arna was caught off guard.

"Yes," Arna stuttered in surprise. Amaryllis nodded.

He started his way upstairs when she asked, "Do you ever hate the Gods?"

Arna stopped walking, the deep oak floors echoing the thud of his steps.

"Ever been mad at them? Angry that only Children are remembered? That all other nonChildren are forgotten?"

Arna's eyes lingered on the image behind her head. His face surrounded by wisteria: haunted, hollowed, confused. Yet, there was something in his eyes.

Understanding.

[Distant chimes sang in harmony.]

"Do you?" Arna asked her. "They didn't give you the Blessing for art."

Arna stood on the stairs looking down at her as she stood in the center of the empty studio looking up at him. He felt the sunlight upstairs heating his back.

Amaryllis pressed her lips together and shrugged. "I can still make art, Blessing or not. A Blessing is one path to skill, but that does not mean there are no others. Why hate the Gods? I made my own choice. Photography is my soul. At the end of the day, They will judge my actions when I go into their embrace at death, but in life it is my decision to do what I want."

But do you? The question was unasked, and Arna hesitated.

For so long he'd done everything for the Gods. He was working for the mortals who loved him, but that did not mean he wouldn't risk everything for the Gods.

No. Not risk. It was a gain.

Arna blinked. Something began turning.

[Birds chirped in symphony.]

"Will you live for them?" she asked him.

"I will fight for them," Arna answered, certain, wanting and ready. For the first time in his life, he wanted it. He really wanted to be alive. Just a few short weeks of actively trying to reconnect with his family, of truly asking for their support, of trying to live, and now he refused to let it go. He was going to hunt for the path for survival and find it.

With them.

She nodded. "I am who I am because the Gods shaped me and gave me life, but my life is mine. Just as your life is yours, Arna. Don't forget that."

What do you want?

He wanted dance. He loved dance more than anything in the world. He loved choreography. He wanted to succeed. He wanted to help others with their dreams. He had done it with Sarcoline. He. . . wanted it for himself.

Arna nodded and headed upstairs to begin working on his mask, taking out his mobile and calling Ebru. Ebru picked up on the second ring.

"Hello?" Ebru was exhausted, as he often was these days. His voice was like something that was close to breaking.

"I want to stop pretending, Ebru," Arna told Ebru again for the hundreth time. He took out the clay in his bag and began to shape it as he had many times before.

"Why?" Ebru asked.

"Because I am done hiding."

(Done with hiding?)

[There was a chorus of bells in agreement, sounding from the back of the room.]

Ebru asked softly, "Where are you?"

Arna blinked confused. "Amaryllis' studio."

"Working on the project?" Ebru asked, voice quick and breathing sharp.

"Yes."

Ebru went silent again. Arna continued to mold features of the mask trying to figure out a way to explain to Ebru what he understood.

"Why does it matter? It won't change anything."

"Do you trust me?" Arna asked him instead. Maybe it was not faith in the others that Ebru needed, but faith in Arna.

"I'm tired, Rosy. I don't want to be let down again," Ebru huffed into the call, stubborn but caving.

"When have I ever let you down, Alis?"

Arna shaped the antlers in his hands.

"What if this is the first time?" Ebru's fear was palpable, but Arna was willing to shape it, to mold it and cherish it. He could do this. He could finally fix it and fix everything else that he'd done.

purpleflowers.

(h u s h.)

"You don't have to be afraid. . ."

Ebru went deathly silent, to the point that Arna almost thought the call had ended. He glanced at the time signal in his augmentations.

"You can say no, it's your choice. But give me an answer tomorrow, okay?" Arna asked.

"Tomorrow?" Ebru asked, his voice shaking.

"Think about it, okay?"

"All because you want them to know I'm Ivumalis? So they accept me?" Ebru clarified, trying to regain stability but failing miserably. His voice quaked at every word.

"No. I'm selfish," Arna said with a deep chuckle. "I want to be able to kiss you in public."

Ebru laughed at the comment, and said a bit more relaxed, "We haven't been hiding that long. . ."

"No, but at some point, they will notice that I'm not coming back late because I'm working on the variation. Now that Ginger is doing my clothes and Amaryllis and Phlox are going to help me with my mask. . ." He had not asked Amaryllis and Phlox yet. He wanted to make the base before he asked them. "The world already knows I love you. Let me finally prove it?"

"No, they already know *I* love you," Ebru corrected, "They're my songs to you."

"Will you?" Arna asked again, staring up into space hoping for the answer.

"I'll think about it. But I need to go. Night," Ebru said, almost excited.

[Silence was a conversation. It worked in many ways.]

Arna shook his head, confused as the call disconnected and Arna was suddenly left alone. It was well past Ebru's final practice for the evening. Arna did not understand but there was a tinge in Ebru's voice that gave Arna hope that he'd say yes. It almost sounded like Ebru was inspired and Arna knew a lot about inspiration.

It drove people to achieve the impossible.

Mortals and Gods, together once more, tethered and tied, bound with the connections of souls, trust, and dance. For the Gods we gift this day. For the Gods we gift this dance. In the Gods we see mortals. In each mortal there are Gods.

— The Prayer of Continuance, how most Ceremonies of Chaos end

Dance 18

Amity

Incarnadine

14 Xeyan

28 Days Left

"I think I have time to do it! I can go and see her. She won't know I'm in the audience, but it's her first show. . . If I made the new schedule, and dance a bit earlier, I would be able to get to – "

"We leave tonight."

". . ."

". . ."

"I'll go buy my ticket."

"Arco, do you want to ruin some dreams with me today?" Arna asked at the end of breakfast, as his mother collected empty plates and their father sat reading over news. Sarcoline stopped eating and stared at Arna, brows furrowed and frown forming.

"What?" Ginger stuttered.

Arna was not sure it would work, but he was going to get Sarcoline to replace him on the stage for the group dance. It was a wild thought, one that came to him unbidden the night before. But the more he thought about it, the more he needed to convince the others. If Arna was going to dance at the Ceremony, he could not be tired from the group dance. While Arna and Sarcoline were not identical, Sarcoline was just as good as a dancer. And the message?

It was perfect: a nonChild dancing with Children. More, Sarcoline was the dancer who had finally taken Arna's rightful place on stage with the greats. It was a hope for a new future. It was a nightmare to many.

It was Incarnate Dreams.

"Sign the nondisclosure, and come with me, Ginger, and Jasi," Arna said, pulling the paper out of his dance bag and sliding it to Sarcoline.

"You mean the group dance practice?" Sarcoline asked through a mouth full of food.

"Arna, Arco isn't allowed on Shadone properties," Zaffre said, disagreeing and eyeing the paper that Arna continued to nudge it towards Sarcoline.

"Really?" Arna asked, still pushing the paper closer.

"Technically no, there was no real legal action," Sarcoline shrugged. "But they hate me."

"They hate us," Arna corrected. He then said in a singing voice, "Which is why you should come."

"And destroy dreams?" Sarcoline tried to clarify, corner of his mouth ticking up in a smirk.

Arna smiled a big toothy grin and leaned forward. While Wenge, Ginger, and Zaffre did ask questions, Arna did not answer. He let their noise disappear around him and he only stared at his brother. Sarcoline met his gaze and grasped what Arna was implying.

This would be like Understanding.

Sarcoline quickly signed the paper and slid it back across the table as Ginger stuttered protests and Zaffre chastised them both.

Taking the paper before his father could snatch it, Arna put it in his bag. He pulled out another and slid it to Rosmarinus who chewed without a word. His eyes widened in surprise. Arna nodded, sliding the pen to him as well. For a moment Rosmarinus hesitated before he signed.

This was the beginning of Arna's revolution.

"Arna," his father said sternly, and for the first time in a long time Arna fully gazed upon his father.

His father's eyes held warning. It was the look he gave Arna often when Arna was a child, as if Arna was about do something that would result in a mess. Arna did not let his smile fade.

"Trust me," Arna said. The whole room went silent. "I got Arco to Understanding. Trust me with this. I'm going to get our studio back this time."

"The Golden Generation?" Sarcoline asked with a bit of humor in his tone.

"We belong together," Arna assured him.

Zaffre's hands tensed. The man looked haggard, albeit it with more weight on him than when Arna first returned, as if he was at least eating enough again. Wenge caressed his arm slowly, and Zaffre finally nodded.

Taking the approval, Arna grabbed his bag. Sarcoline finished his drink and stood, quickly hurrying off to grab his bag. Ginger stood with her own bag, and the two went downstairs. Sarcoline met them minutes later, after Jasi had arrived with the rented car.

"Arco is coming?" Jasi asked. He blinked at his brother. "Rus too?"

Arna smiled wickedly and headed out.

This day was going to be the most important day of his life. He could feel it in the wind, in the way the birds sang, and the way the sun rose. Today was the day that the Golden Generation would be united. It was the day that Arna would be able to finish his variation. It was the day that he and Ebru were finally going to come clean.

The ride to the Shadone studio could not have been longer. Arna was nearly vibrating by the time that they arrived.

"Calm down," Sarcoline grabbed him. "What are you planning?"

"Just trust me," Arna told him with a sly smile. "Agree with me, no matter what I say."

"You are going to make me regret trusting you to begin with." Sarcoline let Arna go and walked beside him. Jasi and Ginger shot Arna concerned looks. Rosmarinus said nothing, unperturbed.

They entered the stark white reception room, as if it praised Xeyaro, but it desecrated the God's memory in its too clean, too orderly nature. The lights were softer than the previous practice, but the people were still as angry, if not more frustrated.

Arna ignored them all and headed towards the practice room, the others in tow. Only one person was on his mind and one goal at the forefront of his thoughts. Today they became a family again.

They ran into Cyclamen as they turned the corner. The man's sardonic smile turned into a grimace as he saw Sarcoline and turned even darker at Rosmarinus. Rosmarinus smiled brightly.

"Hello Cyclamen," Rosmarinus slid his hands into his pockets and said with a jovial tone.

"I was not aware you were invited," Cyclamen said with clear anger. The man then scowled at Sarcoline and spoke, seething. "Nor that I allowed you back."

Arna opened his mouth to say that Saroline signed the nondisclosure just like Rosmarinus had. By the DHS permission that allowed Cyclamen to place random people into their practice room, Arna could bring them both. Two could play Cyclamen's game and Arna knew loopholes better.

Instead, Arna said, "I had a premonition."

Cyclamen grimaced and Arna smiled.

"What are you going to do, stop the will of the Gods?"

"Please don't make a mess of yourself," Cyclamen warned Sarcoline. It was full of hostility that should have been directed at Arna. "I will make you pay for damages this time."

Stunned, Arna looked back to Sarcoline, who looked as if he were ready to stab something.

"What did you do?" Arna asked him.

"Broke a few puppets," Sarcoline answered with a shrug. "They were bad. Dirty, cracked, had to be replaced."

Ginger snorted. Jasi coughed back a chuckle. Rosmarinus laughed openly. Cyclamen glared at Romsarinus who in turn, showed his white teeth more. Rosmarinus stepped between Cyclamen and Sarcoline, and Arna cocked his head using the support to his advantage.

"No fights, Arco." Alabaster's voice startled Arna. He walked towards them, exiting from another room. Cyclamen's face flickered in annoyance. Alabaster said, "Congrats on Blue Rose Fears, Twin Fans, and Holly."

"Yes, congrats," Cyclamen forced the words out. Arna laughed to himself thinking of the supposed meltdown the man had after Sarcoline passed.

"It's to be expected." Arna smiled brighter. "Arco is a good dancer."

"Arna!" Aureolin called from down the hall, peaking out the practice room door.

"Pleasure to see you." *Hope it doesn't happen again.*

Arna walked past the two. As soon as they were far enough away, he said to Sarcoline, "Don't fight with anyone."

"I thought we were breaking dreams?" Sarcoline repeated Arna's words from that morning, with a bit of mischievous joy.

"I meant physical fighting. And we're ruining dreams not breaking them," Arna clarified, but shrugged. He did not care if there were a few things they broke.

"The next time someone calls me great as an insult, I'm not sure I can stop my fist from flying," Sarcoline said, understanding Arna. Sarcoline said sweetly, "But if you so pleasantly ask, perhaps I will listen."

"Arco. . ." Rosmarinus warned him. "Let me handle it."

"I know," Sarcoline sauntered on.

The five walked into the practice room. It was as filled with reporters and audience members as it was before, but instead of the first time they had practiced, the jeering was silent. Instead, everyone was staring at Sarcoline. Some were afraid. Most were filled with hate. Only the reporters and Arna's friends looked confused.

"Why are you here?" Ebru asked.

"Worried?" Arna teased Ebru.

"Arna. . ." Ven warned him.

"You, too?" Arna met each eye individually as he smiled. "He is a master in Understanding, what is there to it? We all are, too."

Phlox giggled, waving her hand. "But he's not us."

"Neither are any of them." Sarcoline walked past Arna and leaned against the railing facing Ebru. "But they don't scare you. I do."

Ebru frowned. "Are you aiming for Holly Understanding too?"

"Wouldn't you love to know," Sarcoline answered, much to the disdain of many of the whispering Shadone students.

Ebru's eye twitched. Every member of the Golden Generation was fidgeting. They were being challenged by an outsider, and despite how much they pretended not to care, they did. Ven and Phlox only had two variations mastered through Understanding. Aureolin now had three. Ginger had four. Ebru, despite being the most secure in his position, looked the most concerned with Sarcoline's taunts.

The tension in the room thickened when Arna shut the door.

"Fair enough," Phlox giggled, dropping the tension by a bit.

The stares continued, pointed at Sarcoline who ignored them. How many of them had told Sarcoline to give up? Yet, Sarcoline had done the unexpected in spite of it. Like a true predator, Sarcoline rolled his shoulders back and gave a lax grin at all of the Golden Generation one by one. A shiver ran down Arna's spine in anticipation.

The vision in his head of his friends and brother dancing was nowhere close to what it was in reality. It became increasingly apparent in the passing seconds that this was the *perfect* introduction for Incarnate Dreams.

Slowly but surely the group began to stretch, and when Arna shot Sarcoline a look, he joined in, much to a set of shocked whispers in the back. Arna ignored them and Sarcoline did as well. After they stretched and warmed up, Sarcoline stepped to the side and the group danced what they had learned before.

When they finished, Sarcoline was looking at them in disgust. The expression was harsh, considering that they were far more unified than they were before, but Ebru was still a problem and all of them were wary. It was not in the way they were apprehensive to Sarcoline: that was rivalry. With Ebru it was a lack of connection and trust.

"What's the dance called?" Sarcoline asked.

"The Unity of Nations," Ebru answered, wiping the sweat from his brow.

"Might as well call it The Shadone Family Presents Government Interference. It reeks of corporate planning," Sarcoline laughed. All of the Golden Children shifted. It was the same thing that Arna said, but unlike before they agreed with Sarcoline. They were standing by him more readily, each of them having opened their hearts instinctually to him, trusting him to protect them. Sarcoline may have been their fiercest competition, but he'd always been their strongest defender.

Before any of them realized what they'd done unconsciously, Arna was going to capitalize on it. Arna nodded at Sarcoline who pretended he did not see, and stepped forward, egging them on further.

"It'll be good for publicity," Ginger sighed to herself. "We need good press."

It was sadly true. The Vivicent family needed good press. Dance itself needed good press. Azza be damned, Arna needed good press. There was a chorus of chuckles from the back at her words.

"It's saying we aren't friends," Sarcoline said.

"It's saying we haven't been in years," Phlox chimed in with a sing song voice, reminiscent of Zaynir. She caught on, as Arna suspected she would. Unlike the first practice, this time Arna would succeed.

"You say that as if it's a surprise." Ebru's leer did not reach his eyes.

Arna and Ebru stared at each other openly instead of in mirrors. Ebru was the first to turn away. He tightened his hands into fists and crossed his arms.

"Last time we suggested making a new dance. Don't tell me you still are set on that incomprehensible solution," Ebru brought up the first practice, offering the suggestion of a new dance. The path to the better future was opened once more.

Ebru begged them to say yes this time.

"Last I checked, you were not a choreographer, Ebru. Or is that another skill you collected?" Sarcoline asked, taking the bait.

Ebru pointed at Arna. "Boy genius, here, choreographed the last dance we did together."

And there it was, Arna heard it in Ebru's voice. This was the moment they came clean. . .

"Or is that too hard?" Ebru mocked him, but there was no mockery in his expression. He was looking at Arna without the teasing, needing Arna to be with him. It was time for Arna to give the Golden Generation clarity on their soul.

liveliveliveliveliveliveliv

"I can't right now." Arna heard the audible groans around him along with a few chuckles. "Alright, I don't know how when we are all hiding things from each other. Is that better?"

"You're one to talk. You're the one who has been withholding—" Ebru wove Arna's words off, like a joke.

"We knew he was withholding information," Sarcoline cut in.

"True," Ebru said quietly. He turned to Arna, more hesitant. "You can still choreograph. Can't you?"

"I can," Arna said, breathless.

Ebru nodded and looked down at the wooden floors, warped in age.

There was a long moment of silence that the others tried to fill but Arna walked up to Ebru and held out his hand. One by one, the Golden Generation's expressions softened. It was no secret that Arna had gone to each of them and had purposely reconnected them. The energy in the room shifted to support. This time it was for Ebru.

"We were born together. We belong together," Arna said to Ebru.

Suddenly, Ebru's head snapped up and he marched across the room away from Arna. Arna did not drop his hand, not this time. Not ever again. His scars were exposed and sparkled in the memory of panic, smothered by defiance.

Amaryllis and Jasi moved out of the way as Ebru tapped at the console.

"This song was made specifically this year," Ebru said as he brought up a new file. "But it was done completely halfhearted. It wasn't meant to be good. But. . ."

All of a sudden, the room was filled with the sound of an orchestra, six notes that immediately faded away into a haunting melody.

Ebru turned ever so slowly to Arna. He was holding himself tight, but he did not look at the others, only at Arna: trusting him.

Arna nodded and shut his eyes. All Ivumalis songs were like dreams. Arna just had to figure out what this dream was showing.

The original version of the song was nothing compared to the new one. It was like looking at an unfinished sketch and then viewing the painting at large. This was fuller, completer and more complex. It was quintessential Ivumalis, from the use of instruments to melody.

There were somehow six separate melodies woven in harmony that worked until one vanished and the other five changed. When the sixth returned everything was in discordance. It swelled and fell, crashed and when the tension reached the peak, the melodies found harmony. It was unity, friendship, family, pain, and overwhelming unconditional support.

It was just like Ebru to express his deepest desires in his music.

When Arna opened his eyes, the song ended.

"As everyone knows," Ebru announced to the world, "I made this and in my good nature, I decided to fix it."

He stepped towards Arna.

Arna may have once been the linchpin between them, but no longer, and Ebru needed to see it was him. Ebru deserved to know what he meant to them.

"Is that a yes then?" Arna asked, hand still raised, palm up.

Ebru approached him until they were almost touching, with eyes that were begging Arna to help him. Ebru bit his lip, the lopsided pout forming. A decision was brewing: the one they both needed.

"Yes."

Ebru presented the words as a vicious attack, but he was clearly somewhere between seasick and crying. Arna examined Ebru, feeling a bit guilty, knowing that Ebru was already at his breaking point.

Ebru's cold expression started to crack. The phantom began to take a tactile form. Arna's heart thumped wildly; he shook off his immediate reaction to take Ebru away and disappear. Arna would support him, just as he always promised he would. He would provide Ebru the space for vulnerability.

"I don't want to force you," Arna said softly, accepting the plea.

"You can't force me to do anything. You only ever give me the support to do what I need to do myself," Ebru said. "And. I don't want him to hold it over me anymore."

"Are you scared?" Arna asked him.

"Of you?"

"Of the pressure," Arna asked. Ebru's eyes glanced to those on his left, the Golden Generation had gathered together to watch. They wanted, needed Ebru corporeal and real. They needed something they could latch on to and believe in. Then to his right, the gallery was pressuring Ebru, keeping Ebru in his spectral form.

"No," Ebru said. "You're here now."

When Ebru took his hand, lacing their fingers together, there was a sharp gasp from Phlox. He finally turned to face all his friends, back to the audience. Arna could tell they'd all seen something happen between Ebru and Arna but did not know what. The Golden Generation, however, stared at their joined hands in scrutiny, knowing that it meant that Arna and Ebru were together for real and not as a joke. Ven was the only one amused and mouthed: *when?*

Ebru took a few deep breaths, sharp and uneven. Ebru and Arna held eye contact with the Golden Generation, without moving. The silence drew long, but Arna did not rush it, did not push Ebru. He simply stood, squeezing the hand that he never wanted to let go of.

Ebru stopped breathing.

"I'm Ivumalis." Ebru's dead pan expression rocked the room.

The room exploded in silent reaction. There was sputtering, failed words, wide eyes, and a deep intake of breath. Rosmarinus stood with a knowing expression, as if he guessed. Ginger pressed up against the dance bar. Phlox nearly dropped her water bottle. Ven's eyes went wide. Jasi's mouth opened in silent shock. Sarcoline dropped his act and blinked rapidly shaking his head in confusion. Aureolin's gaze was blank, and she mouthed *what?* Amaryllis, too, hesitated and her smile cracked as her eyebrows furrowed; she had not seen it.

"Lumak be damned. That's not a lie. Is it?" Aureolin was the only one who was able to speak after a moment.

"Why would I lie about that?" Ebru asked.

A sea of chatter arose from the crowd, and the Golden Generation stood silent. The world's most renowned composer was claimed by a person that no one expected. The Golden Generation, however, saw their friend for the first time as he was: the one who united them before Arna returned.

"The Master will be angry," a student in the back warned. "He does not like lies."

"Cyclamen can cry himself to sleep," Sarcoline snapped.

"It's not a lie." Ebru leaned against Arna, relaxing, arms crossed and nonchalant. "It's my life."

Arna heard Jasi laugh out loud, as the only one who knew that Arna had talked to another person online for years.

Jasi said, "Arna. You're CrimsonFlesh, aren't you?"

"Guilty," Arna admitted to another chorus of surprise.

One by one all of Arna's friends and family looked to Arna as if seeing him, knowing how much he and Ebru loved each other. There was no need to say it out loud. Their music told the world as much.

"That explains. . ." Ven shook their head.

"Oh, my Gods," Phlox exclaimed, "How long have you been together? Did you know this whole time where Arna was?"

"No," Ebru sighed. "We only found out that we were talking when he came back."

Ginger covered her mouth with her hands. "How long?"

Sarcoline pressed his hands into his eyes and shook his head. Amaryllis got to taking photos, snapping out of her stupor.

"Have I been fucking your brother?" Ebru asked and the smile Ebru gave her in the mirror was teasing but kind. "Wouldn't you like to know, Ginger?"

"No more than two weeks," Ven corrected, and Arna laughed as Ebru jolted.

"You knew?" Ebru asked Ven with a tone of betrayal.

"I understand context clues," Ven said, approaching them both. They held out their arms to Ebru, stopping two steps away. "No more hiding."

(No more hiding.)

Ebru hesitated but Arna let him go and gave him a push. Ebru crashed into Ven's arms, hugging them tightly. He was tangible, illusions no longer claimed him.

Aureolin hugged Ebru, as did Ginger before she lightly punched him. Phlox sobbed dramatically in Ebru's arms about why he hadn't told her when she joked about it at last practice. Jasi whispered something to Ebru that caused Ebru to laugh and nod. Rosmarinus shook his hand. Only Sarcoline stood a bit away, at first, until he, too, gave Ebru a hug, the stiffest out of all of them. But when Ebru hugged Sarcoline back, the fighting was over. The Golden Generation was finally back on the same page.

"Now, Rosy," Ebru said when the physical contact grew too much, and he pushed them all away. He was suspended once more between ethereal and the real. Arna accepted it. It would take time for Ebru to feel safe.

"Do what you do best."

"If it's for you, Alis, I can do anything." Arna motioned to Jasi who, startled, raced back to the console, tapped in the air, and pressed play. As Arna activated his A.Reverence Blessing, his mind cleared and for a moment the world slowed. It revealed what the essence of the group dance should be.

His friends watched him, and he watched them. Together they were with him, as united as they had been on the stage when he'd danced Powers for the Ceremony of Chaos. This time they'd dance together, and he wouldn't break the world. He'd fix it.

Amaryllis was dressed in a pink dress. To Arna, Amaryllis was like a camera recording the reactions of the Golden Generation, slowly watching them all. She wasn't looking at him. And like her, he saw them.

Rosmarinus relaxed in his sky-blue shirt with bell sleeves and pants adorned with clouds along the seams. He had had never been one of them. He, perhaps, desperately wanted to be. He gave up his entire life and spent his career taking care of the family Arna left behind. Arna would not leave him behind again.

Jasi was watching Arna, trusting him, supporting him, as if ready to jump in to save them all. Dressed casually in violet slacks and a lavender shirt with violet vest, he was a part of them even if his eyes were purple, even if he belonged somewhere else. He'd chosen them time and time again. He believed in Arna when no one else did. He would make sure that Jasi was able to achieve whatever dreams he made, now that he could make them for himself.

Phlox was a ghost. Dressed in the finest cashmeres and silks, she stood the furthest away. Isolated. Phlox was watching at him as if she were just seeing him for the first time. He saw astonishment and hope. Arna would give her the connection she longed for.

Ven stood next to Ebru. Hair tied up in a bun, they were staring at Arna with a hundred unasked questions, but no anger. Arna saw jealousy, but that, too, was slowly being let go. Arna knew Ven. Ven wanted peace. Ven wanted a chance to carve their own path and Arna would make it possible.

Aureolin stood ever so slightly detached from the group, isolated without meaning to be. She wore an all gold dance ensemble. She was comfortable in her own skin, but she needed help finding her way home. She was looking at him in anticipation. This time Arna would not let her be forgotten.

Ginger, in her baggy hoodie and sweatpants, was looking down at her feet. Her clothes were intended to give off an air of intimidation, but she looked smaller than the rest of them, cowering and trying to hide. There were tears in her eyes but the spark to fight glowed stronger. He would protect her. He'd never let her nightmares come true. Not again.

Sarcoline leaned against the dance bar in the back. He was dressed in a silver and green ensemble reminiscent of winter roses with petal sleeves and iridescent mint leaf adornments. He looked bored, with a million defenses. His eyes scanned over everyone, slowly, doing a wellness check on those he loved. Sarcoline was ready to fight the world if necessary. He was not a Child, but a genius all the same. Sarcoline was breathtaking. He had the ability to drive them all forward. Arna could not let his brother shoulder the burden of a million people ever again.

Then there was Ebru, who stood with Arna. He wore a smoky gray ensemble that threatened to whisk him away. Ebru pretended that nothing could hurt him despite the fact that his face was bright red. Ebru wanted hope. Arna was never going to let Ebru be alone, ever again.

He could not let any of his friends hurt again. They were his Saints, he'd protect them.

In the mirrors, behind where the five Golden Generation members and Sarcoline stood, there were the reflection of candles. They flickered: watching, waiting.

In the far back Arna saw the hate from the observers in audience. They told him that he was a failure, better off dead. To them he was worse than nothing. However, they were blurry images, fading from view. Their opinions mattered little.

"I see," Arna said to himself.

[*Do you?* Xeyaro asked, voice more powerful than it had been in weeks.]

He slipped off his jacket tossing it to Ginger who caught it. All at once all of the dancers flocked away to Sarcoline's side to watch Arna work.

Arna flourished the Blessings that best help him with choreography. A.Reverence, for the dance. Cr.Song, to make sounds with his movement. G.Stillness to draw his focus into a place of creation. Ch.Body to push his body in endurance. B.Body to make him fast and flexible enough to move with his thoughts. Un.Stillness to keep others from manipulating him. K.Reverence so that he could find the correct movement forward when he lost his way.

Then he stood still. Eyes closed, he listened. There were many ways to tell the story, but only one that Arna wanted to tell.

The music repeated itself and he let his body move to the beat. He let himself fall into it, feeling it exactly as he needed to. He moved when he needed to and not a second before, contemplating all the different parts. He thought of what he wanted to see, what he wanted the world to see.

There wasn't much movement in the first iteration, just him playing around as he thought: analyzing, memorizing, and repeating moves in his head. He visualized what he wanted this dance to be, a hundred times, before it ended. The crafting of the group choreography came naturally.

Arna would showcase their talents, complexities, individualities, and stories. It would look easy, entertaining, and incorporate them all. Audiences were going to be more critical because they felt entitled to the Golden Generation. He'd not let them be satisfied. Instead, Sarcoline would dance for Arna.

A spark of thought created sound, and in it, the whole dance was laid out before him.

Arna stepped into the formations for the group dance, picturing the Gods. He saw the Gods in his friends all the time and no one knew the Gods better than Arna. The six dancers would represent them on stage, fully. As his Saints they were the only ones who could.

Heretical thoughts were supported by a chorus of divine cheers. After all, there were no accidents.

Breath out, Arna held nothing back.

The third repetition he did the dance in full, knowing exactly what he wanted, and bringing everything together in his head. He stopped before the music ended.

"Alright." Arna opened his eyes. The others were waiting in anticipation. The five Golden Generation Children stepped up next to Arna, but Arna looked at Sarcoline: he had fought for his spot amongst them and was ready for what Arna was going to throw his way. "You too, Arco."

"Why me?" Sarcoline rose a brow but stepped forward regardless.

Ginger ushered him over. "Just come here."

"Okay. Do you need me to go move by move, or do you want me to. . ." Arna asked them.

"Just go. Show us and if we can pick it up as we are watching then we will. What we don't get, you'll go over after," Ebru spoke quickly, with a higher pitch than usual.

Was he still on edge for having his identity revealed? Their eyes met in the mirror. No, Ebru was finally letting himself express his excitement.

"We can do that much at least," Ebru actually smiled in joy.

The song repeated. With care and dedication to the dance in his heart, Arna showed them. The first part was a solo for each of the six. Next, they came together to shift into the six Gods. They would then dance, moving between mortal and God, as individuals who were split apart until they found themselves together again.

It was the story Ebru wanted to tell, and the story Arna was giving the world.

Exactly as he imagined, they picked up the dance quickly. Arna explained the minute differences between the parts, repeating the song over and over, showing exactly how those distinctions would play out as well as where they'd have to improv.

They had the first minute roughly completed an hour into practice. Arna danced with them, going over the section one more time as Jasi, Rosmarinus, and Amaryllis stood in the wings.

The Golden Generation had fallen in sync with each other. Their energies spun in orbit. His heart soared as they danced together, as if twelve years had never happened.

He was whole. The void was filled. They were one and he never wanted to let go.

[The glowing in the mirrors continued to watch.]

"This is epic," Aureolin said hotly, excited beyond her usually composed nature.

"We are back!" Phlox cheered jumping up and down, no longer refined and caring that the cameras saw her truth.

"It looks good," Sarcoline laughed in agreement.

"Now. . ." Arna said, ready to continue teaching, when all at once mobiles started buzzing. Jasi, Rosmarinus, and Ginger's eyes unfocused and glowed.

"We have to get out of here." Ginger grabbed Arna.

A notification popped up for Arna in the air, sent directly to him alone.

Dad: Get home. Now.

"Is that how you lied?" someone shouted at Arna, holding up their mobile. Lied? Arna's heart began to race. Arna peeled his sister off of himself as images arose in the studio air, projected by the Shadone students who had access to the holotech of the room. There was a video presented to Arna.

Incarnadine Exposed: Watch Me Fake The Relic Ritual

The video started, before anyone could stop it and Arna froze watching the man speak as his brother and sister tugged at him to go.

"Everyone knows that the ritual has not worked since the Splintering, and I am here to show you how Incarnadine's mother, Wenge, faked it." The person showed that he could not make the ritual glow. Then, with the help of others, a combination of Blessings was used to make the ritual glow. "I can control which ones, and when. We know based on public records that Wenge has all three of these individually. It's so easy to do, that she could manipulate the test without anyone noticing, so long as she touched him. It's been a lie since the beginning."

Arna ignored the video and quickly typed it into his mobile, starting into space as he hunted for commentary on the internet. News articles were already posted.

Arna looked through comments on the video and the forums.

> ► I knew it!
>> ► Of course, his mother's the liar
> ► What a waste of life. All of them.
> ► I can't believe the officials were fooled by this.
>> ► It's all corrupt.

Ebru put his hand over Arna's mobile, and snapped his fingers before Arna's eyes so that he focused on the room again.

"Don't read the comments, I know you are."

"I—"

"Don't hurt yourself," Ebru demanded with terrified eyes, shaking hands.

Arna was at a loss for words, unable to speak. He closed all the apps.

THEENDTHEENDTHEEND

Everything was getting tumbled up in his mind around a single thought: *They're going to retest me.*

The government would have to prove he had not manipulated the results when he had. It was not as if he would be lying, so it would be pointless. The video itself was a lie. He had the Blessings. . . but not all of them. . .

Not all of them.

Arna's heart threatened to stop beating. He squeezed his hands tightly, trying to push his Blessings back in place and make the panic silent.

"Ven, Aureolin, get him home. Ginger, make sure he doesn't read the comments because he will if you don't watch him." Ebru did not break eye contact with Arna, leaning close. "Breathe, Rosy. Slowly. Do not read. Do you hear me?"

They are going to test me again. Arna's chest grew tight. His lungs constricted.

THEENDTHEENDTHEEND

His palms were sticky. His Blessings flickered in overuse. His bones threatened to break under the newly remembered pressure.

Arna had not used his Blessings to manipulate the results himself. He'd used all of his Blessings so that the Gods could do it for him. Without them, the testers would know how many Blessings he'd lost. They'd see. He'd see. What if they'd made a mistake in the count? He'd been trusting the Gods blindly.

The air around him became gelatin, impossible to breathe. He couldn't. He couldn't. . .

[*Our connection is too weak,* Ixxzal said.]

I'm going to die. The thought was like Arna falling from a train in the sky, crashing into the religious circle, and turning to flames.

Thousands of dead.

SCREAMING

diediediediediedie

Knowledge he'd held close for years, understood thoroughly, and forgotten in a few short weeks as he tried to fight to live, reverberated. The illusion was collapsing, and the reality collided with him.

Arna's S.Mirrors activated.

"Holy Zaynir!" Ven gasped.

He didn't know how to survive. He didn't know what to do. He still didn't have the path. He still could not tell them about the end of the world.

imposterimposterimposter

"Arna!" Ven yelled. "Breathe!"

He was going to be retested. What if the number was wrong? No. What if it was right?

I'm going to die.

justlikesaffronjustlikesaffronjustlikesaffron

"Look at me, Arna," Ebru said, voice becoming distant to the buzzing in Arna's ears.

[*You will have to do this yourself.*]

"I can't," Arna admitted.

[*You will—*]

"—be okay. You have—"

[*—them.* The God of the Unknown's voice drifted to nothing.]

Eighteen and he died.

Thirty and he had a good chance to survive.

Forty-two Blessings to lose.

If he had touched one too many fans. . . It was all over. He didn't have a chance.

I'm going to die.

DIEDIEDIEDIEDIEDIE

THEENDTHEENDTHEEND

Years' worth of mithridatism with the thought of death was erased in a few short weeks. The fact seeped through him like a poison that he could not stop. The fear of failure roared. The anguish of time spent in vain cackled and burned. The hopes of a life that he'd only began to dream of, were gone: murdered in an instant.

Arna collapsed into Ebru's arms. Ven was there, trying to pull the panic, to shoulder it with him, but each time they tried the panic grew larger and more impossible to carry. The weight of the world came crashing down.

"Arna. Arna, breathe," Ven demanded.

He could only lose twelve. . . He. . .

"Arna? Arna, why are you panicking?" Ginger's voice was distant.

"What hasn't he told us?" Jasi asked Ebru.

"I don't know!" Ebru snapped back as he brought Arna to the floor.

Once more Arna was surrounded by his friends as he tried to center himself. He tried to think of anything else, not the test, not the Blessings. Not the twenty-sixth dance. Not Saffron.

justlikesaffronjustlikesaffronjustlikesaffron

He could not be like Saffron. He could only die after he danced twenty-seven. Not before. Despite the pain.

painpainpainpainpainpain

Oh, the pain.

He thought of every time he'd ever lost a Blessing. He was in every storm he'd ever danced in. He was six minutes of the worst pain he'd ever felt in his life.

He could not fail. He was so close, so close. He was doing everything right. Hands open, hands closed. Nails digging into skin that was not his own, but Ebru's as Ebru refused to let him squeeze the pain away.

"Rosy, breathe." Ebru hugged him. "Breathe."

"What's wrong?" Ginger asked them. Her voice was a distant buzzing. All their voices were static, like a radio, distant screaming at him that he could not comprehend.

"Arna. Breathe. Breathe," Ven demanded of him.

He could not. He didn't deserve to.

THEENDTHEENDTHEEND

S.Mirrors pulled the panic until clariy filled Arna's ears in the form of Ebru's humming of *Serenity's Lament*.

In the gap, Arna flourished his abilities and pushed the panic away. He had to focus on living right now and surviving until the end.

theywereallgoingtoseetheywereallgoingtosee

He could not be the one to end the world. He was so close to saving it. He was so close to finding the way to stay alive.

THEENDTHEENDTHEEND

(No longer hiding.)

(They were all going to see his lies.)

They were no longer going to believe in him.

Their faith in him would be lost.

They'd all know just how much of a failure he'd been.

The worst Chosen since Saffron, and potentially worse.

He would destroy hope forever.

"Incarnadine!" Ebru snapped, and Arna finally looked at him and the others. He took a startled, shallow breath. His lungs ached. His hands, holding Ebru's, were hot and sticky.

"Heal him," Ginger begged Aureolin.

"I'm trying," Aureolin said with her hands on Arna's, attempting to fix the wounds he cut open into his hands. Ebru refused to let him go.

"Tell me this will be okay," Arna said to Ebru as the poisonous promise of death threatened to kill him again.

Ebru shook his head; their vow would not allow him.

Gravity was ripped away.

Arna was surrounded: his father was on one side, their lawyer on the other, and Jasi and Wenge seated nearby. The Cardinal of each religion stood watching him. There were Xeysis Legacy Heritage Foundation officials, the Xeysis LHF President, members of the Chosen Task Force for the World Government Council, and the full Xeysis Government council present. There were video feeds of all the other Governors, the full LHF World Council, the WGC board members, and other WGC high ranking officials. The Governor of Xeysis sat across from Arna. Cyclamen Shadone was there as well.

They had discussed for hours about what to do. The official statements had mitigated most damage, but the public demanded answers. They needed proof.

In six hours, everything had fallen apart. In the first hour, Arna was asked a thousand questions. In the five after, his mother was accused of cheating from the beginning, from the moment Arna was born.

"I didn't fake it," Wenge said again, without a tear in her eye, wearing her best suit and looking colder than he'd ever seen his mother.

"There have been cases in the past where people claimed themselves the Chosen Child. Children and adults who were *not*," the Governor of Xeysis said. "You are the only one with all the Blessings who could have done it."

"I did not do it," she insisted.

"Him having all the Blessings is an impossibility," Mr. Thyme, head of the Chosen Task Force, exclaimed with a fervor that told Arna that the man wanted to see them all suffer.

Not a single one of them in the room could be trusted. They all wanted to tear down the Vivicents, including Cyclamen Shadone, who urged them to retest Arna over and over. They wanted them to pay, wanted to prove it was a lie, wanted repercussions for the Splintering, and now they had their chance.

"Retest him!" the Governor of Ixis demanded. "The cities are going up in protests everywhere. We must!"

"Arrest him!" The Governor of Ludiel demanded, "If he has lied, he must pay for the crime."

"We must believe in the Gods," Cardinal Black disagreed. Cardinal White sat staring at Arna, silently, asking Arna questions but Arna couldn't even think straight. Nor could he try to parse what the old man was asking him without words.

He'd ignored Arna, left him alone. No number of excuses were enough to fix that he, too, had abandoned Arna. They all had.

justlikesaffronjustlikesaffronjustlikesaffron

They're going to retest me.

THEENDTHEENDTHEEND

It took everything he had to keep breathing and not to panic at his mortality that he would be facing at the end of the month.

"I didn't fake it," Wenge said, as stern as she had first been when they began screaming at her hours ago.

"We must be certain. We have improved our facilities and monitored all activity to the best of our ability, but people are constantly learning and changing. There are always new ways to fake the results," the Governor of Podiel said. "We can't let our cities be destroyed because of this lie."

The LHF President of Xeysis glared at Arna. "Yes. We must retest. There are ways that one can manipulate the results through a combination of Blessings."

"Arna, are you okay?" Cardinal White finally asked aloud. He was the first and only person to truly address Arna since the trial of Wenge first started.

Arna blinked.

imgoingtodieimgoingtodieimgoingtodie

He tried to put his emotions into words.

"Should the testing be live?" the Governor of Azis asked, ignoring Arna.

"We can't let the public see," the Governor of Zaydiel protested.

"We must," the Governor of Ixis said.

imposterimposterimposterimposterimposterimposter

Everyone in the room, excluding his family and Cardinal White, hated him. They all had their own reasons. For some, it was because they feared change. For others, they hated the Gods. Most simply hated Arna because of the Splintering. They had wanted to stop him from the beginning but were unable to when the facts slapped them in the face. Now that there was a possibility he lied. . . They were throwing out consequences: imprisonment, mandatory volunteer service, exile from all cities.

diediediediediedie

He is not the Chosen, they screamed at each other.

He is a liar, they declared, in jubilance, finally able to tear him down.

Millions of lives were blamed on him. Millions of people were dead, they said, because of him.

[The blame laid with the stars.]

Even if the Gods said otherwise.

theendtheendtheend

Arna took in a scattered, hiccupped breath. The cascade of the initial damn breaking finally alleviated itself back down to the panic he'd lived with for years.

He was fine. *Focus.*

imposterimposterimposter

Pokk would call it idiocy and near heresy against themself. Other than his family and Cardinal White, Arna was not sure the others ever fully believed he was real.

"You have got to be kidding me. You can't fool the test," Zaffre stated. "That video is a hoax, and you know it."

"Not the test itself, the results," the LHF president disagreed. "You must have paid someone,

taught him how to do it himself when he was older."

"We didn't do that," Wenge said, stern and emotionless.

Arna's head pounded from the noise. He was able to control his breathing this far into the meeting. The moment he was retested he would see his own mortality in its full form.

thisisitthisisitthisisit

His own ego, his own self-preservation, said to run, to ignore it. He should continue to hope without the truth. So long as he didn't see the ones he was missing, was he truly missing them?

Yes, he may not be able to access them, but he never mastered all of his abilities individually anyway. Seeing them gone was completely different than pretending that he'd never had them to begin with.

"We have to retest him." The Governor of Xeysis did not sound convinced. "Our foundation as a society is at risk."

Cowards, all of them. It was what Azza would call them. Lumak would call them fools.

"The results will be the same," Zaffre declared for Arna.

Zaynir would insist on doing something, and Arna would listen. He'd try to find a way out.

Arna prayed to Xeyaro to keep him calm. For a moment he thought they hugged him, until he recognized the embrace as that of his mother.

"Breathe, Arna," she told him.

He took a shaky breath, unsure when he'd taken his last one. He relaxed into her arms, and the room grew loud with fury at her actions. Despite the screaming, she soothed him with her healing.

"Perhaps, they will be the same." The LHF president stared at Arna, as if reading Arna's mind that they would not be. "We will show it live. The public needs to see."

theendtheendtheend

itstheendoftheworldandtheydontevenknow

Ixxzal would mock Arna for being afraid. He was trained for this. He may not have completed their final test to be Chosen, but he was the only one in the world who had the choice.

Hands open. Hands closed. He squeezed his nails into his skin and flourished his Blessings to push everything back into silence.

The Gods had never lied about the count. He repeated the number. It would not be wrong.

He could take the truth. It was not different than all the other truths they'd confronted him with before. He was going to find a way to survive the loss.

It was fine.

"Test me," Arna agreed, standing and pushing his mother a bit away in the process.

There was no way to hide. If everyone had to see, then so be it. His family would not reject him for it. Ebru had not. Ven probably already anticipated it. Those in the room finally stopped talking when Arna agreed.

"Let's go."

Arna left the room first, not waiting for them. In moments, Arna was surrounded by guards, and separated from Jasi and his parents.

"Let us walk with him!" Zaffre yelled, but Arna did not look back as he was led away. He crossed his arms and let himself be directed as necessary.

They were brought to the largest testing room that the Legacy Heritage Foundation had. Arna was kept separate from his parents, Jasi, and Cardinal White, who was deemed untrustworthy as the leader of the Church of the Apostle. The oppressive force of the Un.Guard's Blessings kept his family from trying to assist him. They prepared the room for the live broadcast.

Arna's eyes landed on each relic that lined up with the Blessings he lost.

It was only going to be five.

runrunrunrunrunrun

Arna steadied his breathing. He was fine.

Staring at the five relics was like looking at his death sentence. The Gods always told him never to go past six, that after losing six before the ceremony—even though it was within the gap—things would get difficult.

Mr. Thyme approached Arna.

"Incarnadine."

There were men with him. Without being told Arna suspected that the six of them held the Un. Abilities to counter him.

As they activated their abilities, the pressure grew intense: specialized Un.Ability users. Their Blessings pressed into Arna's bones threatening to break him. His Blessing cocktail to manage his panic, was devoured and the thoughts became screams in his head.

He stood still and straight. The superstorm he'd danced in was worse than this. This pressure and pain were nothing. It was nothing like losing a Blessing. It was nothing compared to Divinity.

Arna breathed deeply and hummed *Serenity's Lament* to himself instead. It drowned out the screams.

Be comfortable with silence.

"You will only activate your abilities when prompted by the LHF officials, and no other time. We shall do this the way babies are tested," Mr. Thyme said as more people approached.

Their faces were blank, but Arna could tell there was smoldering anger beneath.

"Guided into activation." Arna was disgusted that they were treating him like a child, but he understood their vigilance. "Got it."

Children were guided into the process before they learned to use their abilities. They did not need to be a master or use them at full power, just a tiny bit of activation would do to show the capability of the individual. A spark was all that was needed, nothing more.

"Believe me Incarnadine, this is not what I want." The man offered a small smile, but Arna did not trust it. He wanted Arna gone. This man wanted to prove Arna a liar more than anyone else.

justlikesaffronjustlikesaffron

Be able to exist within silence.

"We're ready!" someone called from the cameras.

Orders were called out and all the cameras began to blink and hover in the air. It was made live without any breaks, without any question that it was tampered.

It is serenity.

The Un.Guards led Arna forward with the LHF officials and Mr. Thyme. They approached the circle for Azza where Cardinal Black and The Governor of Xeysis waited. The LHF official yanked at Arna's hands and sliced him open far deeper than was necessary.

His blooded poured in the crystalline water of the bowl that Cardinal Black held. The six guards led him forward as tens more LHF officials with Un.Blessings suppressed Arna. He did not fight back. Without being able to combat it with his own Blessings, he was being crushed by the weight. Still, he did not let himself falter.

It is the story told in moments where sound cannot reach.

He let them lock him down, let them ensure he was not cheating. Arna fell to his knees. When he pressed his hands down to the first circle, they were still pouring blood. The water was splashed to the center of the circle. The pain was but a tickle compared to what he had once felt. The LHF official knelt down and activated Arna's abilities for him. It was as if a knife carved through his skin but over a thousand times worse, the official's Blessings wrecked havoc through his body.

We only think of it after it has passed: when it has come and gone.

This is nothing.

He hummed *Serenity's Lament* louder and used it to stabilize his breathing.

All LHF officials were taught how to activate Children's Blessings through stimulation and a connection. They had to have certain Body Blessings or Mirrors Blessings in order to achieve it. Whatever bedside manner this official had been taught was discarded as their abilities wrought harm upon Arna. It was not an activation by guiding, but by force.

Be with me.

[*We're here*, Xeyaro said.]

He did not flinch and let his Blessings activate in the stimulation, despite the pain that was caused as they did. The Un.Guards continued to pressure him more. The guards did not let up, so the LHF official pulled harder, forcing Arna's abilities to flourish. It was enough, however, to register for the circle.

We long for it.

It lit up in two colors of equal luminance and opacity reflecting his true scores. Except there was one deviation, one relic that was not correct. It only glowed in one color.

[*Hold out. Okay? Be strong.* Azza stood nearby. *We have you.*]

Arna was held there in the sand as the scores were recorded until he was forced to do it again at each of the six circles. They slashed his hands open, threw him to his knees, forced him to obey, and he obliged. Just when he thought it was over, they made him do it again from the beginning.

We hide from it.

[*I will rip them apart!* Ixxzal screamed.]

[*You cannot touch them,* Lumak tried to calm Ixxzal.]

Through twelve full rotations of all six circles, they forced him to repeat the motions, until they were certain he did not cheat. He did not resist, and instead prayed to the Gods. He begged them to help him, to support him, and to ensure he did not pass out in the pain and pressure.

[Zaynir cried in the distance.]

Their anger and sorrow coursed through him each time he activated their circles. He was with them and they were with him, as one. Closer than they had been in months.

The same Blessings were missing in each time, one from every circle except Zaynir's circle.

Fa.Mirrors for Ixxzal, lost the night when he built his fans.

Ch.Insight for Azza, lost the night he burned his eighteenth fan.

J.Body for Lumak, lost when he was twenty-five after years of practicing pain tolerance when he picked it up and was able to run around the city without blacking out.

K.Song for Pokk, lost when he was twenty-one and he was told to pick up a fan, the first time training his body to resist the pain.

N.Song for Xeyaro, lost when he was seventeen and took a fan wanting to break the connection with the Gods.

[Pokk tried to comfort Zaynir.]

We try to fill it when it is not void.

When the officials finally gave up, they reported a number of missing Blessings that Arna knew by heart: five. The Gods had not led him astray, which should have given Arna some comfort. Instead, there was nothing. His head spun from the loss of blood. He could barely make out their figures.

"Can I go home?" Arna asked, healing his body with the Blessings he could use as soon as the Un. Guards and officials stepped away.

In seconds people were at his side. Cardinal White grabbed him and started healing him. Wenge had her hands around him, healing him as well. The silver of her eyes was a smokey gray in fury, and her body tensed like a predator ready to lash out as she clung to him. There were people yelling, but he could not hear him. People tried to pull her away, but she would not budge.

"He is my son!" she screamed at them, righteous and ferocious.

The moments we do not hear, are not lost.

Cardinal White held Arna's hands gingerly. The wounds on his hands stitched themselves back together but Arna was near certain he could see bone before they did.

That couldn't be right. He must have lost too much blood and was hallucinating.

[*Arna!* Ixxzal screamed.]

"Yes," Arna said to him. "I won't pass out."

It is there in our imaginations, in our hopes, in our dreams.

He was trained to never pass out. Handle the pain, swallow it. Ignore the blood, focus on his Blessings. . . His Blessings? Arna tried to activate them but was unable to do so. Why was he unable to do so?

"His system is shocked," Cardinal White said somewhere world. Somewhere far away. "From the overuse of Un. Abilities, constant activation, and blood loss, I'm surprised he's awake."

"I'm okay," Arna said but couldn't feel his Blessings. Panic bubbled in his throat. He didn't lose them all did he? Not yet. He couldn't have yet. No. . .

It is the proof, the support, the essence of what matters.

He sang *Serenity's Lament* louder.

Wenge held Arna, crying to into his ears, like echoes from a distant universe. "I can't lose you again."

"Let's go," Zaffre said, and then Arna was no longer on his knees. He was flying. He leaned his head against the only rock nearby. Otherwise, things were too dizzying.

"Zaffre, we. . . We need to talk." Cardinal Black's voice shook.

"Talk! He is my son! And you—"

"Dad," Arna called. Arna heard his father's voice, though he was not sure where.

There was a rumbling, maybe thunder? Ixxzal was proud and angry. The lights were shattering. The world was breaking. He had no more Blessings.

Silence is not an absence but a reminder of—

"He is an IMPOSTER!" Someone yelled.

imposterimposterimposter
not an absence but a reminder of—

"He is NOT the CHOSEN!"

howmanymorepeoplearegoingtodieforhismistakes
not an absence but—

"HE WILL DESTROY THE WORLD!"

Just. Like. Saffron.

Serenity's Lament died in his throat as he once more tried to use his Blessings and EVERYTHING landed at once. It

bro   ke

a   p   a   r   t   .

His body twisted itself in two, preparing to snap.

His mortality faced him in the form of horrible lightning and thunder that liquified organs. It was millions dead. It was the screams as candles went out. It was the chime-chime-chime of a clock at midnight. It faced him in the form of a crashing train.

The number of days left was the sound of metal crushing itself. The fear of dying and failing was the people screaming at him to help as he leapt from the train. The pain of knowing everyone else would die was his burden to bear alone. The pressure devoured him as the protective shield of the Gods was ripped away.

He only had lost five Blessings.

Every time he danced, he'd lose more.

He was going to lose forty-two more.

He needed eighteen to survive Divinity.

He only had seven left as a buffer. But seven wasn't enough. It wasn't enough. It wasn't enough.

Eighteen was the bare minimum to survive.

To survive.

To live.

He shouldn't have had to lose any of them.

This should have been easy.

He should have been smarter. Been better.

beenbetterbeenbetterbeenbetterbeenbetterbeenbetterbeenbetterbeenbetterbeenbetterbeenbetter

To choose mortality is to choose the Gods.

To choose the Gods is to choose mortality.

Which is the choice?

(He wanted to choose. . .)

Did he have that right?

Five.   Seven.   Eighteen.   Thirty.

Forty-two.

Twenty-Six survive   Die after twenty-seven

notbeforenotbeforenotbeforenotbeforenotbeforenotbeforenotbeforenotbeforenotbefore

Raven was the first.
Watsonia was the second.
Vervain was the third.
Sable was the fourth.
Ilex was the fifth.
Don't be like Saffron.

howcanthingsbeaccidents? howcandivinityberejected? howdoyoumakeacontractyoudonotknow?

howdoyousavetheworldwhenyoubrokeitforadreamandthatdreamistheonlythingthatcouldchangeit?

Arna's brain split apart. His soul fractured. Terror welled up within him.

He was going to die.

He already accepted he was going to die.

He deserved to die.

(He wanted to live.)
Did he deserve that?
whatdoyoulivefor? whatdoyouwantafter? whodoyouwanttobecome?
ifyoucouldgobackwouldyou?
whatwouldyoubeifyoucouldchangeyourchoice?
wouldyoustillbetheChosen?

if it meant destroying the world. . .

(would he still chase the dream?)

Other people were talking in vague voices about going home. Chimes told him it was safe. Birds urged him to sleep.

"The Gods have forsaken us," echoed around him in the form of howling silence.

As darkness consumed him all he could hear was the serenade of the abyss.

The nightmare devoured the dream.

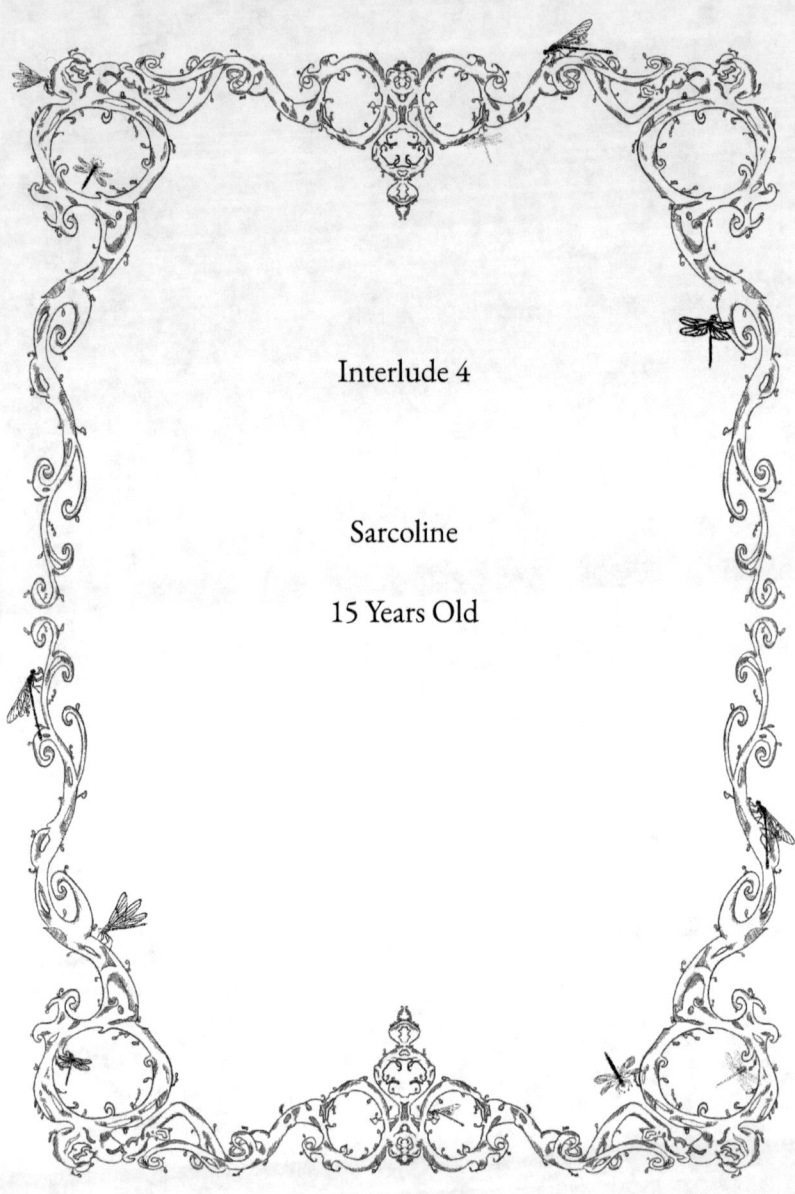

Interlude 4

Sarcoline

15 Years Old

The overhead lights flickered like candlelight, dancing across the mirrors and floor turning their shadows into white. It was snow falling gently from the heavens to cover all that once existed. For a moment the dance studio was not wood and glass, but trees: in a forest, within a city, during a white winter that was artificially created.

Standing there, she met his eye, held his gaze. They were locked in a thousand unspoken words, in the hollowness of the breath between the two of them. Hesitation filled his bones as he held the Blue Rose Fears fans. He squeezed them shut, trying to settle his heart. Her fingers tapped along the lens of her camera, eyes unwavering.

"What?" He tasted the word more than he said it. His heart thudded in his ears. His body swelled with a heat he only recognized after hours of practice: something he had yet to begin. Exhaustion, frustration, elation, and a thousand other emotions tumbled into one. He had no name for it.

This practice was meant to be imbued with anger, too much anger, after a long day of being told no and that he was worthless. It wasn't... She wasn't... Why was she talking? His anger was subdued by a different frustration and curiosity. All his hate was washed away in a few words, leaving him with...

"He died," she repeated, verbatim. "The train crash in Ludiel, three years ago, today."

In the two years and six months that he knew her, he could count on his hand the number of times she spoke more than two words to him. He was certain her vocabulary consisted exclusively of 'yes,' 'no,' 'okay,' and 'do you?' Yet, here she spoke more words than he'd ever heard her say in a single sitting, and she said them exactly the same, twice.

Her thick black hair flickered in the lights. Her brown skin was lightened by the continuous shadows. Her aqua eyes were glowing almost as if there was a spark behind them, some sort of light when he *knew* she was empty inside just like he was.

"There must be a power outage," Arco said, shaking his head of the hallucination. There was no way that she had said the words. "It should end—"

"My heartmate," she said as soon as the lights stopped flickering and held steady. The room was blinding white silver, like the flash of a camera, like the lights on a stage, like snow reflecting the city glow.

Arco hesitated to breathe at all. Heartmate?

He glanced at her left wrist, wrapped in white gauze as it had been since the day, he first met her. A thousand unasked questions were given answers. Why did she only live through her camera? Why did she always look like she was mourning? Why didn't she say anything? Why was she as empty as he was?

Her heartmate died.

"I'm sorry," Arco whispered.

Arco knew nothing about her, not really. Her parents moved to Xeysis for her to learn under Chamomile; Chamomile told him. She had a younger brother who loved her; he was one of the sweetest boys Arco had ever met. Her family was small and kind, not cold like his. For the life of him, he could never understand why she was always on the verge of tears. He did not know why she was sheltering herself from pain at all times. Nor did he want to ask why her left wrist was bandaged as heavily as it was, always.

"I never met him."

Her words sent Arco reeling. What was this? Why was she speaking so much? His heart was racing even though he did not want this. He wanted to get his anger out. He had things to practice. He had to be the best. He had to. . . had to practice so he could fix what his brother broke. Only he could do it.

She said, "It's a lot of pain to lose a heartmate, even when you don't know them. Worse when you do."

Arco tasted sand. His breath was a flame in his lungs. She tilted her head at him, solemnly on the verge of tears *again*. Then it was gone, like snow melting atop the skin, and he was there again.

The day that Arco met her, it was snowing in the Cathedral Forest, on the third petal's south district. He wanted to dance in the snow, far away from anyone and everyone who knew him. He picked two in the morning, certain no one else would be out and as crazy as he was. He wanted to feel its chill against his skin, and maybe—just maybe—he'd feel alive again.

He was slowly losing dance: the only thing that kept him going and the only thing that he lived for. He wanted to feel something, anything instead of emptiness. He didn't even feel angry anymore.

She stood, surrounded by snow. It dusted her collar, shoulders, and black hair like an ethereal cloak and crown. In all the books that Arco had ever read, it should have been a painting: something cut out of time. It was something that was never meant to be his: stories, legends, and enviable beauty. In the world of all white, he was in all black and she was in green.

She always wore green because her parents bought it, and she only wore what they gave her. She only ate what they fed her. She only did what they told her to do.

She said his name that night in the forest. Startled, embarrassed, frustrated: Arco was confronted by a myriad of emotions for the first time in months. Hot like a roaring fire, Arco had left her standing under the trees.

"Sarcoline. . ." she said, startling him from the thought.

They'd never needed names between them. They'd always just existed together, in orbit. He'd only ever heard her use his name twice before. Saying names made the moment real, distracted him from what he had to do.

Once more the unspoken emotions began to swell within him as she stood haloed by the studio lights, like a glowing false moon covered in snowy tears. He tried to focus on the dances he was supposed to practice. He needed to embody the desolation of being worthless. It was in the negativity that he knew could get him to dance well. He couldn't have this, couldn't have. . . Hope had no place in his world. He'd just burn it alive. Goodness did not belong to him, he did not deserve it.

"Why were you in the forest that day?" she asked.

"I wanted to see the snow."

The words sounded false despite it being true. Why was it that between them things always seemed wrong? A lie.

Facts turned inconceivable in Arco's life. *His* father was a drunk. *She* couldn't leave bed most days. *His* mother cried every night. *She* had been bullied relentlessly in her old city. *His* sister was annoying and could never protect herself, so he had to. *Her* brother was injured but wanted to be a dancer when everyone said he'd never be able to with his leg augmentation. The twins who lived in *his* house were a rampage in human form and a struggling coward who was trying to work to support the rest of the house. *She* had no dreams, no wants, no needs. *He* hated his brother. *She*. . .

Her hands were shaking. His anger was breaking. Her words were melting him. They were transforming a relationship that meant *nothing* into something. It could never mean something. He didn't deserve. . .

"I wished my soul would return to me," she said slowly, her voice choking then as the words defrosted and avalanched from her lips. "I *never* knew him. They hated me. All I wanted was to take photos. And everyone was a disaster. Everyone hated . . . Sarcoline. . . It was so empty. I didn't think I deserved anything. I didn't want to be alive."

The second time she said his name—the second time he met her—he was sitting in an alley the day after the forest, bleeding and bruised, trying to find a sense in the pain. The snow on streets was covered in red, turning pink. The other boys had beaten him until he cried and could no longer move. If he were dead, maybe that would give the boys back everything they lost in the Splintering. They were his friends once, no longer. They shunned him for the very things he loved. They hated him for his name.

He was pressed up against a brick wall, huffing and breathing harshly. He wasn't certain but he thought he had a broken rib. He hadn't, but the fear of his father's fury at the injury made him nearly catatonic. An injury of this caliber was career ending for a dancer like himself.

He wished he was dead before an uneasy nonchalance washed over him. It didn't matter if he died in that alley. No one would care. Everything hurt. Nothing mattered. He wanted to close his eyes and stop breathing altogether.

When she had said his name, her voice startled him so much he almost hit his head against the wall. She was dressed in all green, dark as the forest they met in the night before. Her eyes were dull, bags lining them. She leaned down, slipped gauze from her green bag, and bandaged him in silence. She then took his hand and led him to a house. She didn't say another word.

He met Chamomile and danced in the garden until his feet bled. By the time he got home all he could feel was a thick, unspeakable feeling about the mysterious girl who he didn't even know the name of.

He'd danced then, like he should have been here. Yet he was unable to move, staring at her as she stood in his studio. Their images blurred in the mirror as he tried to pull himself back together.

Stop crying.

This was nothing. This moment was nothing. It was not what he had been waiting years for. She was never supposed to ever trust him, to ever talk to him. They were nothing.

He blinked away the tears before they fell.

"Are we friends?" she asked him.

"No," he said, spitting the word before he could process. Friends betrayed him. Friends hated him. Friends hurt her. Friends almost caused her to kill herself. They could never be friends. Friends destroyed everything.

Besides, they had nothing in common. She liked photography, him dance. She was sad. He was angry. He hated people, but she wished for them.

"Can we ever be?" she asked.

"No." He was certain.

Even when she transferred to his Academy; not because she wanted to know him, but because like him, she was lost, and his school was for students who were struggling. Even when she walked with him to Academy each day. Even when she was in the same year as him, despite her being two years older, due to her health. Even when she took all the same classes, and they always did projects together. He did *not* care for her.

Nor did she care for him. She never said more than two words. She never explained anything she did. If he didn't follow her, she'd go astray. With a camera in her hand, she was blind to directions. She would get completely lost and be unable to find her way home.

He should have kicked her away long ago, but for reasons only Ixxzal knew, he could not. He hated having to wait for her but if he didn't wait, she'd be abandoned. He knew what it felt like to be abandoned, and he hated seeing her cry more.

He should have stopped her from intruding in on his private dance practices. Yet she always sat so quietly, and still. It was like disturbing freshly laid snow if he forced her to leave as soon as she sat. He should have never given her access to everything in his life, but she was so careful and never intruded where she was not meant to be.

Their eyes locked. The unspeakable emotion he could not name—would not name, could not understand, would not let himself understand—surged stronger in each passing second.

It was infuriating being near her. Her existing within his atmosphere was enough to drive him mad. Every day she was by him, he found it easier to breathe. Every day that she stood by him, he found it easier to walk on. Every moment with her was another reminder of how worthless he was in other's eyes, but how much he didn't care. Every moment they were together he forgot to hate himself. She hurt him, always, in every way. She made him want.

"Do you know what my favorite color is, Arco?"

"Pink," he said. She always gravitated towards pink items, despite never purchasing them or using them.

"It's green."

"No, it's not."

"Yes, it is."

"No, it's not."

He tried to wrap his mind around the information, unable to reconcile the words with what he'd seen with his own eyes.

Quickly he busied himself, instead, with setting his practice fans away on the rack, away from her. He no longer wanted to practice. He needed to get away and forget this ever happened.

He. . . he could not cry. He struggled to face her again, focusing on the blank wall and trying to blink away the snow until he could see clearly.

"Green is what everyone thinks. What my parents and brother think," she said breathing sharply. "But it is pink."

He *knew* it. He was right. The thought of being right filled him with a lightness. . . Joy spread, and he immediately stopped himself, cutting away the smile that began to plaster itself on his face.

Hiccupping on invisible tears she went on, "But that's a secret. No one is supposed to know."

"It's obvious," he said, waving his hand. This didn't matter. What was happening right now did not matter. It was not real.

"And yours is teal."

The words made him melt, like an icicle about to drop from the branch of a tree.

Spring arrived.

How did she know that? He never looked at it. He always avoided it. No one was supposed to know. He never ever wore it. He didn't. . . His world tilted.

No, no no no, don't think, don't feel. She hates you too. She will never care for you. This is all a lie. It's always a lie, but no matter how hard he tried to convince himself, he could not.

Something had rooted itself deep in his heart without him noticing and now it was the time for it to bloom.

"I see you, Arco," she said. "I know you."

Arco's heart jolted and nearly stopped. Did she call him Arco? No one called him Arco, not even his own family. Not anymore.

"S.Mirrors is a heartmate," she said. "True love. The best match for you. The one the Gods have ordained is meant to be your everything."

"We aren't. . ." he hesitated.

"That's what we're told, about S.Mirrors." she went on, speaking faster, clearer. "It's what I was told when I was a kid. That I had a very special bond, one that could never be replaced. One that could never be replicated."

Despite the pain in his chest, the melting that was trying to overcome him, he focused on the snow, on the cold. Fires were only meant to destroy. Ice was only meant to keep something in perpetuity. He could never be hers. She could never be his. They were supposed to be strangers. He needed to make it clear.

"I'm not your heartmate."

She stepped up to him, facing him. They were the same height and their eyes matched in intensity of the void they both held.

"I know. I don't want a heartmate." The words almost sounded like: *I want you.*

She looked down and his eyes followed. Somehow in the time she got to him, she'd unbandaged her wrist. The white gauze held in her right hand as she drew out his left arm. She held their left wrists next to each other: a faded constellation on hers and nothing on his. When he looked back up, her eyes were sparking with the light of a flashing camera. It was blinding, filling her dull eyes with life.

"Do you still want to die, Arco?" she asked him, cutting into his heart.

He had never told anyone that he wanted to die. Never. Yet, she knew him. And he *wanted* her to know him. How he *needed* this. The feeling was washing through him, and there would never be a way to stop it now. He'd be betrayed again. He'd be left again.

Friends were a disaster. . . Friends would ruin him. Friends would destroy him. The emptiness was easier than this feeling that was resonating. He was. . . He feared. . . He. . . unspoken.

"I like dancing more," he said.

It was the only thing that held him together when his family was falling apart, his brother disappeared, and everyone hated him. Dancing was all he had. It was the only thing he could cling to. But now. . .

She pressed her left wrist over his.

"I like photography more," she agreed.

The two of them stood in the dance studio, punctuated by echoes of their breathing. He thought of snow, and a girl surrounded by it: her breath white in the cold, hair thick and dark as black ink.

She had eyes that saw all. She was covered in so many layers of snow, so pure and white that she glowed. Melting. Growing. Blooming.

Blue Rose Fears resonated deeply in his soul. It was the dance he'd been trying to master in secret, the dance that his father would never approve. He'd memorized all the steps, and in this moment, he swore he *understood* it: the complexity, the love, the hate, the horror, and the beauty. It was within the girl who saw him, and the girl he wanted in his life with a burning unspeakable emotion that she'd stand by his side forever.

Something pivotal had shifted between them. A bristling question rang at the back of his mind as she let go of his arm and busied herself on her camera. He was unable to move away from her as she let the gauze fall to the floor. All he could see was her. All he could feel was her presence in his life. All he wanted was to know if he mattered to her, even when he didn't think he deserved it.

"Amaryllis. . ." He said her name for the first time in his life. It had always been a cherished secret, unspoken. Saying it was like a wish. *I need you.* "Did you find it?"

Amaryllis' head snapped up, camera pulled to her chest.

"Your soul?" he clarified, "That night in the snow."

"Did you find yours?" Amaryllis' voice shook. She stared at him in fear, wide eyed and shaking. What was she afraid of?

The unspeakable emotion began to be named, began to form, began to matter. It was silver slush, warming into an oasis within him and filling the void. As it did, it settled in a way that revealed he hadn't been empty in a very long time; not fully, not for years. Not since. . .

"I don't know," he admitted. "But. . . I met you."

Please, he prayed for the first time in five years, *Ixxzal. . . Xeyaro. . . Zaynir, Lumak, Pokk, Azza. . .* He asked for anyone who would listen. *Am I allowed to have this?*

He wanted this, whatever it was, more than anything he'd wanted in his entire life.

Amaryllis turned her camera around and showed him, the number 00001 was at the bottom of the screen. Arco was in the snow, dancing. It was heartbreaking. It was terrible form. It was horrifying and made him want to scream. It was also the most beautiful photo he'd ever seen.

He tried to stop himself from smiling but failed miserably. He covered his face, trying to bite back the tears at the idea that someone saw him so clearly. Someone had been able to capture what little remained of his heart.

"And I met you," Amaryllis said, voice stable and clear, cutting through her own tears.

Please. . .

No. He didn't care if the Gods would allow him.

He was going to choose her, from this moment on.

"You look better in white," he said what he'd thought since the day he met her. "We should go shopping."

For a moment she hesitated before she began sobbing. Fear coursed through his body as he tried to wipe her tears away. The more he tried the more she cried.

"I'm so—"

"I see you, Arco. I found you." She began laughing, grabbing his hands on her face. Her laughter was bright, loud, filled with energy she never had. She smiled: the first one he'd ever seen grace her face. What he thought was the most beautiful thing he'd ever seen was eclipsed by the sheer magnitude of her joy. Pain and peace, happiness and bitterness: an unspeakable emotion that was impossible to ignore was also one that had a place in his life.

"I found you too, Amaryllis," he said, knowing it and finally giving a name to the emotion: hope.

He laughed with her: confused, incredulous and feeling too much all at one. Their laughter was like the chimes of metronome, settling his heart and filling it with peace. Together they were blossoming.

With her hand in his, with laughter in their lungs and fire within their hearts, the two raced from the practice room. He did not know where he was going to go but he knew she would never care.

Her eyes were a prayer. And so long as she was with him, he'd always find his way home.

the UNDERSTANDING of

Chaos and Creation are abstract, yes.
However, look at how we build, how we destroy, how we hurt others when we know we should not.
There needs to be destruction to have creation. There is no tranquility that chaos can't break.
When we understand this, we can be prepared.

— On Azza

Dance 19

Beauty

Incarnadine

15 Xeyan

27 Days Left

"What do you want?"
"Now?"
"To go home?"
"I'm not sure anymore."

When Arna got home, he was able to walk on his own. Between his Blessings, his mother's healing, and the blood supplements that Jasi stole from the LHF, Arna was conscious.

Not that he wanted to be.

The screams continued to echo in his head.

diefailurediefailuredietheend

His death was inevitable. Because despite everything, Arna was not certain he'd make the right choice between mortals and the Gods. He was not certain he could save the world when a single wrong answer meant the end. He was not sure he could withstand the test even if he did.

Arna was terrified. He was angry. He was petrified by his imminent death. And he was silent.

The Golden Generation, Amaryllis, and Sarcoline, were seated, waiting. Ebru jumped up, and Arna avoided him, all of them, mumbling that he didn't want to be touched as he left the room. When he got to his bedroom, he closed the door without a sound and locked it tight. He struggled to get control over his Blessings.

theendtheendtheend
everythingwasgoingtoendanditwashisfault
imposterfailureimposterfailure

He needed to control it.

The distant voice of Jasi was in a screaming competition with Ebru and Sarcoline. There was crying as well from whom he assumed had to be Phlox and Ginger. Rosmarinus and Ven's voices were a chorus urging everyone to be calm.

Arna lit his alter candles with a prayer, the weak light of their flames flickering ever so slightly. He laid down beneath their alter and slowly began to recite scriptures, clenching his hands tighter as he did. His hands screamed at him as he reopened the knife wounds, digging his nails through the blood, seeking clarity. His nerve endings were shot.

He did not use his Blessings to heal.

Soon the scriptures were not enough.

And his soul cried out in the pain that he'd been concealing.

nomorehiding
allhisfaultallhisfault
imposterimposterimpostertimetodie

Tears ran down his face as he struggled to b r e a t h e.

Even if the world did not end, as the Gods predicted, Arna was not sure that he could imagine a world where the Gods did not speak to him. He needed them, as much as they needed him. Arna could not let them disappear.

He could not let the world die.

> [Xeyaro began to sing to him as they did when he had nightmares
> as a child, their voice shaking.]
> [Azza laid beside him, humming along, as Zaynir held his hands.]
> [Ixxzal and Pokk bickered.]
> [*I want to—*
> *No.*
> *I will.*
> *Stop. He's okay.*
> *They hurt him! He's my—*
> *We couldn't protect him.*]
> [Lumak recited laws that Arna could use to sue the government.
> Making plans.]

When Arna opened his eyes, it was well into the night. His room was a mess of papers on the floor, shredded posters, empty walls, broken iconography, splintered furniture, and ripped clothes. The only thing untouched were the candles for his Gods and their alters, sitting on the floor between his dresser, which was split in two. Sometime in the night his Blessings had gone out of control.

He could not get himself to care.

He sat up slowly, his body aching in a way that it hadn't in a long time. His heart was racing, pounding in his chest threatening to explode. The terror continued to fill his bones and he stared at the candles for a long time.

> whatifhewasthereasonthat—

Ignore it. Kill it. Destroy it. Bury it. Blessings were once more fully under his control, and he wove them until the silence resonated and the thrumming died.

He was fine.

He forced the emotions down, repeatedly over the years. When he first realized he was an imposter? Ignore the sorrow. When he first found out that he could die during the ascendence to Divinity? Kill the fear. When he realized, he was going to lose a Blessing every time be picked up a fan? Destroy the evidence. When he first understood that he could die even if he succeeded because of the storms, the loss of Blessings, and the intensity of the Divinity? Bury the hesitation.

When he first felt the pain of picking up a fan? The second time? The third? The fourth? The fifth? When he first saw the superstorms? When he first had to dance near one? In one? The pain? The suffering? The hate? Say a prayer and never visit the grave.

This was no different.

He was fine.

> makeitsilent.
> (Can it remain hidden forever?)

Nothing new had been revealed to him. He had experienced worse pain before. Sure, the whole world had watched his suffering. Yes, he had been humiliated infront of the world on a live stream. But it did not matter, everyone already hated him. They had hated him since he as fifteen.

Their hate did not matter. The fact that they knew he was missing Blessings did not matter. The fact that many may think he was being rejected by the Gods as an imposter? It didn't matter.

imposterIMPOSTERIm—

It   did   not   matter.

Kill it. Breathe. Breathe. He flourished his Blessings.

Arna counted to six and dug into his wounds, forcing himself back into clarity, before he could spiral. He thought of what was at a stake: of those who had already died for him.

When he was sixteen, the couple in the silver house had burned beyond recognition: faces peeled back in electricity, and a house turned to ash on the ground. The smell of flesh was nauseating and unforgettable.

At seventeen, the couple with the silver door had faded one after another. Their bodies were torn apart from the inside out. They became little more than skeletons as the doctors said there was nothing they could do. Doctors said it had progressed too far.

When he was eighteen, he was wide eyed in terror atop a falling train.

The Gods hated him, he'd once convinced himself. But no, it was an unfortunate fact that the Gods were both coincidence and fate. They refused to be ignored.

The noise was louder right before it was turned off.

By being near him, people were destined to die.

They may have died even if they never met him.

Arna could hear the screams

as the train fell.

as the candles went out.

in protest of him returning.

of the priests that thought they saw him and wanted him dead.

in the Cathedral basement as he stole his fan.

Somewhere in his soul, clawing at him to return and get out and to remember:

(hope)

hopedidnotmatterhopedidnotexist.

hopedidnotmatterhopedidnotexist.

hopedidnotmatterhopedidnotexist.

All cries merged into one.

Threaded with the sound of: lightning igniting the world.

screeching metal

burning corpses

fading memories

the murder of dreams

his agonal breath

Ignore it. Destroy it. Kill it. Bury it. Focus on what matters.

[*We are here.*]

He could not identify the voice anymore. They were scarce because they used too much energy to help him. They were dying.

Everything was d y i n g.

No. Arna let himself bleed and breathe in circular eight counts, gathering himself and his thoughts. He needed to move before he spiraled.

Nothing was new. Nothing had changed. He still had to save the world. He could not fall apart: could never fall apart. He had to keep going.

SILENCE

His Blessings were struggling to work, but they would. He'd make them. He could not fail now. He would never be like Saffron.

Purple flowers died in storms.

Arna got up, and began to clean his room, picking up what remained of some of the posters and throwing them into a corner. He threw the broken iconography aside. The remainder, that which had fallen but were untouched, he sorted by person. He added what was left of the religious quotes into the stacks.

One by one, he took the scrapbooks that he'd stored under his bed and added the stacks into the correct scrapbook. They were simple things, six inches, filled to the brim with everything he'd ever collected. Each scrapbook was a set of three colors, inspired by the Gods that he thought of when he gazed at them from the audience. It was one of his few outlets over the years, that he'd need to complete before he died. Although not this day.

Once they were filled, Arna shoved them against the back wall and cleaned his room. His bed and dresser were shattered.

failurefailurefailure

It   didn't   matter.

makeitsilent

Pulling his bed from the broken frame, Arna pulled out the wood, and tossed it all into a corner. He removed what was in the drawers and pushed the rest into the corner as well. He made a makeshift collection of trash and destruction, piled high. His broken dresser with a slat of wood placed across became a new alter. He set the candles one by one on the thin bridge, hovering over destruction. The remainder of the room was near empty in contrast.

Once Arna picked up his clothes, he grabbed a jacket and walked down to the practice rooms.

Return to normal. He could prove that he was fine.

Move on. Keep going. He did not have time to wait.

The entire house was silent in the early morning hours as it usually was. Narrowly focused on what he had to do, he went to his brother's practice room instead for no reason other than comfort. He said a prayer to activate the practice candles that sat there. They ignited, flickering smaller flames than usual.

With a deep breath he squeezed his hands tight and was blinded by pain. Where his crescent moons used to be were now large and jagged scars as though his palms had been slashed with glass and not a blade. They continued to bleed from earlier when he'd reopened the wounds.

He then flourished all of his Blessings, settling into the sickening pain that filled him at the act. It helped to clear the thoughts, as all he could think of was the darting stars in his vision. Once the pain vanished, only needing six counts to right his mind this time, Arna shook out his hands that were no longer bleeding but the wounds were puckered and red.

Without turning on the light, Arna completed his morning training. He ignored the pain in his hands as he used the practice disks and snapped his fake fans open. He ignored the aches and pains in his knees from having been forced to kneel for hours. He ignored the ways all his bones screamed after the hours of pressure he'd been under, and the way that even using his Blessings felt like his veins were on fire. Dancing through two of the variations, relaxed his body in time.

Nothing had changed.

He was *fine.*

Finally, his Blessings worked for him. Finally, all the screams and echoes and EVERYTHING was silent again.

Arna's hands were shaking when he prepared to go back upstairs. Squeezing them, he let the pain wake him up. He then forced his body Blessings to heal the wounds until they were no more than irritated lines: improperly healed.

It's showtime.

Arna stepped out and headed up the stairs where there was a ruckus. He let his shoulders relax and brought the smile to his lips.

"He's not answering his mobile." Ebru's voice was spun in ire. "You're sure you saw him leave?"

"Yes," Sarcoline said in equal urgency and animosity. "I thought he went to practice, but he wasn't in his dance room."

"I'll search the station. If he left, there will have to be logs." Jasi's voice was slow but clearly panicked.

"He can't go, not again." Ginger was sobbing.

[*We love you,* Pokk whispered.]

Arna walked to the top of the stairs to see everyone: his parents making panicked calls, Ebru and Jasi comparing notes, Aureolin comforting Ginger, Ven, and Phlox. Amaryllis was with Sarcoline, who had a map in hand and a white notebook. Rosmarinus handed everyone drinks and food. They all stopped and turned to him.

An eerie silence filled the room as Arna was examined like being put through a transport machine: scanned down to the smallest molecule.

"I was downstairs practicing," Arna laughed, removing his hood. "Did you not think to check there?"

"Arna. . ." Jasi stuttered and raced over to check him.

"I did!" Sarcoline snapped.

"I was in your room." Arna kept his smile large and shrugged his shoulders, trying to make the other's laugh. "Needed a change in scenery."

Not a single one of them was convinced. If he couldn't convince them, then he couldn't convince anyone.

Believe it. Fake it. He'd done it before.

He was fine.

Arna chuckled and walked into the room, nonchalant and as open as he could fake it. He forced his confidence to the forefront.

"I'm fine. I was a bit shaken up last night, but I'm okay. . . Well, the ceremony left scars." He offered out his hands to show. "But otherwise, I'm okay."

One by one the faces in the room calmed. The tension visibly alleviated as shoulders relaxed, but there was still something that worried them.

Face it and move on. He had to make them feel at ease.

[   ]

"What's wrong?" Arna asked slowly, letting the concern appear on his face. *Keep in control. Do not panic.* He had to keep going. He had to keep pushing forward. The Ceremony was too close. After he danced, he could let himself panic. He needed to prove to them that he could do this. He needed to find the path to live.

(live?)

He was going to *live.*

"We saw the broadcast. We know how many Blessings you're missing. They forced you," Aureolin explained, with a hushed voice.

"Tortured," Phlox corrected, quiet. Her voice broke with the sound of tears. Amaryllis put her hand on Phlox's shoulder and Phlox sniffled.

"Tortured," Rosmarinus agreed.

Arna was not too sure. The word was rather harsh for what had happened, and if he were truly tortured, they wouldn't have shown it live. It was only a little pain and suffering, nothing worth sobbing over.

Rosmarinus continued, "Ebru said that each time you pick up a fan you lose a Blessing."

As he said the words, Phlox cried even harder. Arna had not expected to see Phlox, holier-than-thou-I'm-an-actress-now Phlox, cry real tears.

Ah.

It was a clear look of worry on all of their faces. He turned his attention to Ebru specifically.

"You told them last night?" Arna asked him.

Ebru looked away, and Ven stepped forward instead.

They said, "I told them. I feel it everytime, remember? The first time I went to the doctor, but it couldn't be replicated. The second, I begged them to run every test, but Amaryllis asked me if it could be you. Because it didn't feel like my pain, it was more distant than that, sharp. And the two lasted different amounts of time. The third time, it was agonizing, and it lasted hours. I knew then that it had to be you, but I couldn't understand what you were doing."

Stunned, Arna tried to think of every time he'd lost one. The distance should have made it so. . . that was what S.Mirrors was for, wasn't it? It was an anchor, to keep him from falling apart. It was a connection meant to share.

How bad is it when I'm near?

[Zaynir was a hummingbird.]

Ven was to be his defender. A fighter that stood by him as Arna faced his fiercest battle. Devoted to sharing the burned with him, and Ven had never even made the choice to do it. Ven was forced to stand still by the Gods for him. Were they meant to hover in the storm as Arna danced?

"I told them its why you've been an anxious mess since you got back home."

theendtheendTHEEND

Arna's heart raced again, as fast as a hummingbird. His breaths turned short. He tried to level himself, but the panic was swirling into an incessant need to get out.

No. Hold it together. Hold it together.

(But he wanted to live?)

Arna began to laugh. Hysterically, unable to keep his balance as he did. It wasn't funny and no one else was laughing but Arna found it hilarious. Ven felt everything when Arna lost his Blessings the same way Arna felt them.

After all this time, there was another thing he didn't know. And worse, they all knew it before him.

Arna laughed for a solid minute before he doubled over and then Ebru was there, grabbing him, with Ven and Jasi. They were all pulling him to the couch. Rosmarinus handed Arna a water that he graciously drank, without being satiated.

Arna's S.Mirror was activated against his will, in an agonizing pain, which was then filled with calm and peace. Ven soothed him, but it made Arna worse.

Cut it off. Cut it off. Arna pulled back his emotions. He stopped laughing. He ended the S.Mirrors activation. He sat in silence.

makeitsilent

"I'm sorry. I didn't realize you did," Arna admitted. "I'm sorry."

"Then it's true?" Phlox asked from where she sat. Somehow in his fit of hysterics they were all close to him, sitting, standing, watching him as he sat on the couch. "You will lose one every time you pick up a fan? Even when you dance?"

Yes, and the end of the world is coming and if I don't dance you'll all die. He could not tell her. It would destroy them.

[There is only one secret. You cannot share it, Lumak called far
away.]

"I'm okay," Arna answered instead. The group struggled for words. As if he should have been exempt because he was the Chosen.

"But the Gods will protect you in your dances, right?" she asked as if he had answered her question.

Arna was not sure how to answer the question. He sat for too long and the faces of those around him began to twist and change.

His father knelt next to Arna who sat breathing heavily. "You are, then?"

"The Chosen?" Arna asked, unsure how to answer. He was—

imposterfailuresaffronjustlikesaffron

No. Bury it. Kill it. He was *fine.*

"Arna." His father was soft with the name, a pressing voice that said Zaffre could trust him.

Arna pleaded with his father using his eyes. He needed him to understand. He needed his father to see that Arna could say no more.

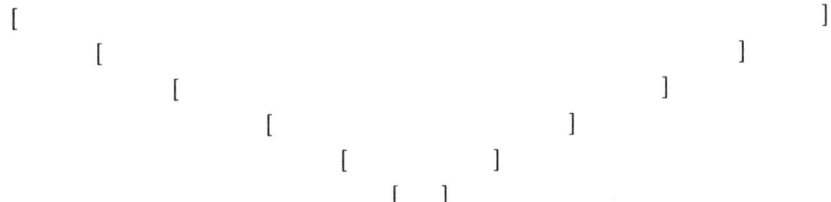

[Still the Gods said nothing.]

It wouldn't be a test if it wasn't difficult, Azza often said. They had tested him and trained him, and they cared. They wanted him to have everything that he had craved for so long. He was going to do what it took to save those he cared about. No matter what. Even though he told it to everyone, and he repeated it to himself, his will to live was fading. Each day chipped away at it.

His father helped him: carefully, delicately, like the father he had always been. The teacher was long gone. Zaffre asked, "Do we need to tell the dancers to cancel the auditions for the Ceremony of Chaos?"

Arna paused.

There were wind chimes.

The ones hanging in the garden were swinging wildly, their sound came through the window that was open next to his father's first fan. The lights began to flicker, like the flames of a candle. The glasses in the room began shaking, clicking in the kitchen. There was a whistle in the air as wind rushed through the house, from upstairs to the downstairs, right through them and into the stairwell.

Arna did not react to the sounds as he had been trained. He was the only one who could hear—

Everyone, save his parents, were reacting, looking around.

"What is that?" Sarcoline asked.

Amaryllis wrapped her arms tightly around herself.

"Did something break?" Ginger asked. "Not the trains, right?"

His friends heard it. They all saw it. It was getting louder, blinking faster. The room was shaking. *It can't be a secret if it's already known.*

Only Rosmarinus' eyes were on Arna, head tilted asking, "Was that. . ."

The Gods sent him back to his family so they could support him. He sanctified them, now he had to trust them. If he was going to live, if he was going to fight, he had to tell them. The Gods were screaming at him: he needed to jump.

Did he need to hide it?

"When I dance, I will lose a Blessing each time I pick one up," Arna admitted at the God's insistence, letting the words fall free. Everything stopped. One by one, everyone slowly looked at him.

"I can check—" Jasi began.

"The Gods aren't *real*," Phlox cut him off, shocking the whole room.

"They're getting weaker," Arna said. "And they're a bit annoyed with me right now so they're trying to get my attention. Sorry."

There was a look of shock across the group.

"But that's not. . ." Ginger disagreed.

[The distant thunder of laughter.]

And then, in the room, Arna closed his eyes and said a prayer: "Of the Gods, hear my call, I sit here before you with prayers that seek to find answers."

There was a set of Everlit candles in the living room, seated behind him on the alter near the stairs. While he could not see it, the others did. When he opened his eyes, he did not need to check.

They were all staring behind him as if there was a ghost, all eyes were locked there, except three. Ebru held tightly to him, grimacing. Amaryllis' eyes were open and staring right into Arna's soul, unraveling him. Sarcoline stared at him with abject horror.

No. Did he. . . What had he. . .

"But you need all of them, don't you?" Sarcoline said, voice shaking. "To dance twenty-six. It's why the Chosen is given all of the Blessings. You need them all to succeed twenty-six. That's the reason regular dancers die."

One by one all of the eyes in the room returned to Arna and the conversation.

Arna did not need to confirm the answer. It was clear that as Sarcoline said the words that everyone else in the room drew the same conclusion that he had. There was a long moment where they all stared at him. Each one wanted to say something, but no words were spoken.

"No," Arna answered, and a hushed expression of relief filled the room. "It's a far more complicated than that. . . But no. I don't need them all to survive twenty-six."

"And auditions?" his father asked.

Before Arna could answer Ven recited, "To pick mortality is to pick the Gods. To pick the Gods is to pick mortality."

Arna's body tensed, accidentally squeezing Ven's hand.

Ven said, "Until you answer that question, you can't dance right?"

Arna slowly but surely nodded. "I won't dance, if I'm not ready."

It was the only answer he could give them.

"The Gods are really asking you to pick between Mortals and the Gods?" Ebru clarified. "Between us and them?"

"It's complicated. . ." Arna sighed. "I have to finish my variation, understand the question, make my choice, and then, and only then, can I dance."

[*We are watching*. Xeyaro's voice was the last to fade into oblivion.]

"We have to hold the auditions," Sarcoline said suddenly. "Dad, Ebru. You have to make them do them."

"Everyone expects him to dance," Zaffre disagreed.

"But until he makes the choice. . ." Sarcoline was speaking quickly, as if he understood something else. "The Dances *must* be danced each year. Right? It keeps the bond strong?"

"The contract between mortals and Gods must be maintained by the performance of the first twenty-four Dances, each year on the solstice. If not, the connection between Gods and mortals will be broken," Arna recited, unsure what Sarcoline was getting at.

"But the connection is already broken," Amaryllis shook her head. "In the Splintering."

"What are you implying, Sarcoline?" Jasi asked.

"Arna has to make his choice. If not this year, then next, the Chosen doesn't have to dance the year they return from their pilgramage, but we have to. If not, we lose our Blessings. And if he has to make a choice, it has to be done without any interference. Isn't that what you said, dad? Isn't that what the scriptures say?" Sarcoline asked and then accused Arna, "You don't know how to answer the question and are struggling. Is that another reason you're anxiety is like the weight of a thousand worlds? Right Ven? That's how bad it is? Let us help you Arna. If we take the burden and give you more time, can you do it then?"

Arna blinked. His brother was suddenly looking younger than he had ever looked before. It was in the way his brother was standing: arms crossed, hands balled into fists, eyes wide, and clear understanding implanted on his face. Suddenly Arna truly saw his brother as someone different from himself.

This whole time Sarcoline was acting as they all did: narrowly focused on the art. But where the others had not cared much for school—they'd picked majors that interested them but did not much care for education—his brother was a scholar. Sarcoline's Blessings were working to put all the pieces together. His brother was smarter than he ever was.

What if Sarcoline pieced together too much?

seethathewasanimposter
seethathewasafailure
seehewasjustlikesaffron

"So long as you support me," Arna said, shoving down every sense of nausea that filled him. "I will dance."

He could not break his brother again. So, Arna grinned instead.

Morning breakfast was filled with fruits and grains, pancakes and sweet tea. Rosmarinus left early for practice, saying he'd return after he finished his charity work and advertisement shoots in the evening. Jasi, too, left for work, irritated by the tasks he needed to complete before he met up with Zaffre and Arna for the task force meeting.

Wenge fussed about Sarcoline and Ginger, who were dressed in their best for the final week of their classes. Sarcoline wore mint and silver; Ginger wore shades of green. Wenge wore a beautiful dress Ginger had made: it sparkled like diamonds and scales, and was mint, an opalescent sky-blue, and white. Arna sat at the family dining table, watching from the living room, facing the kitchen.

"Mom," Sarcoline stopped their mother. "It's just exam week, not graduation."

The worldwide graduation week was the next week. Both Ginger and Sarcoline were supposed to perform for the university graduation.

"It's a performance audition, even if it's just for school," Wenge said, setting his hair.

"We already have the spots." Ginger sipped her tea.

"Are you going to the music festival after the meeting today?" Sarcoline asked Arna, passing him pancakes with banana. Everything had returned to normal, just as Arna wished, but there was something different in Sarcoline. His brother was changed, looking at him and trying to unravel him.

"No, Ebru refused on principal. And I have. . . too much work to finish." Music, dance, fans, almost no time left. "He and I are going to collect sounds later tonight. He has a new song idea, and frankly between that and my own work. . . I don't have the time."

"Yes. *Work.*" Sarcoline passed Arna the grapes, rolling his eyes.

Arna picked at the grapes thinking of a time when he was young. The soft song of the front bell sounded. Arna returned his focus to what he needed to do: actionable steps that kept his mind clear of fear.

His Blessings were working overtime, but it was fine. The noise was gone.

"I'll be right back." Wenge finally left Sarcoline's side.

"You'll be here until dad picks you up?" Ginger asked. "You swear?"

Arna nodded. Ebru and Ven had forbade him from going online, so all he had was hearsay and the sound of the loud protests outside their house. Ever since his testing it was worse. But instead of being called a fake, he was being called a liar. He was being called a failure. He was being told to give up because clearly the Gods had given up on him. . .

justlikesaffronjustlikesaffronjustlikesaffron

Maybe the noise was not gone. He pushed his Blessings harder, but the gap was impossible to fill and the thoughts didn't want to hide anymore.

"Have you told mom yet?" Arna turned the conversation.

Ignore the anger. Ignore the protests. He was fine. Everything was fine. He had too much to do, too much to finish.

"No. . ." Ginger admitted, slowly.

"Ginger!" Sarcoline snapped. "You need to tell her."

"I will. I will." She shook her hands, but Arna didn't believe her. She was too afraid.

"Tell me what?" Wenge's voice came from the archway. The three turned to face their mother, who stood with narrowed eyes and her hands on her hips.

"I—" Ginger hiccupped at the words.

"It's okay," Arna cheered Ginger on, patting her back.

"It's nothing bad," Sarcoline tried to smooth their mother over.

"Gingerline?" Their mother's voice dropped lower, demanding an answer.

"Iwanttochangemymajor," Ginger spat out.

"What?" Their mother relaxed. "That's it?" She practically floated over to Ginger. "To fashion. Is that right?"

"You knew?" Ginger gasped.

"We all knew, baby. Do you need me to go to the school with you? We can do that today." Their mother kissed Ginger's head and fixed the collar of her dress.

"I can do it," Ginger visibly bounced to her feet. She beamed from ear to ear.

"Are you sure?" Wenge asked with a smile that was completely confident in Ginger.

"I am," Ginger said, and Arna believed her.

"Okay." Wenge kissed Ginger's cheek. She walked upstairs,.

"I hate both of you!" Ginger giggled as she stood with her bag.

"Better to say it now." Sarcoline finished his food. "We need to go Ginger. You might be confident in skipping exams, but I need to be there."

"*You.*" Ginger placed her hands on her hips. "Right. You. The one who ditched for weeks and somehow still have the highest grades in school. You're a fucking genius Sarcoline, shut it."

"I'm simply good at research, that's it," Sarcoline laughed as he grabbed his bag off a chair and headed downstairs.

"He's taking more business classes next term," Ginger said, bright and cheerful. Without the pressure of being the heir she never wanted to be. "I guess we'll be graduating together then."

"Why? Won't you still be ahead?" They were both adding majors, but she'd been in university for much longer.

"I'm going to have to get into the design school, and that takes at least a year. Even if he's trying to get two degrees, I will be starting over from the beginning. And if you join us, then all three of us will graduate at the same time. Wouldn't that be something?" Ginger giggled as Sarcoline yelled her name from below. "See you, Arna!"

Ginger raced downstairs. Moments later Arna's mother returned. She walked over to Arna and kissed his head. "Alright, the guards know that I am leaving for Mymy's. Remember to call your father before you go to him."

She then grabbed a few glass bottles of water and went to the door.

"Mom?" he asked her before she could leave.

"Yes?" She smiled brightly but the longer Arna struggled to vocalize his question, the quicker her smile vanished.

"I heard that dad. . . he drank a *lot* after I left."

His mother's expression darkened. "He rejected us all, yes. But he is much better. His therapist is helping and now that you are home. . ."

"I also know that we lost many of our sponsors and allies because of it." Another thing that was his fault.

"They were always fickle, love. Those who were waiting to destroy us did not hesitate, and most others were afraid we were cursed but—" She paused, then smiled lightly. "You don't have to worry, okay? We are better now. You're home."

She kissed his head and told him to stay safe. Then she was gone.

Arna finished his food, alone. There was no sound of Gods. No bickering of people. Truly. Utterly. Alone. . .

justlikesaffronsaffronsaffron

His food tasted like sand the more and more he chewed. The room started to close in on him. His breathing hitched. Everyone was so happy, but. . .

imposterimposterimposter

Arna checked the news despite being told not to. Zaffre had put a lock on web searches in the house, but Arna was good at getting around locks and breaking into things he wasn't meant to get into. Typing in a password, Arna was able to freely access the web online.

What he found was chaos.

Incarnadine A Liar?

The Golden Boy a Golden Failure?

What Does It Mean For Incarnadine to be Missing 5 Blessings?

Incarnadine Vivicent: The Herald of the End?

The END Is NOW

Arna read the articles. Most of them were only reiterating facts, with not much more to be said, or quoting scriptures and citing history. Nothing was particularly interesting itself.

> ► Gods, what does this mean?
> ► Can he even still dance?
>> ► No, the Gods abandoned him, it's why he's missing Blessings.
>> ► I was wondering the same thing.
>>> ► If he does, does that mean the whole world changes?
>>>> ► OR does it mean everything ends?
> ► I'm telling you. Sarcoline would have been less of a disappointment.
>> ► Incarnadine was a failure from the beginning.

Arna glared at the comments and flipped through the boards and forums about him. There was a sense of panic.

> ► He's just an imposter.
>> ► And a failure
>>> ► The Gods hate him.
>>>> ► Mortals hate him too. All of Mortality hates him. If it weren't for him, the world wouldn't be ending.

The End of the World?

What to do if Your Blessings Disappear

Total Number of Blessings Vanishing Worldwide: Live Counter

Have You Lost a Blessing?

Blessings VANISHING En Masse

Azis Hospital Failure

Ludiel Power Outages

Podiel Train Failure: Commuters Cautioned

Zaydiel Petals Technical Failure Truth: Government Mandated Maintenance

Ixis: Map of All Collapsed Sections

Xeysis Warns of Issues in Artificial Weather System

The market was crashing. Priests were on all the stations, talking and leading prayers. The world was in a state of crisis worse than when he caused the Splintering. Arna could find government statements and government announcements, assuring the public things were under control, but Arna knew cover-ups when he saw them.

Arna stopped breathing as he read.

I did this.

theendtheendtheend

andeveryoneknewitwashisfault

He started to shake, terror rising up in his throat. If he did not figure out the answer to the question by the Day of New Dawn, everyone would die. And for what? Because he couldn't figure out the answer to such a simple question?

Terror bubbled. Tears were in his eyes. His hands ached. His entire body was heaving. Bile rose. His stomach churned.

No. Kill it. Destroy it. Bury it. Arna squeezed his hands, and the pain cleared his mind. *Focus on the variation. Focus on the questions and you can save them.*

His overworked Blessings were unable to hold it all back.

Start from the beginning.

The question was Mortal or the Gods. He had to understand the true question being asked. He had to know the true weight and cost of his choice. He had to be willing to accept the choice even if he was wrong.

The issue was that he knew the weight and cost. It was clear. Everyone died if he didn't dance. The world ended if he didn't dance. The Gods disappeared for good if he didn't dance. If that wasn't the true weight and cost of his vow, what *was*?

And how could he accept being wrong? He had to dance. He had to save them all. He couldn't just accept that he could be wrong. He couldn't just accept that he would be the reason the world *ended*.

Arna began to hyperventilate again.

[Sirens were screaming.]

Arna dove to the side, falling off his chair. The gun shots that went off riddled the table in holes where Arna sat. Wood splintered and went flying as Arna rolled over, activating all of his Blessings. Hitting the floor Arna avoided the guards that his father had hired to protect the house from protesters. They had come up from the ballroom, no doubt, not knowing where the hidden staircases were.

There were a dozen of them in the room glaring at him with guns in hand. They all wore masks and jackets with the mark for the god of the One Truth.

"You killed my daughter, you sacrilegious bastard," one man said, leveling a gun at him. There was a malice in their eyes that let Arna know that they did not care for Azza or her greatest taboo: murder. They wanted him dead.

Arna did not think. He reacted. He had to flee fast.

Get to the stairs.

Arna had once almost broken his leg when in a fight in Podiel. At the time, Ixxzal and Pokk had talked him through the self-defense. Lumak had lectured him on the ways to circumvent the laws, how to escape, and how to break into things. They they had sent him out into the world, making him practice by causing fights. He'd done it until he reacted by instinct. Those fights were like this one.

The man closest to Arna started to approach. Arna jumped to his feet flourishing his Blessings. He stepped to the side avoiding a series of shots and dove behind the couch. Crawling on the floor he took a deep breath.

"If you die, the Gods will come back to us. They'll forgive us," someone else in the room said as more gunshots rang out.

The couch was destroyed, and Arna was injured, scratches barely grazing him as he was able to slide across the floor to the other side. The men were caught off guard and Arna took the opportunity. Holding his body low, Arna knocked one man down, spun and grabbed another throwing him at a third. Sliding one foot back to balance himself and spinning to the other side of the man, Arna narrowly dodged a bullet that grazed his arm. He ignored the pain and pressed his Blessings to do more.

Arna once again rotated to the other side and stepped back avoiding a man who yelled and tried to tackle him. When the man ricocheted past him—trying to block him but unable to balance—to the other guard, Arna's path was clear.

He sprinted for the only visible doorway to the upstairs. He could not be caught in the small, secluded staircases of this room. They had guns and were too close in their pursuit. He raced through the halls of the third floor as they shouted after him. He slid to a stop at a door, hand on the panel, revealing a staircase. Before the others could turn the corner and see him, he crashed down the stiars, from the third floor all the way to the first.

[*The back!* Ixxzal yelled from across the house.]

Arna skidded against the floor as he entered the first floor listening. He could not go to the front: protestors screaming. Turning, Arna headed towards the backdoor of the house. He leapt off the hall, through the nanotech wall, and onto the nanotech path that kept him from falling into the garden. He bolted past the center willow tree that swayed and welcomed him. Gun shots splintered the bark of the tree and went through the wall that was meant to protect from the elements not weapons.

Arna leapt again, slid across the floor, and raced down the hall to the backdoor. He threw it open to the small yard. It was only to be used for the air-conditioning, solar panel, and technology units that they did not want stored inside the house. Less than six feet wide, there was no place to hide between the backdoor and the wall that was high above. Arna jumped onto the air-conditioning units, grabbed the branches of the willow tree that tumbled over the back of the house, and yanked himself to the top of the wall. He raced alongside of it and jumped down as soon as he saw a street.

It was only as he landed that Arna's thoughts caught up to him. Arna fumbled with his mobile, looking back to ensure that the guards were not chasing him. He selected his first emergency contact and the call connected.

Before his father could speak, Arna said, "The guards just tried to kill me. I'm not entirely sure how they got guns, but that probably means the government wants me dead? Not sure. The house is destroyed. I'm headed to the government center. Meet me outside."

The real question Arna wanted to know was where the guards got guns. Guns were banned in all of the cities and only the government had access to them. These guards were a private group Zaffre had called, because he couldn't trust the government.

"What?" Ebru enunciated with such ferocity that Arna almost tripped.

Arna glanced into the air to verify the name of who he called. Instinct still driving his decisions, he'd pressed the wrong number. Arna slowly breathed and rationalized. He called Ebru because he always reached to Alis when he was in danger.

"Incarnadine Vivicent, you had better answer me!"

"I meant to call my dad." Arna rounded a corner, nearly certain he wasn't being followed.

"Are you hurt? Where are you?"

"Headed to the government center." Arna winced at the pain as he started to touch his body, checking for injuries. "I'm a bit scratched up, but nothing major."

Arna looked at the blood in his hands and flourished his Body Blessings further. His body knit itself back together in many places. He ignored the pain. He'd danced in worse storms. He'd been stabbed before by debris.

These were just flesh wounds. They were *nothing*.

"Now, I'm going to call my dad and—"

"You'd better call me back." And before Arna could respond Ebru demanded, "Better yet, I'm checking your location. I'm on my way."

"I'm headed to my father. I don't think they'll find me," Arna let himself slip into the shadows and disappear with the right combinations of Blessings that worked better than his forsaken ones that couldn't even keep his emotions at bay.

He pulled up a map for the best route to get to the government center, and the route that would be least suspected. It would take more time but would be safer.

"Next you'll be telling me divine intervention will save you."

"'Guided by the light of Lumak, he rose his fist and declared himself righteous.'" Arna recited, using it to calm himself more than Ebru.

"You Gods damned— Reckless— I swear that when I see you, I'm going to—"

"I'm just your favorite scripture-citing idiot," Arna used the humor to settle his stomach and heart. He was fine.

"When I find you I—"

"I'm going to call my dad. I'll call you back," Arna said, hanging up immediately and calling his dad as he hopped on the bus. He pulled his hood over his head and kept his eyes down. No one noticed him.

"Arna?" his father asked, breathless. "Are you okay?"

"You. . . You know?" Arna was surprised.

"I just got news that there were the sounds of gunshots at the house. Where are you?" Zaffre asked.

Arna quickly resent his father his location. He opened the house chat and the Golden Generation chat sending it there as well: ensuring that everyone knew where he was. He followed it up with the map he'd made to get to the center of town. Then he sent a message to stay away from the house that was liked by all members of the family in one chat and the Golden Generation in the other.

"I'm on the bus now, on my way to you." Arna added, "It may take me some time."

Zaffre was silent for a moment.

"I'll meet you outside," he said sternly.

"Thanks. Bye," Arna said, hanging up and looking at his mobile.

Seconds later his augmentations lit up with Ebru's name. Arna hesitated to answer for long enough that the call ended. A sigh of relief started to form when name appeared again.

Arna answered.

"If you hang up on me again, I swear. . ." Ebru threatened him.

"Your threats aren't exactly convincing. You need me alive so that I can continue to torment you." Arna relaxed into the seat, letting Ebru's voice support him.

"Don't call me next time you need someone to save your ass, then."

"You're right. I should have called Arco, he seems to have a reputation of wreaking havoc," Arna joked, letting his worries slip away.

Instead of laughter, Arna was met by silence.

"Arco isn't. . ." The way Ebru said it was almost too defensive. "He's never done anything that wasn't protecting someone else from serious injury. . ."

What?

"But didn't Arco. . . He's banned from Shadone properties for destruction, isn't he?"

"Ginger almost had her arm destroyed by Shadone students. Arco protected her." There was a long silence on the other end of the line. "How far are you from your father?"

"About an hour," Arna admitted, worried about his brother who everyone thought was violent. The news always reported on it. Was it simply just a combination of how stand-offish Sarcoline was and the one time he defended Ginger? Arna wouldn't have put it past Cyclamen to do something as cruel as to paint Sarcoline as the terrible one.

"Stay on the phone with me until then," Ebru begged.

Arna did as he was told, listening to Ebru's breathing as Ebru went over all the changes he'd made to the variation music. He talked about the internal drama of the DHS small council when Zaffre insisted on the auditions being held. No one understood it, but apparently Cyclamen had agreed, and the two were united on an idea for the first time ever. Ebru talked about his father, who was worried sick about Arna and the other Vivicents.

As he talked, Arna added Rosmarinus into the Golden Generation group chat, and everyone welcomed him.

Every so often Ebru would make a comment, telling Arna not to miss his bus, or to not take the wrong route.

He's following my location.

Just knowing Ebru was tracking him made him relieved. As Arna grew closer, Ebru stopped talking.

"Is it on the news?" Arna asked.

"Don't worry about it," Ebru said. "How close are you?"

Arna left the final bus and headed down the street with his eyes low, towards the government building that housed the task force. When he found his father waiting, he finally felt safe.

"I see my father," Arna told Ebru.

"Get to him before you hang up," Ebru ordered and Arna did as he was asked, walking right up to his father who was searching for him with Jasi who looked terrified. They both looked right past him. Arna deactivated his Blessings and his body heaved. He was exhausted, but he was healed. Jasi winced.

"I'm here," Arna told them and Ebru at once.

"Be safe. I love you," Ebru said.

"I love you," Arna repeated as he hung up the call.

Jasi gave Arna a long once over. "How many times were you shot?"

"Nothing landed solidly. There were scrapes, but they're healed now," Arna said, showing him his arm. Jasi did not look convinced. Arna looked down at his clothes and the chuckle lodged in his throat. He was all scraped up, with cuts across all his clothes. His exposed bare skin was red and purple from recently healed wounds and bruises.

"Well. . ." Arna said slowly looking back up and trying to crack a smile that made Jasi grimace worse. "I'm fine now."

"You keep saying you're fine and I'm starting to believe you don't know the meaning of that word," Jasi hissed, before he sent to the group chat.

```
Jasi: Arna saying "I'm fine" is the equivalent of a lie.
    Make note.
Phlox: I thought we all already knew that.
Ven: Is he okay?
Rus: Based on what I'm seeing, no.
Aureolin: You're there?
Rus: News reports. It's not good.
Ginger: What happened?
Arco: Shooting at the house. Government tried to kill
    him.
Ginger: EXCUSE ME. WHAT?
Ebru: He's with Zaffre and Jasi now.
Ginger: What do you mean the government tried to kill
    him?
Phlox: Quickly now, Ginger. We don't have all day.
Aureolin: Phlox, please.
Arco: Guns, Ginger. Guns.
Arco: Try to keep up. Please.
Phlox: See, Arco does it too.
```

```
          Aureolin: Hush
          Rus: So Fine = Pretty fucking terrible actually, thank
               you for asking? Got it.
          Ven: Yes.
          Arna: I am fine.
          Amaryllis: Way to prove the point.
```

"Let's get inside," Zaffre said, pushing them both inside before Arna could respond further.

The last time Arna had been in the government center where the Chosen Task Force was housed, he had been a bit delirious. This time, when he entered, he was able to truly appreciate the balance between Lumak and Xeyaro that had been achieved in the building: perfectly symmetrical, with floors that were tiled with ceramic shaped like leaves. The room was lined with carefully cultivated garden beds.

The lobby of the building was filled with people going about their daily activities: attending appointments, traveling, going to school or work. He noticed petal dresses from the recent fashion week, and colors that had been popular: citrine and chartreuse. Most people were in short sleeves, skirts, or shorts, of varying degrees of professionalism. All wore soft, natural fibers and some fabrics even drifted as if lifted on imaginary wind.

Arna was pushed away from them by his father, to a series of guards who checked them and let them into an elevator. It was solid chrome with glowing mint buttons. Zaffre picked the ninth floor. When they arrived, the carpets that met them were long and green like grass. The walls were painted in murals of trees and images of what the world should have looked like outside the flower cities: mountain ranges, the great ocean, forests that were not surrounded by homes. There were cities that lived surrounded by nature, not nature that lived within a city.

There were depictions of animals he had only seen in history textbooks when he had tried to identify the shapes the Gods took. Ancient communities of the past that no longer existed, were painted in frightening detail.

Mostly, Arna noted the number of trees: a whole planet of them.

Zaffre lead them to a room with a large table and a slew of people. They all were waiting.

"Pleasure for you to join us, Incarnadine, but I would have expected you to look more put together," the Governor of Xeysis said.

"My son was attacked, Cider. Please," Zaffre said, urging them to sit. Arna did, Jasi on one side, Zaffre on the other: a physical barrier between Arna and the officials.

At the head of the table sat Mr. Thyme, with glasses on his nose and a scowl on his lips.

"Mr. Incarnadine Vivicent," Mr. Thyme began, "Today we have called you to discuss your intention for your variation."

"Before that," Zaffre disagreed. "We need to discuss how it is that private citizens had access to guns and destroyed my house."

All eyes were on Zaffre. Mr. Thyme looking particularly befuddled, glancing back at Governor Cider for guidance.

"We are investigating," Cider, Governor of Xeysis said. "We will—"

"No. I want this fixed now," Zaffre said. "Or I will assume it was you, and I will call for assistance from the church through Apolic Law."

The Governor scowled. It was the only law that superseded all other, but only in matters where the Apostle was concerned. It would force there to be an internal investigation by the Church of the Apostle into the government, which Arna doubted Cider wanted.

"It will be taken care of, and we will ensure additional guards. With the Blessings flickering, the defensive technology around all buildings is failing. It must have affected your home as well. I assure you these rebels had no ties to us. We believe them tied to the One Truth Church," Cider insisted, and Mr. Thyme nodded, convinced.

Arna could only hope that he was telling the truth. Despite having seen the mark, Arna was not sure he fully believed that simple church members could get access to class-zero weapons.

Yet, he did not want to constantly fear for his life while at home. So, he had to trust the man. Zaffre nodded.

"Now, can we get to the conversation at hand?" Mr. Thyme asked, annoyed by the whole ordeal. As if Arna's survival was more of an inconvenience.

"My variation?" Arna asked.

"Your father has put in the request to continue the auditions, which seems strange if you are intending to complete your variation this year," Mr. Thyme explained with a wave of his hand.

Arna seethed. "What are you asking?"

"Are you or are you not intending to complete your variation?" the man demanded in answer.

Arna took an unsteady breath. Thoughts that he had bit back, tried to break free. "Why?"

"I told you, we must prepare. The market of three of the cities is crashing. Everyone is panicking. The Blessings are going haywire. And I believe we all know why..." Mr. Thyme tapped his fingers on the table and all eyes bore into Arna.

Arna kept all his emotions at bay with the poisoned cure of Blessings. He squeezed his palms just enough to sting, but not to bleed. Let them know nothing.

"Due to the Splintering, which you caused, the cities are failing," Mr. Thyme accused Arna. "More so now since your return than ever. I have half a mind to believe the One Truth Church. But they're absolutely insane. However, there is credibility to their claim that your existence or attempt at being the Chosen is causing problems."

Arna tried to keep his expression as calm as he could.

"No," Zaffre corrected. "The Blessings have always gone haywire right before the Day of New Dawn."

"Only since the Splintering!" Mr. Thyme snapped.

"Since forever." Zaffre recited the other points in history that had gotten bad, nearly worse than what they were facing now. Each one was reminiscent of the times since the Splintering, but they were not the same. This time the Blessings would not come back.

"All caused by weak dancers," Zaffre assured the group.

"Mr. Vivicent, are you or are you not the Chosen?" Mr. Thyme ignored Zaffre's whole speech.

"Why?" Arna asked back.

"I, and many of our experts are inclined to believe, that you are not. Instead, we believe that you are an incongruity. That your Blessings are failing you not because of some taboo but due to some other reasoning beyond measures of study so far."

Arna looked at the man as if he were an idiot. Who thought that? Not even the One Truth Church said that.

[*What a fool*, Ixxzal scoffed.]

Ease accompanied Ixxzal's voice.

[*We're here,* Lumak said. *Not all of us. Too much energy, but Ixxzal and I.*]

"The Gods do not make exceptions," Zaffre insisted.

"The Gods are not real, Mr. Vivicent," Mr. Thyme said, and Arna balked at the unveiled heresy.

"How can you think I have this power if not for the Gods?" Arna asked, scandalized.

"History has taught us that there have been individuals of immense power. We do not know how they got it. But I assure you, no God was responsible."

"And the Everlit candles?"

"While our researchers may not know what you did to the Blessings by dropping a fan, science has allowed us to see the truths of the world. We will understand the truth of the taboos, but the Gods are not the answer. We no longer need rely on lies in the face of the unknown."

The man's lecture had Arna in awe. After everything that had happened, he still didn't believe? This was different from Phlox's rejection; it was true atheism.

"And so, you think what?" Arna asked. "That I'm an imposter and I'm just lying?"

imposterimposterimposter

"I think you are an incongruity. If you would just agree to the tests—"

"No," Zaffre said.

What tests? Arna looked at his father.

"You lied to us?" Governor Cider said.

"You were never told about the tests?" Mr. Thyme asked Arna.

Arna shook his head.

"We have a series of tests we'd like you to complete. We believe that by studying you, we can understand the true extent of how Blessings work and function as a whole," Mr. Thyme explained like he was talking to a toddler.

This wasn't a meeting to discuss the future; it was a meeting to tell Arna to give up. They were outright calling him an imposter and demanding that he stop immediately. End everything.

belikesaffronbelikesaffronbelikesaffron

This was a waste of his time. He did not have time to talk to men that did not believe him. He needed to finish his variation and find the answers to the questions from the Gods.

[*Go,* Lumak agreed.]

"No," Arna said, standing and heading to the door.

"Where are you going?" Mr. Thyme asked.

"The Ceremony auditions will happen as my father said, and you will not do tests on me," Arna said, opening the door.

"I take that as your admission that you are not the Chosen," Mr. Thyme said, smugly.

Arna did not answer him as he left the room, headed out and trying to keep his breathing even.

(How much longer could he hide?)

Zaffre and Jasi chased after him. Arna ignored them both, entering the elevator and trying to keep his mind from splitting apart.

theendtheendtheend

You are not the Chosen.

(Was there a reason to hide?)

He was just an imposter pretending to be the Chosen, but he was the only one.

He was the only one.

[*Arna*, Lumak said.]

He was the only one.

Saffron. Saffron. Saffron.

He was the only one.

[*Arna.*]

He was the only one who could do it.

When the Splintering occurred, the Gods only had him. He was the only one that could send them prayers. He was the last connection they had to mortals. If he gave up that, that was it. So, he could not give up. He had to keep going. It didn't matter if he was an imposter. It didn't matter if he wasn't Chosen.

He was the only one.

"Arna."

Arna snapped his eyes open. Jasi was looking at him concerned. Zaffre was not there.

"He went to get a private ride. Look at me," Jasi said, and slowly Arna turned his attention to his friend. Jasi breathed in long, then out slowly. Arna blinked a few times until he realized he was breathing far too quickly. Mimicking Jasi, Arna was able to calm himself down.

"Are you okay?" Jasi asked him.

"Yes."

The lie stung but Arna ignored the pain, just like he did everything else. He shoved it deep and clenched his fists tight. He needed to focus. *Focus. Keep going.* He couldn't let himself fall apart.

Balance is not just Justice. Justice is important for society and mortals.
Balance is between the Gods, knowledge, and the unknown.
Yet Justice is also a prayer, seeking salvation away from Gods giving retribution.
And mortals seek Balance in all things.
The two create stability.

— On Lumak.

Dance 20

Harmony

Incarnadine

18 Xeyan

24 Days Left

"I'm sorry. I truly am. You'll find someone else, someone who will actually love you. I – "
She ran away.
"She's going to hate you forever."
"She's not the only one."

When the door opened to Amaryllis studio's at six in the morning—Jasi, Ginger, Rosmarinus, and Sarcoline at his side—Arna found her with a deep set frown. Her hair was up at the top of her head in a messy bun. She had bags under her eyes and was fuming.

"Were you woken early?" Sarcoline cooed and coaxed, putting his arms around her, letting her stand on his feet, and wrapping her arms around him. He waddled back into the house, towards the kitchen awkwardly. She buried her head into his chest. Arna heard her mumble some things but only heard Sarcoline clearly.

"Yes. Yes. We'll get it fixed, Am."

The others were all there waiting: Ven, Aureolin, Phlox, and even Ebru. They all were looking like they wanted to kill him for getting them up this early when practice was at nine.

Piled high in the center of the room were a series of five boxes.

"What are those?" Jasi asked as they stepped into the house.

"You tell me," Amaryllis snapped from where Sarcoline sat her down. He hurried to make tea. "Delivery men ringing the damn bell at three in the morning. You're lucky I waited until a reasonable hour to call you here."

Arna offered her a small smile. He was not sure why they'd been delivered so early, but from the way that Sarcoline acted, and Amaryllis was calming down, this was not the first time.

"I hate the mail," Amaryllis said with a pout.

"This is why we have strict delivery time rules, Am." Sarcoline rubbed her shoulders as the tea brewed.

"So we can sue them," Rosmarinus agreed. Jasi tapped in the air mumbling something under his breath.

Biting back the question of why it had happened before, Arna approached the boxes and all of his worries were forgotten in an instant. Arna was ripe with anticipation, longing for what was within the boxes, and pride for outsmarting Mr. Hemlock. He jumped from foot to foot.

"Does anyone have a knife?" he asked.

"Yes?" Rosmarinus said, confused. He walked over and handed the knife to Arna, who ripped open the seal and looked inside all five boxes. The contents were exactly as he last saw them. They were glorious and calling him. He wanted to pick them up. His fingers itched, but the pain in his palms made his hands stay away.

Rosmarinus looked over his shoulder as he quickly closed the flaps.

Still, Rosmarinus saw. "Fans?"

"Fans?" Sarcoline repeated. All at once, everyone hurried over and pried open the boxes that Arna tried to keep shut. He was shoved out of the way and fans were pulled out in their plastic packaging.

"Are these machine-made?" Sarcoline asked and everyone gaped at Arna. Ebru looked the most scandalized, giving Arna a look as if he wanted to throttle him. Ginger, likewise, was horrified. They had all been trained as kids by Zaffre to care for performance fans. Arna, Ebru, Sarcoline, and Ginger however, had been official fan apprentices.

"I snuck into Mr. Hemlock's factory. Had them shipped here," Arna said, softly wincing in the predicted ire.

"Did you not think to ask dad?" Sarcoline asked, but he did not sound angry.

Arna was embarrassed to admit that he had but had been too cowardly to ask. It was foolish, but the idea of asking his father was terrifying. He was the last person Arna wanted to disappoint again. But looking at all their faces and knowing just how much he had asked all of them for help, he knew what Ixxzal would say.

"Gods. I'm an idiot."

"Obviously," Sarcoline agreed.

Aureolin attempted to lift one of the boxes, and blinked when she could not.

"Are they all dense and heavy fans?" she asked. Arna shook his head.

"There is some light fabric in there," Arna offered, chuckling under his breath knowing that they would not accept it.

"Some." Aureolin laughed wildly, bright and full bodied as she stopped trying to lift the boxes. "Where did you even get the fabric?"

"I ordered it years ago, but I only got them finalized when I got here. I got access to the factories when I worked with Mr. Hemlock."

"You're kidding," Aureolin said blankly.

"I was working at a fabric design studio. I was loud, boisterous, and intentionally forgettable. A few sweet words and I had his signature." Arna winked.

"Was that before we met?" Ebru asked trying to push one box and being unable.

"After. But I wasn't exactly telling you the day-to-day details of my life at that point," Arna said. "You didn't trust me and to be fair I didn't trust you."

"Manipulative, I adore it," Phlox laughed, hugging Aureolin who was still stunned silent.

"I don't know what you're talking about, Phlox. I was just telling you a story about a time I met a celebrity," Arna feigned ignorance and hurt.

"And I'm a horrible actress," she teased him back, dramatically sighing at the end.

"We really need to work on your self-confidence. You're brilliant."

Phlox stuttered out a sequences of sounds, and Arna laughed. Looking at the boxes, a thought appeared in Arna's mind unbidden. "I'm going to change the group dance."

"Now?" Ebru asked, glancing around. "We've already—"

"You think you won't be able to do it? I can probably get another dancer to replace—" Arna began to mock him.

"Don't you dare," Ebru cut him off. "I'll be fine."

"You all will be. I'm adding fans. One for all of you—" Arna began.

"What?" they all exclaimed at once, stopping him mid-sentence.

"No," Ebru said shaking his head angrily. "No fans. You can't use them."

"Arco will be dancing for me. He's getting two fans," Arna went on as if they said nothing.

"I'm dancing for you?" Sarcoline asked pushing a box with his foot. "Since when?"

"Remember what I asked you to ruining some dreams?" Arna explained, finally able to say it again. It all felt so long ago.

"Dreams. . ." Sarcoline repeated and then began to smile wickedly. "This is what you mean? You were planning it all along?"

Arna responded with a wave of his hand, gesturing across all of the boxes that were too heavy to lift on their own.

"If you're dancing a full set you can't dance beforehand," Rosmarinus filled in for all of them.

"The DHS is going to be pissed, but Sarcoline is the best choice. The only choice." Ebru smiled, sinisterly. One by one they were all grinning in vengeance for what they'd been put through. The only one who seemed at all embarrassed was Sarcoline, who was a bit redder in his cheeks than usual.

"If Arco has two fans, won't the dance be unbalanced?" Amaryllis asked.

"Exactly." Arna snapped his fingers. "It's a dance representing all of the Gods as much as it is representing us. It is already art and nature, emotion and the soul. It is the unknown and the knowledge of universes. Two fans are a symbol of balance. But only one person having two creates chaos. When everyone discards their fans at the end, balance will be achieved."

The others looked at him, unconvinced.

"Well, if we want to be able to test that theory, we had better get moving these to the Vivicent manor," Amaryllis said, motioning to the boxes.

The others grumbled in agreement, and together they created teams to lift the boxes. With the assistance of Blessings and many hands, they were able to get all the boxes to the Vivicent manor before practice.

When they arrived at the dance room at the Shadone Studio, Arna directed the group to pick up the Original Variation Understanding practice fans.

They were of standard weight and opaque. Each fan in nineteen through twenty-four was an ombre of the three colors of a single God: one God per dance. They were hand embroidered with the flower associated with the God and the symbol for the God in a large pattern atop, using only the three colors for the embroidery.

The message was clear, distinct, and exactly what Arna needed for them to hold when they were going to represent the Gods on stage.

One by one the five took the fan that he told them to grab. He turned his attention to Sarcoline, who hesitated, then took the fans from the Twin Fans variation Understanding for Xeyaro. The sets in the original two variations were identical, save the fact that Twin Fans had two fans instead of one.

"What?" a student in the back gasped.

"Since I cannot touch a fan without losing a Blessing, Arco will be taking my part in the dance," Arna announced, nodding at his brother. Sarcoline twisted the fans around. The six nodded at each other and headed to the center of the room.

"What does it matter? The Gods gave up on you," someone else attempted to incite a fight. The Golden Generation turned to say something, but Arna stepped ahead.

"Everyone into places." Arna ignored the jeers. The others listened and followed without a word.

All six, with Sarcoline replacing Arna, stood before Arna with fans. Jasi stood next to Arna for support, leaving the music to Amaryllis and Rosmarinus. The air of those watching grew thick in anger and animosity. Arna could have cut the malice with a blade.

Sarcoline breathed out, saying something to Ebru, who's energy returned bright and hot. His eyes flashed as he scowled at the observers, press, and students in the mirrors. Rivalry bloomed between the five who heard Sarcoline. The rivalry killed whatever anger the others had to the audience and Arna thanked his brother.

Whatever he said, had the group breathing in unison and focused as one, all glowering past Arna in the mirror.

Or maybe Sarcoline simply made them angrier.

Whatever the case was, they were unified. Arna could work with unity.

"Let's go," Arna smiled and stepped up. Arna began to teach them what was changed in the dance they knew, showing them with his hands and snaps, to signify the fans. He taught them the same way he had practiced for years, and after an hour, from start to finish, they got it. Arna turned to Rosmarinus, nodded, and the music began.

The first time through from beginning to end, it was as if Arna had not stepped out of the formation at all. The six danced in harmony, with A.Reverence flourished between them to compensate for the quick teaching and understanding how they had to move: except Sarcoline.

Despite not having the Blessing, Sarcoline fit in perfectly. Whereas the others let their Blessing supplement the memory for them, Sarcoline had memorized it immediately on his own. Arna gained an odd sense of pride watching them all move. The dance formed exactly as he envisioned.

But there were a few things he wanted to change. He could better match Ebru's music. He could better present Incarnate Dreams before he danced it. He could make the dance more complex and thorough, and the story more intense.

Arna noticed Sarcoline grimace.

"What's wrong?" Arna asked him as the song ended.

Sarcoline showed the move. "I'm just trying to understand your motivations there."

"I—"

"No. Not you . . . Arna as the character. Not *you.*" Sarcoline shook his head, closing his eyes. "But would you even understand that? Give me a second before we go again."

Sarcoline stood still for a few minutes. When his eyes opened, he nodded back to Arna who was unsure what happened. However, as the song began again, Sarcoline was different: changed exactly the way that Arna had envisioned moments before. Before Arna even said the changes, Sacroline had made them.

Arna started shaking. Every fiber of his body was reacting to the sight before him. Sarcoline would master Arna's variation through Understanding. He'd understand it and master it first. Sarcoline could possibly be the first nonChild to master three variations through Understanding. Maybe he could master even more.

More.

The idea gave Arna chills. If anyone could master Arna's Variation through Twenty-Five without question, it could be Sarcoline.

In the back, six figures shaped like moths and spiders—much too large to be real—crawled along the walls, speaking in chimes and static. In their wake flowers bloomed and the walls caved. The light around them dimmed.

The Gods were whispering amongst themselves as they often did when he practiced his variations in the past. The Gods were watching not Arna, but the boy who danced with his soul.

They were watching the boy who had not been Blessed.

"I think I want to change a few things anyway," Arna said.

Practice continued after he made the changes. This time it was right. There was much to be refined, but the foundation had been established. "Now—"

"Stop playing around," someone in the back shouted, taking the lull in the lesson to heckle them again.

"Why would the Gods keep their Chosen from touching a fan," someone else mocked.

"Liar."

"Avoiding responsibility again?"

"No. He's just an imposter. He never had the Blessings to begin with."

imposterimposterimposter

Arna froze and glared. His blood was boiling, and he wanted to yell at them, but he couldn't. The cameras were rolling and he. . . his S.Mirrors activated. Shaken, Arna immediately looked at Ven who was shaking their head, and sending him soothing thoughts, telling him he wasn't alone, anchoring him.

All at once, as if struck by lightning, Arna remembered. Ven *felt* his pain. It hurt them the same way Arna was hurt. The storm would destroy him when all of his Blessings were activated. The pain of every time Arna picked up a fan was like a phantom coursing through him again.

Ven winced.

Arna settled himself in the memory of dancing for a few minutes in a superstorm. He focused on the feeling he had as the winds threatened to rip him apart. Ven recoiled and shot Arna a concerned glance.

Ven would feel it every time.

(Ven would feel when he died.)

Arna was there again in the garden watching Ven sob, begging Arna not to leave. He was standing on the stage, seeing his brother's face as his brother saw the Gods in him. He was learning all that he'd left behind, and all that he'd leave behind again.

He had a twelve blessing gap. He'd already lost five, and he could risk one more.

[The candles exploded. Birds screamed.]

One more. And. . . *I need to lose it.*

If the Gods could speak, they would be screaming that he needed to keep the Blessing. The Gods had listed the order they'd take his Blessings, enough times for him to know them by heart. The two he had to keep in order for a chance to survive were S.Mirrors and A.Reverence. However, they'd always told him he could pick the ones he wanted to lose when he touched a fan. Doing so while dancing was not feasible, but right now? He could decide.

While it would hurt, he could not let others hurt for him.

He could not let Ven or any of the others face his pain for him even if they were his Saints. He had to do that himself. He couldn't ask them to die for him. He'd be alone on the stage, and he could not prolong their suffering more than he had to.

[The moths were shedding.]

The lights flickered. The room shook. Everyone grabbed each other, surprised by what was happening as the emergency lights turned on, casting the room in a feint pink glow.

[*NO!* The Gods of the Known screamed.]

[*I stand with you always, but don't do this,* The God of the Unknown begged.]

It was foolish. It was most certainly facing death. Yet, he had five paths before him, and he had to find the single one to survival. If he knew that Ven was getting hurt every time he picked up a fan he'd be distracted. No.

That was not the path that he wanted to take.

Saffron. Saffron. Saffron.

He would not be like Saffron.

Before the idea was full formed, Arna was walking to the fan rack. The pink light flickered urging him to back away. A shadow formed trying to stop him, but he pushed past.

"Arna?" Rosmarinus asked as Arna stepped up to him next to the rack of fans.

He focused on his S.Mirrors connection to Ven. He said goodbye, cut it off, and grabbed a Blue Rose Fears fan, dance twenty.

[Azza and Pokk's screams echoed and bounced across the floors. Somewhere far away Ixxzal and Lumak were shouting. Zaynir and Xeyaro were sobbing.]

Arna's wrist was aflame, the constellation birthmark glowing bright for a second. It then began to flake off like shooting stars as his soul ripped in two. He was left spinning. His vision was a kaleidoscope: oscillating and flickering in a thousand colors. The world around him rang as his head thudded. Pain ran through his body, worse than any other time. The pink light turned orange, blue, green, white, purple, black; it was glowing in a color he no longer knew. The loss of starlight took the oxygen from his lung, warning him that it would never return. It was the fleeting scent of willow trees in the summer.

He hissed. The raw pain from this loss was a thousand times worse than the others, but nothing he could not handle. For in it was the strongest connection to the God's he'd ever felt. They drank in the sacrifice and their light returned from the brink once more.

Besides, he was fine.

painpainpainpainpainpain

It was far less than the superstorms. It was nothing. It was fine.

Ignore it. Kill it. Destroy it. Bury it.

Never remember it again.

Arna gulped and blinked, trying to clear his thoughts but his body weight was shifting.

Gravity rocked and tumbled, threatening to send Arna to the floor.

"No. No! Nonononononononono," Ven cried from behind him.

[*You fool!* Ixxzal lamented angrily.]

Arna was vaguely aware of someone grabbing him and ripping the fan out of his hand. He thought there was another holding him steady and pulling him to the floor; he didn't know.

His body was shaking but he was fine. He was fine.

[*You can't do this Incarnadine. You have nothing to prove!* Lumak cried in protest.]

Arna's vision began to clear, and his hearing returned as the ringing faded. He could count his fingers, his breaths. Breathing felt different, shallower, colder, and harder. His hands were shaking. His vision fully returned to the dim pink room. He was held in Jasi's arms and Rosmarinus checked his pulse.

"You! What did you do?" Ven grabbed Arna's arms, they were sobbing. Their birthmark remained, dulled like those whose heartmate died. Amaryllis grabbed Ven to keep them from falling atop of Arna. Her left wrist, where her dulled heartmate constellation remained, flashed from underneath her sleeve.

"Our connection needed to be cut," Arna said, pulling back from Ven, mind clearing, eyes refocusing past the white spots.

He was already steady and levelheaded. This was the fastest he'd recovered before. Maybe he didn't need to flourish his abilities. That was a good sign for when he had less of them during the Ceremony of Chaos. His body was still weak, but he was fine.

Pushing away from Jasi, Arna managed to get to his feet much to the shock of everyone and glared at the audience, who stared at him in mixed horror. The lights were spinning, not that Arna knew how they could do that. Who made the nanotech do that?

Crossing his arms, Arna said, "Happy?"

[*You needed the S.Mirrors,* Zaynir was crying.]

It will be better like this. Ven won't get hurt.

"You have got to be kidding me," Ebru jumped to his feet as the lights slowly began to return to normal.

"Do you always do this?" Aureolin asked, getting up to her feet as well. She grabbed Arna's face and forced her to look at him. Why were they all so concerned? Why were they all sitting?

"Of course, he does!" Phlox cried. "How did we never notice?"

Other things were said but Arna could not hear them past the partial ringing in his ears that returned. It was like his senses were tied to his heartbeat going in and out, in and out.

"Tell them to give it back!" Ven reached for Arna again, taking his wrist from where they were still collapsed on the floor. They rubbed at his wrist, as if expecting the mark to return. Tears streamed down their face. "Tell them!"

Rosmarinus wrapped his hands around Ven, who was shaking with sobs. Arna stumbled a bit from the spotting and the ringing, trying to find his balance.

I can't fall here. Not after what he just said.

"It's my penance, Ven. I can't touch a fan." Arna peeled their fingers from his wrist. All knew of the taboo, but Arna doubted anyone had ever seen it enforced.

[*The Blessing would give you additional strength and root you in the mortal world!* Pokk yelled.]

This will be better for them.

Ebru grabbed Arna from Aureolin, horror in his eyes. Arna registered Ebru's hands on his face but did not feel them. *Ah, that's a new sensory loss.*

[*It's not negotiable!* Azza screamed.]

[*No! You fool. You utter fool!* Ixxzal was crying too.]

I don't want Ven to feel my pain anymore.

heddiealoneforwhatheddone

If Ebru intended to say something, he did not. Instead, what little Arna could hear vanished as Ebru's face paled significantly. He shook his head to someone behind Arna. Arna tried to look back, but Ebru stopped him from doing so.

"Can you hear us?" Ebru asked.

"Of course, I can," Arna said.

Ven's sobs became louder.

[*No more,* Xeyaro begged.]

No more. He could not risk picking up another. Not if he wanted to have enough abilities to survive the twenty-sixth dance.

[*Don't forsake us.*]

I won't.

Arna winced as his head pounded and the noise suddenly became louder. Before he could fall, Ebru was forcing him to sit on the ground next to Ven. They continued to sob and shake.

"Are you okay?" Arna asked Ven, their head buried in Rosmarinus' chest.

"Me? You! I... I can't feel you anymore. I... It hurts!" Ven stuttered facing him.

"It will be okay." Arna put his hand on their head, moving their hair out of their eyes.

"No! It won't! It won't." Ven began to hyperventilate. Rosmarinus said hushed words to Ven who sobbed into his shoulder. Amaryllis stared at Arna with mixed grief and disappointment.

"It won't be," Amaryllis said. "You do realize that the cut of losing a heartmate hurts the one who is left more than the one who was lost, because to Ven it feels like you *died.*"

Arna reeled. If anyone knew it would be her, and as he met Ven's gaze once more he found great anger.

"It will be okay." Arna had lost enough Blessings before.

"No. You are not okay. Stop saying that," Ven demanded through the tears. They grabbed him. Ebru pulled Arna close as he sat behind Arna. Ginger grabbed his left wrist. Everyone got closer, as if Arna would run again, not that he ever planned to do that. Only Sarcoline stood, arms crossed staring at them all.

Pointed statements were made about Arna by the audience. They were scandalized and aghast in the heresy. Arna focused all the attention of his friends to Ven who was distraught. He did not need it. He... The loss of the connection was like a snapped rope, and he was drifting off to sea.

He was just like Saffron.

All at once there was a break within his soul. As the room became blinding bright and the noises far too loud, his heart threatened to burst from his chest. Gasping, Arna struggled to breathe. Ven grabbed him, but there was a lack in the touch. The usual closeness was gone. The hug was devoid of the weight it once had.

"We're here," Ebru said against Arna's neck and tugged Arna closer to his chest so that Arna sat between his legs. Ven pulled themselves closer, leaning into Arna until Ven was hugging Arna too. The closeness, in such a public space, made Arna's lungs ache.

He didn't deserve this.

No. Focus. Focus. Do not fall apart.

His Blessings were incapable of holding it all back, not anymore.

This was the end.

He was going to die.

(Believing in living...)

was a mistake.

It's fine. They were all reacting badly, but this was necessary. They needed to see the true extent of how far Arna would be pushed. So that they would not interfere when he danced. And he needed to keep his wits about him. He needed to stay strong.

"Why did they have to do this to you?" Ven asked into Arna's shoulder.

"I'm sorry," Arna said and all at once the commotion around him went silent.

"You're sorry?" Ven asked hysterical. Why were they glaring at him? "The Gods did this!"

[It happened all the time.]

This was the end.

It was all for naught.

It was not the God's fault; it was his. He made the choice to drop the fan to chase a dream. He had to deal with the repercussions of that.

"I dropped the fan." Arna insisted.

They all stopped talking, even Sarcoline dropped down to the same level.

"You. . ." Sarcoline began, but Rosmarinus shook his head and Sarcoline stopped .

Ebru squeezed Arna tight, for all the days that Arna had said to him online that he thought he was better off dead. For all the secrets he told a stranger thinking they'd never truly get back to him. For all the moments that were missed. Ebru, this time, was there.

"You really believe this is all your fault?" Ven asked Arna. "Everything?"

It was. They didn't understand. It was.

"You're going to lose a Blessing every time you pick up a fan to dance your variation." Ven finally spoke with clarity. The heaving of their sobs ceased. "This was going to happen either way. Wasn't it?"

"Possibly." When Arna twisted the truth, a shock went through his heart and Ebru flinched. Luckily, Ebru didn't say a word, but held him tighter, nails digging into Arna's arms.

"Is there a way to reverse it?" Ven asked.

The Gods had always told Arna that once he succeeded, he'd get all his Blessings back. It was part of the deal for Divinity. However, that required him making the right choice. Moreso, it required him living through the dances.

"Yes," Arna admitted, and hope lit up in the eyes of all those around him. Ebru relaxed just a bit, at the truth.

But could he live to see it?

Arna sat listlessly in the living room as the others explained to Zaffre and Wenge what happened. Ven refused to let him go and Amaryllis was trying to comfort them.

[*This is the only protection we can offer you,* Zaynir begged him.]

[*Please take it.*]

No one was particularly angry at Arna, even when they should have been.

He wanted it.

He deserved it.

(And. . .)

No. He pressed his Blessings to work.

Arna tried to get himself to focus on his dances, on everything. He had to keep going. Keep going, find the answer, finish his variation, he had to—

"I know that look. I've seen it in the mirror a hundred times." Ebru spoke, words like frosted javelins. Arna jolted in his seat, looking up. Ebru loomed over him. The others said Ebru's name, but Ebru ignored them. "The pressure is killing you."

Ebru was a righteous fury. "You are self-sabotaging. You will not give up on your dream to dance. You would hurt us more, yourself more, by giving up now. Why are you hesitating?"

Arna shook his head. He did not have words for an answer. Not now.

"You picking up that fan was not to make a point, it was to cut Ven out. To cut all of us out! Ever since they retested you, you been pushing us all away again, keeping us distant. Why, Arna? What are you not telling us?" Ebru demanded, voice growing louder.

Arna looked at his hands in his lap and took shallow, controlled breaths.

imfineimfineimfineimfineimfineimfineimfineimfineimfineimfineimfineimfineimfineimfine

"No. You can't avoid me," Ebru said, cupping Arna's face in his hands and forcing their eyes to meet. "What aren't you telling me? Answer me!"

"No."

"Incarnadine! What are you hiding from me?" Ebru yelled louder than Arna had ever heard him get. It gave rise to Arna's own self-loathing. This was what he wanted to avoid.

iftheyknewthetruththeydhatehimtoo

THEENDTHEENDTHEEND

If it was all over, then he had nothing left to hide.

"If I make the wrong choice *everything* will end. The Gods aren't connected to the world because of the Splintering! I'm the one who fucked up everything and I still—" Arna screamed back the answer that he could no longer choke back, the honest truth that only Ebru would ever be able to get out of him. "I don't know the answer!"

Arna's face collapsed into his hands as he understood the gravity of what he said. Now everyone would know. They'd all know.

imfineimfineimfineimfineimfineimfineimfineimfineimfineimfineimfineimfineimfineimfine

Kill it. Breathe. Focus. Focus. Six breaths in. Six breaths out.

(He had no reason to hide.)

"You said you would prove it," Ebru insisted. "Or is Incarnate Dreams not so important to you? Are dreams not that important to you?"

"Ebru. . ." Arna stopped shaking. There was no way to convince Ebru of the truth, not when he couldn't explain the choice itself. And it was clear that Ebru had not pieced together that Arna not being able to pick up a fan meant that he was going to die. "Everything will end."

"This is the one thing you have ever wanted," Ebru said softly.

Arna's thoughts stopped spinning. He didn't get it?

THE END THE END THE END

None of them did. No one heard his admission and heard the truth?

A strange calm filled Arna, silencing the raging thoughts. Maybe this wasn't like his worst fears. "It is," Arna admitted.

"Look at me," Ebru demanded, and Arna did as he was asked, meeting Ebru's eye.

"I've read this self-doubt over the last five years," Ebru said enunciating each word clearly. "I know you better than anyone in this fucking room. Let us help you."

When Ebru had first found out about Arna's fake accounts, he'd had a conversation very similar to this one. Arna was unable to speak, finding the words burning at the back of his throat. The end of the world weighed down on his shoulders. The path to survival was covered by mists at their feet.

Was he on it? Had he found it? Could he ever?

(Did he deserve to?)

He did not.

"Is he getting hate mail, too?" Ebru asked the others. "He's been reading the forums and internet, getting past the blockers. I know he is."

"Mom tries to burn it before he sees it," Ginger offered.

"Which is to say you've seen it. . ." Ebru looked back at Arna, brow furrowed and annoyance plain across his frown.

". . . You know the answer." Arna was irritated. Ebru didn't understand. Arna needed Ebru to understand.

Ebru began his tirade, "I can't believe I have to tell you this—"

Arna followed, "You don't understand —"

"—We are here for you.—"

"—Alis. This is all my fault —"

"—From the beginning until now—"

"—If I can't do it—"

"—You have always done everything —"

"—then there is no point in me —"

"—on your own. No more.—"

"—being alive. I have to fix this—"

"—We are here to stand by you and support you. Let us.—"

"—but I don't know how.—"

"Are you even listening to me?"

But they weren't listening to him. He would never find the path without them but. . .

"I can't do this," Arna said to himself. He couldn't admit to the end of the world again.

"We're here. We can still support you in every other way we can. You don't have to hide and keep secrets from us," Ebru said, and Arna blinked twice, realization dawning. "I will not allow you to harm yourself. I promised you I wouldn't cut myself and you can't do this."

Arna never imagined that he would hear Ebru admit that he harmed himself for years, and that he had wanted to die, let alone in front of all these people.

There was a harsh collective breath that left the room: silent questions, all eyes on the two of them.

"Swear to me that you'll trust us. Swear you'll live for us. Please try," Ebru asked, finally letting go of the death-grip he had on Arna's face, and lightly rubbing Arna's cheeks with his thumbs.

There was a long moment of silence before Arna said, "You're the one who tells me not to make promises I can't keep."

"I swear to Ixxzal!" Ebru dropped his hands and massaged his temples.

There was a few minutes as Ebru calmed himself and no one said a thing, even though there were shifting expressions. Rosmarinus attempted to sedate the tension with blankets and drinks. It worked and everyone settled down, waiting for Ebru and Arna to continue talking.

Because Ebru was right. Ebru knew his everything, since the day that Rosy met Alis. Ebru had been his everything, since they saved each other's lives at twenty-two.

"This is your chance at everything, Arna," Ebru finally said. "You can be anything. You don't have to be afraid. We are here. We can help you achieve your dream."

Ebru thought Arna was giving up on being the Chosen? No. Never.

"I don't want to lose what I've worked for," Arna said. It came from a place of honesty, deep in his soul. However, he did not try to explain the end of the world again.

makeitsilent.

keepithidden.

dontbelikesaffron

They could help but not with this, not with the burden of knowing.

Ebru tried to say something and failed miserably. "You won't."

"He will," Sarcoline's words startled everyone.

"Sarcoline, don't," Zaffre said. Sarcoline glanced at their father and back to Arna. The whole room froze as Arna met Sacroline's eye.

"I told the others last week—" Sarcoline began.

"Sarcoline. No," Wenge repeated.

"It's just a theory," Sarcoline ignored them.

[   ]

Sarcoline sat shifting in his chair looking at Arna with concerned eyes. The world stalled. There was a clarity to Sarcoline's eyes that none of the others had. Arna nodded and Sarcoline gasped out.

"I was doing research on kids like you and me. Talented but without. . ." The words tumbled out of his mouth as he pointed at his eyes. "You know the False Chosen?"

"Arco, no," Rosmarinus said, angrily. It was the first time Arna had ever heard something other than a calming tone from the man.

"What about them?" Arna ignored him.

Arna thought of the meeting with the Governor and Cardinals as they accused him of such. He thought of the online commenters, and how he had once thought it about himself. False Chosen were Children who pretended to be Chosen through veils and disguises.

"There were many in the Third Variance," Sarcoline went on ignoring all the others that were glaring daggers at him. "Which is not surprising, considering how long the Variance lasted. When the tests were changed to the LHF authority and became Government controlled, lots of false reports were stopped. The record keeping for the last Variance has been exquisite."

"You went back and looked?" Arna asked. He vaguely recalled Mr. Thyme talking about it. There were tests and there were records. There were scientists trying to prove why he existed and why he shouldn't. There were people wishing for answers he could never give.

"I did. As a history major, I get access to many private and locked records. I don't think anyone cares about these too much. But there were kids who were like you, with dark brown eyes and all the Blessings," Sarcoline was talking so fast, his eyes darted to the others. They were intimidating him into silence, but Sarcoline had faced worse.

"Some died young. Some were retested in their teen years and their Blessings had dropped. Down to three or four. Others kept more, but they were never Chosen. Usually, they continued dancing. Most never left home. A few disappeared and never returned. Always younger than twenty-four. There were only a handful of cases in this already small number that did disappear and reappeared. But. They never danced past the twenty-fifth dance."

"Never?" Arna asked as soon as Sarcoline took a second to breathe. This was new to him. The Gods had never told him this.

"Never," Sarcoline repeated. Arna pondered it for a moment and then nodded.

"Arco, stop. . ." Ginger pleaded.

"No. Arco, go on," Arna disagreed. Arna's thoughts began to slow. It was like a slow train crash happening with people crying to be saved. Everything and anything Arna worked for slowly returned to *silence.*

Sarcoline understood what Arna had been hiding, and Arna needed to hear it from someone else.

Sarcoline said, "They lived out their lives, with six Blessings. The last one who got as far as you lived about a hundred years ago."

Sarcoline stopped talking and stared at Arna. There was a question loud and clear in his eyes.

Arna was unspeakably calm as he realized that not only his brother, but possibly everyone with him, knew the most well-kept secret he had beyond the loss of his Blessings and the end of the world.

It was why Ebru was convinced he was giving up, why they were all reacting as he did. Sarcoline didn't have to say it because they all believed it to be true, simply based on the way Arna had been reacting since he came home. Here he thought he'd hid it so well, but in fact he had not.

"There are Chosen candidates all the time, but the child has to agree to do what they are told to do, right? You go through a series of tests until. . . Either you succeed or someone else is selected."

Arna sat quietly. Arna may have been one of the best dancers, but he'd known that night that the Gods would have left if he did not say yes. Arna had never been special. A part of him had always known that. A part of him knew that if he had not broken the world, the Gods may have abandoned him. They may have chosen another in the room.

[Distant winds disagreed.]

"And. . ." Sarcoline said softly, "Morality or the Gods? This choice you have right now is one that they always have given, and others have failed, right? This test. . . It's not until you pass this last test that you will go from being a child who was chosen to the Chosen Child. Right now, you can still give up and you'd lose everything. You wouldn't be the Chosen at all."

Mortals or the Gods?

Sarcoline went silent. The whole room echoed the sentiment.

Twelve years' worth of hair tumbled over Arna's shoulders as he leaned forward, until his head was between his knees. Arna's heart lurched as he gripped his left wrist feeling the freezing blue flames beneath the skin of the vow that he had yet to make.

IMPOSTER

HE WAS AN IMPOSTER

THE END THE END THE END

He was going to be exactly like Saffron.

No. No.

He had to keep going. He had to keep moving, but it was too late. He was frozen in time. Everything was converging into this single moment. He was collapsing in on himself. They all knew he was an imposter forcing his way through the prophecy now. He could no longer hide it.

They knew the fans. They knew he was a liar. He knew he was going to die.

No one in the room spoke. No one moved. Arna struggled to regain his breathing as Ebru's hand lightly traced his back.

[You are not alone.]

"Sarcoline, you might be the smartest person I've ever met," Arna said when he could finally speak again. He slowly sat up and glared at his brother, who's eyes were large with terror.

Keep it together. He had to kill the emotions. He had to keep himself together.

But the self-doubts were beginning to swell. He was crumbling under the pressure just as Ebru said. He *was* an imposter.

imposterimposterimposter

He wasn't the Chosen.

diediediediediedie

He was forcing himself to be because no one else could.

Just like Saffron.

But, no one else had the chance. It *had* to be him.

theendtheendtheend

"There was a bit there, when I was on the run, where I thought that I was going insane," Arna said to Sarcoline. "I thought that maybe I'd only wanted to be the Chosen Child and expected it so much, that I'd let myself believe that they talked to me. I thought, maybe it was all in my head. I thought that I was faking it far before everyone else did. That I was convincing myself that the horrible coincidences I'd been through were that: coincidences."

[There were no accidents.]

"Arna." Ebru grabbed him tightly, as if Arna would slip away through his fingers.

His Blessings stuttered and flickered, overdrawn and unable to hold back the flood. Arna tried to avoid the cascade.

Keep it together. He was the only one who could do it. Even if he died in the storm. Even if his Blessings failed him. Even if he picked the wrong choice—no he could not make the wrong choice. He *had* to succeed. *Focus on the success.*

imfineimfineimfineimfineimfineimfineimfineimfineimfineimfineimfineimfineimfineimfineimfine

Arna bit back the emotions and buried them as deep as he could.

They continued to bubble up.

imfineimfineimfineimfineimfineimfineimfineimfineimfineimfineimfineimfineimfineimfineimfine

"Sometimes when I'm panicked, it's all I believe. Sometimes I wonder if being Chosen was truly my dream or just something I assumed would happen; something I assumed I had to do."

The words tumbled from Arna's hysterical lips: the dam had burst.

He could no longer hide the truth.

imfineimfineimfineimfineimfineimfineimfineimfineimfineimfineimfineimfineimfineimfineimfine

Focus. Focus. Keep it together.

The world would end if he did not dance. He would not forsake the Gods now. No. He would succeed.

(He wanted to live.)

"Arna. . ." Wenge said from where she stood next to Sarcoline.

Focus. Focus. Focus. Kill it. Bury it. Never visit the grave.

"You. . ." Phlox said.

"No. . ." Ven whispered from next to Arna.

"Arna, the Gods chose you," Ebru said in a low growl.

Arna swallowed. "I've never thought I was good enough, Ebru. You know that."

"No. Arna," Ginger pleaded.

"Arna, listen," Jasi knelt before Arna next to Ebru. "I did a lot of stupid things as a teenager. Fights. Completed the bucket list. Almost got kicked out of the city."

Arna clung to it as if it were a life boat.

"I finished the bucket list, too," Arna admitted which startled him and he cracked a smile nodding.

"Arco and Rus stopped me from becoming a disaster. And we're going to stop you, okay? We're here. Everything has a reason. There is an order to things. Your disappearance. Dropping the fan. You *aren't* an imposter. Everything adds up. If not, then why would the signs be here? Where is the justice in a lie?" Jasi looked Arna dead in the eye. Arna's hands continued to tremble. Jasi's hands shook too. He didn't want to believe it.

"In the same place where we left it," Phlox said with a bit of snark to it. "On the ground crumpled under our feet with the rest of our childish hopes and dreams."

None of them wanted to believe what Sarcoline was saying, despite how much it aligned with Arna's actions. Here, in this room, their hope and faith was being tested, shattered beyond repair. They were being asked to believe in an imposter, in a lie.

But it was too far gone now, and the lifeboat had too many holes. The secrets were too numerous and impossible to ignore. Arna needed them to see him the way he always saw himself. He needed to face their hate now, before it was too late. Maybe, just maybe, he could fix it.

(Just like he could fix everything else?)

"It's not a lie, Jasi. I won't become the Chosen until the night I dance. If I never do, everything will end. I've known that anyone could do it. . . Since I was twenty-three. . . I've simply clung to it," Arna said, looking up at Sarcoline who was wide eyed in his chair, reeling in terror. Was that what he looked like when he learned the truth? Arna had been a year older than Sarcoline was currently.

"I'm just an imposter in a place I never was meant to be," Arna said to his brother. He hoped that Sarcoline would see that they were the same. "All the same, I'm going to fight for my right to stand here. Just like you fight to dance."

Sarcoline said what Arna feared they were all thinking. "You might never dance."

Arna had to dance. "I have no choice. It's the only way I'll know if I'm right."

The whole room filled with an eerie silence.

"And we will still have the auditions, so you can make that choice in peace," Zaffre said, taking command of the room, as if Arna had not admitted that he was a failure. They pretended as if their faith in him was not for nothing.

Arna was not allowed to be alone. Ebru never left his side. Amaryllis and Aureolin took care of Ven. Sarcoline was lectured by Jasi, Zaffre, and Ginger. Phlox and Rosmarinus helped Wenge with dinner.

By bedtime, Arna curled up on Ebru's bed, in the room he'd once lived in years ago.

Ebru's room was devoid of any personality, with only a bed in the center. Ebru's things for the night were in a bag open on the dresser. A single mirror hung in the room across from the bed. The window faced the garden instead of the outside world, like Arna's.

Outside, past the center of the garden, the sky was lit in streetlights glittering like false stars in the haze of the artificial sky.

Arna swore he could hear the question: Mortals or the Gods?

"Arna," Ebru called to Arna as he exited the bathroom, towel over his head. Ebru's hair was no longer styled. His glasses were on, and his contacts were removed. His piercings were changed from studs in his ears that were pointed, sharp and black, to rounded and bronze. He was softer.

However, he was dressed in a loose, white long-sleeve shirt and sweatpants. As Ebru rubbed the towel through his hair to dry it, black roots showing, yellowed bruises became visible. They peaked out from along the collar and his sleeves, disrupting Arna's nerves.

Arna walked over to Ebru, unsure when the injuries had happened. He'd been with him all day. Was it the day before? When? How?

"Let me see," Arna tugged at the hem of Ebru's shirt.

"It's ugly," Ebru warned him but did so anyway. Arna saw red for a split second, fighting to control himself. The whole of Ebru's body was in quick healing bruises, but they were obviously damaging enough to be nearly black when first caused. There were no visible cuts, but there was a chance those had already healed. Ebru's body Blessing was not nearly as fast as Arna's, but that was because Arna had eleven of them. The injuries had to be horrific if Ebru's body blessing was taking this long to heal.

Arna hissed at the sight, his hands curling inwards, nails threatening to reopen scars. These injuries on Ebru were his fault. He had not gotten back fast enough.

Ebru grabbed Arna's face so that their eyes met. "I'm okay. It's healing."

"Why?" Arna gasped out, no other words able to form. Why couldn't he have saved him? Why did they hurt him? Why did he act like it didn't matter? Why did Ebru love him when Arna continued to break promises?

"I'm pretty sure they just hate me," Ebru shrugged. As Arna held him lightly, Ebru did not wince.

"They did it because of me," Arna said. Ebru did not retort: unable to tell a lie.

Ebru pulled back, eyes searching Arna's face for something. He kissed Arna, pushing them back until Arna tumbled down onto the bed. They were light in their touches, knowing that they could not do much at all. Not when Ebru was this injured. Not when Arna's entire life was slipping through his fingers.

For a moment Ebru looked too soft, too vulnerable, and younger. His eyes were trained on Arna in them Arna saw what he'd been missing. It was not a flicker, or a glance quickly masked away. Arna could recognize it in every interaction before, in the sorrow and taunts, and their lingering stares through mirrors.

For years, it had colored every interaction in the dance rooms, and behind computer screens. It was in every word that Ebru had said to him since he got back. It was in every way that Ebru touched him before he left.

"You said you loved me for three years."

Ebru froze and his smile dropped, caught off guard. This was why Ven and Ebru had fought. Arna didn't need to be told to see. Ven had found out that Ebru had loved him, more than a rival, more than friends, and had been hiding it.

"Arna. Don't."

"You loved me before I—"

"Arna!" Ebru yelled. The room quickly returned to nothing but their breathing. "We are not having this conversation. You need rest, not to think of. . . me."

Ebru was startled as if understanding something that Arna himself did not understand. It was as if Arna always deflected his own pain by asking about others.

"Ask," Ebru hissed through his teeth with much difficulty.

"You should have told me," Arna said. Ebru sat on the bed away from him.

"You were dating Ven," Ebru said sternly. "And then you left, and it didn't matter. Ven yelled at me, got so angry, was so betrayed that I loved you. They left and blocked me, and I couldn't fix it. . ."

"Have you two talked about it?" Arna asked him.

Ebru did not answer at first, the white noise circling the room, until slowly but surely, he nodded.

"And they don't hate you," Arna said holding Ebru. "Why didn't you tell me?"

"I was afraid," Ebru admitted. There was adoration in his eyes as well as desperation. The world condensed into the single moment, as if time stopped and there was nothing but Ebru.

"Did anyone else know?" Arna asked.

"Arco," Ebru said, softly. "I told him the day that we left, when he was begging me for answers why everything was falling apart. I told him so he'd stop asking me, so he'd leave me alone. He knew how I betrayed us all."

Arna pictured his brother standing in his dance room, glaring at Ebru who revealed his heart and ensured that they would always be enemies. Arna had a hard time believing that Ebru was particularly honest in the moment.

When Arna kissed Ebru again, he shut his mind off. He let it slow to a standstill. He ignored everything that happened in the day and thought of nothing but Ebru. He thought of their future and the chance at an after.

It was soft, like a prayer: *I want to live.*

Arna, for the first time, in many years, let himself fully dream.

And its only in dreams where nightmares can spawn.

Revulsion spread through Arna's body, jolting him awake well into the night. He laid in the bed absolutely still. Ebru slept beside him, breathing softly. Arna rubbed his hands over his face trying to understand what was happening. Gasping for air, Arna tried to piece together, who, what, where.

Every thought that he'd been trying to keep at bay was breaking free. Nothing was hidden. The damn was breaking. There was too much noise. Arna closed his eyes tight.

Bile rose in his throat as his heart raced in his chest.

unsafe.run.theyhateyou.gogogogogogo.theyallknow.theyALLknow
THEYALLKNOW
everything is going to end
and it will be your fault

Arna sat up, slowly and trying not to wake Ebru.

The screams were there again, bouncing around him.

In the air.

In the corner.

In his soul, wanting to rip him **a p a r t.**

He didn't deserve it.

`Imposter`

Imposter

Imposter

IMPOSTER

IMPOSTER

imposterimposterimposterimposterimposterimposterimposter.

d   i   e

Gunshots aimed at him.

(who were his Saints?)

He was the reason so many people were dead.

His fault

His problem.

(Why did he keep trying to hide?)

shouldhavebeenbettersmarterbettersmarter.

nooneelsewouldhavedroppedthefanandfuckedup.

Ven screaming. Amaryllis comforting. Amaryllis lost her heartmate in the Ludiel train crash.

BREAKING NEWS: THE END OF THE WORLD
Not so shocking: its caused by Incarnadine Again

(it wasn't his fault. . .)

How could he be so self-centered?

The last few weeks since the day he'd been tested, crashed into him. No matter how much he tried or how much he pretended, he could not hold the emotions back. He could not contain it. It could no longer be buried. It could no longer be drowned. It refused to be hidden.

It scratched at his skin, fighting to live, consume, and destroy him.

Arna raced from the room, headed to his own, silently across the hall.

I don't hear your footsteps anymore.

He

was nothing but a shade.

had no reason to exist.

had no reason to be here.

They **ALL** hated him, *deep down they **all** hated him.*

(was it true?)

stoppretendingstoppretendingstoppretendingINCARNADINE.

It never was meant to happen with you. Shouldn't have been Chosen. What a worthless piece of shit.

He had wanted to be Chosen so bad that he was willing to destroy everything.

How could he be so selfish?

Arna crashed into his room, seeing the candles. They were unlit and precariously placed on the bridge of wood, amongst the mountain of rubble. This was the way Xeysis would be. It was how every city would be.

Torn apart by the storms.

Billions dead.

The survivors hiding and waiting for death to take them.

No salvation coming.

BREAKING NEWS: INCARNADINE WAS SAFFRON ALL ALONG

Arna dropped to his knees before the candles, held out his hands, cupped his palms, and bent his head.

The candles came to light with the faintest, flickering light. He made a wish: "Remind me what happens."

[*You know,* Ixxzal sighed.]

"That never stopped you before." Arna stared into the light of the candles. And he needed to hear it. He needed to center himself. This was the only way now that his Blessings refused to listen to him. It was how they helped him in the past and it would work now. It had to work now. . .

[*The first time you dance your variation will be unique,* Xeyaro whispered. *You will forget yourself in dance twenty-five, completely, and we will separate from you.*]

Remember. Focus Arna. Focus. He tried to keep his mind from spiraling with the facts.

INCARNADINE WAS SAFFRON ALL ALONG

Saffron was twenty-seven when he danced the Ceremony of Chaos and failed. He was Ixxzal's favorite, even if the Gods never admitted it. Ixxzal spoke highly of him, and they were all so disappointed when he failed. Saffron failed and started the Shattering that destroyed the world.

Ilex had tried to fix it.

INCARNADINE WAS SAFFRON

[*In dance twenty-six, the world will become malleable as you fracture the veil between our realm and the mortal realm. If you made the right choice, your Blessings will remain. If not, they will vanish. You will enter the state of ascension, and in doing so, we will be able to rewrite the contract.*]

[*Arna, we don't have to do this,* Pokk said, cutting Xeyaro off.]

"Yes, you do!" They always lectured him when he was unsure. They always reminded him to start over. Whenever he was doubting. Whenever he was struggling. They always gave a lecture. And it always made things **better.** "Please. . ."

[Xeyaro's voice shook. *The universe will attempt to kill you, as no mere mortal may enter Divinity. Your Blessings will have to defend you because we will not be able to interfere. It is not a test, but a transformation of your body and soul.*]

If Arna lived.

SAFFRON SAFFRON SAFFRON SAFFRON SAFFRON SAFFRON

Arna had always been afraid of dying, even as a child. He was so terrified of it, that it made him wake up in night terrors where his mother and Xeyaro had to sing him back to sleep. His own mortality had faced him down for years. He had tried to avoid it, tried to outrun it, tried to defeat it. But it was a mirror, hidden in a mirage. And the closer he got to the Celebrations, the clearer everything became. The likelihood of him living was near nonexistent. With each Blessing he lost the less it became.

(why had he believed in miracles?)

He didn't deserve consecrated friendships.

[If you can survive, you must complete twenty-seven. Twenty-seven is where you'll complete your Divinity transformation and no longer be fully mortal. In this state you'll be able to reestablish the contract on the mortal's side and reconnect the mortals to us.]

"And after the first time, I'll never reach that state again," he said trying to force the emotions

down.

I'm fine. I'm fine.

But they would not back away. He would have to face the emotions whether he wanted to or not.

SAFFRON SAFFRON SAFFRON

[Correct, They said in unison. *Because you will already be Divine.]*

But he never would be.

Focus. The Gods said that the contract took minutes to hours to reestablish. With how weak they were, there was no way that they'd be able to reach him in time.

BREAKING NEWS: INCARNADINE

IT'S THE END OF THE WORLD AND

It was all his fault.

Maybe, in a better world:

(he'd be able to dance again.)

Focus. He was slipping. The world was tilting. Arna stopped breathing.

Maybe in a better world:

(He could Worship without fear.)

(The time for hiding was done.)

Welcome to the end.

In a better world, he was allowed to dream.

[Arna. . . Xeyaro's voice faded like a life cut short.]

[Arna, listen to me! Ixxzal's voice was a screaming nightmare.]

[Arna! No! Arna! Azza's voice was the embrace of death.]

[Arna! Please no, you can't give up! Zaynir's voice was peace that came after all was healed.]

[Arna! Think, remember! Pokk's voice was first sunrise after the catastrophe.]

[Arna! Look at us! Look at us! Lumak's voice was balance when no one could see it.]

He could not be like **Saffron.** He would never be like **Saffron.** He was not like **Saffron.**

Face the mirror.

Arna looked up the candle that were so faint that the light was little more than a pin prick.

In a better world, maybe Arna would have survived to see the future

that one he'd foolishly allowed himself to wish for.

He would not have stopped running, nor allowed the mirage to catch up with him.

But he was and had always been just like Saffron.

No matter how much he tried.

Everything that Arna had ever worked for

S

H

A

T

T

E

R

E

D

The soul and emotion are tied as well. We exist and because we exist, we feel.
We feel and thus we can bond.
Emotions give way to the arts; without one we cannot have the other.
Zaynir ties all mortals together.
Zaynir strengthens the bonds of the world and allows for possibility.

— On Zaynir.

Dance 21

Genesis

Harmony

Incarnadine

25 Xeyan

17 Days Left

"Are you visualizing?"
"What?"
"Your variation? Are you visualizing what that future world will look like?"
"Should I be?"
"Yes. You always should, until the day you know."

It started with a numbness, the Gods   s l i p p i n g   through his fingers.
An apathy formed in his soul as he fully accepted that he was going to die.

Because he was `worthless`.

Because he *deserved it.*

Because he was an ***`imposter`***.

someone better than him would have never been in this position
to begin with
[*Arna, we are still here! Listen,* Azza cooed, their voice distant.]

They were there once: The Gods. As real as mortals, but now they were s m o k e,
lost to the s k y. He could feel them disCON-nec-

ting,

a dying fire in the rage of the sea of sorrow.

They'd go somewhere he'd never be able to find them. THEY **HATED** HIM.
They were leaving him,

because he was terrible.

because he made them use too much energy.

because he was the worst Chosen they had ever picked.

none of the others had jump started the apocalypse.

Except **Saffron.**

Saffron was a flower. Saffron was a spice. Saffron was the smirking, twisted, horror at the core of Arna. For Arna had made sure that the world could never be fixed if he failed. In his own selfishness, he had thought himself so GREAT(!?).

He thought that because he saw the Gods that he was the *o-n-l-y* **one.**

He thought he was   *s*   *p*   *e*   *c*   *i*   *a*   *l*

what a joke

He wasn't! Now everyone knew! They all knew—just like he did, and frankly, accepted years ago, because he was so woefully terrible—that he wasn't anything until he danced.

That he could still fail even after all this time.

That there could have been others.

That it could have been anyone.

He wasn't special.

He was selfish, and he reached for it without a care for anyone else.

Dropped a fan.

Severed the connection between mortals and Gods.

His fault.

Him.

shouldhavebeenabetterChosen.shouldhavebeensmarter.shouldhavebeenbetter. whatawasteofpotential.

Shouldn't   have   chased   a   dream.

I don't deserve it.

[*Talk to Ebru. Call for Ebru. Ven. Anyone,* Lumak suggested, little
more than the concept of a voice.]

Reaching for his mobile, Arna messaged Ebru. There was no response and the feeling of dread continued. The house began to close in on him. It was tearing him apart.

He couldn't BREATHE.

(Everyone here knew.)

Jasione had become violent.

(Knew the truth.)

Aureolin believed everyone hated her. Thought she deserved it.

He was hated by them too.

Gingerline gave up on her dream and cried herself to sleep.

(He had lied to them.)

Phlox lost everyone who ever cared for her.

(About his Blessings.)

Pervenche lost everything.

About the truth that he wasn't Chosen.

Zaffre had drunk himself into a stupor.
Wenge had lost her sparkle.
Alabaster lost his family.

(He had ran from them.)

Rosmarinus had to save a family that was not his.
Amaryllis lost her heartmate.
Eburnean tried to kill himself.

Destroyed them.

And a boy who worshiped him like a God, shattered.
All because of Arna.
Arna could not stay home.

    It was not his home anymore.
    Nowhere was his home.
    He didn't deserve to be anywhere.
    He didn't deserve anything.

diediediediediediediediediediediediediediediediediediediediediediediediediedie

giveupgiveupgiveupgiveupgiveupgiveupgiveupgiveupgiveupgiveupgiveupgiveupgiveup

BREAKING NEWS: WELCOME TO THE END

Arna walked out of his house, searching for air. He walked past the silent guards, out to the street, into the fog.

(what is silence?)

[*Where are you going?* Ixxzal yelled from a window far away. *Go inside. Stay home!*]

There was a way that the cities were built, as if they were the Gods themselves, tripping and tumbling over themselves, blooming and circling further. They were an incomprehensible form in the physical realm. Arna gripped his mobile. It was sharp and broken. Dropping it, he continued on.

Alone.

Arna was there again, in dark rooms without heating.

He was standing, facing down a boss who spat in his face.

He was listening to people cheering at the Celebrations, watching the screen, wishing he could be there.

He was lost in Ixis, trying to find his way home after grabbing a fan, breaking down in a corner, shaking and unable to move.

He was words, orders, suggestions, lectures, and lessons repeated over and over and over and

[*Don't get lost in the abyss, Arna,* Lumak called.]

He was twenty-six, fearing the inevitable when the storms shook his bones, he'd have to **dance** or die. Fear consumed him, but he had to convince himself it didn't matter. **He was not afraid** of dying.

He was twenty-five, holding on to a fan as he ran through a city, **Blessings flourished**. It was the biggest event of the year, everyone was excited in temporary bliss unable to **comprehend** the horror that only Arna knew.

[*What do we do?* Zaynir cried.]

He was crying at twenty-four, afraid to die. Begging for peace, wanting (for a moment) to be allowed to **dream of a future** where he could **live**. But they couldn't guarantee that he'd survive.

He was twenty-three, determined and focused on stopping the end the world, convinced that he could succeed. Even when **he understood that the end was coming. Wishing** that he was a better dancer, that he was smarter, that he was anything but an imposter, but that **was im**possible. He was not alone on his path.

[*Do something, Ixxzal!* Azza screamed.]

He was twenty-two, dancing despite of the storms, wishing to **be happy**. Praying that **he would find someone that would Understand**. Messaging people on the forums even though he was hated, because he was anonymous.

He was twenty-one, wanting to **be loved**. Shaking as the Gods demanded he touch the fan and hold it, understand the pain, **accept it** and push past it, push through it. Pushing through the terror. Pushing through the fear that he was the only one. Because he Understood. And he **hope**d.

[*Don't forsake us, Arna,* Xeyaro whispered, tendrils trying to latch on.]

Phantom spirits rushed through Arna.

He was twenty, screaming at the Gods who he hated. Screaming at nothing, demanding to **go home**. He was breaking into a store. If he did the one thing they told him not to, it would be over. He'd no longer be Chosen. He wanted the connection to be over. He wanted for everything to return to normal. He no longer wanted to **be Chosen**. He was holding the fan. He was blacking out in pain.

He was nineteen, thinking that maybe, just maybe, he would be capable of **saving the world**, but he learned the truth. He was but an imposter. He had broken the world for nothing. He was not **Chosen by them.**

[*Azza! Pokk! Help me!* Ixxzal was little more than a ghost.]

And he was eighteen.

And it was only when he slowed down. It was only when all the truths came to light. It was only when everyone knew and he didn't have to keep running, when he didn't have to keep fighting, when he could finally rest and be seen, that he saw himself for what he was.

He was no longer singularly focused on his variations and completing the task at hand. For a second, he allowed himself to truly dream of a future that he'd never be a part of. . .

He was nothing.　　　　He was worthless.　　　He was the one who destroyed everything.

Imposter.　　Selfish.　　He hated himself.　　　　He deserved to be hated.

be punished.
be smote and hurt and take everything that everyone threw at him.

He deserved it. He didn't matter.

He didn't have the Blessings because he was a fool who didn't understand simple instructions. And he was going to die even if he succeeded at reconnecting the Gods to mortals.

So why did it matter?

(JUMP)

[*Tell me what he needs,* Pokk's voice was splintering into nothing.]

He was eighteen, running from the house with the silver lawn, his name on the wind as the couple chased him. He wanted safety and they had given it to him. He wanted to give them gifts. They wanted to keep him while he tried to fix things. They wanted to love him. He wanted to ignore the Gods' shouted warnings. They told him not to get on the train. He did anyway. The couple with the silver lawn followed.

He was eighteen, listening to the screams as the electrical surge rocked the train. They were falling from the sky as the Blessings holding them up were broken. People were praying, but no prayers reached the Gods. The Gods were laughing in hysterics, debating incessantly, screaming at him to move.

He was eighteen. The couple with the silver lawn were crying Their names were a distant fluttering of dragonfly wings. *Move,* he was told. He did not want to. *Jump,* they said. He was tired. He had been stupid to believe himself greater. *You need to go.* He was willing to die for them, was that not enough?

Live, the couple had said to him.

LIVELIVELIVELIVELIVELIVELIVELIVELIVELIVELIVELIVELIVELIVELIVELIVELIVELIVELIVE

He was eighteen, climbing on the roof of a falling train. The wind whipped his hair around. His tears stung his eyes. There was only one chance. There was one train in their path, when all others had been stopped. He had seconds to make the jump. They would narrowly avoid each other.

Believe us. There were more pleads, more prayers. More.

BELIEVE US BELIEVE US BELIEVE US BELIEVE US BELIEVE US BELIEVE US
BELIEVE US

He was eighteen, in the sky. Floating? Falling? Flying? Landing on a high moving train, Blessings screaming at him as he broke a few bones. Explosions rocked the city. Screams illuminated the night. The death tolls rose.

Nausea from the memory of bodies on the smoke. Too many. Impossible to identify. Missing persons. Missing reasons. Missing funerals. Afraid to show his face.

He was eighteen. Angry. Hurting. Despising everything, everyone, and mostly himself. Eighteen, unsure of where to go. *Blame us. It's our fault.*

But it wasn't. It was his. Arna was not sure where he was, and he did not care anymore. He followed the streets, lights blacking out around him. The city power failed as the Blessings failed and the Gods lost their anchor.

[*Arna. I'm here.*]

When the abyss spoke. Arna knew better than to listen. He knew better than to speak. He knew better than to gaze into its terrible depths for no answers lived there.

Only secrets. Only the unknown.

"What is the point?" he asked.

[   ]

Where do you go when you no longer exist?

When you're a paradox, because you must exist if the world is still turning.
When you wonder if there is an after when you're gone?
Nowhere.

The God of the Unknown did not take you, the God of Chaos did.

The God of the Unknown was too proud.

The God of the Unknown was selfish and terrible.

The God of the Unknown answered no one.

The God of the Unknown. . .

The wind settled around Arna, and Ixxzal stood before him in the form of a six-foot tall creature with antlers and eyes like a spider, spindly and swaying in the street before him. It was tangible as the night and glowing like a million windows. Ixxzal was draped by the sky Arna had seen outside of the cities: entire universes and billions of stars. It was a swirling vortex of smoke and illusions.

[*You exist.*]

A prayer guiding him home.

Ixxzal walked through Arna; he could finally

b   r   e   a   t   h   e

IN

out

How he hated them.

It was like a thorn in his side, impossible to remove.

He despised them.

He hated

their callousness and their despondency.

He wished,

(he always wished)

that he was never given the choice.

(Because he wanted it.)

(They supported him, through every fight.)

(Needed it.)

(Through every storm.)

(Cherished the choice more than anyone.)

(They'd stood by him.)

He shattered the world for a dream.

(Through every harsh night and terrible nightmare.)

Was it worth it?

(They'd believed in him.)

Because as much as he hated them. . .
They'd trusted him and told him over and over that he was the one they'd chosen.

(Even when they gave no answer to why.)
(They loved him.)

And he. . .

[*Start from the beginning.*]

He loved them.
The air he craved.
The future he clung to.
The earth below and the sky above.
The millions of stars, and the essence of laughter.
If they asked, he would die for them: he would.
But, no.
They wanted him to *live.*
[They wanted him to defy.]

Arna searched for his truth, trying to find the melody in the cacophony. He searched for the tempo of his soul, measuring the beat of his heart. Thoughts drifted away, becoming one with the sounds around him until he heard nothing at all.

He was not the words, but

[*What is silence?*]

[*What is Incarnate Dreams?*]

the silent spaces between them.

Again.

Arna stepped. At first, his body was not used to it, displaced in time and space, identity and hope. The second step of his variation was sturdier. With his arms out, he imagined the weight that should be in his hands. He stepped on the cracks, feeling the bumps in the pavement, and listened to the trees. There were the slightest whispers of the world urging him to go, to go, to. . . dance.

[Pokk was the hush of the morning, calling the song for war.]

He glided over roots and stems, discarded things of nature that would be removed by morning as if they never existed. He floated in the night. The universe became a song. He moved slowly at times, quickly at others, his body swaying about as he moved in the way that best suited the world. Down streets, through plazas and alleyways, over hills, through parks, into 'No Trespassing' zones, into buildings with limited security, to the museums, and their courtyards, he went through it all.

[Lumak was the echo of opening flowers as the new day began.]

Each dance was a special thing, something that started in a place he would never be able to articulate to anyone who asked, but that place was everything to him. It moved him forward, deeper, further. Not alone. Everything. All and nothing at once.

Worship, development, hope, memory, change and . . .

[Zaynir was essence of love in tears and fears.]

"Ah." Arna relaxed as he stepped into the religious circle, the Everlit candles before him held the smallest of sparks. It was not enough to make light for the world to see, but he did.

[Azza was the drive to become and to destroy, to change the world.]

The space was his, and his alone. No late-night prayers. No priests to see him. There was a sensation in the back of his mind that he had been followed.

Perhaps? *No. . .* Maybe.

The mist dusted his arms leaving a sparkle of dew upon his skin in the soft breeze.

[Xeyaro was the memory within his soul.]

There was only artificial weather in the cities. Real weather could wreak havoc in the city as it spiraled through the petals and compounded upon itself into an explosion of power. The natural elements could never infiltrate the rose, but Arna swore that the breeze was real.

[Ixxzal was the reminder.]

[*Keep our secrets, Arna.*]

[Do not be afraid of silence.]

Arna walked to The Weeping Stage, observing how it stood in the night with only the softest glow of solar lights to illuminate the stage floor and area around it. No hesitation, Arna climbed up.

He was still afraid of dying.

He was still an imposter.

He had caused the Splintering.

To the audience he turned, focusing on the nothing that was there and the nothing in the world around him.

He was a fool.

He may not deserve it.

He may have been selfish.

Arna stood, arms out in the way he'd start the first dance.

Worship, development, hope, memory, change. Hope once more? *No.*

He knew exactly what to do.

(And all he wanted was to dream.)

So, he faced the nightmare, and allowed himself to change.

All variations were built on a premise. His was built with a demand, blessed by his nightmares. It was the laughter of his friends and family. It was the Gods' cheers and their soft lullabies. It formed as he regained what he lost. It shimmered in the support they gave. It was the promise to dance.

Because he would.

Not because of hope. But because everything was set up for him to die and he yet, a tiny part of him truly wanted to live.

Worship, development, hope, memory, change, *defiance.*

So, he clung to life and was going to fight.

[*You may begin.* Xeyaro's breath were the rustling leaves in the night.]

Arna allowed himself to dream.

Arna danced, and when Xeyaro said [*Next*], he did so, flawlessly. No one dance was completed, never lingering for more than a minute. The darkness welcomed him; Ixxzal was with him. With each movement he was closer to them all. Azza, the moonlight caressing his cheeks. Pokk the light from the solar panels, technology and the sun in one. Lumak was there to balance him, to keep him sturdy and strong. Zaynir let him feel, everything completely, and then let it go until he only had clarity.

With each second, they were stronger. His panic melted. His fears were stolen by the Gods and replaced with faith.

He was reborn.

A lifetime of expectations was no different than a warm blanket. Confidence simmered in his blood. A million years of practice refined his bones until they were sturdier than diamonds.

"I have it," he told them when he stopped. Incarnate Dreams spun across his thoughts. "I know it this time."

It was far from complete, but he had found it: what he was missing. His variation only worked if he lived.

For Sarcoline. For Amaryllis. For Ven and Jasi and Ginger and Phlox and Aureolion. For Rosmarinus and Honeysuckle and his mother and father and Alabaster. And everyone who had ever wished to be something the world did not want them to be. For Ebru. For Alis. For himself.

As Arna opened his eyes, the darkest of night skies was within them. Around him was a sea of flowers, all the same color. That was except for the saffron blooming in the sea of endless black like a path into tomorrow. It beckoned him forward.

[*Yes*, they agreed.]

Arna hesitated looking to the candles. "Can I do this?"

[*What else have you trained for?* Lumak asked.]

But that was not the answer he wanted. The question he was asking was not about training or skill. It. . . it was question unasked in a decade worth of fears, swimming and rumbling, wanting an answer.

"Ixxzal. . ."

[*Yes?* Ixxzal asked.]

The question caught in his throat. It was an answer that could break him completely. It was an answer that could set him free. Make a choice. Will it be worth it?

[*Arna?* Azza asked.]

"No, it's okay," Arna hesitated, not wanting to spiral again.

Jumping from the Weeping Stage, Arna wished it a goodbye. There would be no dress rehearsal. The next time he stood upon it would be the full performance. The sun was rising.

He avoided the path of saffron.

Searching for his headphones and his mobile, Arna remembered he had dropped them both. He cursed himself for his stupidity in the moment. Sighing, he figured no one would have noticed he disappear yet, but he had to get back before they did.

He rounded the corner to find Sarcoline standing a bit further away, able to see the Weeping Stage from where he stood.

Had he been there the entire time?

[*Yes*, Zaynir answered.]

Arna stopped walking. They were all there in jackets and pajamas: all of the Golden Generation including Amaryllis, Rosmarinus, Sarcoline, and Jasi, waiting for him. While it was the hottest part of the year, each one of them looked breathless and chilled.

"What did you see?" Arna asked when he was close enough.

"Everything." Sarcoline was the only one who could speak, his voice broke a bit as he did, and he had to cough.

Had they been following him the entire time? His eyes landed on Ebru, who was glaring at him. Arna vaguely remembered calling him, but Ebru did not answer.

"I always answer," Ebru said as if reading Arna's thoughts. "You didn't *hear* me."

There was an unintentional jab in Ebru's words and Arna recoiled. He then took Arna's mobile and headphones from his pocket and placed them into Arna's bloodied and scabbed hands. Ebru refused to let go.

"We were all at the house. Arco saw you leave. Don't drop your mobile again," he said lightly.

"I won't." Arna searched their faces. *They* saw. They saw *him* at his most vulnerable. They saw what he wanted to do, even if it was a splintered half dance, with him trying things over and over again until it stuck.

[*Yes*, Zaynir was in the wind again.]

"What were you doing?" Amaryllis asked, curious and pressing, wanting him to reveal his secrets again.

"Wandering," Arna admitted, ready to accept their prompting. There was no need to hide anymore. "Like I had Arco do. To find Understanding."

Defiance meant telling them everything.

Living meant relying on them to help him find the path.

"It did not begin that way," Ven called him on his bluff. "You were giving up."

Arna's eyes leveled on Ven. Slowly but surely, Arna nodded in confirmation. Ebru squeezed his hand tightly and everyone sucked in a collective breathe.

"We already lost you once, Arna," Ven said. "We don't want to lose you again. If you need to give up we'll understand, but please don't let it destroy you... We can help you..."

"I..." Arna was not sure how to respond.

[*You are good and that is enough.* Azza almost sounded cruel, the exhaustion clearly taking its toll.]

He had become their blade to carve out a new order. He was their carefully cultivated flower, meant to guide the future. The end of the world was coming. But right here, right now, none of the weight mattered.

He'd been suffocating under the pressure of knowing he had no choice but to succeed. It did not matter what society wanted, or the Gods wanted. Arna had made himself into their Chosen.

Now, Arna was breathing easy, holding himself without fear. He wanted to succeed. He wanted to live. He was Chosen, because while he'd sacrificed the world for his dream... he still wanted it.

[*We are here,* Ixxzal's voice buzzed and popped.]

The contract was crumbling. They'd used a lot of energy to save him, and he wasn't going to waste it. He was going to trust his family, just as they asked him to. He was going to rely on them.

"Arco." Arna turned his attention back to his brother. The brown of Sarcoline's eyes were, deep and rich, filled with abundance of possibility. "We are the same, you and I."

"I know," Sarcoline said after a moment. "It's why you piss me off."

"I may not have passed the test yet, but I will dance," he assured his brother, and in doing so, all of the others.

"Are you sure?" Sarcoline asked. "How can you be certain when you don't know the answer? We see how much it is destroying you. And the pain you'll face when you pick up the fans... Why would you risk all that? Why would you dance knowing that?"

"Because they—" What? *Why* would he risk dancing? Mortals or the Gods? "... Who am I dancing for?"

Arna's left wrist burned.

One of the petals was no longer glowing, but sparkling like glitter that was meant to be rubbed away. When his thumb ran over the mark, two petals remained. Arna rubbed his wrist again and again, until it was gone. Not Mortal or the Gods. *Who* was he dancing for?

"Arna?" Ven called out like the earth quaking.

[*First, you must know the true question we ask,* Lumak was soft and determined.]

All of the God's tests were cryptic. Arna had always danced because the Gods needed him to, because they'd die if he didn't. He always thought he'd dance because the Mortals needed him to, they'd die if he didn't. Both were the same, which meant the question was not about dying. But who he was dancing for? And he couldn't choose either of them. He had to pick neither: something else.

"Arna," Aureolin's voice was soft as the dawn.

[*Second, you must know the weight and cost of your choice.* Pokk was controlled and elegant.]

Arna had assumed it was the end of the world. If he didn't succeed everything would end.

Yet, the petal remained on his wrist.

And the question was asked to *every* Chosen who got this far. How could Saffron have failed when there was no end of the world yet? None of the others had to fight the end of the world. What was the weight and cost if not the end of times?

"Arna," Rosmarinus spoke calmly, the gentlest of breezes calling a person to focus. His voice set all at ease.

[*Third, you must be willing to accept the choice, even if you are wrong,* Zaynir was lush and confident.]

If the vow was not about what could go badly, then what did he have to accept?

He was not sure. But he had two more steps to go, and not much time left. He would find a way to answer the questions now that he understood them.

He had more confidence in finding the path to living as well.

"Arna are you—" Ebru asked, and Arna's head snapped up and he stopped rubbing his wrist.

The world tilted. Everything flickered. The Gods were screaming in warning.

There is only one secret.

"You can't tell anyone you just heard me say that," Arna said immediately.

This was the most important secret of the Gods that he was warned about: the final answer. The statement that could never be revealed. The world could not be changed that easily.

There was a long moment before Arna realized they were all looking at him concerned. Sarcoline walked out and yanked Arna's wrist into the open revealing that there was only two marks left.

"That is part of the answer?" Sarcoline asked, changing his grip from something strong to a lighter one.

"Every part of this question is, and no one can ever know. They have to find their answers themselves," Arna told him as Sarcoline's fingers traced the design. Arna's entire body was shaking. How could he ensure that no one ever found out? He'd revealed the one secret he was never meant to reveal. How was he—

"We'll make a vow," Sarcoline said, eyes narrowing dropping Arna's arm. "That's the only way you can trust us, right?"

"What?" Arna asked, realizing that his face ached. They all stared at him as if they saw through him, as they had for far too long.

"Right here. Right now. This is how we get you to believe in us," Sarcoline said, nodding to Ebru by Arna's side.

"Agreed." Amaryllis said.

"What do you mean?" he asked them all.

"I don't want to hear the words 'I'm fine' from your lips ever again," Aureolin said hotly.

"If this is what it takes," Rosmarinus agreed. "We do it. No debate. No question."

The man turned to his twin and Jasi's expression turned serious.

"I, Jasione Jade, open this concord to the Gods, and invoke a promise by those of us here. We shall unite and protect and ensure a level of trust beyond mortal minds. I call forth a contract to be made. An oath to be bound," Jasi said, stepping directly across from Arna. A tight circle formed with Arna between them. "A Vow."

The winds spiraled around them lightly at their feet. Saffron petals floated through the sky as if they were dancing. The light morning sun cast them all half in shadow and light. Dew in the air froze into scale-shaped crystals, hanging in the air, while glittering and spinning.

"I, Sarcoline Vivicent, hereby swear, under all the Gods and all their Chosen, the Saints and all Blessings, that I shall never reveal a word of the truths of the Chosen to anyone outside this circle, spoken, written, or otherwise. The Chosen's secrets will die with me. The God's secrets will die with me," Sarcoline vowed, holding out his right hand, and placing it in the center of the circle.

The temperature around them rose as the saffron swirled and the crystals began to sing: the melody of a song no mortal could replicate. All the same they tried.

"I, Amaryllis Ink. . ."

"I, Phlox Ruby. . ."

"I, Jasione Jade. . ."

"I, Rosmarinus Jade. . ."

"I, Gingerline Vivicent. . ."

 "I, Aureolin Begonia. . ."

"I, Pervenche Cosmos. . ."

"I, Eburnean Hue. . ."

One by one they all swore, without question, and without hesitation. They each added their right hands to the circle, one by one, holding each other. The sun felt hotter. The lights in the sky of the rose glowed red. Shadows formed all around them as low hanging mists turned to clouds at their feet. The saffron danced across their arms, cloaked them in mirages, protected them from scrutiny.

"As a Child of Lumak keeper of Laws and Vows, I hereby offer these Vows to Incarnadine Vivicent. Do you accept?" Jasi asked.

"I. . ." Arna was not sure what to say, but he wanted to believe in them and wanted to trust them. He wanted them to support him even when he was not sure how. He wanted to live with them.

And a vow meant the truth. He could tell them everything. They'd believe him. They'd never judge him. They'd face their dreams together. And maybe, just maybe, if he trusted them, they could help him find path to defying his fate. Hope clung to him and in it was comfort.

In it he found the words: "I do."

"And your vow?" Jasi asked.

Nine Saints made a choice for themselves and waited on the one they'd Chosen.

"I, Incarnadine Vivicent, hereby swear, under all the Gods and their Children, the Saints and all Blessings, that I shall trust you. With my secrets. With my fears. To support me and to understand me."

Arna placed his hand into the circle.

All of a sudden, Arna was off kilter, as if the weight he'd been holding was suddenly being supported by all of them. It bled through his hand into theirs. The other's winced in surprise as the saffron petals dropped over their arms and the crystalized dew impaled their skin.

Arna hissed as the crystal liquified. The petals seeped into their skin like an acid, creating steam and smoke from where they all held their arms together. Some called out in anguish. Others yelped, and a few cried. No one let go. The acid was a freezing in Arna's vein as his skin bubbled and puckered. It hardened and burned at his wrist. It was harsh and cold, like a star.

When the black smoke rose off their arms and the wind died, a set of dragonflies approached. When the flowers stopped dancing and the sun smiled, the dragonflies weaved through their hands. When the shadows no longer formed scales for balance, and music no longer sounded, the dragonflies vanished as if they were never there. The smoke vanished into sparkles and faded from sight.

Only then did they all let go.

Arna held up his right arm towards the sky.

His veins were visible in a dark, glittering black. Upon his skin something sparkled like gold: almost impossible to see with his eyes. It was shaped like large scales, twisting around his arm in four distinct wings. The massive wings connected to a dragonfly's body in the center of his wrist, marked as a birthmark would be: a shade lighter than his skin. It was cool to the touch.

All of them had the same mark, etched up their arm, with the lower wings reaching up towards their shoulder. It was a powerful vow, based on the sheer size of what they promised.

It was something none of them would ever be able to hide.

It was their promise of unity.

They all boarded a train, much to Arna's insistence. The others argued he didn't need to, but he wanted to try: in part to address the fear and in part to see if he could overcome it. It was terrifying as they headed to Amaryllis' studio, but they distracted him with his variation. They spoke in hushed voices, not wanting to be overheard by the few other patrons who were there. Once they were off the train and walking, it was easier to speak.

"Never again," Ebru told him, and Arna agreed.

He'd set himself into a small panic attack. Nothing Ebru couldn't solve. It was better this time than any of the last, but if Arn did not have to, he never wanted to get on a train again.

Their odd group of young adults dressed in pajamas got a few strange looks from people headed to work. Arna suspected some photographs were taken, soon to be circulated online, and for the first time, Arna was not worried. Who cared if everyone saw their new vow mark? At least it meant he was no longer alone. Despite being incomprehensibly foolish, they were harmonized in their plight.

Once more they spoke about the auditions.

"I told you. There is too much at risk of them trying to change my choice," Arna explained. He needed them to do the auditions. "Besides, the Governor wants me to hold off for a year. The Chosen Task Force doesn't think I'm real. They'd try to sabotage me."

"That wouldn't matter, the Cardinals would interfere," Sarcoline disagreed.

"That's the problem," Arna said. "I can't have anyone make the decision or influence my choice for me. We have to do the auditions."

"I say we fuck it all!" Phlox cheered. "Cause chaos and run!"

"You have the most profound way with words, Phlox. I dare say, you might just be a poet," Jasi snapped back.

"Now, now, Jasi. Flatter me more and I might think you were flirting with me." Phlox winked, nudging him.

Rosmarinus joked with her, "At least we'll be together."

They all laughed and chatted to themselves, trying to figure out how best to assist Arna.

Arna was safe.

"Fuck the Gods!" Phlox said. Rosmarinus and Aureolin joined her. Ven shook their head and Ginger skipped along, happily.

"Keep talking like that and you might regret it," Ebru warned her.

"What are they going to do? Smite me?" Phlox asked, looking up. There was a long moment where they stood watching her, where Arna could hear distant laughter bouncing across the streets and through advertisements that were playing. He swore the wind curled around her fingers.

When they arrived at Amaryllis studio, a man was there. He was dressed in plain, mint clothes, with fading white hair, and wrinkles about his eyes. He was older than Arna had ever seen him. Without his uniform he did not need to hold himself high and mighty above them all.

The man was crouched down looking at the flowers, his back facing the street.

"Cardinal White?" Arna asked.

Unperturbed, the man stood, wiped his hands on his trousers, and gave them his attention. His eyes landed on the mark on their arms, and then he smiled at Arna: *you found your Saints.*

Arna's heart thudded.

"Can we talk, Arna?" the man asked.

Arna was not sure he could say no to someone who had always helped him.

"I thought you couldn't talk to me?" Why now? After all this time of Arna trying to reach out?

"How did you know we'd be here?" Ebru asked, stepping in front of Arna. They all did.

The man pointed at the rose bushes around the front of Amaryllis' house. Twelve dragonflies were flying, gold and black. Ten were large and two were tiny; babies who still needed to grow.

"They called. I followed." The Cardinal was there for Arna. No. All of them. "I believe it's time for me to defy the Church of the Harmonious Six, regardless of the repercussions. No?"

The reasons no longer mattered, he was there, before Arna. Arna accepted him, willingly.

Amaryllis served tea for the group who sat on the floor of the studio, including Cardinal White, who had declined a chair. They sat in silence drinking, as Cardinal White looked around at all the paintings and photographs in the room.

"What do you need to tell us?" Ebru finally cracked under the pressure of the silence. He moved closer to Arna, defensive. When he directed his attention to the Cardinal, Cardinal White's eyes were directed at Ebru, examining the yellowing bruises peeking out from his collar and sleeves.

[*Save him,* Zaynir said.]

If Arna was moving forward with dreams, they all had to.

"I apologize, Incarnadine. The government threatened the church and your father, and I thought it best if I—"

"I don't care." Arna cut him off. "The ancestral home of the Hues is going up for sale."

He was certain they were the words to say. Everyone turned to look at him and Ebru tugged at his sleeve: *don't tell them.* Arna and Ebru had thought they could handle it, but that was under the condition that Ebru continued to suffer.

No more.

Arna continued, "As soon as Ebru switches studios, Cyclamen will sell it in retaliation. I need you to buy it. That'll make up for your radio silence."

Cardinal White contemplated for a moment. "I am not sure we have the funds."

"How much is it?" Phlox asked, calmly sipping her tea.

Arna nudged Ebru, who shifted uncomfortably. He whispered the number, too soft for them to hear.

"Ebru," Ven chastised. They got closer to Ebru and placed their hand on Ebru's shoulder.

"Fine. Six hundred million," Ebru said loudly, gripping Arna's sleeve tighter. "The last time Cyclamen threatened my father."

The whole room crashed into a hush that deafened the room. All those on the floor sat up straighter, and those in chairs nearly fell out of them.

"I don't have to leave the Shadone studio. My father is still there and his contract—" Ebru insisted, trying to dissuade the group from attempting to buy the house. In his insistence he missed how determined all those around him grew, staring at him the way that they always stared at Arna whenever he was trying to deflect and hide.

"Give me the contract and I'll find a way to break it," Jasi cut him off, tapping at the air.

"How long do you need?" Amaryllis asked.

"I can have a plan by auditions," Jasi said, tapping at the sky. She followed suit and nodded.

"We will clean up your rooms," Rosmarinus said with a soft smile and quiet voice, letting the room calm around him as he spoke. They anchored to his tranquility.

"I can do the paperwork for their return." Ginger counted on her fingers.

"No, I'll do it. You need to finish your remedial lessons," Sacroline disagreed. "It's my job anyway."

Ven nodded and spoke quickly, but assuredly. "When we get back to the Vivicent's we can have Zaffre take us all as students again. With Alabaster. We can have the paperwork completed and submit it to the DHS on the day of auditions."

"What?" Ebru asked, aghast. Arna squeezed his hand. "You're all coming back?"

"The Vivicent studio is the studio that trains the Golden Generation," Aureolin explained, as if he should have understood. It was always Arna's intention, but just like Arna, Ebru didn't always see the truth. She said, "We stand united at the auditions. Just like we did before the Splintering."

"Can you help me buy it?" Phlox asked Cardinal White. "That will stop the Harmonious Six and government from harming you."

"Phlox, no," Ebru scolded her.

"Phlox, yes," she mocked, then turned to Cardinal White. "I can liquidate my properties. I can stay with the Vivicents until I can afford another place."

"I'll help," Amaryllis said, a bit distraught. She touched Phlox's thigh and Phlox smacked her hand away.

"Sorry, darling, but I'm not sure you can help much," Phlox said with a wave of her hand and a sarcastic smile.

"I'll help," Rosmarinus said, and Phlox shook her head.

"You are already the money backing the Vivicents, leave this to me," Phlox insisted, a bit more unsure this time.

"We can sell Chamomile's paintings. We always make a lot for charity," Amaryllis added quickly, looking to Arna.

This is the way.

Amaryllis said she wanted to sell more. This was how it could be done.

"I thought you couldn't sell them unless it was for charity?" Ginger clarified.

"Or a purpose I see fit," Amaryllis answered, smile large and bright. "We can get a few thousand each, more if I up the price. People love her work."

"They adore it because they believe it's the work of some lost Child," Phlox warned her. "It's not. What if they find out?"

But it didn't matter. They loved Chamomile's art all the same.

"We can help fund the purchase and gift it the Hues. By ancestral rite it belongs to them," Cardinal White agreed. The man was contemplating something.

"'In their home, they shall pray. They shall live. They shall dance?'" Arna offered the prayer.

"Yes, an enlightenment!" Cardinal White clapped his hands and laughed heartily. "I will have to write my speech for when we present it, but it can be our gift to the world at the Day of New Dawn: returning order to the world."

Each year on the first day of the year, after New Dawn Day, the churches offered a gift to the city's public. Most of the time it was donations to schools, or art and nature initiatives. Arna supposed that this fell under a public restoration, as the Hue house was a National Historic Landmark.

"Why?" Ebru asked with fear in his voice.

"Ebru, we can see your bruises," Sarcoline said callously.

Ebru froze and pulled down at his sleeves. The dragonfly mark glowed on all of them, gold. Arna wrapped his arm around Ebru and leaned his head against his.

"We may have made a vow to Arna," Sarcoline explained, rolling up his sleeve and showing the mark that pulsated and the wings that were moving. "But it's not just a vow to him. It's a vow for all of us. We aren't going to let you suffer there anymore. None of us are going to suffer anymore."

"We're the Golden Generation," Amaryllis agreed, finishing for Sacroline with a voice that drifted mysteriously yet, trustworthy. "We belong together."

There was little noise as Arna moved down to the lower floors, past the wounded walls and destroyed furniture. He avoided the shattered keepsakes and hole-riddled memories. He walked past a willow tree that had been scraped but was ancient and wise: healing as if nothing had occurred at all.

Each studio was empty, save one where there was movement within the mirrors.

Are you with him?

[There was a soft chime in the distance.]

Zaffre was the one person Arna had been avoiding from the beginning: the man who had believed in him without question. Seeing his father cry had been the most heartbreaking thing he'd ever seen, and in his fear of dying, Arna had been unable to connect to his father.

There was one last thing he needed to move forward with his dreams, one more support needed before he could finally defy fate: his father.

Arna watched his father through the glass, looking into the studio. Zaffre's fingers moved with dexterity: years of practice, years of purpose and work. His father's hands flowed like a river, from fabric to binding to structural support. It was as if he were reading a story that only the fan could speak, revealing it carefully and with such focus that Arna did not want to break it. His whole essence glowed silver in fan mastery, just as a dancer did when they mastered The Twenty-Seven Dances. Only his silver was also mint: a grandmaster.

Zaffre was on fan seven of the Original variation performance fans. He always repaired the fans in order of Variance. He said it was a way for him to root himself in the history and fall into faith for guidance. His father worked effectively and efficiently, through the fans and on to Twin Fans. He was quick in his checks. Those he spent less time on were those that he'd made the year before. Those that needed major modifications were set aside to be remade. Those that needed minor fixes he slowed down to alter, making note on a list by his side.

Once through all his checks for all the fans, his father made his fixes. He'd remake all the fans that needed to be new versions over the course of the week. Then the completed fans would be transported to the Temple of Xeyaro, where they would be held until the day of the performance. The day before, the Cardinals would bless all the new fans to consecrate them.

Every few years the fans had to be remade regardless—even the unused twenty-sixth and twenty-seventh fans—and Arna had been lucky to help his father a few times. His own fingers twitched against his pants. Arna had found the rhythm, the melody, and sank into the process.

He held onto the memories, letting them warm him. The year he'd broke the world had been a good year. He'd built his first fans, officially mastered the Holly variation through Powers, and had choreographed their group dance. He had been so careful in the construction of the fans for Blue Rose Fears, and he'd been approved to use them. He could still feel the weight of them in his hands.

They'd burned for his actions, but they had been beautiful.

Zaffre's rhythm dwindled. His father hesitated, picking up the twenty-fifth fan for the Twin Fans variation in anguish: the fans he used for repentance each year.

Arna's stomach dropped to the floor. He never wanted to see his father show that look again, and yet, there it was on his father's face. It had given Arna nightmares for years after the first time he'd seen it. He'd sworn never to do anything that would cause his father to look. . . so sad. And still. . .

His father was both severed and healing, just like Arna was. Arna sighed a bit too loudly.

His father looked up to the door, startled. Arna scrambled to his feet, knowing that even if he did not make much noise, that his father could hear. He was attuned to the world in a heightened way. Arna opened the door.

"Arna?"

"Can I watch?" Arna asked, walking in.

"I'm. . ." his father hesitated. Perhaps due to not wanting to risk Arna's Blessings, perhaps because he was busy. Arna stepped closer.

"Sure," Zaffre sighed and moved the fans a bit further away from Arna. He continued his work on the Twin Fans variation fans, setting the twenty-fifth into the pile to be remade and the twenty-sixth and twenty-seventh into the checked rows. His father stretched and continued on to Blue Rose Fears, examining the fans one by one.

Arna watched in silence, disappearing every so often to get deliveries and return. Blue Rose Fears did not have many that needed to be remade. Roots and Ends had more that needed replaced than were good. Arna's fingers moved along the hem of his pants, mirroring his father.

One day he'd be able to touch fans again. After marrying Ebru and living through the storm, it was the one thing he wanted most.

"There are a lot that need minor changes," Arna observed as his father adjusted the sixteenth fan for the Holly variations. Most of the Holly fans needed light alterations.

"This is my preliminary check. When I dance with them all in the upcoming days, I will feel what I can't see," Zaffre said, making a note and setting the fan aside. "I should have enough fabric for all of these. . . Will you be helping me?"

"I can help to a degree, but I can't. . ." Arna wished he could. He wanted to hold the fans, wanted to know their kindness and support for him. But even if he could not. . . his father could.

"I know." Zaffre nodded. "I won't ask that of you."

"But I do want to help with what I can," Arna insisted, and his father smiled.

"I appreciate it." Zaffre continued working, checking his notes thrice more before Arna got the courage to speak up. His father beat him to the question. "What is it?"

This was his father who could fix a fan without seeing it. He was the only man in the world who could fix one without touching it. The man knew variation fans like he knew his own skin.

Years ago, Arna used to test his father. There were certain skills that the world's only fan grandmaster had, that Arna could use.

"I need your help," Arna said, finally accepting what he should have done from the beginning. Zaffre stopped working and focused on Arna completely. He awaited Arna's explanation, but Arna gave none. Instead, he stood and had his father follow. Arna led them into his studio, where the boxes with his fans were placed in the corner.

His father dragged his feet as he walked in, and Arna turned on the lights. Arna stayed away as his father opened the boxes and pulled out a fan with tentative hands. He looked over the first fan with vigor and tenderness. Arna's heart nearly gave out as his father's smile turn to a frown.

"You got them done in a factory?"

"Snuck into Mr. Hemlock's," Arna explained with a bit more humor than the first time he said the phrase. His father glanced at him and then back to the fans, a smile cracking on his face.

"This is why he was furious. . ." Zaffre chuckled. "And he didn't even know."

"No." Arna let the pride of fooling the man carry him further into the moment, ready to face his father's assessment of the fans.

Zaffre lifted the fans for the fourteenth dance up and down, testing the weight. He swung them around, checking the balance. He snapped them open and closed, testing their durability. He examined the stitching with his eyes and held them up to the light of the studio. After it was all said and done, his father's frown was deep set in his face.

"These won't. . . last."

They weren't terrible? That was fantastic. Arna started speaking rapidly. "They just need to last once. When I actually can touch them, I will properly—"

"Nothing proper about a machine-made fan," his father cut him off, beginning the lecture that Arna had heard a hundred times. "It's not about *should* they fall apart, it's about *when* they—"

"Will. Because otherwise it's a cheap prop, not a symbol of adoration to the Gods. Such a thing desecrates their memory and the dances themselves," Arna completed the statement. "That's why I need your help to purify them."

There was a liquid silence between them beginning to solidify.

"What dance is this for?" his father asked.

"The fourteenth," Arna answered, lightly and a bit worried.

His father's frown steadily began to grow into a soft smile.

"They alternate," Arna took the opportunity to explain the dances to him, wanting his father to understand completely. "Some dances are one, some are two. This excludes Worship, that has two fans for all three dances."

His father hesitated before he started removing the fans from the box one by one.

After signing for another delivery, Arna returned to find discarded plastic everywhere. Zaffre sat in a circle with the fans in an arch around him. He checked them all, one by one, fingers gliding over the fabric, eyes examining the joints. He flicked them open and closed, but without changing anything. He placed them back on the floor without doing a thing.

"This isn't a boning I know."

"It's made of metal for durability, but with the weight of the light structure. Willow bark, willow leaves and my blood, for the coating."

"And the fabric?"

"From Aster Fabrics. They have the rest of what I commissioned, in the event these break."

His father said nothing as he turned from the fans, got up, and left the room. Arna followed without question, knowing what was needed.

His father led them into the large practice room that had once been for the Golden Generation group practices. It was cleaned and pristine, almost as if it was well used. When Arna stepped up next to his father in the center of the room, the investigation began.

His father sized him up, turning him, and checking his muscles. Zaffre's thumb lingered over Arna's wrist and the two petals. He eyed the dragonfly mark along Arna's right arm and said nothing. Zaffre examined him in a way that Arna had not experienced since he was a child. It was almost invasive in the way a parent examined a toddler.

Zaffre used his Blessings to gauge Arna's well-being. A duodecennial of training was revealed in stark clarity.

His father traced the lines across Arna's palms with delicate fingers, wincing externally as he did, and eyes filling with a dangerous anger. However, Zaffre did not say a single word, letting Arna's hands fall, and walking from him towards the front of the room.

"Let me see Original." It was the teacher tone that Arna had not heard directed at him in more than twelve years. It was the voice of the best dancer of the era.

"I've never used the music," Arna warned, shifting on his feet. He stretched and shook out the lingering anxiety in his body.

"Worried you aren't truly mastered?" His father was joking with him, and Arna was lighter at the jaunt. He was confident in his skill, as was his father.

"No."

The reflections of the Gods in the mirrors were floating like dragonflies, hovering in unfelt winds, ready to watch. Arna grabbed the weights for his wrists, needing nothing else. He stood in the center of the room.

[*You may begin*, Xeyaro said.]

Arna motioned to his father. Zaffre pressed play. And then, for his father, he began.

He only danced the twenty-fifth dance in all five variations. Without the mastery of all those prior, it was impossible to master. Arna was tempted to do all the dances, but this was a knowledge check, and Arna was a master with overwhelming proof of it. His father, a master in all five Variations through Worship, would see Arna's glow with or without fans in Arna's hands.

"I take it you know twenty-seven of each variation," Zaffre finally said.

"And twenty-six, yes. But you knew that, when you tossed me Holly's disks," Arna removed the weights at his wrists and placed them back in the cabinet, hands hovering over the weights for twenty-six.

His father nodded, then asked, "Can you?"

"Show you?"

[   ]

"Yes," Zaffre pleaded.

And so, without music and only the pop of the candles in his memory, Arna danced all five variations of twenty-six. Without fans, but with all the meaning and mystery of the dances, he danced them all completely.

Arna collapsed to the floor, breathing heavily. It had been a while since he'd danced so many twenty-sixes in a row. Perhaps he needed to change his training regime to be stricter, and even harsher than before?

"Of course, it's not fully done, because I have no fans." Arna offered a thumbs up at his father.

His father contemplated this.

"That is how the masters said they learned. But all have died upon performing it," Zaffre said, helping Arna sit up. It was a beautiful way to die, so said the world. It was a worthy sacrifice of blood, so said the fanatics.

"Can you fix my fans?" Arna asked him finally, through his gasps. His father helped to guide Arna's Blessings back into equilibrium and out of the dissonance caused by the twenty-sixth dances. Arna flourished his abilities to speed up the process, finding his center again.

"I wish you came to me from the beginning," Zaffre admitted.

"I know. You could have made them." Arna then asked, worried, "How much do you need to fix?"

Silence filled the room and Arna drank it in.

"I'll do it. And Azza be damned, I'll make them the most performance-durable fans I've ever made," Zaffre declared with a large smile and determined eyes.

[Azza giggled weakly.]

His father placed his hand on Arna's shoulder and looked at him with soft eyes. They were the eyes that said he knew that Arna kept running but trusted him to come home. They were the eyes that said he'd support Arna unconditionally. They were the eyes that said Arna could trust him. They were the eyes that said they were family, and Zaffre always loved him.

"I can train you too, if you want."

Arna's heart leapt.

"Only if you need. I know that a new variation is unlike anything else and. . . no. It's alright forget it."

[Invisible dragonflies swarmed around them.]

This was his path, glowing in neon color. This was the way to live.

"Yes." Arna agreed. "Please. I need to do more. It needs to be harder."

"Okay," His father said, tenderly.

Zaffre wrapped his arms around Arna and said nothing about it. Instead, he said, "You did well."

For a few seconds Arna was surprised until the tears welled up in his eyes and began to sob. Arna was there again, at ten years old, in his parents' arms with cake and brownies on the floor. He had said then that he'd never let his father cry again. He'd failed at that. But his father still loved him. His father still saw him. His father still wanted him.

This was his home. Here he was safe.

The dragonflies sang a melody.

With knowing comes growing. With knowing comes action.
That is why knowledge and change are linked.
You cannot change if you do not know.
You want nothing more than change when you do.

— On Pokk

Dance 22

Unity

Incarnadine

30 Xeyan

12 Days Left

"Are you sure you want to be doing this?"
"He asked me to do it. Besides, I can meet her out here, too."
"Too many relationships that don't matter."
"I still have to experience to grow, don't I? I'm a mortal."
"Such is the one issue with mortals. You would already know if you were not one."
"I would not be the Chosen Child, then."

When the Vivicent studio entered The Dance House building, they walked as a united group, chins high and unwavering as the cameras and reporters bombarded them. Tens of questions were sent their way. Wenge ensured they were not distracted.

Arna, Jasi, Rosmarinus, and Ven had borrowed from Sarcoline's wardrobe, dressed in all black. Arna's suit had the adornment of a silver and mint dragonfly while Jasi's suit had dragonfly buttons, and sleeves that were adorned in scales like wings. Rosmarinus wore a black shirt with silver wings off the shoulders blades, like a cape. Usually, Ven liked wearing things that did not cling too tightly to their skin, but to compensate for the wide legged skirt-trousers, they wore a near skintight black silk shirt, with dragonfly wings that hung off the shoulders like long sleeves.

Amaryllis and Phlox raided Ginger's wardrobe for dresses. Amaryllis' was shaped like dragonfly wings, with an empire waist and A-line skirt. Phlox's dress was all black at first glance but it shimmered as it moved and was made of individual sequins that Ginger had cut by hand to mimic a dragonfly's wings. Wenge was dressed in a billowing black dress that fluttered from the sides as she walked, like two dragonfly wings.

Arna's father, siblings, Ebru, and Aureolin walked in all black dance sets, with the name VIVICENT etched on the back of their jackets in all silver thread. Rosmarinus had ordered the dance sets in secret each year, in hopes that a day would arrive when they were united again arrived. When he revealed them everyone cried. Standing with those who wore them made Arna feel powerful.

The group walked in unison.

Zaffre led the charge, headphones around his neck, bag on his shoulder, and jacket open. Sarcoline walked with his hands in his pockets, headphones on, and hood over his head. His bag cut across his side. He had a hop to his step.

Ginger's braids were tied up high on her head with a silver ribbon and she wore her Vivicent jacket tied around her waist, revealing her tank top and vow mark. It glittered gold as she stretched, walked, and listened to her music. Aureolin walked steadily, fingers tapping on her bag, as she held it before her body. Her curls were pulled back into a bun at the top of her head with silver flower clips.

Then there was Ebru, who had every reporter's eye. Arna held Ebru's hand, trying to help him release his tension. Ebru tried to walk nonchalantly next to Arna, but the death grip he had on Arna spoke a different story. Cameras began flashing in their direction, hyper aware of his presence in the circle.

A few of them would have been one thing, but the Vivicents were making a statement by their attire. Just one of the Golden Generation returning would have sparked an international story, but all of them? Ebru let go of Arna's hand and stepped ahead. His hair was once more the color of the darkest ink, and his nails were painted black.

He slipped his headphones off his ears, rose one hand to the reporters and flipped them off.

"Ebru!" Ven chastised.

Sarcoline laughed and flipped the reporters off too. Aureolin and Ginger did the same. All of a sudden Zaffre stopped walking and turned to them all. They dropped their hands, ready for a lecture, but Zaffre motioned them into two lines. They presented themselves for a photo-op.

Past the reporters who were eagerly trying to ask them questions were other dancers and studios standing and whispering. Camera drones flew about, capturing everything for audiences around the world. Advertisements filled their augmentations: they were made for the auditions and were not there for the dance tests days prior.

After tens of pictures were taken, Zaffre returned, pointing Wenge towards their seats, and motioning for the dancers to follow him. Jasi and Arna, who were not dancers, were the only two to follow Zaffre. The others walked towards the Vivicent seats.

Zaffre led them to the registration table. The women sitting at the table looked a bit startled.

"Mr. Vivicent," one said.

"The Vivicent studio is here to sign in," Zaffre said. Before they could ask questions, Zaffre placed down the paperwork, filled out and finalized. "Please enter it into the system."

The woman was wide-eyed and shocked. However, there was nothing the DHS could do to stop a dancer from changing studios. Quickly the woman took the documents and scanned them.

"Aureolin Begonia, has been reregistered under the Vivicent Studio. Your DHS passport has been updated. You are registered to audition for Powers, please take your wristbands."

The room was filled with people from all over the world wearing the wrist bands. There were more competitors wearing the white bands for Knowledge than all the other dances. Understanding took mint, while Worship wore a wristband of all three colors. A couple dozen people wore silver for Appreciation, and only a small few wore white and mint stripped bands for Powers.

Aureolin took her two wristbands: one for Powers and the other for Appreciation. Arco and Ginger were signed in with Zaffre by another receptionist. One by one they were all reregistered into the Vivicent studio: Aureolin, Ven, Phlox, Arna, and Ebru.

"Eburnean Hue," the woman gasped as she read the name twice.

"Yes?" Ebru asked, running his fingers through his freshly dyed hair as he walked forward. The prince-of-dance turned the charm on.

The woman was clearly confused.

"It's not a mistake," he said sweetly. "My father and I are transferring back to the Vivicent studio."

"You are *what?*" Cyclamen's voice did not startle Arna. He nearly expected it. Cyclamen stood with Alabaster who was staring at Ebru with dark circles under his eyes. "First you disappear from home, and then you say this nonsense?"

"It's not nonsense," Jasi said stepping between them and handing Cyclamen a set of papers. "As Lumak's Child, and with my authority of the highest order over all contracts, I have determined the contract by which you have hired Alabaster Hue to be illegal."

"Nonsense," Cyclamen hissed. "Where in the contract—"

"Do you really wish to go into that here?" Jasi stepped forward intimidating the man.

Cyclamen glanced to the sides and backed down.

"We have things to discuss, Cyclamen, Alabaster," Zaffre stepped up, putting himself between the Children and Cyclamen. "Ebru, we are headed to the back. Stay with the others until you are required to complete your DHS duties."

Ebru nodded. Zaffre pushed the fuming Cyclamen and confused Alabaster away, contract from Jasi in hand.

"Is this really going to work?" Ebru asked Jasi.

"Certainly," Jasi told him, hands crossed and confident smirk on his face. "I broke every law in this city. Trust me to know how to break a contract."

Ebru took a deep breath and addressed the woman at the counter. "Am I signed in?"

The woman nodded furiously, and Ebru took his wristbands: one for Worship and the other for Understanding. With them, the group headed towards the chairs set up for the Vivicent studio. All of them were filled for once. Amaryllis set up a table she had brought and placed snacks on top. Ebru plopped down next to Arna, brooding and staring at Sarcoline's wristbands: one for Powers and the other for Understanding. They were taken once their test began, to prevent repeat attempts.

"Arco will win," Arna whispered to Ebru, who bristled at the words and glared at him. They held hands, so that Arna could not hurt himself in the panic of the day. Ebru too was nervous, from how tightly he held on.

"I know." Ebru's eyebrow twitched. "Ginger and I have always been at a near tie."

Each year, their scores had come down to a distinction of a few swing votes. They would still be competing for number one, except for Sarcoline. He was fighting for the second best. As long as everyone agreed Sarcoline was the second-best competitor, then the chances of him being selected were higher than either Ginger or Ebru. Plus, it would be no surprise if Zaffre rated Sarcoline as the best. Sarcoline needed all twos and a one to beat Ebru.

"If I get runner up, I don't want it," Ebru said softly, glowering at Sarcoline.

"Are you going to tell them that?" Arna asked, frustrated.

Ebru sighed dramatically. "Maybe."

They were all nervous. Despite the fact that they were holding the auditions for Arna as a contingency, it was the most important day of the year. They all wanted it.

Past their circle of privacy there were others pointing at them. In corners, people were making bets. It was illegal, due to people attempting to pay off the judges to change the results. Doing it openly was asking for trouble: in the form of DHS officials wearing bright mint suits. The individuals were then escorted out by security.

His father spoke to other DHS members. Zaffre was the lead for all auditions, save his own. All members of the small council had to sit in on all auditions and vote, unless they were the ones auditioning.

"Ebru told me," Sarcoline said.

"What?" Ebru snapped. Arna leaned further against Ebru, signaling him to calm down.

"Nothing. I wasn't talking to you," Sarcoline said. "News flash, Ebru, the world does not revolve around you."

"Last I checked it did," Ebru said, eliciting a few chuckles from the others. Ebru was joking? Arna relaxed a little.

"If you mean Arna, I'm sorry to tell you he's not the whole world." Sarcoline teased back and Arna's cheeks went hot.

"No? Here I thought he was." Ebru's smile was like a liquid fire that ran through Arna's body. He nearly had to turn away from the provocation.

"Oh, hush you two," Aureolin said, stern and a bit too snarky. Phlox leaned her head against Aureolin's shoulder, took her hand and played with her fingers. Aureolin's smoldering dimmed.

"Is it true then?" Amaryllis asked as if nothing had been said at all.

"What?" Ebru asked with a light laugh.

"That the weather pattern changed? A storm is supposed to happen the night of the Celebrations?" she asked, and Arna was confused. Since when?

The mood of the circle shifted. Ebru sat up a bit more directly, glowering at Sarcoline.

"Can't you ever keep your mouth shut?" Ebru asked him.

"No," Sarcoline disagreed. "We share secrets now."

"It's true?" Rosmarinus asked.

"Yes, we got the report this morning," Ebru said softly. "The DHS wants to pick dancers this year that can. . . withstand storm conditions."

There was a long moment before all eyes landed on Sarcoline, who looked as if the news didn't pertain to him. On the night of the Celebrations, during the Ceremony of Chaos, the Blessing shields had to be down. It was required for the contract, and the Twenty-Seven Dances to be completed. Xeysis was like a vortex. Any and all weather changes outside of the rose filtered in, swirled, grew, and terrorized the city. A little rain and wind would become a hurricane.

While a regular storm was city destructive, Arna had a feeling this storm would be a superstorm. This year was for him.

"They're going to pick disposable dancers," Ebru said again.

"You say that as if I'm not disposable," Sarcoline degraded himself. There was a restless anger that spread amongst the group. Sarcoline either didn't notice or chose to ignore it.

"You are not!" Ginger complained.

Sarcoline and Zaffre were the only two dancers who had been consistent in the duodecennial. In every city that Arna had been to, regardless of what was said online, there was only ever praise and cheers when Sarcoline took the stage. The world might have resented Sarcoline most days, but not during the Celebrations. It was as if something flipped when people saw him on stage, as if all the world's problems disappeared and he was their hero. Arna could never figure out why, no matter how many times he watched his brother dance. All the same, the DHS managed the public sentiment on the matter and would never throw him into a situation where he'd be killed.

"They can put up the wards early," Amaryllis suggested.

"'Under a sky of stars and the fading sun, without Blessings of others to protect them, The Chosen will dance.'" Ebru quoted, much to the surprise of everyone. "The shields can't go back until the Ceremony is done. Arco, you will be placed as understudy in both dances."

Arna wanted to say that the Blessing shields could stay up. Pokk used to say that due to the Blessing reset, whether or not the defenses were up, they would come down all the same as soon as Arna began dancing. But he said nothing. The others would not be dancing at all. This audition was just for show, to give him time.

"I won't," Sarcoline said adamantly. "You can't. They won't."

But they would. If the primary dancer got hurt during the storm, Sarcoline would be able to complete it for them. Ultimately, if they insisted, Arna suspected Sacroline would give in. Sarcoline was a good person and there was no way the DHS would place hope into danger.

"Arna. . ." Phlox looked at him, asking him with her eyes as well as her voice. "Are you sure you're dancing this year?"

Before Arna could answer, Ven did. "We can't pressure him, Phlox. We have to operate as if he's not. The choice has to be his and his alone. Whether that is this year or next. It's why we are doing to auditions."

Somehow, him explaining that he needed the auditions so he could hide his choice was misinterpreted to mean that he could take more time, even a year if needed. How was he supposed to correct it?

"And if he needs a year, I'm dancing," was all Sarcoline said when he stood up, got in the center of the chairs, held up his mobile, and snapped a picture.

"What are you doing?" Ginger laughed. Not a single one of them had been ready.

"Amaryllis wanted a photo," Sarcoline said, tapping his mobile to hers.

They all looked at her confused. She had been sitting there the entire time. She blinked slowly with her large eyes.

"Amaryllis gets what she wants," Sarcoline shrugged, collapsing back in his seat next to her. The way he said her name had such a lightness to it.

"I wanted it to be a candid. You should all take them and send them to the group," Amaryllis offered, and in moments Phlox and Ginger began snapping photos.

"Mom! Look! Look!" Arna heard a young girl's voice cut through the sound barrier; as if it was allowed by wind and rain, storms and shine.

Honeysuckle stood with her mother on the opposite side of the room, waving towards them. She wore a bright white ribbon on her wrist, and a saffron necklace sparkling bright in the fluorescents. Her hair was tied up in a high ponytail, just like the kind that Ginger did when she danced, with a matching bow to Ginger's done in white. Her mother looked both furious and embarrassed that her daughter was waving at them.

Before anyone could stop the girl, she was running over to them. She crashed into the circle of chairs, through the privacy shields, and right up to Sarcoline.

"Hi! Hi, Sarcoline!" she said with the world's biggest smile. She glanced around the circle and then tacked on, almost like an afterthought, "Gingerline! Aureolin. Pervenche! Phlox Ruby?" The girl squealed at Phlox. Her eyes landed on Arna. "Hi, Incarnadine!"

And then on Ebru and she went silent. She held her hands up against her mouth covering her wide eyed, stare. Ebru shifted uncomfortably in his chair.

"Eburnean Hue?" she asked softly.

"Yes?" Ebru asked.

"Oh, my Gods! Sarcoline! It's Eburnean Hue!" Honeysuckle tugged at Sarcoline's sleeve. Sarcoline smirked at Ebru, who grew stiff and sat upright.

"Honeysuckle," Sarcoline drew her attention back to him. "What are you auditioning for today?" He asked the question as if it were not obvious that she was auditioning for Knowledge.

"Knowledge! I'm dancing the Holly variation." She stood proudly, unperturbed by the cameras that were surrounding them.

"That's so cool!" Ginger cheered for her.

"It's the first variation that Eburnean ever completed," she said, as if they all didn't already know that. Arna glanced to his boyfriend who was quickly moving, sliding his hand into his dance bag and pulling out a notebook. Before anyone said a thing, he signed his name in the book, ripped out the page, and walked over to the girl, kneeling down and handing it to her. She squealed as she took it.

It was as he knelt that her mother arrived.

"Mom! Look! It's Eburnean Hue! Can we take a picture. Oh, please, can we take a picture?" Honeysuckle begged him.

"Yes," Ebru said, smiling. The two of them posed for a series of photos, as the others snickered to themselves about how cute Ebru was being. He shot them glares repeatedly until he collapsed back in his seat and Honeysuckle, completely uninvited, sat in a the only open chair next to Sarcoline and Amaryllis. Her mother gaped, trying to give apologies and tugged at her daughter who refused to budge.

"That's a cool mark," Honeysuckle said touching Amaryllis' arm. "You all have it. Why?"

"Vivicent group vow," Sarcoline told her.

"Oh! That's so cool!" Honeysuckle gasped, giggling and kicking her feet out. "Can I join? I told mom that we're joining the Vivicent studio as soon as you allow for new students."

"No. You're too young," Sarcoline laughed at her as she pouted angrily. Rosmarinus, who had stood in the commotion, brought over another chair and offered it to Honeysuckle's mother who reluctantly sat, defeated.

"Can I still join the studio?" Honeysuckle asked with a quivering lips, staring at them hopefully.

"Yes," Sarcoline said with an amused smile. "We can add you in today."

"Really?" she brightened. "Truly? *Really*-really?"

Sarcoline nodded and the girl squealed. Sarcoline shot a look to Rosmarinus, who nodded and headed towards the front desk again to get the paperwork that they had not prepared for the girl.

"Your name is Honeysuckle?" Wenge asked.

"Honeysuckle Dawn," the girl smiled. "Your first new student in twelve years!"

What once may have caused a disturbance and anguish instead was met with a joy and excitement. Wenge talked to her about her favorite dances and skills. She sat there giggling, kicking her feet, and completely ignoring how pale and disturbed her mother looked.

"We can talk about her enrollment," Wenge said to Honeysuckle's mother.

The woman froze, glanced amongst them all and then nodded, stiffly.

"How is this judged?" Honeysuckle changed conversations quickly. She leaned forward on her seat, completely starstruck.

The rules and categories had been provided the night before, as an official announcement on the website. It never changed, but Arna was anxious until he saw it.

"It's like the Mastery tests," Arna told her. "You'll be brought to the back, and you'll sit until your name is called. Unlike Mastery, you'll have to dance through your whole dance, start to finish, with only the customary six second breaks between."

She nodded furiously.

"Scores," Aureolin jumped in, calm as a sunset. "Are based on categories—technique, style, artistry, knowledge, awe, and understanding. We're ranked individually by all the judges, and the judges give a score out of twelve in all categories. Once all the auditions are done, the scores are added up together and the final ranking is made."

It was more complicated than that, but Arna supposed it was difficult to explain that there were two ranking lists. The overall lists were compared. There was a ranking list based on the aggregate scores in each category. The scoring system compared all the results together and created a master ranking based on all the score and ranking considerations. Only the final rankings of the top two dancers were announced to the public. Total scores and individual scores in a category were available to each individual dancer and their studio, listed on their DHS passport.

"Mom says that there is a storm predicted for the Celebrations," Honeysuckle said. "Will we be okay?"

"It won't be that bad," Sarcoline lied. He didn't flinch, but Arna knew he should have.

"Incarnadine, I'm sorry you're not dancing your variation this year." Honeysuckle's honesty made her mother pale. "People say you should never dance again." Arna had a feeling that the people she spoke about included her mother. "But you can always try again next year, right?"

"Exactly," Arna agreed. "But I would not recommend dropping any fans. The Gods don't like it very much."

Rosmarinus returned with the application paperwork, and Wenge motioned for Honeysuckle's mother to follow her. The two walked off, leaving Honeysuckle with the group.

Sarcoline gave Honeysuckle advice, telling her what she should do upon entering the room as a nonChild. "You have to capture their attention, okay? They are picking who looks the best and can keep them entertained."

In time Wenge and Honeysuckle's mother returned, paperwork filled out and turned in. They sat, discussing the process. Then Ebru stood suddenly, and the others went silent. He took a deep breathe, pushed his bag to Arna after taking out his dance shoes, and headed towards the front where the other DHS small council members were gathering.

"What's happening?" Honeysuckle asked.

"It's beginning," Sarcoline told her solemnly. The tension in the circle shifted. Even Honeysuckle changed from giggles into severity, knowing that it was time to fight.

"Testing," Zaffre's voice called out through the microphone, and the privacy shields dropped. Talking ceased and like a wave, everyone turned to where he stood near the audition doors. Zaffre was not the head of the DHS small council, but he was the most well-known and the current face of the DHS. He was the head of the Vivicent family, and despite its fallen status, the name held enough power to silence the room.

"Competitors, welcome," Zaffre said when he had the room's attention. "You know the drill. All competitors will be brought to the back waiting room when it is your section's audition. You hurt another? You're barred for life. You miss your name? Automatic failure. Each competitor will be called back one by one to dance. We tell you which dance to dance, and you do it. You drop a fan? You miss a step? You make a mistake? Your test ends there. No questions. No arguments.

"Due to the number of competitors today, we will begin with those going for Knowledge, unlike usual. Understanding will be after Knowledge, then Powers, then Appreciation, then Worship. For now, all Knowledge auditionees follow the woman with the pink sign. She will take you to the back. All judges are needed in the audition room." No one moved. "Families will wait here for the results."

Once again, he paused.

Zaffre controlled the audience as he lifted his hands, held them out as if holding a candle. The motion rippled through the room. Everyone raised their hands. Everyone closed their eyes. Cameramen, reporters, competitors, and families followed; years ago, this would have been unheard of. Azza be damned, even one a year ago it was unheard of; but at that moment, in that room, they all did it. The advertisements disappeared, and the ambient music in the room ceased. Everyone was motionless but Arna, who stood open eyed.

The cameras would see that he did not pray, yet he could not bring himself to. Not when he was certain that if he did it, there would be no response.

[There were no distant bells anymore.]

"'To the God of dance, we seek guidance and hope. Guide us in our struggles and our lives, as we weave stories and speak color into the world. . .'"

The prayer was one from the Church of the Apostle, something Zaffre used to say over dinner. The room reverberated in the sound of Zaffre's voice and the smaller echoes of everyone who repeated the words. Arna did not say the prayers along with the room and instead stood straight in defiance, hearing them, seeing them, and accepting the prayer for the Gods who could not.

"'Yesterday, we danced. Tomorrow, we will dance again. Today, we shall dance for you, and all the Gods beside you. May you see us. May this please you. Be with the Gods. May the Gods' light never fade.' And so, it was. And so, it shall be," Zaffre ended, said final grace, and looked up. Arna locked eyes with his father, who had to have known that Arna did not pray. Without another word, the room began bustling and the privacy shields rose again to mitigate the sound.

Honeysuckle got up, waved goodbye to them all, kissed her mother, and raced off. As soon as she was in line, her mother was collapsing into her chair and apologizing profusely. Amaryllis offered everyone snacks once more, although Arna was the only one to take them.

Shortly after the competitors disappeared to the back, there was shouting between reporters and staff.

Arna's mother turned from the list in her journal to look at the noise. At a glance, the list included the favorite sweets of everyone in the group: rose cakes, lavender milk, special floral chocolates, carrot cake, zucchini bread, banana bread, and frozen grapes. They were all treats for a job well done.

"I'm going to help, you all stay here," Wenge said minutes later, standing and hurrying off to mitigate the conflict.

"What is happening?" Amaryllis asked.

"I'll be right back." Jasi jumped up and followed.

The arguments grew softer, but tensions rose. Jasi stepped up with Wenge. The appearance of a Child of Lumak was enough to get most people to back off, and while Jasi did not appear to be speaking, his presence was enough.

"Does this always happen?" Arna asked.

"No, but mom and Jasi control most of the issues that pop up for the DHS," Ginger explained, sinking in her chair and fixing her hair.

"It looks like One Truth Church members," Rosmarinus grimaced. "Probably trying to cause a scene again."

More DHS members rushed over, getting the One Truth members to leave, as they screamed.

"The dances are a fraud!"

"You'll destroy us all."

The shouts were so loud they cut through the privacy Blessings to mute the sound. All eyes in the room were on them, but no one shouted back.

"Are there always issues?" Arna asked.

"Last year there was cheating," Amaryllis said. "In recent years, some people have tried to injure others, for a chance. Most of the time it's the One Truth Church, although they never get inside The Dance House. The guards usually keep them at bay."

"Its probably the same reason that they got into the house," Rosmarinus offered. "Someone paid off the guards."

The One Truth Church members were glaring at Arna, but they were too far away to get to him. Danger radiated off of them.

"The Storms will destroy us because of you!" someone screamed as they broke from the guards and ran towards Arna. The man was tackled, and Arna clenched his hand. There was more movement, and the group sat silently, all eyes turning from Arna, slowly to Sarcoline, who noticed this time.

"What?" he asked, looking up from his mobile sensing their stares.

"Sarcoline, you shouldn't dance—" Ginger started.

"I'm disposable, Ginger. We all are. We're just doing this so Arna has time," Sarcoline cut her off. "And if Arna isn't going to dance this year, I'm not wasting my chance at Understanding. If they dare relegate me to understudy in both, I won't dance at all."

Without another word, Sarcoline got up and Amaryllis ran after him.

"He means it," Aureolin sighed as soon as they were gone. "And that means he doesn't understand his own value as a dancer."

"He's been avoiding searching himself online," Ven explained. "Am says that he thinks they hate him, exclusively. He doesn't realize how much everyone is dependent on him dancing Powers each year."

He was the world's good luck charm.

"They won't let him dance," Aureolin pressed on. "He's not a Child. He doesn't have the Blessings to fall back on to heal himself and keep him alive."

"No. They'll give him one dance," Arna said, certain of it.

The One Truth members were forced from The Dance House. Peace returned. Everything was held in a temporary stasis as Wenge and Jasi returned to the seats.

"It begins." Aureolin motioned past Arna, where a competitor had returned in tears. Time began to cascade.

They started to debate competitors like when they were kids, deciding who passed and failed before they got to the seating designated for those who passed. After the first two hours, fifteen of the Knowledge auditionees were seated in the special area. Honeysuckle sat in one of the chairs, kicking her legs out, unable to sit still.

"She is so cute." Arna laughed. He remembered when he was that young.

"And the youngest competitor. No matter her score, she's going to get it," Aureolin said. "We haven't had a young dancer for Knowledge in years. She might not have been the best, but they will pick her because they want to remind the world of what can be."

After all the Knowledge competitors were done, a staff member announced that ten minutes of voting had begun. With the voting was underway, the Understanding competitors rose and walked to follow the woman with the pink sign to the back room where they would stretch and get ready. Sarcoline and Ginger left with no one else, taking the air of the room with them.

Amaryllis approached, sitting back down and holding Sarcoline's mobile. She stared at the door while she tinkered with Sarcoline's mobile, but did not press any buttons.

The wait for Understanding was agonizing, despite there only being three auditionees.

whatifwhatifwhatif

Arna began to squeeze his hands.

"Arna do you want to talk about it?" Jasi asked. Startled, Arna met his eyes and saw his dragonfly mark moving. The others were looking at him, and he took a deep breathe, copying Ven. The burden of his anxiety was felt by all of them, and while none of them pushed him to explain—perhaps since they believed they understood it already—their constant reminder that they were with him was enough to ground him.

Arna shook his head and released his hands.

The thoughts did not disappear. But it was enough to distract him and to get him invested in the world rather than hypotheticals.

No one pressed him further. Phlox and Ven changed seats to sit directly next to him. Sarcoline was the first to exit. He was late, according to Aureolin's timing.

"Did you talk back to them?" Arna asked as Sarcoline sat in the circle.

"I wouldn't dare." Which meant he had.

Sarcoline defended himself like a cornered animal, and Arna had a suspicion that someone had said something in the test after it ended. Amaryllis whispered something to him, and he yawned with a smile. He relaxed in his chair, like he was no longer threatened. He was calmer, and scarier in a way, because of how certain he was in himself. Powers was his home field and it had been for years.

Once Ginger walked out, the ten minutes of deliberation were called, and those dancing for Powers were called back. Sarcoline and Aureolin left as Ginger grabbed her water.

"Why were you third?" Arna asked her. They usually went in alphabetical order, with the incumbent going first.

"They wanted to mix up the order, because it's always just Ebru and me," Ginger shrugged. "They may take longer for their decision than normal. They took longer for the Appreciation results, which was why Ebru was called in late."

Ginger then walked over to the successful dancer seats.

The scores were meant to be respected, but the ten minutes existed to work out discrepancies in suspected foul voting. All audition footage was erased before the next group auditioned. What happened in the testing room was never seen by the public, even though the process was common knowledge.

Once more, Arna began to panic, and the others steadied him.

"Fascinating," Ven said when they helped to calm him. "I didn't feel this earlier."

"I think the Vow is balancing the weight amongst us, and the power understands who has the capability of supporting," Jasi said. "Vows are rarely tested, but I would not be surprised if its reacting to our own emotions and what we are doing, just as our Blessings usually do."

Could the path to Arna's survival be in this vein? They couldn't take the Divinity for him, but maybe there was something within it? All the same, Arna felt like his odds for survival were stronger and in it his heart settled more.

Once again, Sarcoline was the first to leave after Powers, this time due to being the incumbent. He slouched deep in his chair with a grimace.

"What's wrong?" Amaryllis asked him. "Did you fail?"

"As if. I'll go over there in a minute just. . ." Sarcoline sighed. "Ebru had a lot of questions for me."

"What about?" Amaryllis asked.

"What dance I wanted more," Sarcoline explained. "I told them that if they put me in understudy for both that I'd walk away and never dance again." He muttered under his breath, "That would probably make them all happy."

"Arco!" Amaryllis gasped.

"And then I threatened to walk out of Powers. I was stopped and they made me dance anyway." Sarcoline shrugged and squeezed his eyes shut in frustration. Sarcoline wanted the dances as much as Arna did.

Ven shook their head. Wenge and Jasi shared a look as Amaryllis chastised him. Arna had nothing to comfort his brother. Rosmarinus tried, by handing him a water bottle. Phlox asked him for more information, and he happily gave it.

Sarcoline had been reckless.

After a few minutes, when Aureolin walked out, Sarcoline and Aureolin walked over to the success seats where Ginger sat.

Knowledge took hours to get through, whereas Worship was just sixty minutes. However, Worship was the tensest hour of the whole day. Neither Zaffre nor Ebru emerged from the doors.

theendtheendtheend

Jasi, Ven, Rosmarinus, Phlox, and Amaryllis talked him through his panic, at least what they could say in public, which was not much. What little was said, was not helpful, but the constant support was.

However, Arna was not alone. The room began to buckle under the pressure when the woman with the pink sign came back. Arna's heart threatened to stop beating.

"Breathe," Rosmarinus whispered.

Both he and Amaryllis struggled to breathe, for she was just as nervous as he was.

"Thank you, everyone," she said after the microphone was given to her. "At this time, the final decisions are being written, and we will have the results soon."

The final politics were now at play. It was rare for this to happen, but not strange. When Arna had gotten the primary position for Powers at age fifteen, there had been twenty minutes of end deliberation.

Five minutes later, the DHS judges emerged. Cyclamen, in all purple as if he were fair and just, held a list in his hands. Arna sat up taller as he waited. The privacy shields for sound dropped around the Vivicent seating section once more.

Zaffre took the microphone and spoke to them and out to the world through the cameras.

"Thank you to all the competitors who danced today. Each one of you is special, and a master in your own right. You danced your best. For those of you who failed, we hope to see you next year. For those of you who did pass, know that even if you are not selected, you have the heart for dance. Do not give up."

The speech was standard, said to give the world time to tune in. There were only two times when most of the world was united. The first was when everyone in the world watched the Ceremony of Chaos at the Celebrations. The second was at the moment the results of who would dance the Ceremony were announced.

Zaffre then handed over the microphone to Cyclamen.

"When called, please come up," Cyclamen said.

Arna's heart raced, and trying to get it to calm, he held his breath. He began to squeeze his hands, but Ven and Phlox smacked his left and right hands at the same time without saying anything. He let go of his fists immediately and breathed in deeply instead.

whatifwhatifwhatif

The presence of his friends next to him and Phlox' arms around his, eased the panic back. They were united.

"Knowledge of the Gods, understudy, dancing the Twin Fans variation: Rose Thistle of Ludiel." A woman in her early twenties stood, a bit shocked. Arna recognized her face as the woman who had danced the level the year before and the one before that. "Knowledge of the Gods, primary dancer, dancing the Holly variation: Honeysuckle Dawn of Xeysis."

Honeysuckle jumped to her feet in shock. Her saffron pendant glowed as she skipped to the line. She was young, had brown eyes, and made a statement by existing. Arna breathed out.

Honeysuckle stood in the front line, before Rose.

"Appreciation of the Gods, understudy, dancing the Twin Fans variation: Pewter Puce of Podiel." The man was in his fifties. He made his way to stand next to Rose. "Appreciation of the Gods, primary dancer dancing the Holly variation: Garance Jasmine of Xeysis."

Garance jumped up and raced over, her hands covering her face. She had a bright smile. Her blonde hair was tied up in a high ponytail at the top of her head.

"Power of the Gods, understudy, dancing the Blue Rose Fears variation." There was a collective gasp in the room, audible and thick. Only one person danced Blue Rose Fears. "Sarcoline Vivicent of Xeysis."

Sarcoline got to his feet slowly, walking to the front of the room, that had gone deathly silent. His footsteps reverberated, with nonchalant and unhurried clicks. Terror bloomed in the audience faces. Sarcoline took his spot in the line, pretending to be unaware of the consequence for where he was standing.

"Power of the Gods, primary dancer, dancing the Holly variation: Aureolin Begonia of Xeysis." Aureolin stood with a grimace and took her spot, forcing a smile. It was obvious that Sarcoline had scored better but had been given understudy. Would the official results reflect it or mask it?

"Understanding of the Gods." Cyclamen acted as if nothing had happened. "Understudy, dancing the Roots and Ends variation: Gingerline Vivicent of Xeysis." Ginger made her way to the front, stepping up next to Sarcoline. She glanced at him, but he did not notice. Arna sat on pins and needles. He tried to clench his hands; Phlox and Ven smacked him again.

Breathe. Breathe.

"Understanding of the Gods, primary dancer dancing the Blue Rose Fears variation." The room erupted into sound: no words, just a collective cacophony of disbelief. This had never happened before.

Ebru always danced Holly or the Original. Ginger used Roots and Ends or Twin Fans. Sarcoline was moving before his name was said. From the back line to the front line, he took his spot as Understanding's primary dancer. "Sarcoline Vivicent of Xeysis."

"Xeyaro, be with me." More than one person prayed. Sarcoline was both understudy and primary dancer. It would not take a genius to know that Sarcoline had averaged best in both, and that his preference had been given to him. Ebru did not stand in the line at all.

"Eburnean lost?" others gossiped.

"Worship of the Gods," Cyclamen continued as if he were giving a lecture in a silent library. "Understudy, dancing the Roots and Ends variation." Once more there were audible gasps in denial, as Eburnean only mastered one variation through Worship. The name did not need to be said, "Zaffre Vivicent of Xeysis."

Zaffre took his spot and Ebru stepped up next to Sarcoline. Cyclamen said, "Worship of the Gods, primary dancer, dancing the Holly variation: Eburnean Hue of Xeysis."

"These are this year's dancers for the Twenty-Seven Dances." Cyclamen Shadone held out his hand to the dancers. "Can we give a warm round of applause for all the competitors?"

The applause given was far from warm: scarce in number, tentative, and slow.

"Scores will be posted. Dress rehearsal is at seven on the thirty-fifth. We will see you all at the celebrations of the New Dawn. May the Gods' light never fade."

The crowd at the front of the room broke apart, some headed to their families, others to collect their things. Sarcoline said something to Ebru and the two began arguing. Zaffre stepped between them, and Ginger grabbed Sarcoline. Sarcoline shook her off and stormed over towards where Arna sat. Zaffre said something to Ebru, and he shrugged it off. Together with Aureolin, they all walked over.

"What did you do, Coco?" Amaryllis asked as soon as Sarcoline was close.

"Nothing, Am. Don't worry about it." Sarcoline stopped walking.

"He gave up his spot in Understanding, didn't he?" Ven asked. "That's why they had to give him Worship."

"No one failed," Zaffre said upon arrival. "The scores were decided as they were. I agreed to giving the spot to Ebru."

Sarcoline shot Ebru a glare and Ebru ignored it, walking over to Arna and taking his dance bag. Ebru then grabbed Arna's hands and turned them over checking his palms. Once he was satisfied, he held Arna's left hand tight and pulled Arna towards the door.

"Are you all headed to Amaryllis' studio now?" Wenge asked. "It's late."

"We have the fitting," Ginger assured her from behind Arna as he was dragged away.

"I'll have desserts when you come back to the studio," Wenge called.

The fitting for Arna's ceremonial garb was not only for the clothes and shoes, but for Phlox and Amaryllis to harp about how the mask that Arna carved looked terrible.

"Hold still," Ginger said, pinning the clothes in place.

"I have to fix it," Phlox shrieked.

"How did you paint it so badly?" Amaryllis asked over Phlox's shoulder.

He thought the mask looked the good: pink and mint for Ixxzal and Xeyaro. He'd even painted the other Gods' flowers onto the mask to represent them.

"He should never be allowed near fine arts ever again," Phlox lamented to Amaryllis.

"There!" Ginger said, backing up. "Ebru! Mirror."

Ebru sighed and helped Ven hold up the large mirror that Amaryllis had bought specifically for the fitting. It was nearly twice the size of both of them, with a silver trim that swirled in the formation of leaves.

No one had said a word about auditions, despite the low hanging fog that swirled around them. No one addressed it, distracted by Arna's variation instead of how catastrophically everything had gone. Arna welcomed the focus on himself, as it put his own running thoughts at ease. He was able to talk through each panic as it propped up, or at least most of them.

theendtheendtheend

One last truth remained: something he continued to bite back, as he was unsure how to explain. It was sour on his tongue and his gut told him that they would not react well if he told them. Whether it was true or not, Arna was not sure.

If not now, then when? he resolved himself.

Rosmarinus and Jasi offered people tea and snacks.

"Should we talk about it?" Arna asked them all. This would be a good approach, he assured himself. After all, they knew how bad the storms were. They knew the danger and—

"No," they all said at once, every single person all with the same tone: *this is not the time.*

"We're only doing it in case you decide to push a year, it's fine. We don't need to talk about it," Sarcoline offered, shooting a mutual scowl at Ebru.

Sure, Arna thought. it needed to be addressed. Arna reminded them, "It's a farce."

It's easy, Arna. Say, 'This is the end of the world so, that's why I'm freaking out.'

theendtheendtheend

"That's the problem," Ebru snarled before Arna could go on. "Because someone thinks he's disposable. That storm will *kill* you Sarcoline."

"And it won't kill *you*? We all know how much energy Worship takes. Arna needs you alive," Sarcoline fought back.

"Me? He needs you!" Ebru snapped.

"I need both of you alive, actually," Arna cut in and both of them glared at him, telling him to shut up. Arna shook his head. What was another approach?

Arna asked, "The storm? What's it classified as?"

"Cat six. Predicted to be as bad as the storm of '96," Ebru admitted.

"What?" Ginger shrieked. "Arco! You have to take it back. People *died* in '96!"

"We'll be fine. Arna is dancing," Sarcoline assured them, rolling his eyes. "No one will die."

What Arna was going to say, disappeared before he could.

diediediediediedie

As they talked about the disaster during the Ceremony of Chaos nearly sixty years ago, it became abundantly clear that they all thought this was normal. The whole world thought the loss of the Blessings, the storm, and all of it coinciding as badly this year, was normal.

It had not been normal before the Shattering, to have the Blessing falter yearly. But they did not know that the Shattering caused the initial divide. How could a world that never knew what it was like not to have the Blessings weaken and disappear yearly, understand that something was dangerously wrong?

There were trends that consistently happened. Blessings faltered, technology failed, especially in years with an Apostle Week. But the tragedies, the storms, the Blessings being lost in mass? It never happened all in one year. Arna was the only one who saw the signs because he knew the truth. That this was not normal, standard Blessing flickering, worse after the Splintering. This was the Shattering happening again but worse.

"Yes. I am," Arna said. However, everyone nodded as if he assured them that all would be well instead of admitting that he'd die.

Not today, tomorrow. He'd tell them when they were less tense and would be better receptive to the news.

everyonewasgoingtodieifhedidnotmaketherightchoice

"Are you okay Arna?" Rosmarinus asked.

theendtheendtheend

"I'm panicked about my choice," he said. It wasn't a lie. "Again."

diediediediediedie

"Done," Ginger said stepping back from where she pinned the alterations for Arna. He examined himself in the mirror.

His clothes were double layered, with a sheer, opal fabric over opaque black. The black fabric was embroidered with the flowers and symbols of the Gods, displayed along his arms and in a line down his legs. The entirety of his torso was embroidered in the designs. The opal fabric was hand painted, with scenes depicting nature and images of the cities: along the cuffs and all the hems. Meanwhile, his pants were covered in the paintings. The two fabrics collided.

He had white arm guards to protect and support his wrists. His ankle guards were more of the black fabric, holding the two layers tight on his legs. All Ceremony clothes were usually tight on the body, to reduce drag. The fans created enough. However, Arna allocated extra fabric to the opal, so that it would billow when he moved. His shoes were not perfect, but they were done well enough.

Arna turned his body, seeing the way that the layers flowed. The two layers collided with each other, baggy on top, tight beneath. As he twisted, the colors changed and the patterns lined up and divided, creating different scenes and patterns.

"The team that embroidered these and hand painted them is good. Did you give them pictures?" Ginger asked him.

"No," Arna shook his head. He had only gave the man a list of locations and very bad sketches.

"Where did you get the fabric from?" Ginger asked instead.

"Aster Fabrics," Arna said. He described where to find it in the city.

Ginger nodded, brightness to her tone, a dream in her words, "I will have to talk to the owner and ask for his team. . ."

"Are you thinking of poaching them for your studio?" Phlox giggled.

"Maybe," Ginger admitted, selfishly.

"Just flash your pretty smile, blink your eyes slowly, and say you're the Chosen's sister," Phlox offered. "I'm sure it will work."

"Stop glaring at me," Sarcoline snapped suddenly and the temperature in the room dropped again. "I'm not backing down on my decision."

"You are the last person I want to hear that from," Ebru snapped back.

"Since when did you care about me?"

Sarcoline approached Ebru, ready for a fight. The two glared at each other and Rosmarinus took the mirror from Ebru as Ebru stepped up to meet Sarcoline's challenge.

"Don't you realize you are the most valuable dancer in this room?" Ebru threw his hand out to point at everyone else.

"That's Arna."

"Only one person in this room can keep up with Children without the A.Reverence Blessing and it sure isn't Arna," Ebru hissed, poking Sarcoline in the chest.

Sarcoline stumbled back, surprised. He centered his weight and leaned forward.

"Stop fighting." Aureolin stepped between them. "Remember, we are only doing this so Arna has more time to decide on his choice. We probably aren't even dancing."

The words did not make anyone feel any better. Sarcoline glared down at the floor. Rosmarinus helped Ven put the mirror against the wall. Ginger ushered Arna away to help him get changed. As soon as he was upstairs he heard more voices downstairs.

How do I stop their fighting?

[   ]

Arna was not sure why he asked. The Gods used too much energy stopping him from forsaking them. He had to find the answer himself.

Just like finding the path to his survival, this too was on him.

tellthemabouttheendandturntheiranger

No. That wouldn't be productive for anyone.

Changing, Arna walked back downstairs with no plan. He found Sarcoline and Ebru in each other's faces. Ven was pulling Ebru back with Aureolin and Phlox. Ginger, Rosmarinus, and Amaryllis held Sarcoline back. Jasi stood between them.

"Why are you fighting now?" Arna asked, exasperated.

"We won't be dancing, remember, Ebru? My life doesn't matter because I won't be on that stage." Sarcoline taunted, ignoring Arna completely.

Ebru lunged at Sarcoline, but could not get far.

"I need to knock some sense into him!" Ebru snapped.

"Arna will make his choice. He'll become the Chosen and then he'll dance," Sarcoline said giddily, but distraught. "We'll be fine!"

Ah. They were all frustrated because they put in so much effort for nothing. Because Arna was going to dance. Because it was a farce. Because none of what they did mattered even when they wished it had.

Sarcoline didn't truly believe he won Understanding. Eburnean didn't truly believe he'd won Worship. Even when it was only the Vivicent studio that knew the truth about Arna dancing, none of them truly thought they deserved what they'd been given.

imposterimposterimposter

Just as he didn't.

And their own reckless self-abandon, the self-destruction that they all hid so carefully, was revealed to everyone: Ebru's self-hatred and Sarcoline's martyrism. They were exposed to each other, and they didn't like what they saw. They all saw each other so highly, and believed the others deserved the world, even if they didn't.

theendtheendtheend

Just like Arna.

Today, he resolved himself once more. They were united. They had to know that they did deserve it, as much as he did.

"We can't force him to make his choice and you can't be so stupid, to think we don't care." Ebru sneered, reaching for Sarcoline once more. Not to hurt him but to grab him and ensure he cared for and loved.

"I will dance, this year. It's the only way I'll know if I made the right choice," Arna said finally ready to tell them about the apocalypse. Widespread confusion filled the air. "Why are you looking at me like that? I told you."

Sarcoline stopped fighting Ebru and faced Arna with terror painting his face. They all looked haunted at his words.

"Repeat that," Rosmarinus ordered Arna, hurriedly.

"I will only know if I made the right choice when I dance," Arna repeated, unsure what was going on.

"Gods. I was too focused on you thinking you were an imposter," Ebru whispered. Quick glances were sent across the room as the nine of them had an unspoken conversation Arna was not privy to.

Slowly but surely they all turned to Sarcoline for guidance. Sarcoline was nearly shaking.

"But I can't be right. I can't!" Sarcoline stumbled back then tottered towards Arna, stumbling forward.

What was he so stunned about? Everyone was looking at Arna like he grew a second head.

"You don't know if you made the right choice until you dance? One or twenty-six?" Sarcoline grabbed Arna's sleeves when he was close enough like a dying man grasping for water.

"Twenty-six," Arna answered. Why was this news?

"And if you made the wrong choice. . . " Amaryllis approachd him, standing next to Sarcoline, "He what? Drops down to six Blessings?"

"Yes," Sarcoline hissed.

"Not until I start twenty-six," Arna explained. What had he said? They knew this. "Until I pick up the fans for that dance, I will still have. . . well the ones I hadn't lost already."

"That makes it worse, Arna, stop talking." Ven hurried over to Sarcoline, who was thinking deeply, muttering to himself under his breath. The others were looking amongst themselves more concerned than before.

Arna's panic was erased by his utter bewilderment. What was going on? Did he still tell them about the end of the world?

Arna opened his mouth but stopped.

"Arna." Sarcoline raised his head, his eyes were filled with desolation.

"Yes?" Arna hesitated, all of their eyes drilling holes into him.

"I need you to answer me honestly, please. Don't make a joke for the first time in your life," Sarcoline pleaded with him. Arna cocked an eyebrow "Because of the Splintering. You have to dance this year, don't you? If you don't make the choice, this year, you lose the chance forever."

"Yes," Arna said, confused. While the assessment was correct the logic was wrong. There was nothing more for the Gods to hold on to and they were dying. "It's the—"

"How high is the probability that you will die dancing?" Sarcoline asked, all in one breath.

Arna let the rest of the word 'apocalypse' fade. He was not expecting that question.

DIEDIEDIEDIEDIE

One by one everyone in the room looked at Arna in abject horror.

"What do you mean Sarcoline?" Ebru's voice was quaking.

"If he goes out there with the wrong answer, the storm will destroy him. He'd lose all his Blessings at once and we saw what losing one did to him. He could survive the loss but the storm will rip him apart in seconds."

Arna had to admit, it would be painful, but he doubted the storm would kill him off that fast. The others were not as convinced.

"And based on my calculations of Arna's fans and how many Blessings he has left. . ." Sarcoline said, voice dropping so low Arna could hardly hear it, "The twenty-sixth dance might kill you even if you have your Blessings, because. . . If you make the right choice, does the twenty-sixth dance still aim to kill you?"

"Yes," Arna admitted. "Or rather. It's not the dance but rather the Divinity. Divinity from the Gods, enters my body and the Blessings counteract that. It's complex and—"

"But even as the Chosen. Even if you're right. The dance can still kill you," Sarcoline confirmed.

"What are you getting at?" Arna asked. Didn't they already know this?

"You can die in twenty-six," Sarcoline repeated, hysterical and breathless.

"I worked much too hard to be destroyed before I can finish twenty-seven," Arna said trying to lighten the mood and failing miserably. Arna tried again, "Look that doesn't matter because—"

"And if the storm is as bad as we think," Sarcoline cut him off. "And even if you are correct in your choice. And even if you survive the twenty-sixth dance that will be *trying to kill you* and you will reach twenty-seven and finish it. . . Do you get your Blessings back immediately? Will you be able to heal yourself?"

[Distant birds were lamenting and dying.]

Sarcoline had figured it out.

THEENDTHEENDTHEEND

"No. The Gods aren't strong enough to give them back to me that quickly," Arna admitted his resolve was quickly depleting.

Everyone raced over to Arna as Sarcoline dropped Arna's sleeves and pulled back, shaking.

Using what little remained of his resolve, Arna said, "Arco, listen. The end is—"

"I WON'T LET YOU DIE!" Sarcoline screamed at him.

"Are you saying. . ." Aureolin choked.

"But the Gods are all-powerful, aren't they?" Phlox demanded.

Saffron.Saffron.Saffron.

"The Shattering, when the superstorms began, was caused by a person named Saffron. . ." Arna tried to explain the apocalypse anyway. Saying Saffron's name was like breaking a curse. Suddenly he existed to the mortals once more, not just Arna.

"The Gods and mortals were fractured because of him. They were almost erased, but Ilex reconnected them to us. The storms are their divinity wreaking havoc: divinity they cannot control. It was ripped from them and left on the earth. Every time someone commits a taboo the energy that used to go to the Gods now goes to the storms. It makes them stronger."

The group looked horrified. It was a common factoid taught in school: how many small taboos that people broke daily.

"What does the Shattering have to do with you dying?" Phlox asked Arna.

"In the Splintering, when the candles went out, the Gods lost their ability to gain power through prayer," Arna said softly. "The dances each year give them temporary power, as it's during the dances when they can receive prayers again. But. . . They are too weak now. When I reconnect them to everyone, it will take time for them regain their strength where they can bestow back my Blessings."

The only sound in the room was the ticking clock.

"But that's why I have to dance, because—"

Ginger screamed, cutting off his words. Ven collapsed to the ground.

"You dance, you're wrong, you die. You dance, you're right, you still might die." Sarcoline clarified, "Or you could give up right now and you'd live?"

"Honestly, I might as well kill myself if I chose to give up now," Arna said and Ginger shrieked again. He tried to explain, "I will succeed. I can't—"

"This is why you were so distant, why there was so much pressure," Amaryllis realized. "We were forcing you to dance this whole time and you didn't even tell us!"

Arna was not sure what to say to it. It was not like he could give up. There was no one else who could become the Chosen after him.

"You aren't forcing me. I have to do it. The Shattering—"

No one was listening to him anymore.

"This is the root of his panic," Ven said. "This is why. He knew this whole time!"

Ginger rocked on the floor in sobs.

"How likely is it?" Ebru asked Sarcoline, alarmed.

Sarcoline shook his head and motioned at Arna.

"Rosy," Ebru took Arna's hand. "Don't you fucking look away from me when you say this."

Arna held the mint eyes steady, Ebru had to hear him.

Answer the question, then finish the explanation.

"What is the probability you are going to die?"

"One hundred, if I'm wrong," Arna answered easily.

"And if you make the right choice?" Ebru asked.

Arna was not sure there was a percentage that he could use. The Gods never talked to him in that way. He was unsure how to answer even if he had one. His dragonfly mark burned, and the other's glowed, urging Arna to answer truthfully.

Arna stumbled over the words. "We can call it a ninety-six. I never had numbers. But there is a path, the Gods told me. They don't know what it is, but they think that with your help I can live."

Jasi grabbed Ginger and Aureolin grabbed Phlox who started sobbing as well. Dissonance filled the air and began to suffocate them.

"Give up," Ven demanded. "Right now. Give up."

"That's a one hundred percent," Arna shook his head, keeping his eyes locked with Ebru. "If I don't—"

"You promised you wouldn't leave us again!" Ven shouted, voice louder than it had ever been. "You promised!"

They'd spent days trying to convince him not to give up. They'd chased him down when he almost had. They'd seen him nearly destroy himself in chasing off the dream. They could not steal it away from him now.

"I can't. I have to do this."

Saffron.Saffron.Saffron.

What little remained of the resolved evaporated into winter mists.

[Arna held the weight of knowing the end of the world was near but was unable to vocalize it. He swallowed it instead.]

Ebru's expression went blank. He drifted, froze solid, and darted for the door. It slammed behind him. The room transformed into a sputtered mess.

Sarcoline was the only one who wasn't crying. He stood in the storm of emotions, completely still staring at Arna as if he were gazing into the abyss and he did not like what he saw back. Seconds turned to minutes, without blinking. And finally, he turned away, and silently left the house, leaving Arna alone with the screams of denial.

Distant storms began to brew, ready to destroy every hope in the world.

Perhaps it is scary not to know; But it is scarier to know and to forget.
Because you did know, and now you do not.
But remember, it is not only fear that lives in the unknown.
There is hope. There is possibility. There are dreams.

— On Ixxzal

Dance 23

Nuance

Incarnadine

"I don't understand how that just happened."
"You – "
"No, I don't need you repeating it. Ha! You know, sometimes you guys are funny."
"I'm happy we humor you. Now, run."

The Omniscient Sextant Enchiridion was written by Saint Citrine and Saint Aubergine and was the foundation for most of the religions in the world. The original collection was lost millennia ago in the wars of the Fourth Variance. The oldest copy dated back to 29 V and was held by the Church of the Apostle, in their Cathedral in Xeysis. Arna had it memorized, despite having never read it. Lectures over long nights, recited to him until he knew it like he knew his own name, ingrained it into his heart.

The first book, the Book of Six, detailed the six Gods. The second book, the Book of Blessings, depicted Blessings, Children, and their rules. The Book of Taboos, was the fifth and longest text: explaining all the taboos, their consequences, and the other natural laws for the world as determined by the Gods. None of them held the answer.

The third book was the Book of the Dances. It designed the details of The Twenty-Seven Dances, the conditions they had to be performed in, the number that had to be performed, and introduced the Celebrations. It had a laid out explanation for the Ceremony of Chaos and held the Scripture of Creation that highlighted the instructions for making true worship fans, and the Blessings that needed to be laid on a fan to make it a divine tool. No matter how Arna searched his memory of the book, it did not hold the answer either.

The fourth book was the Book of Worship, which listed other prayers and practices besides The Dances. There were six additional minor worship practices of significant importance for each God that fell out of practice in time. The last book was the Book of the Chosen. The book was the list of signs to identify the Chosen, the set of instructions for the Chosen, and highlights of how they would be the only person able to dance all twenty-seven dances without dying. None held what Arna sought.

In no form throughout any of the books was the Contract ever defined, despite being referenced over sixty times throughout the texts as either 'the contract' or 'the bond.' Many scholars believed it to be self-explanatory, that the contract itself was to be understood as the Gods provided Blessings and the mortals gave prayer.

The Gods were even *less* helpful.

Lumak explained it as a contract, an agreement between the Gods and mortals: Blessings for Worship. Power for power. Yet, they did not explain how it was woven, written, stated, nor enforced outside of taboos. There was no explanation on how Arna was supposed to fix the contract and little explanation on how it was made.

It began as soon as the Dances began, a dialogue between us and Raven to forge the connection. A conversation is a path and it is never one sided.

Zaynir once explained it as a weaving of souls, mortals to the Gods. The Gods had always existed, listening to prayers, but the contract allowed them more authority. The Dances that Raven danced, thus, were the opening in the universe that allowed Raven to weave the souls to the Gods more explicitly. Zaynir never explained how to open the universe, nor what it meant to weave souls.

It simply is. To dance is to weave the connection. The fans are designed to float through the air and drag the world with them. The contract is much the same. You must weave yourself into life itself.

Xeyaro explained that The Dances were the contract. The message within them, and the decisions made, determined the contract itself. It was why Blessings changed with each variation because the contract was shifted and remade each time Divinity was bestowed upon a Chosen. Their Will and Wants became the basis for the contract. They never explained how Will could make the universe bend. If he believed it enough, it just happened?

Will allows you to shape the world. The universe is your intention, Divinity is a state of being and a power itself. It will happen because it must.

Azza said that the contract was created through chaos. That it simply existed because the dancers danced. It began because the Gods saw it as a way for them to connect to the world and Raven danced as a way to connect to the Gods. The mutual desire allowed for the contract to begin, which was the best explanation of the contract that Arna got if it weren't for the fact that when he asked how he could fix it, Azza said they were unsure.

I can wield chaos. I can craft the world. I will be your link to establish the contract itself, but I cannot tell you how to do it.

Pokk explained that when Saffron failed to accept Divinity, the contract broke because Saffron gave up on the Gods and himself. It did not matter what the rest of the world wanted, the Chosen had decided that the Gods and mortals no longer needed to be connected. By dropping the fan, Arna rejected the Gods further.

However, Arna had rejected them by accident. He had done as they asked and believed in them wholeheartedly to the point of destruction. The only reason that the Gods and mortals were not completely severed again, was because Arna believed he deserved to be the link, and thus he became the *only* link.

In order to fix it, you must merge us back to the rest of the world and heal the wound that has grown.

How did one heal a wound that had happened by accident? It was a wound that was created by a departure and could not be predicted. There was too much uncertainty. There was no forgiveness to seek. There were no actions to make up for what was lost. How did one carve a path to a future?

Ixxzal said, *You just do. You accept the consequences that it won't be perfect, but it will be new. And we can work with new.*

And thus, Arna had no idea how to build the contract at all.

31 Xeyan
11 Days Left

To their credit, not a single one of the Golden Dragonflies told Zaffre or Wenge about the revelation that Arna was destined to die. Arna was not sure it mattered however, when Ginger burst into tears every time that she saw him. Jasi was more solemn than normal. Rosmarinus was dazed, messing up paperwork and burning food. Sarcoline was never to be seen, either practicing longer than usual, staying at school longer than he had to as the year was over, or in his room doing who knew what.

Otherwise, things proceeded as normal. Arna had intensive dance practice three times a day, with his father. He worked on his variation notes and music with Ebru online. He assisted his father with the fans in the evening.

"What happened?" His father asked as he held up the third fan of Blue Rose Fears, pulling the fabric taut and sewing slowly around the boning. He looked exhausted.

"It's hard to explain," Arna said, uncertain how he could break the news a second time.

His father did not press Arna further, his slow hands continued doing meticulous work, looping the thread through the fabric one stitch at a time. He was stitching life itself.

"I am not sure what secrets you are keeping for each other," his father said. Minutes stretched into hours until he placed the fans down. "However, remember that your mother and I are here to support you."

Arna nodded, salt settled at the back of his tongue, threatening to burn his throat.

Rosmarinus stood in the kitchen handing Arna food for dinner, silently and controlled. The two moved about each other through the sweets that Wenge bought for celebrations after the auditions that no one ate.

"You have to dance alone," Rosmarinus stated, in confirmation.

"Yes," Arna said, pushing the desserts from the table to give space.

"You know," Rosmarinus said next, "I've wanted to talk to you for a while. One on one. But I never found the chance."

"Sorry. I was busy."

"I was afraid you'd hate me when I first came back."

Arna stopped moving and looked at Rosmarinus who went on as if he had not said anything at all. A light breeze dusted the table and wove itself around Rosmarinus.

"I always thought everyone here hated me. That they were begrudgingly taking me in because they wanted Jasi, and I was a consolation prize."

Arna balked. His family would never. Rosmarinus chuckled.

"Crazy. I know. But I didn't know anyone then, not really. This was Jasi's family not mine," he said sadly. "But I didn't want to lose him. So, I did everything to make myself indispensable. To be an asset. I made it so they wouldn't want to toss me aside. I stayed out of trouble. Did not ask for much. Made myself invisible, all so that they would love me."

Arna hesitated. How was he supposed to help? What was it like to imagine that you were just another mouth to feed? To feel as if everything rested on you or you'd be forgotten?

"They already loved me," Rosmarinus shook his head. "I just didn't know it. It took loving myself to see that. I didn't need to do more. I just needed to be."

Rosmarinus handed Arna another set of plates and held Arna's gaze steady. Wild winds wrapped around the both of them, no longer contained.

"I'm a very selfish person, Arna. And while, I don't know much about dancing," he said, leisurely despite its heaviness, "I want to help."

Arna paused. How did he find the path? The question was a swirling vortex pulling everything in, uprooting secrets. "I don't know how you can."

The End. The End. The End.

Dragonflies flew through the window and floated in the air above the counter. They drifted up and atop Rosmarinus' head and shoulders. They circled the both of them.

The dragonflies buzzed off back to the willow tree outside. A gust, tranquil but sure, rolled off his tongue: "We'll find a way."

32 Xeyan
10 Days Left

Ginger clung to Arna, crying. He rubbed her back as she sobbed.

"I don't want you to die. You can't die. I just wanted you home. Why do they have to take you away from me again? I just got you back."

He had no idea how to help her. He had no way to ease her sorrows other than to let her cry. They say in the garden under their willow tree. Summer dragonflies—black and lime, black and red, black and the deepest shade of chaos green—floated around them. Each sob was another pointed knife stabbing him until it no longer hurt, and he was left feeling nothing at all.

The flicker of anger he held was pushed away and buried deep until he forgot it existed. He held her close and comforted her, disregarding everything else.

She fell asleep in the flowerbeds, having worn herself out, when Jasi arrived. He said nothing to Arna as he bent down to check her temperature, move her hair out of her face, and kiss her temple.

"Do you believe me?" Arna said.

"I believe that you believe you can survive it. I am not sure you want to," Jasi said, slowly looking at him. The rims of his eyes were red. There were dark circles under them.

Everyone always talks about dying.

The spark of anger returned. After everything he'd done and said? No, it made sense that Jasi believed that. He'd hidden so much, was unable to explain things fully, and even now his tongue was caught in his throat. Did he truly want to live? He could not be angry.

Late in the evening, Phlox dropped her bags down, directing the movers to take her things up to the third floor. She wore a much too heavy scarf for the summer wrapped around her face, a hat so big that it covered everything up to her eyes, and dragonfly sunglasses to hide the rest. Phlox did not say a thing as she walked to her old practice room. She looked around and motioned Arna to place her dance clothes in the corner, near the rack that Zaffre had bought her when she was nine.

When he turned to her, she had removed her scarf and hat. Her hair was unwashed, greasy, and flat. Her face was sprinkled in pimple patches. As she removed her sunglasses she shoved them into her oversized bag that she held. Her bag had fringe similar to the silver branches of a willow tree; they swayed. She wore no makeup and revealed her truth: eyes worn down, cheeks sunken, and flawless complexion splotchy.

Great, she wasn't handling it well either. Had they all missed it when he said that he wanted to succeed and thus live, or did they willfully ignore it? The anger he'd held from earlier bubbled up, and he forced himself to swallow it.

The End. The End. The End.

It's new, they are trying to understand.

"You look like shit," Arna said, trying to calm down, from his unjustifiable anger.

"It's your fault," Phlox said with a glare. "Why?"

Arna cocked an eyebrow at her, daring her to continue.

"Why do you *have* to dance? Say no. It doesn't matter. There doesn't have to be a Chosen and it certainly doesn't have to be you." Phlox crossed her arms. She fumed. Tears welled up at her eyes again. She was putting on a strong front, but the stress was evident on her face.

"Your Blessings mean nothing. Everything you've done: The pilgramage? The practice? The variation? It doesn't matter. You can be *anything* Arna. You can be like us. You can throw it all away and do something else. You can believe in us to help you find a life after it."

Arna blinked. *What?* Was she serious? She thought he seriously was going do that? After everything he worked for? The anger he swallowed began to bubble. His stomach stirred and he wanted to vomit in rage.

maybeheshouldhavedestroyedthem

The End. The End. The End.

"I *am* choosing who I want to be," Arna seethed.

"To be the Chosen? For what? The clout? The money? *Why?*"

Why did he leave at fifteen? Why did he run around the world completing tests? Why did he dance in storms and stand in a superstorm? Why did he train night and day, carving up his body? Why?

The End. The End. The End.

"Because I have to, Phlox." He wanted it more than he wanted everything in his life. He always had. Why couldn't she understand that? What was so hard to understand?

She started crying. Arna ignored her.

33 Xeyan
9 Days Left

When Arna got home from his mandatory Chosen Task Force meeting, he wanted nothing more than to dance until dinner. There were workers fixing the house, patching up the holes and fixing the detailing. New furniture was being moved in as the bullet riddle ones were tossed. He wanted to get his mind off everything. His fingers twitched and his palms ached from squeezing his fists tight. No one was stopping him anymore.

He was trying, so hard, to be patient and to understand where everyone was coming from. Yet, it felt like his sister burst into tears every time she talked to him. The whole house was walking on eggshells around him, like he'd break and just kill himself. This was the exact reason he had kept it to himself for so long. He knew they would react this way.

If they would just listen to him, he could explain the apocalypse, but every time he tried, they wouldn't hear him. It was as if the excuse wasn't good enough.

"Arna," Aureolin said as he walked into his dance room. She was dressed in all tan, with a crown of willow tree branches and a dragonfly broach on her chest. Her face was hollow with eyes red from crying and dark bags beneath them: miserable.

Trying his very best, Arna was civil, despite the fact that she interrupted him. He asked her. "How was your preparation for the celebrations?"

As the Monarch of Flowers, she had speeches to give and needed to be a judge on the celebration's flower competition.

"This whole time, you came back knowing you would die," she said instead. "Choosing to do it over simply killing yourself. And still, you reached out to us to reconnect. Why?"

Arna stared at her with a blank, listless stare. *This is how it's going to be?*

What was he supposed to say? The universe was demanding he pick. Gods or mortals. Living or dying. Everything he had ever worked for or everything he ever wanted.

The End. The End. The End.

"Aureolin I just need you to listen—"

"No. You listen! You weren't going to tell us. You were going to hold this burden on your own and leave us blissfully unaware, and then we'd have to deal with your death without you, thinking *what if,*" she said, voice quaking. "That's why everyone is so mad. That's why we are so upset. Because we can't convince you not to. We want you to do it. We have always believed you would. We were pushing you to it, and you let us."

Arna could not speak. He did not know how. He would have been angry too, if Ebru or Ven had hidden this from him for as long as he had. Whatever he could say would make it worse and there was no way for him to defend himself and his choice, expect to prove it to them. He had no way to do that.

She's justified, he reminded himself. He'd be a fool not to realize what he'd done to his friends. Arna had finally helped them find each other. Then he'd wrecked the foundation again. It was years' worth of knowledge he'd held close; they had to process it all without any real time to grieve. Or maybe there was too much time. It did not matter.

"We're the worst friends. We couldn't even give you the space to admit to us. . . to rely on us. To tell us that you were scared."

She approached and hugged him. Arna blinked back his initial desire to push her away and yell at her to get out.

Let them react. He'd had years to truly process his own mortality. He'd been this depressed and this angry, before. He could control it. He had and he would.

"I'm so sorry." She clung to him, crying. "We want to support you Arna. We do. We are here. You aren't alone. Please don't think you have to die to fix all of this."

Arna held her tightly as she cried into his shoulder. He lightly rubbed her back and expected to find an aching numbness but instead he found a desire to live, growing stronger and stronger. The anger he held was transforming into spite. He would prove it to them that he could live. He'd prove it to the Gods who were terrified. He'd prove it to the universe that was forcing him to make a choice. He had to.

"I've went my whole life thinking this burden was my own," Arna admitted to her, clinging to her as well. He let the rage fill him. He let it guide him. Her tears bleed into his shirt. His dragonfly mark warmed. He said, "It's everything that I am."

"No. Arna. *You* are everything."

The distant call of silence was a scream, wishing to be heard. A passion for life was belligerent and growing.

(Who will he dance for?)

Arna found Ven at the archery range that Ven first started shooting at when they were ten years old. When Ven was a child, trying to get away from their terrible stepparents, they often wandered here, sitting under the willow tree in the front and wishing to disappear.

When they saw Arna they looked down into the grass, knees up to their chest arms holding them close, pulling at their sleeves. After having gone no contact with everyone for multiple days, Arna had made it his mission to find Ven, just as Ven had found him weeks ago. He stood, hands in his pockets, examining Ven.

Was this how I looked when they found me? They were a mess, embarrassingly so. They were withdrawn and trying to become invisible. It was as if the future they wanted no longer mattered, not anymore.

"You said you wouldn't leave again," Ven said as soon as Arna knelt down.

"I'm not," Arna said sitting cross legged, getting as close as he could without touching them.

"If you dance you will leave us. If you don't you will leave us." Ven cried softly. They were smaller, gaunt and distressed. They looked horrible, as if their soul had been stolen a second time. There was no point arguing. Arna just needed them to come home.

Arna picked at the grass and started weaving them together into a chain, like his mother taught him when he was young. He worked at the chain for minutes, sitting in silence, as the two of them breathed in unison.

"How did you find me?" Ven asked.

"You could find me when I was upset," At the tip of the rose staring out into the sky. "I knew how to find you."

"This is where Ebru and I fought. When I destroyed him. You *cannot* destroy him again." Ven buried their head between their knees. Their voice was cracking.

"I know." Arna took in the sight of Ven. The sight of it was heartbreaking. Arna wished he had S.Mirrors to reach out and make them feel better, but he did not. He'd made that choice and now he had to accept it. The void between them was harsh and finite, impossible to bridge. He continued to weave the grass.

"You know, he started composing when I turned sixteen, although his music did not get good until we were seventeen," Arna offered.

Ebru grew as an artist when he began to get popular.

"When. . . he moved studios," Ven said with the faintest of voices.

"And lost you." That had been a year of so much change, and them all falling apart after they had so desperately tried to hang on for a time. This moment was no different.

"I commented on his songs but didn't start talking to him until we were about eighteen. I was in my second city at that point, understood more of what I needed to do and be. We have collaborated ever since."

"I wish I could have been there for him." There was not much of a reaction from Ven. There was, however, a pleading in their voice, "He deserves happiness."

They all did. Arna was going to give it to them.

He stopped weaving and breathing. A thought seeded itself in his mind, hovering there like a dragonfly in the mist. It begged him to follow the logic a step further.

"Just like you do. A large house, laughter, and ease, right?" Ven asked, voice quivering and hands clenching into fists around their sleeves. "It was always your dream, Arna."

Arna's thoughts multiplied. It was the dream he'd had as a kid. A large house. Laughter to fill it. Him in love. Him happy. Him dancing. It was a dream he had not allowed himself for years.

"I don't want to die," Arna said to them, and their head snapped up.

A dragonfly danced between them, black, indigo, violet, and mauve. It waltzed around Arna and Ven, their heads, and darted to between their wrists before flying up. *Chase me,* it called to Arna. But where? Where was it leading him. The answer was at the tip of his tongue.

"I'm not. I'm dancing because I need to," Arna continued. He wanted to live. He needed to dance to save the world. He had worked for this at every step of the way.

[Mortals or the Gods?]

"You don't *need* to. Let someone else be the Chosen. Be with us. Choose *us*," Ven pleaded with him, and the dragonfly disappeared.

After everything he worked for Arna wanted to say yes he would. He wanted to say that he would choose them over the Gods and choose their lives together. He wanted to have that dream more than anything. Yet, something about that answer was the wrong one.

"I don't have to be the Chosen," Arna said and Ven's face grew softer, eyes wider, wishing. "But I want more than anything to be. *I* want this. Can't you help me try?"

Ven shook their head. Arna could ask them anything. *Anything but that.*

Ebru refused to look at Arna as he opened the door. He stood breathless outside of Ebru's house deep into the night. Ebru was once more the withheld diamond prince he'd learned to retreat to.

"Say it to my face, Ebru." Arna said, needing Ebru to repeat himself. Their messages had been short in recent days, until Arna could no longer ignore that Ebru was hiding something. The truth had been devastating.

"It's nothing."

Arna repeated what Ebru said through their chat, "They wanted to cut Worship because the predictions say that storm conditions could kill a person? You convinced them to put you out there anyway?"

Ebru focused on the floor, staring at nothing. Arna's rage flourished into an inferno, threatening to consume the ice and leave Ebru unable to hide.

"Tell them you changed your mind." Arna demanded.

"Each year when the Blessings start to fluctuate like this and people lose them in mass, it's only when we dance Worship that things stabilize." Ebru said with sharp breaths and a soft voice, struggling to hold his own emotions back. "The DHS agreed: I'm disposable."

"That's self-destructive," Arna reached out and Ebru backed away. He turned his head away further.

"That's rich coming from *you,*" Ebru said, clenching his hands but he did not look up. "You're the one who is so dead set on killing yourself for the dances. If you are, I am."

When Arna withstood the superstorm for six minutes, it was something worse than death: unimaginable pain and all consuming. Everything after was inconsequential in comparison. But knowing that Ebru was more afraid of losing Arna than his own death, left Arna feeling as if he had no body at all.

The End. The End. The End.

Keeping them all alive was everything he'd worked for.

"I won't let you die." Arna reached for Ebru and Ebru went to back away but stopped when Arna caught him. Mint eyes meeting black. Neither looked away.

"It's fine if I do," Ebru's words were a slow acting poison, no longer concealed. It dyed his skin gray and killed him slowly. Ebru shrugged nonchalantly, and Arna's fury soared.

Ebru's eyes narrowed and eyebrows furrowed. Ebru ran his hands over Arna's face, checking his temperature and pulling him inside. The house was nice and cool: much better than the sweltering heat outside. Arna touched his cheeks, realizing they were hot, and probably red. Ebru said, "Stay here. I'll get you water."

Arna followed, burning up. They walked into the sterile white kitchen: white tiles, white marble counters, and white cabinets.

"You are scared, Ebru. Of losing everything. I know," Arna struggled to control his temper. "It's the end of the—"

"The world?" He scoffed.

"Yes." Finally, someone heard him. Only, Ebru reacted as if he hadn't by rolling his eyes.

"Stop joking Arna. I'm fine," Ebru said flatly, as if he truly believed that he were.

Joke? Every time that anyone joked that Arna was Ebru's whole world, slapped Arna in the face. THE END. THE END. THE END.

"You die. I die."

How could he not see the idiocy in his own words? Clearly he was unwell. He was ready to die if Arna wasn't in the world with him. He had completely forgot any sense of self awareness and consideration. Not just Arna, but Arna was convinced everyone could see it so clearly; it did not take a genius to see.

(Hypocrisy was a funny thing.)

Arna's heart skipped a beat. Rage mutated to dread as Arna saw in Ebru what the others all saw in him. Golden Dragonfly, buzzed and burned, said: no more.

All his rage? Smothered. His Blessings? Broken. He was nothing. It was a pain he could never replicate and one that he'd never be able to articulate.

This is how they feel. He Understood. He'd always been so focused on his own fear, his own death and the apocalypse, that he'd never had the chance to fully accept the emotions of others. To him, the reactions were justified and obviously correct, but he'd never felt them himself. Now he did.

Arna held the weight of his life. It mattered so much more than being Chosen.

"You can cry," Arna said instead, devastation fizzling out to emptiness.

"Why would I?" Ebru asked.

"You never cry. Ever. Not even when you're hurt. Not when you're beaten. Not when you want to kill yourself," Arna tried to control his tone and keep it even. It was not an accusation but a plead: *trust me. I am here. You can trust me.*

It's not safe, Ebru's entire expression screamed. "No."

"I know you hate false hope—" Arna pressed.

"So then why are you standing there trying to convince me that your personal self-destruction is acceptable, but mine is not?" Ebru slammed the glass of water into Arna's hands. "I don't want you to be the Chosen Child if that means you will die to achieve it. I want you to be because you deserve it."

Why are you asking me to give up on you?

But why was Arna giving up? They finally had each other. They had fought for this. He wanted them to be together long past the New Dawn.

"But I can't stop you. None of us can. You dance and die, and I have to live in the big house *alone*," Ebru snarled. There was pain there that he wanted to express but he bit it back and turned it into a malicious smile.

Ebru's eyes said all that Arna needed to hear: *I cannot be alone again, Rosy.*

Everything that needed to be said was. Ebru would not give him the vulnerability, would not be a mortal once more, until everything was through. He would not, until it was all okay. Until Ebru knew he could trust Arna with his heart unconditionally, this was it.

The spark returned: not rage but passion. Ebru's eyes said, *I won't let you die.*

I will live, Arna would ensure it. He would find a way. His friends would help him. They all said they would. He needed to believe in them. The dragonfly vow on his arm twitched and started to spread its wings further.

34 Xeyan
8 Days Left

Ginger put the Chamomile painting that Amaryllis selected for the Vivicent booth into a box. Load-in for the celebrations had begun for vendors and artists, following the announcement of the Main Stage shows, and the final list of performers for events other than the Ceremony of Chaos.

Between planning, DHS responsibilities, and Zaffre finishing the fans, there was not much time for everyone to get together. Yet, everyone found the time to help Amaryllis move Chamomile's art. The movers were set to transport most of it to the Church of the Apostle for the auction, and despite everyone's expressions, there were only dry eyes.

All of the merchandise and art required blessings before the Celebrations. Arna looked at the program in his hand. The day's events and maps were printed, as well as a full list of all booths and shows. The final programs would be distributed the day of and updated on the website online. The only thing that was not listed was who was dancing the Ceremony of Chaos, as if it would change.

The house was rife with stress as everyone helped to package the paintings to be sold or displayed in promotion at the Vivicent booth. The family had a booth at every New Dawn Day celebrations, where they took sign-ups for the studio. It was the only day that they usually took on new students.

Everyone avoided Arna.

"This one?" Ginger asked holding up The Dancer. "For the booth?"

"Yes," Amaryllis said solemnly.

"Are you sure?" Sarcoline asked her.

"Yes. I want people to see it." She smiled at him, but it did not reach her eyes.

"Is this the last box for the Church?" someone asked, pointing at the one by Arna's feet.

"Yes." Arna helped them lift it and take it to the vehicle. After making sure it was secure, Arna waved them goodbye and turned to find Amaryllis standing with her arms crossed.

The two stood in her garden, surrounded by butterflies and dragonflies. Early summer flower petals danced in the air between them. She examined him a moment, and then sighed.

"My showcase will be in the hall of fans," Amaryllis broke the silence.

She was approved for the showcase in the Temple? It was the most prestigious location for art displays. His mother had predicted it correctly?

"Surprising, I know." Amaryllis beamed. "I got the email a bit ago. They moved me. Times changed, too. Phlox's play is now set to end twenty minutes before Aureolin's second group dance."

What?

Arna tapped at his mobile to open his email. Quickly he imported the times sent to him by the DHS into his calendar. The two continued to stand in silence, until Arna cleared out the screen and found her with the darkest, scariest expression he'd ever seen on her face.

"Are you really that daft? I really thought you were more perceptive," she grimaced. "They are waiting for you to tell them that everything will be okay. Tell them, like I know, that you are trying to live."

Arna laughed. Of course, she knew.

"We both know that's the truth," Amaryllis said. "But like you, they're blind to things that aren't shoved in front of them plain to see. Can you imagine what it must be like? To find out the person that they loved came back from the dead, only to tell them he was meant to die? That you are still going to do the dance knowing so?" Her words were like screams despite how leveled she kept her tone, devoid of emotion.

"Surprisingly, I figured that out," Arna said. "I don't know how to fix it. They won't listen."

Amaryllis contemplated the statement, eying him over carefully for a moment before she shifted her weight and nodded.

"My theme for my showcase is dreams," Amaryllis said like the breaking of a tranquil lake. "I titled it: *The Artists.*"

The word struck Arna directly in his chest. Without her elaborating, he nodded. Her showcase was of them, for them.

"What would you live for?"

Arna reeled at her voice. It echoed both in memory and aloud, in the distant sound of chimes and deepest part of his soul.

"They want you to put your heart and soul into it, but they're afraid that it will ask for more than you can give," Amaryllis told him. Her eyes were melting, the anger leaving her and dissipating like spring warming winter. "They need to know you are going to fight."

Arna wanted to fight for them. He wanted to fight for their dreams. He wanted them to be anything that they wanted to be. And he wanted to fight for his own chance. He wanted a chance at a future. He wanted to defy fate.

Who will you be after?

"Why is it that you like to dig deeply into my subconscious and rip me apart?" Arna asked, recognizing seconds later that he sounded harsher than intended. "Sorry. I—"

"Because I see you," she answered. Arna finally looked up and saw her smiling. "And I've been there. You have a way to prove it, somewhere. Something."

As she said the word, the Golden Dragonflies left the house one after another, looking tired, distraught, and generally horrified.

Sarcoline's eyes landed on him first, solemnly. He said, "The others agreed I should tell you. I've done some research. Jasi and I are coming up with Blessing combinations that can fix you after, so we can give the Gods time."

It was admirable, that out of everyone, Sarcoline actually looked determined. That despite everything, he was going to strive for beauty anyways. He was the only one who believed that Arna could see the day after he danced.

After.

Visualize.

Arna's wrist began to burn: hot, white, pain like the touch of a storm, like the breath of a kiss, like the want and need and drive for *everything*.

"We've seen Incarnate Dreams. We are not going to let you give up everything you worked for. We just don't want you to die. We need time," Sarcoline continued as if his words had not changed everything.

Arna wanted a house with laughter, big and warm. He wanted his friends, to be able to do the bucket list with Jasi, to see go to all of Phlox's premieres, to try on all of Ginger's clothing, and to travel the world with Aureolin. He wanted to watch Amaryllis take over the world. He wanted to become best friends with Ven. He wanted to see his father smile, truly, joyfully, fearlessly. He wanted to see his mother thrive in a sea of flowers and parties and desserts. He wanted to forgive Alabaster. He wanted to love Ebru forever. He wanted to build fans.

He was going to watch Sarcoline become the greatest dancer the world had ever seen.

Arna faced himself in the mirror: *The Dancer* surrounded by Golden Dragonflies. He had walked hand in hand with Ixxzal for years. He had witnessed truths and revered dread to the point that it was implanted on his face. He was an outsider who lived the difference between daring the universe and righteous fear of the ending world.

This time I tell them.

"You have always been amazing, Arna," Sarcoline said. "We need you. *I* need you."

Arna already knew the world was ending. He already knew that he was not the Chosen. He knew he could *die*. He had always known.

Visualize.

It was not a question on what he needed to be, but who he wanted to become. What did he want *after*? Lumak always said that vows were promises made to protect the future. The question that every Chosen got was not about what he could lose, because every Chosen could lose everything.

The cost of his choice was about everything he had to gain. It was not what he'd give, because he'd been given everything. It was what he'd take, what he'd reach for, and what he got after. The cost of his vow—the weight of it—was the world that he intended to make.

His vow would change everything, irrevocably.

The petal on his wrist burned away, like a spark of lightning. A shimmering white smoke rose. It circled around him.

[   ]

Start from the beginning.

"Follow me."

Arna carried two duffle bags, white and black, towards the entrance of the Vivicent manor. They were filled with his scrapbooks. He was not sure what he was doing, but his gut instinct told him that he needed to do this, in this way. He needed them to see. The only way that they were going to be able to stand by him was if they fully saw him: both the good and the bad.

"You are just going to need to trust me, that I'm doing *everything* I can to stay alive," Arna said.

They looked at his bags but before they could say anything, Arna was walking towards the front door.

"But," Arna said as they stepped out into the yard, "I need your help. I'm not sure what you can do to help protect me, but I think you can. We'll have to figure out how together."

"Where are we going?" Phlox called after him. He led them towards the buses without a single word. Everyone else refused to be quiet. They asked him questions and asked him to explain. Their chatter grew distant, like chirping birds in chorus, discussing, debating, and demanding answers.

All he cared for were the thrumming notes on his spine.

The End.

"Be comfortable with silence," Arna said in time with the pulsing panic, shaping it. "Be able to exist within silence."

Everyone stopped walking and stopped talking. They were surrounded by people who looked at them, confused as they went about their day.

"It is serenity. It is the story told in moments where sound cannot reach. We only think of it after it has passed: when it has come and gone." Arna directed the words to Ebru. "We long for it. We hide from it. We try to fill it when it is not void."

Finish.

"The moments we do not hear. . . are not lost," Ebru said hesitantly. "It is there in our imaginations, in our hopes, in our dreams. It is the proof, the support, the essence of what matters."

"Silence is not an absence," Arna joined Ebru to say in unison, "but a reminder of what you have."

Ebru fell silent, but Arna kept speaking. "Ixxzal is terrifying but kind. Just trust me."

He turned and continued to walk. This time as they followed there was not a sound. Instead, they were quickly sending messages to each other using the wrong group chat. He ignored the messages and led them to the train, across the city and ultimately to Ebru's house.

"Why are we here?" Ebru asked finally.

"We need your studio," Arna explained, motioning for him to open the door.

Ebru relented. They walked into the main hall of the house and Arna led them up the metal staircase shaped like vines. The white walls were sickening and pale.

"This is horrifying. You *live* here?" Ginger asked.

"Not for long," Phlox reminded her.

There were boxes everywhere, filled with their belongings, but Arna had faith that Ebru would pack up his studio last. He trudged up the stairs without waiting, and made his way to the studio. Inside it was as lush and green as the first time he'd ever been there.

He dropped his bags on the floor and got to business, moving things aside so there was enough room for everyone. He spoke to each plant as he did, asking for their forgiveness as he disrupted their home. Once there was enough space, he motioned the others in.

"Wow," Phlox gasped as she walked in.

"You can say that again," Aureolin said giddily, unable to hide her excitement. She rushed over to the plants examining them.

"Wow," Phlox repeated.

"Phlox, you might be the most brilliant person alive to take a facetious statement as literal. . ." Jasi said as they stepped into the room, the word catching on his breath, "fact."

"Woah," Ginger said as she and the others entered.

"This is your studio?" Rosmarinus asked, stepping in past them all and helping Arna move the last few plants. "It looks more like a garden."

"Yes. . . It's supposed to be private," Ebru grumbled. The only person who had ever been in it was Arna, but he could not care less. He turned on all of Ebru's speakers, the ones that could annoy their neighbors, and logged on to Ebru's computer.

"Can you tell us why we're here?" Amaryllis asked walking closer.

"Sit down." He shot her a look saying *don't you want to find out?* She bit back a smile.

Amaryllis was the first to sit, followed by the others, leaving only Ebru standing. Ebru walked closer to Arna. Arna pushed Ebru back until he sat down in the chair labeled 'Rosy.'

As the file loaded to open on Ebru's computer Arna walked over to his bags in the center of the room and began pulling out the scrapbooks. He handed them out until only Amaryllis was left without one in hand.

"These are for us?" Jasi asked as he opened it, then shook his head and looked closer. The others were all having similar startled and confounded reactions, flipping through the whole book quickly, staring at pages for too long. Rosmarinus looked the most confused, staring at his book and slowly realizing that Arna had not just been watching those he called friend, but Rosmarinus too.

I always saw you, Arna told him.

Rosmarinus' eyes fluttered with embarrassment as he flipped through the book.

"When I was on the run, I used to collect your stories. I found ways to get your pictures, clipped articles from newspapers, spent way too much money at printers, and I lined my walls in them," Arna said, waving his hands over the walls. "It was a constant reminder that I would one day come home. It was my inspiration to keep going, that if you could all become great, I could keep going."

Ginger looked up at him, heartbroken.

"And every night as I slept, I imagined you were there with me. And when I wanted to give up, I imagined that you were there to tell me not to. And when I was afraid, I didn't have to be, because your stories supported me. Your successes were mine. I would feel whole again."

Ebru wiped his eyes as he read, and Arna approached. Hearing the footsteps, Ebru oscillated. He was a phantom then corporeal: almost revealing but locked away. If Ebru would not give Arna his heart, Arna would give his to Ebru.

First, Arna typed on his phone and sent a list to the group chat.

"What?" Aureolin asked as the notification must have popped up for all of them.

"That's all of them," Arna said without looking away from Ebru. "All of them."

"And you won't make another one?" Ebru asked, eyes dazed as he read the message in his augmentation contacts.

"I can't promise that, but I'm going to try," Arna offered instead. "Everyone can hold me accountable."

"What are they?" Phlox asked.

"The accounts he used to fight with people online," Ebru answered for Arna. He tapped at his computer's keyboard and saved the list. "It won't stop his self-sabotage of reading hate comments, but it is a step."

Ebru blinked back into focus and gave Arna a long hard stare before saying, "You don't have to do this. We will love you even if you aren't the Chosen."

Arna turned his attention to the music file. He opened the filed Ebru had started to make with all the songs combined, with only six seconds in-between each song and twelve between each section.

"Incarnate Dreams is about following our dreams and making them come true. That's my revolution. I'm changing the world to let anyone be anything," Arna said to the others.

"Isn't that too shallow?" Amaryllis asked. None of the others said a thing, but as Arna looked over to them, there were similar looks of contemplation.

"The unknown inspires more than fear," Arna said. He pressed play.

The music of the twenty-five drifted through the speakers in a lull. Twenty-five was a moment of reprieve after the chaos of nightmares in Understanding. It was the moment of bliss before the nightmares retaliated in full.

Twenty-six was beautiful, and the most distant and dreamlike of all the songs. It flourished like a triumph of the heavens finally bringing peace to the planet. It was the Gods descending to save everyone from harm, to erase all pain, and to leave only hope.

Twenty-seven was the collapse and the return of the nightmares. It was dissonance trying to win, fighting to breathe, and ultimately transforming. Dreams and nightmares merged, becoming one: living in harmony, coexisting and supporting each other. Nightmares existed but they did not replace dreams. But dreams did not mean that nothing could go wrong. Everything could.

Paralysis was not an option. Giving up was not the solution. You simply had to hope that when everything could go wrong that it would go right. And live, in defiance of fate.

The song concluded. The others looked at each other in awe, excitement, chattering about what they heard and brimming with rivalry to learn the dances.

"There's a void," Ebru said, cutting off their excitement.

Arna heard it too. Despite what Ebru had done to make it fuller and richer than anything Arna ever could have done—despite it being perfect—it was wrong. There was a void within it: magnified and clarified.

"It's lacking something, but I don't know what," Ebru admitted, and Arna sat in Ebru's chair at the computer, looking at it. The others crowded into the room as Ebru tweaked at the song and played it; it was worse. He tried something else, and it was almost there, but too muddied.

"I don't *understand* it," Ebru seethed at the computer. "I'm better than this, but I can't get it to work."

"What are you talking about? It sounds perfect." Ginger complained.

"No," Ebru, Arna, Amaryllis, and Sarcoline all said at once. Ebru jolted and looked past Arna. Amaryllis tapped at her chin and Sarcoline stood with his eyes closed and arms crossed.

"Can you explain it?" Amaryllis suggested, leaning closer looking at the computer. "More?"

A swell of wind filled the room, dusting across Arna's skin. The others looked back into the main room where the plants were swinging. The dense mist of scents turned to a single one: saffron blooming.

It was time.

The End.

"The dances are complex, the complexity is what allows them to maintain the contract and refine it. We were taught that each of the dances must be able to be described in simple terms. The dedication and worship of the Gods. The new world and a new connection with the Gods. Accepting both horror and beauty in the world and surviving. Allowing things to end and new futures to develop. That while there are things we love, turning a blind eye to suffering cannot be tolerated. And the dedication to chase dreams." Arna leaned back in his chair staring at the computer, searching for the answer of how to fix the void.

"To Understand is to break down the complexity into simple terms," Sarcoline agreed by reciting their father. "And it can be broken down further, into one word."

"Worship, change, hope, worship, change. . . hope?" Ebru supplied.

"No. The way we're taught the root word is wrong. Worship, development, hope, memory, change. . ." Arna corrected. The word lingered on Arna's tongue like a welcomed memory, something sweet that he could no longer ignore. It burned him and cried to be heard.

"If not hope then what?" Ebru asked.

Now?

[Distant bells did not ring.]

Not yet. Instead of revealing his final truth he said, "Defiance."

Ebru's hands began shaking. All at once everyone looked at Sarcoline, but as if seeing each other for the first time, they examined each other.

"This song is for Arco," Ebru said.

"And Amaryllis and Ven, and Phlox, and Aureolin," Sarcoline added, understanding just as Ebru did.

"For Ginger and Jasi and Rus and Arna," Amaryllis squealed. "This song is about change, about being who we want to be."

"This song is for. . ." Ebru hesitated.

"You," Arna said. The creation date was the year they first started talking. The file name was 'for Alis.' Ebru met his eye with so much love and anger that Arna nearly kissed him but refrained.

He took Ebru's hand and said, "There were other ideas that I discarded; none were good enough. Everyone in this room led me to develop the complexities, that is true. But Incarnate Dreams began because of *you*."

[   ]

"That's romantic," Phlox giggled.

Without a word, Ebru pulled out his glasses from his pocket. He removed his augmentation contacts one by one and placed them into their protective case at his desk, before his eyes rapidly blinked. Whenever Arna ever saw Ebru with his glasses on, it meant that Ebru was ready to focus. He slid closer to the computer, glasses glowing.

"I always wondered why we were such oddities," Aureolin said amazed. "I get it now. It was fate."

"It's only coincidence," Phlox assured her.

Arna laughed, knowing there was no difference between the two.

"What was the original idea, before defiance?" Ebru asked clicking to the beginning.

"Sacrifice for dreams. That's ultimately what I gave you because I was certain I'd die. But we've already changed most of that to hope."

"Yes, and before that? Before me?"

"Before that it was a desire to help passions. It was more primal and based on my feeling of what I felt for dance. I started with anything that led me to a new idea, and my love for dance had led me there," Arna provided.

"So, like, just love in general?" Aureolin asked leaning on the chair behind Arna.

No. . . It was like. . .

"The desire and passion for dreams, the love of them," Arna disagreed as he elaborated. "When you care that much, your world spins. It's like you can't stand still, can't keep quiet. . ."

The lights flickered in the room, the computer as well. Everyone jumped but Arna laughed.

This was it. This was what was missing. . .

[*You've got this, darling!* Zaynir cheered.]

[*We're here with you, we always have been,* Pokk said.]

[*Finish it! Finish it! Show them the dream,* Lumak sounded relieved.]

He had added the complexity of the dreams. He had added the fear, the distrust, the worry, the nightmares. He had given them information on the desire for dreams: the passion for it and the love of it. He had led them through the music as if it weren't real.

But that was not all there was to dreams.

[*One more petal, Arna. We can do this together,* Azza encouraged.]

[*We love you,* Xeyaro soothed.]

"We need to add defiance into the music," Arna said.

"Yes, but how?" Ebru asked.

"Silence. More than just between the songs. There have to be breaks, pauses, gaps. It needs to destroy a person's focus." Arna spoke quickly, his heart in his throat. In the frenzy of inspiration, Arna did not care if he made sense. "It needs to make them think: What? Why? Where did the music go? So that I can lead them back in. I need the world to pay attention to what it means to see dreams in the physical realm."

He covered Ebru's hand with his own and pressed play. The first song started, the dance steps playing out in Arna's head. He clicked to stop and highlighted with the keyboard.

"That's the buildup," Jasi warned.

They'd have to restructure each and every song. However, dreams were not all action, all feeling. They were time carelessly spent, and silent progress. They were hope and sacrifice and the defiance of preestablished rules.

Ebru worked quickly, pulling the highlighted section to a new layer. He built up the space around the cut, played the thirty seconds three times then spliced it apart, deleted the rest, and hit play.

"It sounds so wrong," Phlox complained as the disjointed sound echoed through the speakers.

"This is it." Ebru was beaming. Arna let go of the mouse and Ebru worked furiously, typing commands into the keyboard, pulling up the sound archive from *Incandescent* and dragging clips in. He changed more, pulled more out, and replaced it.

He pressed play again and it was clearer.

Chapters were not lost; they simply did not cover what had not been memorable and let the audience guess at what had been erased. What remained was fuller, deeper, more important than what had been there before. In turn, the silences were more jarring, daring, and scarring, pulling the focus to Arna, who would dance.

Defiance rang out in every note.

Amaryllis and Sarcoline leaned against the table on either side of Arna and Ebru. Arna did a double take, confused how Amaryllis had gotten to the other side, but she winked at him instead.

"It needs more. . ." Sarcoline said as Ebru fixed it. "There should be less," Amaryllis suggested, and Ebru fixed it. "I need—" Each change was made before Arna thought it, as the others were saying it, as Ebru was already acting.

No one bothered them until Ebru pressed play and even the others heard it. Ebru dropped his hand to his lap. Sarcoline dropped to his knees. Amaryllis covered her face with her hands. Arna was shaking.

The dance unfolded before him in full clarity: the Ceremonial Garb, the mask, the fans, the music, the lights that he'd shape with his Blessings, the sound that he could warp around him, and the moves that would make dreams into reality. He saw it all now, in harmony, as clear as the screen before him.

"You are creating a coherent story, a focused lucid dream," Jasi said when no one else spoke.

"The world isn't ready for this, Arna," Rosmarinus spoke up with a hint of glee and sedated destruction, ready to tear down the system that contained them.

"Whether they're ready or not, it doesn't matter," Ginger disagreed. His sister's grin in the screen was wild and unashamed.

"It needs to be done by celebrations," Arna told Ebru, "Can we make it?"

Ebru pushed away from the desk and stared at Arna. The whole room went quiet as Ebru looked at him, with anger in every part of his expression: eyebrows raised, twitching lips, and flushed cheeks. The only sound in the room was the second dance that sounded hollow compared to the first.

Six long minutes passed.

"Please don't ask me to accept you killing yourself," Ebru said.

The End. The End. The End.

Everyone winced.

Saffron. Saffron. Saffron.

It's time.

"I'm not asking that," Arna assured him, taking both of Ebru's hands in his own. Despite everyone else in the room listening. Despite them all wanting to hear the words. Arna only addressed Ebru.

This would be simple. It was nothing more than the thousand late night in messages to the void. It was nothing more than spilling his heart out to someone who would always be there.

"Alis." Arna squeezed Ebru's hands. "I want this."

"We can give you a life after, even if you're not Chosen," Ebru insisted. "Your life doesn't just *end* because you aren't making the choice."

"I want a life after I've been picked to be Chosen," Arna assured him.

"Why?" Ebru's voice broke. "Why do you have to be the Chosen?"

"Why do you make music?" Arna asked him.

The answer unspoken: *Because it's my everything.*

"We can be your everything, Arna." Ebru squeezed Arna's hands back.

"Aureolin says that *I* am everything," Arna smiled softly at him.

"You are and—"

"Alis, I need you to listen now," Arna said, and Ebru closed his mouth. "For years I thought I was alone, but you proved to me that I'm not."

The room was silent, but the hushed breaths waiting for Arna to continue.

"I thought I had to do this alone, but you want to protect me. You want to support me. You want to fight for me. And you want me to live."

"More than anything," Ebru admitted. "You don't—"

"No listen." Arna cut him off.

When he didn't respond Arna said, "I did, once, want to sacrifice myself for this. But Amaryllis once asked me why I was so focused on dying. I didn't have to. Since then, all I've wanted was to live. To live for this. To live for you. To live. It was hard at first because I was certain I would die. But now

I want to defy my fate."

Now ask, Arna told him with his eyes.

"If you always knew you would die, then why. . ?" Ebru asked.

"Everything ends if I don't make this choice." Arna used the words he had tried, time and time again.

Saffron. Saffron.

Ebru grimaced at him, contemplating the words and not understanding them.

"Everything. Ends," Arna repeated. Wanting them all to know. The dragonfly mark froze like frost, the room temperature dropped, and Ebru's hands grew cooler as well. "That's my final secret."

"That everything ends," Ebru repeated.

Saffron.

"It's the end of the world. The apocalypse. Everything will be destroyed if I don't succeed." Arna nodded. "It has to be this year."

At first it appeared that none of them heard what he said. It was so silent in the room that a whisper would have sounded like a scream. Ebru's eyes furrowed, puzzled; then the gears began to turn. One by one every expression in the room processed the knowledge: confusion, apprehension, shock, wonder, fear, then brutal understanding.

Finally, every secret Arna held was no longer his to carry his own and the thudding in his spine became a hum between them all. Their vow mark began to shine purple like flower petals and orange like a spice. It glowed golden like a dragonfly at dawn.

A charge ran through the group, electrifying like a storm that was beginning to brew.

"*Everything* ends. . ." Sarcoline repeated, drenched in horrific sorrow.

They had not noticed because they never looked at the press or lived on the internet the way Arna did. They were oblivious to the change because their immediate world had not been affected and everyone was saying it was normal, that everything was the way it had always been.

But it was not.

"Everything," Arna repeated.

The scudding clouds became a vortex.

"You've lived with this, the whole time?" Ebru asked as the storms siphoned off his lungs, somewhere distant and horrid.

Arna slowly nodded, and the burden had been heavy. But with all of them at his side, it was a bit easier to bare. He was not alone in this. Not anymore.

"I think I understand Blue Rose Fears," Phlox whispered.

"Agreed," Aureolin and Ven said with Ginger.

"No one else can do it." Arna told Ebru, ignoring the others. "It's why I have to. It's me or nothing. The Gods are only connected to the world through me."

"But," Ebru choked.

"There has to be another way," Amaryllis said.

The room was filled with a cacophony of voices as verity rumbled like thunder.

The End. The End. The End. The End. The End. The End. The End. The End. The End. The End.

SAFFRON SAFFRON SAFFRON SAFFRON SAFFRON SAFFRON SAFFRON SAFFRON

Arna could not let them get distracted. He could not let it fall apart again. They already did that. He needed them to act.

"Listen to me!" Arna yelled at them all and a hurried hush fell. "I just need you to listen to me. I've gone over all of it. Every thought. Every option. I've had *years.*"

No one spoke as he breathed deeply, letting the rage in his chest guide him. Arna was a storm that burned until little doubt remained.

"When the Gods sent me back they told me they had no way for me to survive the dances, even if I succeeded," he said and Ebru released his hands. Arna snatched them back and before Ebru or anyone could retort he said, "But they said if anyone could find a way it was you."

Ebru froze.

"All of you. That if it were possible for me to live, I needed your help. That you were the only ones who could help me find that path."

"Us?" Amaryllis asked.

"Defiance." Arna repeated.

"We have to save the world?" Ven asked Arna, walking closer.

"No. I'll do that," Arna assured them all. "You just have to keep me alive, while I dance and then after I'm done. How you can do that without interfering with my dance, I'm not sure yet."

"No, Arna," Amaryllis disagreed. "That's what we mean."

The future grew bright, technicolor and real. Nine Saints heeded the call.

"You are *ours,*" Ebru said pulling Arna closer. "You will live."

Defiance was a storm, brewing on the horizon: unpredictable and frightening. Defiance was the song that called for the erasure of stagnation. Defiance was the golden dragonfly floating by the willow tree, showing the way. Arna was going to become the epicenter of the nightmare. He was going to become the genesis of a dream.

Arts and Nature are intrinsically tied, because both are within us all.
We are all a part of this world, and art is fundamental to it.
Xeyaro is the only true God of the mortals, the closest to the mortals.
It is why we dance, for through dance we are with them.
Through dance we can get to them all.

— On Xeyaro.

Dance 24

Rhapsody

Incarnadine

36 Xeyan

6 Days Left

"Has anyone ever told you, that for complete assholes, you are all still my best friends?"
"Gods and mortals as friends? That's a concept. We are your guides. Not friends."
"No. You're chaotic friends. It's less lonely that way."

In typical tradition, the thirty-fifth of Xeyan was the final day of set up, dress rehearsals for performances, and tech for all other technical displays and recordings. In traditional years, the celebrations for New Dawn Day were held on Xeyan 36, however, for the leap year, celebrations for the New Dawn were altered. This year rehearsals and tech took place over two days due to the intensive requirements to host the celebrations for six days.

Arna assumed that viewing it would have been spectacular. People spent decades preparing the technology and systems that would be used for the holocameras to capture the whole event. The DHS and Xeysis government had workers whose entire job was planning the event for the last three years. Apostle Week only came every thirty-six years, and it was when stories came to life. Arna would have loved to see everything being prepared, watching the workers, and the rehearsals of the displays. Unfortunately, he was banned from the Religious Circle until the celebrations began.

Guards surrounded every possible entrance, with nanotech fences that captured anyone who tried to cross in a static electrical cage until officials could have them escorted from the property. Despite his better attempts, Arna had been bared entry twice, and caught three times that morning. On the third time, when he was threatened with more punitive justice, he gave up and returned home to join the task force's meeting regarding the Ceremony of Chaos.

Arna had not asked much about his ban, other than demanding a reason that was met with a mix of looks of disdain. He assumed it had to do with fact that he was the Chosen that they did not choose, and they assumed, rightfully, that Apostle Week would be the time he'd declare himself. They did not want him messing anything up, which made him seethe.

"Arna." Jasi nudged him under the table as the meeting continued, much to Arna's dismay.

All Arna wanted to do was go see his friends practice. Instead, he was stuck in a stuffy, putrid-smelling room: alcohol, cigar smoke, sweat, and spite. All the mortals who did and could hate him were in the room. They were the very people who ignored him every time he tried to suggest a consideration for the Ceremony, when they were all talking about *him*.

"Cyclamen shall handle all affairs regarding the Ceremony of Chaos," Mr. Thyme said to Arna and Jasi, clearly indicating that he knew they weren't paying attention.

Arna glared at Cyclamen. The man sat smugly, dressed in his purple and silver suit buttoned up to the chin. The DHS always worked with the churches to establish control over the Weeping Stage during the Ceremony. It was not unheard of, but the declaration was suspect: choosing to give him the position while Zaffre was at mandatory dance-tech.

"Which is to say what?" Wenge asked as both Arna's mandatory guardian and Zaffre's appointed sit-in for the meeting. "The DHS has always controlled the Weeping Stage."

"This year," Mr. Thyme read his documents slowly. "Cyclamen shall be acting authority for the council and the state regarding all matters for the Weeping Stage. He shall ensure which dancers take the stage, when, and how."

Arna's eyes narrowed. This was how they wanted to play the game? When has he refused to play with their politics? When he refused to pay their taxes or listen to their requests?

"What do you think I'm going to do? Wreck the stage? I'm not allowed into the Circle," Arna snarked back.

"You will be allowed on the first day of Apostle Week, we have told you this," The Governor of Xeysis, Cider, assured him, despite the fact that it was the first time it was said at the meeting, and Arna had commented on it five times prior.

"Yes, yes, but I am not allowed near the stage at all?" Arna clarified.

"You will be allowed on the Weeping Stage for the group performance and that is all," Mr. Thyme corrected. Arna doubted there was any personal guard that would be able to drag him away from the stage, and if they tried, he would not let them.

"The Twenty-Seven Dances of Worship for the Knowledge, Adoration, and Understanding of the Six Gods must be completed in an orderly and controlled fashion," Cyclamen said with a soft voice that claimed innocence. "The storm conditions are too severe."

They were going to try to kick him off. How could he convince them that he needed to stay on? He did not want to get arrested, or worse, locked down. . .

[   ]

Good idea.

"The storm is no worse than the one in '96. Let alone the storm of '82. We may be operating in '96 conditions but we succeeded through it then and will now," Wenge quickly cut in. She used her authorial voice, as if saying she thought they were reckless with their decisions.

"We picked the dancers based on the storms in the past," Mr. Thyme agreed, as if he did not hear her scathing remark. "However, we must ensure our contingencies and safety matters are met."

"That was when the Blessing shields were stronger. We are still implementing the new technology to rectify the gaps. There have been serious damages this year," Governor Cider said.

"I will uphold the values and propriety of our order and by the God's divine light, ensure the Weeping Stage is not tainted." Cyclamen directed the words at Arna as if he'd flinch. "As soon as the Dances are set to begin, only necessary personnel will be allowed backstage."

"If you mean kicking me from backstage while my studio dances, you'd be remiss," Arna leaned forward from where he slouched in his chair, chin on his palm.

"Zaffre will watch the dancers as he has for years," Cyclamen reminded him.

"My father is an understudy. Besides Vivicent studio has six dancers. Per DHS rules, I must stand backstage," Arna smiled, and all at once the looks in the room shifted. For years, the Vivicent studio had been really only three members: Ginger, Sarcoline, and Zaffre. Zaffre had to be leader of the studio for the ceremony *and* a dancer. However, in traditional practice, the dancer was supposed to focus on nothing other than the dance that they'd be performing, and their studio master would worry about everything else.

As Zaffre was the master of their studio, when he danced as lead dancer, the task of managing the studio affairs during the Ceremony should have fallen to the next senior member. In a world where Alabaster had not left the Vivicent studio, it would have been him. However, he had, and he was stuck in the legal battle to break his Shadone contract, effectively tying him to no studio. Sarcoline was next in line as heir, but he was a dancer. After Ginger, Ebru, and Aureolin in seniority was Arna.

He was not officially certified in mastery in any of the dances through Understanding, but Arna was Zaffre's oldest student.

Cyclamen sat in his seat smoldering, unable to say a word. The other officials, who did not know DHS rules as well, glanced to him. Arna smiled at Cyclamen: *it does not matter what you try. I will be on that stage.*

"Especially in storm conditions such as these," Arna sat back, waiting for the man to explode. *Show your true colors.*

"Yes. . ." the man agreed with such audible rage that it made a few of the government officials turn to him in concern. "However. We will ensure that *no one* interferes with the sanctity of the Weeping Stage."

"Agreed." Arna stood. He addressed Mr. Thyme. "Are we done here? We have pre-celebration acts to complete."

"Yes," Mr. Thyme said with a shaken voice. Clearly they would have to talk about things when Arna was not in the room, to scheme about him further, but he and Jasi would do the same.

"I wish I could say I'm sorry for stealing the Hues," Arna said to Cyclamen as he headed to the door, "but I'm not."

Arna left without waiting for his mother or Jasi, and they both chased after him.

"They're going to try to stop you," Jasi said as soon as he caught up, walking in pace with Arna.

"Can you look over the management plans and ensure there are no new laws Arna might accidentally break if he steps onto that stage?" Wenge spoke and did not ask. It was an expectation, not a question.

"I'll study it." Jasi nodded sternly before adding, "We need to prepare for them to try to take him off backstage. I need access to all DHS rule books and will need to restudy them."

"Do you have the time?" Wenge asked, concerned.

"Between me and Rus, we should be able to get through everything, and I can always ask the encyclopedia if needed," Jasi said as they rounded the corner into the elevator.

"Encyclopedia?" Arna asked, arms crossed and leaning against the back as the glass elevator traveled through the air and down towards the bottom floor. He wasn't aware there was one online.

"Arco," Both Wenge and Jasi clarified at once, eliciting a chorus of laughter from all three of them. Of course, it was Sarcoline. The rest of the travel from the government center, back home, was spent discussing all the possible loopholes in the new contract that they had been provided in their emails through the task force.

There were stacks of white and silver crates outside of the house when they arrived. Nanotech and large robotic movers maneuvered the silver crates down the path past the few mortals who stood discussing and talking. Alabaster was wearing a short white cardigan over his plain, flowing white shirt and pants. There were large tables, furniture, and crates. There were plants in glass boxes being set down by the front path. The crowds had been cleared out thanks to the moving trucks, however reporters and cameras were stationed further down the street, recording the whole thing.

The guards let Arna, Jasi, and Wenge through as they approached.

"That all goes to the ballroom," Wenge directed the movers, looking at the furniture that needed to be stored until the Hue's had the manor back.

The movers nodded and tapped in the sky. The robots that were moving flashed green and continued as if nothing happened. Alabaster, looking worse for wear but almost well rested, greeted them.

"Hi, Wenge," he said, kissing her cheek as she kissed his.

"Welcome home," she said, walking into the house. Her voice echoed from inside as she yelled at the mover-bots. "This way. This way. The staircase over here has easier access."

"I'm going to go study this," Jasi said, walking inside and nodding at Alabaster. "Good to see you. Rus is making lavender salmon ravioli for dinner."

Arna came forward, too, anger bubbling in his stomach.

The man grinned, lethargic and sad. "Arna. Ebru said you're the one who helped us."

He awkwardly reached out for a hug but stopped short when Arna continued to level his glare at him.

Arna understood why he left. He understood that Zaffre had broken his heart and that they'd lost their home. He understood the dire straits that Alabaster was in trying to protect Ebru and himself, but he didn't accept it.

"Do you even know how much they hurt him there?" Arna asked, trying not to be hostile, but the knives lashed out in his tone. He was scathing, seething with an unspeakable rage of a near decade. Alabaster flinched. His lethargy disappeared and was replaced by shame and confusion.

"They hit him," Arna tried again.

"I know that now, but Ebru didn't tell me," Alabaster said as if that made it any better, as if that excused him for not noticing.

You didn't even see your own son for years! Arna wanted to scream.

Ebru had been left alone to the point of wishing he wasn't alive anymore. Yet, he insisted that Alabaster was a good father, that he was too stressed and that he was struggling to do what they needed to do. Alabaster was hated, struggled to make money, and had to do things for Cyclamen that he regretted. All Arna wanted was to hurt the man before him.

"How long were you fucking Cyclamen?"

Alabaster expression shifted between six different ones in seconds: confusion, shock, anger, fear, regret, then anguish. They all traveled through his eyes and his twitching mouth. The man's shoulders slumped in defeat.

"It doesn't take a genius to understand that you were," Arna pressed. "You lived at one of his houses that he was always at and kept it a specific way to please him. Did he convince you to entertain others?"

Arna did not mean to say the words to shame or admonish Alabaster. He just had to know: What were the work trips that Alabaster was always on? Why were there always people that Alabaster was meeting that he'd never introduce Ebru to? For years Arna had thought that Alabaster was sleeping around and didn't want Ebru to know. It made Arna furious that Alis' father was neglectful and too focused on his life to notice Alis. Knowing Alabaster, it was an impossibility, unless he was being coerced.

Alabaster was considered one of the most eligible bachelors for decades before he'd knocked up the woman who gave birth to Ebru. She said she loved Alabaster and wished to marry him. She stole much of the Hue's money, using a seven-year-old Ebru as her justification to move it to her bank accounts. Alabaster trusted her, naive as he was at the time. She ran away with almost all of it. Zaffre had to help Alabaster try to find her to get it back. From what Arna understood they never did.

She vanished.

Alabaster had always believed in the best in people, believed that people could change and be better. He believed that no matter what, people were ultimately good. It was why he got used so often. It was why Arna could not hate him for taking Ebru away from Zaffre when Zaffre became a drunk. If Alabaster was pushed that far, then his father had been irredeemable.

"Cyclamen did not force me to do anything I did not agree to," Alabaster said in a voice that was neither confident nor convincing.

It did not mean that Cyclamen did not force it. The man was not above beating Ebru when he disappointed him. He was not above allowing bullying in his studio. He was a man whose philanthropy overshadowed all of the more horrific things that he did, as if that could purify his sullied reputation.

"I did everything I could to protect him." Alabaster was attempting to convince himself more than Arna.

It pissed Arna off to no end that even if it was all real—the abuses, the corruption, the manipulation of authority—that none of it would matter. People would still love Cyclamen and forgive him and say that things couldn't be as bad. They'd say that others were simply over reacting. They'd insist that the Vivicent Family had a specific vendetta against the Shadones.

It might take some of Cyclamen's power, but the men in high places were already in his pocket: giving him complete control over the Weeping Stage.

It would not matter, but that did not stop Arna from wanting to expose it anyway. After he danced, he'd make sure that Cyclamen saw justice.

"You failed," Arna said, softer, anger dissipating. The years of bubbling rage reduced to a simmer and directed where it needed to be. It was not meant for another victim, but at the perpetrator.

"I know." Alabaster hung his head. His arms trembled as his breathing grew ragged. The man was struggling to keep it together, in whatever anguish and pain and disappointment he felt for himself.

For all his faults, Alabaster loved Ebru more than anyone in the world. Most days, Ebru loved his father more than he loved anyone, save Arna. It was why Cyclamen was able to use them against each other so easily. The two would do anything for each other even if it meant facing the rest of the world alone.

Arna was not sure when he could forgive Alabaster, not this week and maybe not any time soon. However, he didn't need to forgive Alabaster for now. Some people needed apologies and forgiveness, others did not. For Arna, he only needed to know that Alabaster was trying to fix everything that he'd done wrong, because he had not done it in malice. He hadn't even been incompetent. He had been negligent and made one too many mistakes, but he was trying. Arna accepted it and trusted Alabaster to change.

The bridge would be healed. It may take time, but Arna was willing to put in the effort. The man who truly deserved Arna's ire was Cyclamen, not Alabaster nor Ebru. They were just trying to survive.

Slowly Alabaster stopped shaking and gazed up at Arna, determined to take on any of Arna's frustration and rage that remained. As mint met black, Arna thought of the man who had first taught him how to properly hold a fan while dancing. Alabaster read Arna children's books, patched up his scratches, and snuck him sweets when Wenge and Zaffre weren't looking. This was the man who taught him how to use his Blessings. He was the one who danced scary stories to make the Golden Generation laugh and scream. He was the man that Arna loved deeply.

Arna hugged Alabaster, crossing the distance in one motion. "This time, I'll help you protect him, uncle. Welcome home."

Alabaster slowly crumbled onto Arna as the hug grew tighter, urgent and desperate. There were years of secrets tied up in Alabaster's body, mind, and heart. Arna was not pressured by it. He welcomed it, for the burden of healing could be shared. One day Arna would know the true extent of what Cyclamen did to Alabaster, and in time things would be better. But for now, this was what mattered. They were broken, but they were now all home.

"Did I miss something?" Ebru asked, startling Arna. He found Ebru walking over from behind the delivery truck, headphones on, eyeing them both. He was dressed in his practice attire.

"Why are you back? You have rehearsal," Alabaster asked, confounded why Ebru, a member of the DHS small council, would even be allowed to leave.

"Cut early. Told them we have dinner plans. I only have one dance for the Ceremony, and I requested to go first. I have music to work on," Ebru said nonchalantly, with a clear disregard to his position.

"Ebru. . ." Alabaster sighed, more authoritative and fatherly in his tone. "This is a punishable offense. You can get kicked off the council. You are required to be on premises for the entirety of the show and rehearsal. The dinner tonight is negligible."

"It's not. And the music is more important." Ebru shifted his weight, hopping between both feet and looking ready to bolt at the single inclination something was wrong. He searched for an answer, between the two, glancing back and forth repeatedly.

"I was welcoming him home," Arna supplied.

Ebru stopped shifting nervously, put his headphones back on, and brushed past both of them, hurrying inside the house without another word.

"I do not know what has gotten into him recently. All he's been doing is locking himself in his room," Alabaster sighed, disappointed.

"He's working on my Variation music, and I sprung a lot of changes on him yesterday," Arna admitted. Arna had given Ebru all the cuts that had to be made and now it was Ebru's job to make it shine.

Between him refining the music and the others rushing to help Arna finish his mask and clothes, they were consistently in discussions. The group chat was constantly gaining notifications as Sarcoline came up with solutions and the others refuted them. Sarcoline was doing the heavy lifting of trying to find the path to Arna's survival but Arna knew they were all invested in coming up with a plan.

Alabaster froze and turned back to Arna, obviously in disbelief.

"Speaking of which, if he's back, and he's working on it, that means I need to as well. We only have six days left." Arna considered his options, and grabbed a few of the plants that were free from a box, shouting back at Alabaster, "Also, I'm sleeping in Ebru's room until further notice!"

Arna did not linger to hear a response.

Arna found Ebru hovering in the doorway to Arna's room on the third floor. Headphones around his neck, staring into the darkness, Ebru was frozen. Arna hesitated to approach him. As decided, they were going to turn Arna's room into Ebru's studio and use Ebru's bedroom as their own. Arna had forgotten, unfortunately, that his room was a mess.

"Is this why you never come in here?" Ebru asked without addressing Arna.

"It's not as bad as it looks," Arna offered. He glanced inside to the disaster that awaited within.

Everything was as it was when it first happened: shattered furniture stacked in a corner, a ripped up mattress sat on the floor and walls littered with holes and slashes from the Blessing backlash.

"How did we not *hear?*" Ebru did not try to walk inside. He instead focused on the candles that were lit in the corner, hovering precariously over the rubble that remained. They flickered like they were living off dying batteries, in and out.

"Where do you want your plants?" Arna asked trying to change the subject. Instead, it gave Ebru the confidence to enter the room. Arna raced after, heart in his throat.

"Put that down and help me. We're getting this all out," Ebru said, placing his stuff down and lifting the mattress. Arna did as he was told.

Together the two lifted it up—old, torn, and falling apart—outside to where Wenge and Alabaster were talking.

"Arna," Wenge gasped as soon as they got out of the house. "Please don't tell me you and Ebru. . ."

"I promise you, this isn't my fault," Ebru said as he pushed the mattress out into the lawn, grabbed some plants, and headed back inside. Arna stood awkwardly facing his mother's punitive stare.

"It's from my panic attack," Arna tried to explain but neither of them looked convinced.

"Am I the last one to find out that our sons are dating?" Alabaster asked Wenge. She laughed.

Embarrassed and not wanting to have any sort of talk about his and Ebru's sex life, Arna grabbed another plant and hurried into the house, cheeks flushed. As if a battle had never been waged, the house was pristine and perfect, with the lingering scent of drying paint.

Ebru chuckled at Arna's fluster as soon as he got back upstairs. Together they transferred all of Arna's clothes and personal items to Ebru's room before removing the broken furniture.

All the while the notifications in the group chat skyrocketed.

imgoingtodiejustlikesaffron.

Ebru placed his hand on Arna's back, and after a moment of breathing together, Arna was able to move again. The hum between them was electric: the panic shared between them.

They'll find a way, Ebru's mint eyes said.

For now, they had to focus on the task at hand.

"The walls are already a mess, so the sound boards should work well in here. It's a different set up from my last studio, but it will work." Ebru pointed out where things would be and sent Arna over an 3D model of the room that had been captured by nanotech while they cleaned up the mess.

Arna opened it and the image overlayed over the real room in a holographic teal. Ebru, holding out his hands, began to mark the walls and sketch out what he was planning. After determining exactly where things would be placed, they got to work. With the help of the mover-bots, they got all of Ebru's instruments, his computer, and all of his plants upstairs. Everything was piled up in boxes, with no display or shelves. Only his computer was turned on and speakers hooked up.

Ebru said nothing more as he began to work, and Arna looked at the layout again. Sighing, he went to order the supplies and the labor necessary to set up the room for them later that night.

"I might not have this done until the day of," Ebru warned Arna from his desk, leaning back and pressing play to hear his changes. "I'm trying, I am, but between the celebrations, helping Arco, and my DHS responsibilities, it will be tight."

"It's okay. Lumak once told me that Watsonia gave the sheet music for her variation to the performers the night of. And that Sable did something similar, but their sheet music was completely unreadable because it was raining, so he had to guide them with his Blessings as he danced. The music is less for us, and more for the viewer and future dancers. I was taught how to use my Blessings to weave and shape the music to my will," Arna explained, thinking of all the times he'd danced without any sound but the pops of candles.

"You can do that?" Ebru asked, amazed. His head tilted backwards, examining Arna in a new way.

"Only while dancing the variations," Arna offered with a laugh, a bit nervous now that it was said. "This song will be on a digital file, it'll be fine."

"And you need it. . ." Ebru agreed, focusing again. The truth unspoken: because Arna would be losing his Blessings progressively over the night. "I'll get it done."

There was a brief moment when things were normal, but Arna understood that they weren't.

Giving Ebru a twice over, Arna recognized the tension in Ebru's shoulders and the way that he held his mouse too tightly. Arna walked over and leaned against the chair. He wrapped his arms around Ebru and rested his chin on Ebru's head. "I'm still here."

"Don't," Ebru said, clicking furiously. "I'm trying to believe you can survive. I *really* am. I want to believe that we can find a way but. . . but it's hard to believe it when the facts are right in front of my face."

"I love you."

"That makes it worse," Ebru grumbled. Arna spun the chair around, forcing Ebru to look at him. Arna pushed his knee between Ebru's thighs and held Ebru's arms down on the arm rests.

Their eyes locked in a fierce battle of fears: Ebru with the realizations that Arna had years to comprehend and accept. Arna with the fear of Ebru pushing him away. The hum between them grew in intensity, as Arna's own fear of death mixed in. They breathed in disjointed harmony, until Ebru's eyes began to water.

"I will not cry," Ebru said holding it back.

"I think you should," Arna suggested leaning closer.

"No," Ebru said, willing his eyes to dry. He glared harder, frown setting deeper.

"I won't be like your mother." Who left him when he was seven. "Or Ven." Who yelled at him and blocked him before regretting it for years. "Or your father." Who left him in a pit of vipers.

"No. You'll just be you, the boy who ran away," Ebru snapped viciously, like a wounded animal afraid of dying. "You would choose to leave me again in a heartbeat."

"When I find you, we'll get married, and I'll never let you out of my sight." Rosy, had told Alis that years ago. "Be mad at me, because it's my fault, due to the Splintering. You don't have to touch me. You don't have to look at me. You don't even have to love me. Just help me."

"Don't say that," Ebru muttered under his breath, clearly not caring if Arna understood him. "We are going to save you. But we have no way how, no matter what research Sarcoline has made, it's terrifying. We're only ten people and we don't have nearly the same amount of Blessings as you."

"When I get scared, I think of the future, of our future. It makes me feel better."

"What's the point of dreaming of a perfect world if you're not there with me?" Ebru asked, soft as a shadow after sunset. "Surviving would be a miracle."

Arna smiled gingerly, leaning in slowly and ensuring the kiss was as light as a feather. "I've stood in a superstorm and survived, Ebru. For six minutes. I'm the only person who ever has."

Arna kissed him: feathers falling to the ground, a symphony before death.

"I'm the only person who survived the Ludiel train crash."

Arna kissed him: feathers like snow, dusting the ground in the most beautiful display he'd ever seen.

"Frankly, this scares me less now that I have all of you helping me. Because I've trained my whole life for it."

Arna kissed him: like transforming mirages into tangible beings, pulling them out from behind mirrors.

"I know miracles are real."

There was a soft few seconds where their breaths merged and turned to ghosts. Arna released the death grip he held over Ebru's arms, which snaked around Arna's neck. Eyes closed and trusting him, Arna let Ebru guide him to what he wanted. When Ebru kissed him it was furious, hungry, and hot.

Anger bled through their lips as Ebru bit at him. Sorrow drenched their bodies as they melted. Pain seeped into every crevice where they did not touch: tumbling to the floor, meeting broken glass that had not been cleaned. Anguish accompanied them, in the hollowed breaths that they gasped, as their souls screamed.

They were all dressed in white, light, and flowy outfits, soft in the summer sun. They walked together, talking about the celebrations the next day. Ginger talked to Alabaster as she had not in years. Phlox spun around, showing off how her iridescent dress glittered. Ebru took Arna's hand as they walked, leaning close to him. Ven and Jasi discussed how to get Arna out of breaking the new temporary law that only authorized dancers could step on the Weeping Stage. Rosmarinus carried the food with Zaffre. Wenge and Aureolin helped Mymy who chastised Wenge. Amaryllis' parents and brother joined the group, as did Honeysuckle's mother and Honeysuckle herself.

All the while, the hymn of the end was a chorus of hums punctuated by a continuous set of messages sent by quick fingers. In the eyes of all those who knew was a stern determination to save the world.

In the light of the late afternoon, they carried baskets to the Cathedral Forest on Xeysis' third petal, the sixth largest forest in Xeysis, and the only one that was set directly above the Cathedral of the Apostle. They found their way to the lake where others were enjoying their picnics and in every direction—spinning, flying, glittering, and glowing—were dragonflies. They danced across the surface of the lake, spun in the air that flowed through the canopy above.

The group found a tree to sit under, laid out their blankets, and began to eat. There were rose cakes, cucumber sandwiches, lavender salmon raviolis, blueberries, and frozen grapes. There were lemon squares, stuffed mushrooms, avocado, oranges, and heavier proteins to fill up the dancers before the celebrations. Ebru's portable speaker played Ivumalis music, soft and peaceful. Each song on the playlist were ethereal and light.

It was the single moment that Arna craved, one that was filled with nothing but talks of life: his coming of age ceremony, Ginger's future classes, and Phlox's next movie. There was no talk of the past. For a moment they were all in a standstill.

It was a tradition, a final prayer before the next year: a thanks to all that had come before. It was a welcoming of the future. It was not a reprieve, but a direct rejection of paralyzing terror.

It was resistance by joy.

"We have two rooms," Wenge told the group. "Honeysuckle, you and your mother will be with us."

Honeysuckle nodded, not seeming to understand that that meant she should be with the parents, whereas the Golden Generation would be in a room together. Whether or not it would bother her in the future was not much of a concern to Arna either as she talked with Amaryllis' little brother.

"Look, Saffron," Honeysuckle said, holding out a chain of twisted flowers.

The boy smiled and held his own up. The two laughed as they exchanged the chains. Ebru left Arna sitting alone next to Sarcoline to get more food.

Saffron, Amaryllis' little brother, had her straight black hair, but cropped short on his head. He had the same dark brown skin as his sister. Unlike her, he had dark brown eyes, and an augmentation for a left leg. The boy wore shorts in the summer, and the skin-colored leg did not appear any different, save the glittering white marks that rippled through it like additional veins. They were only visible as he moved.

"It's his third one," Sarcoline said to Arna. "The first two failed over time, because of Blessing rejection. Without any of his own Blessings, his body gets really sick from the tech."

Arna nodded and a notification popped up before him. He opened it. There was a passcode and room number sent to him by Cardinal White.

"I messaged Cardinal White about practice rooms," Sarcoline gave the answer to the question that Arna did not ask. He was, however, not the only one on the message: Sarcoline was, too.

"Thanks." Arna closed the notification, and another popped up, a request from Sarcoline. Arna opened it and he found a list of all of his Blessings as well as the others. It was followed by a document called: PLAN25.

"This is the current plan. There are too many variables in the Blessing plan," Sarcoline told him. "I've gone over your Blessings. I've gone over all the legends. I've gone over what sort of healing you'll need. But, I can't figure it out: what order you'll lose them in. Without that, we had to change focus to the weather. It's not as good as the Blessing based plan but I assure you I'm going to pull as many all-nighters as I need to figure it out."

"Oh." Arna quickly started typing his Blessing as a list in the document, indicating the order that had been drilled into him for years.

"What? You *know?*" Sarcoline gaped.

"When I dance, I won't have the time to process the thought. The Gods determined it and they have made me repeat it until I memorized it. They'll take them in that order," Arna explained, finishing the order and looking over it again to verify. He placed the 'safe' Blessings in their own category, with A.Reverence as the 'must keep.'

Sarcoline said nothing, staring in open-faced shocked at Arna. As Ebru sat back down, Sarcoline chuckled deeply and fell back.

"What's wrong?" Ebru asked.

Sarcoline shook his head, and pressed his hands into his eyes.

"Arna!" Honeysuckle called.

"Yes?" Arna willingly took the opportunity to scoot closer to the two, trying to ignore the hysterics that his brother had fallen into. Amaryllis and Rosmarinus quickly jumped in but Sarcoline could only laugh at their questions.

"When we get our Blessings, will we be able to fly?" Honeysuckle asked. "The dancers always look like they're floating. Will we be able to?"

Arna glanced at Saffron, who nodded. Both had large, wide eyes: expecting magic.

"Blessings are all internal gifts, and while they have external results at times, they usually are only activated through your body or mind," Arna explained. The two tried to process the information.

"We can't control water? But when Ginger dances, it always looks like the air becomes water as well," Honeysuckle debated him.

"That's an illusion, from the fans and Blessings," Ginger clarified.

"We can't bend the elements?" Saffron asked, scandalized. He turned to Amaryllis in betrayal, who simply shrugged. He whipped his head back to Arna. "Will I still be able to dance on the Weeping Stage? I really want to. I'm certain that once I get my Blessings, I'll be able to. I know I'm not good enough to join the studio, but I'll try really hard."

Before Arna could answer, Honeysuckle took Saffron's hands and nodded furiously. "Yes. Of course. Did you know that Sarcoline first started dancing Holly when he was five and hurt himself so badly he was nearly never able to dance again?"

Arna was not sure how that rumor had spread, as it was factually untrue. Sarcoline had gotten into an accident, unrelated to dance.

"But why not?" Amaryllis cut in, pointedly towards Arna. "We can always believe in a bit of magic. Who knows? Maybe the Blessings will change everything."

Whether it was another one of Sarcoline's assessments that he told her about, or a lucky guess of her own, Arna was impressed. Arna contemplated it for a moment, attention drifting outwards towards the lake where the dragonflies danced in the wind, water, and light.

All of the Blessings changed each variation. Who was to say that he could not give them power over the elements? The superstorms were a byproduct of divinity and powered by broken taboos. A combination of internal and external powers expanding on what they already had would not only sever the connection people had to preexisting expectations, but provide additional opportunities they did not have before.

Arna had never thought of how he wanted the Blessings to look. He'd assumed that was something the Gods decided. But for a moment he dreamt of a future, where they too danced with the elements in tandem and harmony. He was already weaving a world into dreams, adding a bit of magic would not be so strange. If the Gods were the elements, why not mortals?

"Arna?" Zaffre called to him after one too many long minutes of staring into nothing. His father looked haunted and tired. All of the others were showing concern, as if he'd slip through their fingertips again. The hymn between them was loud and most of it was not from him.

"I want to dance in the dragonflies," Arna said, eating a piece of cantaloupe. He stood and motioned for them to follow: all of them this time, Ebru included.

"Me too?" Saffron asked.

"All of us," Arna agreed.

"We're part of the Golden Generation now," Honeysuckle declared to Saffron, hand in hers.

The Golden Dragonflies stood. Jasi and Rosmarinus were dragged out by Phlox and Ginger. Ven and Amaryllis walked with Saffron and Honeysuckle. Aureolin pushed Ebru while he protested. Sarcoline walked in time with Arna, saying nothing. They all smiled bright in the colors of the universe. Sanctified elements began to spiral through their fingertips.

Arna was hyper aware of all those who turned their attention to the group as they walked closer to the lake and deeper into the dragonfly storm. The insects swooped around Arna, through and around his legs and arms. They landed on him as he walked. The others held out their hands as the dragonflies swarmed around them haphazardly.

"What song?" Ebru asked.

"Do you have a song that works for this?" Arna could not think of any off the top of his head.

Ebru contemplated for a moment and played a song that Arna had not heard in full. There was one project he'd forgotten they'd been working. With everything that had happened and changed, Arna was surprised it was finished..

Cinth's vocals began first, deep and low. The breathy and soft baritone voice almost whispered into the air like a wish. The orchestra was rounded with it, airy and fluttering like wings dancing.

"*Incandescent. . .*" Arna said as the music began to swell. Ebru smiled.

"It took forever to edit between projects, but it's done," Ebru said, placing his mobile in his pocket and waiting for Arna to begin.

When Bluebell's voice sounded, powerful and full, it paired with Cinth's vocals in a contrary harmony. The others may not have been ready, but Arna was. He spun: A.Reverence guiding him. Despite having never heard the song in full, Arna stepped into the rhythm.

He made it a partner dance, meant to be danced in a circle. It was a set of six moves and six steps, before they turned around each other and spun to their next partner in the circle. Twelve bodies would rotate in twin circles, in two separate directions. He grabbed Ebru first, coming up with the moves on the fly, trusting Ebru to move as if they shared a soul.

On the first rotation through the moves, the adult dancers were dancing with him, and by the second the others joined: a bit chaotically and stumbling through the moves, but they tried.

Ginger guided Jasi, as Ven guided Rosmarinus. Honeysuckle and Saffron picked up on it faster than even Amaryllis, who struggled to understand despite Phlox, Aureolin, and Sarcoline helping her. The group danced around and around each other, bubbling in delight and triumph.

Arna and Sarcoline met as the partners changed again in the third rotation. The two brothers danced against each other, one with A.Reverence and the other without. Their hands rose, held apart by an invisible barrier.

Black met brown, held in eternity.

They were
> mirrors facing each other.
> lives that could have been.
> moments that could have happened.
> just two boys who would never be loved by the Gods, in a sea of Children who were.

livelivelivelivelivelive

"They love you," Arna told Sarcoline, who tilted his head confused.

Despite what the world said, despite what anyone else thought. The Gods did not only love their Children. They loved all mortals, and they especially loved Sarcoline, just as they adored Arna.

Arna spun away from Sarcoline to Ginger, who smiled at him. Arna caught Sarcoline's eyeing him, but Arna did not care.

livelivelivelivelive

The dragonflies were dancing with them.

> They glided about without swarming and formed two lines with the dancers.

They weaved

in

and

out,

back

and

forth

like the mortals moved.

And when the dancers spun,   the dragonflies spiraled as well.

As the dancers switched spots and around the circle,

the dragonflies crossed paths

all around

before they stabilized in a new location.

It was a complex pattern of trust and support, all without touching. A storm honed by wishing.

livelivelivelivelivelivelivelivelivelivelivelivelivelivelivelivelivelivelivelivelivelivelivelivelivelivelivelivelivelivelive

When the song came to an end, Ebru and Arna faced each other again.

The dragonflies spun around them and with the wind they flew off from the lake into the air. In the glittering sky was the center of the rose, bright with city lights. The sky rails crossed overhead, twinkling like spiderwebs as the dragonflies floated around and through the artificial clouds. They flew past the blue and disappeared into the haze of the illusions.

"Where did they go?" Amaryllis asked.

"Gathering wishes," Arna said. He didn't know if it were true, but he believed in miracles.

Arna leaned against a tree as the others talked, looking deep into the woods, shaded and dark in the fading light of the false sun. There were a few hours left before the celebrations began for Apostle Week. It was just a few short breaths before chaos descended.

The hymn of panic was swelling amongst them all, and the messages in Arna's agumentations had reached the thousands. He refused to read them.

Trust in them.

"Come with me," Sarcoline called to Arna as he walked past, not waiting for Arna to follow him. He stalked into the forest and away from everyone, his backpack in his hand. Arna hesitated.

"Go with him," Amaryllis said from behind. When he turned, he found her watching the other clean up. "We'll be here when you return."

Arna did not need to be told thrice, so he jogged to catch up to Sarcoline. They walked for what started as minutes and turned into what felt like hours, until they came to a slight clearing. The trees were tall, with dark summer leaves. The rich earthy scents spoke of life and the memory of a time long before. The dirt was soft and littered with strangely blooming saffron flowers. For some reason, the holly was still in bloom as well: bright red berries up throughout the clearing.

"This is where I met Amaryllis," Sarcoline said, standing and pointing towards the center. "She was there dressed in a thin green dress. She says that when I found her, I saved her. I doubt that's true, Amaryllis doesn't need anyone saving her. But perhaps it is more like how you saved Ebru. He didn't need you to, but he took your hand when you gave it."

"She took yours?" Arna stepped up to his brother.

"I never offered it." Sarcoline shook his head and dropped his bag. "Who loves me?"

"The Gods," Arna clarified.

"I'm not a Child." Sarcoline squashed a flower in the dirt with his shoe, angrily.

"That doesn't stop them from loving you," Arna said as Sarcoline lifted his foot and the flower still remained.

The two of them breathed in unison without looking at each other. Arna thought of Ebru, and how it was more like they saved each other than anything else. Arna had a feeling it was the same for Amaryllis and Sarcoline.

"She scared the living shit out of me when I found her here. I didn't think anyone would be this deep into the woods at two am," Sarcoline admitted, crossing his eyes and sighing.

"Why were you here?" Arna asked, but it was a silly question. Sarcoline was there to dance.

"I found out that she's not, in fact, some nightmare monster, but a rather clingy girl who, once she started talking, would not shut up." Sarcoline sighed dramatically. "Absolutely harmless and such a soft person that it's almost concerning."

"Soft. . .? Amaryllis is terrifying, Arco," Arna cackled.

People avoided her eyes because she saw everything and peered directly into soul. She said things that cut right to the bone and could read a person to filth without blinking. Amaryllis could break a person down and rebuild them in a series of words as if she was doing little more than planting flowers.

The saffron at their feet was almost a path, forming in the shadows of the trees and fading light.

"No. She's soft." Sarcoline did not elaborate any further. Leaves blew around them, creating an echo of rustling, almost like unspoken conversations. "Are they here?"

Are you?

[   ]

Arna felt the reaction more than he heard it. He felt the weakness, the exhaustion, in his body. The rustling grew louder, reminding him that they were listening, that they were there, that they were watching, and they were waiting. They carried themselves through the trees, taking the earthy scent and mixing it with sea salt and ash. It wafted on a glittering wind that sparkled like gemstones.

"Yes," Arna said, wishing they'd conserve their energy. They had given him the tools to get here. His friends would ensure that he'd thrive after it was done.

"What do the petals represent?" Sarcoline asked.

"Before I can answer the question, I have to understand it." Arna grabbed his wrist and rubbing his thumb across the remaining petals. On his other wrist was the dragonfly mark, fluttering its wings, ready to take flight. He could tell Sarcoline the truth. "Understand the question, understand the weight of the answer, accept the answer even if I'm wrong."

The wind brushed past them both, sending Arna's hair flying and Sarcoline's jacket flittered about him.

"You have to be able to accept that your choice could be wrong?" Sarcoline asked, so softly Arna almost didn't hear.

"If I can't make the choice with my whole being, without any doubt, then I will fail at getting through twenty-six," Arna clarified, no longer feeling the pressure of that choice. Strangely, it was no longer his solitary burden anymore.

"But if you make the wrong choice, that's it. You get no second chance. How can you just accept that you could be wrong, if you won't know that you are until you dance?" The extreme uncertainty started to eat at Sarcoline. "What if we can't save you?"

"What if I fail and end the world?"

Sarcoline hesitated to nod.

"Saffron started the apocalypse with the Shattering. Ilex did what he could to resolve it, containing the storms."

Brown eyes asked, *who?*

"The Chosen before Ilex," Arna explained. "The failed Chosen before Ilex."

"Right," Sarcoline blinked as if remembering, "How did he fail?"

"He rejected Divinity?"

"How?"

"I don't know. It was an accident."

Sarcoline's brow furrowed asking the same question Arna always had, *how does one reject Divinity?*

"I don't know," Arna sighed. "All I know is that I have to try or everything ends."

"And it has to be this year?"

"Yes."

Arna slowly faced his brother, who turned in time with him. The two of them were clones of different ages, twins shaped by circumstance.

"I need you to dance and live, Arna. Not because you have to save the world but. . . Without you, without Incarnate Dreams. . ." Sarcoline said with a broken voice and a half smile torn in pure desperation. "I will be nothing."

Sarcoline faced Ixxzal in the body of Arna, asking to be heard, and speaking into the abyss when he knew better than to ever do so.

Arna spoke back, "You never needed me, Arco. I might be your guide, but you fought for everything with your own two hands."

"Everything changes after your dance."

Arna was unsure how to help his brother. "I am just the spark, Arco. Not the movement."

Saffrons stirred as lightning sparked between them, threading into the bones of mortals.

"I know. Okay? I know that once the Variance is declared we have to work. I get it." Sarcoline picked up his backpack and shoved it at Arna. "I know you just get a new salary, have to do speeches, and have to dance. I know that nothing really changes. Not unless we make it happen."

Arna unzipped the backpack to find folders, binders, cases filled with drives and disks, filled with what Arna could only assume were for him. He pulled out a folder and opened it up to see contracts, highlighted laws with annotated notes. Arna flipped through them. Sarcoline had rewritten the laws, pointed out the inconsistencies, and tried to find anything that could be changed.

In another folder were architecture notes, new ideas for schools, and plans for Blessing reform. Sarcoline had no idea what Arna's path would be. He didn't know the message, but he suspected that Arna would need support. There were contacts and lists of facilities they could use and trust.

Then there was a binder filled with Arna's face printed across the years. There were articles asking if he'd been seen. They were things Arna had never seen about himself.

"You were tracking me?" Arna asked him.

"Just as you were tracking us. I knew you'd need help, and I swore I'd never let you make a vow without my help again," Sarcoline said, pulling at his shirt and lifting it to expose his waist where a mark of a vow lay bare, like a large rotating rose. It was so massive it traveled below his pants. It was something Arna had never known him to have.

When?

The answer was when Arna was ten, when Sarcoline had stopped taking baths with Arna and demanded that Ginger let him dress himself. A five year old child had made a promise that he could never break. The two of them were tied intrinsically, through life and death in perpetuity.

Before Arna could even begin to contemplate the distress he had at the idea of a five year old making such a serious vow, Sarcoline continued talking. "This is the movement. But I'm terrified we won't get you there to see it. I know you are too. And the Gods just expect you to accept it?"

Arna saw his brother for who he truly was. Someone scared, who did not believe in himself, who was still the same five year old child who reached to him for support. He was a boy who had never forgiven himself for not being good enough to help Arna, when he was ten. He'd never forgiven himself for not being strong enough to stop Arna when he was five. He was just a boy who had not made himself trustworthy enough for when Arna returned, to tell him everything.

Sarcoline could not forgive himself for wanting to dream.

It was just as Arna had never forgiven *himself*. He was selfish to want to change the world. He was reaching for a dream, for the future, even when the world said he did not deserve it. He wanted to live, when for years he'd promised himself that he would die.

Arna was not sure that Sarcoline would forgive himself any time soon. Perhaps it would take time for Arna, too.

"How can you accept the fact you might make the wrong choice?" Sarcoline asked. "How can you be okay with risking everyone and still have the chance of accidentally messing up in the end?"

In the forest of evergreen trees, where the clouds hung low, and dragonflies swirled around them. Where the sun was setting and shedding scales rained down upon them. Where saffron grew, surrounded by holly. Where time moved in slow motion, as the wind blew the papers from Arna's hands and Sarcoline tried to grab them before they disappeared into the woods. Arna froze.

Saffron. . . There were no accidents.

Ixxzal.

[*Yes?* Ixxzal's voice was weak.]

It was the question that had haunted him for years. How could he mess up without meaning to? When everything was connected, good and bad. . . He had never asked because he was afraid of the answer, but Ixxzal inspired more than fear.

How do you accidentally reject Divinity?

[*You can't.*]

Had he remembered wrong?

[*You either accept the Divinity or you don't. Saffron rejected it.*]

Then why did Ixxzal say that Saffron did it on accident? Was that not their stance since Arna first heard the story six years ago?

[*He didn't believe he deserved it.*]

[There was the echo of vanishing sound.]

[*I call that an accident.* Ixxzal's voice bounced around as everything and nothing at once. *Because he did.*]

All the years of hate were released. The pain that he wished upon himself, vanished. The years of constant torment he put himself through, disappeared. Yes, he was an imposter. Yes, he made catastrophic mistakes. Yes, he hated himself often enough. But it was okay to love himself, too.

"I don't know yet Arco, it's the last thing I need to figure out," Arna said as Sarcoline returned. He placed both the papers and the folders back into the bag.

They were children again, the two of them, walking to the park. Ten: making a vow. Five: watching his dying brother. They were saying prayers and making wishes. They were making promises never to tell a soul.

They were teaching dances and teaching lessons. They were helping with homework. They were laughing, and falling, and jumping into rivers. They were planting flowers in the garden and sleeping after scary nightmares.

"It's an impossible task," Sarcoline said.

"I believe in miracles," Arna assured him.

They were children getting annoyed with each other because things were changing, and they didn't understand each other. They were crying and yelling and ultimately still saying sorry. They were the warmest hugs the other had ever known.

They were staring at each other: in the audience, on stage, wishing for the other to succeed. They would not break or betray each other. They were watching each other across great distances, believing in each other even when they couldn't say a word.

"I will keep you alive," Sarcoline said. "Even if you make the wrong choice."

And even when he knew that the end of the world was coming, Sarcoline would fight. Even when he knew that Arna could not back down, he was willing to start again as many times as it took. Even when he knew that it was everything Arna trained for, and lived for, and would die for, Sarcoline still wanted to be selfish.

And Arna didn't want to be selfless either.

"There will come a time," Arna said, his voice merging with the trees. "When it looks like the worst. When they scream at me to stop. When they try to get to me. You have to make sure I finish all twenty-seven dances. I need you to believe in me and fight."

The wind swirled about them, changes cascading over them. Darkness descended and dragonflies landed on their arms, glowing like fireflies.

"I think I have an idea, based on the Blessing plan and what you told me about the order you'll lose them in," Sarcoline said softly. "But. . ."

"What?"

"Nothing," Sarcoline shook his head.

Black eyes urged brown: *I'm listening.*

"Just what Saffron said, about Blessings being magic," Sarcoline relented. "Us being able to bend the elements. I thought it was a silly idea from the stories, you know? If it were possible, then. . . I just. . . It's impossible, I know."

Sarcoline looked at him heartbroken the way that Arna had imagined he had when Arna first dropped the fan. Yet, in all fear there was Ixxzal and Ixxzal was the God of Hope.

"Do you remember what I used to tell you about stories?" Arna asked him, as the dragonflies flew away. The wind stopped. The air drifted with the colors of fading shadows and the call of eternity. Ravens and sables were watching. Smoky watsonia, holly, and vervain filled the air. A path of saffron began to glow as a path on the forest floor.

"Good stories tell you, from the beginning, how the story will end," Sarcoline supplied as shadows turned to fog, swallowing their feet and obscuring them in mist. "But that's about dancing."

Trees turned into obsidian, and fireflies flickered like a million stars. Their family's distant voices called, hoping to find them, fearing where they may be. The two boys who lived in the abyss, and called it their friend, stood sharing secrets.

"It's about everything. As long as the stories exists, that means anything can happen." Arna smiled wide. Brown eyes grew large, and faith spread across his brother's face.

They were two. One was the boy who dared to make a choice. The other inspired dreams.

Silence enraptured Arna and Arco, claiming their names and devouring them whole.

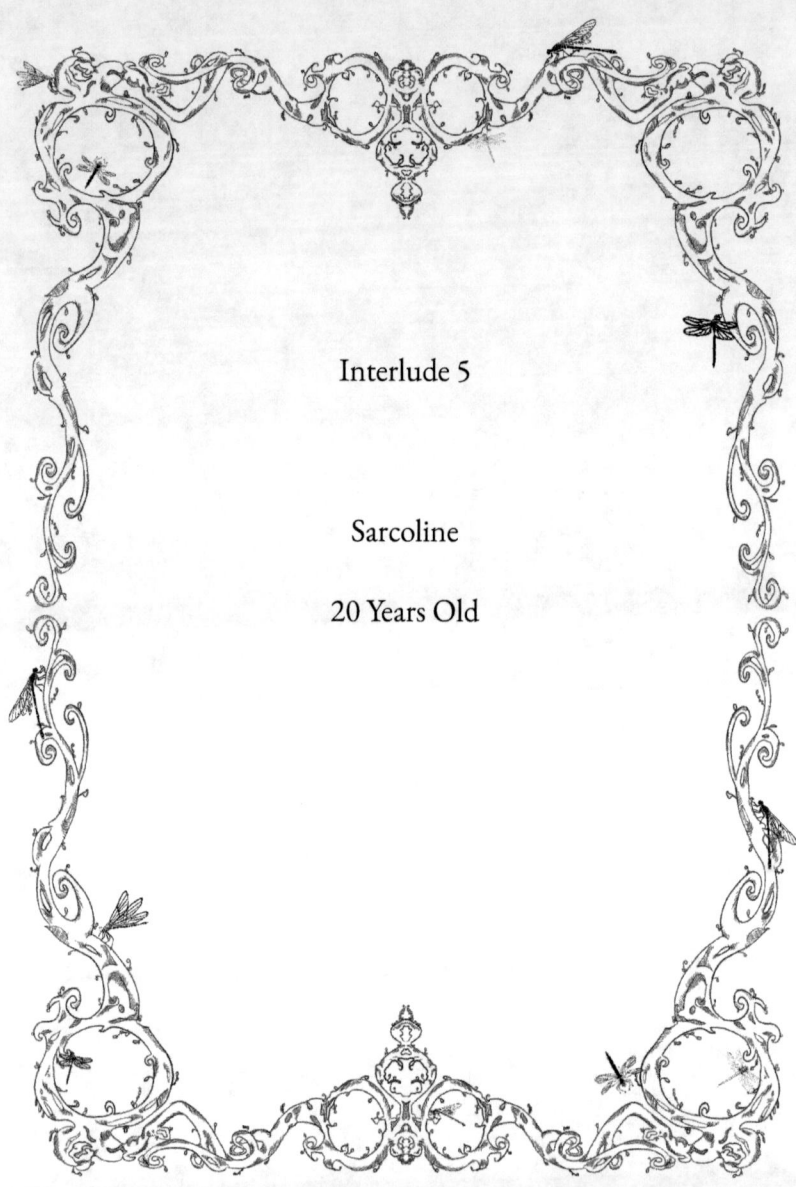

Interlude 5

Sarcoline

20 Years Old

The room hummed with the sound of pen scratches and shuffling paper. The door was locked, and the lights were low. The musk of insanity and intrepid mirth hung like a haze. Walls were littered with lines made of thread and holographic projections attaching pictures across cities. Individual from all over the world had their faces hanging with posted names, titles, roles, importance. Dissertations scattered the floor. History books were tossed about: half open, page-side down, stacks and stacks towering high.

His bed was covered in ink spills, quill pens, Holopens, empty spools, and full ones he'd stolen. His closet was open and stuffed with glittering clothes, hidden behind stacks of boxes, filled with files and papers still to go through. The cabinets near his desk held files in a disarray, pulled partially out, left in stacks, or tumbling to the ground. The floor held a scattering of magazines from different cities, books about the Chosen, and pictures of his brother.

Arco held up the newest plan, fingers black and purple in the ink he'd spilled. Graphite and chalk lined his arms, in white and gray. Amaryllis would be disappointed in him, but he preferred a physical quill and ink to a replenishing false ink pen. It was more official, ancient, like he was a record keeper in some historical castle denoting the passage of time and predicting the future.

Arco continued to laugh to himself, pushing the papers off his bed. Labeled folders—architects, theorists, scientists, artists, teachers, entrepreneurs, wealthy donors—crashed to the floor, and he paid them no heed. Scrambling to his desk, Arco placed the paper down carefully atop it. Every line upon it was written by hand, in his spiraling, curling scrawl.

He tapped at the screen, and it flickered to life: his computer turning on. Clicking on the scanner, nano bots flew from a panel in the wall and spun around him before hovering above the desk. White lines flashed through the air, followed by cyan, magenta and yellow. Then: red, green, and blue. A purple light shined before it solidified to a deep violet. The bots scanned up and down, covering each page in the stack. Again, and again.

On the screen each page flashed individually in many forms. First appeared the original handwritten copy. Then came the digitized version: words pulled out, transformed recognizing his handwriting, and creating a text file in his preferred serif font: Galeri. Pages flashed and disappeared into a new folder. The prompt to name the new folder appeared and Arco named it based on the date. As the scan continued, Arco turned back to his room, fully taking in the state of it.

Fevered insanity trip completed, the real world materialized, and rationality set in. Rubbing his hands together, he got to work. Activating the cleaning bots, Arco began collecting files. The bots pulled his sheets off his bed which sent more papers to the ground. Others collected books from where they were stacked and placed them on shelves alphabetically. His library books were placed aside.

Arco sorted the files that had fallen, ensuring, with a quick flip, that papers were where they were supposed to be. He placed them atop the cabinets and tapped for the cabinet cleaning bots to put them all away. His room swarmed with small, flying tech shaped like moths, picking up and sorting based on the programming. Stretching Arco yawned, glancing over his walls again.

His brother's face was blurry in all the pictures he'd been able to find across the internet. His brother's face had been captured in all five cities at all different ages.

The DHS did not manage to find him. The forums on the deep web had no more information than official sources. The government asked the citizens yearly for assistance, when they remembered to ask and didn't simply believe he was dead. Every trail had gone cold. Every rumor discarded. Theorists and historians were unable to predict him based on principal and on precedence.

Only Arco was able.

He was never able to articulate how or why, but Arco just knew where his brother was. When he first began, at the beginning of the year, he was only trying to see what pictures of Arna existed. He wanted to use it to calm his father and Jasi. While his father was no longer drinking and Jasi was no longer getting into trouble, their religious zeal was beginning to drive even Rosmarinus mad, and Rosmarinus was the calmest person Arco knew. Something had to change, so Arco took on the task himself.

At first it was just to find pictures. Then he read the forums and read the sightings and rumors. He laughed at how silly they were, but he, too, began to play as he collected more: predicting the place his brother showed, as if it were a game. It was a joke at first, until he guessed the timeline correctly and guessed each subsequent locations, precisely. Through the years, from fifteen to the twenty-two, Arco guessed his brother's moves correctly, before he'd found the proof of them in online record. Coincidences, after a time, were no longer fun.

He turned to the official sources, using his name to get access to additional official files not available to the public. At each turn coincidence proved to be fact. Every sighting, every rumor, every indication his brother was alive in the last decade: Arco had been right, at every turn.

So, Arco made a prediction. He wrote it down, told no one, ignored it for weeks, checking the forums periodically, until the rumor popped up. It was a new rumor, the version of Arna as he was currently, the man longer gone than Arco knew him. He checked his journal, and he was right.

The strange fervor that pulled at Arco started at his side, from the vow mark that had laid dormant for nearly two decades. A promise made to himself, under the eyes of the Gods, that no mortal had a record of, called him to act. Heeding it, he dove into tracking his brother without a regret.

For months Arco had scoured maps. He'd outlined and annotated every history book available about the pilgrimages of the five children before his brother. He started researching every historical precedent and compared it with the Omniscient Sextant Enchiridion. Arco had no exact timeline, not yet. Within the record and prophecy, he had two years before his brother showed himself at least. Roughly he had an idea of where his brother should be: Azis.

Arna had been in Ludiel for three years, left after the Ludiel train crash that killed Amaryllis' heartmate. He'd been on it. He'd lived with either two or three older couples. He lived in Ixis for three years, but if Arco was correct, Podiel and Zaydiel for two. The inconsistencies in his spottings was not because he was constantly moving, but rather he was traveling between the cities. More so, he was doing something *outside* of them.

His brother was consistently traveling and consistently learning. It had been harder to track his brother in recent years, which was why there were less rumors. Arco figured that it had to do with his brother's mastery of his abilities, but Arco was also a historian and his Blessings guided him in research and investigation in a way that others in his classes called obsessive.

Pinning Arna's location down was enough for Arco. Finding him had never been an option. The pilgrimage had to be completed before Arna could come home and Arco would not be the reason his brother failed his Chosen training. Instead, after locating he is brother, Arco turned to how he'd *help* Arna.

All of the other Chosen had help. They had those who assisted them with laws, and building new cities, with changing the world. They had allies that they could trust. And they had Saints. Arna would have been alone for too long: he needed those who he could trust to help him find additional allies.

While Arco was not an expert when it came to people, he did listen. He wrote down every name Rosmarinus mentioned in his tours: both those who had money and those who were kind. He made files on those that Rosmarinus found as mentors and those he envied. He highlighted for his brother those he believed were worth asking for support.

He wrote down every name that Jasi gushed about: every litigator, every judge, every Child of note. Arco pressed him with questions. Who would be of use, how, in what ways? Which laws needed to be changed? Why? How could he learn more? Could Jasi help him go through them? Arco spiraled Jasi's fervor into something more useful than rantings and ravings.

He consulted his mother and gathered the knowledge of what needed funding. What projects were on hold? Who were good contacts? What ways could the cities be enhanced? With her help he identified many issues with Blessings in common society.

He listened to his father's ramblings and shaped them into lectures. He reminded his father that someone would need to control the DHS and that their family needed to have the backing to adequately support Arna.

Arco memorized every scripture and dance rule until he dreamt them.

In his bedroom, Arco was surrounded. There were maps, the faces of those who he'd chosen, images of his brother across the world and lines between them. He'd written considerations by hand onto the walls. Most noteably, however were the portraits of the modern Vivicent studio and their roles.

Rosmarinus was in charge of Philanthropy and Outreach. Wenge was in charge of the household. Zaffre was the master of the studio, fans, and ceremonies. Ven, Phlox, and Aureolin were students that Arco needed to convince to return. Alabaster needed to become the vice head of the studio and lead teacher once more. Ginger was the senior student. Jasi was in charge of finances. Ebru would be head student and lead council representative. Arco listed himself as heir to the studio and fan apprentice. He listed Arna as: Chosen.

Amaryllis. . . Her face sat amongst the others with no position listed. He had not determined it, but he'd be remiss to exclude her.

Two years left. They'd all be able to dance together again. They'd build fans together again. His brother, who he missed more than anything in the world, would return. The brother that he had once hated so desperately, would change the world. His brother who had been his everything: home soon.

Letting the programming do its job, Arco walked to the bathroom ready to try to scrub himself clean.

He tried to no avail, the ink staining his skin as if it belonged there. Frustrated, Arco let the hot water irritate his skin while he concealed his emotions, burying them deep.

Sometimes Arco was still angry at his brother for leaving. Sometimes he was distressed and distraught, in anguish at the idea. Most days he was filled with hope. It was terrifying to think about. It was horrid to consider. He still loved his brother deeply, he accepted that, but to hope for a new world? It was insanity. He should have been horrified and filled with fear, just like everyone else was. Even his father was afraid, and his father believed in his brother the most.

But Arco could not feel any of it. He had to remain clam, composed, levelheaded, and get everything back in order so that there would be no chaos when Arna returned. Only then could he be excited for the new world.

Everything would be different when his brother arrived. He'd appear, declare himself with bold words. He'd be just like he'd always been: confident. Arna never hid himself. He never wavered. Arna always believed in himself, and he'd dance and change the world. He'd fix what he broke. He would be glittering, shining, the hero that the stories always talked of. And Arco would stand by, witnessing history firsthand.

Arco tuned off the shower, forgoing anymore scrubbing. He wore the ink like a vow.

One day Arco would be the one to write the novel of his brother. He'd write of his brother's travels and of his Variance. He'd be the greatest historian, and he'd do it all for his brother. He'd help his brother's story glow. He'd no longer have to face the world alone.

Because Arna would be home.

Arco did not know what the future held in store, but he accepted change would come. His brother's Variance would be something that Arco could live by and become. He would no longer be hated by everyone. Finally, they'd see him for what he was, the one who held his family together when Ebru, Jasi, and Rosmarinus no longer could. He was the one who protected the Vivicent name. He may have been a placeholder for Arna, but he was okay with that. Arna would see him for what he did.

Arco placed his head against the cold shower tiles, curling his fingers atop them.

This is the last year.

After this last year, he'd give up. There was too much he had to do to prepare for Arna. If he was going to get everyone back together in time, he couldn't spend hours a day practicing. School already took too much time. It was time to give up dance. It was time to become a historian: the one who would keep the memory alive.

And he'd take over the Vivicent family so his sister could be a fashion designer. And his brother could dance forever. And his father could be happy. And his mother could make the room blossom in a million roses. And he'd finally step aside and. . .

It was all he'd ever wanted. He just had to give up dance to do it.

It was okay, the other dancers could teach. He was only managing for them, stepping out of the spotlight. He was becoming who he was meant to be: a byline, remembered not for who he was but what he witnessed.

Arco began to cry, unable to keep the tears back.

"No, stop, stop," he told himself.

He'd be a teacher, but he would never dance on the stage again. He would have no reason to. It was not his job to do that. He had never been the one anyone wanted on stage. No matter how much he wanted it, it was not the life for him. He would never reach Understanding. He saw it clearly with each passing practice. He would succeed in mastery over all the dances in Powers, but that was it. He was not a genius.

He had to let it go.

This is the last year.

He didn't need dance. He only needed his family together again. He would do everything for them, like he always had. He would be like Chamomile: needing no recognition. This was what his Blessings were meant for.

Arco choked back the sobs and wiped his eyes. *Enough.*

Stepping out of the shower, Arco wiped himself dry. He picked up the sweatpants he'd discarded before and stepped back into them, forgoing the shirt that needed to be cleaned. The pants hung low at his hips as he walked out of his bathroom to see the progress of the cleaning

Amaryllis stood inside, tracing the wall of names and string.

He froze in the doorway.

"Is this why you don't let me in here anymore?" she asked, breathless. It was light and airy, and indicated that at her core, she was pissed.

He did not ask her how she'd gotten in. She had tricky hands, capable to unlocking most locks. She was a phantom that appeared where she was not needed and disappeared when she was. Besides the issue was himself. Despite changing the privacy settings in his room to exclude everyone, he'd left her as an exception. He could never push her away like that, even for his own room, which she never had a reason to be in.

Instead of apologizing, however, he kept his mouth shut. He needed to figure out why she was mad, and quick.

"What are you doing? I said I'd meet you downstairs." he tried to compose herself. Had she heard him just now? He had not found a way to tell her yet that he was giving up on their shared dream and leaving it to her. If she were angry about it, he could sedate it. . .

There were papers in her hands, a familiar report that she no doubt stole from his teacher. His heart sank.

"I should report him to administration." Arco glared at the report that he was proud of. His historical analysis of the Chosen's transition of power had been kept by his teacher so that it could be published.

"He's your advisor and he knows your heart is not in it. Despite how much you pretend." Her eyes were on his side, vaguely making him aware that she could see it. Unnerved he raced for his closet to get a shirt, and she closed the distance before he could reach it. She backed him up to the wall. Her almond shaped fingernails, tipped in white and crystals, traced the vow.

"It's getting published," Arco corrected her, agitated. His advisor had assured him it would be.

"Oh?" Amaryllis asked scandalized. "Are you mad at *me?*"

Arco tried to look anywhere in the room but down at her as she marked every line of the rotating rose that he'd lived with daily since he was five. He knew it by heart: the six layers of petals and the opalescent sheen that transitioned from white to pink to smoky gray to silver. It covered the entirety of his right hip and a good portion of his waist.

"What. Is. This." Amaryllis said the words as if they were the sweetest thing she'd ever said, but Arco heard the wrath.

"I've had it since I was five."

He'd avoided everyone and always changed in secret. He long ago stopped bathing where people could see. He'd concealed it with makeup when he had to. He ensured that no one knew, especially not her.

She clicked her tongue, annoyed.

Arco did his best not to show a reaction knowing she was only trying to get a rise out of him when she poked his side hard.

"Am!" Arco finally met her eye, captured and developed before he could look away.

"I'm going to make an educated guess," she said, stabbing him with her nail and stepping forward. "This. At five? Made for Arna."

"Yes." He hissed at the pain, and she pulled back. She crossed her arms, awaiting an answer, and he relented. "I vowed never to let him make a vow without my help to get him through it, not again. That I'll protect him."

"Are those the exact words spoken?"

"Well, no. I said it in my heart. . ." To this day, Arco was not exactly sure what his vow was for. As a child he'd vowed to protect Arna, and his family based on a feeling, and it had taken. The exact nature of the vow? He was not certain.

"A vow. Without exact protocol to follow?"

"Yes but—"

"At the cost of your own life." Amaryllis spat the words like they were a venom.

Arco did not dignify her accusation with a response, even if it were correct.

"Is that why you're giving up?" she asked him, slamming the paper into his chest. "Why you're serving everyone else's journey but your own?"

I always have. He wished he could tell her.

"Don't!" she snapped, reading his mind. "You are not a martyr, Sarcoline Vivicent. You are a fucking selfish asshole who does not care what anyone else says. You are a *dancer.*"

He wanted to dance so much. He wanted it too much. He wanted it more than anything. He wanted Understanding more than everything. He wanted to be able to dance forever, even if that was not the path for him. He wanted to be the greatest in the world, even when that was impossible so long as his brother lived. He wanted to dance and dance and dance, for himself more than anything else.

It was greedy. It was inconsiderate of what everyone had given up. It negated everything he worked for. It infuriated him that he wanted it so much.

"I'm meant to be a historian, Am. . . " he said softly trying to mitigate her anger.

"Do not patronize me!" she screamed at him.

He balked. He wasn't. He wasn't better than her. She was so much greater than him in so many ways. She huffed at him, radiating a fire he could not quell. The ice within him was melting. Emotions he could no longer keep frozen began bubbling to the surface.

"What do you know?" he snapped, his own volcanic emotion erupting. "You're supposed to be a healer! Everyone *hates* you. Me. They hate *us,* Amaryllis!"

"So what? We give up?" she snarled, glowering, angry, ready to strangle him.

"It is who we are! A historian! A mind healer!" he screamed at her, pushing off from the wall and towering over her. She did not back down, glaring up at him. He was far taller than her now, by a foot. She was tiny. She was nothing.

"No! I am a photographer, and you are a dancer! We are artists!" she shrieked back. She did not cry. She was sweating, turning red, and ready to explode. "It's who we are! It's why we are alive."

"I'm alive because you saved my life," he corrected her, rectifying the lie they'd told each other for years. They had found each other in that forest. They'd saved each other. He swallowed back his anger and chilled himself down the bone. "It's done Amaryllis. I've gone over it enough. I can't do this anymore."

"Our story is not over," she disagreed, grabbing his arm with her left. Her constellation birthmark was dull, but for an instance it almost glowed.

"I never had a story, Amaryllis. I'm just a person who is meant to fade into obscurity. At least by being my brother's historian, I can hope to be remembered."

"No." She clicked her tongue again, anger flowing like slow moving lava. It spread from her wrist that glowed bright. A heat seeped through him where her hand touched his wrist.

"No?" he asked as the ice he tried to build up melted again.

He stepped forward and she did not step back.

"No."

She stepped closer to him, and he retreated with a grimace.

"I—"

"No."

They argued, one word answers, neither relenting. He shrank back, cut down.

"Am—"

"No."

He hit the wall again and slid down it. Their breath became one. Their souls resonated.

"But—"

"No."

He collapsed on the floor. Every dream he thought vanquished reared its head and roared like dragons. Falsities unraveled in his hands.

"What do you—?"

"No."

His vow mark burned. His heart snapped. His entire world tilted into righteous fury, unbidden and uncontrolled. He curled up, pulling his knees close and placing his head between them.

"I am—"

"No."

No tears, only hypocrisy. Only understanding. Only absolutes. He wanted to vomit.

"It's my choice!" he shouted weakly: as the thought died, and the truth was reborn anew.

"No, it's not."

And she was right. It wasn't his choice. If he had truly wanted it, she would not stop him, but he didn't want to give up. He wanted to be a dancer. His choice was always to be a dancer. It was the air he breathed. It was the song of his soul. It was the reason he woke up. It was the reason he fell asleep. It was the reason he existed, and without it he was nothing. But with it. . .

"I'm not special, Am. I'm not worth anything." He pleaded with her to understand why he was doing it. His brother was worth it all. His brother would be everything he could never be. His brother was his inspiration and the perpetual shadow that he would never compete with.

He begged her to understand in the way she always did, instead of peeling him apart and revealing the ugly parts he wanted to hide and discard and ignore. She knelt down before him, taking his face in her hands and getting him to look back up.

"Everything," she amended, smiling and voice settling into cheer. "You are everything."

"But I won't be prepared for him," he said, falling apart to her words, wishing for something he should not. He grabbed both of her hands.

"I'll help you," she convinced him, joyfully knowing that she had won. She'd always win. She was his anchor, reminding him what he wanted and to chase it for it no matter what.

"What if I'm not ready?" he didn't know what his brother was going to do. *What if—*

He wanted it. He wanted it more than anything. But if he chased it. . . if he chose it. . . would everyone forgive him for not being who they expected him to be?

Could he forgive himself for being the person he wanted to be?

"You will be. You are. Always." She said the words without hugging him. He did that. The two of them sat in a swarm of cleaning robots, scanning files, walls of a crazed passion, and another promise spoken between them.

She held him tightly as he sobbed into her hair, cooing him until he began to laugh, and she joined. Their jubilance was a fire within: all-encompassing and ever growing. It was a reminder never to give up. It was a demand to never forget. It was a promise for never again.

It was the prologue to the story of their lives.

the WORSHIP of

Why is it that the entire world decided that one act was superior to them all?
Because it gave results when the world was hopeless, and all was lost.

— The prestige of the Twenty-Seven Dances

Dance 25

Control

Incarnadine

Apostle Week

The Celebrations

"Again."
"I know."
"What's wrong?"
"What happens when I've mastered? When I've perfected my Blessings? What then?"
"Then you do it again. And again."
"And again?"
"Until it is more than a memory, more than a habit. When it is impossible for you to fail."

The Religious Circle had churches for all. Usually small, with the Temple of the City's God in the center, the Religious Circle was the center of every flower. In each city, the Temple represented a unique God in the form of architecture, for Ixxzal it was a puzzle, and for Pokk it was a flame. In Xeysis it looked like a tree, and stood off center, in a circle with the other Cathedrals.

Each Cathedral towered multiple stories, with stained glass and bell towers. It was architecture from millennia ago, built solidly and tested by time. The Harmonious Six Cathedral was made of stone and crystal of all the colors of the Gods; woven and smelted together into intricate interlocking patterns reminiscent of flower petals. The Church of Xeya's Cathedral was white marble perfectly clean for Xeyaro, with silver inlays and emerald tiles. The Church of the Apostle's Cathedral was solid black onyx and granite. There were dragonflies etched into the stone that used to glow in the candlelight, but now the building stood dark compared to the others.

The outer circle of churches were similarly stunning buildings, each with their own flare. Six-hundred-foot tall candles surrounded the district, separating City and secular. Each candle was made completely of stone and gemstones, glittered in the night light. When they were lit, they glowed from within, but now their centers were dark. Their colors were dulled even as they swirled, their patterns unmoving.

Unlike the other cities, Xeysis' religious circle was twice the size of the others. There was a ring of space between the Cathedrals and other churches. The ring held stages for performances, halls for movies and song, and fields for sports. There were gardens and topiaries. Tens of buildings stood tall and long stretches of field were waiting for stalls to be set up. The vast amount of emptiness was filled to the brim with tents, stalls, displays, stages, and temporary structures.

And in the center of this all, where the Temple of Xeyaro should have been, facing the Cathedral of the Apostle with it's Apostle clock and beyond it the candle for Xeyaro, was the Weeping Stage.

The celebrations for the new year began at midnight. Ten minutes before in Xeysis—the last of the cities to experience the new year—the live broadcast started around the world and the transporters opened for all. The moment the clock struck twelve, the fireworks shows lit up the sky. Colored for their Gods, the fireworks were a brilliant show of technical ability and spectacle.

Fifteen minutes later, the festivities for the end of the year began.

Each city had a unique draw. Yet, in Arna's opinion, none were as spectacular as Xeysis. In Podiel, a scientist lectured on new discoveries and medical achievements. In Azis, there were architecture challenges and demolitions. In each city the Children of the Gods would come together for some presentation, celebration, and worship to the Gods. The celebrations were a time of mass worship, of mass entertainment, and of mass wonder and enlightenment. They united everyone from the first firework to the last note played.

In Xeysis, it was the largest art festival in the world. On the smaller stages, musicians played. Artists showed off and sold their work. Photographers were capturing everything. Movie screenings, theater performances live and recorded, and any and all artforms were being showcased.

Flowers rained from the sky. People could get plant readings, leaving the stall with their personal plant pinned to their shirts. There were all-natural drinks and food made by plants and plants alone. Nature was open and free; people communed with it. Famous fashion houses rented their clothes to civilians for use and promotion. Everyone wore their best and most beautiful, regardless of if they rented or not.

Nearly all wore masks: on top of their heads, on their belts, on their faces. Bought or made, it did not matter. Most held fans mass produced for cheering. They were not real: ornate dance fans. To avoid sacrilegious offense, none of the fans were the correct colors, nor the correct sizes. They were not painted or made with the right fabrics of the ceremonial fans. Most were made of paper, and in a few cases, actual fabric. They did not invoke the excessive taboo if dropped, although it was still a taboo to drop one: resulting in a six-second loss of a Blessing, which most people ignored.

Their augmentations were filled with announcements and advertisements. They pointed out which design house someone was wearing and identified where things could be bought. Music played in the moving drone speakers as cameras flew around. Others dropped flowers and flower petals above. Dog shaped robots walked about providing services, delivering food, and giving assistance.

Kids rode around on hoverboards and scooters. In the air, people raced to the floating stages in the sky. Rides shaped like fans, dogs, and flowers floated through the sky delivering people across the vast fields. Tiny orbs twinkled, like stars holding steady in the sky, changing colors as people passed by and creating paths, lines, and light so that everyone could see. Technology and nature were one.

And on the Weeping Stage, the most important stage in the world, from the moment the fireworks ended, there was dancing. With only a few minutes of short intermissions to introduce groups, the dances continued nearly nonstop. Group dances, studio showcases, and performers from all over the world who had gotten a spot were performing—with the exception of the crowning of the Philanthropist of the Year and Monarch of Flowers. It was near nonstop up until the last three hours of the sixth night.

The Ceremony of Chaos was the last performance of the New Dawn celebrations. The whole world coordinated their events around them despite time changes. The Ceremony was watched by all. When programs were running early, due to dropped acts or issues, groups were asked to repeat their performances. The Ceremony of Chaos was only ever pushed back when things ran late. It never started early, due to the broadcasting requirements and the dropping of the Blessing barriers. The latest they could be performed was starting in the last hour of the night before the start of the new year.

Arna's father always told him that so long as The Twenty-Seven Dances began on the last day of the year, it was acceptable for them to end on the first of the new year. However, they had to be danced that day, and twenty-four had to be completed before the next dawn. Arna would have no such luxury.

The Day of Endings
5 Days Left

Flower arches covered the walkways, with dazzling arrays of beautiful, hand-crafted flowers made of paper, clay, and stone among the naturally occurring ones. There were flowers that were only found in greenhouses. Flowers from every season were in bloom and woven into the multicolored arrays.

There was one arch for each God. They lined the main paths to and from the Weeping Stage and guided one into the outer parts of the festival grounds. Wafting scents, sweet and lush, filled the air in a rich aroma that swayed and changed as one moved on.

Food vendor stalls were open, wafting a swirl of different scents that mixed together as Arna walked by them. There was sweet cinnamon as well as savory scents. There were fried zucchini and tofu based dishes on sticks. Fresh fruit on plates were being held. Boiled, seared, fried, and baked vegetables of all types were in bowls. Potatoes in every form possible were held.

Arna wore a mask over his face designed for Ixxzal, blending into the crowd.

Each of the six entrances had a myriad of booths for patrons to shop from, to get into the spirit of the day: masks, Hemlock fans, and glow sticks. The sports showsase centers were assembled in a circle: rinks, rings, ranges, and fields. There were six additional stages: three for music, two for theatre, and one for other performance art. There were hundreds of thousands of people moving about buying food, sticking flowers in their hair, and chatting: celebrating.

Towering trees had been brought in from around the city, to offer shade from the heat. Cameras flew, disguised as flowers, dragging petals behind them as they flew. People were openly dancing and singing, screaming when they saw celebrities and racing to find where they needed to be for events.

The guilds, groups who ran the Celebrations, had their booths set up with elaborate displays of fabric and architecture. They performed dances for history, offered games, mixed potions, told stories, and lead activities.

"I hate him," Amaryllis said as she walked with Arna, face covered by a mask decorated for Ixxzal, as well. She, too, was dressed by Ginger. Ginger had made all their clothes for that day, more beautiful and exquisite than anything Arna had ever worn. Even Jasi, who was on call as a Child of Lumak, was to wear a uniform customized by her.

Everywhere, in all the most visible directions, Cyclamen's name could be seen; in the false sky, and painted by illusions for sponsors. He was in their augmentations, as they passed stalls that had been funded by him. His name was bold in the program and on the Hemlock fans that everyone held. It was disgusting, but the Shadone Studio was the largest sponsor of the day.

Equally, however, there were images of Ebru and Rosmarinus: their faces shining in advertisements and giving pointed reminders to citizens to take care of themselves for the week. Rosmarinus' voice was the prompt for all emergencies, luckily; Arna was not sure what he'd do if he heard Cyclamen telling people to stay calm and that help was on its way.

"I'll beat him," Rosmarinus said, walking beside them in a mask for Zaynir. His glittering iridescent cape flittered about behind him.

"You'd better," Amaryllis seethed. "Another year as Philanthropist of the year and—"

"I did not go on a world tour and dedicate every waking minute of this year to lose. I *will* beat him," Rosmarinus declared, cutting her short. Arna was inclined to believe him, for he could not take another incessant moment of being told to believe that Cyclamen was a good person.

The thrum of anxiety between them was electric and alive, growing as the day progressed. It was as if words were spoken between them: *the end, Arna has to live, how do we succeed?* The messages had all but stopped rising in their chat log. Arna had to imagine that was because Arco was finishing his plan. He didn't ask.

The silent panic between them all was comforting in a way, and in opposition of it, they were united. After all, this could be the last celebrations ever. They could either worry until they drove themselves sick, or they could enjoy what they were fighting for. In unspoken agreement the Golden Dragonflies chose to live.

The three rounded the grounds, heading towards the Vivicent booth where Chamomile's paintings were in wide display: *The Moment,* of Arna dancing when he was fifteen, on one side and *The Dancer,* when Arco danced in Chamomile's garden, on the other. They glimmered in the light of the day as Wenge and Alabaster sat talking to people. Honeysuckle and Saffron giggled to themselves in the back of the booth, as Honeysuckle's mother begrudgingly helped Wenge.

"They're signing up," Arna said, breathless.

"They are," Amaryllis almost squealed.

"Your brother," Rosmarinus said, directing their attention to Saffron, "I didn't know he wanted to be a dancer."

"He only ever told me and Arco because he thought it was impossible," Amaryllis admitted, hands on her hips and humor in her tone. "He always wanted to be a part of the Vivicent studio. And I'll be damned by Azza, I thought he gave up. But I should have known. We Inks, never give up on our dreams, even if we don't tell anyone we're dreaming them."

Not wanting to draw attention to their presence, they waited. They approached once the crowd dispersed. Arna glanced at the sign-up lists.

"Not a lot, but a few," Wenge said without looking up.

"You knew it was me?" Arna asked removing his mask just enough so she could see his face.

"You, your father, your sister, and your brother all act the same," Wenge said, looking up with a slight tilt to her head and the snarkiest, all-knowing smile on her lips. "It took me time, but don't worry. I can hear you again. You can't get past me."

Something about his mother using her Blessings to check for his footsteps warmed his heart, even though it told him he was never going to get away with anything ever again.

"How is practice?" Alabaster asked.

"Good," Arna said. "They're practicing now."

After, Ebru was going to race back to the house to work on the songs more. It was a hellish schedule, but he swore he was going to do it. He said it wasn't as bad as the training the others were doing with Arco, away from Arna.

"Your father said Arco is taking over your training?" Alabaster asked.

Arna's own intensive practice schedule had Arna in a practice room nearly every hour of the day when there wasn't something going on for their friends. This was one of his rare moments of peace, since Arco had to practice.

"Yeah. He's drilling me worse than dad."

Alabaster chuckled. The five chatted for a bit before Amaryllis tugged on Arna and Rosmarinus, pointing towards another direction and dragged them off. Honeysuckle and Saffron chased after them, demanding they were taken too. Unable to say no, they allowed the children to walk with them.

Accidentally they ran into Jasi, though Arna was not sure it was an accident, not when it came to Amaryllis. He was working security off the main stage, but they found him getting drinks for the others. Helping him, they headed back to the Cathedral of the Apostle.

At the entrance, with view of the inside, were paintings on racks and stands, hung in the air by nanotech and protected by Blessing fields. Crowds surrounded them, staring in awe at the art. There were glowing white neon holograms hovering over many of the paintings denoting them as sold.

Arna glanced to Amaryllis who stared at the art that had been sold in teary-eyed happiness. People were buying them. All of her work to get Chamomile's name to be seen paid off. Finally, Chamomile was being recognized by the masses.

"Good job," Arna praised Amaryllis.

"You know it won't last," she warned him. "Someone will find out she's not a Child."

"At that point, it won't matter. They will have bought them. No returns," Rosmarinus reminded her. The wealthy people who bought them may regret it, may even threaten to destroy them, but Arna hoped that they would not.

"We will change everything," Jasi agreed and then hurried them all inside. The priests recognized them and let them through with no question. Inside was filled with prayers by holy followers who had joined the church to preach its doctrine. They were spoken in soft chants like the flapping of wings or a heartbeat. There were not many people inside, however, compared to the numbers outside.

The towering ceilings were filled with depictions of the old world, of stories of the past, and faces of the ancient Cardinals. Massive stained glass depicted the five Chosen. Raven was in all black shadows, with a fan in front of their chest. Watsonia raised her right fan high in the sky like a sword and held her left fan like a shield. Vervain the Blythe held with two Fans extended outwards, roses grew in all directions. Sable stood with a single fan held towards the ground where cities grew out of the ashes. Ilex held two fans, surrounded by holly, and spinning, as the storm clouds parted above.

They were all faceless, black masses, only identifiable by the number of fans they held and the length of their hair. With them were the images of their faceless Saints.

The images around them were beautiful displays of craft and skill, with individual glass, stained, blown, and painted to produce shimmering, prismatic displays. They created dancing, colored lights over the walls as the sun hit the windows. The center of the Cathedral, where mass was held, had a dragonfly statue attached to a massive silver willow. The willow branches and leaves hung around the back corridors, and lightly touched the audience.

"Could you imagine if someone got married in here?" Honeysuckle asked in awe. "It would be so pretty."

"I want to go!" Saffron insisted.

"We need to find someone who will let us!" Honeysuckle rapidly agreed to her own delusions.

The Cathedral for the Church of the Apostle did not allow for anyone who was not a member of the church to enter regularly, let alone for anyone to use the space as a venue. They operated at an extreme margin of loss, relying on donations from their charity work, rather than the tours they could offer or the money they could charge people to enter.

The stone halls were lined with marble tiles. It was an ancient building—as it had been transplanted in the cities millennia ago—but it did not show its age. The stones were worn, depicting a long history of use, but were not cracked or missing. The Cathedral had been completed the year that Ilex was born, and was one of the few Cathedrals from that time that was not destroyed after Saffron failed.

Arna's hand traced the wall as they walked down a back way, past priests who nodded at them, and to the dance rooms in the basement that were built for the Chosen to practice in.

Arco had rented two practice rooms. One was to be used for their Blessing practice, and Arna was not allowed to enter. The other was used for dance.

The DHS, particularly Cyclamen, was not pleased that the Golden Generation requested secret practices. Yet, with Arna's panic attack as well as Ven's, there was enough proof that they needed to be left alone, even if the DHS did not know the source of those panics. With the help of Cardinal White they were given reprieve in a place where no one could touch or see them, and only then did the DHS relent.

When Arna and the others entered the dance room, everyone but Arco cheered. Reluctantly, he allowed them to take the break that was offered to them. They talked for an hour, joking about Arco being a monster with his training. Some of Arna's variation tools were in the room: ceremonial garb, and shoes. His father was not done with his fans; they were still at the manor.

"It's time," Arco said, keeping to the rigorous schedule.

Without a word otherwise, Arna stood as the others remained sitting. He walked to the center and began his stretches. He allowed himself to settle within the space and became one with the black-stained willow floors and ancient silver mirrors. The floors were smoothed with age as if it were impossible for them to splinter.

One. Two. Three. Four.

He took one last deep breath and ignored all the eyes on him save Arco who fractured into six.

Five. Six. Seven. Eight.

"Begin," Arco said.

Arna wove a story under The Dancer's scrutiny.

The Day of Change
4 Days Left

Arna knew very little about archery, other than what he'd managed to read online and ascertain through Amaryllis as she talked about the showcase. Despite that, he adored how much Ven loved it.

Their whole group, including Ebru, who had been easily convinced away from his laptop to attend the showcases of the group, sat in the stands waiting and watching.

Ven stepped up, beautiful as always, holding the bow closely in their hands. The breathed evenly, with hair pulled back and eyes staring at the target far away.

They slowly rose their bow, enrapturing the audience. A collective hush went over the crowd. What Arna read online was that Ven's form was magnificent. It stood sturdy, powerful, like a mountain that could not be toppled.

There was a wildness about them, an intensity that was not there when dancing. As the arrow gave a solid thud, all Arna could do was focus on the Ven. They were different in archery: unknown and powerful. There were many more mysteries to Ven than Arna had ever expected. Ebru did not allow him to clench his hands, so Arna rubbed at his wrist, where his constellation once was.

"Incarnadine," a voice said. Chills raced down Arna's spine.

"Governor." Arna turned to face the man who stood behind the stands with other officials. Some people hissed at how rude it was to talk during the showcase.

"We must speak." He was surrounded by people Arna very much did not want to speak to: Cyclamen, Mr. Thyme, other members of the task force, and some new faces.

"You are interrupting the showcase," Ebru said over his shoulder without turning around. "Leave."

There was a sharp hiss to 'shush,' as another thud sounded. Arna turned wildly. Had he missed Ven? The bow swung in the hand of a different person, not Ven, but Ven was stepping up again.

"Incarnadine."

"The last time we spoke, you tried to accuse me of fraud," Arna said, hovering between watching and glaring at those behind him.

Governor Cider wore a politician's smile and introduced the others. "This is Coral Clay. She has worked with Cyclamen for the city, on the rehabilitation of children without Blessings. As you know. . ."

"Governor," Arna said. "If you wish to speak to me you know where to find me. Have a pleasant day and a wonderful celebrations."

He made a show of it by purposely turning around. He caught Ven's next shot.

"Incarnadine."

Arna refused to budge. Finally, someone made an excuse for them to leave.

"I must apologize. We shall talk more tomorrow," the Governor said.

The man left and Arna swore that he'd do everything he could to avoid the man the next day.

The Day of Hope
3 Days Left

The first of Aureolin's main stage performances with her dance group was held on The Weeping Stage and performed on The Day of Change. It was a dance telling of a battle of the Fourth Variance, where everyone had died and there had been no survivors. It was a harrowing tale that left the audience anticipating the second half of the performance that would come the next day.

When the time for the second half arrived, the Weeping Stage was crowded. History dances were much less adored than the romances, dramas, or the traditional dances that the ballet troupes performed. Knowing this, Aureolin had picked the particularly dramatic dances of the Nine Historical Battles to perform.

The second dance picked up where the first ended, with the war taking place on the battlefield. The townspeople near the battle moved to stop the soldiers from fighting. Inspired by Ilex' new variation, they created peace. All of the Nine Historical Battles were based on real history, but the dances were far less bloody than Arna understood the real history to be.

"Most people died," Arco said as they walked from the seats to find Aureolin. He and Amaryllis ate frozen chocolates and fruit on a stick. Where they got them from, Arna had no idea. Arna didn't remember them leaving.

"Where. . .?" Ven asked staring at the stick.

"Am said she was hungry." Arco pointed at a floating vendor and dog-bots making deliveries.

"Should you be eating that?" Jasi asked him, scrutinizing the food and chastising him in one tonal inflection.

"I'm not Arna, my diet doesn't matter this week," Arco said.

"And you didn't get us any?" Phlox asked. Arco shrugged. Phlox sighed dramatically before she went over to buy more for everyone else.

"What did you guys think?" Aureolin asked, walking from backstage. She was no longer in her performance clothes but a billowing white gown, decorated in handcrafted lace roses.

"Splendid. You did well adapting the historical accuracy like I suggested, save the death count," Sarcoline said, eating a second stick of frozen chocolates. He got halfway through before handing it to Amaryllis and she finished the rest.

"No one wants to see how many more people died, Arco," Aureolin chastised.

"Ready?" Rosmarinus asked when Arco wove his hand to dismiss her.

Rosmarinus, too, was dressed as she was in a white suit with hand crafted iridescent roses. Jasi patted his shoulders, trying to rouse his confidence. Rosmarinus had been made aware he was shortlisted that morning; however, only time would tell if he beat Cyclamen.

She nodded hesitantly before hugging them all, kissing her dance sisters on the cheeks, and then walking backstage once more with Rosmarinus. Together, Aureolin's dance sisters and the older Golden Dragonflies returned to the seats where the audience had dispersed greatly. More reporters and cameras filled the space.

Arna started squeezing his hands, until Ebru pried them apart and held both in his own. The humm between the Golden Dragonflies was ear piercingly loud, but more certain.

Zaffre, Alabaster, Wenge, Honeysuckle, and Saffron arrived, breathing raggedly as if they had run the whole way. Shortly after Mymy, and all of Aureolin's family arrived with Honeysuckle's mother and Amaryllis' parents.

"Are we late?" Wenge asked.

"No. Sit. Sit," Jasi ordered them.

Most everyone sat in varying degrees of unrest and nerves. Amaryllis tapped her foot. Jasi and Phlox clung to one another. The parents talked nervously. Ebru and Arna held each other's hands tightly as Arna leaned into his shoulder. Ginger and Ven played with the hems of their clothes as they assured Honeysuckle and Saffron all was well.

Only Arco and Mymy sat relaxed as the stage lights flashed bright white.

"Hello!" the emcee said, stepping out on stage and continuing the show as if nothing had happened nor changed. He gave a short speech, introducing the city officials, mayors, District leaders, and Governor of Xeysis.

"The Philanthropist of the Year is an award, many aspire to. It is the world's highest achievement in the field of community support and care. This year we name six candidates."

Cyclamen, Rosmarinus, and the four other shortlisted candidates stepped out onto stage. Rosmarinus was the youngest by far, in a suit that made him shimmer. As they were named, their achievements were read out and a short video played, depicting their acts over the year.

"This year, we would like to name. . . Rosmarinus Jade, Philanthropist of the Year," The emcee said.

All at once the Vivicent studio was screaming in cheers, even when the rest of the crowd was not nearly as excited. To his credit, Rosmarinus walked up to take the award without looking at Cyclamen once. The man glowered at him. Rosmarinus shook hands, took pictures, and without a shaking voice gave the speech he'd prepared.

"And in grand order of Celebration tradition. . ." the emcee continued as soon as Rosmarinus finished. "The Philanthropist of the Year shall crown this year's Monarch of Flowers: Aureolin Begonia."

Aureolin walked out and it was as if she were floating. The dress hovered across the ground, not so stiff that it looked immoveable, but as if it reflected the light. The lace flowers danced as she moved, like petals floating in the wind.

Aureolin bowed before Rosmarinus, and he placed a silver grown of willow branches, ivy, and holly atop her head. She turned and smiled to the audience, officially the new year's Monarch of Flowers. Together they stood in matching attire designed by Ginger, like glittering, iridescent roses.

The Day of Stars
2 Days Left

Happiness was abundant across all parts of the celebrations. The energy did not die day to day, instead it intensified. The world acted as if Blessings weren't disappearing at a rapid speed. It was as if they were not running on Blessing power reserves. It was as if public transportation had not been stopped and all the cities were in a state of emergency.

It was a game of pretend for the world: a blissful illusion.

It was a nightmare masqueraded as a dream.

They all wanted to believe that for just one week, the world would be okay. Everything would go back to the way it had been as soon as the Ceremony of Chaos finished. It would work just as it had for the last twelve years. Perhaps, they did not want to admit there was no way to relive the past. The only way on was forward.

The Golden Dragonflies knew this better than all. The hymn of panic between them approached a crescendo. The hours of practice grew tense, and near constant. Everyone operated under little sleep. They were running out of time, and yet they still accepted joy when it was offered.

The group walked out of Phlox's play a bit tired, but overall enthused by her performance. Phlox was stunning live. Arna understood why she was called the Young Queen. He had fully believed he was there, despite the nonsensical plot.

The play was a long-winded drama retelling of a famous romance from the Second Variance. It was considered one of the greatest love stories of all time, about a boy and a girl separated in the burning of a city who had to find each other again. Initially after hearing that she was going to be pining after some guy on stage as she spoke in some old dialect that no one really understood, he had been less than enthused.

However, watching her cry, scream, and fall in love, over and over, had his heart aching.

"It was as boring as I remember," Arco sighed as they waited for Phlox around the back. "I like her movies better."

Phlox's movies showed every day in the viewing theater inside the Church of Xeya. It was one of the best movie theaters in the world. Ebru and Arna managed to watch both late at night while the others were sleeping, after his practice and when Ebru had finished the music edits for the night.

"You just hate love stories," Amaryllis joked.

"Arco is allergic to love actually," Jasi corrected. Rosmarinus laughed under his breath.

"Certified and tested," Arco joked back. "Besides, it wasn't historically accurate. Those events took place centuries after each other."

"It doesn't matter Arco," Ginger elbowed him. "It's about the feelings."

"Sure," Arco said, the word heavy in disagreement.

"I swear one day, Arco, you're going to fall in love so hard you're going to land on your face," Ginger teased him.

"You all say that, because you all seem to put so much value on it." He eyed them all: Ebru and Arna, Aureolin and Phlox, Ginger and Jasi, and Ven and Amaryllis who had once been.

"Did you hate it?" Phlox flung herself over Arco's shoulders.

"It was miserable, but your accent was spot on," Arco said, swinging her around in a hug.

"Thank you for the lessons," she said, kissing both cheeks and then rushing to Aureolin and kissing her hard on the mouth. "I hate kissing boys. Help me."

Aureolin chuckled to herself and kissed Phlox again. Everyone congratulated Phlox for a job well done. Then they began discussing love and the love story, despite how much Arco tried to talk about the history instead.

The Day of Beginnings
1 Days Left

At the back of the Temple of Xeyaro there were multiple rooms where the dancers slept. Traditionally, it was the hall where the performers of the Ceremony of Chaos and their families were able to stay during the celebrations. The Ceremony Dancers were the only performers required to sleep at the event, in order to ensure nothing prevented them from dancing.

The Vivicent Studio was given two rooms. One was for the parents, which included Honeysuckle and Saffron, much to their dismay. The second was taken by the rest of the older Golden Dragonflies. For a full week, they were to sleep in the soundproofed room and get the best rest that they could.

For the last days of Apostle Week, the Golden Dragonflies were cloistered in their room. They only left when they were performing, practicing, working, or enjoying each other's performances. Arna and Arco were rarely in it the first days, using every waking second they could for Incarnate Dreams.

On the day before the last, they rarely left at all, save Arna's mandatory practices which they attended together. There were no performances. Jasi and Ebru avoided work. However, they were not stagnate.

Arco, Ven, and Rosmarinus went over potential ways for Arna to survive and ways the others could use their Blessings to defend him without interfering. Arna did his best not to listen, trusting them to make the path sturdy.

Jasi contemplated how to get around the new contract for the stage that they'd been forced to sign if they wanted to go backstage. Amaryllis was too busy editing photos to notice anyone else. Ginger and Phlox retwisted Arna's hair. Ebru was hunched up in a corner with a blanket over his body, headphones on, and editing music. Honeysuckle and Saffron played card games and occasionally went out to play, but usually they hovered close.

Aureolin forced everyone to leave the room periodically.

"You all can't stay in here the whole time," Aureolin huffed when they all refused to move, despite her prompting for the third time in the hour.

Before, being amongst the declaration of dreams had been inspiring. For that was what the celebrations were: an expression of everything a person loved and lived for.

"We can try," Arna suggested.

Now, the hum of fear was resounding amongst the Golden Dragonflies. There was still so much to do and even less time.

"This is the biggest celebration of art in the world!" Aureolin reminded them, "We won't get another Apostle Week for thirty-six years."

There was a banging at the door as Phlox finally let go of Arna's hair, finishing the locs. Aureolin groaned when she was the only one who moved to open the door.

"Hurry! Fast, hurry!" someone yelled.

"What's happening?" Aureolin asked.

"Amaryllis' collection—" The man said and in seconds Arco was up, off the floor, and running before anyone else could react: including Amaryllis herself. Arco bolted out the door by the time Arna was on his feet.

Arna crashed through the back halls of the Temple past people visiting private display rooms of the different indoor showcases. He raced out into the main hall: a large circular room that held only the statue of Xeyaro.

The main hall was reserved for those deemed Xeyaro's best of the year: six artists who were given different sections and the walls, floors, and sky to hang their art in creative ways. Amaryllis' collection, in the far back, was a selection of hanging photographs in a variety of sizes: hand developed, digitally printed, on canvas, and on photo paper, glossy and matte. Most of the photos hung from near-invisible wires that sparkled like spiderwebs when they caught the light. They hung artfully at different levels around twelve massive prints, held up on stands and partially covering each other in a circular display. The display was meant to be walked around, to be viewed in multiple directions.

All of it was being ripped from the ceiling.

Arco stood frozen, and like him, Arna was unable to fathom what was happening.

Guards tried to stop them, but there were too many and the Temple did not have that many guards as people didn't think that anyone would purposely destroy art during the celebrations. It was a taboo on normal days, far more grievous during the celebrations for the New Dawn. The pictures were picked up and torn apart, all to no retaliation.

The taboos were no longer working, just as the Blessings were dying.

"Even Xeyaro doesn't care!" one of the instigators yelled at a guard.

"The taboos don't even count for her!" another laughed. "Even they despise her art."

There was a level of rage in the voices that was misdirected. It was not just about her art. It was about the billions who had lost their Blessings overnight. Much of what remained for public service was running on reserves, his father said that morning. The governments were acting as if nothing had happened and silencing the news. People were acting as if nothing had happened, afraid to admit it. This was not like previous years.

This was fear, the fear that Arna had sat with for years. The world was ending and Arna suspected everyone now saw it.

"Why aren't the taboos stopping them?" Ginger shrieked.

Amaryllis. Arna turned but it was too late. She stood, expression devoid of thought, in a sea of horrified expressions. Her eyes traveled with the photographs that were destroyed and stomped on the floor. The crowd that had gathered were watching, interested but uncaring. A few glared at Amaryllis rather than the people who caused the destruction. The guards pushed the majority of the instigators away, but still a few continued their havoc.

"Who are you?" Arco stalked forward before Arna could grab him.

"An actual artist," the blonde haired instigator said proudly. "What right does she have to be here when I cannot? This is a ceremony for the Gods. It's for us to show them how we have made use of their skills!"

"She's not *Blessed*," the instigator in a dress criticized.

"How dare you call yourself an artist!" a third screamed at Amaryllis. The woman who yelled had mint eyes, and a righteous fury directed at Arna rather than Amaryllis herself.

"How dare you!" Arco yelled. "She *is* an artist."

"She is not a Child. It is not—*should* not—be allowed," the mint-eyed woman said. "But you, too, have not done what the Gods have asked. By ignoring your nature, you have condemned the world. You dance where you should not! It's because of you!"

She pointed at Arco, but she meant Arna. There was an odd swell in the energy around them. People spoke in hushed voices saying how they agreed and how the Golden Dragonflies' actions could offend the Gods.

"What, do you think you're *great?* I'll show you great!" The blonde instigator picked up one of the large canvases about to break it.

Arco lunged, snatching the painting away, as Jasi jumped to pull Arco back. The man stumbled and fell, even though Arco had not made it more than an inch.

"Stop this nonsense!" Cardinal Black yelled, and people made way for him. Arna made eye contact with him. The Cardinal helped the artist up.

"Incarnadine," Cardinal Black said. "This has become an issue. She must leave. We cannot have her presence interfering with this scared day. And your actions on this day, Sarcoline, are serious. We may have to revoke your position for tomorrow. You were warned. No violence."

Arna blinked at the man. *What?*

The room around him was filled with the scorn from the crowd.

There was ire at the Child who had went into a sport instead of staying in Dance. There was frustration at the worthless Child who continued to dance despite being from a ruined family. There was spite towards the Child who was not a great, who danced with a group of nonChildren, and was the presumptive Monarch of Flowers. There was scorn towards the Child who claimed music in his soul, and dance in his veins: choosing both.

They showed apathy towards the girl who had become a fallen family's first student when no one else dared. They showed a disregard for the boy who wished for magic when he had no Blessings at all.

They held malice for the Child who chose to act when the whole world wished she remained silent. They held animosity for the Child who chose the arts over balance and justice, over his own God, because of love. They held rancor for the man who chose to defend a family when everyone told him not to.

They showed enmity towards the Child who believed himself a God, despite him having destroyed the world, despite their being no proof that he was.

They hated the Child who had done photography instead of healing.

They were scared of the boy who held a painting close in his arms.

"No." Arna glared Cardinal Black down. "He will dance. She will remain."

"Incarnadine, see reason," Cardinal Black pleaded.

Arna smoldered at the man, trying to formulate the words. Why did she need to leave? Amaryllis had been selected by a blind panel. There was a reverberating silence that filled the hall.

"I may not be a Child, but I am good."

Amaryllis' voice echoed across the floor, the ceiling, bounced and grew louder as she stalked forward in her heels, clicking across the tiles. She walked up to the group, bent down, and started collecting the photographs. Phlox, Aureolin, and Ginger hurried to help her. Amaryllis whispered something to Phlox who nodded quickly.

Arco and Jasi forced everyone to get out of the way as she ripped the wires down. They fell with ease and she arranged the lines on the ground like a true spiderweb, a blank canvas upon white marble floors.

"I don't take photos because I want people to like me," Amaryllis' voice reverberated as she took all the photos from the others and began laying them down. "I don't do it because it's easy, either."

On the ground she placed the photos, using the shards of destruction to create something new. It was a mosaic of ripped up photographs: technicolor, sepia tones, black and white, and everything in between.

"If I wanted easy, I wouldn't develop them by hand. I would take photos that didn't make people angry."

There were images of them all. There was Arco over the years in different places, dancing. There was Ven in places all across the city, a smile on their face. There was one particular photo of Ebru working on his laptop, with his headphones on and eyes on his screen with a soft smile.

"I don't do it the hard way because I want to punish myself. I'm not a tortured artist who believes suffering is the only way art can manifest."

There was Arna standing laughing with his friends. There was Jasi studying a book and Ginger dancing. There was Phlox in a candid, laughing loudly, on stage and bathed in the limelight.

"I do it because when I learn a new skill, the adrenaline feels like a miracle. When I spend hours on a project and it turns out exactly how I envisioned, the relief I feel is euphoria. I do it for the catharsis."

Amaryllis moved her big prints into a semi-circle around the arrangement on the floor that looked more and more like a dragonfly as Arna continued to stare at it.

The Believer: Saffron was holding a fan in his hand and making a prayer to unlit candles in a makeshift dance room.

The Watcher: Honeysuckle was standing in a set of people with wide eyes, contemplating, smiling, and glowing.

The Archer: Ven held their bow in hand, starring off into the distance, hair in the wind, and shining determination in their eye.

The Actress: Phlox mimicked the infamous photoshoot, this time older and more mature, but just as vulnerable.

The Designer: Ginger held needles in her mouth and fabric in her hand as she made lace look like it could be a real flower.

"Even if it's not perfect. Even if others can do it better." She walked up to Arco and took the canvas that he held.

The King: Rosmarinus stood with cameras flashing behind him. His form was spotted in light and shadow.

The Composer: Ebru looked up to the sky in the midst of chaos. The bodies around him were blurred. The aerial shot made him look tiny and alone.

The Guide: Jasi stood in his uniform at a school, teaching kids, purple eyes bright, and holding fans as if he, too, were a dancer.

The Monarch: Aureolin was in a garden, cultivating ancient flowers back into existence, a soft smile on her lips.

"I'm not making art because it's going to change the world. I don't even care if you like it," Amaryllis said, placing the canvas down in the center.

The Dancer: Arco had his eyes closed. He was in the midst of spinning with his hands lifted high. It was the image of a person who wished for everything.

The Chosen: Arna was in a forest of wisteria looking haunted. The image reflected a person who knew nothing.

"I do it because it makes me happy, and I share it in hopes that it will make someone else feel something, too." She turned to look at them over her left shoulder, standing next to the portrait of herself: *The Lens.*

The self portrait of Amaryllis had her in a white dress on a stool surrounded by all white walls. She was sitting profile, looking over her right shoulder, and staring directly into the camera.

The only color in the black and white photo were her bright Aqua eyes: all knowing, all seeing.

"My display is fixed." She turned her attention to the assistants who were in charge of controlling the Temple. With her words the room bustled in movement. The guards escorted the instigators out and the crowd was dispersed.

Amaryllis headed to the back without saying a word.

The Day of Dreams

Arna woke after dawn on the sixth next to a sitting Ebru, who rubbed his eyes and looked exactly the same as he had the night before. His laptop was open far too early in the morning.

"Have you slept at all?" Arna asked him, lightly touching Ebru's hand.

"I'll sleep tomorrow. Today is the most important. Get up."

Startled, Arna did as he was told. Everyone else was already awake and dressed. Phlox tossed him a bag from across the room.

Confused, Arna held it gingerly and unwrapped it to reveal his mask.

The mask was not so much a person's face as it was a curved frame with two large holes, much too large for eyes. The paint danced across the surface, with dusted petals of actual flowers mixed in to create a three-dimensional display. Glitter and resin created three layers of rivers spiraling, through the eyes and past the end of the mask. The design was more beautiful than Arna could have ever created himself, but also exactly the way he'd envisioned.

The artist had taken what he'd painted and expanded, made it grow and pop. They'd created a display of surrealist representations of the Gods, in the way Arna saw them. Some flowers looked like birds. There were twigs like deer antlers around one eye, and rose petals around the other. The rose transformed into a sun, then into the moon. The antlers transformed from slick and untouched to scaled with what looked like actual dragonfly scales, then into the clouds at the top of the mask.

"This is beautiful," Arna said in awe.

"You created the bare bones, we had enough to work with. And my contact knew I needed it done quickly. She worked nonstop for days," Phlox beamed.

"I'm done too," Ebru said, holding a tiny chip. Arna stared blankly at it, trying to process what was said.

"It's time to practice, Arna," Arco ordered and Arna stumbled to his feet, throwing on his practice clothes.

The older Dragonflies moved in the dark of the morning, from the Temple of Xeyaro to the Cathedral of the Apostle, past the priests, and into Arna's practice room. Ebru loaded the music, and like it had been for the last week, Arna began to practice, guided by Arco who called him out for being sloppy. It was the first time the music and dance came together, but it felt as if it was the millionth time he'd done it.

"This is going to make the world explode," Phlox said, breathless as Arna finished Worship.

"That's my intent." It was his variation's nature. Despite the awe, however, the looks of expression in the room were that of deeply resigned terror and anguish.

"You still have one more petal," Ginger finally voiced the hum's melody aloud. "You can't dance until it's gone."

Arna nodded. He'd figure out the last part. He had to. Everyone looked at him as if he were walking to his death sentence. They were also worried about their own.

"We will defend you," Arco reminded them of the task. "We'll dance until you have the answer, and protect you when you do. Our plan will work, so long as you can shape the Blessings right."

Arna hoped it would be so simple.

Are you with me?

[In the breaths of those who slept there were whistles and chimes.]

"Let's enjoy the day then," Arna suggested and no one voiced a question or complaint.

For the majority of the day the others followed Arna through the celebrations, having fun, as friends. They were floating on the wind, living and breathing and telling stories of times when they were kids. They wove themselves through crowds, who were blithely unaware that they were the harbingers of change.

"The Golden Generation dance is still scheduled for dusk," Ven said, noting the time when it grew late.

"A state of emergency might be issued," Ebru warned the group as they returned back to reality. "The storm intensity has increased. It's suspected to last six hours. . ."

The sky was gray and misty as the Golden Dragonflies walked through the crowds, making their way to the Cathedral of the Apostle. When they arrived, they gathered Arna's things. A dissonance spread amongst them all as they hovered in the dance room, slow and lethargic.

"Arna," Arco called to him before they left.

"Yes?"

"The future is uncertain," Arco said, reminding Arna of his one last fear. "Don't let it be an accident."

"Accident?" Ebru asked.

"It won't be, I'm dancing," Arna said unable to smile.

"Amaryllis always tells me," Arco said, all eyes on him, "That every time we put art into the world, we can never anticipate the reaction it will bring. We never knows what the future holds. But we must be intentional in it."

Mortals or the Gods?

Arna stopped moving as the voice bounced across the floor. Who would he dance for? The weight and cost of that choice was the future he wished to build.

Oh. It was so simple.

"For that's what it means to be an artist," Amaryllis supplied.

livelivelivelivelivelive.

He'd been too focused on death again. It was not about the risk of dying for his future.

"When you make your choice," Arco said, "believe in it with everything you've got. Leave nothing up to chance. Let's defy fate. Let's see tomorrow."

Was he able to accept the chance that his future would not work out like his dreams? Would he dance despite knowing that? Could he accept that it wouldn't be perfect?

"Yes, because I'll be alive."

Like a drop of ice water, the last petal melted from his wrist.

When the group got backstage, dressed for the performance with makeup and hair done, the group before the Golden Generation dance was already on. The Dragonflies were filled with an intensity that was impossible to match, and an uncertainty that their plan would even work.

"Where were you?" Zaffre hissed at them, standing next to a set of white and black bags. Arna knew they held his fans. He had dark bags under his eyes, as if he hadn't slept in weeks.

They offered no apologies. Zaffre's lecture faded as he saw Arco, dressed for Arna. Protests were ignored as Arco called the Golden Dragonflies together, including Honeysuckle and Saffron.

"We are Vivicents," Arco declared. "We belong together. We die together. We will build the path together."

The dragonfly mark on their arms began to move.

"We go out there, no questions, no qualms, until the choice is made," Ebru said, glancing to Arna. Honeysuckle and Saffron agreed, despite not knowing what they were agreeing to.

"Show me a dream that only you can create," Arna wished. "Show me what it means to change the world."

Show me who I should dance for.

The music ended for the other group and the announcer went out. The performances were running late, which was a bad sign in a race against the weather.

"All performers accounted for the Golden Dance," the Assistant Stage Manager reported into their microphone. "Go."

One by one the members lined up, Ebru at the front of the line, stepping out only after the group was presented. The performance began with Ebru's first step and the audience was struck with it, in awe of it.

Arna watched from the shadows next to the Assistant Stage Manager, who gave him a twice over, startled.

"I'll tell you when to start the music," he told her.

It had taken them hours of debate and justification to pick their colors. Ginger had designed simple outfits to best suit the dance, and to represent that ambiguity of the Gods. They were nondescript, but each costume was defined by the colors of a single God. Each dancer had a black dragonfly stitched on their back. Everyone but Arco held one fan.

Ebru was Ixxzal, both known and unknown: pink, gray, and bronze. The swirls that billowed through the fabric were a shimmering gray, like a starry sky. He was the one people would be curious to see and interested in watching. He gave them hope. He gave them fear. He was everything they expected, and nothing they could comprehend all at once. He was the mystery that everyone wanted to keep, and the answer to every one of Arna's questions.

Ven was Lumak: balance, justice, humility, and the centering force. Violet, indigo, and mauve alternating scales and lavender flowers were across their clothes. It was strong to look at, but Ven's personality dimmed the intensity. Ven was their counterbalance and their anchor. They were the calm and the just: a mystifying safety that created an ache. Ven was the trust that gave Arna peace.

Aureolin was Pokk of knowledge and change: orange and yellow, with golden suns. Like a sunrise, she was the first to adapt and grow. Aureolin had moved on when she had known everything was over. She came back to them when she knew that there was a new beginning. She faced each day welcoming the new. She was the confidence Arna needed even in the face of danger.

Phlox was Zaynir, the one who hid everything. She was in aqua and sky blue with dark blue clouds, shimmering like a divine sky. She was emotion. She was drama. Phlox was so much soul that the world wanted to contain her, box her in, and make her into something that she was not. She reminded Arna that emotions were meant to be free.

Ginger was Azza, chaos and creation, in a shimmering forest green and red base with lime green moons. She dazzled and surprised. She supported others and opened doorways, especially for those who would wreck everything the world knew. She was selfless and selfish, life and death. She was Arna's backing to face the world, no matter the cost.

Arco.

What were cheers turned to silence. Confusion. Desperation. Fear. They were the sounds of a people who were having their world views changed. Where was Arna? Why? Why was *he* there? Was Arna leaving everyone again? Why Arco? Who did he think he was? He was not a Child. He did not belong to the Golden Generation's stage. *He* was not one of them.

And he wasn't; he was a Dragonfly.

Arco was Xeyaro of art and nature: dressed in white, silver, mint, and the leaves of a sturdy willow tree. The God of Dance stood on the stage. He was the one true manifestation of art. By being named Xeyaro, the message was clear: A nonChild was equal to the Children. That he, too, was a Child of Xeyaro. Arco was the embodiment of Arna's dream.

They moved to place their fans on the ground. One by one they froze and posed. Only Arco looked to the audience, daring them to complain and offering them nothing in return. Walking slowly, meticulously, powerfully, he sized up the crowd. The others stood still as he made his way across the stage. He did not take his eyes off the audience. He took longer than practice and was more ethereal by the minute.

Arco stopped walking, challenging the audience to look away. Then Ebru called to him—"Arna"—in a voice that was like the softest pin breaking silence against a hardwood floor. Arco was not just dancing for Arna. He was Arna.

Arco took his spot in formation and snapped his fan first open. Arna gave the Assistant Stage Manager the cue, and the music began.

Breathtaking. Arna was entranced.

History roared to life.

The softest whistle.

Chimes in the sky.

Glee filled Arna.

The dance was everything they had worked for and everything he wanted it to be.

a controlled statement.

a raving shriek.

a ravenous hope.

a shattering change.

This time dreams would not be pushed aside in the books and records because they were only
good.

They would be remembered,
celebrated,
known,
loved,
just like the greats.

Because, perhaps, they were better.

A thousand words tumbled into one, transforming and becoming more.

What is the point of the future if one clings so heavily to the past that they forget to see and believe in possibility?

A dragonfly—
even those whose wings flapped in a prehistoric past
that caused a rippling change through time
until it cascaded to the present
—is but a dragonfly, nothing more.

There will be thousands after just as there were before.

The now was but a myriad of choices made until they fused into one.

They are made consistently,
little ones in the moment,
while big ones come and go.

People could change their mind due to new facts, opinions, or values, and revoke decisions of the past.

When fear stagnates the waters of choice,
progress is not a suggestion, but a duty, regardless of the odds.

What is faith if not believing in the impossible?

What is living if not dreaming of the world after the impossible has been achieved?

There on the stage, in the bodies of a those who loved dance and loved each other more than anything, a story was woven. It was indestructible and rooted itself deeply, leaving no heart untouched. They gave three minutes to prepare the world for change, and to present the terrified with solace, before the end of all they'd ever known.

The lights will fade.
The audience will grow still.
The music will begin.
And you will know what to do.

— Another reminder that all will be well.

Dance 26

Creation

Incarnadine

Apostle Week

The Ceremony of Chaos

"It is time to decide, sweet child."
"Decide what?"
"We are giving you the opportunity to be our Chosen. If you wish to be, listen carefully.
When the clock strikes for the turn of the year, you must ensure you are not holding a fan."
"And then I'll be the Chosen Child?"
"You must give your soul so that you may learn to live without it. You will give your family
so they may see without you. You shall give your dreams so the world may dream without
being held back. You will give your all."
"I am Chosen?"
"Trust in us and we will not fail you. Ignore us and the opportunity will be lost. Before you
there is a single choice, nothing more: mortals or the Gods. The choice is yours."

The group walked off stage, passing Honeysuckle, who stood in her custom-sized ceremonial garb and mask on the back of her head: customary for the Original variation. In her hands she held a box. On stage the emcee stalled for time, waiting for the Assistant Stage Manager to send on Cardinal Black.

"I had my mom prepare these." Honeysuckle offered a box to all of the Golden Dragonflies. Inside were eleven necklaces just like hers with a stone of amber encasing a saffron flower. Saffron was the first to grab one, Arna second. He held it to the light.

Saffron. Saffron. Saffron.

He placed it around his neck, no longer needing to be afraid of being like Saffron. He deserved this.

The others followed suit without much complaint, following Arna's lead. Honeysuckle smiled back to her mother, who was surprised they took them at all.

"It is almost weightless," Ginger said in amazement. "This won't affect our dancing at all."

The others nodded, solemn. There was a surge of the thrum of panic amongst them. Arna rubbed his bare wrist as the whistle of true wind ripped through the city, high pitched and free of the Blessing shields.

"It begins," Arco said, taking a deep breath.

The hymn finally reached its peak.

"We can do this," Jasi reminded them. "We've gone through it tens of times."

"So long as it works," Rosmarinus said, reminding the all of the likelihood of it not working. Regardless of what he said, however, the way he said it was a taunt, a dare for them to achieve the impossible.

"It will," Ven insisted. "Are you ready, Honeysuckle?"

"Yup!" she nodded and hurried to the Assistant Stage Manager, leaving the others behind. The older Dragonflies shared a look.

"Focus on your choice, Arna," Ebru insisted. "You have to make the right one."

Arna nodded.

"Until then, we dance for you," Ginger reminded him. "We're prepared for this. Just. . . don't choose too late."

He wouldn't.

"And now, at this time of the night, we ask for you all to pray." Cardinal Black's voice called their attention back to the stage. His hair was tossed a bit by the wind that was beginning to form. Cardinal Black led the world in prayer: "'And they said, upon you we grant bodies so that you may move, and live, and grow.'"

Arco, Ebru, Aureolin, and Ginger all traded outfits for their ceremonial clothes, getting dressed in silence. As Cardinal Black spoke, attendants and fan apprentices rushed on stage to check the Ceremonial Regalia: clothes, fans, and masks. At the back of the stage were five cases made of glass, holding the ancient but preserved remnants of the original Ceremonial clothes worn by the five Chosen before him; and inside were their original fans for Worship. The most important national treasures in the world were on display for the Ceremony of Chaos.

"'And they said, upon you we grant voices so that you may communicate, and change, and bond.'"

Arna closed his eyes, and rested his hands, palm open, at his sides.

The only thing he'd ever wanted was to be the Chosen Child. There was nothing he wanted more. He'd followed every part of the Apostle prophecy. He broke the world chasing the dream. He did it all, because he had wanted it, selfishly.

When they told him to run, he listened. When they told him to jump, he did as he was told. When they lectured him. When they isolated him. When he screamed at them to let him be and leave him alone. . . It was still all he ever wanted.

"'And they said, upon you we grant intelligence so you may know our divine nature and worship our benevolence.'"

When he hated everything and wanted to forsake the Gods. When he had learned he was an imposter forcing a plan that may have never been meant for him. When he thought the Gods a false figment of his imagination. When he did not care if he was killed, wanting the pain to end. He still wanted it.

This would not be the havoc wrecked on his body in six minutes of a storm. It would not be the bleeding of a Blessing being exsanguinated. It was not the hiding secrets from those he loved. Nor was it helping them process the inevitability that he had already come to terms with. Everything paled in comparison to the potential of this failure. This was going to be worse.

"'And they said, upon you we grant Blessings so that you may thrive, and so that our brilliance may shine through you.'"

The Gods were terrified, fading, flickering, and dying. The mortals were afraid of the same. To protect them both had once meant he'd die for them. Now it meant he must live. The split-second decision Arna made at fifteen to cause the Splintering was to be rectified with arduous contemplation after twelve years. Arna knew the question, knew the cost, and accepted whatever choice he had to make.

He had spent years training. He was prepared to make the vow to them to be their Chosen. He was willing to rebuild the contract despite not knowing how or what it meant. He was going to do it because it was his everything. Now he had to make his choice.

"'And they said, upon you we ask of peace, between your kind and to the world around you. Balance and life are what we require.'"

[*Mortals or the Gods?* The voice was little more than a memory.]

The Gods were not back. Their voices unsteady, like a recording, echoing and chanting, offering him the vow he needed to make.

Who would he dance for?

[   ]

Arna opened his eyes.

"'And they said, upon you we ask for reverence in the form of Twenty-Seven Dances given each year on the solstice, so that the bond between us may be strengthened and continued.' And so, it was. And so, it shall be," Cardinal Black finished, walking off stage.

"We're cutting the introductions for dancers between Ceremony sections," the Assistant Stage Manager said to the emcee before he could walk out. Instead, she motioned to Honeysuckle.

She glanced back at them all, took a deep breath and walked on stage. As she did, her straight honey-blonde hair, tied up in a high bow the same color as Ginger's, whipped around in the air. She held steady and walked to the center of stage where the fans were finished being placed by the fan apprentices, ready for her.

Honeysuckle danced perfectly, without missing a step. She was brilliant for a nonChild, and someone unBlessed. There were cheers from the audience until there was not. They must have realized how old she was: part of the generation that the world forgot. She made them face it.

"Why is the wind early?" Zaffre asked someone in the back.

"Arna," Arco grabbed his arm. "How much more time do you need?"

He and the others were all changed into their clothes for the Ceremony.

"As much as you can manage." Arna told him, still contemplating, entranced by Honeysuckle. "I'm thinking, but I don't have it."

[*Arna, your choice?* Gods? Something else? Someone?]

Hands open. Hands closed. *Don't squeeze.*

The winds backstage berated him for his inaction. Thunder crashed somewhere far above.

Honeysuckle continued to dance, the wind lifting at the hem of her clothes, adding a flourish to her moves. She nearly stumbled but held her balance; she was an excellent and practiced dancer. Her moves were learned, trained, and mastered into muscle memory through hours of intense study.

"She should have been a Child," Honeysuckle's mother cried to someone else, and Arna disagreed. She didn't need to be a Child to dance; she was already doing it. She was already proving it, because she wanted it. When Honeysuckle walked off stage, she was windblown but otherwise okay.

"I think the winds are too powerful, something is wrong," she said as soon as she could. The apprentices hurried to set up the next section.

"Nothing is wrong, sweetheart," Cyclamen said, cooing her, but she rushed away to Arna's side, without acknowledging his existence.

"I'm a Dragonfly, too," she said.

"And you help us," Amaryllis said from next to Arna. "Arna hasn't made his choice. Everyone dances until then."

"The storm is too powerful. . . It could destroy the city if the shields aren't put up in time. It's worse than even our latest predictions," someone said much too loudly to Governor Cider, back against the walls.

"Get everything cleaned up," Governor Cider ordered.

From where Arna stood in the wings, the damage was clear. The trees were beginning to sway in the distance. The lights in the sky above flickered and started to glitch in and out: night and then a blinding city of light. Night, then light pollution again.

"Order a vendor clear-out," Governor Cider said.

The apprentices returned and Assistant Stage Manager signaled for Garance to go out. The girl walked on stage, glancing at Aureolin who gave her a thumbs up.

"Is everything going to be okay?" Saffron asked Arna, walking over to Honeysuckle's side.

Arna closed his eyes once more.

"No," Honeysuckle told him. "We have to help Arna."

Hands open. Hands closed. He traced the scars.

Arna could dance for the mortals; those who tried to use him and had ignored him when times got hard. He could dance for them, and then what? Trudge forward? Slosh through the mud of politics and bureaucracy? Inadequacy? Doing what they told him to do forever? Working every moment of his life to make up for the thousands of lives that had been lost because he'd been selfish enough to want to be the Chosen Child?

He got one chance, one answer. He had to make it count.

Arna opened his eyes as the winds ripped through backstage with a horrid tearing sound. Electricity buzzed within them. The Rose cried as she was forced to move. Lights overhead flickered. Roaring sounds of metal crashing reverberated in the distance as the entire stage began to shudder.

There was a soft gasp and clatter behind Arna. Aureolin was near the door, on the ground, holding her ankle with a disarray of items around her. Everyone turned to Arco. He couldn't dance both Powers and Understanding.

Still as an icicle, Arco said under his breathe, where only Arna could hear, "Please just give me this."

"I'm fine. I'm fine." Aureolin laughed loudly, trying to dissolve the tension. She did not struggle to get up. Despite this, she was not okay; Arna was certain.

"Arco?" Honeysuckle tugged at his sleeve.

"Nothing changes," Arco said loudly, and the Golden Dragonflies all nodded. Arna would die for them, but they were a mirror reflecting it back: they, too, would die for him.

Arna's breath caught in his throat.

"We are with you," Arco reminded him. Arna forced himself to nod.

Despite the horror at the idea of them dancing, Arna accepted it with the cruel and cold rationality that they accepted the end of the world. For weeks they had proven it, time and time again, that they were a team. They were going to fight this together. They were born together, and they belonged together. It was painful to accept, like a part of his heart was snipped away and he'd never get it back, but he had to honor it.

"It's fight or die now, boys." Amaryllis stepped up, camera in hand, snapping photos where no one could stop her.

They were choosing to fight.

He was no longer alone, they were with him. He was afraid of dying, but they all were. He was afraid of being an imposter, but he already was one. He did not want to face the pain, but neither did they. And yet they stood there staring at him, asking him to trust them.

He did.

The Weeping Stage creaked, and there was a gasp and shriek from the audience. Garance fell: between two songs. She was unable to get up, leg twisted in a horrific direction. She did not have the Blessings to assist her, nor was she a good enough dancer to dance in the assault.

"Aureolin, take over!" Cyclamen ordered.

"I'm—" the understudy said when the man was pulled back by the guards.

"Not a Child," Cyclamen disagreed. "I am the master of this stage."

The contract they all signed took effect. Cyclamen's word was law. They dragged the understudy from the backstage and away.

"Aureolin. Go."

Aureolin walked forward, hand on Arna's shoulder. She squeezed. "I will buy you time."

The assistants helped Garance off stage. Garance tried to say something to Aureolin, but Aureolin ignored her. She stepped forward to the fans for Holly Appreciation that fluttered, their fabric lifted in the wind. She adjusted them, picked up two, and then began to complete Appreciation starting from the ninth dance. She was perfect.

"They're going to throw me out there," Ebru said, walking up to Arna, tracing Arna's scars with his fingertips. "Whatever choice you make, it will be the right one."

When their eyes met, Ebru's were sparkling. *I believe in you.*

"What are you whispering about?" Cyclamen called to them as they stood near the wings. No one answered him, but they all turned their attention to the stage. Phlox watched Aureolin anxiously.

As Aureolin danced the winds did not look dangerous. Yet, the stagehands backstage struggled to hold the curtains back as they began to float and whip about. The fan apprentices quickly changed the fans to Holly Powers for Aureolin.

As she began the Powers dances, Aureolin grew sloppy. Her arms were heavy, lethargic, and not nearly as clean as she should have been. She was almost a bit slow, struggling to keep up with the dances. Her right leg dragged and when she dropped to pick up the fans between thirteen and fourteen, she did not get up.

The curtains had to be tied back. The creaking of the rose grew louder. Entire sections of the city were blacked out, like pits of a void. The Weeping Stage cried in protest, replicating those who died in the Shattering. There was a thousand-year history in the wood.

"She sprained her ankle. She can't dance," Arco walked on past them all before Cyclamen called his name. Cyclamen did not stop him. No one called him to stop, as he was the understudy and despite not having the Blessings, much like Garance or Honeysuckle: they believed Arco capable of anything.

The temperature dropped to a chill, breath a white vapor. Arna's hair whipped around his shoulders. Aureolin refused to move, holding her ankle even as pebbles and sticks began to land on her. The music of her variation droned on and on, before the Assistant Stage Manager cut it short with a click of the portable console, only to be used in emergencies. An eerie silence overtook the stage, marked by the sound of her ceremonial clothes whipping against her body.

"Ginger, get ready," Cyclamen agreed. "You are dancing Understanding."

"Yes." Ginger hurried to the back, stunned out of her stupor.

When Arco stood before Aureolin, then and only then did she look up, tears in her eyes.

Her voice was carried on the wind, "I'm sorry, Arco. I'm sorry."

"It's okay, get up. I'm here now."

Arco helped her up and quickly. The stagehands and Phlox rushed out to help her off the stage, and Arco took her spot. He nodded to the Assistant Stage Manager, who called for the fourteenth dance to be restarted.

The entirety of backstage took a collective breath of relief. The audience, those who were not racing away for cover, cheered for Arco. Arco was the embodiment of peace. He danced as he had been trained to do, in the spot they knew him to inhabit. The serenity that came with that was jarring compared to how they had treated him less than an hour earlier. His shirt lifted from his waist, exposing his bare side.

When the song began it was the Holly variation. In his hands he held the same fans. And despite being known for Blue Rose Fears, the dance about hope, Arco gracefully danced Holly: capitalizing on the destruction to fully embody the variation's terror.

"The audience is being moved to shelter," Governor Cider told Cyclamen. "Sports fields and stages are coming down. Everything that can be closed. We need to hurry this up."

"We cannot rush this," Cyclamen disagreed.

That was when the rain began. At first Arna did not believe his ears, the light patter of drops on wood. Then it grew and pelted the stage, drenching Arco in water. Makeup bled from his side, drenching his clothes in brown. Spinning, his vow mark was visible to all.

Arna turned to his father. He was on the mobile talking to their mother. His eyes were on Arco, furrowed in confusion. He glanced to Arna, who shook his head. Now was not the time.

"What is going on?" Honeysuckle asked Arna. "Why is it raining?"

"Honeysuckle, we need to go," her mother called over the loud music. Honeysuckle did not move. Saffron stood by her side, despite Amaryllis' parent's urging.

[*Do not forsake us,* Gods cried, somewhere far away.]

"Wenge and Alabaster are on their way. The standard lights will be going out soon, and the emergency lights will go on. Some booths have already been destroyed in the wind," Zaffre approached the Golden Dragonflies, staring directly at Arna. "This is for you, isn't it?"

Arna slowly nodded.

I have to go. But what did he choose? He couldn't choose Gods or Mortals.

The mortals saw him the same way he saw the Gods. They wanted him to step in. They wanted him to give them the correct answer. They wanted him to fix everything, as he had before. They wanted him to change the world. However, they had let him go home because he was ready to decide without them.

Hands open. Hands closed. Ebru took his hand.

The Governor of Xeysis argued with Cardinal Black and Cyclamen. "We need to redirect all power to the wards, too much is going to be destroyed if we don't."

"The wards must stay down. The Ceremony of Chaos must be done under the open sky, without interference," Cardinal Black insisted. "We will force you if we have to."

"This can destroy the city! They must go up."

"You might think you hold the power here, Cider, but you do not. I do. The wards will stay down."

"People will die!"

[*For whom will you dance?* they yelled in the form of a whisper.]

In the audience a few people stood as if the wind did not matter. Arco walked off more exhausted than Arna had ever seen him. He had danced as if the wind had meant nothing to him, but Arna could see it in the way that the trees were moving: the winds were a disaster. Everything was being thrashed about and the curtains had to be lifted and tied to the walls. There were the sounds of snapping wires. In the sky above, the web of the rails was swaying and flickering.

Luckily, or perhaps not, Arco had no injuries.

[There were no accidents.]

Ginger walked out as soon as the crew cleared the stage. All eyes were on her as her music began and she started to dance Roots and Ends Understanding. Perhaps they would do it after all. Perhaps they would be able to. . .

There was an earth-shattering sound of metal moving that cut through the music. Arna stepped up and stared up. The metal rose petals were swaying.

[*Arna. What is silence?*]

"There is only so much movement they can take!" the Governor shouted behind him.

"The wards stay down, so help me, Cider! I call upon Lumakic Law," Cardinal Black snapped back, invoking the law that stated the capability of a Church to take over the government, if deemed necessary.

"You wouldn't dare!" Governor Cider screamed as if this had not been Cyclamen and Cardinal Black's plan from the beginning.

"Under the sight of the Holy Gods, it is already done," Cardinal Black said.

"You! You have not! The Gods will not abide by it."

"My people are already in control," the man said. Cyclamen was smiling wildly.

Screams erupted from the audience. Branches, glass, and broken parts from the booths were being thrown about in the wind. Sand and dust had been kicked up along with dirt and water to form a thick mist. Tables began flying towards the stage, slamming against the base of it. People dove out of the way. The nanotech barriers that were meant to activate when the stage was in danger, did not turn on.

Ginger continued to dance, unable to stop. She trusted Arna to make his choice. She believed in him and the time she was providing him. She was hit in the leg by a rod. It ripped open her pant leg and spiraled away, impaling the glass behind her. The pole stuck out of the box, a clean insertion with cracks that surrounded the hole. It did not shatter. The barriers still did not turn on.

Ginger stumbled but did not fall. Blood drenched her clothes, dying them crimson. More rocks, branches, celebration fans, and discarded glow sticks, hit the glass boxes behind her. She continued to dance as the glass dust dyed her brow red. Gravel cut up her cheeks and neck. She continued to dance, eyes ahead, as if nothing could stop her.

The dancing had to be ferocious, and what little control the dancer had had to be maintained. Each one of the performers had done their best to complete the song that was set before them. But. . .

Arna squeezed Ebru's hand. Ebru squeezed back.

Arco's dream was his dream. Amaryllis' dream was his dream. Ven was the peace they had when they held a bow. Phlox was the brilliance when she stood on stage. Aureolin was the passion when she cared for flowers. He wanted Ginger to be able to fashion design. He wanted to see the world with Jasi, carefree. He wanted to be there for Ebru in the depth of the night, talking of music and hopes.

"I'm—" Arna began, knowing that he had to go out there, even if he had not yet made his choice. He needed to save them, to protect their futures.

"Eburnean, you are going out there," Cyclamen said as Arna did.

Ebru's eyes were wide in a stunned silence. Cardinal Black and the Governor continued to argue.

"No?" Cyclamen asked him. "I hold complete authority over this stage, and you will do as I say."

He wanted this, this power over Ebru, and Cardinal Black had easily given it to him.

"He can't go out there. . ." Arna started but could not finish. This was the support he needed. The others were buying time for him: long, agonizing minutes where they hoped and prayed that he would come up with an answer. But if Ebru went out there, he was not trained to dance in a storm; worse, a superstorm that was forming. They may not have known, but there was electricity in the air.

"He's going," Cyclamen insisted. He had never believed in Arna, even less now, as his guards surrounded them and picked Arna up before he could protest. "But I do believe that by subsection eight of the contract, all non-required individuals are to be escorted off stage now that Lumakic Law has been established."

Ginger screamed as dance twenty-one ended, and quickly everyone was moving. Ginger was moved backstage as Wenge and Alabaster arrived.

"Emergency vehicles can't get here." Wenge saw Arna's sister and without a sound she rolled up her sleeves. "I'm going to have to heal what I can until they arrive."

She got on the ground next to Ginger who was breathing heavily and began to help.

"Get the Chosen's ceremonial regalia out of there," the Assistant Stage Manager yelled to the crew. "Everyone nonessential, evacuate. All people are being escorted out of the Religious Circle to the surrounding buildings."

Jasi and Rosmarinus. Honeysuckle and her mother. Saffron, Amaryllis, her parents. Ven. Phlox. Aureolin, who was injured. Alabaster. Arco. All of them were grabbed from where they stood by the guards backstage.

"What are you doing, Cyclamen?" Zaffre shouted.

"By the Gods' will, we have to dance all the parts tonight, and your golden boy will not dance." Cyclamen glared at Arna. For once, the man wore spotless white, as if he had no fear of the storm leaving a stain upon him. He smiled wickedly at Arna. "All other dances are completed."

With only Zaffre and Ebru remaining, Zaffre would be the senior member of the Vivicent Studio overseeing them. The rest of them were negligible.

"Remove them! Zaffre, Wenge and Ginger can stay," Cyclamen ordered, and Un.Abilities showered down atop of Arna, dragging him from the backstage, into the wind. Ebru stared at Arna, unmoving, a vast emptiness filling Ebru's form as Cyclamen patted his shoulder. Ebru was a void, a blank space, the inspiration, and Arna's reason. Once again, all Arna saw was him.

"Ebru! Don't go out there!" Arna shouted at him, as he was dragged offstage. *I can't lose you.*

Within seconds they were berated by the winds off of the stage. Rain, dust, and the audience chairs were spiraling about in the beginning of a vortex. Sand and smoke pelted their bodies as they were forced through the haze. Arna struggled to activate his abilities as he was held down by tens of men, all with Fa. and Un. abilities specifically hired to combat him. The others screamed for Arna as they were dragged in the opposite direction.

As Arna was hauled away, there were shadows on the stage, visible through the haze of dust and fog. A singular figure walked to the center, melding and becoming a phantom himself.

Arna was thrown to the ground with a thud. Spitting out dirt, he glared up at the guards who surrounded him, recognizing familiar faces from those who had attacked his house.

"Here to finish the job?" Arna asked as the music for Blue Rose Fears Understanding began.

"The One Truth will be pleased that we stopped your heresy," one man said.

Arna was not sure what bothered him more: the fact that Cyclamen had stooped so low in his attempt to destroy Arna that he hired crazed religious fiends, or that they called him a heretic.

Arna rolled in the dirt, trying to get away from them. His Blessings refused to trigger under the pressure of the abilities, all too familiar.

"So, you tried to kill me *and* you were hired by the government for my retesting," Arna understood. He never should have trusted any of them: the governor, Cyclamen, Cardinal Black.

The rain turned the dirt into slush, covering Arna in filth as he scrambled to get away from the men. Some drew knives. Others held guns. There was nowhere to hide and nowhere to flee.

Survive.

> [*We are with you!* the Gods screamed, their voice melding with
> the broken world.]

Arna pressed himself up, trying to get leverage as the first gunshot went off, masked by the shrieking of the swaying petals. Lightning lit up the center of the rose, rushing along the skyrail. It glowed hot blue. He twisted on his feet trying to avoid the next shot that grazed him, searching for his Blessings. He was not fast enough. He was not strong enough. He was not—

Lightning struck between them all, white and soundless.

Arna crashed to the ground rolling over and over. He tried to make sense of what way was up and down. His ears did not ring. Through the mists figures rushed towards him. Arco knelt down, grabbing him, and their eyes locked.

"The One Truth shall be heard!" the man yelled, raising his gun again.

"No!" Phlox screamed and the wind around them knocked the man over, ripping the ground asunder.

"Hurry over here!" Ven stopped running, beckoning Arna and Arco closer. The storm began to shake open cracks in the ground. The mud grew thick. A singular path of flowers formed in grass towards the others.

Arco pulled Arna to his feet, and they raced over across solid ground towards Alabaster and Rosmarinus. Jasi helped Aureolin. Honeysuckle and Saffron, their families, Cardinal White and Mr. Thyme looked breathless. He and Cardinal White were accompanied by security that rushed to help. Mr. Thyme shouted orders Arna could not hear as an ear-rupturing S C R E E C H claimed the air.

"Watch out!" Aureolin screamed, pushing past Jasi as Arna ran close. She leapt for him, grabbing him and Arco, pulling them back as a flying car landed in the grass between them and One Truth guards. It caught on fire. Groans and screams of the One Truth guards erupted.

"They had guns!" Mr. Thyme shouted. "This is an international incident! We cannot allow this to stand!"

Arna glanced at Mr. Thyme who was caught halfway through an apology and great disdain. The man still may have disliked him, but he was on his side. The task force was made, at the end of the day, to protect the Chosen.

Cardinal White helped Arna up.

"How are you here?"

"I thought there was trouble," Cardinal White said.

"The Governor tried to separate us," Phlox said. "He wanted to kill you!"

"Not the first time." And Arna imagined it would become an investigation in the future. For now, they had a task to complete.

"Where is Amaryllis?" Arna asked them.

"Don't focus on her! Ebru!" Arco snapped back and Arna's attention turned to the stage. In the mists Ebru danced to Blue Rose Fears instead of Holly, calling Arna home.

His face was cut, bleeding from many places. The lights were flickering. His clothes were ripped. Ebru had not stumbled, but his legs were bleeding in six places each. The metal of the rose creaked louder. Ebru danced harder, bleeding from his neck. His breath was visible in the mist.

Deep breath in, deep breath out. Hand open. Hand shut.

Mortals or the Gods? The voice was Ginger and Saffron, chaos and creation in one.

People often mistake selfishness for selflessness.

"Run," Arna said, turning back to the stage entrance, and sprinting. He did not wait for anyone, sensing his Blessings and flourishing them. He pushed through the pain.

He had to get to Ebru.

All he had ever wanted was to be the Chosen Child, to dance forever, to be with his family, and to be loved. For years it was the closest dream he held to his heart: to be loved and to accept love. He wanted it in all its forms. Old love. New love. Platonic and romantic. Unconditional, undying love that would support him through anything.

Mortals or the Gods? Ven and Jasi's voices swelled together creating harmony and security.

What are you willing to live for?

Arna crashed back onto the stage, Cyclamen glowering at him as Ebru screamed. A collective gasp took over backstage as Ebru crumbled. A large branch had embedded itself into Ebru's stomach. Nothing that large should have gotten to him, but the barrier malfunctioned. Despite it, the fans did not fall from his hands. Instead, he collapsed to his knees. He placed the fans down, without toppling.

"Get him off!" Zaffre yelled, lunging to get on stage. And somehow, disturbingly, Ebru grabbed the next set of fans and stood. Zaffre was pushed back by the guards that remained.

"I will have everyone who fights arrested!" Cyclamen yelled at them. "It is the Gods' will."

"Why do you pray to Gods who want this?" Phlox yelled as she collapsed into Arna. He was frozen, watching the love of his life die before his eyes.

"We have gone against their word for too long, pretending to be things that we are not," Cyclamen hissed at Arna, and Cardinal Black nodded.

Mortals or the Gods? Phlox and Rosmarinus' voices were confident, charming, emotional, and searching for Arna to answer.

What are you willing to fight for?

Ebru moved. His back was drenched, all his clothes scarlet, but Ebru was dedicated to completing the dance. He would never fail, could not fail. Arna's heart ached. Ebru was dying. For him.

Just like Arna, Ebru would die for the Gods, but he'd also die for his friends and family. He'd die for all mortals if it meant they survived. And yet as much as he'd die for them. He wanted to live for them, too. Arna had always been able to convince him to live because he wanted to.

Ebru continued to dance. Screams reverberated backstage as the debris started to shower on them, and the entire stage began to crack. Ancient memories of the storms it withstood seeped into the air as a pink haze.

Zaffre struggled to get past the blockade on the stage with Alabaster. Arco went running with Phlox and Aureolin. They were tossed back. Arna was pushed back to the wall, far from the curtains and the stage. No one paid him any heed. He was forgotten, erased. One last breath and he too would disappear with Ebru forever.

"He's not your student, Cyclamen!" Zaffre yelled.

"He's my son!" Alabaster cried.

Mortals or the Gods? Aureolin and Honeysuckle were a fire, raging and passionate, demanding for the known to be realized.

And what will you become after?

Arna dreamed of saffron flowers and loud music. He pictured a future that he did not yet know, but accepted would not be perfect. He wanted to be what he thought he was, what they hoped he was. He wanted to help others achieve their goals. He wanted to save Ebru and Arco and everyone who had ever dreamed and been told no. He wanted to figure out who he was meant to be.

Ebru continued to dance, as his inspiration continued to bleed out. Dreams were powerful, but fragile and forgotten when one woke up. Nightmares were different. They were corrupted, etched into the soul and remembered in perpetuity.

The world around them had shattered. Staff cowered in corners. Others were praying. The Assistant Stage Manager wiped her eyes. City lights were down. The Rose was shrieking.

Screams were calling through the wind, from far off petals.

Hands open. Hands closed. Hands opened. Hands closed.

What is silence? Amaryllis' voice was a litany, a path that did not exist: one that would guide him true.

Near Arna's feet, untouched by the wind and the fighting, were bags of white and black. The dance as the Chosen Child was a vow. It was one that could never be broken. But how did one craft a contract they didn't know? How did they gain forgiveness when there was no apologies given or needed? How did one build a path to live?

You just do.

Nightmares were just corruptions. They could become dreams once more. The world slowed, seconds taking minutes, lasting an eternity, clarity enveloping Arna. He addressed the abyss within himself and called, expecting no answer, "I understand."

Only Cardinal White watched him.

"You couldn't discipline your own child," Cyclamen snapped back at Zaffre. "This is the Gods' retribution. He should be the one dancing, but he refuses. He would already be dancing if he wasn't a *liar*."

Arna looked at Cyclamen Shadone, and then back to Ebru. Ebru missed a step but did not stumble. Fury spiraled through Arna.

Mortals or the Gods? The voice was both Ebru and Arco, supportive and sarcastic in their provocation.

"Or rather he can't." Cyclamen Shadone glared at Arna. "Because you are not and have never been the Chosen."

A thousand words. A million lessons. Dark nights and hidden voices. It was the statement made by a dreamer who wanted to dance. ***You've worked your whole life for this.***

It was the comment by a God who never lied. ***He didn't think he deserved it. . . He did.***

The decision had been made long ago, in the flashing light of midnight. It had been made on the rail cars that were crashing. It had been made when he was watching from the caves as killer storms screamed. It was behind the shadow of silver leaves. With each agreement and each lesson. Years of scars. Years of tears. Effort. Practice. Time and time again.

Ebru continued to dance. The music played but was consumed by the sound of Arna's beating heart.

Mortals or the Gods? From years ago, young and overconfident, Arna asked himself. He was the moonlight through the willow tree. He was death in the form of a lie.

Cyclamen Shadone continued his tirade. Tens of people avoided looking at Ebru, who bled for them, who had always bled for them. Arna's feet were moving too fast for anyone to stop him. He threw his fist at Cyclamen Shadone, knocking the man down. When Cardinal Black tried to stop him, Arna pushed him back as well.

"More than anything. . . You will *never* touch him again," Arna said, calmly: the epicenter.

Ebru was breathing heavily, moving between songs. Ebru stood after dance twenty-four, chin lifted to the sky. There was no chance Ebru's body could dance twenty-five. It was a miracle he'd gotten as far as he had.

"That is illegal under the Contingency Clause!" Cyclamen screamed at him, scrambling away. He pointed at the guards, who approached Arna. Arna wanted to rip the man's spleen out through his throat. He flourished his Blessings before they could stop him.

"The Contingency Clause states that you have full authority of the Weeping Stage and undermining it during Lumakic Law is treason." Arna had listened to Jasi lecture him on the rules that the task force had shamefully crafted and knew the loophole just as well.

He had worked his whole life for this storm. He had spent years studying scriptures, working with only two hours of sleep, and practicing until his bones ached and his brain screamed. He'd done everything for the world, to make up for his mistake. He had spent restless nights online, trying to prove that he existed to someone. He had spent years visualizing, sweating, crying, bleeding, and preparing to die for the dances.

"But Lumakic Law is built to protect the interests of the Chosen," Arna said. Arna didn't care if it were the correct answer. He was going out. He was dancing. He was too prepared, too ready. The whole world may try to kill him, but he would survive.

Because he was the Gods' damned Chosen Child.

Mr. Thyme was backed up against the only sturdy wall he could find. His guards tried to retain order against Cyclamen's, but it was a stalemate. As their eyes met, Mr. Thyme, terrified and shaking, stepped forward.

"The task force stands by you," his voice quaked, but it was all Arna needed. "We revoke Cyclamen's rule, under Lumakic Law."

"I name Cardinal White, witness and ruler," Arna spoke, claiming the final section of Lumakic Law: that while any church could call it to order, the Chosen could change who held control at any time.

A collective breath formed.

"You are not!" Cyclamen sputtered, but it was enough to give everyone pause. "You are an imposter that the Gods spurn! You will destroy us all!"

"And under Apolic Law," Cardinal White said. "I hold all power, while the Chosen dances."

Arna ignored Cyclamen, and shoved past the guards to get onto the stage. He grabbed Ebru's hands before Ebru could pick up the Holly fans for the twenty-fifth dance, that had been placed with the Blue Rose Fears fans. The wind was hostile, threatening to rip Arna's clothes from his body. The petals overhead were swaying back and forth with an ear shattering screech. Most of the city was dark. The glow of the lighting far above the flower illuminated the city, bouncing over metal and glass.

"Arna?" Ebru's eyes were cloudy, like smoke that swirled and dwindled. Shadows formed to consume the light.

"I'm here." Arna said the words knowing they were the only words he needed. He placed their foreheads together.

"You found me." Ebru's words dusted Arna's skin like promises made in foggy mornings. It was the symphony that came with silence.

[   ]

"Yes." The answer was neither. He would dance.

For himself.

Arna quickly picked up Ebru as Ebru's eyes went dark. He was as light as a feather and with little breath in him. Arna rushed him backstage as the Holly music was cut short, madness descending across the group. Arna laid him down near Ginger and Wenge in the wings. There was a small pause as Arna got to his feet. He shrugged off his bloodied and muddied jacket, tossing it to Arco.

"We begin?" Arco asked, with an odd sort of mixed glee and radiant vindication.

Arna took one last deep breath in, filling his lungs.

"We begin," Arna exhaled.

The Golden Dragonflies swarmed about the stage past the guards, moving as they had practiced, without another word from anyone. Arna struggled out of his clothes. Ven quickly assisted. Phlox and Rosmarinus grabbed Arna's fans, racing to the stage.

"Incarnadine?" asked his father, hope in his voice. Arna tossed him the chip file that Ebru had completed that morning. The exhaustion in his father's contenance lifted.

"Give that to the sound board. The file is titled: The Incarnation of Dreams Upon the World Variation of the Twenty-Seven Dances of Worship for the Knowledge, Adoration, and Understanding of the Six Gods Danced with Alternating Fans." It wasn't necessary, but Arna wanted to say the title in full so that everyone heard him. He needed them to know his claim.

Zaffre, without being prompted, raced to the Assistant Stage Manager, accessing the portable console that connected her to the Stage Manager and sound technician at the top of the Cathedral of the Apostle. Jasi approached Cyclamen and Cardinal Black with Mr. Thyme and Cardinal White.

"What are you doing?" Cyclamen yelled.

"Cyclamen, you are to remove yourself." Cardinal White's voice was softer but demanding.

Arna stripped from his shirt as Ven rubbed a towel along Arna's arms, silently cleaning the mud off of him. They helped him into the top as Ginger had shown them, buttoned each clasp with fingers that did not shake. Their eyes locked, and Arna removed his pants.

"By whose authority? I called the Law into action," Cardinal Black yelled. "He simply cannot change it! He is not Chosen!"

"But the Chosen Task Force under Lumakic and Cardinal White under Apolic, have claimed him. Their law is above yours," Jasi said to Cardinal Black in a mocking tone.

Arna pulled on the bottoms as Ven adjusted the cuffs around Arna's wrists and ankles. As Arna slipped into his shoes, Ven wiped down his hair, fixing it and retying it up in the ponytail elastics that Ginger always used with her own braids.

The commotion continued as Cyclamen and Cardinal Black lost power. Jasi ordered the stagehands to move. Honeysuckle and Saffron hovered nearby, awaiting their orders, despite how the other adults tried to move them away.

"Go help Phlox and Rus," Arna ordered the younger Dragonflies. They nodded and raced off before anyone could stop them. Honeysuckle's mother glowered at Arna, but Amaryllis' parents held her back. He paid them all no mind as Alabaster pulled them to the back.

"The stage is drenched. The conditions are horrible," Ven scolded Arna.

"I know, but we have to try anyway," Arna assured them.

"It's going to be okay," Ginger's voice called from where she was struggling to sit up.

"Ginger. . ." Ven shook their head.

"It's okay. I can do this," she said, her eyes glowing as she struggled to stand. All around them the water stopped. Arna's eyes went wide. She blinked and it all fell, but for a second. . .

"The veil is thin," Arco told Arna. "Do you think the God's know our intention?"

"Let's make a story," Arna said.

The mortals were becoming Gods, and the Gods were turning mortal. They were going to make magic real.

Arna began to stretch as Arco knelt next to him.

"You've done this a hundred times," Arco praised him.

"More," Arna said, certain.

They recited the list of lost Blessings together like a mantra.

"Get through twenty-six," Arco breathed in unison with Arna as the stretching continued.

"Finish twenty-seven," Arna added.

"Live," They said together.

Soon the clothes beautifully tailored by Ginger would be in tatters. The mask expertly crafted through the assistance of Phlox would shatter. His shoes would fall apart. He'd potentially lose all his hair. It would be the worst pain he'd ever experienced in his life, nonstop, without reprieve.

The time was ticking down in his head. He did not have long before the height of the storm. There was not much left before everything was too far gone to save.

When broken up, including the breaks and the emcee talking about the dancer, the twenty-seven dances in total usually lasted three hours. For this Ceremony they had skimped on the breaks, due to the storm. The first sections were always the shortest. The last section, the longest. The timing depended on the variation being used, but most everyone had danced Holly, which was the longest of all the dances.

Through his augmentations the time flashed and Arna took a breath: determined. His variation set was one hour and forty-five minutes with no breaks. He would finish his dances before midnight.

"Arna," Ebru called, and Arna turned all his attention to the figure on the floor. Ebru was looking at him on his side.

"You're awake?" Arna asked as Arco pushed him towards Ebru.

"Circle up!" Arco called the others.

One by one all of the Golden Dragonflies but Amaryllis, formed a circle. Arna looked for her, but still Arco shook his head without a word.

"Are you going to dance?" Honeysuckle asked him, tears in her eyes, voice breaking.

"Yes," Arna answered.

"You will succeed?" Saffron asked, equally scared.

Arna looked at them both. "I'm dancing."

"We've checked everything twice," Rosmarinus assured him. "Everything is in order."

Arna turned to the original Golden Generation. They had been with him the day of the Splintering when Rosmarinus had not, and Honeysuckle and Saffron had yet to be born. Once more like a twelve years prior, they were in a circle. This time they wished luck not just to him, but for themselves.

"I'm not sure I trust that the Gods are real. But I believe in you. So. This time. Come back," Phlox said sternly.

"We will defend you with *everything* we have, Arna," Ginger said fixated, supported by Aureolin. She was not crying but smiling wide and bright.

"Dance, as if nothing will touch you." Aureolin nodded from next to her, looking stronger and sturdier by the minute. Dirt and mud caked her skin. Her curls laid flat on her crown, but in her eyes, there was a fire preparing for war.

Jasi squeezed Arna's shoulder. He said, enunciating every word, "Trust your instinct."

"Just because you've practiced for this more than anyone, I will not let you die," Ven said again, holding onto Ebru to keep Ebru from getting up. Concern, with rage bled into their face. "I don't care what that means for anything else."

Ebru glared at Arna. His eyes flickered between light and dark, mist and smoke; there and not as Wenge healed him. He was a miracle and a wish all wrapped into one.

"Even if you break every bone in your body," Ebru tried to joke and ended up coughing. Wenge hissed and her eyes glowed brighter. Ebru gasped out the words, "You better come back to me."

"Fight." Amaryllis said from where she sat next to Arco. She held a crown of vervain, wisteria, and willow branches over his head. It glittered with fake dragonfly wings—silver and black, white and mint—like iridescent kaleidoscopes shifting in color.

"Where did you get this?" Arna asked.

She smiled, placing the crown over Arna's head. "I saw it in the sky."

"How will it help?" Rosmarinus asked.

"It won't," Amaryllis giggled, tapping at her camera, "But it sure will make for a great picture."

"Are you ready Arna?" asked Arco. Black eyes met all the colors of the world.

"Honestly? No. The whole plan is reckless, but I trust you all, for you're my Saints." When Arna said the words, all of their eyes began to water. "And this is what I was born to do."

"Done!" Zaffre gasped from the front and Arna stood out of the circle, staring at the stage.

He adjusted the crown, swallowed everything else he wanted to say, and walked forward, facing the stage where his fans lay waiting.

"What about the lighting?" the Assistant Stage Manager asked Arna.

"Don't worry about that. Once I go on stage, I'll flourish my Blessings. Everything from that moment on will be on me. Just press play for the music and stand back. Do not stop me, no matter what. If I die, I die." His father blinked confused. The Golden Dragonflies started moving, Arco hurriedly urging Arna onstage as he finished saying, "But I must finish the dances."

"And when do we know that you are ready to begin?" The Assistant Stage Manager called as the two walked on stage.

"Don't worry. You'll know," Arna called back as he and Arco walked to the threshold of the known and unknown. With one more look back to all those he loved; Arna cleared his mind of everything.

Then with a long breath, he stepped out to the unknown.

His arm was caught.

"I'm not sure I'm right." Arco said quickly, stumbling over his words as he held Arna.

The winds ripping around them encapsulating them in their own bubble of time.

"But you said you picked to get rid of S.Mirrors. That you can choose."

"I can, but not when dancing. I won't be able to focus," Arna explained, confused by the sudden change. "The order was predetermined so I—"

"They made you memorize it like the dances, so it becomes instinct. Override it and get rid of A.Reverence at nineteen," Arco demanded, cutting Arna off.

Black and Brown mirrored. One with. One without.

Their dragonfly mark glowed.

"But I need it. . ." Arna whispered, eyes widening, fear bubbling. It was the one Blessing he had to keep. It was the one he needed.

"Follow the order otherwise, but drop A.Reverence at nineteen," Arco insisted. *You aren't like them. You're like me.*

"But. . ." Arna tried again.

"I know you don't believe me. But this is the way. Trust me." Arco repeated Arna's own words back at him, leaving Arna in a standstill.

The Gods would disagree. The world would call him mad.

But he trusted his brother more.

Arco let go of Arna, stepped back, and smiled. Two mirrors met, crossed in time and space. A legacy to forget. A legacy to remember. Understanding to be found. Learn it. Feel it. Dance.

Arna slipped his mask over his face, turning to the unknown, the weight of a billion stars discarded. The stage echoed with his footsteps as he walked. Click. *Click.* **Click.** The hush overcame the creaking winds and swaying rose petals. Entire districts were dark as night. Light exploded across the city and across broken railways. Rumbling clouds spiraled in a vortex of real and unreal.

The audience before the weeping was empty. What remained were knocked over chairs and floating cameras thrown about. Wind whipped trellises in the distance. Dirt and grass turned to slush and mud. Bodies were on fire. Stage light burned hot overhead, threatening to fall. Stationary cameras drilled into the stage, blinked red: live. Speakers buzzed and popped.

Twelve years ago, the audience would have been filled with cheers for his arrival. Now there was the silence of chaos. The Stage splintered and shook, threatening to break.

Amaryllis raced out to the front, hair whipping around her as she knelt down in the empty audience, camera in hand. Ven followed behind holding a bow with a quiver filled with arrows. Phlox and Aureolin chased after with practice fans in held in both their hands. Backstage, Rosmarinus and Jasi controlled the people, keeping them far away. Arco waited in the wings.

Eyes down, Arna dropped to his knees. He glanced at the fans before him. Zaffre's familiar hand stitching was obvious. These were not the ones made by machine. No. They were made by hand. With little time to contemplate the change, Arna flourished his Blessings.

He began as if it were any other practice: with the final vow he'd been taught the first day on the run.

"To my loves and my Gods, I pray to you that you hear me. I signal that I am here and that my words are yours. My body is here. My mind and heart heed your call."

The rose screeched. Thunder rocked the stage. Horrified screams echoed from distant parts of the city as embers coated the slick rain.

"May Lumak give me peace as I do what is right and Azza grant me the courage to accept change."

Distant yelling said it was time to prepare. Confusion that was not his own reverberated through Arna's bones. Distant chimes and birds were dying. Rain scratched his cheeks like tears.

"May Pokk inspire me with the knowledge of the past and Ixxzal give me guidance as I face the unknown."

Feathers fell. Animals cried. Flowers sang and sang and magic that was beginning to realize. Elements wrapped around dragonflies.

"May Zaynir calm my mind and soul. And Xeyaro, may you give me this, so that I may thank you in the only one true way that I can."

Arna sat up straight, hands out towards the Everlit candles that did not shine. They flickered. Their patterns swirled. Power growing. Storms brewing. The end arriving.

"I vow to bleed for the mortals and speak for the Gods."

A thunder CLAP.

A raging inferno.

"I vow to eternity and ethereal guidance, that I shall be."

The s t r e a k of silver lightning,

causing parts of the skyrail to shatter and fall with a sickening

thud.

"I vow that I know the risks and the weight."

Buildings collapsing.

Sirens sounding.

Emergency lights fli-fli-flickering mint and aqua and violet and bronze and gold and green and black.

Black.

Black.

"To pick mortality is to pick the Gods. To pick the Gods is to pick mortality."

Arna pulled his hands to his heart and closed his eyes. His skin glowed in a radiant hue of obsidian, from the inside out.

Rain dripped off him like oil.

"I vow to you, that I shall dance."

As he announced the last words loud and steady, Arna stood and took his position. His fingers dusted the tops of the first fan he'd take. A hum of fear coursed it's way through him and was met by the hymn of support.

His family would protect him.

"This is my choice," Arna said softer, to the Gods only.

[*You may begin,* Xeyaro said like it was all the lessons before.]

One. Two. **Three. Four.**

The lights dimmed with the storm's power. The music drifted through the speakers like a midnight lullaby. Arna's mind drifted away.

*Five. Six. Seven. **Eight.***

It comes from within, as a moment matched with tempo and rhythm.
It's a story told through silence and action.
When you know what it is saying, the world opens up for you.

— all first lessons end like this.

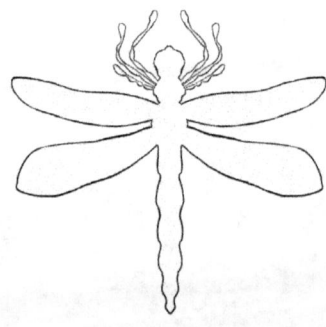

Dance 27

Choice

Incarnadine

"And then what do I do?"
"Dance."

The Sixth Variance

The first dance started with no fan. He moved slowly, dreading the moment that was inevitable. They were familiar steps in a practiced pattern, repeated in sequence until change was demanded.

When Arna grabbed the first fan, he gasped at the pain running through his body. The connection between him and the Gods sputtered, stronger for a moment, before once more beginning to drain. Yet, in that moment they gifted him the elements.

Instead of electricity burning him from the inside, Arna thought of it as starlight, seeping out of him. Power bloomed within him and fed the world. What was once pain turned into a familiar friend, one who would stand by him until he completed the song and put the fan down. The fan was a feather in his hand, lighter than any practice disk or weight. It gave him confidence. His father had made them, and they would not fail him.

Arna snapped open the fan and spun.

The steps were conservative in movement, as all the **Knowledge** dances began. It was easy to learn and to mimic. The first dance was the beginning of the world and mortality, a simple story that Arna crafted. When the thirty seconds of silence rang out, he hoped everyone panicked.

Then audiences would focus, for that was when the listening began.

That was when Arna wove the dream for them. He crafted infinity, slowly shaping the wind so that it worked with him, rather than against him. The stage stopped rumbling and the noise dissipated to little more than his music. The rain hovered around him, swaying in time with him. The lights flashed, following him. The fabric of the fan created a haze of illusions: captured shadows of his form cascading in six directions.

History was simple, yes, but it was far more complex than taught, so much of it unknown. In each of the variations, Knowledge was changed to reflect what had happened since the last, told in a new way that helped the narrative. Through each dance, dedicated to an individual God, Arna told the history of the world through the dreams of others, embodying them. He moved in a way that made it so that the world was unable to take their eyes off him.

The first dance was a call to wander, to gaze upon and within, to investigate what was known and confront a new reality. Chaos wrecked the creation: silent dissociation.

Amaryllis snapped pictures of him in the audience as he spun. Ven shot flaming arrows towards the sky, lighting up invisible dangers. Phlox and Aureolin faced the flames and activated the barriers around the stage manually. The stage floor lit up blue as the override was switched on from the front.

Nothing could hurt him then. Not the harsh winds. Not the empty audience. Not society's panic. Everything was light, and buoyant.

The second: a journey home, through the past, touching on everything that was missing, everything that was to be gained. Balance and justice being sought. Expectations laid plain.

Arna slid across the stage, steadying himself, and memorizing where the floorboards were cracked and where the puddles formed. He tugged at the connection with the Gods for the split moment where he lost his Blessing and the shock of it strengthened the Gods. Tossing his fan's weight around his body—both too heavy with rain, heavier than he predicted they would be—Arna focused on the connection. It was dwindling out like an old fire.

Live, so there would be an after.

Form the contract.

His Blessings flourished harder, brighter. The air crystalized into fractals, snow in the summer.

The meaning of these early dances were simple. The complexity was saved for later dances, but Arna added passion and anguish. He used the wind to aid lightness, airiness, and freedom.

The third: the arrival. Silence hopscotched with sound. A dissonant harmony spoken in parts and missing fractions. Hidden melodies twisted harmonies. The synths mixed with the orchestra and the off-beat drums. Almost together and yet, not.

It was imagination solidifying, a new world order taking form. He bounced the music around from speaker to speaker, moving it with his powers, creating sound from his body and warping the noise around him into harmony.

Four: inquiring, investigating, digging deeper into the past and revealing an uncertain future.

There were six seconds between the dances. He'd calculated every transition, each movement in between, to keep the dream swirling.

Five: loss and revelation. New, never told before. The old in conflict with change. A desire to return.

He controlled the lights, the colors and the intensity. They were a spotlight one moment, and dimmed the next. He did his best to avoid the debris around him and to move it with the powers that remained, clearing the stage, and creating an image of perfection.

Six: the hysterics that could never be returned. A rejection of the known and the dive into the abyss.

Arna heaved. His arms ached. The wood creaked beneath him. Beyond the Blessing-tech barrier were piles of debris and dust, and fire consuming the fields, untouched by the rain. Eerie shrieks filled the sky above where there was nothing: devoid of all light entirely.

Ven was out of arrows. Jasi rushed out with more. Rosmarinus screamed and pointed at something. The elements twisted around them. Arna reached down. Nine Blessings gone. *Keep going.*

Appreciation.

It was a deep dive into examining how the world was perceived to dreamers: the love, the desire, the hope, the fear, the carnage, the sorrow. Knowledge was the establishing of the rules and expectations: rejecting them. Appreciation was about crafting acceptance of the message, of the world, of the dream.

Seven: The return of everything. Every instrument. Told without silence at all. A symphony that rocked the stage, with all of the accompanying melodies half a measure off. Dissonant notes trying to bypass and supersede each other. Hints of harmony within.

He grabbed his next set of fans and placed the others down, trying not to break the trance. Keeping everything in his control, he wielded his Blessings. The stage cracked beneath him. Snow covered his fans. The wind lashed out at him. *Control it.*

Eight: interrogation of the message. Silence blurring the truth.

He showed how the relationship between Gods and Mortals, between Mortals and the Blessings, had created restrictions. He showed how in history there were those who pushed against it. He depicted how dreams shaped the world, and how they did not have to exist in the status quo that they currently had.

Nine: a revelation. A gap. A chance. A loss. A promise. *This is the way.*

The temperature dropped. The snow continued to fall, covering him layers. His body steamed. Breathing labored, it took everything in Arna not to slip, not to be knocked back by the wind, not to jump at the clap of the thunder, and not to rock with the stage as it shook.

Ten: overwhelm and clarity. It was the first time the melodies came together in synchronicity.

He had gone a year—morning, night, and day—performing an entire variation from start to finish before attempting to work on Incarnate Dreams. He had practiced in storms outside of the cities. He had stood on plateaus to learn balance. He'd been stark naked in the dead of winter and bundled up for frost in the height of summer, dancing for hours upon hours.

He could do this.

Eleven: the music slowed. Examining the facts. Taking stock of what existed. Visualizing a future.

Arna twisted his fans around him, watching as the stage's nanotech shield started to crack under the pressure. Not much longer and it would collapse completely. Stamina? This was nothing. Pain? No big deal. The elements? He could take them.

Twelve: the rush. Silence that consumed the song, the longest section yet. The message began. The contract formed. A vow took shape. Dreams.

Arna twisted the fan around him creating the song with his steps. With the snap of the single fan, he shaped the Blessings in his hand. It was not pain but power. He lashed out, casting the snow away, leaving the stage bare. His other fans were untouched. The Blessing-tech shield shattered.

Powers.

Thirteen: the song of new. Of powers that had never been. Accepting the dream in every facet of the body.

As the wind lashed out at Arna, with the debris and dirt that it carried, Arna wielded the fan in hand to create a vortex around him. He brandished his Blessings at full power. Weapons at his disposal, Arna carved out an image for the world. He shaped the dust into memories that danced with him like shadows on a wall. With his body, he became the message. He called upon nature and the elements. He granted new powers to the Saints who danced. Together, they made twelve.

Fourteen: determination and an ideology. Rooted, proven, acting and reacting. Growing.

The sky lit up in fire, cast out by Aureolin's fan as she burned the twigs and trees back. Phlox danced with her, shaping the wind and pushing everything away. Ven shot another arrow that tumbled with the dirt in the air. It became a drill, demolishing the vehicle headed directly to the stage. It split in two and crashed with a large thud on otherside of the stage.

Arna jumped but had no time to react. *It worked.*

Fifteen: the harmonies came together. Finally. Nearly. Hiccups where silence cut in. Dissonance unstable. No dream was perfect, but it could be.

He did not flinch. One by one Blessings turned to starlight, seeping from his wrists. Moonlight ran down his face. He was loud; he was wild. He was a symphony of a million voices, conducted by one.

Sixteen: the truth of dreams. They had to be wanted. They had to be chased. That anyone could be anything. But without work, it could not come to be. Face the mirror.

Jasi stood behind Amaryllis, whose hair was going wild. He held up his arms and pushed outwards, screaming. The earth rumbled. The fire in the grass, that was headed their way, was pushed back. Honeysuckle raced out and with Aureolin, fans in hand, they forced the fire into embers.

Seventeen: the full meaning. The acceptance. The joy. The love of the new. Everything would be okay. The dream would occur. Change was scary but needed.

The music swelled in a triumphant forte. It appeared in the illusions, surrounding him in a million colors: one for each note. Through shadows on the floor, flowers grew out of the wood beneath him.

Eighteen: the message in full. The powers and changes. The unity. The dream: real. And a shatter.

The music stopped. It was cut out of the speakers as the metal petals made an ear piercing sound. A rumbling cascaded through the rose. The entire city shook. Arna's crown slipped. He ducked a bit lower than normal to ensure it did not fall off. A light fell from above. What would have scalped him became a light graze, taking the majority of his hair with it and leaving no injury. The glass shattered behind him.

Vervain and wisteria fell over his shoulders, a crown split in two. The music picked back up as if it had never been lost.

Understanding.

Dance *nineteen*, in turn, was silent after the first six seconds.

A.Reverence

A.Reverence

A.Reverence

A prayer that people wished for.

A prayer he no longer needed.

The world fractured as Arna lost A.Reverence. The music lost its glow. The storm became heavier. His body was strange. It was as if he lost the guiding light that led him forward. The path that had once been so clearly marked vanished into thin air. He was shaken, ungrounded, and unsteady as he moved through the steps, by muscle memory, drilled into him by a boy who never had the guidance to begin with.

In six steps, Arna's shaky foundation stabilized. He stepped into memory. The phantom of inspiration—of everything he learned, of every lesson the last few months had taught him—was ingrained into his very bones. He willed himself to dance. Not because he had to. Not because he needed to. But because he wanted to, and he knew his variation like he knew his own heart.

Music memorized, Arna provided what needed to be seen and heard with only the Blessings. There was a music file for nineteen, for those who were not him. No one would ever be able to replicate what Arna could do. Ebru had said it was crazy. Arna knew it was necessary. It was the horror that he needed the world to see before he continued forward.

As he danced without A.Reverence it became increasingly clear how correct he had been in giving it up. Everything turned thicker, more daring and more intense. The Gods were slipping but the loss of something so important revived them. It was a sacrifice so significant in weight that divinity strengthened and roared.

Not for long, however. Without A.Reverence, he could see. In time he'd have to give it all or nothing would remain. Without A.Reverence, he was no longer blithely unaware of the truth.

Still, he faced it no matter how ugly it was.

When he stopped—when he gazed out to the abyss of the world with less than a minute left in the song—the world was forced to gaze back.

They were forced to see what he gave, what they'd all given. He'd had danced without A.Reverence and would continue to do so. There had been no music, and every sound had been in their heads.

For that was where fear lived.

Dying world

Dying Gods

Everybody talks about dying.

What will you live for?

The realization could not set. He could not ignore how petrification was caused by terror's haunted gaze. Arna pushed through and guided the audience towards a better world: the future he designed where they experienced life outside the confines of their individual minds. They could not remain in world built on fears.

The music returned in the speakers and the last six seconds came a close.

Make a choice. Make a wish.

Understanding was built from the foundation set before it, and was danced as one near continuous movement.

Twenty: the disillusionment of the dream, presenting all the counterarguments, the issues and horrors.

Twenty-one: the abandonment, forsaking the dream and returning to it in a cacophonous explosion. The vow remembered to one's self. A step forward to combat the horrors.

The movements to grab each new fan was choreographed. Fans in and out of his hands, as if he had never let go of them at all. Fans up, fans down. Fans opened. Fans closed. Lights on. Lights off. Shadows danced. Paint glowed. Music waltzed across the speakers like a thousand forgotten memories. Falling lights crashed into the stage. Puddles were made of mud and slush. Curtains raced past and up into the abyss above. Blood streaked across the sky from wounds that could not close and would no longer heal.

The loss of Arna's Blessings were continuous supernovas yet invisible. Power slipped like star dust from his veins. Voids formed where his abilities once were. Phantoms circled and threatened to kill him, should a single thought deviate. Pain echoed through him, no longer controlled by the Gods, as they flickered like fast melting galaxies.

Arna did not falter, training had led to this moment.

Each dance flowed to the other, with no noticeable breath between them. The shift had to be gradual, but obvious in hindsight.

Twenty-two: a combination of forces contrasted with deeper considerations, pressures that could not be ignored.

Twenty-three: acceptance. The dream in full, combining the known and unknown, panicked wishes, aspiring dread. Craving.

It was the moment that manifested the intense desire for change.

Understanding set mortals apart from the Divine. It was the realm for masters to discover. Thus, it was rich. It was complex and messy. There were things that people would forget and have to rediscover, layers upon the layers. The deeper one fell into the dream, the harder it was to get out without suffocating on passion.

He wanted to scare them.

He wanted to love them.

He wanted them to cry and to cheer.

Branches and fire entered the vortex. The storm was too strong to combat. The others shrieked in pain as they were berated by the assault. Wind ripped clothes. Arna's shorn hair flowed around him as he moved. He took their pain and their screams, and made it his own, echoing it outwards, louder and stronger. He did this all while dancing, without faltering.

And when he was done, they would forget, just as the details of a dream were never remembered upon waking. The idea's essence implanted itself onto the subconscious instead.

The last dance, *twenty-four,* was the cumulation of all of Understanding: the simplest in movement, but the most profound in intention. It was slow, deliberate, and the actions were the silence that the world so craved. The music played on, but his dance was the pause. The breath. The moment to almost wake up.

Worship was set to begin.

The dream started to decay as the stage floor rocked. Parts of it had already collapsed around him with gaping holes and entire pillars fallen. Without the Blessing-Tech to protect it, the stage was crumbling.

Arna could no longer control the lights that still hung. The sound blasted from the speakers, out of his grasp. Breath ragged, he was surprised by how calm he was.

Keep going.

There were screams of roaring metal as it wobbled and swayed, whistles in the wind, and chimes somewhere in the distance. Flashes lit up the gray sky. Pouring rain twinkled like stars. Lightning lit up the stage, crashing down before them. Amaryllis was knocked to the ground and the others raced towards her. She shook them off and leveled her camera at Arna.

Lighting hit the Rose, causing ripples of blue across the whole sky. It ran down rail lines, snapped and hanging in the sky, threatening to fall. Thunder shook the Rose, and Arna's entire body relaxed.

He focused on his breath and the three steps he took to place down the two fans from twenty-four. He grabbed the twenty-fifth fans and let his mind draw a blank. Whatever happened from there was practice. It was years of experience. It was everything he had trained for.

He was going to dance.

Worship began with the loss of Arna's mind. He let himself forget who he was and step into the Divine. The twenty-fifth dance picked up the energy, where the twenty-fourth had been a break. It was vibrant and radiant. It was the last bliss. It was the beginning of what everyone was going to remember when the rest was forgotten. For it was always the end of a dream that was remembered the most vividly.

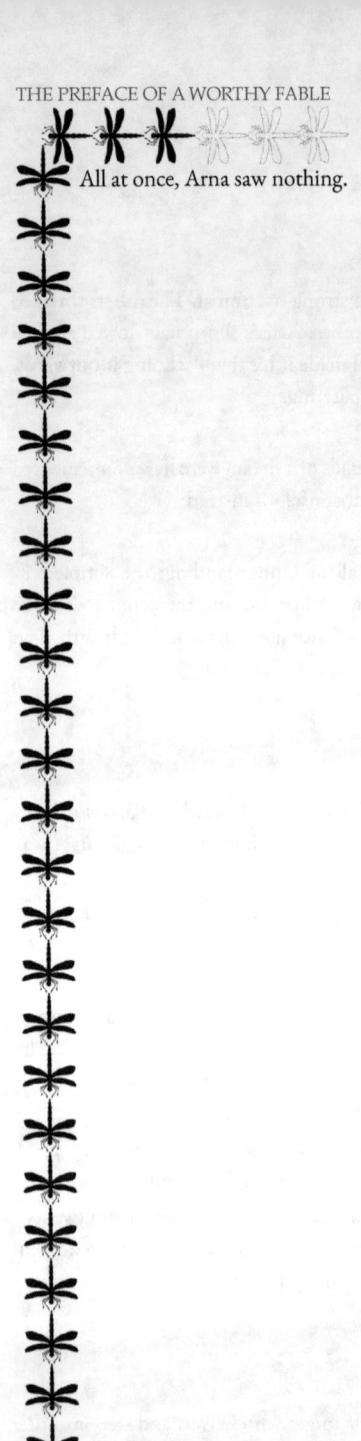

All at once, Arna saw nothing.

[Arna was all.]

Shadows danced under the single light that remained. The rest had shattered or fallen. One body cast six figures on the stage. A mirage threatened to disappear at one moment. It glowed in the next.

The rain hovered and stopped. A field of water became a river in the sky. The Designer held out her hands, stably controlling the waves. The Believer raced across the stage in the back, hands up and yelling that he would get the snow. The Chosen danced.

The Archer and The Guide heaved. The Guide tried to stabilize the rumbling as the Archer directed it outwards, with a single shot. Uncertain in their abilities, they did so believing in themselves. The Chosen danced.

The Watcher and The Monarch waved their fans and burned away the dust, stepping in sequence with one another, determined. The Chosen danced.

The King and The Actress mastered the wind. The Actress, with her fans, dissipated the gale the best she could, as The King used the redirected wind to knock falling speakers and stage walls from The Chosen, who danced.

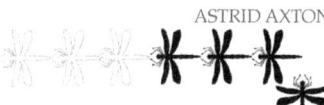

The Chosen noticed dangers that were flying towards him but did not care. He danced as if they did not matter. The audience breathed out in awe and relief as he danced and avoided each one. The glass spiraled around him in jagged massive pieces, within the whirlwind, and joined his shadow.

The sanctified path-makers took the pain that was offered by the Gods, who could no longer aid The Chosen. Burning starlight filling their lungs, their bones, their muscles, and their veins. Powers that were new, that they did not know how to use, became theirs. Eleven Golden Dragonflies believed in magic and miracles. Pushing themselves to their limits—unsure how long they could go on as the blessings burned them from the inside—they prayed and acted. It was the least they could do. This burden was theirs to bear and they would.

The Chosen was the epicenter of a vortex, debris flying about him, mists and dust making a haze. His shadow split. The glass refracted his image. A kaleidoscope of color spun around him. When he moved, he took the light with him. Every movement was visible, glowing. He was a phantom: invincible.

The Chosen saw those on the side of the stage who watched. A mother who screamed. A father who gaped. An uncle who wished. A Cardinal who cheered. An official who believed. The Composer who struggled to see. The Dancer who stood without moving, snapping his fingers in tempo. The story was woven about him. He was a stillness, singular in the chaos. A nod.

The Lens continued to see, continued to capture, and refused to look away. Smoke billowed around her, illusions twisting past her. What she saw was GROWING, mirroring The Chosen in all directions. And he saw through her.

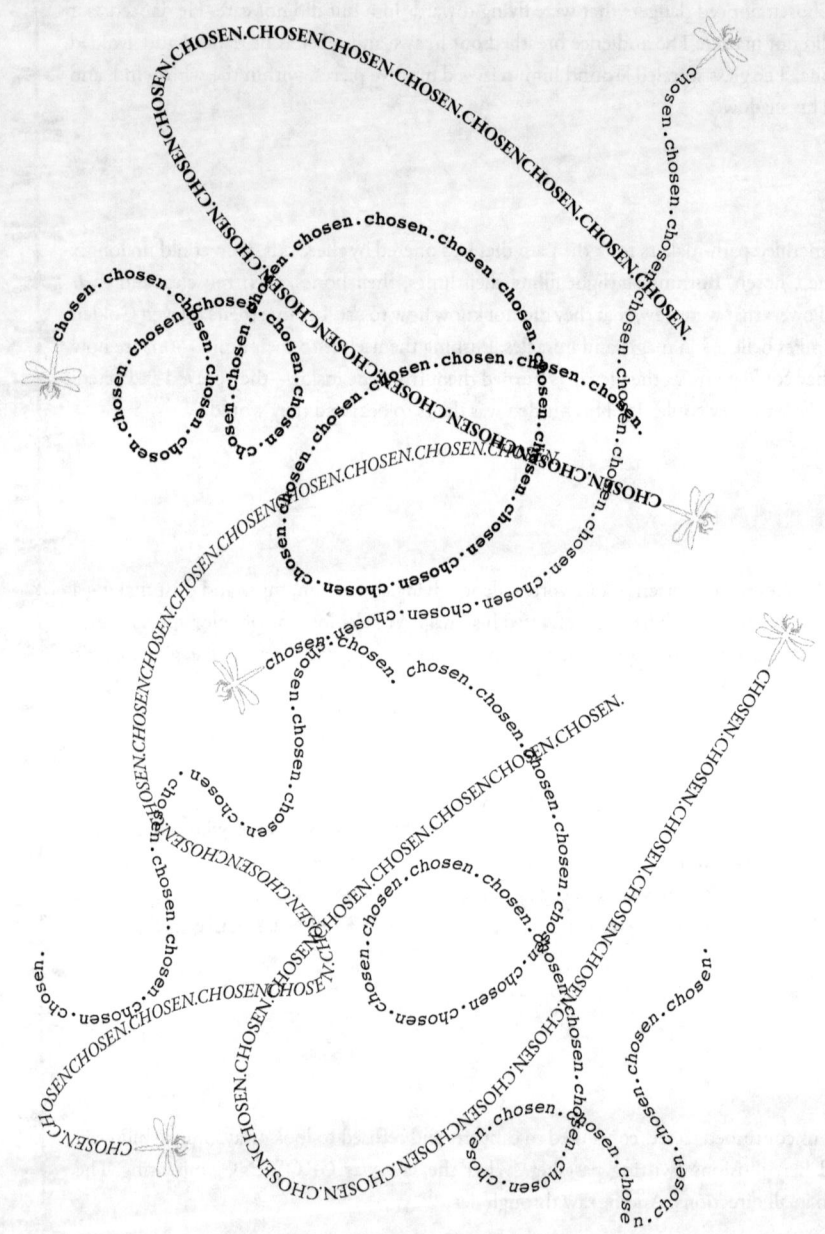

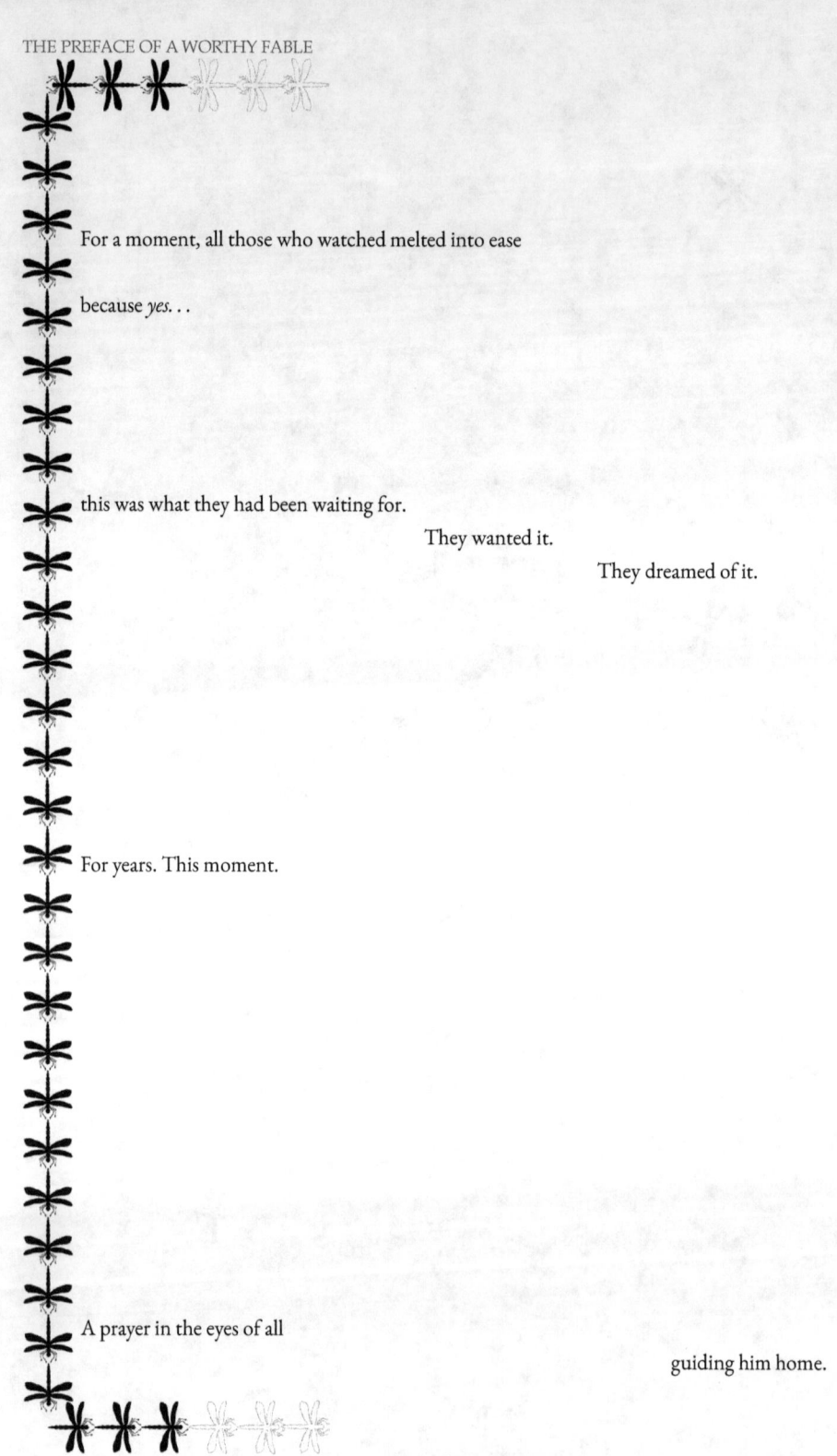

For a moment, all those who watched melted into ease

because *yes. . .*

this was what they had been waiting for.

They wanted it.

They dreamed of it.

For years. This moment.

A prayer in the eyes of all

guiding him home.

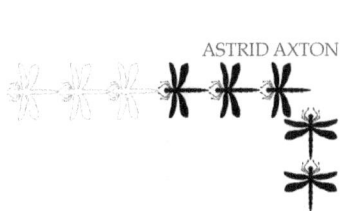

His actions **s p a r k e d** their

desires
hopes
wishes

Tears.**Fears**. *Smiles*. `Trials`. Actions.***Shouts.***
Screams.**Chants.**Cheers.**Practice**.Joy.*LOVE*.
Hate.***Drive.*****Motivation**.`Ambitions`.Resilience.***Yearning.***
ANTICIPATIONS.expectations.*Prayers.*
Silence.Defiance.
AFTER.

Incorporeal upon the earth.

Tangible in the beyond.

Gods who were mortal. And Mortals who were gods.

Mares were evicted from the bodies of flesh.

Dreams scratched through to thrive.

At the moment of twenty-five, none but eleven thought of twenty-six.

Most did not remember that in Worship, there were three stages:

>Deprivation,
>**Destruction,**
>*Destiny.*

When The Chosen discarded his ego, the mortals relished.

They desired. They craved. They yearned:

>Control,
>**Creation,**
>*Choice.*

A new world was o p e n i n g before them.

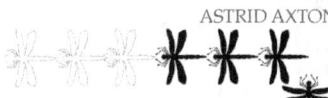

Eleven noticed when twenty-six began.

All at once, everything became too much. Powers were overdrawn. Miracles were no longer enough, and the elements were beyond their control.

Water crashed as it slipped from the fingers of The Believer and The Designer.

The earth shook and splintered the land from the stage, collapsing.

The stage floor teetered dangerously over an open pit that

The Archer and The Guide could not close.

pleasepleasepleasepleasepleasepleasepleasepleasepleasepleasepleasepleasepleasepleaseplease

Flames lashed out at The Watcher and The Monarch.

Fans began to burn.

A tempest spiraled out of the hands of The Actress and The King.

The Lens ignored it all, as she was berated by being too close.

Knees over the ledge.

Camera snapping.

The Dancer snapped his fingers. One. Two.

Three. Four.

The Dance of Destruction began.

Divinity descended.

The Dancer was not immune to the dance, but he Understood it. He had lived it, and he knew that in order to reach the end, he had to face the nightmare. He stopped anyone from getting any closer to The Chosen from backstage.

The Golden Dragonflies dragged The Lens back, the earth crumbling as they did.

She was bleeding but The Dancer ignored her. She ignored him.

Camera up.

Fingers snapping.

This was what they had worked for. They would bear witness.

When The Chosen began twenty-six, the universe turned against him. He was bombarded from all sides and the stage floor was dyed red. Glass became scales along his arms. Fire burned his skin. The air threatened to suffocate him. Thunder rolled.

The Chosen danced.

It   was: *flickering*   like   a   candle.

A million colors, iridescent from the blood and light and glass.

A pained scream through lips that could not control the sound.

Electricity that sparkled and flew.

Dust that shined.

Creaking from a breaking city, forming a harmony to the song in the speakers.

The Chosen's dancing was as enticing as before and, in some ways, more ethereal.

It was the horrors of facing a dream.

They all were privy to the pain, suffering, anguish, and sorrow.

They became acquaintances with

> the desire to give up,
>
> the desire to never try again,
>
> and the ways in which others would savor their failures.

Despite the carnage the Chosen danced on.

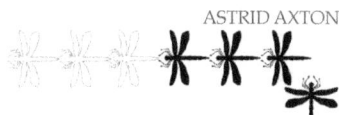

His shoes dissolved off his feet.

Razor sharp winds aimed to blind him. Instead, his mask was pulled from his face, shattering and joining the disarray.

```
Dreamy: Expression
      Mind: Peace
     True: Horror
```

His body was torn: opal turned crimson and wine syrup began to drip from oil-slick sleeves. Yet they were woven by those who believed in him and stitched together with love; by them he was mended.

Terror **dawned.**

Silence *reverberated.*

His steps were soft taps against the stage.

> He did not stop.
> He did not falter.

```
Was he dying?
```
They did not know.

```
Was he going to survive?
```
They hoped he did.

There, on bated breath from enthrallment and horror, they watched the Chosen.

Their heartwishes took root.

He stepped down, blood in his wake, and a collective hush overcame the universe.

The Chosen was sleeping, lost in a dream.

None of the ceremonial fans had moved.

The Dancer counted.   Snap.   Snap.   Snap.

When the rest of the world was grasping at comprehension. He understood.

Five. Six.

Seven. Eight.

```
Music: in abundance
It was: beauty.
```

And as the world fell apart:

The silence was a reminder of what he had.

Don't let him die, the Dancer prayed.

He will not, the Gods wanted to tell him.

The Chosen would die: reborn Divine.

He would survive: no matter what it took.

He would live.

And after?

Dance for the dream.

Create when all there is, is doubt.

T   H   R   I   V   E

Selflessly, thought those who did not know him.

Selfishly, thought those who did.

The twenty-seventh dance fans were picked up by The Chosen's visibly shaking hands, as all the others began to fall to the abyss. The Dancer smiled. The Golden Dragonflies chanted his name. In time. On count.

The Dance of Destiny began.

The twenty-seventh dance was the waking. It was the longest of them all. It was everything that came before and everything that came after. The when. The now. The here. The there. Change.

The Gods were leaving. What was once there, to be no more. Even in the burst of the connection gained from the loss of a gift, they were little more than an echo. For they had given all their power, redirected it to the mortals, in hope of seeing the world beyond.

Goodbye. A melody that swirled.

[*No.*]

Twenty-seven was the lucidity between dream and reality, the moment of change. It was beautiful, and yet simple. As it progressed, those who watched realized they'd forgotten everything they'd seen before. Each moment transient, incapable of remaining forever.

He was Divine in a way he'd never be again. In that was power.

The stage began to cascade into a field of fire. Ash dropped into the abyss. The fans that were left behind were burning, falling, disappearing into the void. Glass dropped from his body. The last light fell, directly aimed at the last remaining stretch of stage, that would send the Chosen careening below.

[*When I was a child, all I wanted was to dance.*]

The Composer stood, clinging to The Dancer.

[*I loved every part of it.*]

[*The hours of practice. The sweat. The tears.*]

The Dancer lifted their hand and lashed out, not knowing what he could do but drawing upon all of the power within his body.

[*But the fans were always my favorite.*]

(In all other variations, dancers tossed the fans. But not in his.)

Lightning streaked from his fingertips. The falling spotlight exploded and transformed into glitter, raining around The Chosen.

(He never could risk it. For the loss would be too great.)

(It had always been his favorite move. The one he was best at.)

Children's innocence, when it comes to that which they love, is the most sacred.

For they are capable of anything.

The first toss was unscripted. A risk done before the consequences could be fully rationalized.

BOOM

The radiance of stars was willing given as a gift.
A sacrifice was made when it was not needed.
He traded one gift for another.

No! Live!

The Chosen spun and tossed both fans. BOOM

In retaliation, they protected him from the storm that wanted him to die. Blessings flashed through the sky, as he pulled the world back together. BOOM

He had jumped when the mortals said jump. Had run when the Gods said run. BOOM
Now the Gods would return when he said come home. BOOM
The mortals would survive as he said *I will not let you go.*

For a dream was not complete if there was no happiness after.

With each spin, and turn, The Chosen gave up the Blessings time and time again. He did not so much as gasp.

Do not forsake me. Do not forsake me. [*Do not forsake me.*] Do not forsake me.

Eyes were like prayers for they were windows into the souls: connecting all into one.

Slowly.
Slipping.
Tossing.
Spinning.
Sacrificing.

Myriad.
Kaleidoscope.
Cascade.
Bond.
Choice.

Each Blessing a martyr: pulling harder, surviving longer, a magnetism stronger than even death. The Chosen gave it all until there was nothing left to give.

The universe clung to the fleeting seconds. They did not want to wake yet. They did not want him to stop.

Mortal and Divine.

Death and Life.

Both?

Neither.

All was nothing.

Nothing was all.

the   same   in   everyway.

He was stronger in the embers of the new.

For every galaxy that was swallowed, another emerge.

Choices expanded into eternity.
Possibilities emerged even as others collapsed.

There was an unknown ahead.

Dive
Headfirst

That was where he would be waiting.

Never
Hesitate

That was where they would find the dream again.

Create.

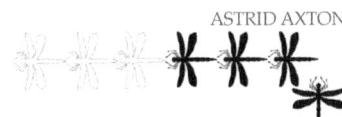

and

— when they embodied their dreams, unapologetically —
that was when the chance would be theirs.

Six seconds to midnight. The Composer raced to the stage, shadows spinning about him as the remainder of the roof collapsed and The Chosen lost his final Blessing. The Composer lifted it, shifting the gravity so it would hold. He took on the pressure of the universe.

For *just* **six** **seconds.**

Every healed injury burst open as The Dancer blasted the roof away.

Twelve shadows like dragonflies, drifted and hovered over settling winds, condensing into

the last

six

steps.

When you have the freedom to choose, it is your choice to decide.
Defy fate.

That was Incarnate Dreams.

Arna slowly knelt down to place, not drop, the twenty-seventh fans on the bit of stage floor that remained. He was deliberate and precise. His body was mush that could topple over at any moment. His heart did not beat. Haphazardly, his mind became his again and he gasped as the night air filled him. Spasms of pain were an unrelenting pressure. The taste of copper stained his mouth.

Do not fall. This practice was not over.

"These Dances are my vow. May your benevolence smile upon the world for this Variance and all Variances to come," Arna said the final words.

[*We accept.* A whisper of a memory. *Finish the ceremony.*]

"Mortals and Gods, together once more, tethered and tied: bound with the connections of souls, trust, and dance. For the Gods we gift this day. For the Gods we gift this dance. In the Gods we see mortals. In each mortal there are Gods," Arna recited, kneeling, hands out towards the candle of Xeyaro that he could not see. He couldn't see anything, but it did not matter. He finished the practice.

Only it was not practice.

Sobs sounded in the form of wailing wind. Worry cascaded through rumbles.

Burning. Sticky. Red. Ashes.

[*Rest, Incarnadine.*]

The wind stopped. He blinked away the sand and darkness until he could see the outline of the candle behind the Cathedral. The first strike of the Apostle clock sounded. Dust and mist collapsed around Arna. The candle before him roared to life.

[*We will take over from here.*]

"Did I. . ." The words hurt too much to formulate, his vision fuzzy. His brain was a heavy slush. Thinking was difficult.

[*Yes, you incessant fool,* Ixxzal begged him. *Now stop talking, please.*]

[*Lay down now,* Azza said.]

Arna did as he was told.

[*Your taboo will be lifted,* Pokk spoke as if they were kneeling next to Arna.]

[*We will return your Blessings to you,* Zaynir's voice came from the other side.]

[*Your vow has been accepted, Chosen,* Lumak said.]

The starlight return to his veins and bones, crystalizing into strength.

Chosen.

[*You are home.* Xeyaro placed their hand on his head.]

Sleep took him in the form of a warm blanket.

A beautiful prayer was held in the eyes that loved him.

1 Axid 1 VVVVVV

The beep of the heart machine was the first thing Arna recognized as he woke up. Stiff and aching all over, Arna slowly opened his eyes. Where was he? There was a tightness at his side that tugged in an unfamiliar way: stitches? How bad were his injuries? How long had he been out?

There were no clocks in the room but there were copious types of flowers throughout: covering the floor, the tables, and every part of the otherwise empty space. Arna's bed was the only one within the soft golden glow.

"You're awake." His father's voice came from behind the flowers. He stepped into Arna's line of sight. He was dressed in all black, sheer and light, drifting like a mist as he approached. Arna struggled to turn as his father approached his bed, but his neck screamed at him. He wore a brace to keep him looking straight and up.

The bed moved slowly after his father pressed some button, and Arna was able to see more. He was alone, with the privacy curtains drawn. He assumed the figures on the other side of the glass windows were security guards.

"How long?" Arna's tongue was dry. He smacked his lips, searching, with the little movement he had, for water. His father handed him an ice chip instead. Reluctantly, Arna took it.

"Six days," his father said from the side, out of Arna's sight. "Your spine was nearly pulverized into dust under the pressure of the dances."

"That's it?" Arna struggled to laugh. His body felt strange, as if it were not his own. He was in it, but he did not feel it fully. There was a damper placed on his senses.

"Incarnadine," his father chastised. "Serious lacerations, pulverized bones. For a moment the doctors claimed your organs had *liquified.*"

"They probably did," Arna admitted, running the ice through his teeth. There was a surge of power racing through his veins, flourished without his control. Otherwise, he could not feel much, save the tightness and limited mobility. The aches and spasms that suddenly rushed through his skin vanished as soon as he noticed them.

"We thought we'd lose you for a minute there, when no one could use their Blessings, but. . . You've been showing signs of waking for the last hour." His father sat on the bed, so that Arna could see him. He looked just as exhausted as the last time Arna saw him. Arna heard arguing outside the room. Zaffre grimaced. "Everyone is here. Cardinals, Governors, the Chosen Task Force. They're bared entry but they will try."

"Thanks." He groaned. "Even Cardinal Black is here?"

"He and Governor Cider are currently in custody, with their actions being reviewed for conspiracy. Mr. Thyme was appointed the Vice Governor and head of the city in the meantime. Apolic and Lumakic Law are still in ordinance, with Cardinal White overseeing everything." Zaffre sighed. "The Children of Lumak and Pokk have descended on the city, and they are investigating *everyone* that could have been involved."

"Cyclamen?" Arna hoped the man would get punitive justice.

"Last I knew he was at the Shadone studio, considered not a conspirator," Zaffre said disgusted. They both knew it not to be true. "Regardless, for now, focus on healing."

Arna nodded and his father handed him another piece of ice.

"I can't really feel my body to be fair," Arna admitted.

"Between the pain meds and your Blessings, which are apparently flourished against your control," Zaffre cocked his head in confirmation. Arna tried to nod, unsuccessful. Zaffre accepted it. "I'm not surprised."

"If I'm going to have to dance in a storm each year, I think I need to have a permanent residence established here," Arna joked.

His father stared at him in opened faced disappointment and terror before breathing extremely deeply and massaging his brow.

"It's a joke," Arna whined.

[There was laughter clear as crystal.]

"I know," Zaffre chuckled. "Only you could joke about having to stop the apocalypse."

"Arco told you?" He supposed that it wasn't much of a secret after the fact, or perhaps even during it.

"The damage and timing are hard to ignore, and there were too many miracles last night. Although most people assumed after hearing the Gods. . ."

"You heard them?" Arna sat struck by the words, ice falling from his mouth.

Zaffre laughed. "No one can explain it, because it's not a voice or a sound we should understand, and it cannot be analyzed. The recordings say it was just you talking, but it is there. Everyone can hear it if they play back the performance. It wasn't in your music files. It is only in the performance videos of that night. Perhaps, in a way, it was their way to legitimize you. Regardless the Sixth Variance was declared, and your variations are being scrutinized and analyzed."

"What about the candles? How many people died? Are the Blessings back?"

"You don't remember?" Zaffre asked, concerned, and Arna struggled to shake his head in the brace. "Don't. . . Just, hold still. Okay. No. No one died."

"Bullshit," Arna gasped.

"I told you, miracles. There were injuries, however any form of serious disfigurement? Maiming? Death? None. Everyone who was injured, healed in hours. Whatever you did worked. Experts haven't tracked a single superstorm since you finished dancing," Zaffre said.

A melody of success reverberated through the room and harmonized with Arna's healing.

"The candles are lit again. Everywhere. Everyone who lost a Blessing has them back, albeit changed. Those who never had them before are lining up for their Blessing Revelation Ceremonies."

"Changed?" Arna asked. His father snapped his fingers and a breeze rushed through the room, through the petals of the flowers.

Arna gasped. "Magic."

"We don't know the full extent of what you did, but that is the most I can do so far," Zaffre said adjusting Arna's blankets. Arna pictured his father sitting close, watching and having nothing to do but worry and practice.

"What do you remember?" Zaffre asked.

Arna thought back. His memories were fuzzy but slowly coming back.

"I remember little after I started. I know they said I was good to go and that I completed them, but. . . I vaguely remember the sound of the bell from the Church of the Apostle. That the weather shields went up? Midnight. . ."

His fans.

"You rebuilt my fans. From scratch?" Arna asked. His father must not have slept.

His father sighed and said after a moment, "I didn't trust the machine ones. I had to try."

"They felt different."

"I got the owner of Aster fabrics to assist with fixing and altering the boning. He tightened them, recarved the prayers, and fixed the coating. Cardinal White reblessed them."

"Thank you." He doubted machine made fans would have survived the tosses.

The the door opened, accompanied by a chorus of shouting. It shut and Wenge walked in. The sound vanished as nanotech turned blue for quiet. Wenge's irritation drained from her face. For a second, she hovered near the wall, before she placed her bags on the ground and rushed over, lightly touching Arna's face with delicate fingers.

"My baby," she cried, tears streaming down her face. She left butterfly kisses on his cheeks, and a light dusting on his forehead from her lips. She sat on the bed and refused to completely let him go, holding his hand with the dragonfly mark instead. "The apocalypse, Arna? Truly? You could have told us. You didn't have to do it all alone."

"I told Arco," Arna coughed, and his father handed him another piece of ice. Arna sucked on it quietly. "And the others. . . I wasn't alone. I had them."

Zaffre and Wenge shared a look before smiling at him. Wenge said, "But you have us, too. Not just your Saints."

"I know now. . . But, I had Arco and he knew what to do," Arna explained. Arco had always understood. Arna wondered if, unconsciously, Arco always had.

"How are the others?"

"In recovery," Wenge said solemnly. "Ebru is in the worst state, but the doctors predict he'll make a full recovery. Although, he is still asleep."

Arna laid his back staring at the ceiling. His head pounded and his eyes were heavy.

"You must rest now." Zaffre's voice was a buzz drifting off and away. "We're proud of you, Arna."

"We love you so much," Wenge said, like the sound of spring birds calling in the morning.

"I'm home." Arna meant it when he said it, as sleep took him into its vast expanse of everything and all.

2 Axid 1 VVVVVV

The neck brace was removed with a debate about medical protocols. Arna was shown scans of his bones, scared up and refracting like crystal: impossible but fact. However, he was confined to his bed until the doctors were certain it were not a mistake.

Arna sat in his empty room humming to himself, hoping that whatever smoothie his mother brought him had strawberries in it.

Are you there?

[   ]

They were much too busy to answer him. There were too many prayers and calls to respond to. Arna did not mind. He'd had them to himself for twelve years. They'd return to him in time and provide another lecture about how he could not grow lax and lazy.

There was a knock at the door but before Arna could answer, it opened to a chorus of unrelenting arguments. Ven stepped inside holding a smoothie. As they approached and the noise cancelation activated, and they examined Arna in detail.

"You owe me an explanation," Ven said, placing the smoothie in Arna's hands.

"What?" Arna asked.

Ven leaned close with a large frown, livid, "If I didn't call you back, you would have left us."

Arna did not remember that in the slightest, but as Ven's wore a sinister grin, he shivered.

"I'm sorry?"

"No, Arna," Ven laughed, breaking the charade and relaxing onto the bed. "Were you scared?"

"Have you been learning from Phlox?" The expression had been heart-ending.

"She's a great teacher, and we've had little else to do in our room the last few days other than listen to Jasi or Aureolin's lectures," Ven sighed, running their left hand through their hair. The constellation birthmark on their wrist sparkled and rippled in light. Arna lifted his left hand, attached to wires and IVs. His mark laid clean without the petal overlaid on top, shining like it had for years before he'd shattered the vow.

"You anchored me," Arna said. It was the weight in his soul: the constant flourishing. Only one person could control his Blessings other than he could. "You. . ."

"Thank you will suffice," Ven said with a loving smile. "It was the first one back, I think. I could feel your soul before Ebru and Arco were at your side on the stage. I could feel your other Blessings being poured into you and I tugged. I held on. I haven't let them go."

"Will you?" Arna asked.

"Not until I'm certain you're healed. It does not feel like you are yet," Ven assured him, and Arna did not ask to be released. "Jasi, Rus, Honeysuckle, Saffron, and Aureolin will be released today."

"Arco?" Arna asked.

"He was never hospitalized," Ven assured him. "Ginger will be released in two days. Ebru and Amaryllis need to wake up. I will leave as soon as I'm not having to constantly help you."

They looked drained, from the color in their cheeks to the bags under their eyes.

"Thank you," Arna said to them.

"You made the right choice," Ven said, not asking for what it was.

None of them would ever ask, for it did not matter: he made the correct one. Even with their mark of bearing secrets, without the fear of it being exposed, Arna would not say.

After all, they had to know what choice he made. It was the same one that they all would have made. It was the one he made for himself.

He would have to dance for the rest of his life. He'd have to spread the word of the Gods as well. Perhaps there would be more tests, more stages to the quest; but finally, he was free to dream. His story was his to create, and the world's story was ready to be shaped by them all.

3 Axid 1 VVVVVV

On the day of their release, Phlox and Aureolin were the first to leave. They arrived bearing kisses and left with bouquets in hand, promising to decorate the Vivicent manor for his return. Then entered Jasi and Rosmarinus. Jasi reminded Arna of his legal right to not be bothered, and Rosmarinus assured Arna that the fees were covered by the church.

Cardinal White was the only Cardinal given entry. Without discussing world politics and considerations for the future, he showed Arna the deed for the Hue's ancestral home.

"It took some time to get it, but Thyme assisted." Cardinal White smiled brightly. They had not been able to present it as scheduled without the deed in hand, but a few days late was not never. "I will present it to Alabaster and Eburnean at the end of the month, when you all have had enough time to recover."

"Thank you." Arna truly meant it. Cardinal White may not have been there from the beginning, but he had helped. He nodded and left Arna to his own devices.

4 Axid 1 VVVVVV

On the day that Ginger was to be released from the hospital, Mymy arrived with a big basket of fruit and Aureolin in tow.

"Look at you," Mymy said, hovering over Arna's bedside. "Have they got you walking yet?"

"Not yet," Arna admitted.

"Nonsense. Nonsense. I'll tell those doctors that you need rehabilitation now!" the woman announced. "Can't be dancing if you can't even walk."

Arna laughed as the door opened and Ginger walked in with their mother.

"Wenge!" Mymy chastised. Wenge backed up looking for a way to flee, unable to return back outside. As Mymy scolded her, Ginger approached Arna's bed. Her long braids were gone. Instead she wore braids, tight against her scalp. Her long hair curled right under her chin at the back of her neck.

"You look terrible," she said to Arna with a cocky smile.

"Mom did your hair?" Arna asked her.

"My braids got cut," she motioned with her hands. "We're going to try a new pattern later. For now mom said this is best, so I can focus on healing instead."

Arna agreed. The bruises across her skin were an indication of her strength.

"Amaryllis and Ebru woke up last night," she told him. Aureolin gasped. Zaffre had told Arna that once they arrived at the hospital, Arco had never left Amaryllis' side. Likewise, Alabaster had been with Ebru. Although Arna was not sure what had happened to Amaryllis, her injuries had been great. She had completely disregarded her safety to capture his actions in real time.

"The Cardinals *and* Governors are demanding to speak to you," Aureolin interjected. "Your father had to invoke the wrath of Zaynir to keep them from disturbing you just now."

"He's done it twice. I'll have to give them some divine message to think about at some point," Arna laughed before saying softly, "Sorry that it took so long for me to get the right answer."

"You got it in the end." Ginger smiled like a thousand oceans and million rivers. "Now there are endless possibilities."

There were endless futures that they were all willing to fight for.

5 Axid 1 VVVVVV

When Arna awoke, Ebru was next to his bedside in a wheelchair. Alabaster hovered close by, talking to some nurses. Their eyes met, mint and black. Arna smiled at him and sat up.

"Dad, leave," Ebru demanded. Alabaster stopped talking, abruptly.

"Arna, you're awake," The man approached with a smile. He hugged Arna. "You did well."

"Thank you." Arna glanced at Ebru. He was staring at him, paying no attention to anyone else in the room. Arna looked back at Alabaster. "Can you. . .?"

Alabaster chuckled and nodded. "We'll be outside."

The nurse and Alabaster left. Outside there was only a clattering of voices, most of Arna's critics seemed to have left for the night.

"You, Amaryllis, and Ven will get discharged tomorrow," Ebru started after the door shut.

"So long as I can walk and control my own Blessings, yes."

Arna was not sure how seriously he took it, considering they did not want him moving at all. According to the experts he was perfectly healthy, but no one believed it based on the state he'd arrived in. Arna could not believe it either, but he supposed that was the perk of being Divine. Arna reached out for Ebru with his right hand, dragonfly mark pale and unmoving.

"You should be resting. . ."

Ebru's gifts weren't as powerful as Arna's and Ebru's injuries had been devastating. The fact that Amaryllis would be released the next evening was startling, considering she, too, had been knocked out.

They sat there in silence for a while. Ebru observed the flowers in the room and Arna stared towards the sky. The light of the day shifted in color.

"They're saying I can't be discharged until next week, that it took them too long to get me. I refuse to stay in that room alone. I'm leaving tomorrow, whether they want me to or not," Ebru finally spoke angrily, with a hint of despondency.

"No. You will stay," Arna scolded him.

Ebru simmered in his seat as their eyes locked in a battle. According to Arco, Ebru had waited for Arna to finish dancing. He had forced himself to his feet. He had run and used elemental Blessings that he did not know. He had been the first to Arna's side after Arco. All of this he had done, despite being on the cusp of death.

"You held the weight of the world for me."

"The whole world bent to you," Ebru said with a quivering voice, breaking uneven and ragged. "We all did what we could to defend you. When the roof came down I—"

"Thank you," Arna squeezed Ebru's hand. Telling him it was okay. He did not need to hide any longer.

"I didn't even realize how injured you were until you collapsed. I thought we were winning," Ebru's voice became a sob.

He broke down in the contemplation of what could have been. He finally released years of sorrows: vocally and outwardly. He was safe enough to be vulnerable. Safe to express. Melting.

"We did," Arna said, tenderly.

In the end, the results were all that mattered. Perhaps they could have been better, stronger, or smarter. They could have worked together from the beginning and prepared longer. Perhaps the plan could have gone exactly the way Arco wished. But it didn't. All that mattered was what remained.

"Because I'm alive."

Ebru latched onto Arna's arm, pulling it to his face as he sobbed, pressing the heat against his cheek. Arna sat up, leaned over, wrapped his right arm around Ebru, and did not care about the tug of the IV and machines that checked his vitals. Ebru solidified in his arms: no longer an image behind a mirror, tangible and real.

"You're alive," Ebru clung to him. "You're with us."

"I'm here." Arna breathed Ebru in. *I will never let you go.*

"You were always the best of us," Ebru cried revealing his late night nightmares and deepest fears.

"No," Arna said pulling back, lifting Ebru's chin to look at him. "I was only as good as I was because of all of you."

Tears fell. Lips locked. All and nothing merged into one.

"Don't make me ever regret loving you," Ebru threatened and hiccupped between kisses.

Arna chuckled. *That's my Alis.*

Soon they'd return home, begin practice in the Vivicent studio for the new variation. He and Ebru would work with fans, dance, and music. They'd have the Hue house, which they'd fill with the laughter of their friends by day. And by night, Ebru would never be alone again.

Arna would be Chosen for the rest of his life. He'd spread the word of the Gods and help lead the world into the future. He would accomplish all his dreams. He would dance in all the places he couldn't. He would eat all the things he craved. He would be supported, loved, and seen.

His leading moment was ending, and he had a whole, new, unwritten path to explore.

His story, the one the history books would remember, was over. What happened for him was all inconsequential. But in a way it had never been about him. It had been about all the lives he touched and the moments that had yet to come that he could not fathom. This was just the beginning.

And like all good stories, Arna knew exactly how this one was going to end.

6 Axid 1 VVVVVV

Wearing only a pair of pants and no shirt, Arna struggled. The doctors and nurses watched him with flying scanners, checking his diagnostics through his exposed skin. He had seventy-one Blessings: most had returned but one, which he suspected would remain missing, forever. Arna accepted that.

His shaved head was cold. His dragonfly mark flapped its wings. The snake on the back of his neck glistened like scales. The spiral on his chest pulsed like a heart. The constellation birthmark on his wrist shined.

The room was filled with the faces of all those that loved him. Ebru sat in a wheelchair next to Amaryllis, in her own. Mymy was in the back with Cardinal White who reminded her to be quiet. Alabaster stood behind Ebru, hand on his shoulder in support. Zaffre held Wenge back so that she could not lunge forward and simply fix it. Honeysuckle and Saffron clung together, wide-eyed in awe and shouting their supports.

"You can do it Arna!"

Ginger clung to Jasi, keeping him from leaping forward to help. Rosmarinus stood close by Ven, arms crossed. Phlox was in Aureolin's arms, the two watching confidently. Ven's fingers curled around their sleeve as they finally released the hold they had over Arna's Blessings.

Arna heaved as the Blessings snapped back to him in full force. Pain, that he had not been able to feel, weighed heavily on him. Pressure, that he could not understand, threatened to drown him. His body was foreign. His senses were strange. Everything was a technicolor spiral.

[Pokk reminded him to take it slow.]

[Zaynir was the wind at his back, supporting him.]

[Azza was the drive that coursed through his veins, rooting him.]

[Lumak was the one who centered him and provided balance.]

[*You can do this*, Xeyaro sang.]

[*This is nothing*, Ixxzal agreed.]

Arna stood a bit shakily with the help of the nurses that supported him. Arco watched with stern eyes, hands on Arna's arms. He wore plain white, low-rise pants and a cropped, white turtleneck without sleeves. The mark over his hip and waist was completely exposed. He was no longer hiding it.

Arna dove in without hesitation, activating all his Blessings and flourishing them himself. Pain once more spiraled, ravaging him.

"Breathe," Arco demanded of him, and Arna did as he was told.

And it got easier, every moment surer. The pain slipped away. The Blessings coursed through his body. The power was once more his to control and contain. His vision cleared. His hearing got brighter. Everything was greater than before.

"You have to get walking if you want to teach us," Arco pressured Arna. Arna looked up at his brother, haloed in the light of the room.

His journal for his dance had been destroyed. His fans had fallen into the hole in the center of the city. His clothes were tattered beyond recognition. The music chip shattered. His mask fractured into hundreds of pieces.

However, Arna had created all the steps. His sister had made two versions of the outfit, one that needed to be tailored again. The music was saved on Ebru's computer. The mask could be remade. This time, he could make his fans by hand.

Despite all that was lost, there was infinitely more to be found.

Arna stepped with his brother. One step forward. Sturdier. Stronger. Certain of himself.

He took another, accepting the new weight of his legs and the way the world made him feel. There was another and another until the two of them were able to cross the whole room and there were cheers.

"Again." Arco demanded him and Arna relented. He followed Arco across the room six times until Arna could walk on his own, master of his own body once more.

Blessings and magic worked in tandem throughout the unknown.

"Now. . . Are you ready?" Arco asked, with a fan in his hand.

It was the first fan his father ever made.

Twelve years of panic was unable to fathom what he was being asked to do. Arco did not drop his hand, did not pressure Arna to try. The room held a collective breath, waiting and watching.

"Arco. No."

Arna was not sure whose voice it was, but it did not matter.

"Where did he even get it from?" another asked.

"Arco, stop."

"Is that my first fan?"

But Arco never stopped when he was asked. He always presented Arna the choice when Arna needed to hear it. He applied pressure when Arna needed to have it. He believed in Arna in a way perhaps no one else would ever know.

Arna reached out, fingers tracing the fabric. His hands were no longer bandaged. His palms held scars that were properly healed and ready to fade in time.

Arco wasn't asking him to jump. Arco wasn't asking him to take it, no matter the cost. Arna was not being forced. He did not have to make the choice today, nor any time soon.

Not if he didn't want to.

Brown eyes, the color of the richest earth cultivated for growing and nurturing. Black eyes of the darkest night devoid of stars, but holding the lingering wishes sent to them.

Arna took the fan, flinching in anticipation as he did. He was fully prepared for the spiral that was to come. He centered himself so that the agony would not knock him over.

Nothing.

Blessings deactivated. Staring at the fan in his hand. Distant cheers that he did not register. Excitement in other dimensions.

Nothing.

Arna stood still without question or pressure, letting nature take its course.

For, what is silence?

The story in-between.

Arna let it weave its tale.

In his hand was just a fan, heavy from the billowing fabric that draped to the floor. It was just a fan that he opened with a SNAP. It was just a fan that gave no pain, that brought no sorrow, that was no longer an agonizing reminder. It was a fan, a bit heavy, soft to the touch, and finally home, in his hand where it was meant to be.

Tears filled his eyes. A sob scratched at the back of his throat.

The future was ready to be written.

And on his back, covering most of the skin—prominent, bright, consistently shifting in color and form—was a flower.

At times it was a rose of trust and love, retribution and storms.

Sometimes it was an orchid for wrath and knowledge, war, and change.

It could be a lotus for the home and emotions, family and souls.

Then it could be a lily for loyalty and happiness, destruction and creation.

For a moment it was a lavender stalk, for justice and friendship, stories and the truth.

But it was mostly a tulip, smoky and bronzed on his skin, sparkling like a galaxy. In it there were miracles and illusions. In its light the shadows of the unknown were contained.

It held defiance: magic in all its forms and hope in face of the greatest fears.

The LEGEND of

SHE Who Saw All

&

HE Who Wove Stories

Chapter 1

At the Epilogue

After the apocalypse, what came next? When dreams were achieved, what came after? What happened to the story when the hero was done? Arco had asked himself these questions a thousand times in the days after his brother saved the world.

Arco stood, masked by the light of the doorway, stepping into the shadows the room and gliding across the floor until he was at the window. The sunset bathed him in the flames of radiant color. His brother hummed to himself, unaware of Arco's presence, surrounded by monochromatic shadows. He gathered his things into his bags at the side of his sick bed.

Twelve days since the end of the world and he was finally discharged. He was ready to go out in the world and do what one did after they were the savior.

His brother's injuries shined as bruised badges on his skin. Everyone else had fought. They'd been injured from debris, and Arco was the only one that been clean of injuries. He was the only one who did not have the luxury to fight alongside them. He would have died if he went into the storm that his brother had faced.

"Can we talk?" Arco asked.

His brother jumped, an unintended consequence of Arco's silent steps. It was another mistake. It would be another thing he'd have to repent for.

"Sorry."

He came to find out what miscalculation he had made, so he would not make it again. His brother had nearly died, and it was his fault, of that he was certain.

"Arco? What's wrong?" his brother asked.

"Did you have to give up all the other Blessings because you lost A.Reverence?"

The list they'd created sacrificed his brother's A.Reverence ability in place for A.Body, so that he'd stay alive and heal as he danced. After his brother had given up A.Reverance on his suggestion, it should have been easy.

Yet, his brother spun his fans in the air, over and over after he reached the last dance of the

Twenty-Seven Dances and bridged the mortals to the Gods. In doing so he'd fixed the contract of the world and saved them all, but the tosses were not a part of the original choreography. He'd changed the dance on the fly. Arco had counted each fan that his brother threw, losing a Blessing each time he did, until his brother hit zero.

His brother should have died without all his Blessings, without the powers to protect him from the divinity of the Gods.

"When you suggested it, before I went on stage, how did you know I needed to give up A.Reverence?" his brother asked.

Arco reeled in his own oversight. He'd done it out of greed. It was a hope that his brother could succeed in the dances, while being like him. Arco did not have A.Reverence that connected him to the Gods and gifted him in dance.

"I didn't," Arco admitted. "I just knew that in the perfect world you'd have all the Blessings, and it wouldn't be a problem. And that this was not the perfect world."

He never wanted his brother to die. He didn't want him to risk everything.

There was a heavy silence that filled the room. A truth spun between them that neither wanted to face: his brother's mortality. Another reared its head with unspeakable urging.

"A.Reverence is the link to create the contract," his brother moved through the white and black, like a mirror. "It bridges a person to Understanding."

Then why. . .? If his brother needed it, if it was necessary for the contract, how had anything happened? How was he alive? How as the world still standing? Why didn't he have it back now?

"But. What was the foundation of my variation?"

Hope? No. To survive? No.

"To defy," Arco stepped into the white glow, his shadow growing across the mint floors. A warmth flared between them. Elements swirled. Refracted light danced on the wall in the form of rainbows.

"And I already Understood my own variation," his brother explained. "I did not need it to complete the contract. The Understanding first and foremost, is what is needed for the contract not A.Reverence. Like the first Chosen who created the Blessings, who had none, I did not need it."

"But you gave up everything."

"You guided me home." His brother's breath was as white as snow, in the midst of summer.

Arco reeled. What? Arco was not some beacon of light that guided his brother through the darkness. He had simply kept time and watched.

The Chosen stared at The Dancer. Between who was Chosen and who may have been, a lingering question remained.

"We've always been more than our Blessings, you proved that."

"The dances could have killed you!" Arco tried not to yell and failed.

"And yet, you never believed I would."

The two were mirrors, the same in more ways than one. They accepted each other and all their faults. They believed in each other in a way no one else would understand.

Arco shut his eyes and inhaled deeply.

In many ways Arco did not expect much. He had experienced so much failure and rejection in his life that supporting his brother in silence was more than he could have wished. He was content. He needed to be content. It was enough.

But.

For forever he had fought. He battled wars that were not his to wage. He supported everyone else. He had given up his time to listen. He sacrificed everything for their happiness. He demanded nothing in return. He searched for a path, for an answer, and held everything together; not because he had to, but he wanted to.

He stood unyielding when thousands wanted him to fall. He transformed himself hundreds of times. He found his soul in a forest covered in a blanket of snow. He had accepted giving up for the greater good of the world. He did it all while wanting it, clinging to it, and knowing he couldn't.

But now. . .

What came next after the apocalypse was over and the savior did his job? What did the story become when the hero won? What came after?

"Xeyaro. . ." Arco finally prayed aloud to the Gods who would never answer him, knowing that through his brother they would hear. The Gods gifted his brother with their voices, with their visages, and with their love. Not him.

Yet. . .

Arco wanted to chase after the dream with everything he had if he could. He wanted the life he'd never allowed himself to fully strive for, the hope he'd never let himself fully wish for. He wanted the chance. It was all he needed.

Just a chance.

"Am I allowed to choose this? To try?" Arco asked, voice as light as leaves drifting in the wind. "Please. Give me this."

A pause. A thousand memories. A thousand answers.

Captivating and deafening as the silence grew

longer,

lingering,

twisting,

transforming.

Promising solutions. Pushing others to chase their wants and desires.

A brother like a mirror showing: all he could be and never would become.

And, he already had the chance.

Arco opened his eyes.

As his brother smiled, Arco no longer needed an answer. He never needed one before. Arco had guided the world in defiance of Blessings. He had stood where no others could and claimed the titles that were withheld from him.

He was going to chase his dream to do it regardless of if the Gods let him or not.

Just as he always had.

"You can be anything." His brother said.

It was not an answer but a promise.

The choice had always been his to make.

A thousand mint-colored flowers bloomed within Arco's soul as he smiled. The cracks of his heart—filled time and time again by sheer will and motivation—solidified into silver. White light filtered through the window and became a storm within his veins. Lighting sparked at his fingertips as the hope that entangled his soul rooted him firmly in dreams.

He needed to practice.

"Are you leaving?" his brother asked as Arco wordlessly headed to the door.

Without another consideration, he left.

Without another prayer that would never be heard, he went on.

He would keep trying, no matter how hard it was. Maybe he would not succeed, but the only one to decide that was himself. Maybe everyone would resent him for trying but he didn't care.

He had his life back. He had his brother back. He found himself in the cheers of those who needed him. He found his soul and would never let her go. He pulled his family together. And when the rest of the world had given up, he believed.

Arco walked from the room, past Archbishops, Cardinals, and doctors debating scriptures and medical miracles. He walked past his parents who waited for the Apostle, saying nothing to them at all. He hurried through the protective shields and guards. He left the hospital behind with the crowds of believers, nonbelievers, priests, and concerned citizens.

In the streets children and adults tested their newly found elemental powers, gifted to them through his brother. It was power in a form it had never been before. And there past the magic, past the holograms and advertisements in the sky and the bodies that filled the street, was the girl who was his soul.

She stood, camera in hand, hair tied up high, and aqua eyes seeing all. She wore a soft white dress with a hem made of crystal, radiant and glowing. Her soft pink almond shaped nails tapped at her camera as she stared up at the willow tree by which she lingered. She was waiting.

Amaryllis.

She turned as if hearing his wordless call and met him halfway. Arco walked on without stopping, lightning sparking in his hands. Amaryllis skipped ahead with a bright smile, smoke and illusions cascading in her wake.

The world was their stage. Their history was to be written. The story of the beginning was over. The ending had yet to come. One day the world would know their names without fear, spoken only in hope. And they'd create.

They'd create in the morning, as the petals peeled apart to skies where no storms brewed.

They'd create in the night, in the middle of nowhere, kissing the future that had yet to be tasted.

They'd create through every emotion, through every crisis, through every argument and pain. Through every occasion, through every love, through every change and joy.

They'd finally be unburdened and free to make the same choice again and again every day.

For themselves.

What comes after, when everything is said and done?

"Ready?" Amaryllis asked with her camera raised. Her voice was made of knives: sharp, cutting, and unyielding. Her eyes refracted and reflected but never revealed.

Between them was a promise and an unspoken vow. It was a want and a need. It was Anything and Everything all at once. It was hate and spite, love and trust, faith and fight condensing into one. It was an uncompromising hope in unrelenting uncertainty.

"Always." He smiled, as he began to dance. Each action he made was deliberate. Each moment was dedicated to what he wanted.

Two shadows split into twelve, moving almost as if alive.

Chimes rang from distant gardens and bells sang from distant homes. The wind billowed. The dew in the air crystalized. The warmth between them was the heat of a thousand suns. Stories were unraveling, weaving, woven.

White like snow. Silver to heal.

Flower petals swept up from the ground.

For a moment Arco believed that he was capable of bending starlight.

Because they were artists.

And when they created, the result was legendary.

[   ]

Glossary

The following is the glossary (or the abridged world building guide) for *The Preface of a Worthy Fable*. For the full glossary and world building guide, please visit foxfairyfont.com for more information.

Important Symbols and Colors

God	Primary Color	Second Color	Third Color	Symbol	Flower/ Plant
Azza	Green (Forest)	Green (Lime)	Red	Moon	Lily
Ixxzal	Gray (Smoke)	Bronze	Pink	Spirals/Stars	Tulip
Lumak	Violet	Indigo	Mauve	Scales	Lavender
Pokk	Gold	Orange	Yellow	Sun	Orchid
Xeyaro	Mint	Silver	While	Leaves	Rose
Zaynir	Aqua	Blue (Sky)	Blue (Navy)	Clouds	Lotus
Apostle/ Chosen	Black	N/A	N/A	Dragonfly	Willow

Blessings

A.Reverence	
PREFIX is A.	CENTER is Reverence

PREFIX

Whether it is in spoken, or written language, the Blessing's prefix is denoted with either one or two letters. Each prefix glows a different color during the Blessing Revelation Ceremony.

Azza – Pronounced "Aye-zah"

      Ch. – Short for Chaos. Pronounced "chuh." Shows as Forest Green.

      Cr. – Short for Creation. Pronounced "kur." Shows as Lime Green.

Ixxzal – Pronounced "Ix-ix-zz-al" (like six-six-zal, but no s)

      Un. – Short for Unknown. Pronounced "un." Shows as Grey.

      Fa. – Short for Reality. Pronounced "fah." Shows as Bronze.

Lumak – Pronounced "Lu-mak"

    B. – Short for Balance. Pronounced "buh." Shows as Violet.

    J. – Short of Justice. Pronounce "juh." Show as Indigo (almost Blue).

Pokk – Pronounced "Paw-ck"

    K. – Short for Knowledge. Pronounced "kuh." Shows as Gold (shines).

    G. – Short for Change. Pronounced "gur." Shows as Orange.

Xeyaro – Pronounced "Zay-arr-oh,"

    A. – Short for Art. Pronounced "arr." Shows as Mint.

    N. – Short for Nature. Pronounced "nuh." Shows as Silver.

Zaynir – Pronounced "Zay-near"

    S. – Short for Souls. Pronounced "sur." Shows as Aqua.

    E. – Short for Emotions. Pronounced "eh." Shows as Sky blue.

The "assumed" nature for an "A" Blessing will be in the arts. All "Fa." Blessings are power amplification abilities. Un. Blessings are the most regulated Blessings as they can negate other Blessings.

CENTER

The Center is the aspect by which the prefix manifests. There are six.

    Song (symbol: fan) – These centers revolve around the word, spoken or written.

    Mirrors (symbol: mask) – These centers revolve around mimicking other abilities.

    Reverence (symbol: Candle) – These are the most blessed and powerful, their abilities usually involved worship.

    Body (symbol: flower of specific the God) – These centers revolved around the body.

    Insight (symbol: book) – These centers revolved around knowledge.

    Stillness (symbol: sundial) – These centers revolve around the mind and peace.

Taboos

Greatest Taboos

    Azza – Murder

    Ixxzal – Revealing Secrets

    Lumak – Lies

    Pokk – Withholding Knowledge

    Xeyaro – Destruction of Art

    Zaynir – Apathy

Second Greatest Taboos

    Azza – Upholding the Status Quo

    Ixxzal – Exploitation

    Lumak – Breaking Promises or Contracts

    Pokk – Stopping Change

    Xeyaro – Destruction of Nature

    Zaynir – Breaking Souls, People, or Torture

Mentioned Organizations

Dancers of the Harmonious Six, The (DHS) – The dance organization who manages all dancers and the Ceremony of Chaos.

Floral Association, The – They are in charge of the Floral Festival and manage all plants, flowers and natures inclusion at the celebrations. They name the Monarch of Flowers each year.

Legacy Heritage Foundation, The (LHF) – The organization keeps a record of all Blessings. They issue most tests for Blessings, as well as verify those they did not initially test.

Maple Rain – A named famous pop group.

World Government Council, The (WGC) – The international government created to oversees trade, and peace agreements between the six cities.

Characters

The Golden Dragonflies
The Golden Generation

Aureolin Begonia (27) – She is the Captain of an all-girls dance team. She is called "Lila" by her grandmother.

Eburnean "Ebru" Hue (27) – He is a skilled dancer and badboy.

Pervenche "Ven" Cosmos (26) – They are Arna's S.Mirrors partner and an excellent archer

Phlox Ruby (26) – She is a skilled actress who has won multiple awards.

Gingerline "Ginger" Vivicent (25) – She is Arna's younger sister, an excellent dancer and a fashion designer.

Incarnadine "Arna" Vivicent (27) – The Chosen Child of All the Gods.

The Dragonflies

Amaryllis Ink (24) – She is the best friend of Sarcoline Vivicent. She is public enemy number one of all those trying to hide their deepest emotions from the world.

Honeysuckle Dawn (11) – She is a girl born after the Splintering, who learned the Dances and was inspired by Sarcoline and Eburnean.

Jasione "Jasi" Jade (27) – He is Incarnadine's former best friend and boyfriend of Gingerline.

Rosmarinus "Ros" Jade (27) – He is Jasione's twin brother, a swimmer, and the main breadwinner of the Vivicent family for six years.

Saffron Ink (11) – He is Amaryllis' younger brother who lost a leg in a taboo accident.

Sarcoline "Arco" Vivicent (22) – He is Arna's younger brother. Arguably he is the best dancer in the world.

All Other Modern Characters

Alabaster Hue – He is Eburnean Hue's father and former best friend of Zaffre Vivicent. He is in a generation with Cyclamen and Zaffre.

Bluebell – A powerhouse soprano singer.

Cardinal Black – The leader of the Church of the Harmonious Six.

Cardinal Song – The leader of the Church of Axis.

Cardinal White – The leader of the Church of the Apostle.

Cider, Governor – The Governor of Xeysis

Cinth – A baritone singer

Chamomile Gladiolus – A deceased teacher of Amaryllis. She was a blind woman who loved painting and is considered quite good by some mortals. Not a Child.

CrimsonFlesh – Arn'a online persona and the friend (husband) of Ivumalis. He is called Crimson (by strangers) and Rosy (by Ebru).

Cyan – A mezzo-soprano singer

Cyclamen Shadone – The head dancer of the Shadone Dance Studio and the Shadone family. He has been Philanthropist of the Year for about a decade and member of the Dancers of the Harmonious Six for about three decades. He leads the DHS small council. He is a member of Alabaster and Zaffre's Generation.

Mr. Hemlock – A Fan Master who created factories to make performance fans, believing that fans made by mortal hands contain error and are imperfect.

Ivumalis – An online composure, Eburnean's online persona, and the friend (husband) of CrimsonFlesh. He is called Ivu (by strangers) and Alis (by Arna)

Garance Jasmine – Friend of Auerolin, in Aureolin's dance group. She was Knowledge dancer for Ceremony of Chaos, mastered in the Holly variation.

Myrtle "Mymy" Begonia – She is Aureolin's great grandmother.

Pewter Puce – He is the Appreciation Understudy for the Ceremony of Chaos, prepared in the Twin Fans variation. From Podiel.

Rose Thistle – She is the Knowledge Understudy for the Ceremony of Chaos, prepared in the Twin Fans variation. From Ludiel.

Mr. Thyme – World Government Council Member, head of the Chosen Taskforce

Wenge Vivicent – Arna's mother. She is a former conservationist.

Zaffre Vivicent – Arna's father, best dancer of his generation. He is in a generation with Alabaster and Cyclamen.

All Characters From the Past

Hevona Reed – A former non-Child who learned to Understand the Dances.

Ilex – The 5th Chosen of recorded history who started the Fifth Variance. He healed a part of The Shattering caused by Saffron and reestablished the connection between Gods and Mortals. He ensured that mortals could continue having blessings and living.

Raven – The 1st Chosen of recorded history who started the First Variance. While this is not the person's name, it is the name used by the Gods as their actual name was lost to time. History before Raven is scarce, as it is a time before the Gods and mortals made their pact.

Sable – The 4th Chosen of recorded history who started the Fourth Variance.

Saffron – Saffron ultimately failed to dance the complete form of his variation of dances, resulting in the creation of the superstorms that began to decimate the world. This act was called the "Shattering" by the Gods, as it ripped apart their connection to mortals.

Saint Citrine – One of the Holy Saints of the religions

Saint Aubergine – One of the Holy Saints of the religions

Vervain the Blythe – The 3rd Chosen of recorded history who started the Third Variance. She almost died from a plague and spent the most amount of time creating her variation (as opposed to the other Chosen).

Watsonia – The 2nd Chosen of recorded history who started the Second Variance.

Acknowledgements

When this novel first began, I was blissfully unaware of the undertaking it would become. It was simply a coming-of-age tale, not meant to be anything more extravagant than that. It was never necessarily supposed to become *this*.

Writing Preface has taken me everywhere.

It was born in Scotland, halfway through my Creative Writing Masters, and ended with me back in the States. It began as a presentation to my writing workshop group, the first piece in our long form, and ends now in the modified and expanded group.

When I first started writing Preface my goal was to be published professionally. I queried the book across agents hoping to get a hit. It ends with me self-publishing, with my own publishing company, ready to take on the world the way that I see fit. Now, I have absolutely no plans to sell to an editor at a major house. For this book is not meant to be about the money; it's about the art. It's about the soul. It's about silence.

The word "silence" did not end up on the page in the form that it is here until draft seven, where I was asked to push it and to really contemplate what silence is as a concept. The word is what transformed this book from what I'd consider traditional epic fantasy into its current poetic, might-be ergodic, nearly Arthouse (yes, the film term), form. I began to play with space, with spacing, with alignment and really examined how words appeared on the page.

I started considering the dances as more than just a part of the plot but the chapters themselves.

What would it mean for the book if I structured the arcs of the novel like the sections of the twenty-seven? What would it be like to structure the chapters like the dance that it referenced? How do you create a tempo in your words, on the page, and across spread to make it look like the text was dancing?

From the beginning, I knew the frame narrative had to begin and end with Arco. This book is the preface to his and Amaryllis' journey, but it was "silence" that solidified that. It was what frankly, I believe, allowed that intention to shine through. This is the prologue to their story, the silent memory that is often referenced in the main narrative. It is the same narrative you will never receive, as that, too, is silence.

Building this novel was hard. In many ways I wish it were perfect, although I am never quite sure that it is. Yet, it doesn't need to be perfect. It just needs to exist.

This story is as much me as it is the people who reminded me and pushed me to never give up. If is for the ones who stood by me and gave me hope even when things seemed bleak.

Thank you to my parents and brothers who have stood by me through every crazy writing endeavor I have made. You understood when I said this was what I wanted to do, even if you were a bit terrified by what that meant.

Thank you to my aunts and uncles who have called me up and sent me messages. Your constant encouragement has helped me soar.

Thank you to my grandfather who reminds me constantly, that if I'm not working towards writing then I'm not myself. Your belief in me is unwavering and means more than you will ever know.

Thank you to those of original workshop group, who left: Angela and Ellie. Thank you for giving me the time, and your kind thoughts as you helped to push this project into the direction it needed to go.

Thank you to the new workshop group members: Elisha, Liz, and Hanna. I know that you were thrown in at the end of this journey, trying to provide the best feedback that you could. All of it was extraordinary.

Thank you to Elana Seplow-Jolley of New Moon Editorial for providing guidance in the process of editing. Your edits and feedback helped to inspire this book to where it is now.

Thank you to David Leahey who not only designed the book cover, but taught me much along the way. Thank you for your patience with my questions and changes.

Thank you to Savannah Drews who designed my companies logo and did all of the inner art found on the page. Your art elevated this book in a way that I could have not done on my own. I know that this project means as much to you as it does to me.

To Kendra Penn. Thank you for staying up with me late at night as I went down spirals talking at you rather than with you. You sat with me as I tried to understand and rewrite the book in my mind before I even touched the page. Thank you for every text of love and every word of encouragement. Thank you for being ready to fight with me ten-toes-down about the meaning of a word, because it matters.

To Kate Rogan. Thank you for helping me grow this project from the beginning. Your hands carefully cultivated each chapter. Your willingness to throw hands when I was about to give up was pivotal to my success. Thank you for the memes and the jokes and the insistence that Phlox and Amaryllis are your babies and needed to be loved. Thank you for every line check and vibe check. It was necessary.

To Juliette Morazain. Thank you for Carnation. Without it, I think that this book would not have become what it is. Thank you for every demand and deliberation. Thank you for asking the questions I knew the answers to but did not want to write on the page. Thank you for asking for more, even when I was certain I needed to give less. Thank you for pushing silence even when all I wanted to do was explain.

Thank you all for reminding me what it's like to dream.

Thank you all for reminding me what it's like to believe.

And now, I present to you, dear reader, my manifesto. This is the introduction to my career. Regardless of if I get better (or worse in your opinion), I have laid it all out, here and bare. The themes and messages are my battle cry. The hopes of the characters are my prayers.

Thank you, reader, for reading this book. This novel is as much for me as it is for you. And even if we never meet. . . Even this is our only chance encounter. . . Thank you for joining me in this journey.

For what is silence

if not the story in-between?

Never stop creating.

Learn more about Astrid Axton and Fox Fairy Font at:

foxfairyfont.com